INVISIBLE SCARS

By

Emma Lidgett

ISBN-13: 978-1976260506
ISBN-10: 1976260507

DEDICATION

I thank all my family for their support with this book. I dedicate this
book to my Nana who passed away in 2016 from Cancer.
She is my role model.

CONTENTS

ACKNOWLEDGEMENTS

I'd like to thank all my readers on Episode Interactive for making me think that this was possible.

Chapter 1

Today is the first day of my new school. My family and I travel a lot. My Dad says he is protecting me, whatever that means. I got to pick where we went this time. I love the sun, it makes me feel calm, relaxed and happy. So I decided to move to Spain, it's sunny all the time. I remember coming here for a holiday. It was perfect, all our family together, although we live here now, I wish that we could go back to the holiday.

I lie in bed wishing this day would go away. I love school, it makes me forget my life. My dad has always enforced good grades. I don't like to think of my punishments over that. I live in this house with my Dad and my overprotective brother. I love my brother but he is annoying, but all brothers are, aren't they?

I decided I better get dressed as Dad would kill me if I didn't go to school. I put on a dress for school, luckily we don't have a uniform. Uniform sucks. I look at myself in the mirror, I hate what I see. I brush my long wavy black hair, trying to get it under control. I get serious bed hair, this will have to do. I'm so nervous to start a new school.

"Emmie, are you ready? You'll be late." Urgh, my Dad is so annoying.

"Coming Daddy!" I yell, annoyed. I grab my school bag and run downstairs. Danny, my brother, is waiting for me.

"Hey sis, how are you today?" he says with a huge grin on his face. I love my brother, he never fails to put a smile on my face.

"Oh bro, it's such a lovely day. Did you know the sun's out? I want to feel the sun on my face." Danny laughs at me, he does that a lot.

"You and the sun, I will never understand your fascination with the sun."

Dad enters the living room, he smiles and kisses me on the cheek.

"Have a good day at school princess."

Dad and I have a love-hate relationship, I hate him and he loves me. You might be wondering where my Momma is. Yeah, she left me when I was 8, I'm now 18. Dad says that she didn't love me anymore, so she left me. I ache for her every day, I love my Momma. But she obviously doesn't love me. I dream that one day she will come back for me. Free me from this painful life.

"Emmie, are you daydreaming again?"

"Huh, what?" I'm confused, I guess they were talking to me.

"I said do you want a lift to school. I'm leaving for work."

I don't want to be seen with my Brother on the first day of school. That would be embarrassing. "Thanks, bro, but I'll walk. I want to walk in the sun."

"Fine, I'll see you later sis. Have a good day." He kisses me on the cheek and leaves.

I don't like being left here with Dad, so I make an excuse to leave. "Daddy I'm going to be late. I'll see you later." I turn for the door.

"Ahem, where is my hug and kiss?"

He strides up to me and hugs me tight. I feel awkward when he hugs me. I quickly peck him on the cheek and I make a run for school. I am definitely going to be late now. The school isn't far, about a 20-minute walk. I like to walk, it helps me clear my head.

I finally get to school, the halls are busy. I take a look around, I can identify the usual crowd. The smart geeky ones, the popular ones, the bad boys. It's the same where ever you go. You get the bullies and the victims. People are so cruel sometimes.

"Hey, I'm Jade. Queen Bee. You must be new."

"Err yeah, I'm Emmie." I hate meeting new people, they always look down their noses at me.

"Well Emmie, as long as you don't get in my way, you'll be fine."

Jade walks off. She has long blonde perfect hair, she's beautiful, a complete opposite to me. She wears tight clothes that show off her flattering figure. She has two little minions that follow her around. Behind every bully is back up, they're too scared to walk around alone.

I go to class and I only see one seat free, I gingerly walk to the seat. "Hi, do you mind if I sit here?" The pretty, friendly looking girl looks up and smiles.

"Sure, I'm Jessie." She has lovely natural black hair. She's skinny, unlike me. I take a seat.

"Thanks, I'm Emmie." My first lesson is maths. I love maths, it's my strongest subject. The teacher clears his throat.

"Class, settle down," he says with an irritated voice. "We have a new student that's joined us at Lady Elizabeth. Please make her feel welcome."

He glances at me and gives me a friendly smile. Damn, he's hot for a teacher. He has a little button nose, blue eyes and messy blonde hair. I bite my lip.

"Her name is Emmie Salvatore, Emmie would you come up please?"

Oh no, really? It can't get any more awkward. I stand up and walk gracefully to the front. All eyes are on me.

"Hello beautiful," says one of the guys.

I roll my eyes, I get this wherever I go. All the guys flirt with me. They never get the hint. I don't see why they bother.

"Thanks Emmie, take a seat." He gestures for me to sit down. I walk back to my seat, all eyes are still on me.

"Hey Emmie, I'm Brody." I look around next to me on the next table. I have to admit he was pretty damn hot. He has spiky black hair with blue eyes. I just melt at the sight of him. He winks at me. Boys, they are only out to get one thing.

"This is my school, I run it. If you need anything then I can help."

"Dude you're desperate," says the pretty blonde guy next to him. Must be a friend of his.

"Shut up," he says disappointingly.

I need to put him in his place, I'm not interested.

"In your dreams," I said confidently.

"Haha you got burned man," the blonde guy says whilst laughing. Brody looks pissed, he glares at him. He looks offended. I imagine he doesn't often get rejected.

"Shut up you idiot."

Boys and their testosterone. The class flew by, Brody was quiet during the rest of the lesson, but something tells me I haven't heard the end of him.

"Emmie, it's lunch, would you like me to show you around?" Jessie is so sweet. I have a feeling we are going to be great friends.

"Sure, thanks, Jessie." We get up from our seats and I follow her to the cafeteria. I have to admit I was really hungry.

"I'll go get some food, would you like anything in particular?"

"I'm not fussy as long as it's vegetarian. Thanks." She looks at me with a smirk on her face.

"You're a veggie?" People don't understand me being vegetarian. I shrug.

"Yeah, I am." She laughs, and nods and heads to the line.

I see Brody enter the cafeteria, I see him scanning the room, our eyes meet and he gives me a big sexy smile. Oh great, now he is walking over.

"Hey Emmie, I'm sorry about earlier. I wanted to apologise. Can we start over?" Did I not make myself clear before?

"I know guys like you. You go around flirting with all the girls. Getting as many as you can. You're trying to add me to your trophies, am I right? But hey, just a heads up. It's not going to work." The look on his face was as if he just accepted the challenge.

"A guy can try." I roll my eyes at him.

"I guess I'll have fun watching you try."

Jessie walks up behind me. The food smells great. "What do you want?" I can tell Jessie doesn't like Brody. I can't say I blame her, he's an ass.

"Nice to see you too. I was just apologising to Emmie about earlier." Jessie burst out into laughter.

"You don't do apologies." He looks a little offended.

"I will succeed, you will want me eventually." And with that, he walks off.

"I got you a pizza, I hope that's good." I love pizza.

"Pizza is great, thank you."

"Brody is the school's biggest douche bag. He thinks he's god's gift to women. Every girl is head over heels for him." I've seen people like him often enough.

"Yeah, I've seen a lot of people like that. He looks like a tool." Jessie giggles.

"I like you, Emmie, I think we are going to get on very well."

"Yeah, I think so too."

We chatted all of lunch whilst eating our food. It felt good to find a friend. I didn't have many in my old school. The bell rang for class.

Jessie tells me she doesn't have the same lesson as me next. Kinda sucks to go into class alone. I take a seat, I have the same teacher, I guess that's something. He is very easy on the eyes. I look at the door and Brody strides in. His friend calls him to sit next to him but he ignores him and comes over to the empty chair next to me.

He winks at me, "Hey beautiful." I roll my eyes at him.

"That seat is taken," I lie.

"Ouch, that hurts. Anyway, it's taken by me." So with that, he takes a seat.

"Moron."

"Emmie, I really would like to be friends."

Is he serious? "You have done nothing to make me want to be friends with you."

"Well let me try to get to know you?" He looks at me, pleading me with those dreamy eyes.

"You can't…"

"Miss Salvatore, you have been here 5 minutes and you are already disrupting my class," the teacher says, interrupting me. How rude.

"Not her fault you are boring." Did he really just say that? He looks very smug. Mr Dudley shoots him a glare.

"Mr Rivers, enough of your big mouth." I have to say, Mr Dudley is so hot.

"He's such a loser," he scowls.

"Whatever. Sure."

"What were you going to say before he interrupted you?" he says with a cheeky grin.

"Did you not hear him, he said be quiet?" He is so frustrating.

"Does it look like I care?" No, it doesn't, but it should.

"Obviously not…"

"Right, I've had enough of you two. Principal's office now!" He screams. Wow, he gets angry quickly. I can't believe Brody got me into trouble. Dad's going to kill me if he finds out.

"Alright, don't get your damn knickers in a twist." Brody looks shocked at what came out of my mouth. He looks impressed.

"How dare you speak to me like that?" he looks very mad. He crosses his arms in annoyance.

"I dare because I don't care," I say with a sarcastic voice.

"Wow girl you have balls, I love that in a woman." He eyes me up.

"Get out of my class now!" Oops, I guess I offended him. We walk to the principal's office. We don't say a word, I'm still mad at him for getting me into trouble.

Brody knocks on the door. And there was a husky voice. "Come in."

Brody took the lead, it looked like he was very familiar with going to the principal. I stand awkwardly next to Brody. The principal has long shaggy blonde hair, he is quite old, maybe 50 odd. Well, it's not old but he definitely hasn't aged well. He looks mean and strict.

"Mr Rivers, why am I not surprised you are in here? And Miss Salvatore, your first day and you're already in trouble." He looks disappointed.

"I just thought I'd let myself be known."

"You have a mouth on you," he says sternly.

Brody looks uncomfortable, like he can't believe what he is hearing. "Well, you are both receiving detention after school. 3.30pm."

Yeah, I don't think so. I have plans," I scoff.

"Well unmake them. I'm serious." He crossed his arms, trying to intimidate me.

"Anything for you sir." I give him a wink. He looks put off, awkward even. Emmie 1- Principal 0. Go me.

"I have a feeling you are going to be a handful, Miss Salvatore. I will be contacting your Dad."

I know my Dad will be pissed. But I will deal with that later. "Well, tell him I said *Hi*, will you?"

Brody and the principal's mouth drops open. Was it something I said? I giggle and walk out of the office. Brody Isn't far behind me. I enter the hallway where Brody's friends gather. The blonde dude is there. And another guy with dreads.

"Hey new girl, I heard what happened in class, you are a total badass."

What is it with these guys and flirting with me? What had gotten into me today? I'm never this bad. Because I know the consequences. "Sure, whatever."

"See you around hot stuff." Brody and his friends wander off. Jade walks towards me she looks angry. Drama, I don't do drama. Bloody girls, they are so emotional.

"Stay away from Brody. He's mine. If I didn't make myself clear earlier, I'm queen bee. Everyone knows Brody is mine."

"Aren't you full of yourself? You must feel very insecure if you're threatening me. I'm not interested in Brody. But your man keeps chasing me. I guess you're not woman enough for him." Her mouth drops open. I can tell I've just added fuel to the fire. Oops.

"You bitch, how dare you speak to me like that?!" Someone is having a paddy. I giggle.

"No queen Bee tells me what to do. Why don't you get your head out your ass?"

One of her minions pipes up. "I like her, she has courage."

"Milly, stop admiring the new girl before I tell everyone you are gay."

She made Milly look really uncomfortable. She's such a bully. "Nothing wrong with being gay Milly." I give her a reassuring smile. She smiles awkwardly back.

"Of course there is, everyone will make fun of her," she scoffs.

"No they won't, it's the 21st century." She stamps her foot on the ground. Childish much?

"I hate you. Come on Milly." They storm off. She's such a drama queen.

"Hey, girl you're on fire today." I turn around to see Jessie. She seems excited.

I giggle, "It's a gift." We both laugh together. We go to class. I'm advanced compared to most people. So, I don't need to pay much attention.

It was soon the end of the day. Detention, the word in itself is the devil. I make my way to detention. I take a seat. Brody follows shortly behind me. Of course, he sits next to me. How stupid could I be? "What's your favourite colour?"

"Shut up."

"Colour?" he says imploringly.

Fine. "Pink."

He smiles like he has achieved something.

"What's your hobby?"

"Horse Riding."

"Wow, horse girl, nice. What's your favourite thing?"

"The sun." He continued to badger me with questions. I guess he's not so bad. He seems genuinely interested in getting to know me. "So are you finished asking questions? It's only fair you return them."

He looks disappointed. "Fine, blue, sleeping with girls and smoking."

Seriously? Is this all I get to go on? "Really? I already knew most of that." He shrugs. The bell rings.

"Great, time to go. See you tomorrow beautiful." He winks and walks out of class.

I guess it's time to face the music at home. He's going to be so angry. I walk slowly home. I wonder what mood he will be in. I walk through the door and I see him standing there with his arms crossed. He glares at me. Great, unreasonable Dad, here I come. "What the hell have you been up to Emmie?"

"Oh you know, I've been in the sun soaking up the rays." And now I've put my foot in it. Why do I have to test him?

"Don't give me that crap Emmie. The Principal phoned, he told me everything!"

"Why did you ask if you already knew?"

His face turned deadly. "You are in so much trouble, Emmie. Get to your room, I will deal with you later."

Oh shit. As he said those words I knew I was getting it bad tonight. "I'm sorry Daddy," I say terrified.

"Get to your room now." I know he is serious. So I ran to my room. I know what was waiting for me when he came up to my room.

Morning comes too soon. The sun is peeping through the curtains. I don't do mornings, I'm very grumpy in the morning. I groan, my body aches today. I'd better get up, Dad will kill me if I'm late for school. I roll my eyes at the thought of school. After yesterday's fiasco, I hope it's not the same today. But somehow, I know it won't be true. Seeing all the guys all over me makes me sick. My phone beeps, I pick it up from the bedside table. I don't recognise the number. I open the text.

Good morning Beautiful. Brody.

He better not turn out to be a stalker, how the hell did he get my number? I know I agreed to let him try, but he seriously has no chance. I'm not interested in a relationship right now. My life is too complicated as it is. I get dressed and brush my unruly hair. I drag my feet downstairs. I hope Dad is in a better mood today. He was so angry. Danny is waiting for me in the hallway again. He smiles at me, I love him.

"Hey sis, you okay? You don't look yourself?" Perceptive, isn't he?

I don't feel myself but I shouldn't have misbehaved. I'm not going to blame anyone but myself. "Hey, Bro, I'm okay," I say half-heartedly.

"Are you sure?" Oh, here comes the brotherly concern, if only he knew.

"Yes, I'm fine. Jeez." I love how protective he is but it gets annoying. I know he doesn't believe me, but he chooses to let it slide.

"Okay, I'm off to work. See you later." He kisses me on the cheek and off he goes. About time I make my exits before Dad comes. Oh shit, too late, here he comes.

"Hey princess," he says with a smile on his face. He seems extra happy today.

"Hey, Daddy." I look at the floor rather than look at him.

"Have you learnt your lesson?"

Why did he bring it up, he knows that I have? But he likes to rub it in. "Yes," I say awkwardly.

"Yes what?" he says sternly.

"Yes, Daddy." He insists I call him Daddy, I don't know why.

"Good, but I like disciplining you. It's fun," he says and I know he is picturing last night.

He enjoys punishing me. I frown at the thought. I need to get out of here. "Bye Daddy." I quickly peck him on the cheek and leave.

The walk to school did me some good. The sun is my therapy, helps me clear my mind. I get to school in time. I see Brody and his friends in the hallway, I look at the floor trying not to be noticed. But it didn't work, I saw them all gawk at me. Brody winks at me and makes his way over to me.

"Hey beautiful, did you get my text?" He is such a stalker but a cute one.

"Yes, how did you get my number. Are you a stalker?" I say irritated.

He chuckles. "Only with you beautiful."

Wow, if this is how he picks up girls then I'm disappointed. "What a cheesy line."

He seems to shrug it off. "So, I've got a party tonight. Will you come?" he looks hopeful.

I haven't been invited to a party in a long time. "A party, sound great. Can I invite Jessie?"

"I suppose, see you at 7 pm beautiful, I'll text you the address." He looks pleased with himself. And he wanders off.

I walk to the classroom and see Jessie at her seat. She looks up at me and waves, she's also happy. Everyone is happy but me. Oh well, I take a seat next to her. "So guess what?" I say teasingly.

She looks at me genuinely interested in what I had to say. "Spill..." she says impatiently.

"We are going to a party tonight."

"Whose party?" she looks confused.

Second day and I bag us a party. "Brody's," I say casually. She looks shocked.

"Omg, Brody is lame, his parties, however, are not!" She looks like she's going to explode with excitement. I giggle at her.

"How did you get an invite, his parties are very exclusive?"

"Oh you know, being the hot new girl has its perks." We both giggle.

"Full of yourself today, aren't we?"

"We better take notes before we get in trouble." She laughs.

"God friend, getting me in trouble."

And that's what we did. We took notes and concentrated for the rest of the lesson. It's my second day and I feel like I've known Jessie a long time.

"Hey Emmie, I noticed some bruises on you. You okay?" Jessie says with a concerned voice.

"Yeah, course I am. I'm just clumsy, that's all." I lie. I hope she believed me.

The day dragged on and it was finally time for Brody's party. I put on a tight black dress with heels. I tie my long wavy hair up and apply some makeup. My phone vibrates, so I read the text.

Hey beautiful, look forward to seeing you tonight. Brody.

Will he never give up and get the hint? His texts are really sweet. I'm meeting Jessie at the address so I make my way there. I can't wait to let my hair down.

I arrive at the address, maybe heels weren't a good idea. I may have to get Danny to pick me up later. Wow, this house is huge and very posh. I see Jessie waiting at the front gates for me. She waves, we head to the front door together. She looks amazing, her straight hair falling down her shoulders. She's wearing a really sexy looking short red dress. Guys will be falling for her tonight. We were shown to the entertainment room, there is a pool table in the middle of the room. There are loads of people here, some I recognised, some I don't.

Some people are already drunk.

"I'm getting us some drinks."

"Thanks, Jessie." She heads off to the bar where all the drinks are. I catch Brody's eye and he strides over. He looks hot tonight, he's wearing a white shirt with black jeans. The white brings out his blue eyes. He has the top few buttons undone so you can see his chest. I think he catches me staring because he smirks at me.

"Hey Beautiful, you look amazing." He eyes me up from head to toe, obvious much. "I'm glad you came."

"Me too, I love parties," I say because it's the truth.

"My kind of woman." He winks at me. He has a way of affecting me, why?

"You don't get the hint, do you?"

"I won't give up trying. I'll catch you later for a dance beautiful."

He wanders back to his friends. Why do I feel myself falling for him? I told myself I wasn't interested. But he is everywhere. And I honestly love it. Jessie comes back with drinks, I don't know what she got us but boy is it strong. We have drink after drink, and we let loose on the dance floor.

"Brody is staring at you."

I look around at him, I have to say I've drunk so much that I am more confident. He is looking at me so I give him a cheeky grin and wink at him. Why am I flirting with him, I'm not interested? I can see him laughing, he looks like again he's just achieved something. Maybe he did.

"Want to send him wild bestie?" She is just as tipsy as I am but I can't help but play this game with her.

"Absolutely," I say with a huge smile. She grabs my face and pulls me in for a kiss. So this is what she meant? I play along and kiss her back, I look over at Brody who's gobsmacked. I feel a sense of an achievement too. In fact, all the guys are staring with their mouths wide open. Brody looks slightly pissed actually, is he jealous?

"Did you see their faces?" she says whilst giggling.

"I did, it was priceless." We carried on dancing the night away.

I feel really drunk, Brody walks up to us. He is so handsome.

"Hey Emmie, could I speak to you in private?" he says.

"No she can't, she's dancing with me," Jessie says annoyed.

We were having a lot of fun together.

"You're hot." I can't believe I just said that. Oops.

"And you're drunk," he says laughing.

"And? It's a party isn't it?" I giggle. I really am drunk.

"Will you take a walk with me in the fresh air?" he sounds hopeful.

I can't resist him right now. "Anything for you sexy." I wink at him.

"I love it when you're drunk, come on," he chuckles. And so I did, I followed him to the roof.

It is beautiful up here. There are pretty pink flowers growing up the vines. The smell is delicious. If he was trying to be romantic, he definitely succeeded. The fresh air helps me think more clearly. But I am still mesmerised by his beauty. The moonlight makes him look mysterious. "Wow, this is beautiful Brody," I say in awe.

"Beautiful like you," he says with a smile. And before I knew what he was doing he kisses me. This was new for me, he sent pulses down my spine. I completely surrender to him. In this moment, he could have me if he wanted.

"Let me take you to bed," he begs. I knew he felt what I did. I nod, he takes my hand and takes me to his bedroom.

I want this, I do. He starts taking my clothes off exposing my skin, I tense up. I couldn't have him see my body. I disgust me, I'm not ready. "I'm sorry, I can't do this." I truly am sorry, I want to for him.

"Okay but it feels right though? Because it does for me?" he says worriedly.

It does feel right, but I can't. "Yes it does, but I can't, I'm sorry." I hope he will forgive me. He gives me a smile as if to reassure me.

"Are you a virgin? Because if you are it's totally cool." He is being really understanding, maybe he isn't as bad as I thought. The alcohol is making my head fuzzy. This just makes me feel more awkward him asking me this.

I feel so exposed standing here in my underwear with him. "No I'm not a virgin, but I wish I was." I sigh. He takes a step back and starts to eye me up and down. He frowns, he obviously doesn't like what he sees. I feel awkward under his stare even with alcohol in my system.

"Emmie, has someone hurt you? These bruises are really bad."

I shake my head. I have to get out of here.

"I can protect you if someone is hurting you."

And I believe he would try but he wouldn't succeed. "No, you can't, no one can. I have to go." I grab my clothes and flee the room. I am pulling my clothes on as I run out. I'm so embarrassed. I run home and went straight to my room. Looks like everyone is asleep, I'm going to have a hell of a hangover in the morning. That night like most nights, I cry myself to sleep.

Chapter 2

I am mortified at how I acted at Brody's party, I don't get that far with guys. Not because I can't, rather because I don't like to get that attached. I drank way too much. I've stayed in bed all weekend, and as you can imagine Danny has been fussing. Over protective Brother gone overboard. He knows something happened at the party, but he respects my privacy. Brody and Jessie have been texting me all weekend asking if I am okay. I totally bailed on Jessie, she should be pissed at me, but she's not, she's concerned. I've been alone in my own little bubble for so long I don't know how to let anyone in. I've ignored them, I can't deal with them right now. I'm slowly falling deeper into the dark deep black hole. All alone.

Monday morning came too soon, I can't face seeing Brody so I'm going to stay here. I can't gather the energy to get up. Someone knocks at the door. Danny comes in, and he frowns at me. He knows I've been crying. "How are you feeling today Sis?" he says with concern in his voice.

"I'm not feeling well at all Bro." He comes to sit on the bed next to me where I lay.

"Shall I tell Dad to ring the school for you?" I know he is dying for me to open up to him. But I can't, it's just been myself and my thoughts for so long.

"Yes please, bro. Tell him not to disturb me either."

"Okay sis, but you know if you want to talk I'm here," he sighs.

"I know, thanks Bro." I give him a reassuring smile. He kisses me on the forehead and leaves for work. The day drifted by, I laid in bed watching the day go past with the sun on my face. I don't know if I can ever get out of bed. This is one of my low days, I get them sometimes when life builds up on me. Danny gets so worried, I don't like to see him so hurt. But I can't help him right now, not when I can't help myself. My phone goes off, and I pick it up to read the text. It's probably Brody or Jessie asking where I was. I couldn't believe what I was reading on this screen. I must have been added to a group message.

Emmie is a slut who will sleep with anyone. She is so desperate. From Queen Bee.

Argh, I hate that girl, I need to put her in her place once and for all. Who spread this around? I can't imagine Brody would do this, but how well do I know him really?

My life couldn't get any worse right now. There's a knock at my bedroom door. "Go away," I shout. I don't want my Dad coming in.

"We are coming in whether you like it or not."

We? Who is we? I know that voice was Brody's, why the hell is he here? And that's what they do, they walk in. I cross my arms to show how pissed I am.

"Hey friend, how are you?"

She's pushing for something, just beating around the bush. "I'm fine, I'm just ill." I lie. I don't like lying to my friends but again I'm not ready to open up to them.

"That's bull and you know it. We've been worried about you." He seems angry but I know he is genuinely worried. His concern catches me off guard. Why would he be worried about me? We hardly know each other.

"Brody says he saw bruises on your body, I noticed some too. Can you explain them?" What is it to them?

No, I can't. He will hear, they need to be quiet. "Shh be quiet," I say worriedly. They look confused.

"Why?" he says with his arms crossed. I know they won't leave without an answer. All this pressure from people, it's too much.

I jump out of bed, I feel exposed again in my PJs. "He will hear you. I can't talk now."

"Well will you take a walk with us?" he says softly.

Now he's definitely going to know something is up. "No, you need to leave now," I say angrily. They need to get as far away from me as they can.

"Either you come with us or we stay here. Your choice." He is not going to take no for an answer.

I just need them out of my house. So I agree to go with them. "Fine, but I need to get dressed. Wait for me outside." He looks at me with those dreamy blue eyes.

"I like you in your PJs." Is he flirting with me now? God, men! I'm panicking and he is flirting.

"Get out, meet me outside," I say sternly.

"Are you sure I can't tempt you to stay." He winks at me. He truly is irresistible.

"Get out Brody." I roll my eyes at him.

"See you in a minute beautiful."

And they leave. He is so annoying yet dreamy. I throw on some clothes. I need them away from my house. I run outside. They are waiting outside of my house. "I can't talk here, where do you want to go?" I'm still new to the area.

"Let's go to the coffee shop," Jessie says reassuringly.

So we walk to the coffee shop. It isn't far, I feel more relaxed when away from the house. I have no intention of telling them anything. But having coffee with friends is maybe just what I need. We take a seat by the window, I feel safer when I can see the sun.

"Emmie, what do you want to drink?" Jessie asks.

"A caramel latte please friend." She is just like a sister to me, one I never had. Although we haven't known each other long we seem at ease with each other.

"Brody?" I can tell she doesn't like him but is being polite for me.

"I'll have what Emmie is having, thanks." So she goes and orders the drinks.

"Please Emmie, I can help you. Just tell me who is hurting you." He looks so concerned. He grabs my hand on the table and I pull away.

Why does he care so much? We hardly know each other. "No, you can't help me, just drop it," I say angrily. I stare out the window, wishing someone would take me away from this life. Everyone looks so happy walking down the street or driving their cars.

"No I won't drop it Emmie." He is irritated at my stubbornness.

Jessie comes back with our drinks and takes a seat. I feel like I'm being questioned by the police. I roll my eyes at them.

"Emmie, can I get you some food?" Jessie says.

"No thanks."

"Have you eaten anything?" Brody asks.

He is getting on my nerves. It's none of his business. Only mine. Why is he pushing me? "Why do you care so much? You're not my boyfriend. I get enough of this crap from my brother." I look into his blue eyes, he is hurt by my words. And for the first time, I feel hurt by his eyes. Why do I care about his feelings?

"Emmie stop pushing me away. Please," he begs. I push everyone away, it's what I do.

I know I have to tell him now. My heart is aching to tell him, what is he doing to me? "Fine, but you can't repeat it," I say awkwardly. How do I put it into words? They both nod, reassuring me to continue. "It's my Dad," I say, covering my eyes. I'm ashamed of what I'm going to say. Jessie looks confused

"What about your Dad?" she says.

I take a deep breath. "He did this to me." Tears start falling down my face. Do I feel relieved? Or do I feel repulsed? I don't know. They both look at me with pure disgust. They don't believe me. I feel I need to explain more as the silence is killing me. "He gave me the bruises, because of my attitude with the principal." I shrug. I'm used to it, I know I should be good.

"Emmie, I'm sorry. I feel so bad. I got you into trouble." Brody seems so sad.

"Brody this isn't your fault, it was just a matter of time before he found an excuse to do this." He gets kicks out of it. I can see it on his face.

"So he hits you?" Jessie says shocked.

I got this far, I should tell them the rest. "Yes, and more, he has hurt me really bad in the past. He's a doctor, he knows what he is doing." I shrug. I guess it isn't so bad, he is my Dad and I love him.

"What do you mean and more Emmie? Hang on. You said the other night that you wish you were a virgin. Don't tell me he...?" he looks so angry.

But I'm used to it, this is the life I was given. I learned to live with it a long time ago. "Are you serious?" Jessie says shocked.

I wish I wasn't but it is what it is. "I shouldn't have told you. I don't expect you to believe me. Anyway, it's my fault for misbehaving." It's true, if I didn't misbehave then it wouldn't happen. He's my Dad though, he hasn't left me. He is my constant.

"Emmie, this is not your fault. He makes me so sick. He is disgusting. Just wait till I get my hands on him."

"Brody no, please. Calm down." I say, scared. I don't want them hurting each other.

He takes a deep breath, "You are not going back there." I wish that were true.

"He's my guardian Brody, a well-respected Doctor. There are no medical reports because he always nursed me at home. No one will believe me."

"Fine, but you are staying with me. Until I get this sorted." There is nothing to sort, this is my life.

"Brody there is nothing you can do, I didn't tell you for you to do something." He looks at me like he doesn't believe what I just said.

"Let's go to my house," he says.

"I will see you at school Emmie." Jessie hugs me and she leaves. I hate to be hugged so I just stand awkwardly while she hugs me.

Brody and I walk in silence back to his house. I am exhausted. His bedroom is your typical teenage boy bedroom. His theme is red. Double bed with red sheets, a desk looking out the window.

"I will take the floor Emmie, you take my bed."

How sweet of him. But the truth is, after what happened today I just want to be held. "No, please share the bed with me."

He smirks at me. "Anything for you beautiful."

I love the way beautiful rolls off his tongue. I've never had someone affect me the way Brody does. I have had my walls up for so long, I don't know how to let it down. We get into bed and I have my back to him. He snuggles up behind me and puts his arm around me. I love being in his arms. I don't feel completely comfortable with him touching me but it makes me feel better. I fall straight to sleep, no crying tonight, which is rare. I wonder what tomorrow will bring.

I wake in Brody's arms. I feel warm, maybe too warm but I feel comfy in his arms. It feels strange to me, alien. Should I be letting him so close?

"Good morning beautiful. I could get used to waking up to you."

I have to admit, I could too. "Strangely me too, even if you are a moron." I turn around to face him. He strokes my face.

"How are you feeling today?"

I am terrified, I know my Dad would come for me. "Scared," I admit. He kisses me gently on the lips. They are so soft, who knew he could be so gentle and caring?

"Don't worry, I'll protect you. You're safe with me."

His words soothe me, I know they aren't true but it feels good to have someone on my side. "I need to tell my Brother today, it's time he knew. He will be freaking out right now."

"Do you want me to come with you?"

"No, I need to do it on my own," I say. I get up and get dressed. My little safe haven was now gone, and I have to face the world. It was something I did every day. Why should this be any different? He comes up behind me and hugs me tight. Mhmm, this feels good.

"We need to go to school."

He sighs and gets dressed too. "It will be okay beautiful."

If only he knew what my Dad was capable of. I just hope Brody doesn't get caught in the crossfire. "I will be down in a minute." He nods and heads out the door. I need to write a letter to my Momma.

'Dear Momma, I know that you will never read this. But it helps me to write to you. I miss you so much. Life has gotten very hard, Dad still hurts me. I hate that you left me. I need you, if you were to come back...I would forgive you for leaving me. But I know you won't, I'm not worthy of you. I made you leave... I know that. Doesn't stop me loving you. Love your Daughter x'

I put the letter in my pocket and head to find Brody. He is leaning up against the breakfast table. He looks mighty fine as usual, he catches me staring and smirks. How does he do this to me? We head to school together. We find Brody's friends in the car park. The blonde one winks at me.

"Hey, new girl you're looking smokin' today." He takes a puff of his cigarette. How he is wrong, I haven't even done anything to look reasonable today.

"Can I have one?" I ask.

"You smoke?" Brody says shocked.

"No, but I want one." I shrug.

"Here, have one of mine new girl." I take one from him and light up.

"Honestly, my name is Emmie." I roll my eyes at him. I don't want any special treatment, I'm just plain old Emmie.

"I know that, but new girl is better," he shrugs. Why is it?

Brody looks at me, "You know you are turning out to be my type of girl in every turn." He's flirting again and I don't mind, he is growing on me. There could be something between Brody and I in time. I will need time and patience though.

"Get a room you two."

Brody laughs, "We already did."

I can't believe he said that, when I say he is growing on me what I meant was that he's a Moron. "Brody!" Why would he say that? I know he is just joking around with his friends but I'm not that kind of girl.

"I don't blame you mate, I'd have some if I got the chance." He winks at me.

Men, who would have them? "Hello, I am here you know and anyway you wouldn't be so lucky."

Brody smirks. "I love your mouth, let's get to class."

I sit next to Jessie today. I told her about last night, how nice Brody was. She never expected that from him. Apparently, he is a player and doesn't settle for any girls. I feel special in a way. The teacher tells us all to be quiet and to settle down. She is older than the first one. Meaner, harsher even. My stomach drops as I hear the tannoy system.

"This is your principal speaking, Miss Salvatore can you see me in my office?"

I'm freaking out, I know my Dad has come to take me home. I look nervously at Brody who also seems worried. "You heard him, Miss Salvatore, off you go." She sounds pissed.

"Do you want me to go with you?" Brody says reassuringly.

"No, I'd better go on my own," I say. It will be better if I'm on my own.

I make my way down the hall dreading what will happen next, my heart is pounding. My palms are sweaty. Man up Emmie, you've been through this before, you'll be fine. I take a deep breath and knock the door.

"Come in," he says.

I walk in, and I see Dad. He looks mega mad. I am in big trouble. My face drops, I look at the floor and walk over to them.

"Your dad is here. I hear you've been having problems at home. He has come to talk to you. Very irresponsible to stay out all night. At the very least you should have contacted him," he says sternly. I have to fight my corner. Problems at home? That's an understatement.

"Please Daddy, don't do this. Not now," I beg him, scared.

"I'm so disappointed in you Emmie." He's angry. Tears fall down my face. Of course he is disappointed, I disappoint everyone. I ruin everything.

"I'm sorry Daddy." I know nothing I say will help.

"It's so not good enough." His words send shivers down my spine.

Someone barges through the door. I can't see with the tears in my eyes. But as soon as their arms were around me, I know it is Brody. I don't know whether I'm relieved or sad, he could make this worse.

"I want you home now!" he shouts.

I feel Brody's grip get tighter. "She's not going anywhere with you." Brody is mad too. Brody has no chance against my Dad. But I feel comforted by him being here. I am very conscious and sensitive about where Brody touches me.

"Mr Rivers how dare you barge in here. This is private." The principal sounds mad too. Everyone is mad.

"Who the hell are you? How dare you speak to me like that. I'm her Dad, she will go where ever I tell her to."

"Brody please," I beg him to keep quiet.

"I'm Emmie's boyfriend, I know what you do to her, you sick pig." I can't believe he said that. He said boyfriend, he's not but it's not such a bad idea. Dad looks pissed. Dad is definitely going to retaliate at this.

"Emmie isn't allowed boyfriends, she knows this..."

It's true, he always forbid me to have boyfriends. Quite frankly I never wanted one. I couldn't handle being that close to someone. I meet Dad's gaze, it is cold and icy. It cuts right through me. I am terrified.

"Mr Rivers, what are you talking about?" he asks questioningly.

"Brody, don't." You'll make things worse. But of course, he doesn't keep his mouth shut.

"He has been abusing Emmie." The principal looks shocked, in disbelief. He doesn't believe him, why would he?

"Don't be so ridiculous, Mr Salvatore is one of the most respected Doctors," he scoffs.

"As the principal, it is your job to investigate any complaints that arise," Brody demands.

The principal takes a deep breath. "Emmie, do you have anything to say?" he demands. I am speechless. What could I possibly say? Brody stands in front of me and hugs me tight. He steps back and strokes my cheek. He lifts my chin so I look at him.

"Get your hands off my daughter," Dad screams.

"You're safe, beautiful. Trust me."

I look into his eyes. I do trust him but why? I take a deep breath. "I'm sorry Daddy. It's true." The principal gasps.

"Can you prove this Miss Salvatore?" he asks.

I have no proof and Dad knows it. "I guess not," I say looking back at the floor. I wish someone would just take me away.

"See, they're just lies," Dad says with his arms crossed. Brody looks at me.

"Show him the bruises."

I can't do that. No. "I can't Brody." I don't like showing people my body.

"What bruises?" Brody nods at me with encouragement. How does he do this to me?

I take my t-shirt off. Underneath are black and purple bruises around my stomach. I've had worse but they are there. I stand awkwardly in my bra, I can't look at anyone. I just stare at the floor. I feel disgusted with myself.

"Wow, I don't know what to say..." he says, shocked. I guess he believes me now.

"That wasn't me," Dad says defensively.

"I have to pass this on to the police Mr Salvatore. I can't keep this to myself. The evidence is there," he says.

"That's if they catch me."

Dad turns on his heels and makes a hasty escape. "Daddy, where are you going?" He left me. He said he would never leave me. I guess I pushed him too far this time. I'm not worthy of him staying.

"I hope the police catch him quick before I do," Brody snaps.

"I'm sorry I didn't believe you, Miss Salvatore. I can't believe someone would do that," he says apologetically.

"It's okay, I never expected anyone to believe me. I don't let anyone in." Brody puts his hand in mine.

"You're safe beautiful."

And I do feel safe, even though Dad is on the run. "I need to speak to my brother. I need to be the one to tell him." I put my T-shirt back on to cover my fat.

"Take the rest of the day off Emmie," he says reassuringly. We walk out of his office. I feel a sense of relief.

"I'll be back in a minute." He kisses me on the forehead and walks off.

Oh great, I see Jade in front of me. This is all I need, she looks angry. Why is everyone angry today?

"Here comes the desperate slut," she calls.

"Go away. You may call yourself the queen bee. But you're last year's news. Bitch I'm the new girl every wants." This girl needs putting in her place and I'm going to do it.

"You bitch, how dare you?" she screams.

She slaps me on the face. I laugh so hard. "Haha, only little girls slap." She looks so mad. I'm definitely pushing buttons. I punch her hard in the face. She looks like she's going to cry. Crowds start gathering around us. They are all chanting, "Fight." Most people are saying, "Go, new girl." She throws a punch. It was pathetic. I hear Jessie call in my favour. I punch her again, hard. Before I know it, Brody is behind me.

"Guys stop."

I threw one more punch and she falls to the ground. The crowd cheers. "You did good beautiful, but we have to go." He looks pleased that I put her in her place. It feels good to let my emotions out.

We walk to the local cafe shop in town. Brody places his hand in mine, it feels different but good. I decide to call Danny on the way. He sounds worried on the phone but that is probably because I sound off. He will be along shortly.

"You'll be fine," Brody says, I guess he knows I'm worried.

We take a seat at the window. I can't handle this waiting. The door opens, I look up and Danny strides in. Concern floods his faces. He strides over and takes a seat. My heart is pounding. I don't want to lose my brother.

"Be the strong girl I know you are, I will be over there if you need me." He kisses me on the forehead again. I love it when he does that. I nod and he strolls off. How would he know? I'm not strong.

"Who was that? Was that your boyfriend? You've never had one of

23

them?" He seems shocked but also happy. Here comes the overbearing brother.

"He's not my boyfriend but I do like him. But that's not what I wanted to speak to you about." I take a deep breath. He is the hardest to tell. I love my brother, but he will be pissed that he didn't know.

"Is everything okay?"

"No, it's not. But don't hate me." I can't lose him.

"I could never hate you, sis. What is it?" he looks really worried. I look at my hands on the table.

"It's Dad." Is all I manage to say. Come on Emmie.

"Is he okay?"

"Yes, he's fine."

"Then what is it?" he looks confused.

"You know when I used to get bruised or break bones, and Dad used to say I was clumsy and fell over?"

He nods. "Yes but I never believed it."

It is now or never. I look into my brother's eyes. Be strong Emmie. "He's been abusing me, Danny."

Chapter 3

Danny sits there staring at me, rage is building inside of him. Is he angry at me? I look at my hands on the table. I glance over Danny's shoulder to see Brody watching, the sight of him gives me the confidence. He smiles at me. How does he affect me so much?

"Emmie, what do you mean he abuses you?" Danny says angrily.

"I'm sorry, Danny." This is so hard.

"Mentally, physically and..." I can't say it. The words won't come out of my mouth. Tears start to stream down my face.

"And what Emmie?" he is definitely mad, but is it aimed at me? Does he not believe me?

"Please Bro, don't make me say it." Because I don't think I could. Shock enters his face, this is new.

"He rapes you?" he says in disbelief. I can't look at him.

"I'm sorry Bro, please don't hate me, I understand if you don't believe me." I wouldn't believe me either. Silence fills the table, he takes a deep breath obviously gathering his thoughts.

"I don't hate you, sis, I hate myself. I know you are telling the truth, I can tell when you lie and this isn't one of them. I wish you were." Oh Danny, you only see what I want you to see. You don't know me, you can only tell if I'm lying if I want you to know.

Oh thank god. He believes me. I feel relief. "Oh Danny, I was so worried you wouldn't believe me. I've been trying to tell you for so long." I wanted to tell him so many times, but I could never find the right words.

Dad has always drummed into me that no one would believe me. He got so mad sometimes, one time I said no to him raping me. He got really angry and beat me. It was so bad, I was losing consciousness but before he fixed me up I felt him take my clothes off first and he had what he wanted from me first. After that day, I never tested him again. I just let him do what he wanted with my body. I was alone. I didn't want him hurting Danny.

"How long?" he says sadly.

"What?" I'm confused.

"For god sake Emmie, how long has he been doing this to you?" he is irritated.

"I don't know. I don't remember a time when he didn't." He bangs his fists on the table. It makes me jump.

"What a bastard, I'm going to kill him."

"Danny, can I ask you something?" he nods.

"Did Momma leave because of me? Dad said she did leave because of me." Dad wouldn't let me talk to Danny about this before.

"Are you serious Emmie? She loved you more than anything. She didn't want to leave you. She didn't have a choice." He is very surprised by my question. I'm glad to hear my Momma didn't want to leave me.

"What's going to happen now with Dad on the run?"

"I will look after you now Sis, I'm sorry I couldn't protect you before but I will protect now. Shall we go home?"

I take a look at Brody. "Actually I was hoping to hang with Brody today. I couldn't have got through this without him." He looks strangely happy.

"I understand Sis. I wish you could have opened up to me but I'm glad you found someone you could trust. Can I meet him properly?" He wants to meet him?

"Umm okay?" I catch Brody's eye and invite him over.

"Danny this is Brody, Brody this is Danny," I say awkwardly.

"Hi, I'm Emmie's Brother. I just wanted to say thank you for what you have done for my sister. I truly wish she would have confided in me sooner. But she seems to trust you, so thank you." He sounds grateful.

"I'm glad she trusts me too, I care about her," he says as he winks at me. I have butterflies.

"Just to warn you, if you hurt my sister, I will hurt you." Here we go, protective big brother. Thank god Brody finds this funny.

"Haha okay, I hear you."

"Hey, Brody can we get out of here?" I say hopefully.

"I was going to meet up with friends if you want to join?" he sounds happy for me to tag along.

"Sure, sounds good. I will see you at home Danny."

"Does that mean I don't get to wake up with you anymore?" he's teasing with me.

"You're not that lucky." I giggle.

"Remember I will hurt you," Danny says annoyed.

"Chill, I was joking. Anyway, Emmie can handle herself."

Danny laughs. "I know she can."

"See you, Bro."

We walk to the park hand in hand. We aren't officially together, but I feel closer to him than I have with anyone. How much time am I going to need? Will Brody give up waiting?

The blonde one says, "Hey Dude, where have you been?"

"I've had things to do. What's up?"

The one with the dreads gawks at me "Hey, hot stuff."

God, men are so annoying. Brody finally introduces me properly, the blonde one is Sky. And the dreads is Max.

"Hey new girl, you're looking mighty fine today, you look more beautiful every time I see you," Sky says, admiring me.

"Such a smooth talker, why don't you find someone in your own league?" I roll my eyes.

Max starts laughing, "You got burned, dude."

Brody wraps his arms around me. I feel good to be here.

"Guys stop flirting with my girl already." His girl sounds so good.

"I'm no one's girl, so you should all quit trying," I say teasingly.

"Wow someone's sassy today. I like that in a girl," Sky says, still flirting with me.

"Seriously, back off already." Brody is irritated.

I feel warm inside from him fighting over me. I look out onto the park.

I notice some older looking dude staring right at me. He is so creepy, I wrap my arms around Brody, I feel protected here, snuggling up into his arms.

"So what's everyone doing tonight?" I say, trying to forget about the creepy guy. Sky mentioned that they are all going to hang out and get drunk and I should join. I'm totally in, I love being one of the guys. I know they only want me around because they think I'm hot. But I don't care right now. We started talking about how we all wanted to get back at Jade for her little stunt with the text. They are all on my side which feels good. So we leave the park, the guy is still staring. I make a hasty exit.

We make our way to the school. We grab alcohol on the way, drinking as we go. I feel like a badass, it's getting dark. I don't like being out at night but I feel safe with these guys. Safe with Brody.

"You do surprise me beautiful," he says as he leans in for a kiss.

His lips taste like whisky. We stand outside the school, "Come on new girl, show us what you got," he's egging me on. Does he not know that I'm up for being bad?

"I was born for this, let's go." We manage to sneak through one of the windows, Brody gave me a leg up whilst Sky helped me from above. We find Jade's locker.

"Who wants to do the honours?" Sky asks.

She did this to me, I should be the one to do it. "I do, this bitch deserves what she gets. This is karma."

"Wahey, go new girl."

"Honestly." I roll my eyes.

"Maybe you should join the gang, you have balls."

I'd love to be part of the gang. Brody shoots Sky an icy stare. Maybe he doesn't want me to hang out with his friends. "Shut up Dude." Brody is pissed.

I feel sad that he doesn't want me to be one of the guys. I walk up to her locker and plant this sweet revenge. I can't wait to see Jade's face when she opens her locker. This is probably the most badass thing I've done. And I like it. I love being one of the boys, even if they do flirt with me every chance they get.

"Let's get out of here before we get caught." Brody grabs my hand and leads me out of the school. We walk back to my house, Danny will be pissed I'm home so late. But I enjoyed tonight, I had so much fun.

"That was so cool new girl, you're such a badass," Sky says.

Even though Sky flirts with me a lot, I like him. He's cool. I think we are all nearly drunk.

"I hope to hang out soon new girl. You are amazing," he says, totally eyeing me up.

"You're drunk."

"Yeah, but I'm not blind."

Seriously? He may be slightly more annoying whilst drunk.

"Dude." Brody sounds angry.

I hear a call from the house. "Emmie!" Oh no, Danny knows I'm back.

"Someone's in trouble new girl," he says teasingly.

I call back, "I will be there in a minute." Jeez, he's such a buzz kill. Sky and Max say their goodbye's to us, typically flirting with me. And we watch them walk away drunk.

"Seriously... They're unbelievable. I know you're beautiful but they don't need to be all over you. Jeez." Bless him, who knew he would be so bothered?

I giggle at him. "Aww is someone jealous?" I say, teasing him.

"Well actually, yes I am," he agrees.

He pulls me in for a kiss, this is passionate, the perfect ending to the day. When I'm with him I forget myself. It's nice to feel like a normal person, hanging out with friends. Kissing a boy in the street.

"Emmie!" Danny shouts again.

"Your brother has bad timing."

"Yeah, I know. I'm coming, Danny!"

"I had such a great night tonight, I don't want to leave you." Wow, those words, he's not being a tool right now, he's been a genuinely nice guy. This guy in front of me is hot, and he wants me. Can I give myself to him? Am I ready?

"Emmie if I have to drag you to the house then I will," Danny shouts.

I hate him right now. "I'd better go in." He nods and kisses me goodnight and he leaves. I don't want him to leave me either. But I'm not ready to lift this wall. I walk to the house where Danny is standing with his arms crossed.

"Where the hell have you been Emmie?"

"I've been hanging with Brody and friends, chill out."

"Don't tell me to chill Emmie, I've been trying to call you." I roll my eyes at him.

"I was safe, I was with Brody."

"Emmie, with Dad on the loose you can't do that. How can I know you're safe?"

I didn't even think about Dad all night, I can't believe I was so stupid. Brody makes me feel normal.

"Danny I'm so sorry, I didn't even think."

He takes a deep breath. "I'm just glad you are safe. You reek of booze, how much have you drank Emmie?"

I giggle, I am drunk. Oops. "I love you, Bro, I'm tired. I'm going to bed." He giggles.

"I love you too sis. Sleep well."

I stagger upstairs, bumping into things. I finally find my room, I'm too tired to change so I just strip into my underwear. I climb into bed and think of what happened today. And that night, I dreamed of Brody. And another night I didn't cry myself to sleep.

I wake up feeling hopeful today. My phone goes off, I read the text.

Good morning beautiful. I can't wait to see you today. Brody.

How sweet. I guess I should reply. Things are looking more hopeful for me. Something is sure to come crashing down on me, it always does.

I miss waking up to you. YOUR Emmie.

That will send him wild. I'm so bad. I take a shower, I reek of booze. The water feels so good on my skin. I feel fresh after the shower. I dress in jeans, long boots and a baggy shirt. I shove my wet hair up in a ponytail. I don't have time to dry my hair. I grab my stuff and run downstairs. I kiss my brother on the cheek and leave for school.

I can't wait to get to school to see Brody. I am practically running, I've never been so hopeful before. And he has made that happen. I reach the school, I take a moment to take in the sun before I go and find Brody. I hear someone walks up behind me and I turn around. It's the guy from the park, is he following me? He eyes me up and down.

"Hi," he says, flirting with me.

"Are you stalking me?" I say with my arms crossed.

He moves closer to me. "Pretty much," he says laughing at me.

"What?" I'm scared now, who am I kidding? I'm terrified walking out my house. He hits me hard around my head. I fall instantly to the floor. I can feel everything go dark. I can't see anything. I feel him pick me up and put me in a car. I've been kidnapped. Oh hell no. I lose consciousness.

I wake up slowly, I hear muffled voices. Where am I? It smells damp and mouldy in here. I slowly start to regain vision. My head hurts so bad. I can't see the sun. There are no windows in here. I begin to panic. "Hello... What Idiot put me in here?" I sound strangely confident. The stalker enters through the door.

He crosses his arms. "I did, now shut up."

"Who the hell do you think you are?" Moron.

"Be quiet or I will make you." How rude.

"I'd like to see you try, if you touch me I will scream the place down."

A younger looking dude comes in. He has bright pink hair, he looks kind. He has big muscles. He's huge. "What the hell is going on in here?" he crosses his arms.

"This one has a mouth on her. And Lady I'd love to," he smirks at me.

Urgh, men. Why do I have verbal diarrhoea? I'm making things worse. "Bring it, you idiot."

The Big Guy laughs. "Beautiful AND feisty."

"I can't say the same for you. Why are you keeping me here?"

"Boss wants to see you, let's go." Pft summoning me really?

"Well, you tell your boss." He's laughing at me. Jerk.

"You're kidding right?" I wasn't actually but whatever.

The stalker grins. "You may do the honours."

Big Guy's eyes light up. What's going on? "My pleasure."

He walks towards me, I step back. He grins at me and moves towards me again. My back is up against the wall. He bends down and picks me up and puts me over his shoulders. What the hell? I don't like people touching me. Get off.

"Put me down, you idiot. I do have my own legs." He laughs.

"Yeah I know, and mighty fine legs too. Especially from this angle." He slaps me on the ass.

How rude, this is all a game to him. "Don't touch what you can't afford, how dare you loser?"

31

"Your smart mouth is so hot."

Urgh. "Put me down," I scream. And so he does, in front of a door. I guess this must be the Bosses office. He opens the door and strides in.

"I put you down, now come in here. Don't make me put you on my shoulder again," he calls.

So I walk into the office, cross my arms and glare at him. "Jeez, keep your hair on Big Guy."

"What's been going on?"

I look over to who must be the boss. He is hot. Blue eyes, sandy coloured hair. I can see his abs through his shirt. He looks pissed but alluring. "Why the hell don't you tell me, you idiot?" I'm mad, but he looks shocked. I can't stop looking at his beautiful face.

"Sorry boss, she's got a hell of a mouth on her. She's been a handful, to say the least," he says awkwardly.

"Looks like your guys can't handle one little girl. You may want to seek your staff elsewhere." I laugh. He looks pissed. Oops.

"Shut up! You do have a mouth on you. Thanks, Sully I will handle her from here." Sully looks awkward. Idiot.

"You're not handling me... not any shape or form." He glares at me.

"Shut up before I make you. I'll have to teach your pretty mouth to behave," he says with a grin on his faces.

Bastard. "You can try," I say teasing him back.

Big Guy laughs. "Are you sure?" he says doubtfully.

The boss chuckles. "I will certainly have fun trying."

Big Guy nods and leaves the room.

"What the hell is going on, wise guy?" I seriously can't stop looking at his handsome face. Why am I admiring the guy that has me hostage? What's wrong with you Emmie?

"I won't tell you again. I ask the questions. I got my men to kidnap you," he says, chuffed with himself. I roll my eyes. Whatever you say.

"No Shit Sherlock." He has a cold look in his eyes. It takes me by surprise. He walks towards me, so I take a step back. He smirks at me. The wall is against my back, I have nowhere to go. I can feel his breath on my throat. My heart starts racing, but not with fear, with lust? He whispers in my ear to keep still. I'm not going anywhere. This is turning me on. He starts kissing my neck, teasing me. I tilt my head back to give him better access. This is torturing me, his soft lips. What the hell am I doing? I can smell his scent around me, it's like nothing I've ever smelt. I feel safe.

"That shut you up, did I hear you moan? Was I turning you on?" he says teasing me.

He knows he did the bastard. Why did he stop? Concern fills his face. "You're bleeding."

My head really hurts. He steps towards me again and this time I don't move. I crave his touch. My breathing is rapid. He grabs a tissue from his pocket and dabs my wound to clean the blood. He smells so good, his left-hand cups my face and he gently strokes my cheek with his thumb. His touch is soothing. Our eyes meet, his eyes are dark and cold. But I feel myself being lost in them. They are dreamy and hot. His eyes soften, his pupils dilate like he is desperate for me. Why does he affect me so much? He leans down and pulls me in for a kiss. I'm kissing a complete stranger, and I like it. It's like we were made for each other. I know he feels it too. He's holding back, I can tell. I don't feel like I want to push him away and that is a strange feeling for me.

"I'm so glad I found a way to shut you up. I'm having so much fun. What, nothing to say?" his eyes are playful. I was having fun too.

"I want answers, what am I doing here?" I demand.

He smirks, "At the moment you are keeping me amused."

"Don't play dumb." It doesn't suit him.

"Your mouth, what I'd like to do with it. You're a means to an end," he shrugs.

What I'd like him to do with my mouth, I get lost in thought. I take a deep breath, he's messing with my thoughts. "And that means what, tough guy?"

He shrugs, "Your boyfriend. He's my arch enemy."

I don't have a boyfriend. "I don't have a boyfriend so it looks like you are dumb enough to kidnap the wrong person." It looks like I hit a nerve.

"Wind your neck in, I'm not afraid to hurt you even if you are a girl." I gulp, he's threatening me but I can't help but feel turned on. "Brody Rivers, you know him?"

Brody? What does he want with Brody? Brody seems like a nice guy once you get to know him. What did he do?

"I can see by your face that you do know him. I've had you both watched."

He's been watching me? I feel the need to protect him. "What do you want with him?"

"His gang fucked me over. I'm out for revenge. The thing he cares about most is you. So that's why you're here."

There is a promise in his words. Brody's not in a gang, he would have told me, wouldn't he? "Brody's not in a gang. You're insane."

"I'm not lying. You're just a means to an end. But... you've turned out to be a pretty fun one. What am I going to do with you?" he says playfully.

"Nothing, you better not hurt Brody," I say with my arms crossed.

"What are you going to do if I do?" he says questioningly. What will I do? "I have to say you are a pretty decent prize. I suppose... If you make it worth my while then I might consider not hurting him."

What the hell does he mean by that? "Are you serious. What sort of sick moron would propose this?" I'm mad.

"I guess that would be me. I guess the question is how much do you care about him?" he shrugs.

I care about Brody, I do. But how far will I go to protect him? He put me in this situation, why should I help him get out of it? Who am I kidding? He saved me from my Dad. I owe him my life. Of course I will protect him. I can do this for him.

"So what's it to be?" he says, begging me to take his proposal.

"Don't hurt him," I beg.

"You have balls lady. You made a good choice. SULLY!" he seems happy with my choice.

What will happen to me now? Sully enters the office. "Yes, boss?"

"Change of plan. I've had payment for River's mistakes. Leave him, stay off the radar. Take her back to her room."

Sully looks at me, obeying his orders. "Don't touch me," I shout.

"I will put you over my shoulder again little lady."

I roll my eyes. "Whatever."

I can hear the Boss sigh. "Sully."

And so Big Guy picks me up and carries me to the smelly room again. I take a minute to think. I'm not scared. Why not? And then it dawns on me, Dad was worse than kidnappers. Dad was never this... nice. Big Guy puts me down in the room. He tells me to stay put. Seriously, where am I going to go?

I miss the sun already, I miss how it feels on my face. I don't even know what time of day it is. I lay on the smelly bed and close my eyes. I dream of the sun on my face. I slowly drift asleep. I don't know how long I was asleep for but I feel warm arms around me. Pulling me to their chest. Whoever this is they smell safe and delicious. I'm too tired to open my eyes, so I drift back into sleep. Although I am here against my will, I feel safe for the first time in a long time.

Chapter 4

I wake, not because of any other reason than my head is pounding. It hurts so much, I feel before I see. There is a big heavy arm around my waist. Against my back is muscly sternum. I feel the sun on my face, this is what I've been dreaming about since being here. Where am I now? I vaguely remember someone carrying me, but I was so tired I just drifted back to sleep. I feel so safe in his arms. He's cradling me in his arms and I don't want to move. Why would a kidnapper bring me here and sleep in the same bed as me? I know he hasn't touched me, I know how that feels, I've experienced it often enough. Although I know what my Dad did to me was wrong, I feel hurt that he left me. He promised he never would leave me. I know I shouldn't care. But I was my Daddy's girl. He said I was special, I don't feel very special now. He left me, I feel abandoned. My eyes are still heavy, I drift back to sleep again.

"Mmm," I moan, I'm so comfy. The sun is still on my face, I'm comfy in this guy's arms. My head still hurts. I'm going to hurt him for punching me. I'm just a weak girl, he could have just dragged me to the car. He didn't have to hit me. I turn around in his arms so I'm facing him. I realise I don't even know his name. But I stare at his beauty, he is topless and in his boxers. He's still sleeping so I sneakily touch his abs, tracing the outline with my fingers. He stirs, I guess I woke him. Oops. For the first time, I feel like I can comfortably touch someone else.

"What are you doing?" he asks still with his eyes shut and his arm around me.

"Nothing," I lie. He smirks at me, he's so cute in the morning. He seems more carefree in the morning.

"Of course you weren't, good morning sexy," he grins.

"Hey, yourself," I say confidently. Why am I so comfortable with this guy? He opens his eyes, they're even more beautiful than I remember. "What am I doing here?" I ask.

"You're here to do whatever I want with, and I wanted you here. And as you're running rings around my men, I thought I should watch you."

So that was why he was cradling me, so I didn't move. Not that I want to move. Danny will be so worried about where I am. I hope he doesn't get into any trouble, I can't lose my Brother. And as for Brody, I miss him but I can't have him hurt. I'm doing this for him, it's not so bad anyway. I feel safe for the first time in forever. I shouldn't feel safe, should I? But I do. "What's your name?" I ask curiously.

He chuckles, "You spent the night with me, and you don't know my name?" he says, teasing me.

"Nothing happened, and I didn't have a choice," I say, mocking him. He lifts his eyebrow at me. How am I supposed to know his name when he hasn't introduced himself and, well Sully calls him Boss, he can think again if he thinks I will be calling him boss.

"How do you know nothing happened?" I know because I've woken up enough times after my Dad raped me to know how it feels. My Dad had me at every opportunity, most nights he would sneak into my room. At first, I tried to pretend I was asleep, but that didn't stop him. And every time I woke in the morning and he was there next to me, I knew he had his fill of me. But he was always very clever, he'd get up before Danny got up.

"I just do, and if you did I would kick your ass," I snap. He's touching a sore subject.

He chuckles, "Oh would you now Miss Salvatore?"

I love how playful he is. I make no attempt to break out of his grip. I'd be happy if I stayed in this moment forever. He lifts his arm from my waist, he puts me on edge because I'm never sure what he's going to do. But I'm not scared of him. I don't move, he strokes my cheek and my hair. I love it when people stroke my hair. He smirks at me like he has accomplished something. He leans towards me and his lips lock with mine, I respond to his kiss. This time it's different from before, it feels more demanding, urgent, hot! He breaks away. What! He's leaving me wanting more. What's wrong with me? This hot stranger making me want more. I told myself I wasn't ready for anything like this and here he is making me want more. I didn't even want more with Brody yet. I don't know if I ever will.

"My name is Rider," he says.

"Like riding a bike?" I giggle. He looks more serious now. Have I done something wrong?

"Tell me something?" he says. I tease him, trying to get playful Rider back.

"What do I get in return?" My breathing is still rapid. He strokes my cheek again.

He frowns, "Why are you not scared of me? I'm holding you here against your will and here you are at ease, teasing me."

That is a difficult question and one that I'm not happy with sharing with a stranger. I guess I feel safer with Rider than I do my own Dad. "I don't know," I respond with a half-hearted lie. It's half true, I guess.

"I know you're lying to me, tell me."

He doesn't know me, how can he know I'm lying? My family could never tell if I was lying. They only see what I show them. He gets out of bed, leaving me cold and alone. I sit up on the bed, watching him. "I don't want to talk about it, let's just say I've been through worse." I shrug. I can tell he's not satisfied with my answer, I like that fact he doesn't know my past.

"What's that supposed to mean?" he looks confused, obviously frustrated with my secrecy.

I sigh, "It means I don't want to talk about it." Get the hint dude. It's painful to think about the past. Dad hated secrets, I eventually got good at lying. But he once pushed me down the stairs for lying to him. I broke my arm, I had to say that I was clumsy and fell down the stairs. My lies had to be convincing to my Brother, to my teachers, not that they usually asked. He looks like he was on a mission to find out, well he won't hear it from me. He kisses me on the forehead.

"I have work to do, I'll take you back to your room."

After last night, that's it, he's gone back to being an ass. "Fine," I say with my arms crossed. He gets changed in front of me.

"Just because you stayed with me last night does not mean you get special treatment."

Yeah, I get it. "Whatever."

He sighs, "Fine, you can walk around the basement level, but don't annoy my staff," he says. Wow, that was easy.

He's trusting me to walk around? I'm not going to complain. "Would I?" I tease.

He chuckles, "Yes you would." Not going to lie, I probably would.

"I've put clothes over there for you, pick something and come downstairs." He turns on his heels and exits the room. Wow, his ass is sexy as he strides out the room. Urgh, stop it Emmie, concentrate.

He got me clothes? Or are they second-hand clothes? It doesn't matter, I just need to change. These are actually my style, I'm surprised. I pick a dress to wear, it's a casual light blue one. It will do. I suppose I'd better go downstairs. I follow the corridor to the stairs, it's bigger than I thought. The basement level is grubby and smelly, but I guess it's better than the small confined space. I see Rider talking to Big Guy, all eyes are on me as I walk in the room. God, men and their gawking. I stand awkwardly in front of them, I look at the floor.

"Sully will watch you whilst I'm working, there better not be any trouble." He crosses his arms.

I like to tease this guy. "Of course, there won't be, I'm just the innocent girl you kidnapped." I smile sweetly at him.

He chuckles, "Whatever you say." He leaves us in the room together. What shall I do?

My head is so painful, I've been through enough pain before but this seems different. Dad always looked after me, prescribed me the right pills. But now Dad isn't here, I have to fend for myself. "Hey, Big Guy!" I call. He strides over to where I am standing.

"Yes?" he asks.

"My head hurts, please can I get some painkillers?"

He looks awkward, "Sorry Miss, I don't have any and I can't leave you." He genuinely sounds sorry.

"Please call Rider." I don't know how much longer I can handle this pain.

"I can't disturb him miss," he says apologetically.

Argh. "Fine whatever, thanks for nothing." He apologises and walks off to what he was doing. What am I going to do? I glance over to the other side of the room and I see Danny standing over there. Oh my god, he has come to save me.

"Emmie, be careful, hold on. Keep fighting," he says worriedly. What's he talking about? Be careful? But I feel safe here.

"Danny, what's going on?" I'm so confused.

"Keep fighting," he demands. Keep fighting what? I blink and he disappears. Where did he go? Sully walks back up to me.

"Miss do you need something?"

No, I just... "I was just talking to…" I'm not sure now.

"Miss, there is no one here. Just me and you. Are you okay?"

Am I losing my shit? I hope not. "Umm okay, I'm okay, thanks Big Guy." He looks confused and concerned. He's not the only one. Sully leaves me once again.

I shut my eyes and take a deep breath and clutch my head where it hurts. When I open my eyes I see… my Momma. I must be dreaming. "Momma, is that you?" my vision is slightly blurry now. Maybe this is how I imagine she'd look like. I haven't seen her in ten years.

"Hold on princess, don't let the darkness take you," and then she disappeared too. What darkness?

"Momma don't leave me." I'm so confused and in pain that tears fall from my face. Everyone is leaving me. I see a figure in front of me, I have to squint to see who it is, and I wish I hadn't.

"What have you been up to? Your big mouth has got you in trouble." His voice sounds so real. Dad is here to punish me.

"I'm sorry Daddy, please don't hurt me." I know this does no good. But I have to try, right? "I promise I'll be good. Don't hurt me." I feel hysterical right now.

"You will never learn, will you?" he walks towards me, he looks so mad. Tears flood from my eyes I'm so scared. How did he get to me? He grabs my arms. I will never learn because I always do the wrong things.

"I'm sorry Daddy, please don't hurt me," I sob.

A familiar voice surrounds me. "Emmie, you are safe. Emmie, look at me."

I look up and squint again. Oh, thank god, it's Rider. Rider is hushing me, hugging me. He strokes my hair calming me down. He brings me back to the here and now. He pulls back, looking at my face. He kisses me softly. His scent is relaxing me.

"You're safe, baby." He called me baby. I like that.

"He was trying to hurt me." He strokes my cheek.

"No one was trying to hurt you. No one is here," he reassures me.

The room starts spinning. "Rider?"

"I'm here."

"Rider please stop moving, I can't focus." The darkness is surrounding me. "Don't leave me."

"Emmie I'm not moving, I promise I won't leave you." He sounds worried. I fall in his arms. I can't hold myself up anymore. All I can hear is Rider shouting Sully. Rider asks him if I've been in pain. Of course, I asked him for painkillers. Sully explained what happened. Rider sounds mad. I feel Rider scoop me up into his arms, I feel safe and I slip away.

I can hear voices, one of them is Rider, he sounds so angry and worried. That figures, why can't I wake up? I feel so groggy, heavy. I can't open my eyes, I try but nothing happens. I want to see Rider's face, it soothes me. I feel scared here, alone. Darkness takes me again. This has been happening a lot. But I can never seem to wake no matter how hard I try.

"Mrs Grey, we are going to try to wake you now." Who is Mrs Grey? Who is talking to me? I'm scared.

"Hey baby, you are still up to mischief. Follow my voice." It's a familiar voice, it makes me relax. Rider is here. He wants me to wake for him, he sounds so hopeful. His voice surrounds me, I try to follow but the more I do the more pain I feel.

"Mrs Grey open your eyes." I'm going to punch him if he calls me that again. "Mrs Grey." That does it, my name isn't Mrs Grey.

"What's going on?" Rider asks worriedly.

"I'm sorry Mr Grey, she's not responding. She's not ready." What do you mean I'm not ready? Shut the hell up.

"No baby, fight for me. Get her to wake up. Come on beautiful, fight!" He's begging me to wake up, his voice is scared. He sounds so hurt. I can't have him hurting for me. I try with all my heart to wake up.

"Yes, come on Mrs Grey." Yes, I will just to punch you. Idiot.

"What's going on?"

"She's fighting for you."

I wake to Rider standing over me with tears in his eyes. Why is the big idiot crying? Some smart looking dude is checking machines and things around me. He tilts my bed so I am sat up. Where am I? And why was I brought here? Rider looks relieved and he puts his forehead on mine. His touch soothes me. Is he not worried I will tell this man about him kidnapping me?

"Who is Mrs Grey?" I ask curiously. The smart guy with blonde hair in a suit frowns at me. Why? I look around me, I guess I'm in the hospital.

Rider laughs, "Feisty as ever." I love to hear him laugh. Not so much that it's at my expense though.

"Mrs Grey you are in the hospital, I'm your Doctor. You are lucky to be alive," he informs me. Lucky to be alive? I'm still living the same nightmare.

He seems kind and friendly. "I'm going to slap you if you call me Mrs Grey again. And gee, I don't feel very lucky," I say matter of factly. The Doctor looks slightly intimidated by me. Oops.

"I've missed your smart mouth, what happens now Doctor?" he asks.

The Doctor's facial expression changes, what's going on? "She needs more tests, she needs to stay here. I need to make a phone call," and he exits out of the room.

"Rider what's going on, I want to go home." I don't feel safe here at all. There are people everywhere, Dad could be here for all I know.

"You slipped into a coma Emmie because of your head injury, I will kill Larry for hitting you. And you can't go home Emmie, you know this." He seems hurt. Why would someone want to kill someone because they hurt me? I'm just his hostage.

"No need, I'm going to hurt him myself when I see him. I know, I meant home with you." He seems shocked with my confession. Is he happy or sad about them? He takes a deep breath. I don't see one place as home. My Dad's house isn't my home, it never was.

"You need more tests," he sighs.

The Big Guy comes running into my room. He looks worried about something. "Boss we got to go. Now!"

"She can't leave, she needs more tests," he says angrily.

"The doctor is on the phone to the cops, you need to make a choice now."

No, he can't leave me. He promised he wouldn't, I can't be left here alone for my Dad to take me. I grab his hand and he turns to face me. "Don't leave me," I plead. Concern fills his face.

"I should leave you, it's better for you. You need tests Emmie." He's going to leave me. What's better for me is to feel safe.

Everyone always leaves me. What do I do wrong? "You promised you wouldn't leave me, but fine, whatever. Just go." I turn over and curl up in a ball on the bed so he can't see how hurt I am. I feel his arms around me, he picks me up and pulls me to his chest. This is where I crave to be, safe in his arms. His scent sends me into a daze. I bury my head in his neck.

He whispers something that comforts me. "I will never leave you," and it sounds like a promise. I fall asleep in his arms as he carries me out the hospital.

I'm back in my house, in my bedroom. This bedroom is filled with bad memories already. We haven't been here long. The night I got in trouble because of school. He was so angry, he walked in my room with a deathly face. I knew I would get it bad. He was always careful not to get my face. He said he loved my face. Danny was out, just me and him. I had nowhere to run, and hey, like I'd have the chance to call for Danny even if he was in.

"Get to the wall," he says, angry but quiet.

Of course, I obey, I knew better than that. He takes off my shirt and sniffs it, this happened quite often. He seems satisfied and throws it on the floor. He ties my hands up with his tie, he is a smartly dressed guy because he is a Doctor.

"Put your hands above your head," he commands. I obey in a second.

"Now you are here because you misbehaved, you disappointed me, do you understand?" he says calmly. I nod, not having a voice. He takes his belt off in one swift move and he hits me with it across my ribs with the buckle end. I cry out.

"Answer me when I talk to you, I like to hear your voice," he growls.

I drop my arms so I can clutch my side where he hit me. I scream out in pain. "Yes Daddy, I understand," I whimper. I will never get used to the pain he inflicts on me.

He steps closer towards me so he is touching me, he pins me up against the wall. He strokes my cheek and kisses me on the lips and says, "Good girl."

"Please, I don't want this, don't hurt me, Daddy. I only want Rider to touch me." Anger fills his face. I repulse his touch more now that I have felt Rider's touch. I didn't think that would be possible.

"Hands up now," he screams. He hit me again across my stomach. "You are mine, do you understand?" he growls.

I see Rider enter my room. He looks pissed at me. "I'm disgusted with you Emmie," he says and he stands there while Dad hits me over and over.

"Rider please don't leave me. I love you," I confess. "I know I'm disgusting and broken, but please," I beg. I look into his eyes while my Dad rips my underwear off. Staring into his beautiful eyes calms me. I don't expect him to help me, no one can help me. But he can't leave me.

"Emmie, wake up." Rider's voice floods the room. He sounds sad and worried. "Baby, wake up, you're dreaming," he says, reassuring me. I'm dreaming? No, I'm having a nightmare.

I jolt awake, Rider is holding my hand and stroking my hair. I love people stroking my hair. He cups my face and gently kisses me. I instantly relax at his touch. He pulls away and looks into my eyes. Tears fill my eyes.

"How are you feeling?" he asks. My head still hurts.

"My head hurts, why didn't you leave me?" I ask. He looks taken aback by my question.

"Because you asked me not to," he shrugs. There must be more to it than that.

"So you follow requests from all your hostages?" I say doubtfully.

He sighs, "Only you." I feel special to think that I'm the only one, but why? I don't understand. He starts to kiss me, I can't deny this connection anymore. I need him, and for the first time, I found someone that I want to go further with. I don't feel scared with him. "I want you," I plead.

"You have me baby, all of me." That sends butterflies to my tummy. I have all of him. It makes me feel complete for the first time in my life. He gets on top of me, I pull his shirt off revealing his abs. Wow. This feels so natural, he is gentle with me. But I honestly don't want him to be. I want this, he feels my body, and I wrap my arms around his neck and stroke his hair. He groans in my mouth, this feels so good. He is like a drug, my therapy to life. I can return this love. We are making love, I can touch him. I want to and I want him to touch me.

I wake up, it must be morning. Last night was amazing, better than I ever imagined, I never thought I would enjoy being with a guy after Dad. What he does to me is sick, forcing me to do this. I used to get jealous when I saw him with Momma. I knew it was wrong to feel that way, but he said I was his and I was his special princess. I used to wish Momma would leave, and that is exactly what happened. I blamed myself for her leaving and Dad only confirmed my suspicions. I was a bad daughter. I wished my Momma away because I wanted Dad to myself. But I also didn't want him to touch me either. I'm going to need counselling for life I think.

Rider is curled around me, I get up out of bed. Rider is still asleep, or so I thought. Me moving must have woke him up. "Where do you think you're going?" he says still with his eyes shut.

"I was going for walk." Clear my head. He climbs out of bed wearing his boxers, the way they hang from his hips. Yum. I stare at his body. He comes towards me and kisses me hard.

"You look beautiful," he says, breaking our kiss.

"Yeah, you don't look too bad yourself. Stood there in your umm..." He chuckles. I bite my lip.

"Fighting talk this morning, I love it. Put some clothes on and meet me downstairs." He kisses me on the forehead and leaves with his clothes. Leaving me hanging again. I want something comfy to wear so I grab one of his shirts from his drawer. And I go in search to find him.

I hear shouting, Rider is shouting. I slowly enter the room where the shouting is coming from. I'm not eavesdropping at all. Oops. I see Rider shouting at a pretty blonde girl.

"What the hell are you doing here Lara?" he growls. Wow, he's mad.

She's definitely flirting with him, "I wanted to talk to you about our night the other day." What night?

"We slept together once, it was a bit of fun. It won't happen again. Now leave."

"What?" I say before I realise what was coming out of my mouth.

Chapter 5

Rider is staring at me speechless, sad. Tears run down my face, he slept with her whilst I was in the hospital. I know we aren't together and our relationship is fucked up but I feel hurt. Hurt and betrayed. I let him touch me because I trusted him, how stupid could I be? I've been let down enough, I should be used to it by now. Rage boils over me. "What the hell did you just say?" I yell. This bitch isn't getting away with this.

"Emmie, please, I'm sorry," he begs.

I can't handle this betrayal, I love him and he's hurt me. "Shut up, shut up, shut up." I put my hands on my head trying to gather my thoughts. I walk up to this blonde-haired slut, "What do you have to say for yourself?"

She giggles, wrong move, "What can I say, he wanted a bit of me?" she says, eyeing up Rider.

"If you mean a bit of you, you mean absolute slapper, then you are totally right." She is offended at my words. Good, I am glad. No one apart from my Dad hurts me and gets away with it.

"You bitch, who are you anyway?"

Psht, please. "I'm the one that is going to humiliate you." She looks confused.

"What do you mean?" she asks curiously.

"Emmie, take it easy, don't forget your head," he says.

"Shut up you idiot," I yell.

"Emmie please," he begs.

I know he technically hasn't done anything wrong but I'm still hurt. His voice is sad, my heart aches for him. All I want to do is curl up in his arms but I can't. All I can do is teach this bitch a lesson. I punch her hard in the face.

"You bitch, how dare you?" she's horrified.

I giggle. "Stupid cow." I punch her again. She screams like a little girl.

"Boss, please help me."

Is she for real? "Are you kidding me? He wouldn't dare." I glare at her. I get lost in anger, I punch her over and over until she falls to the floor.

"Ow, please stop. I'm sorry okay," and she genuinely does seem sorry.

"Get out. Now!" I yell. And she gets up and runs out the room. I hope I never see her again.

"Emmie, I'm sorry." Tears fall down my face once again. I punch him hard in the face. He looks surprised by my strength.

"Jesus Emmie, that hurt." He clutches his face.

"Good, that's only minimal compared to how much you've hurt me. Leave me alone." He tries to close the distance between us, but I step back. If I let him touch me I will lose myself. I need to make a stand. He hurt me. His eyes are in pain, I know he's regretted his actions.

I run out of the room, instead of going upstairs I went to the room that I woke up in on the first day I came here. I don't know why I come here, I need to get out of here away from him. I need space, not even Brody is worth this pain.

Rider walks into the room, "Baby, please."

"I'm not your baby, I'm nothing to you, you've proved that." This pain hurts too much.

"You are everything to me," he confesses. I shouldn't be though, I am just a girl he kidnapped. I am nothing special but he is something special to me. Even in this short time.

I can tell he means that, but it's too late. "I can't do this, let me go, let me go back to my family," I beg.

"And go back to him... Brody?"

I know he cares about me and worries I'll go back to Brody but honestly, I was Brody's first and he kidnapped me. "That has nothing to do with you anymore." He looks in so much pain.

"Okay." He looks defeated.

What? "Okay, what?" I ask confused.

"Okay you can go." He looks at the floor, not looking at me.

His words stab me in the heart, he's letting me go too easy, he doesn't care about me. I hoped that he would fight for me, I want to leave but I also wanted him to fight for me. "Are you serious?"

"Yes, go live your life, you deserve it, never stop living," he says reassuringly. Those words sit heavy on my heart, he's so confusing.

And I do, I leave, I go straight to Dad's house. I wonder what's been going on since I've been gone. It was quite a way to Dad's house but I got there eventually. I walk in the front door and shout, "Danny are you home?" Before I know it I hear feet pounding down the stairs. I see him running downstairs and he runs straight over to me and hugs me tightly. I'm taken back by his affections. We are hugging for what seems like ages.

He finally breaks the silence, "Oh my god sis, you are alive. I've missed you, you okay? What happened?" he says all too fast without taking a breath.

"Danny you are squishing me, and Danny you're an idiot. Go soft did you?" he releases me and blushes. Aww, my big brother is blushing.

"You and your sharp mouth, I've missed it," he chuckles.

"Is that all you've missed?" I tease.

"Seriously where have you been? What trouble did you get into?" he asks. So I start from the beginning and finish with just now. He asks why I woke for him, he doesn't understand but neither do I. I don't understand why him? What makes me attracted to this man? Why am I at ease with him touching me? So I explained the best I could.

Danny looks awkward. "Sis there is something I need to tell you," he says worriedly.

"What?" He takes a deep breath. It can't make me feel any worse, surely?

"When you were missing and the Doctor called, I went to the school to tell Brody the news. Emmie, he was kissing your best friend."

Say what? Brody kissing Jessie? I thought Jessie hated him. Everywhere I look there is betrayal. I can't handle this, I can't. My breathing becomes rapid. I can't breathe. I risked my life for this guy. Everything is boiling up inside of me, I'm so angry and hurt. Everything goes dark. I can't breathe. After everything, what I need now is Rider. He calms me.

I wake up in a strange place. Why does this always happen to me? This room reminds me of the same room Rider kept me in, although this one is cleaner, lighter and nicer. But there still aren't any windows. I need the sun. "Hello, where am I? Let me go," I yell.

Danny walks into the room. "Emmie calm down," he says, concerned. I try to get out the door but he holds my shoulders, keeping me still.

"What the hell happened?" I'm so confused.

"Emmie, calm down." My breathing starts to become laboured. It's hard to breathe, my chest is tight. "Doctors reckon you had a mental breakdown. They think you're a danger to yourself. They are keeping you here until you're better." I've always been a danger to myself, no one has noticed before.

I can't stay here. No. "You better be joking. I'm not staying here. Danny, get me the hell out of here." I'm freaking out, how could he do this to me?

He looks sad. "I can't, I'm sorry," he says. I fall against his chest in defeat and he strokes my hair. I prefer it when Rider does it.

"I can't cope in here. Danny, there are no windows. No sun... My healer."

"I'm sorry, I'll come back to visit." He withdraws away from me. Don't do this, please.

No, he can't leave me here. I scream at him whilst he is walking out the room. "Don't leave me. Everyone leaves me."

Someone familiar walks into the room, like from a dream. "Momma is that you? Or am I ill again?" God, I'm ill again and I'm stuck here. I miss my Dad, I was never this ill when he was around.

"No princess, I'm actually here," she says, reassuring me.

Curly black hair falls around her shoulders like I've seen in my dreams. She has big black glasses that make her pretty blue eyes stand out. She's smiling at me. I've missed her, and now she's here and she wants me. Her presence calms me. "The world is crushing me Momma." Tears fall from my eyes. She walks towards me and wraps her arms around me. I love that she is here, but there is only one person that can calm me right down. I miss him so much. There is nothing like a mothers' love, it feels alien to me but I hope to get used to it.

"How did you find me?" I ask.

"I've been looking for you for years. Your Dad kept moving you. Every time I got close to finding you, he would disappear. After that didn't work he managed to get a restraining order against me." He was trying to keep me from her? Restraining order?

"What? He told me you hated me. That you were ashamed of me. I believed it for years. I felt so alone." She looks hurt, she looks broken like me. I still feel alone.

"I hate him. I love you baby girl. I hate what he did to you. I didn't know. If I did I would have done things differently. I'm sorry." I only have myself to blame.

My Momma came back to me. I said I'd forgive her for leaving me. "I wouldn't give up finding you. My motherly instinct kicked in. I could feel you needed me. But I broke the restraining order. He had me put in jail."

Oh my god, no way. "He did? How did you get out of jail?" I ask. I can't believe Dad did this.

She looks happy. "I didn't baby girl. Some guy named Rider got me out of jail and he brought me to you."

He did? Why? He doesn't care about me. "Why?" I ask, confused.

"He loves you baby girl. I can see it in his eyes. He's so worried about you. I don't know how he found me. Your dad made me disappear without a trace." Why would Rider do this? I was just his hostage.

He doesn't love me. No one can love me. I'm ugly and worthless. "Momma, I can't stay here. I need to get out of here." I'm so scared.

"You're not well Emmie, you have to stay here." No, I can't. I haven't been well for a while.

"No, I need to leave. Don't make me stay here. Don't leave me. Help me, Momma. I can't, I can't, someone save me from this pain." My chest is tight again, why can't I control my body? My breathing? Everything goes dark again. My Momma has slipped away again. My world is crumbling around me.

I wake up alone in this awful room. I don't know how much longer I can take this. I start to sing because music helps me. It's one of my favourite songs.

'A silent tear. An empty smile. So insincerely, but so gently in denial. And me the thief. So selfishly. All the moments meant for you, I made them mine. How was I, so blind to miss you, crumbling inside? Is it too late now to fix you? Let me make it right! Cause there'll be no sun on Sunday. No reason for words to rhyme. Cause if you're bleeding, so am I, a wishful look. A hesitate. You're hoping I will notice that you're not OK. And me a fool, you turn away. It's only then I feel the weight of my mistakes. And if I cut you, if I bruise you, then the scars are always mine. Cause I love you, so to lose you, would be worse than if I died.'

Tears fill my eyes again. When will this pain end? "I didn't know you sing," a soothing voice surrounds me.

I turn around to see Rider standing in the doorway. I run into his arms, I've missed him so much. He pulls me in tight, I know he's missed me too. I don't want to let go of him right now. I feel safer, calmer. Why am I so weak? He hurt me but I don't care right now. I need him more. "You came back to me," I say, still hugging him tightly.

"I would always come back to you baby." His words comfort me. He pulls away from me to see my face. He wipes away the tears with his thumb. He leans in to give me a soft gentle kiss.

"I want to go home Rider," I beg.

He sighs, "I know baby." He looks broken too.

"Please take me home," I beg even more.

"I can't baby."

"Why? I promise I will get better if I have you. I will be okay." I feel safer as his hostage than I have at any time of my life.

"You need to get better without me."

I can see in his eyes how hard this is for him. "You promised you wouldn't leave me." My words seem to hurt him.

"Emmie, I'm being arrested."

No way. "For what?" I mean he's a gang leader, but still.

"For your kidnap, taking advantage of you. For your mental state."

He's getting arrested because of me? He hasn't done anything that I didn't want him to do. "I'll tell them you didn't do anything." I can't lose him.

He sighs, "You're suffering a mental breakdown. Your word won't stand up in court." He takes my hands in his.

"I can't stay here Rider."

He gives me a reassuring smile. "Stay strong baby."

He cups my face in his hands and he runs fingers through my hair. He sends chills down my spine, his touch means so much more than anyone else's. How can I lose this beautiful man? He places his forehead on mine, I could stay in this moment forever. "I'm going to miss you," I confess.

He smirks at me, "I'll miss you too baby."

He kisses me more urgently, like this is going to be the last time. "Thank you for finding my Momma." He smiles at me.

"It's the least I could do for you beautiful." His scent smells so good. I'm so tired, I can't say goodbye yet.

"Please stay with me until I fall asleep," I beg.

"Okay baby." I climb into bed and he climbs in behind me. He hugs me tightly and strokes my hair, sending me into a daze. I feel calm and safe and I drift quickly to sleep.

*

Doctors tell me one month has passed. My recovery has been rocky and slow. Rider never got in contact. My Momma visits me every day. She has been my rock through all of this. Brody and Jessie tried to visit but I refused to see them. Danny feels guilty for putting me in this place so he doesn't visit often. I haven't been eating. I miss the sun. Doctors feel it will be good to be at home. Bit ironic because my home is with Rider. But I know home should be with family. My Momma arrives and she takes me home, we sit in silence in the car. I feel anxious about being out of the hospital, I feel anxious everywhere. I get out the car and I feel the sun on my face. I've missed this. "You coming inside?" Momma calls from the house.

"I'll be in, in a minute." I need a minute to think.

"Hey, beautiful." I turn around to see Brody. He knows I don't want to see him, so why is he here? I'm angry, all these emotions are exhausting. I punch him hard in the face, how dare he come here and act natural.

He holds his face where I hit him, "I know you're hurting but please let me explain." He looks sad.

"All you guys do is need to explain. Why do you guys always do stupid things that you need to explain? Do you know what I did for you?" I'm screaming at him, why?

He sighs. "Yes, I know this is my fault."

I need someone to be mad at, he got Rider locked up. "I suffered a breakdown because of you. Not Rider!" he looks hurt. Well good, I am struggling to get better, he deserves a little pain.

"I'm sorry," he says sadly.

It looks like something inside of him snapped. "I wasn't the one that kidnapped you, held you against your will, attacked you and brainwashed you." No one brainwashed me, they kept me safe.

How dare he? Is he serious? I wouldn't have been kidnapped if it wasn't for him. "How dare you, you don't understand. You never will." Only Rider understands me. He didn't brainwash me, I just fell in love with him. I know it was quick, but there was an attraction I couldn't deny. I trust him with my life. Which is why I let him have me. I felt sick at the thought of someone touching me. But Rider's touch was so much more, it was like he was healing me with every touch.

I was deep in thought and I suddenly feel Brody's lips on mine. That spark that was there before is still there. He kisses me and sends electricity through me. He still has it. The guy that I protected at the cost of myself. This is him, this is what I was protecting. I'm so angry with him but he's taking my breath away.

"Brody, stop." He takes a step back. My walls are still up and my body is screaming to stop.

"Emmie I'm sorry, I got carried away."

I take a deep breath. "It's okay, so did I." I felt it but I can't go any further than this. Brody just hits my wall. My wall won't lift for him.

He grins at me, "You felt it too?" I love his smile.

I sigh. "Yes, after all this time and anger," I confess.

"Please let me spend every day trying to fix things." I don't know what good it will do.

"You can try." I shrug.

"That's what you said to me at the beginning. I told you that I wouldn't stop. And I won't this time. I will win you back. Are you going back to school?"

It brings back memories. When things were less complicated. "Yes, Momma says routine will be good for me." The thought of school makes me feel sick.

He winks at me, "Well see you at school beautiful." He still affects me, I can't deny it.

I walk to my bedroom, I just want to curl up in my bed. It feels like ages since I've been in here. It feels empty, this isn't my home. I feel really dizzy. What's going on? I feel sick. "Danny!" I yell. He will protect me. I'm scared, I thought I was getting better. Danny is running into my room, shortly followed by Momma. They both look worried.

"Emmie, what's going on?" Danny asks.

"Baby girl talk to me."

I can't get any words out. Everything goes dark and I fall, some strong arms catch me.

I wake in the damn hospital again. I'm sick of hospitals, each time I think I'm getting better I end up taking 3 steps back. I look around to see Momma and Danny next to the bed, looking worried. I've been back one day, and I'm still causing them pain.

"What happened?" I ask.

"You fainted," Momma says.

"I'm not sick again am I?" I am terrified at the thought of it. I don't think I've got better but I'm out of the mental health clinic so that's all that matters.

"The Doctor is running some tests," Danny says, reassuring me.

The Doctor enters the room. He smiles at me.

"It's nice to see you again Emmie." I wish I could say the same.

"What's wrong with me? Am I sick again?" I dread the answer.

The Doctor shakes his head. "No Emmie you are not." I don't get it, so what's going on?

"Emmie, you're pregnant."

Chapter 6

I'm pregnant? How is that possible? Dad always took care of contraception. One day he came into my bedroom and told me he had to put this rod in my arm. He said it wouldn't hurt, he explained the procedure. I trusted him to do medical stuff, he is a good doctor. He told me it was called the implant and told me why I needed it. Every 3 years or so he would perform the same procedure. He was always very happy with himself once he'd done it. The first time he did it I was too young to understand. But I wanted to make him happy so I complied. "Excuse me, what did you just say?" I demand.

"You're pregnant Miss Salvatore," he says calmly.

How is he so damn calm? I'm losing my shit. Dad is going to be so mad if he finds out. The Doctor was talking but I wasn't hearing anything. My head is fuzzy.

"Baby girl."

Me, be a mother? I can't even look after myself.

"Emmie."

Rider is going to be pissed at me too. Maybe I shouldn't tell him, he won't want me or the baby. Not that he is likely to contact me.

"Emmie!" Momma shouts at me.

I guess I zoned out again. "Yeah?" I respond. All eyes are on me, what did I miss?

"Have you been listening to the Doctor?" Momma asks.

"I can't do this Momma." I'm so scared. Danny reaches for my hand. He looks me in the eye.

"Sis, you're okay. Just listen to the Doctor, he will give you the options." I'm so glad that Danny is here. I love my brother, I need overprotective Danny right now. I nod and look at the Doctor.

"As I was saying. You do have options. You can either have an abortion. Which we suggest to do it sooner rather than later. Or if you want to keep the baby we need to start you on folic acid and other vitamins. Then we would book you in for a scan later on. There is also adoption to consider."

This was way too much to think about. "I heard you, can I go now?" I need to get out of here, breathe the fresh air and feel the sun on my skin. Yes, this will help.

"Emmie, don't push us away. We are here for you whatever you decide. Emmie, honestly how could you be so careless?" Danny says.

Ugh really? Careless, is he really doing this? "I'm sorry I'm not perfect bro. And besides, I'm on the implant, I guess it ran out. Dad normally deals with that. I need to take walk." I climb out of bed. They all seem speechless, shocked at what I said. I guess I've dealt with this for a long time, they are still getting their heads around it. I storm out of the room and run outside.

I walk for what seems like ages gathering my thoughts. I can't imagine the thought of Rider hating me. Brody will hate me too because I never told him we slept together. He knew how I felt about going that far. He was willing to wait for me, but he's going to hate me now. Everyone will hate me when they find out. Rider is in jail, he hasn't contacted me. I don't know what I want anymore. I end up at the park, why I ended up here I have no idea.

"Hey, new girl."

Jeez, why do people sneak up behind me? I turn around to see Sky and Brody standing there. Sky has a cigarette in his hand, blowing smoke all over me.

"What's up beautiful?" Brody can tell something is wrong, he always can.

"What's wrong? What's wrong is that idiot smoking around me." They both look at me shocked and confused. What is it with people today, is there something on my face? Jesus.

"I thought you didn't mind?" Brody asks softly.

"Well, I do now." I cross my arms. I guess they just caught me at a bad time.

"Okay, no more smoking, you okay?"

Sky puts out his cigarette. "Just my life..." Because my life is painful, it just seems to be getting worse. I thought once Dad stopped hurting me my life would get better. But it hasn't, my Dad kept me safe from harm. Except from him. I need to calm down, I can't keep losing myself.

"Emmie take a deep breath, talk to me," Brody pleads with me. He used to calm me but now I'm not so sure. I'm not even sure he truly calmed me to start with.

"I'll catch you two lovebirds later." Sky walks off.

"Emmie breathe, what's going on?" he's worried.

I can't, he sweeps me off my feet and kisses me. How does he do this to me? Just two seconds ago I was angry. Sad, worried. And now being here with him has made me forget. Taking me by surprise. How can I hate him when he is doing everything he can to win me back? Deep down I know this is not his fault. I'm so fucked up. Not because of him. But because of Dad.

"Wow, you take my breath away." It feels good that I affect someone in this way.

"You are my safe haven, Brody." He smiles. Maybe I should give in to Brody, he has been trying so hard for me. He's been understanding and sweet. But all I can think of is Rider.

"I feel the same way." He does? He seems to say all the right things.

Something catches my eye, I look over Brody's shoulder to find someone standing behind Brody. My heart sinks when I realise who it is. He is wearing a hoody with the hood up covering his face, he is on the run after all. I don't think I've seen him so scruffy, he hasn't shaved in a while and he looks tired. "Daddy?" I say, terrified. He's come for me, I know it and Brody won't go down without a fight. But the difference is my Dad will fight harder for me. Brody turns around to look at him, he puts himself between me and my Dad. He's protecting me.

"Stay the hell away from her," Brody growls. Dad crosses his arms he looks at me sadly.

"How could you do this to me? I've given you everything. I forgave you for cheating on me. But this? I have to fix this. I can't sit back and watch you anymore."

What is he going on about? He's been watching me? But did I really expect anything else? I know how much I mean to him. "What do you mean?" I say awkwardly.

"You sick pig. She's not yours. You need help." Brody is really mad. This isn't good.

"Shut up. You've hurt her, she will never go back to you. If I didn't have more important things to do. I would kill you for doing this to her," he says, angry and accusing.

He's right, I don't know if I ever could go back to him. But I should try? "Dad please," I beg, I don't want him to hurt Brody. After what I went through last time, I still find myself protecting him. His eyes turn icy cold.

"What have I told you about that? You call me Daddy. You're my little girl. Remember that."

Yes, I do remember, the time when I called him Dad instead of Daddy. He pinned me up against the wall, put his hands around my throat and choked me. I felt the life draining from my face. I didn't think he was going to stop, he terrified me that day. More so than any other. Fighting for your breath like that is life changing. From that day, I've always called him Daddy, no matter how much I hate it. "Sorry Daddy, don't hurt him." I don't even know what I'm going to do with the baby but I naturally hug my tummy. To protect him or her. I know my Dad will take me. I need to protect my baby. "Okay Daddy, I will come with you. Just please don't hurt anyone." I see his eyes light up.

"Good girl, princess. That's my girl." I go to walk towards Dad but Brody puts his arm in front of me and pushes me back.

"You must be stupid if you think I'm going to let you take her," he scoffs.

Dad laughs. "Oh I will take her, I need to take care of this disgusting thing in her tummy." He scowls at my tummy. I hug my tummy again, he wants to kill my baby.

"You're pregnant," he says in surprise. His face is hurt. I didn't want him to find out like this.

Dad punches Brody while he is off guard. That was unfair. "Stop. Please," I beg. I hate violence. I don't want Brody hurt. Brody throws a punch.

"It's okay beautiful." He seems calm, I thought he would hate me once he knew I was pregnant.

Dad punches Brody again but Brody falls to the ground. "Brody!" I scream. I kneel down to see if he is okay. He's still breathing but unconscious. Deep down I know if this was Rider with me, he wouldn't let Dad take me. He would die trying.

"Come on," Dad demands. I can't leave Brody like this.

"No!" I protest. Dad punches me hard in the face. I fall to the ground, he doesn't normally hit my face. He picks me up and carries me to the car. The scent of him sends flashbacks. I feel really sick. What is he going to do with my baby? He throws me in the car. I know better than to make a run for it, so I sit in silence.

We reach an abandoned building. It looks creepy. He gets out the car and comes to my side of the door. He opens the door and reaches in and pulls me out. He grabs my hand and leads me inside. We enter into the damp bedroom. I know it's wrong but I've missed my Dad. Not the abuse, but my Dad. I will always love my Dad.

"I've missed you, princess. I've been waiting for so long to have you back." I've missed your protection. I missed you Dad.

Has he been staying here all this time? No wonder he looks scruffy. "I've missed you too." He frowns at me.

"I'm not sure I believe that. You slept with someone else," he growls.

He punches me in the face and I fall to the floor. "Get up!" he orders. I obey. "You are mine, do you understand?" I nod.

He hits me again, I can feel blood dripping down my face. "Daddy, please stop," I beg.

He pins me up against the wall, grabs my chin and turns my head. He whispers in my ear, "That's what you should have said to that idiot."

He's jealous and he's taking it out on me. He kisses my exposed neck. He rips my clothes off leaving me in my underwear. It's cold in here. He leaves the room, why? I stay put, not daring to move. He comes back in with a first aid kit. He addresses my wounds on my face. He seems to take extra care. He really is good at his job.

"I can't believe what they did to you. Your head injury. I was so worried. I tried to get to you but that idiot had people everywhere. I was angry, I'm going to be more careful with you in future." So that's why he is treating my wounds before he has me. He's worried about my health.

I've missed how well he treated me with my injuries, I know he was the one who injured me but I never needed any operations or anything and he made me recover each time, kept me from school. He finishes nursing me. He picks me up and places me on the bed. Tonight he is very gentle with me. He tucks me into bed and climbs in behind me. He pulls me close to him. It feels strange, why isn't he forcing himself on me? It's what I'm used to. I'm not used to this with him. I think of Rider, and me being his hostage. I drift slowly to sleep.

Days pass, I know no one is coming for me. Rider is in prison and he won't know I'm missing and even then, why would he care? Well, Brody, he couldn't find me last time. I knew I must protect myself the only way I can. I start to lose myself. I just slipped away from my body, I still feel some pain but it's easier this way. I'm in my own little world, drifting in space. I feel light as a feather. It's just me here with my thoughts. I'm going to be stuck like this forever, no one is coming. Which is fine because I feel safe here. Dad got really angry when I left my body but he carried on as normal. He's a Doctor so he knows what's happening. I feel cold all the time.

Time flew past, I honestly don't know how much time. I'm lost in deep thought when I hear a door slam. Dad is always very quiet, even when he is mad he never slams doors. I hear shouting. What's going on? The voice is soothing, what is he doing here? It's Rider, he came for me. He found me. I feel hope, he's angry as usual but I'm not scared of him at all, I feel comforted by him being here. I hear a gunshot followed by a stabbing pain in my side. I want to clutch my side but I can't move. I feel paralysed. Who shot me? I hear another gunshot but without the pain. Who else was shot? Please say it wasn't Rider. I pray to god it wasn't him. I feel hands on mine.

"Hey baby, come back to me." He strokes my hair. He's okay. Thank you, thank you.

"Is she okay?" Brody's here too? They're working together? I never thought I'd see the day.

"She's alive, let's get her to the hospital. Call her family, get them to meet us there." Rider scoops me up into his arms. I feel warm and protected. His scent surrounds me. I just want to bury my face into his chest but I can't move.

I feel sore, very sore. It smells clean and sterile. I guess I'm in hospital again, I hate being here but I guess it's better than being in that damp cold building. I feel Rider again, he's stroking my hair again. I feel really groggy.

"Hey baby, please come back to me." His voice is hurt. I hate to know he is hurting.

"Hey beautiful, come back to me." Brody is here too. They both want me to come back, but I can't. I'm not ready to wake up to all the pain and heartbreak. I'm protected here.

"Why isn't she waking up?" Danny demands.

"I'm sorry, it looks like she's not ready." There is that annoying Doctor again. At least he knows my name isn't Mrs Grey.

"Why isn't she coming back to me like she did last time?" Rider says sadly. I don't want him sad.

"That was a miracle. I guess so much has happened, she doesn't feel safe. Some patients stay in this state for years. Keep talking to her. She may come around. Reassure her," the doctor says calmly.

"How is this happening?" Rider says whilst crying. Rider crying? I feel hurt, when he is hurt, I'm hurt.

"I think we all need some rest," Momma says. Yes, I need them all to take care of themselves.

"I'm not leaving her, I will take the first shift watching her," Rider says stubbornly. I like that he doesn't want to leave me.

"Okay, call if you need anything," Momma says.

"Do you want a bed made up Rider?" the Doctor says.

"No thank you." He needs to sleep, I need him to look after himself.

"What will happen when she wakes up?" Brody asks. What does he mean?

"She will have to make a choice," Brody says matter of factly.

"Honestly, I just want her to be okay. If she's happy and wants to be with you, I will accept that. I just want her to be happy," Rider says. I can't believe how understanding he is being but I guess he doesn't know about the baby.

"Wow, dude. Better than me. I couldn't stand to lose her," Brody says, shocked. Why are they doing this now?

"The difference is, I'd rather her alive and happy than she be dead. I will cope as long as she's alive," Rider says. His words are so sweet, maybe he does care about me more than I thought.

"I'll be back later." I guess Brody left.

"Hey, baby. You're still causing mischief as usual. Where's my smart mouthed girl gone? Our baby is okay. Stay strong for our baby. I love you. I will never leave you." Oh my god, he knows about the baby? How did that happen? I love those words. He says he loves me, I feel warm and fuzzy inside. I can't believe they were fighting over me. At least they weren't fighting each other. I'm so glad my baby is okay. I don't know what is going on, I have so many questions. I love you too Rider, and I wish that were true. That you would never leave me.

Wow, I can smell him all around me. He's lying behind me, cuddling me. No wonder he didn't want a bed made up, he wanted to share mine. I guess he wants to keep me close, and I love it. I love that he is here with me, protecting me. He's my drug. My home.

"Hey, beautiful. I'm back. I hope you're fighting in there with your smart mouth. Come back to me, beautiful. I love you. I can deal with the baby. We can be together as a family. I was so worried I was going to lose you. I hope you're dreaming of the sun on your face. With horses surrounding you. All the horses are gay because you dressed them in pink! I don't think the boy horses like pink." Brody's back.

Rider is still with me, he is breathing softly in my ear. I guess he is sleeping. I feel his arm around me. He loves me? Two guys love me. What did I do to deserve this? I'm no one. Haha, this guy is nuts. Pink on horses? Not such a bad idea haha. Enough with the come back to me crap, I would if I could. He remembers that day I answered his questions. I can't get back to them, will I stay here forever? I stare at the stars, they are really pretty. And I drift away in space.

"Is there any change?" Momma says. When did she come back?

"No, not yet," Brody responds.

I feel a shift of weight, the warm arm protecting me has gone. I guess he is awake. I don't want him to get up. I can't smell him anymore, it suddenly makes me panic.

"I'm going to go home and change." Wait what? He said he wouldn't leave me. No, please don't leave me.

"Okay," Momma replies.

"I'll leave you guys to talk. I'll be back later too," Brody says.

"Why hasn't she woken up yet?" Momma cries.

"She's still hurting Mom. She will come back to us," Danny says reassuringly.

They are both leaving me. What if Rider sleeps with someone else again? What if Brody runs back to Jessie? I can't take this anymore, he said he wouldn't leave. The anchor that was keeping me here is gone. So I slip away, I'm too tired to fight anymore. It all goes black. I feel like a weight has been lifted. I feel peaceful.

I feel a sudden shock. Ow, what the hell was that? I felt peaceful, now I just feel pain again.

"Emmie is stable now," the Doctor says. I am? I wouldn't use that word to describe myself.

"What happened?" Momma says crying.

"Seems like she gave up fighting, her heart stopped. But we managed to get her back." Why bother? I wanted to slip away. I was peaceful.

"Give up fighting, why did she do that?" Danny sounds shocked.

"She heard them leave. She heard Rider leave... Call him," Momma demands. Yes, the pain I felt when he left. He promised he wouldn't leave me. I knew it was a matter of time before he left but it doesn't mean it hurt any less.

"Okay," Danny agrees. I zone out again, blocking out the noise of the hospital. I want to be alone. I'm always alone, it's what I'm used to.

"Hey baby, I'm sorry I left you. Please don't scare me like that again." He's back again. Time seems to be flashing before my eyes. His words comfort me. I begin to relax again, how does he affect me so much?

"We will go grab a coffee, we won't long," Momma says.

"Did all the words I never said hurt as bad as those I did? You know I never even cared, not before you. If I could go and turn back time, if I could only press rewind, I would bleed this heart of mine just to show you I'll be the first to say I'm sorry, the first to say I'm stupid. Why do I always take it there? Is it hopeless or maybe you still want to meet me at the altar? And I will lay it all to bare, and I told you all my secrets, all my fears, I've let go. And it's flawless, you are the only one, you are the only one, don't you know, don't you know? Am I fading from your mind, has the distance blurred the lines? They say all things heal with time, but it's untrue, I will linger on every word, I know it's more than I deserve. Chances are I'll make it worse, but I need to. And I told you all my secrets, all my fears, I've let go and it's flawless, you are the only one, you are the only one, don't you know? Don't you know that the hardest part's not having you to hold? Don't you know, this old heart of mine can't bear to see you go?"

Wow, he's been softly singing to me, I feel hope for the first time in my life. I love his voice, it's surrounding me. Who knew he could sing? He has a lovely voice, I must get him to sing to me more often. He's my home, these lyrics mean so much. My heart aches for him. I start to drift. Where am I going? I manage to open my eyes, I see Rider's beautiful face. He has tears falling down his face.

"Stop singing already, you're making my ears bleed." I giggle. But stop because it hurts. He looks up at me and he looks like a kid at Christmas. I smile at him. He hugs me tight. This feels so good.

"Baby you're awake. Is my singing that bad?" he laughs.

"Haha. No, your voice is beautiful. You're my anchor to this world.

You pulled me back to you with your singing, your lyrics. You brought me home." I stare into his eyes. I get lost.

Chapter 7

I sit up in bed and Rider hugs me tightly, please don't ever let me go, that's my biggest wish. Being in his arms is so good. He sits on the bed in front of me, we both sit crossed legged. Knees to knees, with my hands in his. We sit like this for ages in silence, soaking each other in. Until he breaks the silence.

"Hey Mi Chica Bella."

What is he going on about? "You're a Moron." I glare at him. He smirks, I love it when he does that. His eyes light up and make them irresistible.

"I've missed your insults."

I love messing with him, "Is that the only thing you've missed?"

He laughs, "I can think of something." He leans forward and kisses me. I love playful Rider, I love every part of Rider, even the angry Rider.

"What happened Rider?" his face drops.

"You know what? Why don't you call me by my first name?" he says.

I'm confused, "I thought I did?"

He shrugs, "Rider is my last name, my first name is Damon. Not many people know that and only family calls me by my first name."

He's opening up to me and I feel warm inside. Does that mean he sees me as family? I love that he is sharing but I also know he's stalling. I play around with his name, "Damon... Yes, I like it but what the hell is going on?"

He laughs at me, "Demanding aren't you?"

I try to act sweet, "Who me? I'm just an innocent girl and you are stalling."

"You keep telling yourself that, you are the most beautiful, bravest badass I know."

He's flirting with me and I can't help but blush. How can he think these things about me, I don't see it. "Thanks, I think. What the hell happened?" I demand, something really bad must have happened if he keeps stalling.

"What do you remember?" he asks, frowning at me.

"I remember my Dad taking me, that first night Damon. He was different." Damon frowns.

"What do you mean different?"

"Well he was gentle with me, he seemed worried he was going to break me. He punched me so hard in the face that I fell to the floor. He shouted for me to get up. So I obeyed." I take a deep breath gathering my thoughts. "He hit me again, I could feel the blood running down my face. I got back up, he used his body to trap me against the wall." Damon's face is in pain, I know he doesn't want to hear this but he wants me to be open to him. "I begged him to stop and Dad growled at me and said yes, that's what you should have said to him." I leave out the idiot part because Damon isn't an idiot, not to me anyway. "He was jealous, he thinks I should have said no to you Damon." He's listening to me intently but he's hurting.

"God knows what was going on in his head baby," he sighs.

"Anyway, he ripped my clothes off and he just walks out the room." Damon looks shocked.

"Why would he do that?"

"I was so scared that I stayed where he left me, he'd never left me like that before raping me, it was new to me. He came back with a first aid kit."

"A first aid kit?"

"Yeah, I was shocked too, for the first time he looked in pain. Like he was sorry for what he did. Maybe the time apart made him appreciate me more."

"Baby don't feel sorry for him. He doesn't deserve it," he says.

"After he cleaned the blood and took care of the wound, he took me to bed." Damon holds his hands up.

"Baby I don't want to know any more, maybe you can talk about it like it's normal. But I can't get my head around it."

"Damon, you don't get it, he didn't rape me that night. He just hugged me and I drifted asleep, it felt normal. Like I had the Dad I always wanted." I know he won't understand how I'm feeling but I'm not going to lie.

"He didn't? I don't get it. But then I don't get why you felt normal. The guy just hit you."

"I love my Dad, Damon. Even if it is wrong. I know he loves me too." I can see the pain in his eyes.

"Your Dad shot you, Emmie." He did what? Why would he do that? Maybe I didn't know my Dad like I thought I did.

"Why would he do that?"

"Brody and I worked together to find you. We finally got a tip-off. He was in a hospital getting the abortion drugs. He had obviously been laying low for the week. We followed him back to where he was keeping you."

I'm shocked. "A week? I was gone for a week? I still can't believe you two worked together. I heard you."

He frowns, "What do you mean you heard me? We had a common goal, Emmie. To save you."

"When you came to save me. This past week I've been drifting, it was safe. It was a pretty place. Like my own safe bubble. I heard you, it brought me back to the here and now. Your voice. Brody's voice. I heard a gun shot. I was so worried that one of you got shot."

"I tried to save you but I wasn't quick enough. I was terrified as you were awake but you wouldn't respond, lifeless. I couldn't imagine what pain he caused you. The last time I looked in your eyes, your spark was gone. But this time it was like you were gone. Just an empty body."

I remember the last time I saw him. I was at rock bottom. I didn't want him to leave me. "You tried to take a bullet for me? How are you out of jail anyway?"

He shrugs, "I would give you my life. I've been having you watched by Sully. He rang me to tell me about the baby. He said that you were so unhappy, his words, like you, were alive but you weren't living. You needed me, so I used my connections to get out of jail. And I find out you'd been taken. My heart ripped out, even more than it did when I left you in the mental hospital." He strokes my face, I love the way he looks at me. It's like I'm the only one in the world. Like he could look at me forever. I do need you Damon and that scares me.

"So is my Dad in jail now?" He takes a deep breath.

"No Emmie, he shot himself in the head. Probably lucky he did as I would have killed him myself. I think he killed himself to be with you." He looks angry but in pain at the same time.

My Dad is dead? I don't know whether to feel pain, sadness or relief? Tears start rolling down my face. My Dad's dead.

"You are safe now baby. Don't cry." Damon kisses my tears that roll down my face. He takes my face in his hands and kisses my lips urgently. Damon makes me forget everything. We hear the door of my room open and Damon pulls away.

"Oh my god princess, you are awake." Momma comes running to my side. Talk about awkward timing. Danny comes striding over to me too with a huge smile on his face.

"Hey sis, you sent us all mad. Don't do that again okay?"

I giggle. "I like sending people mad." They all laugh, the bastards.

"And don't we know it," Danny says laughing.

"Let's take you home," Momma says reassuringly.

Home isn't that place. All I know is abuse. "Okay," I respond with a sigh. I guess I would rather go there than stay here in the hospital. Danny and Momma leave the room, Damon helps me out of bed. I feel sore. I look down at the floor but Damon places his hand on my chin and lifts my chin so my eyes meet his. It's like he knows what I'm thinking. He takes my breath away. He kisses me urgently, his hands find themselves on my back, pulling me close. He pulls away, leaving me craving more. What is he doing to me? "Have you finished taking advantage of me now?" I smile sweetly.

He raises an eyebrow, "It's not taking advantage if you are enjoying it."

Oh, that's so true. "Who said that? I hated it, you aren't a very good kisser, you know." I toy with him. He comes closer to me but not touching me, my breathing becomes rapid, anticipating what he is going to do.

"Your body is telling me something different Emmie, maybe I should get more practice," he says with a quiet sexy voice.

I swallow and bite my lip. "Maybe you should." I look into his eyes they are playful and happy. What I wouldn't do for this man. He reaches up and strokes my hair and kisses me. I feel his tongue caressing mine, the torture he inflicts on me. These feelings are new to me and they honestly scare me. Damon scoops me up into his arms, I snuggle up to his neck. He smells so good, I'm home right here right now. I feel safe, protected. I love being in his arms. He carries me to his car and places me in the front passenger seat. He climbs in the car on the other side. He leans over to get my seatbelt.

"Safety first Emmie," he laughs at me.

"Is that because you are a bad driver?"

He frowns. "No Emmie, it's because you are so accident prone."

I guess he is right, I am. I never used to be, my Dad was always so strict. I wasn't allowed to breathe without his say so. I watch Damon drive all the way back to the house, there is something I find sexy about watching him drive. Maybe it's the pregnancy hormones. The car journey ended all too soon for my liking. I go to climb out the car but Damon is already at my door. I love being in his arms but I'm not a kid. He leans down to pick me up. I must be really heavy but he seems to pick me up like I weigh nothing. He gently puts me down and knocks on the door, Momma opens the door to let us in. She gives us a smile and walks off to the kitchen.

"Make sure you take it easy, maybe I should carry you to bed," Damon says, flirting with me.

I roll my eyes. "I'm fine, stop fussing. I don't think you could control yourself," I say, teasing.

"Not where you're concerned, shall I take you to school tomorrow?" he asks.

"No it's okay, I can walk," I shrug.

"Emmie, you do realise I'm not letting you go out alone," he sighs.

Argh, I'm not a kid. "Seriously Damon. Stop fussing, I'm pregnant not a cripple." I'm angry. Why am I angry? He's actually being pretty sweet, caring about me but I'm shouting at him. What's wrong with me?

"You are going to be one tough cookie to handle, especially because of our baby," he says, winking at me.

"If you can't handle me at my worst, you don't deserve me at my best," I say, crossing my arms.

He raises his eyebrow. Damn, he is sexy when he does that. I can't help but bite my lip. "Your mouth, what I'd like to do with it, and trust me, I'd take any part of you that you'd give me. Can I ask you something?" he says. It sounds like a promise.

I can't help but think, what would he like to do with it? I shrug. "Umm sure." He takes a deep breath and sighs. He looks in pain, sad even.

"At the hospital, you came back to me, you followed my voice. You fought for me. The Doctor thought it was a miracle. Why didn't you fight this time? After all, I was only your kidnapper then."

His question pulls on my heartstrings. He is hurt I didn't wake for him but he hurt me, does he not understand that? "Damon I did fight for you. Your voice surrounded me. I could feel you when you slept next to me. I tried to fight. I tried to fight for Brody too but you both hurt me. You betrayed me, both of you." I don't think he liked my answer, but I don't want lies between us. He seems to be processing the information I've just given him.

"So how did you come back?" he asks curiously.

"You said you wouldn't leave me. I felt safe. I heard every word you had with Brody. How you both felt about me. Both of you declaring your love for me. I was ready to forgive you both. I didn't think I could ever get back to you two. I wanted to." I try to reassure him.

"So what happened?" he asks.

"You both left me. It hurt like nothing else. I knew my anchor, you had left me. I was worried you would sleep with someone else like you did last time. I felt rage, anger, sadness. I thought Brody would seek comfort in Jessie again. The pain was too much." Even Dad never made me feel this sort of pain.

"So that's when you stopped fighting?" he asks.

"I suppose. I thought you both could get on with your life. But then I heard you come back. Your voice, your singing. It was like nothing I'd ever heard. The lyrics were so true. You pulled me back," I say matter of factly. He looks hurt by what I've just confessed to him.

"But who did you choose?" I take a deep breath.

"I don't know." I hate not being able to choose and I know by his face that he is hurt. I'm so torn between these two guys. Before Brody, I never felt anything towards guys. I couldn't allow myself and now I have two guys who care for me. I will never understand why. I am nothing, I'm worthless.

"I'd better go," he says.

He's leaving? Those words seem to rip my heart out. I've never been this dependent on someone before, it terrifies me. "Fine, just go, you moron." All I want to do is jump in his arms and make him stay. But why would he want me?

"Emmie please," he says. What? He's the one leaving me. He steps towards me. I look at the floor not wanting to make eye contact, not wanting him to know he's hurt me. He places his hand on my face and gently lifts my chin to meet his gaze. The way he looks at me, it's like he can see right into my soul, like he gets me. It makes me feel warm and fuzzy. He leans in for a kiss. We start off soft and gentle, but we can't hold back, he becomes more demanding with his kiss. I know he wants this just as much as me. He strokes my hair with his hands and runs his fingers through my hair. Damn, what does he do to me? He breaks away from me, leaving me wanting more. "Goodbye Mi Chica Bella." He waves and leaves the house. Leaving me alone.

I go in search of my Brother. I walk into the kitchen where Danny and Momma are sat at the breakfast table. They are deep in conversation as they don't notice me come in. I head for the fridge to get some water. I'm so thirsty, as I open the door I see a hand on the fridge door. I spin around, "Jesus Danny, don't do that. You made me jump." What an idiot. I slap his arm.

"Emmie, sit down, I will get you whatever you want."

"Danny I can get myself some water." God, here comes overbearing Brother.

"Emmie, sit down." He glares at me. I roll my eyes and head for the chair. I wince as I sit down. I guess I'm still sore. I watch Danny as he moves gracefully around the kitchen fetching a glass. I hate to have people running around after me. I'm not a child. Danny places the glass on the table and takes a seat next to me. I down the drink in one.

"Do you want me to get you some food?"

Food? No that's the last thing on my mind. "No thank you."

"Emmie I don't want you lifting a finger. Anything you want you just yell okay?"

I roll my eyes at him. "Do you know what I really want?" I say.

"You name it and it's yours," he says reassuringly.

"Okay, well I want you to stop bloody fussing. I'm fine." Danny sighs.

"Emmie we are just worried about you," Momma says.

"I'm going to go lie down," I say and Danny jumps to his feet.

"Sit down Danny," I say annoyed. Is he going to follow me everywhere?

"Let me just get you into bed Emmie and then I promise I will leave you alone."

"Fine, whatever." Danny helps me up the stairs and into bed. The one thing I love is this bed. It is so comfy. Danny leaves the room, leaving me to it. I am exhausted even though I've been in a coma for a week. I drift to sleep.

I wake with a jolt. I feel soft hands on my face. I feel very disorientated. I'm hot and clammy. Urgh, I must have had another nightmare. I look up to see Damon's face peering down at me. He is sat next to me on the bed.

"Hey, baby. Are you okay?" he asks curiously.

"Yeah, I guess I'm okay. What are you doing here?" he strokes my cheek. God, I must look awful and here he is looking at me like I'm perfect.

"I came to take you to school, but I got here and you were very restless." He looks sad.

"I get nightmares, Damon. It's nothing new." I shrug.

"What are your nightmares about?" he asks.

"My Dad mostly." They're often of the past where Dad used to hurt me. Flashbacks, they feel very real. Sometimes they are the anticipation of Dad hurting me.

"Baby your Dad is dead, he can't hurt you." Of course I know that when I'm awake but I can't control my fears when I'm asleep. I climb out of bed.

"I need to get dressed Damon," I say with my arms folded. He lifts his eyebrow up in that way that makes me warm and fuzzy inside. Damn, he's hot and he knows it. "Get out Damon."

He smirks, "Do I have to? I've seen you naked." He eyes me up from head to toe.

I squirm under his gaze, he knows exactly what he's doing. Keep cool Emmie. "I know but get out Damon."

He chuckles gently, "Spoil sport. We could have some fun." He winks at me.

"Out, now! Anyway, I thought I should be resting?" I say, teasing him.

"Oh baby, I would make an exception," he says, flirting with me.

"I won't tell you again," I say angrily. Why do my moods seem to change so quickly? He laughs.

"Okay smart mouth, I'm going." I watch him as he strides out the door. I put on some blue denim shorts and a black top with some dolly shoes. I love Spain, I love the heat, the sun. I brush my hair and leave it to hang over my shoulders. I stagger to the bathroom to wash my face and brush my teeth. I feel exhausted before I've even done anything. I take one last glance in the mirror before deciding that will do. I make my way downstairs.

I'm greeted by Danny and Damon standing in the hallway. They seem to be talking freely. They both look up and smile. "Hey Sis, I've got to run but take it easy, okay?"

I roll my eyes. "Yeah, whatever." I huff. He kisses me on my cheek and heads for the door.

"Wow, you look amazing, you'll be sending all the guys wild." He looks jealous.

"Nothing new there then, this school is like dogs on heat." I hate how guys flirt with me. I'm no one special so why do they do it? Are they making fun of me or what? I don't get it.

"I can't blame them. Come on, let's go."

We walk to his car. He drives a black BMW, god, men and their cars. He holds the passenger door open for me to climb in. What a gentleman. The school isn't far from home so the journey isn't long. We climb out of the car. He places his hand in mine, this feels so natural with Damon. We walk to the main hall. I turn to face Damon. "So are you going to enrol in school Damon, so you can watch me?" I say with my arms crossed.

"I'm tempted just to keep the guys away. But no, I've got work to do." He smiles.

"Hey, new girl." God, one guess who that is. I turn around to face Sky who seems to be drooling slightly. Awkward.

"You are looking hot today, nice to see you back," he says, winking.

"What did I tell you about calling me that?" I fold my arms. Damon takes a step towards me and places his arm around my waist pulling me close. He's jealous and he is marking his territory. Really?

"Maybe I should find a different name," he says, toying with the idea.

"You think?" I sigh.

"Someone's sassy, I love that in a girl. You know I was the one that told Brody you'd got kidnapped."

Huh, he was? Shame Brody couldn't find me. Instead, he was busy kissing Jessie. "What, do you want a medal?" I say, annoyed.

"More like a kiss," he says.

"I don't think so buddy," Damon says angrily.

Wow, who knew he would be so wound up by this? I try to lighten the mood. "You'll be lucky Sky," I say with a giggle. Sky crosses his arms, he looks pissed.

"Who is this guy anyway?" he says while eying up Damon's arm around me.

"Someone not to be messed with," Damon growls.

"Damon, chill." I roll my eyes.

Sky looks startled, "Hang on, he's the guy that kidnapped you, isn't it?"

Jeez, does it really matter? It's happened now and who cares? "That's none of your business Sky."

Sky takes a deep breath, "I'll catch you later new girl." He winks and wanders off.

"Is that guy for real? Maybe I should stay just to fend off the guys."

"What, is someone jealous?" I say, teasing.

"Emmie he was all over you."

I hear before I can see. Jade's annoying voice coming from behind me. She appears in front of me and glares at me. If looks could kill, I would be dead.

"Oh, it's you. I'd like to say I'm glad you're back but I'm not." Straight to the point. I guess I admire that.

"Aww is queen bee worried that I will humiliate her again?" I giggle.

"You're a crazy bitch, you knocked me out," she says angrily. The only one that looks crazy is her.

"It didn't take a lot, you and your girl slaps wouldn't get you anywhere. So are you afraid that I will be the one the guys all want?" I shrug. She looks awkward, she's definitely worried. "Yes you are or you wouldn't be here threatening me."

"I can see my girl is a total badass in this school." He grins at me. I almost forgot he was here, he's been rather quiet. Jade deliberately moves between me and Damon and starts giving him the flirtatious eye. Really? She's unbelievable.

"I haven't seen you around here handsome."

"I don't go to school here."

"Damn, it would have been nice to hang," she says, getting closer to him.

"Hello, I am here you know," I say annoyed. Yes, this is pissing me off. They are both ignoring me. What is Damon doing? Getting me back because of Sky?

"So you must work out a lot huh?" She's totally eye fucking him right now and he's not pushing her away.

"Yes I do actually, I have to keep in shape." His strong muscles whilst he made love to me. The way they were gentle with me yet I could feel how strong he was. How much he wanted me.

"I can tell." She touches his biceps. That's it, I've had enough of this.

"Are you kidding me right now? What the hell is this?" I yell. I storm off to class, leaving them to flirt behind me. I hear Damon yell my name but I just keep walking. I feel the anger rising inside of me. Brody catches my eye.

"Hey beautiful, what's wrong?" concern runs through his face.

"Nothing, whatever, doesn't matter," I mumble under my breath looking at the floor.

"It matters to me when you are upset," he says, reassuring me.

"I don't want to talk about it," I growl.

He closes the gap between us. I'm too angry to move. His hands find my face, he looks into my eyes and he moves in for a kiss. I return the kiss, his soft lips calm me down. I am so fucked up, I'm jealous because Damon is flirting with Jade. Yet I'm here kissing Brody. He pulls away and smiles.

"Better?" he smirks.

I nod. "Yes, better," I agree. What's wrong with me? Why can't I pick one?

"Good, I will see you in class beautiful." He winks at me and walks off.

I feel someone push me from behind. I fall into the classroom in front of me. I fall flat on my stomach. I hear the door slam behind me. Ouch, sharp pain reaches my back and stomach. God please no. I climb to my feet, I'm in agony. What the hell happened? I walk to the door clutching my stomach. I pull the handle but it's locked. Did it lock when it slammed? I see smoke coming from the door. Is there a fire in the school?

"Hello, is someone there?" I scream. I can't get out, I'm trapped. I hear the fire alarm go off. I start to panic, my heart beating rapidly.

I fish for my phone my hands are all sweaty. I drop my phone, I'm such a clutz and a nervous wreck. I slowly bend down to collect my phone. Tears fall down my face. I ring the only person who I need right now, the first person who comes to mind. He answers on one ring.

"Emmie?" he says worriedly.

"Damon. Please help me," I beg.

"Where are you baby?" he demands softly. Trying not to worry me. But I can tell he's worried.

"I'm locked in the science lab, Damon. I fell on my tummy. I'm scared." I'm a blubbering mess. I start to cough as the smoke starts to get thicker.

"Shit, I will be there soon baby."

Chapter 8

It feels like a lifetime since I've been trapped in this classroom. I just want to be safe in Damon's arms. For him to stroke my hair to smell him all around me. But instead, I can't breathe. Coughing from the smoke. I start to see flames coming from the door.

"Baby, can you hear me? We are both here." I hear Damon and Brody outside the door discussing strategy. I'm scared.

"I can't breathe Damon," I yell but I end up coughing. I'm starting to feel light headed.

"We need to get this door open. Something could be wrong with the baby," Damon informs Brody. I slowly drop to the floor, not having the energy to hold myself up. I curl up in a ball.

"What the hell is going on? Who locked her in?" Brody says angrily. Someone locked me in?

"I don't know but I will soon find out. Baby talk to me," Damon calls out to me.

But I can't find the air to respond. I hear them kicking down the door. Takes them a good few blows to get the door open. Look at them working together. Lights me up inside. Damon rushes in, I look up at his face. He looks mega angry but he always has a reassuring smile just for me. He picks me up into his arms and I drift asleep knowing I'm safe in his arms.

I wake to the suffocating sterile smell. My throat is very sore. I start to cough, I feel warm hands on my free hand as I cover my mouth with my other hand. I look up to see Damon giving me one hell of a smile. He makes me melt under his gaze.

"What have you been up to this time? I should reserve this bed just for you," the Doctor says questioningly. He is pretty handsome in his own way. But isn't there something appealing about a Doctor anyway? How smart they are.

"How is she?" Damon responds almost immediately.

"She's suffered minor burns and smoke inhalation. She needs rest. But she will be fine," he says matter of factly.

"And what about my baby?" I say breathlessly. I stroke my tummy with my free hand. Damon still has hold of my other hand.

"Your baby is fine, strong like its Mom," he smiles. Oh, thank god. Damon puts his hand over mine on my stomach, I meet his gaze and he smirks at me. I can't believe how into this baby he is. I mean he's a bloody gang leader.

"So why the pain? What happened?" I look up to see Brody sitting in the corner of the room. He's been here all this time silent. I hadn't even noticed he was here. He winks at me sending butterflies to my tummy.

"Most likely the jolt of falling. Stress? Emmie, were you stressed before this happened?" Of course, I bloody was.

"Yes, someone was being a complete idiot." I glare at Damon but he tries to ignore me.

"That's why you were mad? Oh well, I enjoyed the kiss anyway," Brody says, thinking out loud. Oh shit.

"What, you kissed her? You're unbelievable," Damon says angrily, raising his voice.

Brody shrugs calmly at Damon, giving me another wink with a smirk on his face. I know what he's doing and it's working. Damon is mad. Really mad. "You were flirting with Jade, how do you think that's supposed to make me feel?" I cross my arms. At the end of the day, it's happened now, they both saved my life. It's over but I'm stubborn, I like to make them sweat a little bit.

Damon holds out his hands in front of him in denial. "Emmie I wasn't..."

I cough trying to clear my throat. The Doctor hands me some water. I take small sips. "Yes, you were. You completely ignored me. You're a jackass."

He laughs, mocking me. "Am I now?" Why is playful Damon so hot?

The way his lip curls up on one side. The sparkle in his eyes.

"Why would you be interested in Jade? I don't get it." He scoffs. Crossing his arms. He is so carefree, so different from Damon. Damon is angry all the time but he does show me glimpses of fun, playful Damon. But Brody, he is calm most of the time, his presence and whole demeanour. The way his hair falls close to his eyes. He is beautiful.

"I'm not interested in Jade. Give it a rest already," he growls, giving Brody a cold icy stare.

How does he change moods so quickly? "Stop it, both of you." They are like little kids arguing over a toy. Now I'm angry. They both crumble under my gaze.

"Emmie, take it easy and I can discharge you." I sit back against the bed. I can do relaxed, so long as I can get out of here sooner. I go to climb out of bed but Damon puts his hand on me stopping me getting up. The Doctor leaves the room and I look up at Damon.

"I need you watched 24/7," he says like he's not to be messed with. Has he not met me?

"I'm not a kid, I don't think so." Damon's face turns cold. I don't think he's used to be argued with.

"Emmie I agree with Rider." Again, I forgot Brody was here. The way he lays down the law. It's so casual like you could trust him. He is calm but you can tell he means it.

"What's going on?" I know there must be more to it than me being accident prone.

Damon takes a deep breath, "I think someone is trying to hurt you, Emmie."

Hurt me? Who? "Who would hurt me, Damon?"

"I don't know. But I will find out and so help them when I do." He is pissed. I know I shouldn't push him as he's only trying to look out for me but it's just been me, myself and I. I'm not used to all this attention.

"The fire and the locked door all seems strange to me," Brody says in deep thought.

"Me too, let's go," Damon shrugs.

I get up from the bed. I cross my arms. "No, I'm not a child. I'm not being watched 24 hours a day. You can forget it."

"You are acting like a child. I swear to god Emmie if you don't do as you're told." He is super angry. Maybe we aren't a good match, it looks like we wind each other up.

Brody gets up from the chair and strolls towards me. "Think of the baby beautiful."

It just takes that one word. Baby. How am I supposed to be a good mother when I don't even think of the baby at a time like this? I sigh. "I'm sorry, this pregnancy thing is messing with my emotions."

Damon chuckles, "Yeah, that's what it is."

"Hey." I can't resist him when he is like this.

"Why don't you both come to my safe house and we can talk to my team," Damon says, it's more of a command than a question though. Like I have a choice anyway but I think it was more for Brody's sake than mine. Brody nods in agreement. Damon scoops me up into his arms again.

"I can walk you know?" I huff against his neck.

"I thought as you were acting like a child, I would treat you like one. But mostly I love you in my arms, means I have you and you are safe." I smile against his neck. I love being in his arms too. Brody walks off ahead, getting the doors as we go. I start to tease Damon on the way out, slowly kissing up and down his neck.

"Emmie," he says breathlessly, warning me. I know I've affected him. I lean up and gently plant a soft kiss on his lips. I start to play with his long shaggy hair, twirling it with my fingers. He looks down at me with dilated eyes.

"God Emmie, what are you doing to me?" he confesses.

We reach Damon's car. He places me in the front passenger seat and does up my seat belt. Safety first with Damon. I roll my eyes at the thought. I watch him walk to the driver's seat. Brody climbs in behind me. It's awkward to have both of these people together in such a close proximity. Damon puts some music on to soften the mood probably. The car journey doesn't take long.

I take off my seatbelt and open the door. I climb out, coughing unladylike everywhere. Lovely. I push the door shut. Damon grabs my hand and leads me to the building shortly followed by Brody. He types in a code on the keypad. '641993'. He leads me into the building where we are greeted by the Big Guy.

"Hi Boss," he says.

"Gather up Larry and meet us in the lobby," Damon says with no pleases or thank yous.

I know he is the Boss but he could at least be polite. Sully nods and walks off. My eyes follow him whilst he walks away. I feel a gentle tug on my hand. Damon is pulling me into the next room. This feels exactly how I remember. Dark, gloomy and damp. We reach the room where I met that blonde-haired bimbo that Damon slept with. God, I hope I don't see her. Damon takes a seat on the sofa and gestures for me to sit next to him. So I do, he places his arm around me. Brody takes a seat next to me on the sofa. Sat side by side with the two people I care about.

Larry, the guy who hit me, walks into the room with the Big Guy. They look ready to take orders. "Boss, what's happening?" Larry says.

"Emmie got locked in a classroom and a fire started. I want her to have 24-hour security. Someone's after her," Damon says calmly. I tense at the thought of someone hurting my baby. I place my hands on my tummy. Damon pulls me onto his lap and puts his arms around me and places his hands on top of mine.

He whispers in my ear, "It's okay baby, you are safe." The way baby rolls of his tongue lights up my heart. He's protecting us both. And I do feel safe here with him.

"I will make some calls and see if I can find anything out," Larry informs. Damon nods and Larry leaves on his phone. Why would all these people help me? I don't understand. They don't know me. I'm not worthy of being protected. I miss my Dad so much.

"Sully, unless I'm with her, you are. Do you understand?" Damon says with his no-nonsense tone.

"Not the Big Guy," I groan. If I were to choose out of Big Guy and Larry, I would pick Sully every time. But hey, I like to be difficult. Sully blushes slightly, his cheeks matching the colour of his hair. I giggle.

"The Big Guy?" Brody asks.

"He's very strong." I shrug.

"Do I even want to know?" he asks.

"Probably not," I confess. He probably doesn't want to hear about when I was kidnapped.

"Well, you were having a tantrum. So I thought I'd give you as good as you give," he says, slightly embarrassed. I can tell he doesn't often have to deal with people like me. Or it may just be because I'm a girl. Who knows?

"You couldn't beat me," I scoff. He may be big but I could take him on.

"True, you are a total badass," he smirks.

Damon lifts his hand to his head in annoyance, I think? "Emmie, stop flirting with my staff," he growls. This guy is so jealous. I'm not even flirting. I don't know how to flirt. I've never had to nor wanted to. I cross my arms, offended. I turn my head to Brody, he seems annoyed too. Maybe I was flirting? I don't know. I always do things wrong. I look at the floor.

"I'll leave you to it." Sully retreats out the room. He must know what Damon is like.

My phone starts to ring. I grab it from my pocket and look at the caller ID. It's Jessie, I haven't spoken to her since Brody and her kissed. But I forgave Brody, I guess it's time I forgive her too.

"Hello?" I say.

"Hey, Emmie," Jessie says nervously. "Look I know we aren't getting on right now but I wondered if you wanted to go to the movies with me? Girls night." She sounds hopeful.

I want to go. But I know there will be arguments. "Sure, I'd like that." I get up off Damon's lap and turn to face them. Both their faces are like thunder.

"Great, see you at 7 pm at the movies." She hangs up. I place my phone back in my pocket.

I look up, anticipating what's to come. "Are you kidding me? You aren't going anywhere," Damon shouts.

Even in his angriest moments, he doesn't scare me but I imagine he scares other people the way his eyes glare at you. "Yes, I am." I shrug.

"Emmie, I thought we agreed?" Brody says calmly. He's annoyed but he knows he needs to be gentle with me.

"We did, that I couldn't be alone. Not that I couldn't go anywhere." I shrug. I'm not being locked up inside all day.

Damon sighs, "Fine, then I'm going with you."

I cross my arms, "Sorry, it's girls' night."

"Then you aren't going." Now who's being childish?

"I'll take the Big Guy," I shrug. Damon looks hurt but he obviously trusts Sully enough to do this. Anyway, what's the worst that could happen? That I could trip over my clumsy feet?

"God, you are so frustrating, woman. Fine," he agrees.

Brody says goodbye and he makes his leave. I head upstairs to shower quickly and change. Damon still has clothes here, again I don't know if they are for me or they are some old clothes from ex-girlfriends. I try to shrug the horrible thought from my mind. I hate the thought of him having other girlfriends. We aren't exactly official and I haven't even decided who I want yet. So why am I letting it get to me?

I grab a pair of jeans and a tight fitting blue top. It shows all my curves, when I say curves I mean fat. I hate my body, I hate my face and everything about myself. I use Damon's toothbrush to clean my teeth and use his comb to brush my unruly wavy black hair. I just stare at myself in the mirror wishing I saw something different. I get lost in thought when arms find themselves around my waist. I frown in the mirror.

"You look beautiful baby." I blush at his kind words. If only that were true. He kisses the back of my head. "Are you sure I can't come with you tonight? You are making me jealous of my staff."

I giggle but he was obviously being serious. I turn around so I am facing him, I run my fingers through his hair. I tug at his hair, giving me easier access to his lips, he's taller than me. He smiles against my lips and kisses me. This man feels like he was made for me. He knows how to make me feel special. The kiss, the electricity between us is breath-taking. Our kiss becomes more passionate, urgent, our breathing becoming rapid. His hands find themselves at the top of my legs. He lifts me up and pushes me against the wall. He is all I can think of at this moment. I need him more than I've needed anything else in this world. He lifts my top over my head. He kisses my exposed neck, nibbling as he goes.

I can't get enough of him in this moment. I grab his shirt and lift it over his head, he breaks contact so I can remove his shirt. His hands explore my hips, my hair. He isn't exactly being gentle but this is exactly what I need. He undoes my jeans and slides them off me in one swift movement. My breathing is loud, his touch sending me crazy. I groan as he cups my breasts in his hands over my bra. He quickly removes my panties and proceeds to take off his jeans. Before I know it, he is inside me. I hear him groan in my ear. He keeps up a punishing rhythm and it doesn't take long before we both surrender to each other. We both fall to the floor, I lie on top of him with my head on his naked chest, breathing him in. He strokes my hair, I close my eyes.

"Baby wake up." I feel Damon shift underneath me. I must have fallen asleep. I look up at him and he smiles. "As much as I'd love to stay here with you. You need to get up. It's 6.30pm."

"Oh, crap." I kiss Damon quickly before I get up. I grab my clothes and hide my body with them. I see Damon get up and walk towards me naked.

"Don't be embarrassed by your body baby. You are beautiful."

I proceed to get dressed, ignoring his comment. I'm ugly I feel disgusted anyone would have to look at me like this. Damon's eyes are sad. I head for the door but Damon grabs my hand and pulls me back. I fall into his hard abs. I trace them with my fingers. He grabs my hands and I let them fall.

"If you do that then I will want round 2," he says with a sexy voice.

I bite my lip. He leans down and kisses me. Why does my body crave this man? I can never get enough. "Give me a sec to get dressed and I will see you out."

He picks up his clothes that are discarded on the floor. I've never had such hot passionate sex before, I have to say it was better than expected. Before Damon, I couldn't handle anyone to touch me. Would I let anyone else touch me? I just don't know. I watch as he gracefully puts on his clothes. The way his muscles flex as he does so.

"Come on before I hold you hostage, again," I giggle.

"I love it when you are so carefree and happy," he smiles. Those eyes, I get lost in thought.

Chapter 9

Sully and I are sat in the car, there is something I find sexy about a guy driving. I don't know what it is. "Are you sure I can't put pigtails in your hair?" I ask.

Sully lifts an eyebrow, not taking his eyes off the road. "No Emmie."

Such a spoil sport. We pull up outside. I see Jessie waiting outside the movie theatre. I wave at her. I climb out of the car and close the door. Sully obviously pissed because he didn't get the door for me in time. It's just a door, I'm not going to break. I roll my eyes. We walk over to Jessie and we hug each other. Jessie is a hugging type of girl. I'm not used to physical contact so I probably look really awkward. I feel awkward.

"You made it," she blurts out excitedly.

"Of course I did." I shrug.

"I thought it was girls' night?" She looks at Sully who is by my side.

"I tried to put pigtails in his hair but he wouldn't let me. This is Big Guy. He's my bodyguard." I roll my eyes at the thought of having a bodyguard.

I start to cough again. God damn it. Sully walks off somewhere. He doesn't seem to be taking this very seriously.

"Oh, Emmie you are so funny. I heard what happened at school. Are you okay? But why do you have a bodyguard?"

Sully comes back with a bottle of water in his hand. He holds out the bottle, I grab it. "Thanks, Big Guy." He's so sweet. I take a gulp of water, soothing my throat. "I'm okay, Brody and Rider insist on me having 24-

hour protection. They think someone is after me." I roll my eyes. They are being paranoid. Jessie gasps.

"Emmie Salvatore doing as she's told. I never thought I'd see the day." I can tell she's worried about me but nobody has anything to worry about and what would it really matter if I died anyway? Apart from my baby.

"I was outnumbered for one." I clutch my tummy. "And I have to protect this little one." Her eyes light up as she looks from my tummy to my face. She screams and hugs me.

"You're pregnant? Congrats Emmie. I can see why you are doing as you're told," she smiles. "But if you go all hormonal on me, you are on your own." She crosses her arms.

"Gee, thanks friend," I say sarcastically. I look at Sully who has yet again turned the colour of his hair.

"Well nice to meet you, Big Guy," she waves at him.

"Emmie, you could have introduced me by my name," he huffs.

I hold my hands up in defence. "I did, your name is Big Guy," I giggle.

"Well at least it looks like I'm your date," he smiles.

I cross my arms at him and glare.

"Don't let Damon hear you say that." Emmie -2, Sully -1, go Emmie. He looks sheepish. "So what are we watching Jessie?" I asked curiously.

"Fifty Shades Darker of course." Oh, how silly of me.

"Really Jessie?" We both giggle. Sully looks really uncomfortable.

We went to take our seats in the theatre. We managed to get my favourite seats at the back corner. I sit in the middle of Jessie and Sully. I loved the trilogy books to Fifty Shades but I have to say the films aren't as good as the books, but they never are. I do love to read.

"Emmie?" I hear Sully call my name. Looks like I fell asleep on his shoulder. Oh, sweet Jesus. I fell asleep on Big Guy's shoulder. Good job I don't snore. I remove my head from his shoulder. I don't sleep very well anymore and from today's drama, I guess I was just exhausted.

"Sorry Big Guy," I whisper. I look at the screen and it's finished. Exactly how long have I been asleep? The lights flicker on. I turn to Sully who gives me a reassuring smile.

"How good was that?" Jessie asks.

"It was good," I lie.

"It was, wasn't it? God, Christian Grey is hot." She starts talking about the movie. I just nod in the right places. We head outside. I need fresh air, it's hot in there. Jessie hugs me goodbye. "I had a great time. We should do it again soon."

"So did I. And yes we should," I agree. It's nice to have a normal night with a friend. I haven't had many friends and Dad never often let me go out anyway.

I hear a car zooming towards us. Why do people need to speed? What do they get out of it? Nothing, yes that's right. Sully pushes me behind him. Ow? What the hell was that for? There is a black limo in front of us and skinny dude gets out the limo. I move to the side of Sully so I could see what is going on. The guy lifts his hand and points at me? Wait, I look carefully at his hand. He holds a gun in his hand. He seems to take aim at me. What the fuck? I hear the gun fire as I shut my eyes. I'm anticipating the hit, the pain, but nothing comes. I hear Jessie scream behind me. I manage to prise my eyes open, Sully is on his knees in front of me. I see blood pouring from his chest.

The guy comes towards me. "Does this bitch never die?" he curses. Excuse me? What does he mean by that?

"Don't you dare touch her," Sully warns. Sully took a bullet for me. The guy takes his gun and hits Sully round the head. Sully falls to a cold bundle on the floor. I'm an idiot. Why the hell did I make him come with me? I just stand still, not being able to move. Jessie is crying behind me. The guy grabs my arm and drags me into the Limo. The only thing I could do is follow him into the Limo. I hear Jessie call out my name. This guy, he isn't easy on the eyes at all. He has long black hair that's in need of a haircut.

"Give me your phone."

"No."

"Give it to me, or I will take it."

"You dare." I hold up my hands to reject him. He slides towards me on the seat, he holds me down with his weight. Although he is skinny, he's still heavy. He feels around my body for my phone. I just keep still, tensing at the touch of someone else. I feel sick as he touches me. I feel trapped, out of control. He eventually gets my phone and releases his grip on me. He moves away from me. I slowly sit up from where he pushed me down on the seat. Watching him as I do. He opens the window and lobs it out the window. I sit in silence just watching this guy, he mostly just texts on his phone.

The limo pulls up. He puts his phone in his pocket and he opens the door. Before I have a chance to move, he grabs my arm once again and drags me out of the Limo. I fall to the ground on my hands and knees. He grabs my arm and lifts me to my feet. He pulls me to the building in front of us. He fishes through his pocket and gets out an ID card and swipes it. The door clicks open and I step back trying to evade his touch but he is quicker on his feet than I am. He grabs me and pulls me in. We are greeted by men with guns at the door. My heart is beating double time. If it wasn't for the fact that this guy is dragging me forward, my feet would be stuck, frozen to this spot.

We enter a big room that looks like a pub. There is a bar where people are spread around the room. They all seem tough and strong. The skinny dude walks over to the bar where a blonde guy stands, leaving me by the door. He is pretty good looking. I guess he is the boss.

"Is it done?" the blonde guy asks.

"Not exactly."

"What happened?" he sounds angry.

The skinny dude looks worried, he puts his hands on his head, "The bitch won't die, Rex."

How rude, I walk up to them, crossing my arms. "Who the hell are you calling a bitch, you idiot?"

"What the hell is going on? Why is she here? She's supposed to be dead?" Rex growls.

"She just won't die. She had a security guard and he took the bullet for her. So I thought I'd bring her here to die." He looks nervous.

"How hard is it to kill one girl?" He rolls his eyes.

"Trust me, she's difficult."

"Hey, I am here you know." Ignoring me. Something catches my eye. I look up past Rex and I see... No way.

"She's supposed to be dead. I want her dead," she yells. Of all people, she wants me dead. Her whiney voice. What is this a stupid childish vendetta? Is she serious?

"Really Jade? You put this death sentence on my head? What's wrong with you? Is it because I kicked your ass?" I cross my arms.

Rex glares at me, "Shut up." He's angry.

"Okay T-Rex." The little voice inside my head is covering my mouth to shut me up. The other is shouting with a megaphone. I'm an idiot.

Rex raises his eyebrow at me. "Gobby little thing, aren't you?" I shrug.

"I want her Dead. Let me do it," Jade whines. God, she's so annoying.

I can see Rex thinking things over. "Quiet baby, all in good time."

"Go run along little girl," I tease. Rex slaps me hard across my face. I stand, stunned, I clutch my face. I can't let him know he's hurt me. I straighten up and smooth my clothes.

"Shut up before I change my mind," he growls. Change his mind about what?

"You get her baby."

"You do know how pathetic you look hiding behind T-Rex?" Jade is getting more and more annoyed. She doesn't hide her feelings well at all.

Rex faces Jade and smiles sweetly at her. Jesus, it makes me sick. "Baby, would you leave us?"

"Fine." She storms off. I hadn't even realised the skinny dude had left either. It's just me and him.

He turns towards me, he has a dark look in his eyes. "How dare you disrespect anyone from my gang?"

I shrug, "You all seem a bit pathetic for a gang, don't you think?" He hits me again across my face. I glare back at him, crossing my arms.

"You will learn girl."

"Sure, whatever you say."

He grabs my arm and drags me to a basement. It's cold and spacious, there isn't much here. A bookcase and a sofa. He faces me, "You are going to stay here, you are here for anything I see fit. Do you understand?" he demands.

"Whatever." I shrug.

"Now for my first pleasure."

He pushes me against the wall, pinning me against the wall. His weight keeping me still. He strokes my cheek. I can't stand him touching me, I try to push him off me. My hands push against his chest to get him away from me but he doesn't budge, he's too strong. Tears run down my face. He wipes them away, and then he kisses me. Forcing his tongue into my mouth. No, I can't go through this again. I can't. He pulls away, thank god.

"God, all you men just want one thing from a woman. What the hell would your girlfriend say?"

He hits me again. Why must I provoke this guy? Damon and Brody will never forgive me if I end up dead. I can't imagine how Danny and my

Momma would feel either. I don't care much for my life but I should protect my baby, right? "You will learn to behave eventually and that's none of your business what me and Jade are."

"Well if I have to put up with you using my body like this I think Jade should know," I say angrily.

He seems to think for ages. What is on his mind right now? "What Jade doesn't know won't hurt her," he shrugs. I can't imagine he cares deeply for Jade or he wouldn't be doing this. So why would he offer to kill me? I don't understand. He walks towards me, I'm stuck, frozen in this spot. He removes my clothes so I'm just in my underwear. I feel cold and exposed. I hate people seeing my body, of all people a stranger. You can see all my fat, my scars that had once been given to me by my dad. The bullet wound is still healing. I stand awkwardly.

"I want you to wear this, and only this," he says while looking at my body up and down. He seems pleased with what he sees, but why? He pins me against the wall once more, but this time he doesn't stop. He proceeds to invade my mouth. He pulls my panties down my legs. My whole body is screaming at me to move but I can't. I close my eyes, shaking, hearing my heart pumping. I dream of Damon holding me in his arms. Stroking my hair. Tears stream down my face. I hear him remove his clothes. I shut my eyes, picturing Damon's perfect face.

Rex finds his release and he pulls away from me. He steps back, leaving me in a quivering mess. He puts back on his clothes and leaves the room. I retrieve my panties from the floor and place them back on. Rex enters the room with some rope. He throws the rope over a beam above my head. Without speaking, he grabs my wrists and pulls my arms above my head and ties them together. I am stuck, tied up, I'm defenceless. It's cold and I feel uncomfortable. Am I supposed to sleep like this?

"Good night," he says as he leaves. "Have fun dude," he says whilst shutting the door. I look up in horror. The skinny dude comes towards me. What does he mean by have fun?

"Boss likes to share things here," he says, staring at me.

"No. Please." I can't go through this again. How much longer until they break me?

"Don't worry, I will be gentle and quick," he shrugs.

He removes his trousers and boxers and comes towards me. I close my eyes tight shut. He feels my body, gripping tight as he goes. He is really hurting me. I can't move even if I wanted to. He removes my panties. I feel like such a whore. My body feels used. He is breathing really loudly in my ear. His breath stinks of liquor. He kisses down my neck to my chest. Ow, he bit me. I pull against the restraints. Is he marking me? I try to block everything out.

He seems to be nice enough as he places my panties back on before he leaves. My eyes are sore from crying too much. I haven't eaten for a while, which is probably a good thing or I would be sick everywhere. I close my eyes, I'm exhausted. My mind drifts back to earlier this evening, the passion Damon and I had. How he made everything feel natural, the way he makes me feel safe.

I feel warm hands on me. I jolt awake. How the hell did I fall asleep like this? I search the room around me. Rex is here in front of me, but there are a few other guys in the room. All eyes are on me. This can't be good. Am I having a nightmare? "Keep real still baby," he whispers in my ear.

"I can't fucking move you moron," I say. He punches me in the face, I must look like a big purple grape by now. Maybe it's a good thing Damon isn't here. I think he would die if he saw me. Rex puts his hands on my hips and spins me around so my face is towards the wall. I stick my knees out to protect my tummy. I feel tender after last night.

"Tommy, really?" Rex sighs.

"What?" he laughs.

"If I'm nice enough to let you share my girl, don't mark her," he growls.

His girl, really? I'm no one's girl. I'm all alone. It's the way it's always been. Why is he so pissed that he marked me? His hands find my panties and he pulls them down. Really? I tense at his touch.

"Hush now baby," he whispers in my ear. What is this? Why is he letting them watch?

"I love you," he whispers when he makes his release. Wait what, he loves me? I'm so cold, especially when Rex pulls away. I hear Rex gather his clothes. I get pulled back around. I see Rex sat on the sofa watching me. I stare at him, not taking my eye off him. He seems to be thinking things over. Tommy is standing in front of me. He marks me again. I pull against the rope.

"Fuck sake, Tommy," Rex roars.

"Come on, it's fun," and he carries on.

I meet Rex's gaze I beg him to stop with my eyes. Tommy continues to suck and nip around my neck. I call out in pain when he does it too hard. Rex jumps to his feet and walks towards us and puts his hand on Tommy's shoulder. "Enough," he demands.

"I was just getting started Rex. Lighten up."

"Get out. Leave us," he screams. Everyone makes a hasty exit, all bar Tommy. Tommy stares down Rex, he's pissed. "You ruined it. Don't mark my girl."

"Why do you care? Shouldn't it be Jade that you don't want to share?"

"Fuck Jade, I'm bored with her. Emmie, she's special. Now get the hell out." Wow, he's mad.

"I'll come back later then."

Rex places his hand on Tommy's chest. And stares him in the eyes. "No, you won't touch her. Do you understand me?"

"Fine." He leaves the room and slams the door. Rex takes a deep breath and turns towards me. He skims his thumb over the marks from Tommy. He collects my panties from the floor and puts them back on. He leaves the room. I'm so cold. Time has passed, I'm exhausted. Rex enters the room with a tray of food. He places the food on the sofa and makes his way to me. Kisses me on the lips and undoes the rope. My weight drops but he catches me. He carries me to the sofa. I look at the food and stare at it.

"Eat," he demands.

"No."

"Why? You must be hungry."

"I'm a vegetarian." I shrug.

"What the bloody hell is one of them?" he scoffs.

"I don't eat meat."

He laughs, "That's funny. Now eat."

"I'm not eating it."

"I will force it down you if you don't eat it voluntarily baby." He raises an eyebrow.

I knock the tray on the floor and the food goes everywhere. "Oops, such a clutz." He looks really angry. He grabs my wrist and pulls me back to my feet.

"Why can't you just behave?" I shrug. He goes to tie me up.

"Wait," I beg.

"What?" I look at the ground. This is awkward. "What Emmie?" he strokes my face, imploring me to answer him.

"I need the loo," I say, blushing. He grabs my hand and leads me out the basement. I pass all his staff in my underwear, I'm so embarrassed. We stop outside a door.

"Go on, don't lock the door."

I go in and shut the door behind but I do as he says. I'm so desperate. Once I've finished I look at myself in the mirror. I hardly recognise myself. Bruises everywhere, my face, my body. The ones I hate the most are the once on my breasts. I sigh. I hear the door open and arms are around me. I get a flashback of Damon's safe arms around me at his safe house. His scent, I miss him so bad. I look up sad to be met by Rex's gaze. Is this how he likes his woman? Broken, powerless?

"Come on let's go." He takes my hand and leads me back into the cold basement. He ties me up again. I am so exhausted that I try to block things out. Who knows how long I've been here? He rarely shares me with his gang anymore. He likes to save me just for himself. I've obviously got under his skin.

I'm so cold, I smell before I see or hear. That scent I've been craving, the scent that makes me feel safe. I feel dead to the world but I prize my eyes open and I smile at the face my eyes meet. Warm arms make their way around me. His hands undo the rope, he catches me before I fall. He strokes my face, pressing his forehead against mine. I think he is soaking me in. I've missed this guy. He carries me to the sofa and I sit curled up against his chest, not speaking a word.

"What have they done to you, Mi Chica Bella?" I've missed his low soft sexy voice. He takes off his jacket and puts it around me. He feels so warm and comfy. I could stay here forever.

"What are you doing here Damon?" is all that would come out of my mouth. I look up and see his perfect face. Am I dreaming?

"This was the only way, Emmie. I'm undercover, I will get you out but I can't just yet." He looks hurt. I know this must be killing him right now. He's usually so in control. I make him out of control. He examines my body, skimming my skin with his fingers. I feel really sore. The pain in his eyes. I grab his hand.

"It's okay Damon. I'm okay." I lie but knowing he is here and he came for me, that's all I need to keep me going. "I've dealt with worse." That's totally debatable but he needs to know I'm okay.

"Baby he will be back soon. I'm sorry, I need to tie you back up." I don't have the energy to stand anymore. I rest my head on his shoulder, soaking him in one last time. He kisses my head. Damon pushes his jacket onto the sofa and he stands up with me in his arms. I kiss him before he puts me down. The spark I remembered, what I've been holding on to is there stronger than ever. He gently puts me down. I lift my hands up so he can tie me back up.

That's good timing, the door creaks open and Rex appears. He bounds up to me. "So you've met our mascot?" he smiles, admiring me.

"Yes, and a beautiful one too," he looks at me with sorrow in his eyes. Even in this situation he still makes me feel special.

Rex looks at me and winks at me. "Yes, isn't she just? Lucky she has looks and her uses or she would be dead."

Damon looks angry. "What do you mean uses?" What do you think he means Damon? Are you really that naive?

Rex seems deep in thought again. "Untie her will you?" Damon looks at me, he is so close to me. He has to press against me to reach up and untie me. His touch means so much more, I look into his eyes and bite my lip. He catches me when I fall. Supporting me once I can hold my own weight. "Us guys need a treat, she has all my guys begging for more," he shrugs.

I see Damon's whole body tense up in front of me. Oh shit. He could literally kill him right here and now. But that's not going to do either of us any good. Damon's fists are clenched behind his back. I take a step forward and reach for his hand. He seems to relax at my touch. "Well she does look like something special," he says through clenched teeth. Rex moves in between Damon and me.

"I can say that she is." He winks at me. He strokes my head with his right hand. I close my eyes, I've found this is the best way to deal with this.

"I can't say the same for you T-Rex." I know what's coming but I'd honestly prefer him to hit me then to touch me and there it is. The blow to my face. I see Damon lurch forward. I look at him and beg him to stop and he does, he looks so helpless.

"Will you never learn to behave?" he whispers in my ear. I shut my eyes, I hate him this close to me. I feel his breath on my neck. I open my eyes and find Damon's gaze, he looks pissed at me for opening my big gob. I can't help it. It's who I am.

Before I knew what I was saying, I just blurt it out, "Hey T-Rex, he looks like a good one. Are you going to share me with him?" Again I'm met with Rex's fist. At least it keeps his hands away from my body.

"No, you're mine. I don't like sharing. New guy, get out." Shit. What did I do? I feel Damon's eyes burning into me so I look at his face. He looks so afraid like he can't leave me here. I've never seen this side to Damon.

"Are you sure you don't need anything else, she looks like a feisty one?" Oh, Damon you know I am. But he's beat me down. I'm tired, I can't fight anymore.

"Huh, don't want an audience this time?" I scoff. Damon looks shocked. Oh, Damon, do you live under a rock? You should know what happens in gangs. Some are just more ruthless than others.

"Sometimes I wonder how you're still alive. You know what happens when I get mad." I roll my eyes.

"You're in love with me, that's why I'm not dead and yes I do, you go all red and your vein pops out of your head," I giggle.

Embarrassment floods his face. "I-I-I don't," he stutters.

"You've told me many times, you hate that I don't return the feelings." I shrug.

"New guy, out!" he growls. I can see Damon thinking this over. I wish I could help him with this but instead, I just give him a reassuring smile. He hesitantly heads for the door. He takes one last look before he shuts the door. My poor sweet Damon. I just stare at the door.

"Why won't you love me?" I look at Rex. He looks genuinely sad. Is he crazy? Yes, I think he is.

I love Damon. "You aren't my type and what did you expect?"

"What do you mean?" he asks. He's lost it. Unless this is normal behaviour for him?

"You lock me in here. You don't feed me. You and your friends use me for your own pleasure. You tried to have me killed." I stand here cold, beaten and he doesn't know why I won't love him?

"What If I let you out of here? Be part of the gang. Then you'll be my girlfriend?" he asks hopefully. I think this is the only way. Play on his emotions.

"You are so desperate. I guess it will be a start," I say. I can see I am driving him crazy. He ties me back up. I hate being tied up like this.

"I will get the new guy to bring you some food." He walks briskly out the door. He seems impressed with himself.

I wait patiently to see Damon walk through the door. Seconds, minutes passed? I hurt so much. I rest my head and I hear the door creak open, I feel too exhausted to lift my head. But I know its Damon, he strokes my face, lifting my head as he does. "Hey baby, I see you are still a total badass."

I giggle, "Of course, Damon please untie me. It hurts," I beg and he doesn't hesitate.

"We have about 10 minutes before he comes back." He pulls me to the sofa. I sit on his lap, he's so warm, I snuggle up to him. Exploring under his jacket and his shirt. "So Damon what do you want to do in 10 minutes?" I say, teasing him.

He takes a deep breath. "Oh baby, what am I going to do with you? I want to know what's been going on," he demands. I'm not sure that he does.

"Fine, I guess you know how I got here. Is Sully okay?" I start thinking about how Sully took a bullet for me. He was fighting till the end. I hope he is okay. I can't have him die because of me.

"Yes, I know someone tried to shoot you and then they took you. Sully is fine, he got shot in the lung. But he's going to be fine. He's so angry with himself that he didn't protect you."

I frown, "Damon, he took a bullet for me. He did protect me. He was still fighting to save me when he was on the ground. I'm so glad he's okay."

"Me too. Yes I know. I'm angry, but not at him. He kept you alive. So what happened next?"

"Well, the idiot dragged me to the Boss and there I saw Jade." He tenses underneath me.

"What the blonde girl from your school?" he says in disbelief.

"Yes her, she was the one who put the death sentence on my head."

"Why?"

"She's pissed that I humiliated her at school. Rex obviously has a soft spot for her so wanted to make her happy. Anyway, I guess when he saw me he couldn't resist me." I shrug.

He kisses me playfully on the lips. "I don't blame him, you are hard to resist."

"He shared me with his friends. My mouth getting me into trouble as usual. He's been trying to control me. Somewhere down the line, he's fallen for me. I thought after you, I could accept other people touching me. But I can't stand it, Damon. I'd rather he hit me than touch me."

He strokes my hair, "Is that why you wind him up? Baby, I'm sorry. I could tell you were repulsed by his touch. He loves you?"

"He wants me to be his. He will do anything to make that happen. I'm so cold and tired Damon." He hugs me tightly I wince at the pain but it's a nice pain. "I'm playing on his emotions to get out of here Damon."

"You are one smart cookie you know?"

"What are you doing here Damon?"

"Well, I found out where you were. But there was no way I could raid the place. Security is too high. So I thought I would work for him. Get him to trust me. I wasn't expecting to find you on my first day. But I'm so glad to see you."

"I've missed you."

"I want to ask you something."

"Fire away." He could ask me almost anything and I'd give it to him.

He slides me off his lap so he is facing me. "I can't lose you again. You've turned my world upside down. I need you in my life, I hate not being in control. I love you," he confesses. Is this the first time he's said he loves me to my face?

"I love you too Damon."

"Emmie, will you marry me?"

Excuse me, what did he just say? I just stare at him, I look down at my hands. He places his warm hands around my cold ones. "What did you say?" I must have heard wrong.

"I said marry me, Emmie. Choose me."

Chapter 10

How am I supposed to process this? It's too soon. Why on earth would he want to marry me? I'm nothing. I'm fat and ugly, why would he want me as his wife? This is some sort of joke, this is all a nightmare I will wake up soon. "I…" I'm speechless.

"Way to keep a guy hanging Emmie."

"Damon. We haven't known each other long. We don't know each other that well. We aren't even together."

"You can't deny the connection we have Emmie. You said it yourself, you can't stand anyone else to touch you. I feel like I've known you forever. Every day without you is painful. I need you in my life."

He feels like he's known me forever? Does that mean I'm boring? That's what happens when you get used to something, isn't it? "Well, I can't say this is very romantic. What with being in a cold basement. Being held hostage."

"Emmie, please. I know it's not romantic but I can't lose you. Knowing you will marry me will help me get you out of here. Please marry me." I can see he needs this. But I can't give him this.

"Why don't you ask me when we are out of here?"

"Fine okay, I will accept it for now. Now, will you eat something?" I climb back onto his lap again. He lifts his arms so I can snuggle up and once I'm settled, he holds me tight to his chest.

"No," I say simply. He pushes my head away with his hands so he is looking at my face.

"Why not? Think of our baby." Our baby. I love it how he says our baby.

"All these guys and Rex coming in here trying to get me to eat. I'm a bloody vegetarian. Because they're blokes they don't get it." I push his hands away from my face so I can once again lean against his chest. Hearing his heartbeat soothes me.

"You aren't eating because you are a vegetarian?"

"Yes." I can feel him take a deep breath.

"You need to be better looked after, baby."

"It's okay, I'll be out of here soon enough."

"I will go get you some food." I hug him tighter. He kisses my forehead. He stands up and carries me over to the wall. He ties me up again. Damon leaves the room, I watch him as he leaves. His sexy ass, the way his jeans fit around his ass… I stare at the door waiting for his return, I hear the door go and to my disappointment it is Rex.

"Hey T-Rex," I say sweetly. He looks worried.

"I'm going to let you out okay? Please be my girlfriend." He needs professional help. He must be so insecure if he has to beg me to be his girlfriend. I get a marriage proposal and now this in one day. I must be popular. Under normal circumstances, I would rudely decline. But if I have any chance of getting out of here, I need to agree to his terms. No matter how hard this will be. At least it will just be Rex touching me and not the rest of his gang. "Fine, just let me out." These restraints are so uncomfortable.

He takes a deep breath. "Thank god for that."

He is such a big girl's blouse. He was scared I would decline him, if you compare Damon and Rex, Damon just proposed to me, yes he was nervous but our relationship is deeper, more meaningful and here is Rex, terrified that I would turn him down. I need a guy who will take care of me, protect me from harm and someone that will keep me from ruining my life. Pushing me to better myself. That's what I see in a boyfriend/husband. Rex just doesn't cut it. He reaches up to undo the restraints, brushing up against me as he does. His arm wraps around me as I'm released. I flinch at his touch. He looks at me deeply. He walks to the sofa and grabs me my clothes. I quickly dress, I feel much more comfortable in clothes, hiding my fat, my awful body.

"Come," he demands.

I follow him out of the basement. We enter the main room again that has a bar. Why doesn't Damon have a bar? I think it's pretty cool. I scan the room of people feeling nervous and awkward, knowing they all probably had their fill of me or seen me in my underwear. I smell really bad and probably look awful, as per usual. My eyes seem to be fixated on Damon, he stares at me questioningly, he must be wondering how I pulled this off. He's talking to her, talking to Jade. She's like a leech that gets everywhere. Luckily Damon seems to be ignoring her whilst he is staring at me. Rex grabs my hand and I instinctively flinch and withdraw my hand. The feeling I get when someone touches me is like I'm trapped, frozen in time. I feel sick all the time, I'm repulsed by people's touch. I look up at Rex whose face is mad.

He grabs my hair and pulls it tight and pushes me up against the bar. Fuck that hurts, I'm leant over the bar with my head being forced on the bar. "Boss, what are you doing?" Damon is already by my side.

"If I want to hold my damn girlfriend's hand I will do so, okay?"

"Girlfriend?" Damon says in disbelief.

"Yes T-Rex, we all know you are the Boss." I roll my eyes knowing full well he can't see me. He releases his grip. Damon helps me stand up straight. I know this is killing him.

"What the hell is going on Rex?" Oh god, here comes miss whiny. It pierces through me like a high pitch ring.

He turns towards Jade. "Shut up."

"You said she was dead, what is this?" she stamps her foot. God, what did he ever see in her?

"I won't tell you again. I never said she was dead. I just said I sorted it." Rex seems really angry, even I don't know what he is capable of. There is only so far that I'd push Rex and she's crossing the line.

Jade's face screws up like she's going to explode. "Maybe I should kill her myself."

I couldn't believe my eyes, Rex closed the gap between him and Jade. He places his hand around her neck and proceeds to strangle her, Jade's feet dangling in the air. Jade's face is turning red and then white like the life is leaving her face. I just stare in horror.

"No you won't, you touch her and I will kill you. Do you understand?" he growls. Jade tries to agree but she doesn't have any breath and he lets go, leaving her to fall to a bundle on the floor. It takes her a good few moments to gather herself and stand up. Tears are falling down her face. I half expected her to run for the hills but she doesn't. I respect that.

"I get it, Rex, why are you protecting her all of a sudden?"

"She's my girlfriend," he shrugs.

Jade's mouth drops open. "Aww is someone upset?" I mess with her.

"How could you even like her? She's not even pretty." Okay, we get it. We all know I'm not pretty. I'm fat and ugly. He's mentally unwell, he doesn't know what he wants.

"Ha, is that why every guy here has been begging to sleep with me? They've all had me and they've been begging for more?" Damon is shocked at what I've said. I stand awkward, I love that he's here but I'm also disgusted at what he may find out about me. I'm worried he may get to know me and he will walk away. I don't know why he hasn't already, I dread the day when he does. I know there will become a day when I will fuck things up. It's what I do. I always loved my Dad, he never left me. He was always there for me even when I didn't deserve it.

"What, so that's what you've been doing? You're such a slut," she says in sheer disgust.

I shrug, "Considering I didn't have a choice, it's a moot point."

"She's the most beautiful woman I've met. She's got looks, amazing personality and she's got balls." He turns to me and he seems to get lost looking in my eyes. I break the eye contact because it makes me uncomfortable. He reaches up to stroke my cheek, I go to step back but my back is met by the bar. So instead I close my eyes. I feel his hand reach my face, I am frozen once again. Feels like an eternity until he removes his hand. I slowly open my eyes and I see Damon's face he is hurting. His eyes search mine like he is giving me some sort of secret message.

"I think I should get Emmie some food," Damon breaks the silence and awkwardness.

"No need, I'm taking Emmie out for a meal." He seems very smug with himself.

"Yes, Boss," Damon is gritting his teeth while he says those words.

"You don't have to do that T-Rex." I hold my hands out in front of me.

"Yes, I do. You haven't eaten since you got here and I want to treat my girlfriend." I can go a long time without food. Me and food don't get on and if I do eat, I usually end up puking it back up.

"Come on." He grabs my hand before I can retract it. He holds it tightly so I have no choice but to follow him. I turn my head so I can see Damon before I leave. He is wearing his heart on his sleeve, he can't contain his emotions here. He is usually so composed, if anything always angry. But I've never seen this.

Rex opens the car door so I can climb in his silver Porsche sports car. It's really low and I pretty much fall into the car. I have no grace about me. I can't believe he is taking me out like this. I look a complete and utter mess. He opens the glove box whilst driving, I look in to find a small bag.

"Jade's makeup. Why don't you use some?" My first thought is that he doesn't want to be seen with someone like me. So I need to cover my face, I mean I semi like myself with makeup. I loved to wear makeup to mask my face, it was like a shield that I could hide from the world. But Dad didn't like it. He said I looked better natural. Rex could want me to cover these bruises on my face, maybe he doesn't like them now I'm his girlfriend. Or maybe he's worried he might get arrested.

I pull the sun visor down in the car so I can see in the mirror. I'm pretty good at applying makeup. I carefully apply concealer, powder and mascara. I look decent enough. Thank god Jade has concealer. She does need it I suppose. I fish around the makeup bag to find a pop out hair brush. My hair is greasy and messy. I brush it and let it fall around my shoulders, covering my hickeys. I take one last look in the mirror and sigh. I close the visor and sit back in the seat.

Rex pulls up outside a restaurant, it's stylish from the outside. I feel the sun on my face as I climb out the car. I've missed this, if I ever get away from Rex I think I may just live outside. Just soak up the sun. I straighten my clothes. Rex grabs my hand and leads me inside. We are greeted by a young male waiter who is dressed in a shirt and a pink tie and waistcoat. He looks at me and stares at me up and down. I look down at the floor, I don't fit in here. I'm wearing jeans and a top that shows my chubby fat.

"Table for two," Rex demands.

"Yes, sir. Right this way." He grabs some menus and escorts us to the table. The waiter holds out a chair and gestures for me to sit. God, this is way too posh for me, never in my life have I been treated like this and nor do I want to. It's too much attention, I'd rather people ignore me. I take my cue and sit on the chair.

The waiter hands us the menus. I take a look and I gasp at the price of these meals. He could have taken me to McDonald's and I would have been happier. "Can I get you some drinks?"

He looks at me, I guess it's polite to take the woman's drink first. "Water please."

"You don't want wine?" Rex asks.

"No thank you." He doesn't know I'm pregnant and I think it's better that I keep it that way.

"I'll have a whisky."

"I will be back to take your food order shortly." The waiter takes his exit. I scan the menu, there are things I haven't even heard of.

"So what happens now?" I ask curiously.

"We order food Emmie," he shrugs.

"No, I meant with us."

"You'll stay with me," he says calmly.

"Forever?" I cringe at the thought of forever.

"Well yes..." he admits. I can't stay with him forever. I'd rather die. Considering I don't value my life anyway.

"Why?"

"Because you are my girlfriend, you can't leave me." He's crazy, what does he want, for me to surrender myself to him?

"I have a life T-Rex." Well, not really but I have people I'd like to go back to.

"You are going to have to start a new one."

The waiter arrives with our drinks and to take our order, damn that was quick. Umm, what do I want? "Emmie," he sounds annoyed.

I pick the one at the top of the list, "I'll have the macaroni cheese please."

"I'll get the steak, rare." I go to hand back the menu but I drop it in my nervousness.

"Crap, I'm so sorry." I jump up to retrieve the menu.

"Miss, it's okay. I can get it."

"Emmie, sit down," Rex growls. I sit down and hand the waiter the menu that I picked up from the floor and my cheeks get really hot in embarrassment.

"Is there anything else I get for you?"

"Apart from not eyeing up my girlfriend. No." The waiter glances at me and blushes awkwardly. Rex must be mistaken, why would anyone eye me up? The waiter nods and leaves us.

"Really T-Rex? Embarrass the guy."

"Emmie he was checking out your ass, he couldn't have made it more obvious." He crosses his arms and glares at me. Was he really? I was too busy making a fool of myself.

"Anyway, I can't make a new Momma or brother." Or Damon or Brody.

"Enough of this, I'm not negotiating. You are mine forever." He has issues. I keep quiet, there's no point in pushing this. I wouldn't win anyway. I try to excuse myself to go to the loo but he refuses to let me go. Where would I go? I'd probably trip up and break my neck if I tried to make a run for it anyway.

The waiter arrives with our food. Now it's here, I've suddenly lost my appetite. Not that I had one before. The waiter excuses himself and leaves. I pick up my fork and start to play with my food. My stomach is in knots. I don't do well under pressure.

"Emmie, eat. Now. Don't make me force feed you," he threatens in a low voice. I take a mouthful of macaroni cheese. It is pretty tasty but then I'd expect it to for this price. I force the rest of it down. Rex seems satisfied. He makes short work of demolishing his. Rex holds his hand up to get the attention of the waiter.

"The bill," he demands. Why is he so rude and abrupt? The waiter leaves to go fetch the bill.

"T-Rex I really need the bathroom," I confess.

"Just wait, Emmie," he scowls. The waiter hands Rex the bill. Rex fishes out his wallet from his pocket and pulls out a few notes. "Keep the change." I imagine this is not to be kind, it's so we can leave.

"Thanks, sir. Enjoy the rest of your day. Bye miss." Rex shoots him an icy stare. I wave goodbye to be polite. Rex is so uptight. Rex grabs my arm and pulls me to the bathroom, but instead of waiting outside he comes in with me. Luckily it's just one toilet and not cubicles. He locks the door behind him.

"What are you doing?"

He stays silent and forces himself on me. He's more demanding than usual, he pushes me against the wall. I did actually need a wee. I guess he doesn't care about this right now. He undoes my jeans and slides them off in seconds. Kissing my neck as he does it. I close my eyes to try to block him out. I hear him undo his belt, he lifts my legs around him. Just like Damon did and he slams into me. I wince at the shock of him inside me, so hard. He kisses me on the lips. Invading my mouth with his tongue.

"Kiss me," he demands. It's so much easier to just try and block this out but now he wants me to reciprocate. I don't know if I can. Is this punishment? Is this what it means to be his girlfriend? He grabs my face with his hands and holds tightly, demanding me to kiss him back. This is what I do. Tears stream down my face, I hate my life. This guy needs to be locked up so he can't hurt anyone else. My body is screaming at him to stop. I feel dirty inside and out. He finds his release and growls my name. He pulls out of me and starts to do up his trousers.

"You are mine. Do you understand?" Was this all because he was jealous of the damn waiter? He is unbelievable. I nod in agreement. Daddy tried to claim me as his and now Rex wants to claim me. It's too much pressure.

"Good. Hurry up. Don't lock the door." He leaves the bathroom. I can't seem to move. Just stuck against the wall. Tense and scared. Come on Emmie. I go to the loo as I am desperate. I wash my hands and place my jeans and panties back on. I stare at myself in the mirror. I just stare for I don't know how long.

"Emmie, hurry the fuck up," Rex calls through the door. I compose myself and leave the bathroom. He grabs my hand and storms out the restaurant. I'm practically running to keep up with him. It's dark when we leave the building. He marches us to his car and I manage not to fall into his car this time. The engine roars to life and he drives away. I curl up on the seat and close my eyes thinking of Damon. Being curled up in his arms.

I jump awake when I feel hands on me. I feel groggy. I fell asleep? I look up at whose arms I'm in. To my delight, it is Damon's. I close my eyes and snuggle up into his chest. He doesn't say a word, just carries me back inside. I guess Rex is too lazy to bring me back in himself, who knows. I'm so exhausted, I feel safe in his arms so I fall to sleep instantly surrounded by his scent calming me.

"Emmie wake up." I wake suddenly, feeling disorientated. Rex is looking over me. I sit up on the sofa where I've been lying alone. I rub my eyes.

"I have work to attend to. I won't be long love." He woke me just to tell me that? Really? I nod and he retreats out of the room, probably to his office. I feel the sofa dip next to me. I jump out my skin and turn my head in a panic to see who it is. Please say it's not Tommy.

"Marry me." I'm happy to see this hot guy. But not to hear those words. I frown at the thought. I know he means well. But I can't do this now. I cross my arms in frustration.

Chapter 11

"I'm going to keep asking until you say yes. You're driving me crazy. How have you got him wrapped around your little finger?" he asks.

I roll my eyes at him. "I don't know, everyone seems to love me. I just don't get it." I start fiddling with my hands. Anyway, I'm not completely wrapped around his finger, because if I was I could stop him hurting me.

"I do, anyway, did you have a good meal?" The meal? Yeah right. I look at my hands in my lap. He places his hands over mine. I look up at him. "What happened, did he hurt you?"

"It's nothing he hasn't done before Damon," I mumble. Well, it's sort of true I guess.

"What are you hiding from me?" he implores.

How does he know when I'm hiding something or lying? I'm usually a good liar. I've had to be. Unless it's that I trust Damon and I too, wear my heart on my sleeve. "Well, it all started when I dropped the menu on the floor."

"What's so important about a menu?" he asks questioningly.

"I felt so out of place there that I scrambled to pick it up and Rex shouted at me to sit down. He accused the waiter of staring at my ass." I don't know if he did or Rex is just a psycho.

"You have a nice ass, Emmie. But carry on," he smirks. Bastard.

"At the end of the meal the waiter said goodbye to me, Rex grabbed my arm and dragged me to the bathroom." My eyes start to well up. I can feel tears drop down my face. Damon wipes away the tears with his thumb. His touch still sends me wild. "He had me in the bathroom, but instead of letting me block it out. He…"

"He what baby?" he demands.

"He commanded me to kiss him back. I guess it's what it means to be his girlfriend. All I could think of was you," I confess.

"Oh, baby. I'm so sorry."

"Please tell my Brother and my Momma that I love them."

"I will but why do you sound like you aren't going to see them again?"

"Damon, he's never going to let me go. He's insane."

"We all know that. But you'll be out soon," he promises. From the corner of my eye, I see the door to what is probably Rex's office open. I quickly withdraw my hands from Damon's. I try to compose myself. Rex smiles at me and walks over to me.

"You ready to go my love?" he seems in an extra good mood.

"Yes, T-Rex," I nod. Rex leaves the room.

"Stay safe Mi Chica Bella."

I can't promise that I already feel broken. "I promise I will protect our baby," I reassure him. I stand up and follow Rex out. I hear Damon call out to me.

"Emmie that's not what I meant." I know it's not. I don't turn around to see him as I leave. I hate to leave him like this. I am met by Rex in the hallway by the main entrance. He grabs my hand and holds it tight and we make our way to the car.

As we drive down the road, I guess we are going to his house. How he trusts me to be there with him alone, god only knows. He places his hand on my inner thigh and I flinch at his touch and grip my legs together. "When will you learn Emmie? Just wait till we get home and I will be more than happy to teach you that I will touch what is mine," he threatens.

He glares at me. "Keep your eyes on the road T-Rex."

"No need, we are here now." We pull up into a fancy driveway. I always feel uncomfortable with all this money. Is this sort of home really necessary? I hesitate to get out the car, I just sit and wait. But obviously, I'm not able to do such a thing. Rex opens my door. "Get out." I can't seem to move. He sighs and reaches in and grabs my arm and pulls me out of the car. "Why must you defy me? I want, no need, you to behave." He drags me into the house.

I take a look around, I see a big entrance hall with huge stairs. The flooring is oak. It's rather stylish but not my taste at all. He takes my hand and leads me straight upstairs. We reach a door and he opens it and ushers me in. He shuts the door behind me and walks to the dresser by the huge bed. He rummages around in the drawer and picks up a key. He walks back to the door and locks it. Really? He puts the key back into his pocket and looks at me.

"Stand by the bed," he growls. He is starting to sound a lot like my Dad but at least I knew what to expect from my Dad. I loved my Dad, my Dad never hit me across the face, well only once before he died. My Dad would always take care of me after. Rex hits me in the face and I fall to the floor. "Get up and stand by the bed," he orders.

I scramble to my feet and walk over to the bed. He takes a seat on the chair by the door facing me. I stand here awkwardly while he sits there staring at me. "Take off your clothes," he demands. My clothes? No way. He is sick. "Don't make me ask you again Emmie," he growls.

I slowly start pulling my t-shirt up over my head. I discard it on the floor and proceed to undo my jeans. I stare at the floor not wanting to look at him. I slide my jeans down my legs and step out of them. I use my arms to cover up my body. "All your clothes."

"Please don't make me do this T-Rex. As your girlfriend, I should get a say in this," I beg him but I still don't look at him.

"You agreed to do this. Is this not better than being tied up in restraints?" I don't know. I thought it would be, that I'd only have one guy to worry about, but this one guy is difficult to deal with. He really is.

"Yeah, I guess."

"Then carry on." He sits back on the chair and watches. I reach behind me and undo my bra, sliding the straps down my arms, dropping it on the floor. I place my thumbs in my panties and slide them down my legs and step out of them. I look up and see Rex smiling from ear to ear. "Come here."

I walk slowly to where he is sitting. He lifts his hand and skims my thigh with his fingers, watching my face as he does it. "Undress me," he demands.

I take a step forwards so I'm closer to him. I reach forward to grab his shirt and lift it over his head. I drop it to the floor next to him. I stand awkwardly, thinking of how I should proceed. He grabs my hand, gestures for me to undo his trousers. My hands are shaking, my hands won't obey. I fumble around to undo his belt. It seems to take me ages, I'm not used to this at all. My Dad would always do the undressing for the both of us. I haven't been with Damon that many times to experiment. This is alien to me. I undo his trousers and he lifts up so I can remove them along with his boxers. He sits back down, grabs my hand and pulls me on top of him. I hold the back of the chair so I don't have to touch him with my hands. He lines me up and pushes me onto his erection. I've never been on top before, my Dad always liked to be in control. My heart is beating really loud, feels like it may explode.

"Move my love," he whispers in my ear. I start to move, it's deeper this way and makes me wince. He grabs my hips to assist me. "Yesss," he hisses in my ear. I cringe at his reaction and being so close to him. I can't handle much more of this. He stands up whilst holding my legs so he stays inside of me. He carries me over to the bed. He gently places me on the bed and climbs on top of me. He carries on this hard, punishing rhythm. I close my eyes in desperation that he would finish. To my luck, it isn't long. He pulls out and demands me to lie on my side, he moves behind me so he can hug me from behind. I silently cry myself to sleep, praying tomorrow will be a better day.

I wake laying naked on the bed. Rex stirs next to me. He groans. "Morning my love," he mutters.

"Could I possibly grab a quick shower. Please?" I beg.

"Seeing as you asked so nicely. It's just through that door. Don't be long, we have to go shortly." He nods at the door the other side of the room. I grab my clothes from the floor and make a quick retreat to the bathroom.

I turn on the shower and climb in, the water is hot on my skin but I honestly don't mind. I need to try to wash Rex off me. Wash his men off me. I look around the shower to only find men's shower gel. This will have to do, it's better than nothing. I try to scrub my skin, wash all these bad things off, but scrubbing myself doesn't make me feel any better. I start to cry in a panic that nothing is working. I fall to the floor of the shower wishing that my Dad had killed me that day. That I was with him right now.

"Emmie, hurry up," he yells through the door.

I pull myself up using the walls, I find some shampoo and wash my hair. My legs feel weak like jelly. This will have to do. I turn the shower off and climb out. I grab a towel off the rack and wrap it around me. It feels soft on my skin, fresh. I look in the mirror, it is all steamed by the heat of the shower. Probably a good thing but I wipe the mirror with the towel anyway. What I see disgusts me. I am met by the usual ugly self, just been made worse by the bruises. The mascara has streamed down my face, I look terrible. I wipe the mascara with the towel. Making me look semi normal. I quickly dry myself and dress in my old clothes. At least Damon gave me fresh clothes when he kidnapped me. I find some men's deodorant and spray my clothes with it. I smell of a man now. Oh well.

I walk out of the bedroom to find Rex already dressed and waiting. He's on the phone, he looks up when I enter the room. He gestures me to follow him, I follow him out of the bedroom down the stairs to the big hall. I feel like a zombie being controlled. I don't have any fight left in me. So I obey. He ends his call and looks at me. He closes the distance between us and he kisses me. I without hesitation kiss him back even though my body is screaming at me.

He pulls away and walks out the house, holding the door open so I can follow. I walk outside feeling the sun on my skin. It gives me hope that today will be a better day. He locks the door and heads for the car. I follow like I'm attached to him by an invisible piece of string. I climb in my side of the car and curl up on the seat. Rex doesn't care about seatbelts, so I don't wear one. It would be a blessing in disguise if we had a car accident. I look out the window watching people getting on with their lives. Some happy, some tired, others sad.

Rex pulls up at the safe house. My first thought is that I hope Damon isn't there because I don't want him to see me so broken. I climb out the car and follow Rex inside. He greets his men on arrival. He puts his arm around my shoulder and we walk together into the room with the bar. I see Damon pacing by the bar, how long has he been waiting for us? He looks up and his face drops. I can't even manage a smile for him. Instead, I just stare at the floor. Rex leads us to the bar where Damon is standing.

"Good morning new guy."

"Morning Boss, what has you so happy today?"

"Oh just my girlfriend made me a very happy man last night." He turns to look at me and pulls me into a kiss.

"Too much information Boss." I know what he's trying to do. He's trying to get Rex off me but Rex isn't ready to pull away just yet.

"Look at her though." He steps back to admire me. I just look painfully at the ground.

"Okay T-Rex. No one needs to see what I look like. Do you not have work to do?"

"Someone's snappy today. Do I need to teach you how to behave again?" he raises his eyebrow.

"No," I whisper, fiddling with my hands.

"I will see you later love. Hopefully, you will be in a better mood. Or I can teach you again," he says calmly and he retreats to his office.

Damon grabs my arms and looks at me. "Emmie come back to me. Don't let him break you."

"Leave me alone Damon, I can't deal with this right now."

He sighs, "I'm getting you out of here today. Just hold on," he begs. Oh, Damon, I've already gone.

"Yeah, yeah. You said, you Moron," I snap. I can't have him near me right now.

"Your Mom and Brother loves you. They can't wait to see you." I know he's trying to make me feel better.

"You saw them? Are they okay?" I sound hopeful.

"I said I would Emmie. They're worried about you."

"I'm fine," I lie, I need them to know I'm okay.

"Don't shut me out, baby. It's nearly over," he begs.

"So you keep saying but I don't see anything happening," I shrug.

"Marry me." Really? This feels a lot like a pity proposal. He can't actually want to marry me for real, he's just trying to give me hope. I'm nothing special, he would have better luck with a blonde bimbo. They will be less broken than I am.

"No."

"You are so frustrating." He sighs.

"You don't give up, do you?" He is nearly as stubborn as I am.

"Not where you are concerned." He seems to say the sweetest things but I can't help but wonder that he's just telling me what I want to hear. I see the door open to Rex's office and I pull away from Damon's hold. He looks at me like he hasn't finished the conversation but accepts it. Rex wanders over to us.

"Hey, love."

"Hey T-Rex." I hear gunshots from the entrance hallway. I freeze, I see police officers surround us in the big room. I feel arms around my shoulders, pulling me back. Rex is using me as a shield from the police. Guns are pointing at me from all directions.

"Put the gun down and let the girl go," the policeman barks his orders.

I glance at Damon who looks like he may die inside. He waves the police officers down. To just wait I guess.

"No you aren't taking her," he sounds terrified. Terrified of losing me. Damon moves closer to us and Rex draws a gun and points it at my head.

"Please let her go," he begs.

"Stay back."

"Damon I'm okay, just go." I want him far away, away from harm.

"I'm not leaving you," he scoffs like he remembers the time when I begged him not to leave me.

"She's not leaving me, I can't live without her." He's nuts, he doesn't even know me. How could someone get such a fixation for someone in a small amount of time?

"Me neither, so I guess we have a dilemma," he shrugs. What the hell is he doing? Is this the plan to get me out? I told him Rex wouldn't give me up without a fight. If Rex shoots me then it will be better than living here as his girlfriend.

"You don't even know her."

"Of course I do. Do you really think I'd work for someone like you? I run my own gang." Damon's angry, he needs to calm down. But I know he's scared that Rex will hurt me.

"You're him from the fiery wolves aren't you?" Rex sounds surprised like he's only just noticed something.

"Yes, and you have your hands on my girl." Oh damn it Damon, don't antagonise the guy. Again, I'm no one's girl.

"You can't have her, she's mine," he growls. He pulls me further back.

"Damon you aren't helping," I say.

"I can't lose you." Damon holds up his hands in front of him. He seems to truly believe that.

"You are going to have to, she's mine," Rex contests.

"Damon just go," I beg, they are just going to keep fighting over me. Someone is going to get hurt.

"No," he says simply. Plain old no. Like he wouldn't even consider it.

"Please, he won't hurt me," I beg.

"How can you be so sure?" he asks in disbelief.

I shrug. "Because he loves me, as do you. Would you hurt me?"

"Of course not," he says defensively.

"And neither will he."

"I wouldn't be so sure. You love him?" Rex demands. Wait, this isn't going to plan. I can't lie.

"Yes."

"And do you love me?" Oh crap. I can't lie god damn it.

"I…"

"That's all I needed to know."

I close my eyes, I feel the gun move from my head to my side. I hear the piercing ring met by the pain that fills my body. I drop to my knees and I hear another gunshot but I don't get the pain. Unless I've gone numb, who knows. I hear Damon scream my name, and he catches me before I fall completely to the floor. I open my eyes to see Damon crying, his face filled with sadness. He pulls me into his lap and strokes my hair. I feel darkness surrounding me and I drift peacefully in Damon's arms.

Chapter 12

My whole body aches, disappointment enters my body. Knowing I'm still alive makes me sad. All these events that have happened have made me fight for my life a little bit less each time. I wake in the hospital room alone. I can hear shouting from the hallway. Sounds like Momma and Damon. I roll my eyes at the thought of them arguing. I honestly don't know who would win. I sit up and gasp at the pain. I want to feel the sun on my face, I need to. So I carefully climb out of bed and stagger to the window, ignoring the pain. I pull the window open so I have the breeze and the sun. I soak it all in for a while. I hear the door open but I don't look around.

"Emmie, what the fuck are you doing out of bed?" Damon growls. I roll my eyes knowing he can't see me. I ignore him, I feel arms around me and he lifts me up and places me carefully back into bed. I wince at the pain. "Jesus, are you trying to give me another heart attack?"

I look around the room to see my Momma and Danny. They seem relieved to see me. Their eyes lightening up, the pain in their faces lifting. The Doctor enters the room. "Emmie, you really do need to stay in bed." He fiddles with the bed controls so I'm sitting up. He gives me a big grin. I think I'm warming to this Doctor.

"Hey Princess, I'm so glad you're okay," my Momma says in tears. I'm not okay, but I need to stay strong for my family.

"I wouldn't say I was okay. I was shot again," I say disappointedly.

"I'm sorry," Damon says, ashamed of himself.

"It's okay."

"It's not okay, he puts you in danger wherever you go." She is mad.

"Momma this isn't his fault. This would have happened with or without him. He got me out of there. Even if he was a Moron."

Momma crosses her arms. "Yeah you got that right." She glares at Damon.

Damon laughs and holds his hands out in denial. "Hey."

"What, you are a Moron. Whose stupid idea was it anyway?"

"Mine, the plan should have been fool proof." The pain enters his eyes again. He looks tired, stressed.

"Are you serious? You think a guy like that would let me go so easy?" I scoff.

"Well yes. I had to get you out of there," he shrugs.

"Would you let me go?" I know it's slightly different but I need to get my point across.

He processes this for a minute and he finally says, "No."

"Exactly." Hallelujah, he's finally got it.

I hear the door go, I look up and see Brody walk in. He gives me one hell of a smile which makes me grin. He walks straight over to me and gives me a big strong hug. Which he holds for a while. "Ow," I say as he grips too tight. Not that I really care, pain is good. Brody seems to ignore my protest.

"Put her down. Be careful," Damon disapproves and narrows his eyes at Brody.

Brody pulls away and kisses me on the forehead. "Don't do that again okay?" Brody takes a deep breath.

"I'll try." I shrug.

"What the hell did he do to you, Sis?" Danny crosses his arms.

"It's not something you all want to hear." Nor do I want to think about it. I sit thinking about what he did to me. The way he made me obey him, the fact that I'd rather him hit me than touch me. I shudder at the thought.

"Emmie, what is your pain like?" the Doctor asks. My pain? Physical or mental? I frown.

"Emmie?" Damon says, looking for an answer.

"Fine." I guess. I can handle physical pain, it's not as bad as my mental pain.

"On a scale of 1-10 Emmie?" the Doctor raises his eyebrow.

"5." I shrug.

"Emmie." Damon glares at me.

"What Damon?"

"You forget I can tell when you are lying."

"Emmie, please tell the Doctor," Danny pleads.

"Look I can handle this pain. I'm okay." I cross my arms and wince when I forget about my side.

"Damn it, Emmie, so help me, if you don't tell the Doctor," Damon argues.

"Keep your hair on Damon. I guess it's about an 8ish," I confess.

"I will give you some more morphine. I want you to rest though." I start to laugh but immediately stop as it hurts too much. Me, rest? That's funny. I can see them all glaring at me. They need to lighten up.

"We will come back tomorrow baby girl, okay?" Momma comes over and kisses me. It's starting to get dark out. Danny hugs me tight, I don't think he wants to let me go but he does eventually and they both leave out the door. The doctor injects me with morphine and leaves the room. Here comes the awkwardness again. This love triangle between us. I still don't know who I want. I hear a phone ring, and Brody fishes his phone out of his pocket.

"Yes?" he snaps. What's eating him?

"Fine, I will be there soon." He ends the call and puts it back in his pocket.

"I have to go Beautiful."

"Sure, you should go." No one should be obliged to stay with me. Brody walks towards me and kisses me on the lips to say goodbye. Feeling someone else's lips on mine after Rex feels good. He smirks and looks up at Damon, he looks super pissed but stays quiet. I'm sure Brody did it on purpose to wind him up but he leaves the room. I start to feel nauseous, and I can't run to the bathroom. I cover my mouth.

"Damon." He grabs a disposable sick bowl from the side dresser and gives it to me. I vomit in the bowl. Damon grabs my hair out of my face. He is so cute sometimes. Why would anyone want to be this close to me when I'm sick? This must be morning sickness kicking in. I hate being sick and it hurts more when you've been shot. I nod to him when I finally finish.

"Damon?"

"Yes, baby?"

"I'm tired," I say sleepily.

"Then sleep, baby."

"You aren't leaving, are you?" I don't want to be alone right now. I don't feel safe alone right now.

"Of course not." He uses the bed controls to make the bed lay down. He removes his shoes and his jacket.

"Slide over." I carefully move over so he can lay behind me. He is very gentle with me but holds me close.

"I don't know what I'd do if I lost you." He kisses the back of my head and strokes my hair. "What did he do to you baby? When you left you were still strong. Then overnight, you were gone. I was pacing all night worried about you."

"Damon, please. You don't want to hear what he did," I whisper.

"I want to know everything about you, if you don't want to tell me then that's fine. But I want you to know I'm here." How is this handsome guy so perfect? So understanding, protective, sweet and kind? To top it off, he wants me. Why?

"He took me to his house and we went straight upstairs to the bedroom. He locked the door so I couldn't leave." I pause for a while. "He sat on a chair, he told me to stand by the bed." I still remember the sheer revulsion I felt. The sick feeling I felt in my stomach. "He ordered me to take my clothes off. I begged him, as his girlfriend I should have a choice."

"And what did he say?" He nuzzles his nose into my hair.

"He said that I should be happy I wasn't still tied up. That it should be better. So I did, I stripped for him. I couldn't look at him but I knew he was pleased."

"You are beautiful, baby, but I'm sorry you had to do that." He starts to stroke my hair, calming me.

"That wasn't the worst. He ordered me to stand in front of him, he demanded me to take off his clothes. I have never had to do that. My Dad always did that for me." I feel Damon tense, he still isn't comfortable with my Dad. I can't blame him. "We were both there naked and he pulled me on top of him. He made me take him on top. It wasn't something I had done before. I hated myself."

"Oh, baby. You shouldn't hate yourself." I hear the pain in his voice.

"In that moment, I wished…"

"Wished what baby?"

"I wished that my Dad had killed me that day."

"What?" I turn on my back so I could see his face. Shock and pain runs through his face. He strokes my face and leans in for a kiss. I love his lips on mine, so soft. My body reacts to his touch with the same charge as before. Tears run down my face.

"Marry me?"

"No," I whisper.

"Why?"

"Why would you want to marry me?"

"Because I love you. You are beautiful, strong, brave. I could go on."

"I'm tired." His smell, his soothing touch, his calming voice is making me tired. I'm relaxed for the first time in ages. In his arms.

"Sleep baby, I'm not going anywhere." He strokes my hair and just watches me. I close my eyes and drift asleep.

*

A week has passed, the Doctor is letting me go home today. I wake up feeling disoriented, I suddenly panic, Rex will come back for me. My heart is pounding. I feel an arm around me. "Baby are you okay?" I turn and face Damon who looks concerned. He lifts his arm sleepily and strokes my face. "You're fine. I'm here." I instantly relax at his touch. He is so cute when he is sleepy. He closes his eyes but holds me tighter. I put my hand on his cheek and lean in to kiss him. Damon groans and responds instantly. I need him, I need to be closer to him. Although I've showered I still feel dirty. He pulls away and sighs. He sits up and climbs out of bed. I know he's trying to restrain himself. He still sees me as fragile.

The Doctor walks in the room. "Hey, Emmie are you ready to leave today?"

"Yeah, I hate it here. No offence." I smile sweetly.

"I can understand that. Well, you can leave when you are ready Emmie. But remember, you need to take it easy." I nod, relieved that I can leave the hospital. The Doctor leaves the room. I climb out of bed, changing into my clothes so I can leave.

"Are you ready baby?" I nod. He lifts me up and pulls me close and proceeds to carry me out the door.

"I can walk you know," I half-heartedly protest. The truth is, I love this side of him. He has many sides, but I love them all.

"I know, I know." I hope he won't see me as some fragile person soon. I hug him tightly as he carries me. We reach his car and he places me on the seat. He shuts my door and walks around to his side. I stare out the window, remembering being alone in the car with Rex. I jump when Damon puts his hand on my leg. I look at him.

"Sorry," I mutter, he gives me a reassuring half-hearted smile and leans over and buckles up my seatbelt. I forget he's such a safety freak. He starts the car and drives carefully down the road. I'm deep in thought when he grabs my hand. He lifts my hand so he can kiss it gently. My heart melts at his sweet gestures.

My heart fills with disappointment when we reach my house. It's not home, I don't think it ever was. Damon pulls up in the driveway and climbs out of the car. I don't want to get out, I feel comforted by his car. My heart is pounding, I'm just stuck, frozen. Damon opens my door, he frowns at me probably contemplating on how he should proceed. He holds out his hand to encourage me out the car. I take a deep breath and take his hand. We walk hand in hand to the house. We pause outside the front door. I know he's leaving me again, he hasn't left me for long since I've been at the hospital and I've been grateful. I love his company and I feel safe. He embraces me into a passionate kiss, exploring my mouth with his tongue. The charge I felt before is stronger than ever.

"I will see you later Mi Chica Bella." He kisses me on the forehead and walks to his car. I watch him as he gracefully strolls over to his car. The way he moves with ease, I just stare at his ass while I bite my lip. Jesus, these pregnancy hormones are raging. I walk into the house, I'm greeted by my Momma. She hugs me quickly.

"Baby girl you need to pick one. You can't keep stringing them along. It's not fair." She's watched me at the hospital loving them both, not pushing either of them away. I just can't imagine my life without either of them.

"I know Momma, I just don't know what to do." I shrug.

"I think you do, you just don't want to lose the other." She carries on speaking about who I think of when I think of home. Who brought me back out of a coma. I just nod in agreement.

"Baby girl, what do you want to eat?" I hold my hands up in rejection. I can't eat now.

"Nothing, thanks though." I smile sweetly.

"No Sister of mine is going without food. Especially a pregnant one." I turn around to see Danny walk up and hug me. I love my brother, he's so protective and sweet.

"Honestly Bro, I'm not hungry," I groan.

"Honestly Sis, I'm not taking no for an answer. We've been through this before. You must eat and I'm here to enforce that." I roll my eyes.

"Fine," I say annoyed.

"Come, let me make you your favourite - cheese and bean toastie. That always gets you eating." Momma places her hand on her chin as if she's missed something but chooses to ignore it. We walk into the kitchen and I take a seat at the table. I watch Danny make my toastie. Many times during my early teens I've refused to eat. Dad always said I will eat when I'm ready, he didn't like it but it wasn't something he felt he had to push. Danny wouldn't take that crap from me. He would always make a cheese and bean toastie, my favourite, to get me eating.

Danny places the toastie in front of me, and I just stare at it. "Eat Emmie," he snaps. I proceed to eat the toastie, it tastes really good and once I finished I kiss him on the cheek.

"I'm off out," I call while leaving the kitchen.

"Emmie, you should be resting," Danny yells. I choose to carry on out the door.

"Emmie, I want you home for dinner," Momma yells. I carry on in my tracks. I walk briskly to my destination, I just have to get this off my chest. I've made my choice and I have to do it now, while I have the courage.

I stand outside the safe house. I put my hand on my chin trying to remember the code. I think long and hard. I proceed to type in '641993' and the door clicks open. Thank god I paid attention. I walk in and it's all quiet, it creeps me out being here. Shouldn't there be guards or something? There was at Rex's place, I shudder at the thought. I walk down the hall to Damon's office, I hear voices. Sounds like Damon and Sully. I guess I should knock, seeing as I'm uninvited. So I knock at the door. I hear Damon shout to come in.

I open the door and walk in trying to act confident but truth is, I'm shaking like a leaf. Damon's face drops in surprise. "Er, Emmie what are you doing? You should be resting."

"Shut up," I snap. I walk further into the room and stand between Sully and Damon. I turn to look at Sully who is looking embarrassed, sad even.

Damon is laughing at me. "Yes Miss," he says, mocking me. Bastard.

"Hey, Big Guy," I say with a grin on my face.

"Hey, how are you?" he says, still hurt.

"Sore but I'm getting there," I shrug.

"I wanted to say I'm sorry," he says. The pain in his eyes makes me sad. Certain people make me feel what they're feeling and Sully seems to be one of them. I don't let him see that.

"Sully, you saved me. I owe you my life." I do owe him my life, even if I didn't want him to save me. The mental pain I had to go through with Rex is excruciating. I walk up to him and hug him. Sully doesn't respond straight away but soon pulls me into a tight embrace.

"Okay, put my staff down." I pull away from Sully and roll my eyes and Sully smiles.

"Shut up, and jealous much?" I say, still not looking at him.

"You're on form today." Sully winks at me.

"Anyway, I need to talk to Damon. For future reference, you can take a bullet for me anytime," I play with him.

He laughs, "Noted." Sully leaves the room.

"Emmie you really should be resting." I turn around to see Damon slightly pissed but concerned all the same. "How did you get in here?"

"You should be more careful with your security, I remembered the code," I shrug. He raises his eyebrow, he looks impressed I think, I'm not too sure. "Yes, " I say awkwardly.

He looks confused. "Yes, what?"

I shrug, "Yes." He seems to contemplate what I've just said.

"Emmie, are you saying what I think you're saying?" he has a grin from ear to ear.

I nod, "Yes, I'll marry you."

He comes towards me picks me up and spins me around while hugging me tightly. He puts me back down and fishes around in his pocket. He produces a small black box and opens it, it's the most beautiful ring I've ever seen. Simple yet elegant. I couldn't have picked a better ring myself.

"Wait, you already have a ring?" I asked awkwardly, shuffling my weight.

"What can I say? I hoped you'd say yes, eventually, you did keep me hanging," he smiles, it's so good to see this handsome guy smile. It lights up his eyes, which lights up my soul. He makes my heart beat. He takes the ring from the box and places it on my finger, skimming my finger with his.

Oh wow, it sends pulses deep down within me. I bite my lip, and he kisses me. He lifts me up onto his desk, he stands between my legs. Pushing my legs wider. We are both caught up in each other, and he pulls away. No!

"You like to keep me hanging, don't you?" I say disappointedly. He thinks I'm fragile, which is true, but I need him.

"Emmie, please. You've been shot and god knows what damage Rex did." He's trying to compose himself. I know I've affected him.

I grab his hand and he looks at me and strokes my cheek with his free hand. "Please Damon, I need you. It sounds weird I know, but I need you. I feel dirty, I want you to be the last person who touched me." Tears stream down my face. I hate how emotional I am. He thinks over what I've just said. He kisses me, our breathing becomes rapid. He quickly removes my clothes and then proceeds with his. He makes this feel natural, I don't feel so exposed with him. The way he looks at me, I feel loved. He is being very careful but I feel relief when he's inside me. I can finally try and put Rex behind me. We are both lost in each other. I finally look forward to the future with my fiancé. That feels so weird.

We fall to the floor, I lay on his chest, soaking him in. He kisses my forehead and I smile into his chest. I could lay here for hours with this man. I stroke his hairs on his chest. "I have to go," I sigh. Momma wants me back for dinner. I don't want to leave this moment.

"Why?" I think he's as disappointed as I am.

"My Momma has a meal planned. I think she has some news to share." I get up and gather my clothes, covering my body once again. I don't think I will ever be comfortable naked around anyone. Not because of Damon, but because I don't love myself.

"Oh okay, I'll see you later?" Yes, he's definitely disappointed. He finds his clothes and dresses. I watch as he gets changed. Now that he's my fiancé it's allowed, right? He closes the distance between us and protectively cups my face. Placing his forehead on mine. I love it when he does this, we breathe each other in. I don't want to say goodbye to him. Not yet.

"Why don't you come?" I say hopefully.

"Are you sure? Your Mom doesn't like me much."

"It will be fine," I shrug. My Momma loves me. She will want me to be happy.

He grins. "Okay, sure."

He rifles through his drawer in his desk and pulls out a phone. He hands it to me, it's one of the latest iPhones. Why is he giving me this? I look at him questioningly. "Don't argue, just take it. I know you don't have a phone, and I need to be able to contact you," he says in his not to be messed with voice. I thank him awkwardly and kiss him on the corner of his mouth. His soft mouth that I want on me.

He takes my hand and we walk to the car. Once in the car, he asks me how I got here. "I walked Damon, I do have legs."

"Do you not drive?" he asks.

"My Dad never let me drive Damon. He said I would be putting myself at unnecessary risk." I cringe at the thought. But deep down I'm sure it's so that I didn't try running away. Not that that had stopped me before. I stare out the window, remembering the time that I did try and run away. I cringe. I couldn't handle it another night so I waited until he'd gone to bed and I snuck out the house. As soon as I was out the house, I just ran. I didn't know where I was going, I just wanted to be away from him. I was 14 at the time, I took refuge in a bus shelter. I was cold and I was drifting in and out of sleep. A nice lady in her forties appeared in front of me. She had a kind face and sparkling eyes. I stayed with her for a few days, she looked after me.

She was one of these people you could trust instantly with her kindness. I eventually told her who my family was, and she went behind my back and contacted my Dad. He was so mad, it was the first and last time I ran away. He even had the lady arrested for kidnap just so I wouldn't risk going back there. He took me home and he gagged me whilst he hit me non-stop. Danny was at work when it happened. So he didn't really need to gag me. I hated myself, I hated life so when he finished I went to the bathroom. I locked the door and I cut my wrists, I watched as the blood oozed out of them. I felt relief. That was the first time I'd hurt myself but it wasn't the last. I fell to the floor and just watched the blood. Dad was pounding on the door, demanding me to open it. But I was frozen, I saw the door kick open. I saw Dad's shocked face. "Jesus Emmie," he said. It still haunts me. He grabbed my wrists and looked at me.

He hugged me tightly, this was strange for him to show such affection. But this is what I craved, my Dad. Not the monster he showed me. But in that moment, I had my Dad. He dressed my wounds, and that night he was the Dad I wanted him to be. But it didn't last long. I found myself doing it a week later. I don't know if it was because I wanted my Dad, I really wanted to hurt myself, or both. It helped me for a while, but Danny found out that I'd been hurting myself. Seeing my Brother hurt like that, he helped me deal with my issues. Yes, I slipped from time to time but my Brother was always there to pick me back up. It has always been me and my Brother.

Chapter 13

"Baby?" Damon grabs my hand and kisses each of my knuckles, skimming his soft lips over each one of them. I turn and face him as I'm brought back to the here and now. I frown. "We are here. Are you ready?" he asks softly. I nod and open my door and climb out. I take a deep breath from the pain. Damon is with me in seconds, taking my hand, leading me to the door. I take out my key from my pocket and open the door.

"Momma, we are back," I yell. I walk in and Damon closes the door behind us. Momma comes striding from the kitchen. She frowns as she looks at Damon.

"Good, you're back. Emmie, what is he doing here?" She narrows her eyes at Damon. Mom!

"I'm sorry Mrs Salvatore, I said you wouldn't want me to be here. I can leave." Damon turns to leave but I grab his hand.

"Momma," I scold. She can't do this.

She takes a deep breath, "No, it's fine you're here actually, she may need you."

I may need him? What's going on? "What's that supposed to mean?"

Momma looks awkward, she pats her long curly black hair. "Let's go to the kitchen." She turns and walks to the kitchen. We both walk to the kitchen after Momma. Momma and Danny stand side by side. What the hell is going on?

"Sis, I love you. But don't freak out okay?" Danny says like I'm a child.

"Will someone please tell me what the hell is going on?" I demand. I'm angry, why? Damn hormones.

"If this doesn't work, then he is gone, okay?" Momma says nervously. She's gauging my face for a reaction. Fiddling her fingers in front of her.

"No Mom, you need this, you deserve it." He puts one arm around her before he glares at me. I look up to Damon who looks as confused as I am. He looks down at me and shrugs.

"Seriously Bro, I will punch you. What is going on?" I demand again.

Danny laughs at my reaction. "Okay, okay, don't get your panties in a twist." He holds his hands up in defeat.

"I'd like you to meet someone," Momma says, still looking at my face. On cue, a man in his forties maybe walks through the far kitchen door. He has black wavy hair that reaches his ears. He hasn't aged well at all. He is smartly dressed in grey trousers, a white shirt, grey waistcoat and a red tie. Damon's arm wraps around my waist. I just stare dumbfounded at this man. Who is he? There is something about him though that I find off and slightly creepy. Am I reading too much into this? He walks towards me with a smile and leans forward to give me a peck on the cheek. I tense, realising his intentions, anticipating someone else touching me. I guess Damon noticed my reaction and pulls me tighter.

"Sweetheart this is Desmond. My fiancé." Say what? Fiancé? My mouth drops open. I close it, then open it to say something. But close it again, not finding any words.

"Sis, don't freak out," Danny says, sensing my reaction.

"Why would I freak Bro?" I'm screaming. God damn it. Emmie, keep your emotions in check.

"It's nice to finally meet you, Emmie," Desmond says with a smile.

"Can't say the same about you considering I didn't even know you existed," I scoff, crossing my arms.

"Emmie calm down." Danny rolls his eyes at me.

"Don't tell me to calm down. I'm not even mad," I yell. Okay, maybe I am but I don't know why.

"Emmie look at me," Damon's soft voice surrounds me. I turn to face him, to see his beautiful face. Just the sight of him calms me. It's like it's just me and him in the room.

"Just relax," he says whilst looking deep into my eyes.

"I am relaxed," I whisper barely audible, getting lost in his eyes.

He reaches up and grabs my face with both hands. I close my eyes at his touch. "No, you're not. No one here is going to hurt you. Your Mom deserves happiness. I'm sure your Mom has done a lot of thinking about this." I keep my eyes closed, carefully considering his words. I need time to think about this.

"Sweetheart, I really like him. I've known him for years," she confesses. She sounds genuine, I think. I haven't seen my Momma for years so I don't really know her, do I?

"Your Mom told me what happened to you. I wanted to say that I would never hurt you." I can't believe my Momma told him. I shudder at the thought of yet another person knowing my life. They can't understand what happened to me. I lean into Damon's soothing hand and open my eyes. I turn to face my Momma.

"Please just everyone be quiet. Momma I love you and want you to be happy. I do. But I need time. Please start dinner, I need to lie down." I put my hands on my head trying to process all this information. The pain is ripping through me. My wound is hurting, throbbing. My back hurts. I need to lie down. I stagger to my bedroom and clamber into bed. I sink into the soft mattress and shut my eyes. Moments later I feel the mattress sink behind me. I smell Damon around me. He places his arm around me and I wince at the pain but ignore it. He holds me close, stroking my hair. He moves my hair from my neck and places a soft kiss.

"I'm a horrible person, aren't I?" I sniff. Tears slowly building in my eyes.

"Of course you aren't. You're hurting. Your Mom knows this was a big step for you," he says with his soothing voice.

I turn around to look at him and gasp out in pain. Shit, what is this pain? "Are you okay?" he says, concerned.

"I'm fine," I reassure him. How could I be so selfish? I need to stay strong for Momma. She deserves this.

"Emmie your life has been tough. More than anyone should have to go through. You deserve a little time." I love how this guy is on my side, here supporting me through this. It feels good to have someone fully on my side for a change. Someone to protect me, to challenge me and tell me when I'm being unreasonable.

I sit up, screwing up my face in pain. "I know, I'm ready." I stagger to my feet and make my way back downstairs. I hear Damon close behind me.

We are all seated around the dining room table. I'm sat between Damon and Danny. Dinner is served, they all have steak whereas I have veggie pasta. "Momma, I wanted to say I'm sorry. I shouldn't have been so selfish. These hormones are sending me crazy." I sniff, why am I crying now? For god sake.

"It's okay sweetheart. No one would blame you if you weren't okay with this," she says, reassuring me. Damon places his hand on my thigh, his touch feels so good right now. I look up at him through my eyelashes and bite my lip. He smirks at me and shakes his head in amusement.

"Yes they would, you deserve to be happy. Anyway, I'd better be a bridesmaid," I giggle.

"Actually I was hoping you would be my maid of honour," she shrugs. Wow, maid of honour. I don't know how I feel about that. I don't like the thought of being that open to attention. But my Momma seems to be happy with the idea.

"Are you sure?" not believing she wants me to be maid of honour.

"Yes, Darling."

"Shall we eat?" Desmond says, interrupting my thoughts.

"Yes, I'm starving," Danny says and I giggle. Everyone digs into their food. I can't face food. I hurt too much. I feel sick.

"I hope you don't mind, but we have news," Damon says with a grin on his face.

"Well, it can't be any more of a shocked than Emmie being pregnant. So go ahead," Momma says with a half-smile. Danny nearly chokes on his steak.

"Emmie has agreed to be my wife." Silence fills the room. Awkward. Damon grabs my hand and kisses it. I melt at the sight of him.

"You finally chose one sweetheart. Although isn't this a bit quick?" I can't tell if she's happy for me or not.

"I love him, Momma, I'm having his baby. After Dad, I can't handle anyone touching me. But Damon, he's different. He makes me want to live." I look down at my untouched food.

"Sis, look at me." I turn to face Danny next to me, wincing at the pain.

"Tell me you haven't been getting those thoughts again." How does he know? I shrug.

"What thoughts?" Momma asks.

"It doesn't matter," I try and brush them off.

Danny sighs, "Look if you hurt her, I will kill you."

"She means everything to me. I want to look after her, protect her," Damon reassures him.

"Emmie, what is he talking about?" she says irritated. Danny is keeping his mouth shut. He knows it's our secret.

"I used to hurt myself." I don't feel ashamed or embarrassed. I feel gasps around me.

"What do you mean?" Momma demands.

"I used to cut my wrists," I confess.

"Why?" Momma asks. Really, why? I know she will never understand my life, or understand me. But what a silly question. Danny grabs my hand to support me. I love my Brother.

"There's times when life gets too much. It helps me cope, but the way Dad reacted..." I pause.

"The way your Dad reacted?" Momma asks.

"He was devastated when I cut my wrists. He acted the way Dad should. He was the Dad I always wanted. A real father's love. It didn't last long. So I would cut my wrists to get his attention."

"Oh Emmie, your Dad was a coward of a man. He didn't deserve your love."

"It was me who didn't deserve his love. Do you not understand at all?" I feel the lump in my throat burning. Why do my emotions keep changing so quickly?

"I hate what he did to you," Momma growls.

"I will spend the rest of my life proving you are worth it," Damon says. I look at him, his jaw is tense, searching my eyes for what? I don't know.

We all started to talk at ease during the rest of the meal. Desmond and Danny are talking about football. What a bore. Damon is teasing me with his fingers up and down my leg. I love playful Damon.

"Emmie, will you eat something? Please," Damon whispers in my ear. I don't want to argue with him so I batter my eyelashes at him sweetly, lift the side of my mouth and shrug. We had a nice family meal, well the company anyway. Damon can't stay so he walks me to the door and kisses me goodbye.

"Thank you," I say sadly, looking at the ground. I don't want him to go. But he has been great and he's not forced to stay with me. He's probably fed up with my company. He lifts my chin so I'm forced to look at him.

"For what?"

"For everything," I shrug.

"Oh my sweet Emmie, I would do anything for you." I smile at his confession. He grins back at me, kisses me on the forehead and leaves. I stare at the closed door where he left. Tension seems to fill the room. I start to feel anxious, and empty. Why is that? I head straight to my room. I decide to have a shower before I go to bed. What a day. I've accepted to be Damon's wife. Met Momma's fiancé that I knew nothing about. There is still something about him that freaks me out. But most men do, so I should give him a chance. Right?

I carefully remove my clothes, I examine my wound. It has been bleeding, oops. It's become very red around the area. I shrug it off and climb in the shower. I am brought back to the memory of being in Rex's shower. How helpless I felt, how broken I felt. Will I ever get over this? Maybe in time, with Damon by my side. That's if he doesn't leave me, I'm bound to ruin things like I always do. I wash my hair and body and leave the shower. I feel better after the hot water cascading on my skin. I dry myself and dress in blue PJ pants and a black top. I clamber into bed and like most nights, I cry myself to sleep. Feeling the warm tears fall down my face.

My alarm jolts me awake. Oww, that hurt. I reach over and grab my alarm clock and switch it off. Yes, I can manage school today. I shuffle out of bed wincing at the pain. Physical pain is good, I chant to myself. Yes. I proceed to my dresser and pick out a loosely fitting top and some shorts. I dress carefully, avoiding contact with my wound. I place on some of my heeled boots. I look in the mirror and brush my hair. God, I look awful, puffy eyes from crying again. I look like a zombie. This will have to do. I wish I could change what I could see in the mirror. But nothing will change how ugly I am.

I wander downstairs and into the kitchen. I'm startled at the sight of Desmond. I guess he stayed over, he's still dressed smartly. He gives me a creepy smile. "Hey, Emmie."

"Um, Hey." Why am I so nervous?

"Can I get you something to eat?" He wants to make me food in my house? I don't think so. Maybe he wants to secretly poison me.

"No thank you."

He narrows his eyes at me. "You really should eat something."

"I'll grab something at school."

"Emmie, someone's at the door for you," Momma calls. I smile and quickly make my way to the door to see Damon. But when I get to the door there is a pang of disappointment when I see it's not Damon. But instead, it's Sully.

"Umm hey Big Guy." I smile at him.

Momma looks at me confused. "Big Guy?"

"Yeah, that's what I call him," I giggle and Sully blushes again. Bless him.

"Why?"

"Because he's big, duh," I say, staring at his muscles.

"Who is he and what's he doing here?" she demands. I guess she doesn't trust other people where I'm concerned. I guess I can't blame her.

"I don't know why he's here. Why don't you ask him? And Big Guy took the bullet for me," I shrug.

"This is him?" she says with her eyes alight. She steps forward and hugs Sully. "Thank you," she says. Sully looks at me over Momma's shoulder giving me a help-me-now-please look. I giggle at him. Momma steps back.

"You're welcome Ma'am." He looks at me. "I'm here to take you to school."

I roll my eyes. Of course he is. "Where's Damon?"

"He has things he needs to take care of. He doesn't want you to be alone. He says danger follows you." Sully chuckles.

"That's ridiculous, danger doesn't follow me," I scoff. Does it?

"I think that's a good idea and who better to do it?" she says, winking at Sully. Wait, is she... flirting with him? Mom!

"Thanks, Ma'am." Sully goes bright red again.

"Please call me Esme." I roll my eyes at her.

"Sure, Emmie are you ready? Or do I need to carry you over my shoulder again." He winks at me and I grin at the memory of him doing that. Bastard.

"I'm ready, I have my own legs." I cross my arms in a playful protest.

"Fine ones too." He cocks his head to one side.

"Don't let Damon catch you flirting with me. He will probably castrate you," I giggle.

"I'd like to see him try." Sully chuckles, I think Sully is one of few people who aren't scared of Damon.

"Have a good day at school darling." Momma kisses me on the cheek and leaves us to it.

"Seriously, get your butt out the door, Emmie, before I spank you," Sully says with a straight face.

"I'm going…" I giggle and head out the door. I'm glad Sully and I get on well. I climb into the open door that Sully is holding open for me. I put on my seat belt and wait for Sully to get in.

"Hey Big Guy, how long have you worked for Damon?" I ask curiously.

"Since he started the gang about 4 years ago."

"So you've known him for 4 years?"

"No Emmie, I went to school with him too. We are great friends. I have a lot of respect for the guy."

"That explains a lot."

"What does?"

"Well, you don't seem to be scared of him. You don't take any crap from him. Yet you do as you're told." I shrug.

"He can be a real pain in the ass sometimes but he's done a lot for me."

I giggle, "Yeah you can say that again." It doesn't take long to get to school, it's really not that far. But Damon insists on me being driven. Is this what it's going to be like? Him bossing me around. I groan at the thought.

"Have a good day Emmie," Sully says, opening my door. I clutch my side as I climb out of the car.

"Bye Big Guy," I smile and head for the school.

I enter the hallway and catch sight of Jessie by her locker. I just stand immobile in the corridor. It's overwhelming being back here. So much has happened, this feels unimportant compared to what I've been through. Meaningless. Jessie looks up at me and frowns but strides over to me. She hugs me which makes me flinch. I still can't accept touch yet, even from my best friend. I've never been a hugger. She steps back and looks at me. She shrieks, making me jump. She grabs my hand and admires my ring. Oh, that.

"Emmie, you kept that quiet." She's excited. "Who's the lucky guy? I'm guessing Rider?" I nod in agreement. "When? How?"

"He asked me when I was kidnapped. When he came undercover to save me." I shrug. "But I said no, I needed time."

"I don't understand. I think it's romantic."

"I had to know he didn't just feel sorry for me in that place. Besides, I didn't know who I wanted, him or Brody," I scowl.

"So what happened?"

"He asked me at every opportunity he had and then once I was out the hospital, my Momma made me realise who I wanted. So I went to find him and I said yes." I smile at the thought of the aftermath when he made sweet love to me.

"That's romantic. Wow, Emmie. We have prom coming up soon too. We need to go shopping." Her enthusiasm is too much for me at the moment.

"Sure," I nod. She frowns at me but chooses not to push me, which I'm grateful for. My phone vibrates in my pocket. It's a text from Damon. I smile.

Hey baby, have a good day at school. Damon x

I miss you. Your Emmie I smile at myself at my response.

I like the sound of that baby. I could text playful Damon all day but I'd better get to class.

It's P.E next. We head into the changing rooms to get dressed in our gear. I groan, I hate it. We both walk arm in arm to the fields. I can see Mr Dudley in the distance, he looks mega pissed. Once we reach him he crosses his arms. I cross my arms in retaliation. "Salvatore, Hawkins you're both late," he scolds.

"Sorry, sir," I say, curling my hair with my finger. God, is it wrong that I think my teacher is hot? His blond hair sticking up. His bright blue eyes that stand out from his face. I'd say he was in his late 20s. He seems to be taken back by my apology. His face seems calmer, I think. He's difficult to read.

"It's her fault," Jessie says, nudging my good side and giggles.

"Sure, blame your pregnant best friend." I giggle too.

"Pregnant?" Mr Dudley raises his eyebrow. He looks kinda pissed too. Why? It's none of his business.

"Looking good Salvatore." I turn to see Brody and Sky waving at me in their football gear. My mouth drops open at the sight of them. I close my mouth instantly, trying to compose myself. Jesus little baby, what are you doing to me? I hug my tummy, I've started to develop a round bump that must only be noticeable to me as no one has mentioned it. God, I can't deal with getting fatter. I decide it's only polite to call back at them.

"You too." Although I don't know who I'm talking about, maybe both? But they both seem pleased and they go back to their football.

"Enough, you are a troublemaker Salvatore." He raises his voice at me, trying to intimidate me.

"Yeah, and what are you going to do about it?" I wink at him. Because this sort of confrontation makes him uncomfortable or at least calms him down a bit.

He raises his eyebrow as if he's accepted a challenge. "Both of you, run a lap of the field. Move it," he yells. I groan and we both start to run. Jessie is fitter than I am and seems to effortlessly take the lead. I soon find myself slowing down. I'm all clammy and hot. I don't feel well at all, but I don't want to give Mr Blond God the satisfaction of not completing the lap. I start to feel dizzy as I near the end. I reach Mr Dudley and put my hands on my knees. I look up at him.

"Huh, Sir?"

"Yes Salvatore?" he says.

"Why are there two of you?" I'm seeing double of him. One's enough of him. Even though he is good looking, his mood is not something to be desired. They both frown at me.

"Emmie, are you okay?" he seems concerned. I hold my head which is hot. Real hot.

"Emmie?" Jessie is scared. Why?

"I'm okay," I reassure them. Before I know it, I'm falling to the ground but strong arms catch me and then I black out. I don't know how long I've been out for but when I wake, I'm lying on the ground in Brody's arms. I guess he caught me.

"Emmie?" Brody says calmly. I blink up at him, the sun bouncing off his beautifully tanned skin. He looks like an angel.

"Hey Beautiful," it comes out of my mouth before I can stop it. There goes my verbal diarrhoea. Shit! Pull it together Emmie.

"You okay?" he says with concern on his face but he grins at what I've just said. Embarrassed, I get to my feet with the help of Brody's strong arms. I dust myself off.

"I'm fine, why are you all fussing?" They are all gawking at me like I've just dropped from the sky.

"I think I should take you to the nurse," Mr Blond God says with his fingers on his chin.

"I'm fine, jeez." I cross my arms in annoyance. I'm not but I don't want to go back to the hospital. I'm hot and clammy, my wound is pounding.

"If you won't go to the nurse then take the rest of this class off," Mr D says worriedly.

"Yay, no class," I cheer but instantly stop when it hurts and walk off the field.

"Emmie, wait up," Jessie calls. And she's soon by my side. We walk in silence to the cafeteria. Once we take our seats, Jessie hits me with her disapproval.

"What the hell happened out there?" she demands.

"What?" I shrug.

"Don't play dumb, it doesn't suit you," Jessie scowls at me.

I feel backed into a corner. "I don't know what you want me to say? Probably doesn't help that I'm pregnant," I say, pissed at her for putting her nose in my business.

"You don't go and pass out because you're pregnant."

"I guess I may have skipped breakfast." It's not a lie, but then I always skip meals. It's nothing new.

"You can't go skipping meals when you're pregnant." She scolds me. I feel like a damn child again.

"Whatever." I roll my eyes at her. I get up and stomp out of the cafeteria. I walk into the corridor and end up bumping into her of all people. Jade. I groan. "Urgh, not you," I scowl.

"The feeling is mutual," she says in agreement.

"Seriously, your face is like a slapped fish." I must keep my emotions in check. I hug my tummy, what have you done to me? You've turned me into a green-eyed monster.

"I hate you," she screams.

"I hate that you're a bitch."

"What's got up your skin?" She seems genuinely interested.

"You, you're just like a damn leech that gets everywhere and no one wants you there." I'm yelling, I'm screaming. I'm angry. What the fuck? Hands are on my shoulders, they calm me. Brings me back to the here and now. His scent is overpowering me once more. I relax at his touch. I don't even need to look to know it's him. My fiancé. I take a deep breath.

"Emmie, calm down," he says firmly but kisses the back of my head.

"Honestly you are such a stress head." She glares her eyes at me.

"Don't you remember me kicking your ass?" I lurch forward towards her but Damon's hands are still on my shoulders and he holds me back.

"I'm out of here." She walks briskly out of the corridor.

Damon spins me around so I'm facing him. "Emmie, what's wrong?" I need to close the distance between us and I walk into his arms and snuggle his chest.

"What are you doing here?" I say, breathing him in.

"Jessie called to say you fainted. What happened?" He pulls me away so he can examine me. He touches my sweaty forehead and frowns.

"Nothing, I'm fine."

"She said you missed breakfast. Emmie, you didn't eat your dinner either," he says disapprovingly.

"Desmond offered to make breakfast. He could poison it, so I passed." Once again, I make my way to my favourite place in his chest and he doesn't stop me. He just holds me close and strokes my hair. I've relaxed again, I've been so uptight since he left me last night. Why am I letting a guy make me feel like this? I feel so helpless. I should be standing on my own two feet but I'm relieved to find comfort in life. Something that makes me feel safe.

"Emmie, why would he do that? No one will hurt you. Not eating doesn't fully explain why you fainted." He starts to play with my hair with his fingers. I close my eyes, enjoying his soothing touch.

"How should I know?" I sigh. "I'm fine Damon."

"I knew I shouldn't have let you go back to school," he growls. I pull away from him wanting to leave this place. I walk briskly out of school. I can hear him calling from where I left him, but I carry on walking. Outside I'm pleased to see Sully, he must have driven Damon here. I smile at him and he returns the smile.

"Hey Big Guy."

"You okay Miss?" Miss? Is he being polite or is he playing with me?

"Sure, can you take me to my Momma's?" Momma's house is not home. I don't see a single place as home. I don't feel safe anywhere.

"Where's Damon? I think we should wait for him," he says awkwardly.

I roll my eyes, "Trust me, he will be here soon."

He chuckles, "What did you do?"

"Nothing really." I smile sweetly.

"Seriously Emmie?" Damon is behind me. He sounds pissed.

"What?" I say whilst climbing into the car.

"Where are you going now?" he's exasperated.

"I'm going to my Momma's." As I shut the door, I see them both give each other a look. Damon walks around to the other side of the car and climbs in the back with me.

"I don't think so," he says softly.

"What?"

"I'm taking you to the hospital," he says and I know it's his not to be messed with voice. "Sully."

"Yes, sir." Sully starts the car and drives. I guess towards the hospital and not my house like I asked. I'm angry, what gives him the right to tell me what I can and can't do? We both sit in silence, both too stubborn to say anything. Sully pulls up outside the hospital so we can get out. Damon gets out the car and walks around and opens my door.

"Emmie, get out," he demands.

"No." He shrugs and leans in the car and picks me up. "Ow," I protest. But it hurts to struggle so I fall back into his arms. He walks silently to the ward. We arrive at the reception desk. A young pretty brunette girl looks up. She flashes her eyes at Damon.

"Can I help you sir?" she's flirting with him even though I'm still in his arms.

"I'd like to see Dr Grey please."

"Have you got an appointment sir?" she asks.

"No but this is an emergency."

"What sort of emergency?" She raises her eyebrow.

"Look, I'm not taking this crap. Will you just page the Doctor?" he snaps. He's his usual grumpy self.

She seems to wither under his gaze. She's intimidated. "Yes sir. I will do that. Take a seat." She makes a call and Damon takes a seat. But he still doesn't put me down.

"Are you scared I'm going to run off?" I giggle.

"Something like that." His jaw is tense. I put my hand under his shirt so

I can feel his bare chest. He groans. I continue to explore his chest with my fingers, feeling his abs and muscles.

"Emmie, what are you doing to me?" He looks down at me and strokes my cheek, I stare into his dreamy eyes.

"Rider? Emmie?" I hear the good old Doctor and Damon stands.

"Hi, Doc," Damon replies.

"Come with me." We follow into a side room. Looks like an examination room. The Doctor closes the door behind us. Damon carries me to the bed and puts me down.

"Ow," I wince. The Doctor frowns at me.

"What's going on?" he asks.

"Nothing, I'm fine."

"We will let the Doc decide that, shall we? She fainted at school today, so I brought her here to be checked out." Damon crosses his arms.

The Doc puts his fingers on his chin like his thinking. He looks very smart and intelligent when he does it. "What were you doing? When you fainted?"

"Running, in P.E." I shrug.

"You really shouldn't be pushing yourself, Emmie. You need to be resting."

"I wasn't."

"How's your wound doing?" Why did he have to bring that up? Okay so I haven't checked it since last night. But it hurts.

"It's fine." I fiddle with my fingers in my lap.

"Emmie what is it?" Damon demands. God, how does he know when I'm hiding something?

"Just been a bit painful. But it's fine." Ish.

"It really should have healed by now. Let me look, lie down," Doc says. I wince as I slowly lie down.

Chapter 14

"Lift your top up, Emmie," the Doctor says. I hesitate, this is going to end badly.

"Emmie." Damon lifts his eyebrow as if to ask what I'm hiding. I do as he asks and I lift my top. I see the Doctor's eyes widen. Crap.

"Emmie, you've pulled the stitches out and it's infected."

"What? Emmie," Damon shouts.

"Emmie, why didn't you come back? You must have known," the Doctor asks while cleaning my wound.

"Honestly, I'm fine. I saw it was bleeding. I had a shower and it felt better."

"I can't trust you to take care of yourself, can I?" Damon's pacing the room. "God damn it, do I have to chain you to a bed?" He can chain me to his bed anytime. Although he wouldn't have to chain me, I'd probably stay there of my own accord.

"I don't need to be wrapped in cotton wool Damon. You are over reacting."

"It seems as though you do. I'm totally supportive of that," the Doctor chuckles.

"Emmie, you are soon to be my wife. I need to know you are safe."

"Wow, congratulations. You make an excellent couple," he says approvingly.

"Thank you. I think so when she's not so stubborn." Damon grins at me. It's only a matter of time before he won't want me. He's just said himself 'when I'm not so stubborn.' I frown at the thought.

"Okay, I've removed the stitches. I'm going to leave it open so the infection can draw out. You'll need to take antibiotics." He removes the pads and instruments he was using from the bed.

"Are they safe?" I hold my tummy. I love this baby already. What I wouldn't do for this little small person. I will do everything to protect my Bambino.

"Yes Emmie, now don't take this the wrong way, but I don't want to see you in here again."

"Are you sure you won't miss me?" I giggle.

Damon takes my hand. "Come on, let's go." He leads me out of the room, out the bright white corridors. Out to the car where Sully is parked up outside. Damon holds the door open for me. I climb in and scoot over so he doesn't need to walk around the car.

Damon climbs in and puts his seat belt on. I hate him being mad at me, I can't help being this way, it's who I am. He looks over at me. "What's wrong?" I climb onto his lap closing the distance between us. He doesn't look amused but he doesn't question me. "I'm sorry." I curl up into his chest.

"For what Emmie?" like he doesn't understand.

"Being stubborn." I place my hand under his shirt again. I love to feel his skin.

"Oh baby, it's who you are and I love you for it. I love your smart mouth." He nuzzles his nose in my hair. He grabs my hand and he starts to play with it, stroking it with his thumb. We sit and soak each other in whilst Sully drives us to my house. It all comes too soon when Sully pulls up outside. Sully gets out and opens the door. Damon gets out, keeping me in his arms. He playfully places many kisses on my neck and I squeal like a girl. He laughs and continues. I move my head back, giggling, giving him better access. We reach the door and he puts me down.

"I love to hear you happy and carefree."

"You make me happy and carefree," I confess, smiling at him. I grab my key and enter the house.

"Seriously Emmie, take it easy."

"Yeah, yeah." I smile sweetly.

He sighs, but he can't hide his grin. "What am I going to do with you?"

I bite my lip thinking about what he could do to me. He steps towards me and sweeps me off my feet and he holds me, I'm close to the floor and I squeal again, laughing. He kisses me softly. I could stay in this moment forever. But he brings me to my feet all too soon, and I know he's leaving again. "I have work to do, I'll catch you later." He winks at me and leaves. Leaving me full of tension again. Maybe I have always been this tense and just didn't notice until Damon came along.

"Momma, I'm back," I yell. I expect Momma to come and greet me but instead, it's Desmond. Shit.

"Your Mom has popped out. She will be back soon." I stand awkwardly, looking anywhere but at him.

"Oh okay." I hope she's back soon. Being here with Desmond alone creeps me out.

"She won't be long." He smiles.

"I'll be in my room." I run upstairs, ignoring the protest of my side. I take my shoes off and get into bed. I'm so tired, I don't know if it's this wound, the fact that it's infected or that I'm pregnant but I will just shut my eyes for a while. I wrap the sheets around me, feeling the comfort of them around me.

"Stand by the bed." Oh no, please no. Rex is sitting by the door on the chair. Bile works its way up my throat burning as it goes. The sight of him sets me on edge. He's looking at me with his fingers on his chin. I look down and I'm naked. What? No, please. His room is just the same, huge bed in the middle of the room. The smell is the same.

"Sweetheart, wake up." I jolt awake, I'm soaked with sweat. My heart beating rapidly. I scan the room. Momma is by my side, stroking my forehead. I start to come back to reality. What the hell was that about?

"You okay baby girl? You were having a nightmare." Am I okay? Yes, I think so.

"Yeah, I'm okay." I frown and fiddle with my hands in my lap.

"We'd like to speak to you." I scan the room to see Desmond in my room. God, why did she let him in here? While I was sleeping? Really?

"Okay?"

"We would love to have a new start. I'm worried that you are still traumatised from the past and being here... well, can't be easy for you." Why does nobody let me forget? That's what I'd like to do. Just forget it all happened. But It was my life, I will always remember the good times and the bad. Hell, there was a lot of bad.

"What are you getting at?"

"I'd love it if you would all move in with me. I have a big house. New start," Desmond says with a smile on his face. It's a smile that on the outside you can trust but something is nagging at me on the inside, screaming for me not to trust him. But I don't trust any man, except Damon. They want me to move in with this man? I can't. It's too much. I've only just met the guy. They're crazy. No.

"What did you say?" I must have heard wrong. My Momma can't expect me to move in with a stranger, surely?

"Emmie, you heard what he said. What do you think? I think it will be good for us." Momma crosses her arms. I can see she really wants this, but can I do this for her? I just don't know.

"I would love it if you would move in with me," Desmond says. Of course he would. I shiver at the thought.

"I-I..." I stutter, I don't know what to say. My phone vibrates so I check it. Party tonight. Cool, I need to get away from here.

"Are you listening? Can you talk to us, please?" Momma demands.

"It's rude to use your phone while talking to us," Desmond scolds.

"Who do you think you are, my father? Well, guess what, he's dead. He was a pretty shitty one. So I do not require a new one." I'm angry again. This is exhausting. I storm off into my bathroom and lock the door. Calm down, Emmie.

I decide to run a bath, I need to relax. I reach to run the taps. I take a look at my reflection in the mirror. I frown whilst taking my clothes off, discarding them on the floor. The bathroom is steaming with the hot water. I clamber into the bath, wincing at the heat. But I like hot baths and quickly get used to the heat. I turn off the taps and lay back and relax. After all my Dad did to my Mom, she deserves to be happy. I have to give this to her. I must. If she loves Desmond enough like she seems to, I must give her the benefit of the doubt.

I wash my hair and body and climb out the bath. Grabbing a towel off the rack, I wrap it around myself, shielding me from any harm. Yeah right, like a towel can protect me. But it's welcome on my skin. I unlock the door and peer out. Oh good, they're gone. I walk over to my wardrobe and take out a black dress with a brown belt. At the bottom, I find some high heeled calf boots. Yes, this will do. I dry myself and get dressed. I decide I will apply makeup, it's so much easier to face life with makeup. I apply mascara first, then concealer followed by powder. I apply some blusher and jobs a good'un. I smile, yes this is what I like to see in the mirror. I grab my hairdryer and sort my unruly hair out. I'm ready, I just need to leave.

I walk downstairs and head for the door. "Where do you think you're going, missy?" Oh crap, I turn around startled, like I've been caught sneaking out late at night. Well, I guess I have.

"I'm going out, there's a party tonight." I shrug.

"You're not going out. You're not too old to be grounded, Emmie." God, where has she been my whole life? She hasn't been here so she hasn't the right to boss me around. I'm pregnant and engaged. I don't need this crap anymore.

"That's what you think, see you later." I turn for the door. Desmond grabs my arm and swings me back around. He touched me, and he touched me hard. His fingers are digging into my arm. Tears spring into my eyes.

"Let me go. Please. I'm sorry." Tears are free falling down my face. "I'm sorry, don't hurt me," I beg. Desmond releases me in an instant. They both look horrified. I run out the door. I hear Desmond calling me that he's sorry. I can't see in front of my face. I hear a car door opening and Sully steps out of the car with concern on his face. I run into his arms.

"Emmie, are you okay?" he says, holding me close. It's not the same as Damon's hold. But I feel happy and safe in his arms. I can't find the words. "What happened?" he implores. I stand back and wipe my tears from my face with the back of my hand.

"I don't know if I'm reading too much into it. Could be my hormones, I'm just being silly."

"You're clearly upset, tell me what happened and I can tell you to man up or not... Or should I say Emmie up because you're a pretty scary woman you know?" I giggle, he has a way with words.

"You're funny. My Momma and Desmond want us all to move into his place."

"And you don't want to?"

"Honestly he creeps me out. I want my Momma to be happy but he's still a stranger to me. This is too much too soon for me." But I know I will do this. Just for my Momma.

"It is very soon, you wouldn't be human if you weren't ready for this." He holds the door open for me to climb in. He walks to his side of the car, slides in and faces me.

"We got in a fight, I'm off to a party. I said I was going out. My Momma said I was grounded and not to go out. I needed space so I went to leave anyway and he grabbed my arm. I freaked out."

Sully grabs my arm gently to examine it. He looks horrified. You can see fingerprints forming already. No doubt I'll bruise. I bruise easily. "He grabbed you? He must have grabbed you hard." He can't stop looking at my arm. Like he's hurting, a look Damon would have. Although Damon would probably be in there murdering him.

"Honestly I shouldn't have pushed him to it. I'm a bad person, I deserve this." I shrug him off.

"Emmie relax, you're safe. You don't deserve this." I'm so anxious, I feel better with Sully. But I'm still freaking out. I need a distraction.

"Hey Big Guy, do you think you could drive me to a party?" I smile sweetly.

He laughs at my question or my smile, who knows? "Sure, considering I'll be going anyway, least I can do is give you a lift." What's that supposed to mean? He seems to answer my unspoken question. "Don't shoot the messenger but Damon wants me to follow you. Wherever you go just to make sure it's safe. He knows how you like to walk into trouble." I frown, I don't know what to make of this. Of course he's having me followed.

"Well, you might as well enjoy the party then. Good job I like you Big Guy or I probably would shoot the messenger," I say with a straight face but fail as I end up grinning.

"I'll keep that in mind." He laughs, I like Sully. He has a funny side. I'm glad to get away from the house. I give Sully the address and it doesn't take long to get there. He pulls up in a parking bay. The sun is setting. It looks beautiful here at the beach. Sully doesn't hesitate to get my door and I climb out. Beach party and I'm in heels. I remove my shoes and place them in the foot well of the car. Sully smirks at me and shuts the door.

I put my arm in Sully's, and we walk across the road to the beach. I feel the sand beneath my feet, between my toes. "You know, it looks like I'm your date again."

"You aren't that lucky Big Guy," I grin. The party is in full swing when we arrive. There are a few faces I know.

"This looks fun, I'm going to get a drink." I clap my hands.

"Emmie..." Sully looks at me sternly.

"Yeah, yeah, non-alcoholic. I remember." I roll my eyes and join the queue at the bar. I rest my arms on the bar. A young attractive guy winks at me taking my order.

"I'd love a wine but, it seems that's forbidden. So I'll get a Pepsi please."

"Coming right up sexy." Hmm, sexy. Emmie, stop it. Jesus. Hormones! I feel an arm around me and I flinch. I turn my head to my left and Brody is giving me a sexy smile. Oh wow, that smile. I melt.

The barman frowns when he returns with my drink, probably because Brody's arm is around me. "Here you go gorgeous." I smile. I catch Brody glaring at him. I roll my eyes. I take my drink from the bar and let Brody lead me to where everyone is dancing. We find Jessie dancing. She hugs me. We both dance together, whilst Brody dances next to us. Watching us. I look over and find Sully on the phone. He looks concerned, but he's here all the same.

"You two are nuts," Brody shouts above the music.

"Yeah but it wouldn't be a party without us," I call out. Jessie grabs my hips and starts to dance down my body. I giggle, yes this is what I need. To have a laugh with my friends.

"True," he says in total agreement. I don't know how long we've been dancing for but I start to feel exhausted. Jessie and Brody seem to be drunk.

"I love you, Emmie," Jessie says with her arms around my neck.

"I love you too Jessie." I giggle. She looks wasted. She moves forwards to kiss me. Although I'm not gay, it's fun to send the guys wild. She pulls me towards her to deepen the kiss.

"Okay, Emmie. Jessie, please put my fiancée down." I pull away from Jessie shocked that Damon is here. "Hey Mi Chica Bella," he says, half pissed half amused.

"Hey." I've gone really shy.

"You know, you drive all the guys wild when you do that." He's jealous. Wow.

"I know, that's why we do it," I giggle.

"We will leave you two lovebirds to it," Jessie says, dragging Brody away with her.

"I'm happy you're here," I confess shyly. I've missed him, although it hasn't been long.

"I'm happy to see you happy, baby."

I shrug, "I needed this."

"And I need you," he says and closes the distance between us. He caresses my face and I close my eyes and lean into his delicate touch. Wow, he's hardly touching me and I want to pounce on him. Oh, Bambino what are you doing to me? He leans down and kisses me like his life depends on it. I'm pretty sure I didn't do anything to deserve an amazing fiancé like Damon.

"I don't know what Jessie felt kissing you but I have to say it's pretty damn good."

"Right back at you," I say breathlessly.

"Do you want to stay here for a while or go home?" I frown at the thought.

"It depends."

"On what?" he pushes a strand of my hair behind my ear.

"What place you are calling home."

"Emmie, I know you don't feel home is at your Mom's. I don't blame you after what's happened. I know why you wanted to get out of there today. I was going to take you to mine tonight. But you should let your Mom know what you're doing. She will probably bury me alive."

I giggle, "Yeah she probably would. I will text her."

"Great, let's go." He takes my hand and leads me towards his car.

"Damon I left my shoes in Sully's car." He cocks his head to one side considering my protest. He shrugs and picks me up so I'm in his arms.

"What's the problem?" he laughs. I squeal with delight.

"No problem dear fiancé," I say sweetly. He unlocks the car and opens the door, and places me in the seat. He strides around the car and slides in the car. I bite my lip and he reaches up and he runs his thumb over my lips to get me to release my lip. He looks down at my arm and his face drops. I instinctively cover my arm. He grabs my hand away from my arm so he can examine the bruises that have now formed.

"It's fine Damon." He shuts his eyes to process what I've said. He lets out a deep breath that he must have been holding in. He opens his eyes and starts to kiss each small fingerprint bruises. Oh wow, that's making me squirm. That feels so good. His lips on me.

"You know? When Sully told me what he did to you, I wanted to beat the shit out of him," he sighs.

"I'm glad you didn't." I give him a reassuring smile. I grab my phone from my small bag that is placed over my shoulder and type a quick message.

I'm staying at Damon's tonight.

There is an immediate response.

Baby girl, I'm sorry about earlier, stay safe. I love you.

I need space from them right now so I place the phone back in my bag. Damon focuses back on the road, starts the car and heads to his place. I suddenly sag with relief and curl up on the seat How is it that when I'm with him I feel so relaxed. "What are you thinking about?" he glances at me for a moment to gauge my reaction.

"Stuff." I shrug.

"Like?"

"You."

"What about me?"

"I've noticed whenever you leave me I get tense and anxious. But just your presence has calmed me. I feel safe with Sully but not relaxed. I was just thinking how did I end up so lucky?" he seems to think over my words for a while.

"You are tense and anxious without me?" he seems hurt.

"I think I've always been like that and then you came along. You leave so often I guess I just feel it more." I don't want to sound too needy. God, he may leave me if he really knows how insecure I am.

"Baby you deserve the world and I will give it to you. Don't doubt that." He grabs my hand while he keeps his eyes on the road. His touch makes me stop breathing. "Breathe Emmie." He grins at me. How does he know? "Have you eaten today?"

"No."

"For fuck sake Emmie. It's not just you anymore," he shouts.

"Calm down, Damon."

"Am I going to need to force feed you?"

"I'm not a child Damon."

"Then don't act like one." Damon pulls up into a driveway to a stylish building. Not huge like Rex's.

"Where are we?" Damon gets out the car and walks to my side. Is he ignoring me? I get out the car when he opens my door. He leads me to the front door and opens it and ushers me in. He leads me into a kitchen. It is very modern, black worktops and cupboards. Exactly what I'd pick if I'd been given the choice. Worktops surround the edge of the kitchen. In the middle, it has an island. To the left of the island are a table and 4 chairs. Damon drags me to the table.

"Sit." I take a seat whilst watching him wander around the kitchen. He puts bread in the toaster and gets beans out the cupboard. Places them in a bowl and heats them in the microwave. Hmm, I like to watch him. "We are at my house, Emmie. I don't live at the safe house." Oh yeah, course. How stupid. I guess he's talking to me now.

"Finally found your voice, did you?" I tease.

"Emmie, you infuriate me. This is new for me. I've always been in control what with running my own gang. But you, I feel so out of control, you never listen. Yet I love you, and I'm drawn to you. I like a challenge Miss Salvatore but you test my patience."

The toaster pops up making me jump. Damon grabs the butter out the fridge, collects the toast and butters it. The microwave pings and he tips the beans over the toast. Picking up the plate, he collects a knife and fork from a drawer and strides over to me and places the food in front of me. He sits opposite me. I stare at him awkwardly. "Don't push me, Emmie, if you tell me you've gone vegan or anything I will lose my shit. Eat." I do like beans on toast. I just hate eating on my own. I feel fat. He takes a deep breath.

"What's wrong?" he says gently.

"I er, don't like eating on my own." He laughs. Why? Am I funny? He reaches over and grabs a piece of toast and takes a bite.

"You aren't eating on your own now Miss Salvatore. Now eat." Even chewing his food is hot. I just stare at his mouth. "Emmie."

I pull my eyes from his mouth and pick up my knife and fork. I dig in, slowly chewing my food. I look up at Damon who seems to have relaxed. I didn't even know he was tense.

"Do you kiss your friend a lot?" he asks amusedly.

"Only at parties. Why? Are you jealous?" I smile at him through my eyelashes.

"When I arrived, Sully told me that all he heard was you were the heart of the parties and then I saw you two kissing. I didn't know whether to laugh, be angry or join you both."

I pause with my food mid-air, mouth open shocked processing what he's just said. He grabs another piece of toast and takes another bite. "Keep eating Emmie."

I do as I'm told. "So did you decide?" I say, teasing him.

"Oh baby, I only want you. I'm a jealous guy, but Sully reminded me that you're my fiancée." His words melt my insides. I need him right now. I quickly finish my food.

"Good girl," he praises. He stands to collect my plate, but I stand up and kiss him before he gets the chance.

"Emmie. You need to take it easy."

"Please," I beg.

"Here or the bedroom?" I giggle at his response.

"I don't care." Because I don't, I just know I want him right now. He undoes my belt without breaking our kiss. The way he makes love to me seems to mend my broken heart for a while. Makes me feel like I'm special. I'm his. He reaches for the bottom of my dress, skimming my skin as lifts it over my head. He goes to undo my bra but I stop him. He breaks away looking at me, confused.

"I want to see you, baby, don't be ashamed of your body. You're beautiful. Trust me?" Of course I trust him. What a stupid question. He reaches behind my back and unclips my bra. Using both hands to remove the straps down my arms. I cover myself with my arms, damn I should have said bedroom and have the light off. It's too bright in here. He grabs my hands and pulls them out so I'm exposed. He steps back to gaze at me and I blush. "Beautiful and all mine."

"Yes, yours." He kneels on the floor, keeping his eyes on me and pulls down my panties, I step out of them not taking my eyes off his. He slowly starts to kiss my thighs, going higher up my tummy. He pauses at my tummy and places both hands on my tummy and kisses me between his hands. I squirm under his lips. He stands up and removes my hair from my neck and places sweet delicious kisses. I reach up and grab his face so he's forced to kiss me on my lips. He slides his hands down the backs of my thighs and lifts me up and places me on the edge of the table. Damon lifts his shirt over his head in seconds and I grab his belt pulling him closer to me, undoing it as I go. He kisses my neck while I struggle with his jeans. I frown, will I ever get used to this?

"It's okay baby, take your time. You can do it," he murmurs against my neck. Wow, his confidence in me warms my heart. I manage to undo his jeans and pull them down along with his boxers. He kicks off his shoes and sinks into me. I put my arms around his neck to steady myself. He picks me up but stays inside me. I wrap my legs around his waist, he walks out of the kitchen turning off the light as he goes. He climbs the stairs and we find ourselves in a big bedroom with a king size bed. I glance at the room, it's green. I hate green. Damon carries me to the bed and gently lowers us both down. I guess he didn't like sex with me in the kitchen. I shrug off the thought and we start to really move. All my tension from the day, all my problems are gone. It's just him and me together.

He's it when I think of husband material, this is him. He makes me feel safe, protected he pushes me to be better, he's not afraid to tell me when I'm wrong. I still don't know if he will actually want to marry me later on down the line. But I'm all in. We both find our release and I lose train of thought. I'm in a world of my own.

When I come back to the here and now he's on his back and he's pulled me close to him. "I don't think I will get enough of you baby." He kisses my hair.

"Hmm." I curl up into him and close my eyes.

Chapter 15

My body feels heavy as I'm being drawn back to the faint voices I'm hearing. I was so comfy and peaceful in my sleep but as the voices get louder, I jolt awake. Damon's arm is around my chest but he doesn't let me up. I guess he must have woke when I did. "You okay baby?"

"Yeah I guess, who's that?" Damon sits up and frowns. He has his boxers on already, when did that happen? I'm also under the covers. Hmm, did he get up and move me last night? I sit up and hold the sheets around my chest. Damon strolls over to some chest of draws and pulls out a t-shirt. He throws it at me and grins. Playful Damon's back.

"Put my T-Shirt on," he orders. I do as I'm told, welcoming the cover over my naked body. I climb out of bed and stand behind Damon, wondering who will come through the door. Within the second the door opens, Sully and Danny stand in the doorway. Sully looks really angry, I don't think I've seen Sully so angry. He's usually so calm, sweet and thoughtful.

"You can't come barging in like this, I'm sorry Boss." Sully glares at Danny.

"I need to speak to my Sister." Sully goes to grab Danny's arm but Danny shrugs him off. What does he need to speak to me so urgently about? I glare at him. How did he even know where Damon lives? I don't even know.

"If the idiot needs to barge in here and see me in my boxers then he can go ahead." Damon seems strangely calm this morning.

"Yes, Boss." Sully glances at me and blushes and quickly retreats out of the bedroom. What was that about?

"What the hell are you doing here Bro?" I'm mad, god damn it.

"I've come to speak to you." He crosses his arms in annoyance, I think.

"No shit Sherlock." I narrow my eyes at him.

"Look, I love you Sis but you have Mom in tears." Have I? What did I do this time? I'm such a bad person. I frown.

"What?"

"What you said to her has hurt her." Of course it has. Because I always say the wrong things. But I miss my Brother since Momma came back. It was always him and me against the world. But now it feels like he's putting her first. Why wouldn't he? She's beautiful, kind, caring and our Momma.

"I'm sorry Danny. I never meant to hurt her." Tears are forming in my eyes. Bambino, this is no time to make me emotional. Pregnancy isn't treating me well. But I do love you, Bambino.

"You need to give this guy a chance. For Mom's sake. You need to stop being so selfish." Ouch, selfish? That hurts. They think I'm being selfish. Maybe I am. I just don't know anymore. All this is too much for me. I wish Dad was back, he would always put me on the right path. I didn't have to think much, he would just demand and I'd obey without hesitation. Damon puts his arm around my waist, I can feel his muscles are tense. Oh shit, here comes angry Damon.

"You need to watch what you say before I damage your pretty little face. Emmie, you don't have to do anything you don't want to." Damon's using his don't mess with me voice.

"Okay," I say in defeat.

"Okay, what?" Danny is confused.

"I'll move into his house." What's another house anyway? I don't feel safe in the house we already have. What's another one? I don't want Momma to hate me or leave me again.

"You aren't a very good Brother, are you?" Damon growls. I hug Damon tight with both arms, feeling the security of his warm body. I stare at Danny, I'm broken and he's breaking me even more.

"Excuse me?" Danny is horrified.

"After what he did to her yesterday the least she deserves is some time to think about this. Now you've just made your insecure, self-hating sister agree without thinking about her. I know you love your Mom, but do you not care about your sister?" Damon thinks I'm insecure? Oh no, this is worse than I thought. If he thinks I'm insecure he won't want me. I pull back but Damon doesn't let me go. Oh.

"Of course I care. I feel so awful about not knowing what my Dad did to her. My sister doesn't feel like that, I'd know." Oh dear Brother, what I'm able to hide from you. I've done it for years, I've had to. But how does Damon know?

"You're manipulating her feelings like her Dad did." Wow, that's a bit strong of a word. I'd made up my mind anyway.

"I did? Emmie, I'm sorry. Is this how you feel?" I can't tell him the truth. He'd be crushed, and Momma needs this.

I take a deep breath and close my eyes to think. Damon's right-hand moves the hair from my face, stroking my cheek as he goes. Hmm, what his touch does to me. "You're right, I need to stop being so selfish. I love Momma I need her to come first." I open my eyes to gauge his reaction.

"That doesn't mean your feelings don't matter. I'm sorry." He looks so hurt, why? My feelings really don't matter. I sigh.

"I will move in, I've made up my mind," I say, reassuring him.

"Emmie you really don't need to do this," Damon says softly. Oh, sweet fiancé of mine that won't want me soon, yes I really do.

"Yes, I do." I bury my face into Damon's chest so neither one of them see my face.

"I want you to leave now!" Damon raises his voice.

"I'm going, I will tell Mom the good news." He seems very excited, hmm maybe just to know my loved ones are happy I will be okay. I have time to process this though.

"Emmie." Damon pulls me away from his chest and looks at me with pain in his eyes.

"No Damon, I've made up my mind." He just doesn't understand. No one understands me.

"Fine, get dressed. I'll take you to school." Damon grabs his clothes and retreats out the door. Last night was... great and now I get don't talk to me, Damon. My clothes are still in the kitchen. I'd better go retrieve them. I walk out of the bedroom down the stairs into the kitchen. Damon's house is spacious but very plain. It seems to be just a shell. No personal items like pictures or anything. I wonder why that is? Does he have family?

As I walk into the kitchen, Sully is sat on a chair at the table reading a newspaper. A newspaper, really? He looks up at me and blushes, is it more noticeable because of his hair colour or is this just who he is? I stand awkwardly in the doorway. Aww man, my underwear is all over the kitchen. I hesitantly gather up my clothes, Sully's eyes just stay on me, making my cheeks redden too. Why is he here anyway? I run back to Damon's bedroom and quickly change. I hate to wear dirty panties so I rummage through Damon's drawers to find some boxers. He won't mind, surely. I find the bathroom and look in the mirror. My makeup has smudged, damn it. I grab Damon's toothbrush and start to brush my teeth.

The door clicks open and our eyes lock in the mirror. Damon walks over to me and hugs me from behind, still keeping his eyes on mine. He grabs a flannel from a shelf and puts his arm around me to make it wet. What's he doing? He lifts the flannel to my face and starts to rub off my makeup. I pull away. "What are you doing?"

"I want to see what's underneath. You don't need makeup baby." I do, it's my shield from life. It makes me prettier. I frown. "Emmie, you are beautiful, why can't you see that?" He holds the back of my head with his hand and proceeds to wash off my makeup. I don't stop him, if this is what he wants then I will give it to him. "There, that's better." He leans down and briefly kisses me on the lips. "Come on, are you ready?" I nod and he grabs my hand and leads me downstairs. Instead of leaving the house, he takes me back into the kitchen again. Why? "You don't think I'm going to let my fiancée leave without breakfast, do you?" Oh god, more food. Is this what it will be like when we're married? I will turn into a fat whale. I groan at the thought.

"I'm not hungry."

"Hungry or not, I can't trust you to feed yourself. So at least this way I know you've at least eaten today." I love him for trying to take care of me, I do, but the food thing may be the end of us. Danny is the same, we argue about this too. "Jam on toast?" I love jam on toast. I smile and nod. He grins too. This time he puts in 4 bits of bread in the toaster. I hope he doesn't expect me to eat 4 slices. "Sit." Always so demanding. I take a seat next to Sully.

"Is this what you do all day? Read?" I giggle.

I love Sully, he has a good sense of humour. He laughs too, "Something like that."

"What good use of your money Damon, pay for your staff to read." I glance at Damon to see his reaction, he looks amused. Thank god. Damon brings over two plates and he places one in front of me and one for himself.

"What?" Damon raises his eyebrow.

"Nothing."

"You said you don't like eating on your own." He shrugs. He did this for me? Oh wow, I melt inside and I start to eat my food. Damon and Sully start talking about work. Something to do with a shipment coming in today. I zone out and stare at my fiancé eating his food. It's so sexy. Damon looks at me and raises his eyebrow, I've been busted for staring. Oops. He grins. I finish my food and go to clear my plate.

"Leave that, my housekeeper will do that." Of course he has a housekeeper. What money can't buy.

"I will see you at the safe house Sully." Sully nods. Damon leads me to the front door where my boots have been placed. Oh wow, Sully brought my boots back. I put them on and we walk hand in hand to the car.

When we are both in the car I ask, "Does Sully live with you?"

"No he doesn't, but he has a key. He comes and goes."

"Why is he here today?" Blushing at the memory of my clothes all on the floor.

"His job at the moment is to keep you safe. So that's why he was there."

"But I was with you. I'm safest with you," I confess, relaxed, comfortable in my own skin. Hmm, the way he made me feel beautiful whilst making love to me.

"That's good to hear." My favourite song comes through on the radio. I turn it up and start to softly sing.

"Say, go through the darkest of days. Heaven's a heartbreak away. Never let you go, never let me down."

He grins at me. "Let me love you? Very apt song baby."

We sing the chorus together. *"Don't you give up, Nah-nah-nah. I won't give up, Nah-nah-nah. Let me love you. Let me love you. Don't you give up, Nah-nah-nah. I won't give up, Nah-nah-nah. Let me love you. Let me love you. Oh baby, baby."*

"I love to hear you sing." He is his carefree self.

"Back at you," I grin. His voice is so soft, he sings really well. I love to hear him sing. It's very soothing. Damon pulls up outside of the school.

"Be good and stay out of trouble today, okay?" he says whilst grabbing my hand and skimming my knuckles with his lips. I close my eyes, relishing his touch.

"I won't promise something I can't keep," I grin.

"What am I going to do with you?" I bite my lip.

"I can think of something."

He laughs, "Oh my brave fiancée, you do like to keep me on my toes." Fiancée sounds good, although I will prefer the sound of his wife.

"Are you going now?" I hate that he leaves me, I can feel the tension rising in my body again.

"I am going. I have work to do. I mean it, stay out of trouble. Can I take you out to dinner tonight?" He wants to see me again tonight? That's a good sign, right?

"Err sure."

"Good, I'll pick you up at yours later. Say 7 pm?" I have to go back to that house again. I smile and nod. I go to leave the car but he doesn't let go of my hand, instead, he pulls me back and embraces me into a kiss. He catches me off guard sometimes. How can a gang leader be so sweet and caring? And be all mine.

"Goodbye Mi Chica Bella." I smile on the inside and out and leave the car. I turn and wave to him as he pulls away. I walk to my first class with Mr D again. I swear I have him a lot. I walk into the classroom and see Jessie. She waves and calls me over.

"Hey," I say.

"Hey, great party huh?" She looks as though she's suffering today though.

"Yeah, great party," I agree.

"You know we are the talk of the party." She grins.

"When aren't we?" I giggle.

Mr D clears his throat, "Settle down class, I wanted to inform you all that we have a camping trip this weekend. And it's compulsory." Oh shit, not camping, I groan. Loudly.

"I hate camping. I don't do camping," I sigh, putting my head in my hands.

"You do now, it will be fun." She's excited about this. Why?

"I suppose it means I can get away from them." Alone time to think about moving.

"Away from who?" Jessie asks, concerned.

"Nothing, it doesn't matter." I shrug her off.

"Miss Salvatore, why are you always disrupting my class?" Mr D roars, making me jump. What's his problem? What does he have against me?

"Maybe because you are so boring," I shrug.

"Total badass, as usual," Jessie whispers.

"Salvatore, leave now. I'm sure the principal would like to deal with you," he sighs.

"Is that because you can't?" I tease.

"Go now. Your attitude is appalling. I can't stand the sight of you." Bit rude.

I stand and head for the door. "You must be the only guy that can't." I turn to see all faces, including Mr D's to see they are all stunned. Ha Emmie 1 - Mr D 0. I giggle and make my way to the principal's office.

I knock on the door and I hear Mr Beale call me in. I open the door and walk in, closing the door behind me. Two sets of eyes are on me, Mr Beales and Brody's. He gives me that sexy smile that melts me inside. What is he doing in here? "Miss Salvatore, what trouble have you got into this time?"

I shrug, "Mr Dudley didn't like my sense of humour. Hey, Brody."

"You are a total badass as usual." He winks at me.

"Of course."

"Enough, Miss Salvatore when will you learn to behave?" He seems angry.

I cross my arms, "We don't have long left of school, so you're not going to teach me that quick."

"Detention after school for the both of you."

I love to mess with Mr B, "Sure, I'd love to join you after school sir." I wink at him. "Anyway, what did you do?" I turn to face Brody.

"They caught me smoking on school grounds." He rolls his eyes.

"This isn't a social break. You need to start thinking about your actions," Mr B roars.

God, what is it with people trying to control me? "Whatever." I straighten out my dress. A bit overdressed for school. Oh well.

"You, young lady," he points his finger at me, raising his voice.

"Yeah, what are you going to do about it?"

"I'm going to call your parents." He sounds exasperated.

Call my parents? Really? "My Dad's dead, thank god. So you can't hurt me," I scream defensively.

"Emmie, I didn't mean hurt you." He's shocked.

Brody grabs my shoulders so I'm looking at him. "Emmie, he didn't mean he was going to get anyone to hurt you. You're safe." Life is building up on me. I feel anything but safe right now. Rex and my Dad still loom over my life.

"Whatever," I say, not believing them.

"I'm going to inform your Mother of your behaviour. We can discuss the way forward." Momma is going to flip her lid.

"Great, can I go now?" I need fresh air. I need the sun on my face.

"Yes, but I will see you after school."

"You'll be lucky." I turn on my heels and storm out of the room. I hear Brody call out my name, but I need to get out of here. Everyone is a threat to me. They all push me down a little bit at a time. Once I reach the comfort of the outdoors, I stand and soak in the sun. 'No one likes you, Emmie, only I.' I hear Dad's voice in my head. It's clear as day. 'They are all out to get you. I will protect you.' I miss my Dad.

"Emmie, are you okay?" I jump out my skin. Damn it, Brody.

I turn and face him. "Yes, I'm fine," I say, placing my hands on my head. Too much is happening in my head.

"You don't have to shut me out you know." It's the way it's always been, I can't change now.

"I know, I just want to go home." Yeah home, I don't have a home.

"But it's not even half way through the day." He seems to look out of his depth like he doesn't know how to handle me.

"I know, I just need to go." I start to shift my weight uncomfortably.

"Well, I'm always here if you need anything. Shall I walk you home?" Walk me home? Where is that? I just feel lost right now.

"No it's okay, I'm sure Sully will be around somewhere." I search around outside scanning the cars but I can't see him.

"What do you mean?"

"Damon gets Sully to watch me as he thinks I walk into trouble." I shrug.

"That is so true," he smirks. I pull my phone out of my pocket. Damon has already entered Sully's number on my phone. I press call.

"Emmie?" He sounds confused.

"Sully?"

"You okay?"

"No, can you come get me?" I feel better with Sully. He can keep me safe.

"Sure, I'll be there in a minute." He hangs up and I put my phone back in my bag.

"He's on his way," I inform Brody.

"Good, so how's your Mom?" My Momma, she's happy in love.

"Happy in love. I just need to keep it that way." I shrug.

"That's good and what do you mean?"

I shrug. I can't do this now. "Emmie," he says sternly.

"The guy creeps me out, that's all. He wants us to move in with him." I cross my arms, protecting myself.

"Do you want me to go over there and give him what's what?" he smirks, flexing his arm to show how strong he is.

"Thanks, Brody, but no." I giggle.

"I can be pretty scary." I'm sure he can. I see Sully pull up and I start to walk over to the car. Brody follows me to the car. Sully has gotten out the car to open my door.

"You ready Emmie?" he says with concern on his face.

"Yeah, Bye Brody." He hugs me tight, and then releases me so I can get in the car.

"Bye Emmie, hope you are okay," he calls as I climb in the car. I wave as Sully closes the door.

Sully slides into his seat and looks at me. "Where would you like to go?"

"I don't want to see my Momma yet, so Damon's?"

"He's at work at the moment, but I'm sure he won't mind you going there."

I shrug, "That's okay, I need to think anyway."

He looks into my eyes, for what? It looks like he's searching for something. But he chooses not to say anything and starts the car. "Emmie, put your seatbelt on. Damon will kill me if you died in a car accident." He smirks at me. I roll my eyes but I do as I'm told.

I stare out the window, watching buildings go by, watching life go by. Before I know it, we are at Damon's. Where did that time go? I clamber out the car and follow Sully to the house. I take off my boots at the door. "Thanks, Big Guy."

"No problem, I'll let Damon know you're here." I nod and go to find my own time. I haven't explored his house yet. It's quite an open plan. I follow the corridor and find his living room. It has a huge white corner sofa against the wall under the window. There is a large flat screen TV on the wall in front of the sofa. I grab the blanket that is folded on the sofa and curl up on the sofa. Hmm, it smells like Damon. I shut my eyes, I'm always so tired these days.

I wake to his hand stroking my hair. My head in on his lap, how did that happen? How long have I been here? I groan, relishing his touch. "Hey, beautiful."

"Hmm." I'm too comfy to wake up yet. I hear him smile. I feel protected by this man, just the little things he does. "Hey. What time is it?"

"Noon." I open my eyes to see him looking at me like I'm a cherished item. His bright blue eyes.

"What are you doing here?" He should be at work.

"I could ask you the same. After all, you are in my house. Sully phoned to say you were here. I wanted to check you were okay." That's cute. Maybe he does truly love me.

"That's nice of you. But I'm fine now." I'm only fine because I'm here with him. The security of him, his house, his scent.

"What happened?" He frowns at me. I turn into his chest so he can't see my face. Putting my hand under his shirt. "Emmie, don't shut me out. I'm soon to be your husband."

"Everything just got on top of me. The thought of going back there." I cringe.

"Back to your Mom's?" I nod into his chest. "Why didn't you say?"

"I didn't want to make a big deal out of it." I don't want you to find out I'm a totally insecure, needy, crazy person.

"If something upsets you, I want to know about it okay? When you're sad, I'm sad. Your brother came round, said you're in trouble at school. What did my smart mouth girl do this time?"

"The teacher didn't like my sense of humour," I giggle and Damon raises his eyebrow the way that makes my insides melt. Oh, I love playful

Damon.

"I love your sense of humour. What did you say?" He looks into my eyes, searching for something.

"He said I was a troublemaker and said I should leave as he couldn't stand the sight of me. So I said that he must be the only one that couldn't."

"Oh, Emmie. You are probably right."

"So I got sent to the principal. Brody was there, and Mr Beale said he would call my parents because he didn't know what to do with me. I got angry and said my Dad was dead so he couldn't hurt me and he would have to try something else." I feel like everyone is out to get me. Or things remind me of Dad. It just feels like a vicious circle.

Damon takes a deep breath and closes his eyes for a moment. Is he annoyed with me? Because I'm so insecure? "Oh, baby. No one's going to hurt you. You're safe," he says in a soft reassuring voice. He's going to get sick of me soon. I know it.

"Only safe when I'm with you," I shrug.

I can feel him tense beneath me. "Is this how you really feel?"

Shit, this feels like make or break time. Do I tell him the truth or lie? But then again, he can tell when I lie. I still don't know how. But he knows me better than anyone in such a small space of time. "Kind of. I feel safe when I'm here with you and I feel safe with Sully as he took a bullet for me. That's why I rang him. After everything that's happened, I see danger everywhere. I don't know if it's my pregnancy hormones..." All this could be hormones, isn't it a mother's instinct to protect their baby? As I'm always in danger, this could be my body reacting to that? I'm just so confused.

He strokes an escaped lock of hair and tucks it behind my ear. I close my eyes, enjoying the touch of his skilled hands. "Well, I'm glad my staff make you feel safer. I thought you'd kill me for having you watched."

"I considered it, but knowing Sully or you are nearby, it makes me feel better. What did my Brother want anyway?"

"If he wasn't your brother, he would be out of our lives by now. Your family want you to go to the house as soon as you wake." He seems angry and distracted, what did he actually say?

"Well, let's get this over and done with." I cringe at the thought. Life would be so simple here with Damon. I wish I could live with him. I'm 18 now so technically Momma doesn't have legal responsibility for me. But

160

Damon hasn't offered and I don't want him to feel obliged and Momma really wants us to be a family.

I sit up and look at Damon. He pulls me in for a kiss, he pulls me on top of him. I feel the pull towards him that's always been there. I pull away. "What?"

"Is Sully here?" He always seems to be here or near me. Which of course I feel safer but in this moment, I don't want him here.

"No baby, he is on a job." Oh good. What sort of job? I push it to the back of my mind and kiss him again. I want to try something, I'm not sure how it will go, or how I'll feel but I don't want this memory lingering. I still get nightmares.

I pull away and stand between Damon's legs and start to lift my dress over my head. My eyes meet his when my dress is discarded on the floor. His eyes are wary. "Are you sure you want to do this baby? There is no pressure." He puts his hands on my hips and looks up at me. How does he know me so well? He is so understanding, he knows how hard this was for me to do this for Rex. But he is my fiancé and things seem so natural with him.

"I want to try Damon, no, need to try," I say but I don't sound very confident.

"Okay baby. You're wearing my boxers? Nice." He winks at me.

I reach for my bra behind my back and let the bra fall to the floor. I reach for Damon's shirt and he lifts his arms up but keeping his eyes on me. I lift it over his head, he pulls me closer and starts to kiss my tummy.

I giggle, "Boss, if you don't keep still, I can't undress you," I say playfully, yes this is working to plan. I can do this. I feel Damon smile on my tummy. He leans back so I can have better access to his jeans. I bend forward to undo his buttons. I manage them quite easily and I smile to myself. I lift my head up and kiss him on the lips whilst my hands find his jeans and boxers and I pull them down. Damon lifting to help me. They fall to his ankles.

"Now Miss Salvatore how are you going to please me?" he teases. I bite my lip, wow, please him? Yes, this is what I want to do. This is so hot. I am so turned on and it looks like he is too.

"If Sir wants pleasure he should be quiet." I giggle.

"Oh Emmie, you are so beautiful. You are killing me right now." I pull his boxers off me and climb onto his lap, my legs either side of his. He puts his hands on my hips.

"Are you sure you want this?" he says breathlessly.

"Yes," I whisper. He lifts me up and gently eases me onto him. I tilt my head back and groan. He kisses my neck, I start to move up and down. I will never get enough of this guy. I feel beautiful in this moment. It's a new and different feeling, he sure knows how to make love. He makes me feel top of this world.

"I love you, don't ever doubt that," he whispers in my ear and tugs my ear with his teeth. In this moment, I don't doubt his love for me but is that because he has me wrapped up in a spell? Right now, I don't care. It's me and him and I will fight for this man. I close my eyes, knowing I'm close to my release. He grabs my face and kisses my lips, his tongue torturing mine. We both find our release together. I collapse against his shoulder and hug him tight. He lies down on the sofa, pulling me with him. I'm laid on his chest again. I close my eyes and seem to drift asleep.

I wake to Damon kissing my forehead, my nose, my cheek. I'm on his shoulder, his bright blue eyes staring down at me. "Hey," I say nervously. Why am I nervous again? I think it's because he leaves me so often. I just want to spend all the time I can with this guy, get to know him, grow old with him.

"Hey, Mi Chica Bella. You made me a happy Boss." He grins. Hmm, our role play, that was fun. "How do you feel?"

"I'm glad I made the Boss happy. I feel good, I'm hoping I've buried something." I hope Damon has healed this pain for me. I certainly feel better anyway.

"I want to heal your pain and I won't give up trying. Come on, get up. Your Mom will skin me alive if I don't return you," he laughs but slides off the sofa and gathers his clothes. I frown, I love being in our own little bubble.

"You have no complaints from me." I sit up and bring my knees to my chest, protecting myself. He puts his clothes on quickly and strides over to me and kisses my forehead.

"I'm glad to hear it. Get dressed, I'll make you a sandwich before we leave." I watch him as he walks out the room. I put my head on my knees trying to gather my thoughts. My heart starts to beat double the speed as I think of going back there. I love my Momma, I do, but I'm terrified of this change. I don't know her, I've had 10 years without her. But I feel like I should make her happy, obey even? Is this my Dad's doing? He's still controlling me even now. I feel sick, how did I end up with this life?

I feel Damon's hand on my shoulder, I look up at him. "Baby, it will be okay. I'll keep you safe." His words reassure me. I half smile in return. He kisses my forehead. Every kiss seems to strangely mend my broken heart. I stand and dress myself and take a seat back on the sofa. He hands me a plate with a sandwich on. I take a bite. Oh my god, my eyes light up.

"Chocolate spread sandwich? My all time favourite," I say excitedly. "Cadbury, my favourite."

"I will keep that in mind Miss Salvatore," he grins. He watches me while we both eat our sandwiches. It doesn't take long for me to finish my sandwich. That was delicious. "I love to see you eat, with no arguments."

"Well, when you make me my favourite, how can I resist?" I smile. He stands up and holds out his hand. I put my hand in his and follow him to the front door. I pull on my boots, Damon holds the door open for me. I walk to the car whilst he locks the door. I open the car door slide in and buckle in. I watch out the window as Damon pulls out the driveway into the traffic. Tension building through my body, even with Damon I still seem to be anxious. What do they want?

"Emmie, stop it." I jump as he pulls me back into the car, away from my troubled thoughts.

"What?"

"Don't overthink things, you'll be fine. You'll keel over with stress or a heart attack. Relax." He grabs my hand and I stop breathing again. I relax at his touch, knowing he's here with me and not some blonde bimbo makes me happy. We arrive at Momma's house. I take a deep breath and walk to the house with Damon. He grabs my hand before we walk in. "You'll be fine." I nod and open the door.

"Oh good, you're back. You are in so much trouble." Momma comes from nowhere. Was she hovering? Waiting for me? Desmond appears too. What is this, gang up on Emmie day? I turn to close the door. Placing my forehead on it for a second, gathering my thoughts. I turn back around.

"The school phoned. You've been running wild. It's not good enough." Momma crosses her arms. She's angry, will she hurt me?

Chapter 16

Momma is glaring at me, I crumble under her stare. "I know you, you're a good person. You're out of control." Out of control? I've been out of control my whole life, why am I more so now? No one noticed before, so why now?

"Your behaviour is unacceptable," Desmond says.

"Things need to change. What do you have to say for yourself?" Momma asks.

"Oh, you're going to let me talk now are you?" I shout back. Mood swings again. Whoever says pregnancy is a great experience must be lying. I don't think I would willingly do this again.

"Enough of this. What the hell is going on with you?" You wind me up too tight, give me a freer rein and maybe I won't recoil so badly.

"Don't speak to your Mother like that," Desmond raises his voice at me. Who the hell does he think he is? I'm not his daughter, he has no right. I can't do this. I turn around to leave but I am met by Damon's chest.

"You aren't going anywhere, Emmie," Momma says sternly.

"Damon, get out the way. I can't do this." I rest my head on his chest.

"I'm here, you're safe. You need to talk this through with them." He strokes my hair and rests his chin on my head.

I take a deep breath. "Okay," I say. I feel like I can do anything with him here. I turn around and Momma's face seems to have softened. "I'm sorry Momma."

"What is going on in your head? I'm here for you," she says reassuringly.

"We want to understand," Desmond shrugs. What is he a parrot? He seems to be repeating Momma's words, just changing it slightly.

"I just freaked out about moving. But I'm okay now."

"If you are not comfortable, we won't move."

"I'm fine, you deserve this. I was just being silly." I'm not comfortable with it, but I never will be.

"Are you sure?" Momma says. I nod. "Well, in that case, we are moving tomorrow." What? Moving so soon. Why?

"What...?" I whisper. Damon wraps his arm around me and pulls me close.

"Why wait? I want us to move forward as soon as possible." She's happy, really happy.

"I'm so happy. I can't wait," Desmond says, he comes over to hug me, Damon has to release me. I don't move, just hoping he will let me go. I'm repulsed by his touch like everyone else's.

"Can I go now?" I demand. I need to think.

"Umm sure." Momma frowns. I pull out of Desmond's hold and run upstairs to my room. I shut my door, not that this will do much good. I curl up on my bed, tears falling down my face. I hear the door creak open. I don't look up to see who it is, but I soon know who it is when I smell him all around me.

"Hey," Damon says softly. He hugs me from behind.

"Hey," I sniff.

"You know I admire how brave you are for your family. But it kills me to know how much you're hurting," he says softly.

"I need to do this." I turn to face him.

"I know, I don't understand. But I will support you."

"That's all I ask."

"I love you, Emmie Salvatore."

"I love you too Damon."

"Now, is my badass girl turning up to her after school detention?"

"I suppose I must but I want a quick shower and change first."

"Okay baby. I will be here waiting for you." I kiss him on the lips and walk to the bathroom.

I deposit my clothes on the floor and climb into the shower. I wash my hair and body quickly, a lot has happened in the last couple months or so. I feel lucky to have Damon in my life but I can't help but feel ill-fated. But if it means I have to go through these hard times to have Damon, then I will persevere. I climb out the shower and grab a towel and place it around me. The towel smells of washing powder. Clean and fresh.

I walk back into the bedroom and walk straight over to Damon who is sat on my bed, focused on his phone. He looks up with a raised eyebrow, I ignore him and close the distance between us and curl up on his lap. He doesn't say anything, he just wraps his arms around me. Everything is okay when I'm with Damon. I feel the pressure returning when I know he's going to leave me. He places soft kisses on my hair. I don't know how long we stay like this in our own world but eventually, he sighs. Guess I'm boring him.

"Baby, I'd better get you to school." I nod and slide off his lap. I find a pair of jeans and a shirt, along with underwear and walk to the bathroom to change. I should be comfortable about changing in front of Damon but he shouldn't have to look at my body more than he needs to. I dress quickly and brush through my knotty hair. My hair is just unmanageable. With one last glance in the mirror, I frown and turn for the door.

Damon is up and waiting for me when I get back into my bedroom. This will soon not be my bedroom after tomorrow. I'm not sure whether to be sad, happy or relieved. I guess it's just a small piece I have left of my Dad. I know it's silly to see it that way.

"Are you ready my badass?" Yes, I'm yours, I've only ever been yours. I belong to you in every way I know how. This is new for me, it's scary but this seems to be the most right thing I've ever done. Every single atom of my being seems to draw to him like a magnet. Like gravity, it's hard to explain because I don't understand it myself. I take his offered hand and follow him outside.

We arrive at the school, I go to kiss Damon goodbye but he's already out the car, walking to my door. That's weird, but I get out and he puts his arm around my shoulder and we walk into the school. I see Brody and Sky play fighting ahead of us in the corridor. Damon turns towards me, blocking my view to the guys.

"I'll see you later for our date." Hmm, date.

"A date now is it? I thought it was just dinner," I grin playfully.

"A date sounds better, I'll see you at 7 pm." He looks over his shoulder, Brody and Sky are casually watching us. Damon smirks and kisses me hard. It's a long time until he breaks away. If it wasn't for the fact that I'm enjoying this, I would accuse him of winding up the guys. But honestly, I don't care right now. He kisses me on the forehead and I watch him leave.

Within seconds, Brody and Sky are either side of me. They stare at me like I'm some sort of alien, it makes me feel awkward. Finally, Brody breaks the silence. "Hey Emmie, you came back." State the obvious.

"No, I'm at home." I roll my eyes and laugh. "Duh." They both grin at me but they don't laugh with me.

"Full of yourself," Brody says.

"Hey, Cara De Angel." I guess he found a new nickname for me.

"Is that my new nickname?"

Sky has the biggest smile on his face like he is proud of himself. "Totally." He winks at me.

"And how long did it take you to come up with that one?" I mock him playfully.

"A while actually." He looks irritated. I'm good at doing that, I breathe out heavily. "It means-"

Before he has time to continue, I interrupt him, "I know what it means, it means angel face. Someone who has an angel face but is far from an angel. To look at an angel face makes you happy." The definition doesn't describe me well but I guess I should be honoured that he gave me such a thoughtful nickname. Although it sort of frustrates me that it's not true.

"So what do you think?" He looks hopeful, his eyes are sparkling, his stunning blue eyes standing out from his face. The blue eyes and blond hair is an attractive sight. Any girl would be lucky to have such a catch like Sky. I know he wishes it was me, but I can't give him me. I just wish him to be happy.

"I'm not sure Sky, I mean it's a lovely name. I'm just not sure it fits me." I look at the ground rather than assess his disappointed face.

"Well too bad, it's totally stuck now." He nudges me and grins at me. It's the little things that people do like this that makes me grin like a Cheshire cat.

"So are we going to detention?" Brody seems slightly annoyed. This is exhausting, I always end up making someone unhappy wherever I go. I nod and take Brody's arm and we walk towards the classroom.

He looks down at me, "I'm glad you came back. How are you?"

"I'm okay, just issues at home. But I'll be fine."

"Well, you had better be. You are the bravest person I know." Cheesy much? He's not good at these lines. Although maybe normal girls dig this stuff. I'm just not a normal girl.

I push him with what little strength I have, he barely moves, "Tough enough to take you on."

He laughs as we take a seat. Mr Beale, the Principal clears his throat, "Settle down guys. You all know why you're here. I want complete silence from all of you. All of you must write lines of why you are here."

We all stay silent, we know better than to speak in front of the principal. I take out a pen and chew the end of the pen, thinking of what to write. I peer up and look through my eyelashes at Brody. He is engrossed in his lines, the way he frowns when he is concentrating. His lips are apart and his chest is slowly breathing in and out. I try to match mine with his but my breathing is rapid as usual. The only time it's normal is when I'm with Damon and sometimes Sully. Brody looks at me and laughs quietly, my cheeks go really hot. Shit, caught staring. I look back down at my paper.

I write *I am here because I have a good sense of humour and Mr D doesn't.'* Yes, that sounds about right, I smile at myself. I write it over and over.

"I'm excited about the camping trip," Brody whispers so only I could hear him. I groan.

"Don't remind me."

"Is the badass not a camping type of girl?"

"No, I hate camping."

"It will be fun, we can all hang out. We are taking vodka."

"Yeah because that's good for pregnant women."

He puts his fingers to his chin. "Well that sucks, but you're fun without alcohol anyway, so it's all good."

"Rivers, Salvatore. What did I say? I see what all the teachers are talking about Salvatore. Another word from you and you'll get detention for a week."

"Anything for you sir," I say, twirling my hair around my finger while looking him directly in the eye.

"Sucking up to the Principal I see."

"You got to know how to play people." I shrug. A shadow catches my eye, I look up and Mr Beale is standing over me. He seems to be reading over my shoulder, so I grab my lines and hold them against my chest and glare at him.

"What do you call that?" he growls.

"Lines." I shrug.

"Miss Salvatore, you aren't here for your sense of humour. You are here because you can't follow rules and respect your teachers."

I shrug, "Huh, well if that's why I'm here maybe you should have written my lines for me."

"I will be calling your parents AGAIN! I'm going to call a meeting. Your behaviour is unacceptable." He walks back to the front of the classroom and sits at his desk and watches me. I cross my arms.

"Stop getting me in trouble." I elbow Brody in the ribs.

"Girl this is all you. You're a badass."

The bell finally rings and I stand quickly and walk out of the door. Brody runs to catch up with me. He doesn't say anything just walks at my side. I head back to the house, Brody escorting me home. I place my arm in his again, our relationship seems natural now that I've decided to be just friends. I can treat him like a friend. Can't I? I do hope so. I say goodbye to Brody and he wears his sexy smile, white dazzling teeth that bring out his eyes. I move my eyes away from his mouth and walk into the house.

I am greeted by hostility. I groan, waiting for them both to pounce. Momma's eyes are looking tired, she's starting to show her age. The wrinkles around her eyes. Momma is 51, it's not old but she's not as young as she used to look to me. Desmond stares me down with his creepy eyes, his big blue eyes. His black wavy hair covering one of his eyes. He crosses his arms.

"How was detention?" Momma asks. I know very well that she knows. It annoys me how she does this. Why can't she just be done with it?

"Boring." I shrug, it's not a lie. It really was.

"Anything happen?" Yes, a lot actually, I got caught staring at Brody. I wrote lines, I got in trouble with the Principal. But nothing new, right? Momma glances at Desmond. What's he going to do? That's right, nothing. I roll my eyes.

"Not really, why?" She hasn't been here for over 10 years of my life, and she chooses to do this now? The only one that could truly control me was Dad. I don't think a little bit of attitude towards a teacher is too much of a big deal. School's nearly over.

She balls her hands up into fists in frustration. "Why must you lie to me? The principal phoned to say your attitude stinks." Well, of course, I know that she annoys me with this clueless act, so I annoy her with the lying. I'm pretty sure if Mr B didn't ring her she would have believed me. My lying became a habit, like I believed it myself.

I scream, "Why ask me if you already knew?" Why am I shouting? I feel out of control.

"I wanted to give you the chance to come clean. You've changed so much, you never used to lie to me." Oh Momma, I always lied to you. You just didn't see it. And you still don't, I'm glad she doesn't know what I'm thinking. It makes me feel safe and protected.

"Maybe growing up thinking that your Momma hated you, your Dad abusing you, feeling alone, will do that to you. You were never there, I love you but you can't expect to have things go back to normal. Things will never be the same." This is not what I need or want. She's suffocating me, if I could run away I would. I want to be alone, all this pressure of people around me makes me want to crawl into a hole for the rest of my life.

Momma's face changes from anger, to sad, to hurt in seconds. She looks at Desmond and he places his arm around her waist. She half smiles at the gesture. "I know sweetheart, but this behaviour is not acceptable. I can't stand by and let you do this." She must, this is my life, if I make mistakes on the way then that's my problem.

I take a deep breath. "Your Mom has been nothing but supportive and caring and you treat her with such disrespect." Desmond's words slice through me. I hate him, I don't hate easily, I'm usually quite an non-judgemental person.

"Who asked you anyway?" I cross my arms and glare at him.

"Don't speak to him like that," Momma snaps. He is allowed to speak to me like that. One rule for one and one rule for another.

"You enjoy your freedom while it lasts. This won't happen under my roof." Did he really just say that?

"Are you threatening me?" Both their faces drop. Desmond strokes the back of his neck.

"No one is threatening you," Momma says softly, almost a whisper.

"Certainly sounds like it," I growl and run upstairs to my room and slam the door. I cringe waiting for Dad to come and tell me off for slamming the door. But I wait and no one comes. I take a deep breath and walk into the bathroom.

I need to wash this day off me. I undress and climb into the shower. I wash with strawberry body wash. The cool water cleansing my body. Tears fall down my face, pressure building inside of me. I'm trembling, what the hell is wrong with me? I feel sick thinking that I miss Dad's control, I miss not having to think for myself. I miss him. I scramble out of the shower in a hurry to reach the toilet. I vomit over and over until there is nothing left. My body heaving, still trying to vomit. I hate being sick.

I slowly sit up and close the lid of the toilet and sit on it for a second. The room is spinning. I clutch the sink for support. Breathe in and out. My vision becoming black around the edges. I stand and grab a towel and wrap it around me. I sink to the floor, bring my knees to my chest and put my head on my knees. I start to rock slowly back and forth. I hear the bathroom door click open but I don't look up. There is only one person it would be today.

I feel an arm around me, I've missed this brotherly love. Since Momma has been back, he seems to be keeping his distance and that's okay because he shouldn't have to be here for his 18-year-old sister. I won't be that type of person, even if deep down I need him now more than ever. I come back to reality, the room has stopped spinning. I look up and open my eyes, they've been screwed shut for a while. I hadn't realised I was that tense.

"Sis, are you okay?" I look at him, he keeps his arm around me. I nod, words don't seem to be forming. He frowns.

I manage, "What are you doing in here?" it comes out as a squeak. Oh dear lord, man up Emmie. I clear my throat.

"I heard you fighting with Mom, I wanted to speak to you." He looks at me with concern on his face. But I doubt the concern is for me, it's for Momma.

"Do you mind?" Could he not have waited for me to get out of the bathroom? Although he could have been waiting a while. Was it him, the distraction that brought me back to reality, or was it time and steady breathing? Who knows.

"We grew up together Sis, nothing I haven't seen before." He lets out a chuckle. That is true, we used to bathe together when we were younger. But that's exactly it, when we were younger. I've matured since then, become more closed. Become more self-conscious.

"You're gross, can I help you with something?" I say defensively.

"Can you not try to be more reasonable?" I don't look at him, instead, I stare at the tiles on the wall in the bathroom. Reasonable? What does he want from me, my soul? Since when did he turn against me, like everyone else? Why can't people love me for who I am? I always seem to try so hard to get people to like me, it's exhausting. I am not a very likeable person, so this makes it harder. It wears me down bit by bit.

"I am being reasonable. I'm moving to his house tomorrow. Do I need to sell my soul and everything else I own?" I feel sick again, but I can't let him see me like that. I stand up and face him. I concentrate on his face, his jawline, his blue eyes like mine. He is perfect, Momma made a perfect child. Why could I not get some of those looks? I frown.

"Sis stop being clever. Is everything okay? Since Dad's gone you've gone off the rails. I'm worried about you." Off the rails, I test those words. No, I'm just free, and I'm not sure I like this freedom. Being independent is hard, why is it so hard? Should it be?

"Not worried enough obviously." I cross my arms, protecting myself. As much as I would love to carry on with this conversation, not, I walk out of the bathroom and into my bedroom. Danny follows after me, he grabs my arm and pulls me around. I still hate being touched, that hasn't changed. I pull away from his grasp and he lets his hand fall to his side. He is staring at me with his sad eyes, I become aware that my face is what he's reacting to. I am shocked and slightly panicked that he touched me.

"What does that mean?" he whispers.

I scratch my forehead and look down, "Before Momma came back it was you and me against the world and now it's you three against me."

"Sis, is this how you feel?" he reaches up to my face and strokes my cheek. I step back out of his reach. I know he is trying to comfort me, but I can't bare it.

"Just get out Danny. I get it, I'm a trouble maker that's out of control." I need to shut the small windows to my wall keeping people out. He could never get through those windows, but I want him out.

"I want to talk about this." I go to my wardrobe and take out a tight blue dress that looks half decent on me. I dress in front of Danny, shielding myself as much as I can.

He doesn't move all the while I dress, "Well I don't, you're never going to be on my side and why would you? Momma is back and it's the best thing that's happened. We've both wanted this. We can't risk losing her again. I get it. Now leave," I shout.

He crosses his arms and glares at me. "This isn't over," he growls but proceeds to walk out my room. I decide makeup would be best for tonight if I have to go out in public, people need protection from my face.

I am just about finished when I feel arms around me, I flinch but in a second I sag with relief. All the tension dissolving from his presence. I apply a bit more mascara.

"Wow, Mi Chica Bella. You look breath-taking." Our eyes meet in the mirror. How does he find the sweetest things to say? He strokes the back of my hair, I close my eyes and try and contain this electricity pulsing through me. He grabs my shoulders and twists me around so I'm facing him. My back against my dresser.

He lifts me up so that I sit on the dresser, and he pulls me into a kiss. My body relaxes even more at his skilled hands cupping my back, my waist, my hips, my legs. I let out a moan into his mouth and he smiles against my cheek. He pulls back and looks at me, he frowns. I look at the ground, hurt by his expression. He doesn't like what he sees again. Is this what our life would be like, me being a constant disappointment?

"Don't get me wrong, you look beautiful. You are the prettiest woman I've ever met. But you don't need this." He strokes my cheek, I know he is referring to the makeup. The prettiest woman he's ever met? He can't have met many people then. But I do manage a smile at his flattery.

"You okay?" he asks.

"Sure." I nod. I hug his waist so I don't need to look at him. I've missed him, and it's only been a few hours.

"I know that's a lie, you are so tense. I mean, when I came in and hugged you, your whole body just relaxed. It was weird." I continue to hug his waist. Pulling him closer, I want him to be closer to me. It's just there is no way physically possible for him to be any closer.

"I'm okay now you are here," I mutter into his shirt. His scent is making my head spin, in a good way. Not like it did earlier. He pushes my shoulders away so he can look at my face. I frown.

"What's happened?"

"Oh, you know, this screw up gets in trouble at school. My brother hates me for fighting with Momma and Desmond. Desmond threatens me but apparently, he didn't. I should be more reasonable." My mouth speaking what my brain is thinking. I should think before I say. He picks me up and carries me to my bed and he sits down with me on his lap. I bury my face into his neck. Yes, this is my favourite place in the whole world.

"Calm down. I leave you for a few hours and you're freaking out. Your brother needs a face readjustment I think and you're not a screw-up, you're a perfect, beautiful, smart woman." I giggle at the face readjustment. Why? I'd never allow my brother to be hurt. So why is that funny? "And what do you mean Desmond threatened you?"

"His words were 'enjoy your freedom while it lasts as this won't happen under my roof.'"

"Everything will be okay," he says between his gritted teeth. "Are you ready to go?" I nod in agreement, I want out of this hell hole. Why can't he kidnap me again? Oh yeah, because he got arrested last time. Damon takes my face into his hands and kisses me. What was I thinking about? I don't know because Damon overwhelms me, makes me lose track of thought. But it's a welcome distraction. I place my legs either side of his and he pulls me down on top of him so I'm lying on him. I still don't like being on top like this, it makes me feel fat and heavy. But Damon's expert hands distract me from that thought too.

"Shall we skip the meal, and stay here?" He smiles a big sexy smile. The one I can't resist.

"I'd be up for that, if…" I sigh, "if I didn't want to get out of here." He laughs and lifts me off him and gets off the bed. He grabs my hand and leads me outside. The cool air feels good in my lungs. I can breathe again.

Chapter 17

We reach the restaurant in 20 minutes. It's nice, but not too nice. Damon requests a table outside, the night sky is gorgeous this time of night. The waiter holds my chair out and gestures to take a seat. I hate this sort of attention, I start to play with my hair and squint my eyes and shift my weight. I take a deep breath. Damon looks at me, he walks over to my chair, "Allow me," he says to the waiter but not taking his eyes off me. He points to the proffered chair. He smiles that sexy playful smile and I can't help but grin back at him. I take the seat Damon has offered.

"Can I get you some drinks?" the waiter asks.

"I'll have a whisky, Emmie?" He looks at me expectantly. Eyes are on me, stop looking at me.

"Water please." I haven't drunk or eaten anything since I was sick, so I'd better take it slow. He frowns at me but doesn't say anything. The waiter nods and retreats, leaving us with the menu. I scan the menu. I keep it in front of my face, shielding it away from Damon.

"Are you feeling okay baby?" he asks, peering over his menu.

"Morning sickness, I think."

"You think?"

"Yeah well, I was stressed at the time and I had a thought that made me feel sick." I shrug. Not that he can see me because I'm still hiding. I'm looking at the menu but the writing is just black blotches. I'm too nervous to concentrate.

"Explain baby, please." His words are soft and gentle.

"I just realised that I miss the control my Dad had over my life. I miss him, I miss the way he decided my life for me. I miss feeling safe. And I got sick at the thought that, that's how I feel." Damon reaches for my menu to look at my face. He doesn't seem shocked but he's not happy.

"How can you miss that? Do you not like being free?"

"No, I don't like all these choices I have to make. Everyone thinks I'm going off the rails, Damon. But really it's just me thinking for myself. I've fucked things up, I never had to worry about hurting people or making bad choices. Because Dad always made the right ones for me."

He looks repulsed. He understands me most, even in the short time. I would never share this stuff with my family. I wouldn't share it with anyone, so why him? The one that means so much to me, why would I risk losing him by sharing this stuff?

"You are only human, people make mistakes. Don't beat yourself up. If people don't like you the way you are, the real you, then they don't deserve you." His words shock me to the core. Sends shivers down my spine. Don't deserve me?

"Oh Damon, I wish that were true. I mean, I make more mistakes than most and it's me that doesn't deserve them. Can you not see that?" I cover my mouth, stop confessing these things. Stupid, stupid.

The waiter returns to take our order, I haven't even had time to study the menu. My hands are sweaty, I can't concentrate. Damon looks at me and grabs my hand that's under the table on my lap. He squeezes it and smiles at me. Oh, he's reassuring me. I love how he does this. How does he know I'm losing my shit?

"What can I get you both?"

"I'll have the steak." Figures, that's all he seems to eat.

"And you Ma'am?" I put my other hand that Damon's not holding on my forehead in annoyance to the term Ma'am. I mean, how old do I look?

"What's your chef's vegetarian special?" Damon asks. What's he doing?

"Vegetable lasagne." He looks at Damon with his hand on his chin.

Damon puts his fingers on his nose and looks at the waiter. "She will have that." The waiter nods and goes back to the bar. Huh, he ordered for me. I guess that takes pressure off of me. It's like this handsome god was made for me. How lucky am I? What penance will I have to pay for him?

"Where were we?" He twitches his lips. "Ah yes, your ridiculous issue that you think you don't deserve them." He frowns and pauses for a while.

"You are worth more than a million people. How can I get it into your head?" Million people? I'm not worth more than half a life let alone a million. Is he crazy? "Stop it." He removes his hand from mine. "Overthinking things. You are talking yourself into thinking you aren't worth it. Aren't you?" How the hell does he know these things? He must have super powers. What am I bringing into this relationship apart from negative things? He's bringing frickin' super powers into it.

Our food arrives and we fall into easy conversation. My tension disappears completely. He makes it disappear. Again, with his super powers. He finishes his steak and mutters in appreciation. "Such a bloke thing to choose," I say, teasing him.

"What can I say? I'm a sucker for steak." He shrugs and winks at me. "Among other things." So, this is the game he is playing. I twirl my hair with my finger and smile sweetly at him.

"And what are the other things?"

He laughs, "I think they better remain a secret. Can't have you using them against me."

"Would I?" I giggle.

"Yes, you would." He looks at me in awe. Why? I look back at the food I'm still eating and blush. I take another mouthful. It's actually really good. It feels good to fill my stomach after being sick. I finish all that's on my plate. I lean back on my chair and look at Damon. He is still staring at me.

"You are my little troublemaker." Yes, I am, I'm his in every way. That's if he does want me, and if he doesn't, well even then my heart would still belong to him.

"Nothing little about me."

"I love to see you so happy and carefree. I seem to leave you happy and then when I come back you're sad, stressed. You know it makes me never want to leave you." He frowns and then sighs.

"Then don't leave me," I say. I would give anything to stay in his company, his protection forever.

He looks shocked and processes my words. "Oh trust me, I wouldn't." Wouldn't? What does that even mean? I don't understand. It sounds like he will leave but he doesn't want to? I'm confused.

Everything goes into slow motion as I watch Damon bend down on one knee. What the hell is he doing? He grabs my hand that's in my lap. "Emmie I love you, you're beautiful. Smart, funny, everything I could ever want. I can't imagine my life without you. Emmie Salvatore, will you marry me?" He seems nervous, why is he nervous? He's already asked me and I've said yes. His words make me smile. All eyes in the restaurant are on us and I can't handle the pressure.

"No, I don't think I will." I keep a straight face. His face falls.

"Why?"

"Because I changed my mind." I shrug. The silence is deafening. "You're a bit of a Moron, did you forget that you proposed already?" I say.

"No, you said it wasn't very romantic, so I thought I'd try again." Is this what this is? I feel guilty for messing with him now. He's trying to do the whole sweep me off my feet bit and I'm being mean again. "Jeez Emmie, talk about keeping a guy hanging." He really is sweating, I've never seen him so nervous before. What happened to my strong protecting fiancé?

"Of course I'll marry you. This is perfect, thank you." I giggle. He sags with relief and then grins his big sexy smile that I love.

"You're welcome, only the very best for my girl. It's perfect, like you." He leans forward and puts his hands on my legs and leans up to kiss me. Everyone cheers, I honestly forgot everyone was watching.

"Are you finished?" I nod, he leaves money on the table and grabs my hand and leads me outside. We reach the car, but instead of opening the door, he pulls me in for a kiss. My back pressed against the car. His hands curl into my hair. The smell of the evening breeze, the smell of Damon. His lips crushing mine. I can't think straight, I just know I want to stay in this moment forever. I place my hands under his shirt to touch his bare skin on his back. He groans, was that an achievement? I smile against his lips. His tongue slowly evading my mouth. He pulls away from my lips, trailing kisses down my jaw, my neck and my collarbone.

"Stay with me tonight," he says between each delicate precise kiss.

"Yes," I say breathlessly.

"Text your Mom, though. She'd have my balls," he whispers. His forehead on mine, catching his breath.

"Can you not talk about my Momma in this moment?"

"I need my balls intact. Why would I not?" He laughs. "Don't worry, you are all I think about." I like the sound of that. I'm all he thinks about. I feel like he is fixing me from the inside out, all my invisible scars. He seems to heal them, while he is with me anyway. When he leaves they seem to crack open again. He places his hand on my right hip and pushes me over so he can open my door.

We arrive at his house. I take my shoes off at the door. He does the same.

"Ma'am," he says, offering his hand with a smile. I slap him on the arm. He obviously knows it annoys me. He laughs and grabs my hand and leads me to his bedroom. Instead of stopping in his bedroom, he takes me straight into the bathroom. He removes his clothes and starts to remove mine. I stand perfectly still, watching his face as he makes short work of my clothes. He steps back and smiles. He takes my hand and pulls me into the shower.

The water is warm, Damon and the shower is a heady mix. I hug him around the waist and bury my face into him. I know tomorrow I'll have to say goodbye again. I should be enjoying the here and now, but instead, I am dreading him leaving me. He pulls away from me, cupping my face in his hands. He nudges my nose with his. I close my eyes and soak him in. I feel something soft on my face. A flannel? He wipes it over and over on my face.

"That's better, I have my Emmie back." My eyes fly open. What does he mean? Oh yeah, the makeup thing. I know I can be comfortable around Damon without makeup because he makes me feel special that way. He reassures me all the time.

He kisses me, letting his hands explore my body, my shoulders, my breasts, my hips and my legs. He lifts my legs so I am wrapped around his waist. I feel more sensitive in the shower, every touch feels like electricity pulsing through me. I didn't think his touch could mean any more to me, but I was wrong. I tilt my head back so I am resting my head on the glass wall. He kisses my neck, sending me wild. My hands ball up into fists in his hair. He gently bites my neck and I scream quietly. Wow, what is he doing to me? I'm lost, lost in him.

I come to my senses when I feel him carry me to the bedroom, and places a towel around me and lowers me onto the bed. He slides in next to me, we lay facing each other. Silent but it feels loud, space surrounds me with him. He is everywhere, I feel so safe and protected. He gives me butterflies when I stare into his eyes. His big blue eyes that sit perfectly on his face.

I dream of Damon that night, no nightmares. Just Damon and I together forever, our life together. Our perfect life together, walking in a meadow hand in hand, giggling like kids. The moment is interrupted by a phone ringing. I check my pockets and I don't have a phone. Not in my dreams, I wake up in a daze. I gather my thoughts before I answer my phone.

"Wakey wakey Sis." I groan into the phone. What is the time? I glance at the ridiculously overpriced phone that Damon got me and it says 6.30am. Argh, what's his problem?

"What do you want?" I perch the phone between my shoulder and my ear. I walk into the bathroom to retrieve my clothes and dress myself.

"Someone's not a morning person." I can sense him grinning down the phone. He is in a good mood today.

"You know I'm not, what do you want?"

"You need to get over here now. We're moving remember?" No, I didn't remember, I lose time with Damon. He makes me forget my problems.

"I'll be there soon," I snap and hang up. I walk back into the bedroom, Damon is still fast asleep. He looks so young and peaceful. I kiss him on the forehead before I leave. I don't want to leave, but I know I must. I walk downstairs and straight to the front door. I put on my shoes, and I have a weird sense someone is watching me. I turn around to see Sully watching me. Not in the way that most guys do, but just watching me. It doesn't annoy me like it would if he was gawking at me.

"Hey, Big Guy."

"Hey Emmie, are you okay?"

"Yeah, we're moving into Desmond's today and my family request my presence."

He frowns, thinking something over, but what? "Do you want me to take you?"

"Yes please." I smile.

"Where's Damon?"

"He's asleep, I didn't want to wake him." I shrug. He looked so cute sleeping, I couldn't bear to do it.

"I don't think he will be too impressed if he wakes up to you not there. I'll let him know when he wakes up. Let's go." I never thought about that, he is protective after all. He worries that I get into trouble a lot. I nod and follow Sully to the car. As usual, Sully is as ever the gentleman and gets my door.

"You know, you are different." I look at Sully to wonder what he means by that. He keeps his eyes on the road.

"What do you mean?"

"I've been Damon's right-hand man since the beginning. Out of all his girlfriends, he's never been this protective." He pauses for a while. "He gets cranky when you are in trouble, more so than normal. He is good at what he does and he has always been happy doing it. But now he is happiest when he is with you. It is amazing to see." I frown thinking about what he's just said. That can't be right, can it?

We pull up in the driveway. I take a deep breath feeling the pressure building. I look at Sully who is looking at me with concern. "If you need anything, just call me 'kay?" When Damon's not around I always need you. You keep me safe, safe from myself. My door opens and it makes me jump. Sully frowns in annoyance, I spin to see who it is. Of course, it's Danny, he looks excitable. Danny grabs my arm and pulls me out the car. He shuts the door and pulls me to the house. I look back at Sully who is glaring at Danny. I wave apologetically, he nods and reverses out of the driveway.

"Danny, let go." He releases me and smiles. He is too lively.

"You need to get packing." I nod and head for the stairs. My feet feel like steel, every step makes it impossible to move. I reach my bedroom, I decide I should change into something more comfortable. I dress in sweats. I start packing my clothes into boxes, some clothes I don't think I can wear again. I'm just not that comfortable in my own skin. I move on to my dresser, my makeup, perfumes, hair brush. My phone buzzes so I check it. A text from Damon.

I missed you when I woke up. I hope everything goes okay today. You know where I am if you need me. I love you.

I need you always. *Thank you, I love you.*

I go back to packing, before I know it two hours have passed. I am just about done packing.

Danny walks into the bedroom without knocking. "Hey Sis, are you nearly done?"

"Yeah, I'm done." I walk and perch on the end of my bed. I feel dizzy.

Danny kneels on the floor in front on me, placing his hands on my knees. "You don't look so good."

"I'm fine." I close my eyes and breathe in and out.

"Have you eaten today?" he says gently.

"No, stop fussing."

"Sis you need to eat. Skipping meals isn't good for my niece or

181

nephew." Is that all he cares about? Well, I know that's not true. He cares about Momma.

"So you care about my baby and not about your sister?"

He rolls his eyes, "That's not what I meant, of course I care about you."

I push his hands off my knees. "Get out."

"No, stop pushing me away."

I stand up and he does the same. "Pushing you away? It feels like you're pushing me with a stick off a cliff. And you're telling ME not to push you away?" I growl.

He holds his hands up in defence. "Sis...I..." He's speechless for once. His face shows pain.

"Just get out." I back away, trying to protect myself from him.

"We are ready downstairs so come down when you are ready." He grabs some of my boxes and carries them downstairs. I take one last look at my bedroom. I won't miss it, but it doesn't mean it isn't a part of me. A part of Dad. I take the last box from my room and carry it downstairs.

I hear them all squabbling over photos. "I don't want them coming with us," Momma says.

"She might want them," Danny argues.

"I might want what?" Danny looks at me and glares.

He walks over to me and grabs the box from me. "Don't you let me catch you carrying anything again, do you hear me?" I roll my eyes at him. I walk over to Momma and grab the photo frames from her. I haven't seen these before. Pictures of me and Dad. I remember him taking some of these. I look happy, he looks happy. I was happy because he was my Dad in these pictures. Of course I want them. I need something to remember my Dad apart from my memory. I clutch them to my chest.

"Of course I want these," I snap.

"Sweetheart you need to move on, your Dad keeps holding you back."

"No, you keep holding me back. Dad was part of my life and I can't change that. Some things I wouldn't change. Now please, I want to keep them."

"Okay sweetheart." The phone starts to ring. Momma goes to answer it. I start to look at the pictures again. Stroking Dad's face with my thumb.

"Sweetheart, it's for you." She looks confused, I'm confused too. If they want me, they call my mobile. I walk to grab the phone off Momma.

"Hello," I say weakly.

"Hello, Miss Salvatore?" A male's voice comes through the phone. His voice is hoarse.

"Yes, that's me."

"Miss Salvatore, I've been trying to reach you for a while. I was starting to give up hope." Who is this guy? He creeps me out. "I'm Mr Declan. I am your father's attorney." Attorney, why is he contacting me? "Miss Salvatore, are you around today for a meeting? I really need to speak to you regarding your father's assets."

"Er, okay," I whisper.

"Can you come to my office, at Sun-Lawyers in La Zenia?"

"Yeah, I know where that is."

"Say 3 pm?" I look at my phone, that's in 3 hours.

"Okay, see you then." I hang up.

I text Damon. *I have a meeting with my Dad's attorney. I don't want to go on my own. Can you spare your right-hand man?*

Momma asks me about the phone call, I shrug her off until I have more information. I feel sick, I run to the bathroom downstairs. My head is in the toilet, I hate being sick. The smell is awful, making my eyes water. Danny walks in and holds my hair back as I'm hunched over the toilet. I haven't eaten today, yet there is still something in my stomach. He strokes my hair but says nothing. It soothes me, I feel exhausted. Danny has knelt next to me. I flush the toilet, wipe my face and lean against Danny. I'm so tired, pregnancy does me no favours. He hugs me tight. I drift slowly asleep. I feel arms around me, Danny is carrying me to the car. I fall back to sleep.

I wake to Danny stroking my hair. "Sis, wake up. We are here," he whispers. I feel worse after that nap. My head is in Danny's lap. I sit up slowly. I can still smell sick, I know I wasn't sick down myself. So I guess the smell has lingered in my nose. Momma has got out the car. Desmond pulls up in the hired van next to us. I grab my phone from my pocket. Another text from Damon.

I'll do one better than that. I'll send his Boss.

I giggle at the phone.

Is the boss not too busy? Meeting at 3 pm La Zenia.

I get out the car, Danny holds my hand and leads me to the house. Normally I don't like Danny touching me, but after today I need my brother. I think he's thought about what I said and he is trying to look after me. The house is huge from the outside, a joining garage. The house is grey, with a big front lawn. Danny leads me into the house. It feels darker in here than it looks from the outside. Desmond and Momma join us in the hallway.

Desmond puts his arm around me and Momma. I flinch at his touch, did he notice? He certainly doesn't let on if he did. "I'm so glad you are all my family and moving in with me," he says.

Danny and Momma both agree, but when I think of family, this isn't it. I love these two, I do. But I always feel like I have to sell my soul to please them. They make life hard, whereas when I think of Damon, he is my family. Now deep down I know I regret the decision to move into Desmond's. But I still wouldn't go back on that.

"Would you like a tour?" he says, peering down at me. I nod. He removes his arms from my shoulder and I relax a little. Danny lets my hand go and lets Desmond show me around. I guess he has been here before. It wouldn't surprise me. We walk into the living room, it's dark. There is flowery wallpaper. Cream sofas surround the back walls. A large cream rug in the centre of the room. It has oak flooring. It's nice, but not my thing at all.

"It's nice," I say. He smiles and sets off to the next room. We enter the kitchen, again it's dark. Why are all the rooms dark? It's a rectangle kitchen, there are work tops all along the left side of the room. In the middle, there is a kitchen island, dark brown theme. American style fridge freezer. I don't like it. But hey, I don't like a lot of things I have to. This will be an easy one to live with. He sets off to the next room. It's a large bedroom. It is dark and goth-like. A king size purple bed sits in the middle of the room. Black silk sheets, black silk curtains. Purple carpet.

"This is your room," Desmond announces. My room? I like it, I do. I just wouldn't choose this for myself. Although I can see myself getting lost in this dark room. Matches my soul. I laugh.

"I like it," I admit. He goes through another door in the bedroom. It leads to a bathroom. It's very pink, pink is all I see. Pink tiles, pink toilet, pink bath. I love pink, and this is very me. But something I would choose? Maybe not.

"And this is your bathroom," he says.

"What happens if I don't like pink?" It was meant to come out as a joke but it came out sarcastic. Desmond looks awkward.

"Your Mom said you liked pink," he cringes.

Momma has been following silently behind us. "Stop messing around Emmie. Desmond is trying to make things perfect for you." Perfect? Perfect would be not his house and him not with us. Even then it wouldn't be perfect. Is that because I have high expectations? Am I being a horrible person again? I sigh.

"Sure, it's great. Thanks, Desmond." I try to muster up a smile, I'm not sure if one reaches my face.

"You're welcome, Emmie. We will leave you to get settled in." They leave me in the bathroom. I drop to the floor. I'm exhausted and the day isn't over yet. I wish it was. I put my head on my knees. Hold it together Emmie, you've been through worse. I stand up and head to the bedroom. I find some boxes of mine, Danny must have carried them up for me. I don't feel safe here at all. Nothing has happened but there's a feeling I can't shake. I grab my phone and call Damon.

He answers on the second ring. "Hey, Beautiful. Everything okay?"

I take a deep breath, "I wanted to hear your voice." My voice is trembling. Shit.

"Emmie, what's wrong?"

"I don't think I can do this." I sit on the floor cross-legged.

"Baby, you're okay. Take a deep breath. Has something happened?" No, not really, I'm just lacking your soothing presence.

"No, I just don't think I will ever feel comfortable in this house. It all feels so... wrong."

"You're my brave girl, remember why you did this. Like I said, you don't have to do this." But what will I do? Let my Momma and Danny hate me for being selfish, no way.

"I know. I just wanted to hear your voice. It soothes me."

I sense him grinning. "I'm so glad I could help." Oh Damon you did, but you'd help me more if you were here so I could curl up in your lap. Feel your warmth.

"I'll talk to you soon," I say.

"Bye Beautiful." I hang up. Danny enters my room, without knocking again. He sits in front of me.

"I want to talk," he demands.

I cross my arms, "Well I don't." I've had enough talking, it just gets me into trouble.

"Well just listen then. I've been thinking about what you said. Do you really feel that way? About, you know, me pushing you over a cliff?" I bring my knees up to my chest to protect me. He moves closer and he hugs my knees, waiting for an answer.

I try to reassure him, "Danny it's okay. I need to do this for Momma."

"It's not okay. I love you, Sis. I forget that although you act and look tough. Underneath you're not so tough. I'm going to try and put you first from now on okay?" He doesn't take his eyes off me. I love it when we can be close like this. When I don't want to push him away.

"Okay, Bro, I love you." He kisses me on the forehead and leaves my room.

Moments later I see Desmond stood in the doorway. I jump up, uncomfortable at his presence, just me and him. "If this is actually my room, then I want you to get out," I say defensively.

"This is my house. You'll respect me and my rules." He's angry but he doesn't raise his voice. Rules?

"Excuse me?" How dare he speak to me like that. The only person that could do that was my Dad. The Dad I'd replace him with any day.

"Yes, excuse you. Rule number 1. You'll respect your Mom and me. Rule number 2. You will start being good at school. Rule number 3. No boys staying over. Rule number 4. If you do stay out, text your Mom or me. Rule number 5. You will help around the house. And finally, you will do anything you can to please me."

That's a long list, one that I need to process in my mind. "What?" I whisper.

"I'm sorry, did I stutter? Did I speak too fast for you?" What, stutter? No.

"I'm sorry, I heard you loud and clear." He is glaring at me, I can't handle his piercing eyes. If he had superpowers he would definitely have some sort of laser eyes that could cut through anything. My body is shaking, something about him scares me.

"Good." Desmond smiles and leaves the room. I drop again to the floor. My body feels like a tonne of bricks. I curl up into a ball. I can't breathe, his words swim around in my mind. My lungs are empty. I feel myself slipping again, I can't see anything. I find nothing to anchor me back. Why am I so weak?

"Emmie?" I hear someone calling me. But all I see is black. I can't breathe.

"Shit Emmie, you're safe." I am? I don't feel safe. I feel the warmth around me, I smell his scent. Damon is here. His voice soothing me.

"What's going on? Is she okay?" Momma asks.

"I don't know but she never wanted to be here so we're leaving," Damon growls.

"You can't take her," Danny argues.

"I will do the hell I like. Especially if it's best for her." Best for me? No, you should do what's best for them. I can't be selfish. But I can't find my voice, I concentrate on my breathing. Trying to match mine with Damon's.

"Well call me when you get some sense out of her," Momma says.

"I hope you're okay my girl. See you later." Desmond's words are icy. My body instinctively moves away from his voice, into Damon's chest. I lose all meaning of life. I feel nothing, everything goes black.

Chapter 18

I wake to Damon stroking my hair. He never left me, that gives me comfort. I open my eyes, we are in his living room. He is staring at me, he looks like he has aged in a few hours. He looks angry, hurt and tired all at once. My head is on Damon's lap.

"What's going on? How did I get here?" I say but I don't move.

"You're safe. I went to see you and you were on the floor in a state. You wouldn't respond to me so I brought you here." He frowns. "What happened?"

"Everything just got on top of me." I lift my hand and place it under Damon's shirt to feel his skin.

"I know there's more."

"It's nothing."

Sully clears his throat, "Er, Boss." I didn't even hear him come in. I go to sit up but Damon doesn't let me move.

"What's wrong Sully?" Damon asks.

"We've finally received that Document we were waiting for. It's bad Boss." I move my legs so Sully can sit down on the sofa. Sully takes his cue and sits down, he takes me off guard. He grabs my ankles and places them on his lap. Damon doesn't seem to notice, if he does he doesn't say anything.

"What do you mean bad?" Damon asks curiously. What document?

"I think we should talk in your office." Sully looks worried.

"Stay where you are. Why is everyone so worried? What's this document?" I demand.

Sully looks down at me and then to Damon. "Boss?"

Damon shrugs, "I guess she has a right to know," he says.

Sully looks at me again. "After the day you came out your house crying, that Desmond put his hands on you." I remember, how could I forget, he freaked me out that day. "Well, I was worried about your safety. So I ran a background check." Why would he be worried about my safety? Background check? Is he allowed to do that?

"So what did it say?" I whisper.

"I was very concerned as it was taking a while to come through. Turns out he was suspected of murdering a young girl."

"What?" I squeak.

"Suspected?" Damon shouts, making me jump.

"They never convicted him. They had no evidence. So he walked free." No evidence, I can live with that.

"But that doesn't mean he did it?" I'm lying to myself. "No evidence..."

"Well no..." Sully puts his hand on his chin thinking.

"I'm not taking the risk where you're concerned," Damon says. What's he going to do? Keep me here against my will? Except if he opened his arms I would stay there anyway.

"Me neither," Sully agrees.

"This is not your choice to make," I shout.

"Excuse me?" Damon is angry but he doesn't shout like me.

"This is my life. There was no evidence. Nothing to worry about." Except there is, Damon would freak if he knew what he did earlier.

"Why do you have to be so stubborn?" He looks me in the eyes and strokes my cheek. I shrug.

"Because that's who I am." He said I should be myself. This is me. Except I'm not being stubborn for me, it's for my family.

"You drive me crazy." In a good way, I hope.

"What time is it?" I ask

Sully looks at his watch, "2.30 Emmie."

"Time for your meeting then." I stand up. I wonder what this meeting is about. My Dad has been dead for a month. Why now? Did I do something wrong? Damon grabs my hand and leads me to the car. Instead of opening my door he stops me. "Stop overthinking things. I will be with you, you'll be fine."

"Do you know what this could be about?"

"I have an Idea." He opens my door and I get in.

We arrive outside the Attorney's building. It's 2.55pm. 5 minutes to spare. Damon grabs my hand and lifts it to his lips. I gasp at his touch, he grins. He knows exactly what he does to me. He kisses my hand and then leaves the car. He opens my door. "Come on baby."

We walk hand in hand into the building. We reach a reception desk. A young pretty lady looks up from the computer. She does a double take at Damon. "Can I help you?" She flutters her eyelashes at him. He seems oblivious to her flirting. Good, I smile at myself.

"Miss Salvatore has a meeting." He looks at me. "Do you remember who with?"

"Erm Mr Declan," I say, my voice is shaky.

"Yes, I see. Take a seat. He will be ready shortly." We take a seat. Damon keeps my hand, stroking the back of it with his thumb. I start shaking my leg, waiting. I hate waiting. Damon places his hand on my knee to restrain my leg from moving. He looks at me and mouths the word stop.

"Miss Salvatore?" Another woman enters the reception area, in a short pencil skirt and a smart white blouse. I stand up and nod. Damon is right behind me. She knocks on a door and walks in.

"Miss Salvatore is here for your meeting sir." She waves us in. The room is huge. Much bigger than necessary. His desk sits by the big floor to ceiling glass windows that looks out onto the town. Must be nice to sit in the sun all day. He looks at me and smiles. He is a middle-aged man who is rather handsome actually. He has short blonde hair, green eyes. He's wearing a grey suit. He looks at me a little too long and then looks at Damon and frowns.

He moves around his desk and walks to me and shakes my hand. I tense at his touch. The lady retreats and shuts the door behind us. "It's nice to meet you, Miss Salvatore. Please take a seat." He points towards the chairs in front of his desk and then releases my hand.

"Please call me Emmie," I say, walking over to the chairs.

"So who is this gentleman? I really did expect only you to visit," he says disappointedly.

"I'm Rider, her fiancé," he snaps. What's wrong with him? Mr Declan takes a seat at his desk.

"Well Rider, as you aren't family yet, you shouldn't be here," he says sternly. Damon's hands make fists. I put my hand on his leg.

"Mr Declan, all due respect but Rider is my family and he will be staying regardless of the fact that it's allowed or not," I say calmly. Damon looks at me and smiles.

"I see, well shall we begin?" He looks pissed. Why? He should be more professional. "I've been trying to contact you for weeks. I have your father's will." His will? He made one of those? What does that have to do with me? But of course he did, he was a control freak. "Your name is the only one written in the will. He wants you to have everything."

Everything? What does that entail? What about Danny? My mind is swamping with this information. Why me? I was always so bad, I know he loved me, but this much? I don't know.

"What is everything?" Damon asks.

"Well, he has 5 million in savings. He owns one house and a car." 5 million pounds? Jesus Christ, no I can't have that much money. I didn't do anything for it, I didn't earn it. It feels dirty money to me. I can't accept it, no way. "Emmie, you'll need to sign this paperwork to have it signed over to you." No, this is too much. Why couldn't he leave me his favourite pen or something? That would have been a more suitable gift for me. What would I do with that sort of money? "Emmie, did you hear me?" Mr Declan snaps.

"Shut up a minute, will you?" Damon growls. I am staring at my hands. Damon's hands reach my face and tugs gently at my face so my eyes meet his. He is calm, he takes everything in his stride. I wish I could do the same. I frown at him, he's perfect and I am not. "Emmie, you can do this."

"No Damon. I feel like this is dirty money."

"As much as I hated the guy Emmie, he loved you in his own weird way. He wants you taken care of."

"Mr Salvatore was rather insistent that you take everything he has. He left you a letter too." Mr Declan hands me an envelope with my name on it. I can't read this now. What can it say that I don't already know? I stare at it in my hands. I guess I can donate it all to charity, that would be good, right? I don't need it. I don't want it. "I have to say most people just accept the money and go." Mr Declan shrugs.

"I'm not most people," I say calmly. "But I will sign." Damon looks at me confused. But chooses not to say anything.

"Okay Emmie, sign right here." He points on the dotted line on the paper in front of me. I take his pen from his hand and our fingers touch briefly, I'm repulsed by his touch so I snatch my hand away. I sign on the line. I push the paper back to him. He holds out his hand to collect the pen but I place it on the paper so I don't have to risk touching him again.

"Well, Emmie it was a pleasure to meet you. If there is anything else you need, don't hesitate to call." Mr Declan, I will never need your assistance, I can assure you. You are slightly unprofessional in my opinion, unless that is just my biased opinion. He moves around the desk and Damon and I stand. Mr Declan extends his hand, I stare at it contemplating what I should do. Damon steps in front of me and takes the proffered hand, much to Mr Declan's disgust. I smile, how does Damon know these things, unless he doesn't and he didn't want him touching me? Either way, I don't care.

Damon and I leave, walking past the reception desk. The young woman looks up and waves at Damon. Damon rolls his eyes. Did he notice that time? We walk outside and I take in a deep breath, feeling the sun on my skin. Damon grabs my hand and brings it up to his face. He smiles at me. "You never fail to amaze me." I frown, what did I do this time? "I didn't think you would accept the money, I know you aren't like that."

"You'll take the car right? Sell it, keep it. I don't care. The rest will be donated to a charity." He laughs.

"Oh, baby. So that's why you accepted it. You don't have to decide right away. I will support you in any decision you make. But you may want it for the baby." Of course I want my kids well cared for but with this money? I'm not so sure. Am I overreacting? "Did you want to come back to mine baby?"

"I would love to but I have a camping trip at school. All weekend, I need to collect clothes from..." I cringe, "Desmond's house."

Damon laughs, he's in a good mood. "You camping? I'd love to see that. But you know..." He leans towards me so we are nose to nose, "I will miss you."

"Will you? Because I'm not sure I'll miss you. What with all those guys." He pulls away, he is mad. I was joking. "Damon, I'm joking. I miss you the minute you leave me."

His face softens, he leans in and kisses me urgently. "Miss me the minute I leave huh?" I nod, I'm too breathless to answer. How does he change moods so quickly? I have my favourite Damon back, the playful one.

"You're always leaving. Which means I miss you often," I confess, why did I do that? I could push him away. He frowns.

"Well, you are leaving me too now." He raises his eyebrow. That's not what I meant and he knows it. We walk hand in hand to the car.

"So will Sully be coming on this camping trip?" I giggle. We are driving towards Desmond's house. How did he even know where he lived anyway? I didn't even know.

"I don't think the school would be too impressed." I feel a pang of disappointment, I've grown confident knowing one of them is around. I shouldn't need to rely on bodyguards.

He looks over to me and raises an eyebrow, "You aren't planning to do anything stupid, are you?" I never plan to do anything, it all just seems to go wrong.

I laugh, "Who me? Poor old innocent me?"

"I think we have already established you are not innocent."

We reach Desmond's house. "Do you want me to come in with you?"

"No, it's okay, I won't be long." I run to the house. Should I knock or just walk in? I decide to just walk in. Besides, that's what you would do at your own house. I want to be as quiet as possible but Danny has already seen me coming. He pulls me into a bear hug. Lifting me off the ground as he does it. I stiffen at his touch but he ignores me.

"Danny, what are you doing?"

"I'm so glad you are okay."

"Of course I am, you idiot."

He laughs, "That's my sister." He releases me and looks at me. "So what was that meeting?" I shush him and tell him to follow me upstairs. I get lost so he walks in front of me and leads me into my bedroom. How can I get lost, stupid? I close the door and he turns to look at me.

"Is it bad?" he asks.

"Look, I want to keep this quiet but I wanted to tell you."

"Okay Sis, I won't say anything. You can trust me."

"Well, I had a meeting with Dad's attorney."

He frowns, "About?"

"Danny, he left me everything. I'm sorry." I look at the floor. I feel so guilty, why didn't he share it with Danny? I wouldn't be so bothered about it. He pauses for a while, processing I guess. He walks over to me, closing

193

the gap between us. He grabs my head and pulls me in for a hug. My head on his shoulder, stroking my hair. I wrap my arms around his waist.

"Don't be sorry Sis. You deserve everything he has."

"I don't want it."

"Why not?"

"It feels dirty. He left me a letter too."

"What does this letter say?"

"I don't know, I haven't read it."

He pulls my head away gently. "Why not?"

"I can't face it." I shrug.

"Shall I read it to you?" I nod and he pulls me over to the bed. Danny sits on the edge of the bed and I sit crossed legged next to him. I hand him the letter from my pocket. He carefully opens it, examining it as he goes. I watch him, that's all I can do.

Danny clears his throat, "Dearest Emmie, if you are reading this it means I'm dead and you are here. If I had my way I would never leave you. What a bastard." Danny is adding his own commentary. "I wanted to let you know that I love you. Please accept my gift to you, build a life for yourself. No, you will accept it, don't be stubborn. I hope you realise now what I did to you was for your own good. Wait, I'm not reading this if that's what he has to say," Danny growls.

"Danny please, I want to hear it," I beg. I shuffle towards him, place my arm through his and study the letter.

"I kept you safe, safe from the world. Safe from you, you are your biggest enemy. I'm so proud of you Emmie. You are a smart, beautiful woman. With this money, I can make your dreams come true, I have worked so hard to make a life for you. It's my dying wish to have you safe. So accept the damn money, Emmie. The car though, sell it. I don't want you in unnecessary risk. Of course, you wouldn't be having kids because you belong to me. You still aren't allowed boyfriends Emmie, even when I'm gone." Danny curses. "Emmie, he is a sick waste of space. Don't listen to him." He looks at the paper again.

"I want you to be happy and remember you are my princess and don't let anyone treat you any less than a princess. I love you, Daddy."

I love you too Daddy. Tears fall from my face. I miss you, Daddy. Danny shifts so he can look at me. "Emmie, Dad didn't deserve to be in your life, so don't listen to this letter." He wipes my tears from my cheeks.

"I will throw it away."

"No!" I snatch the letter and hold it to my heart.

"Emmie, you don't believe any of that, do you?" He looks at me like I'm unstable. He doesn't understand. "Emmie."

"Yes, get out Danny. You don't get it," I scream.

"What's wrong with you?" What is right about me?

"Everything. I'm broken."

"Yes, broken because of Dad."

"Get out!" I scream. He gets up and walks out the door and slams it behind him. I reach over to my bedside cabinet and grab the picture of us both. I curl up on my bed and clutch the picture and the letter to my chest. I sob, is grief finally hitting me? I miss my Dad. He has been my constant.

The door clicks open. "Get out Danny." I sob into my pillow but I don't look up. I feel arms around me. His strong scent. My Damon is here.

"Danny told me what happened." I don't say anything, just continue to cry. Damon strokes my hair, soothing me. Eventually, I stop crying and turn to face him. "Can I read this letter?" Damon asks.

"You won't tear it up?" I want to keep this letter. My last piece of my Dad. I clutch it tighter.

"Emmie, it's yours, I wouldn't dream of ruining anything that means so much to you."

I prize the photo and the letter away from my chest and hand him the letter. He doesn't remove his hand from my hair, but with the other, he reads the letter. He frowns. "Can I see the photo you are holding?" he asks calmly. I nod and hold out the photo. He examines it.

"You look so happy here." I nod, I remember feeling happy. "I understand why Danny reacted the way he did." I sniff. "But, I also know you. The way your mind works." Sometimes I'm glad that he does and sometimes I hate that he can. I've always been on my own. "He loved you Emmie, and you loved him."

"Yeah." I did, I still do.

"I'm not going to tell you what to do, but after everything he did to you, you need to put yourself first, don't let your Dad hold you back." I love how Damon is so patient with me, making things black and white. He probably wants to scream at me like Danny did, but here he is calmly talking things through with me. Damon gives back the photo and letter and I place it on my bedside cabinet.

"So, you got side-tracked? Do you need help packing for your camping trip?" I sit up and look at him. I wipe my face and smile. I stand up and walk to one of the boxes that's labelled clothes. I bend down to pick the box up but Damon is already behind me, he puts his hands on my hips and pushes me to the side. "I'll take that," and he picks it up. "Where would one like said box Ma'am?" I slap him playfully and point to the bed. He chuckles and does as he is told.

I open the box and start pulling clothes out. I make a pile of clothes to take. Once I'm done packing, Damon takes my bag as we make our way downstairs. Danny runs to the door. He hugs me tight and whispers, "I'm sorry Sis. I love you." I sigh.

"I love you too Bro."

He smiles, "Now remember, the spiders are probably more scared of you. You are pretty scary." He chuckles and so does Damon. I glare at them both. Momma comes from nowhere. I guess I need to explore this house more, I've forgotten where everything is.

"Stay safe sweetheart." She kisses me on the cheek. From behind Momma, Desmond appears taking me by surprise, I involuntarily step back into Damon. Who puts his arms out to stop me falling.

Desmond walks towards me holding his arms out, maybe making it clear to me what he's doing. Doesn't make it easier though. Damon's hands are on my shoulders, he must feel me tense but he doesn't let go. It keeps me calmer. Desmond hugs me but I don't return the hug. I just stay paralysed till he releases me. I wave and say goodbye and then I walk hastily out the door straight into Damon's car. He stays close by me.

"What was that all about?" he says whilst pulling out of the driveway.

I shrug, "What?" I know exactly what he's talking about.

"When Desmond walked towards you. Has he done something?"

"No," I lie. Was that convincing enough? "I'm still adjusting, still getting to know him. You know how I feel about people touching me. Like when Mr Declan wanted to shake my hand."

"He was a creep, Emmie. I didn't want him touching your hand, especially after I saw you flinch when he lingered his fingers after giving you that pen," he growls.

"Lingered?" I gasp.

"Yes, Emmie. Did you think he touched your fingers by accident?" Well yes, I did actually. He noticed me flinching? Damon definitely has super powers.

I shrug. We reach the school for 4.45pm. In the car park, there's a coach, I see everyone waiting. We both get out the car. Damon grabs my bag, I offer to take it but he wouldn't let me. Rah, I'm pregnant not an invalid. We walk over to the coach. Damon kisses me goodbye. He walks up to Brody, what's he going to do? He shoves my bag at Brody which he takes with no questions asked.

"Make sure you take care of her," Damon says to Brody in his no-nonsense manner. I roll my eyes. Brody crosses his arms and stares at Damon.

"What do you think I'm going to do, let her get eaten by bugs?" Brody says defensively.

"You know what I'm talking about." Damon rolls his eyes.

"Honestly, I can take care of myself," I say crossing my arms.

They both look at me and in unison, they both say, "No you can't." Jessie laughs at us even though she's not with us. I glare at them both and poke my tongue at them. Brody walks to the coach and places my bag in the under storage compartment with all the rest. I find Mr Dudley and Mr Beale the principal with clipboards at the front of the coach. Really, them two? This is going to be fun.

Damon grabs my hand and kisses it softly. "Behave, okay?" I stop breathing at his touch. "Emmie, breathe."

"I will," I say, trying to reassure him, he sounds nervous. He can't be that worried about my safety, I'm not that bad. He kisses me softly, I put my arms around his neck to deepen the kiss. He groans, ha another achievement.

"Alright class line up," Mr B shouts but Damon doesn't break the kiss and I don't want to either. Two days seems a long time without seeing him. I put my hands on his hips, his strong sturdy hips. I feel a hand on mine and before I know it Jessie is dragging me to the coach. I wave at Damon. He's not happy but he waves back.

"What was that?" I demand.

"Looked like you were going to eat each other's face off." She rolls her eyes.

"And?" I cross my arms. She laughs. "Maybe we were hungry." I laugh too.

It looks like Mr B is taking a register. Mr D walks down the line that we've all created. He stops just in front of me and starts staring at me. "Where were you today?" he scolds.

"What's it to you?" I mutter. He crosses his arms and goes red with anger.

"I missed you in my class today." Bit inappropriate, I thought he didn't like me anyway.

"That's good to know, well we have all weekend together." I wink at him. His mouth drops open for a second then shuts it again. He shakes his head and starts walking down the line again.

"You really do have a death wish." Jessie turns around to talk to me. I shrug. We all start piling onto the coach. I sit next to Jessie. I take the window seat so I can be closer to the sun. I hold my tummy thinking of my baby.

"Hey, Cara de Angel." Sky pops his head between the gap of the chairs in front of me. I smile at him to be friendly. "You want a lollipop?" He pokes one through the gap. I take it.

"Thanks, Sky," I say while sucking on it. A hand pushes Sky's face out the way and Brody's head looks through.

"Hey, Jessie," he says.

"Hey, Brody." What's going on? I block them out and watch out the window. We are on the move now. Watching cars go past, buildings. I pull my knees up to my chest. I can feel the tension rising again in my body. I shut my eyes and lean my cheek on my knee. Breathing in and out. I eventually finish the lolly and put the stick in my pocket. I take up my normal position. Closing my eyes again.

"Emmie, shit Emmie wake up," a voice demands. Go away I say in my head. I feel hands on me and I jolt awake. Sweat dripping off me. What the hell is going on? Brody is leaning over Jessie and his hands on my knees. All eyes are on me.

"What are you looking at?" I say sleepily. Brody relaxes in front of me. I frown.

"Emmie, you were screaming, what were you dreaming about?" I don't know. I wasn't really, I just know I don't sleep well when Damon isn't here. I'm never safe. I shrug but Brody doesn't move, he's looking for an answer.

"I'm sorry okay? I get nightmares all the time. I can't help it. Whatever I said just ignore me. 'kay?" Everyone goes back to what they are doing.

"Jess, do you mind for a sec?" He looks at Jessie who shrugs and slides out her seat and she takes Brody's seat. Jess? Since when does she go by that? Brody takes the seat next to me. He grabs my hands, I frown and pull them away from him. They're all sweaty. My heart is beating frantically. "You can't get much peaceful sleep if you get nightmares." He scratches the back of his head.

"I wake up sweaty most mornings unless I'm with Damon and then I don't get my nightmares." I lift one side of lips.

"Why do you think you don't get them with Damon?" he asks, genuinely interested.

"Because I feel safe with Damon," I say without thinking.

"Do you feel safe now?" I shake my head and his face drops.

"Brody, I spent my whole life not feeling safe. It's like a habit. I'm damaged." I wipe my palms on my legs.

He puts his hand on my shoulder and he frowns. He must feel how tense I am. "I won't let anything happen to you," he says softly, Brody is always so calm, so much that it nearly calms me. He reaches up and strokes my hair. I think about pushing him away but I'm too tired. I sag against his side and he puts his arms around me. We're friends, we can do this right? I don't want him in a romantic way, I just need him in my life. I close my eyes and he continues to stroke my hair and I drift off to sleep again.

"Emmie we're here," he says softly, I can feel his breath on my face. He smells like sweets. He must have had a lollipop too. I sit up straight and he releases me. He smiles at me and strokes my cheek.

"Everyone off the bus," Mr D calls.

Brody looks up and takes his cue. As we walk off the bus, Mr D is outside of the coach. He grabs my arm on the way out and pulls me to the side. I snatch it back and glare at him.

"Are you okay? I heard you screaming." What's it to him? I continue to glare at him.

"I'm fine. Just a nightmare," I say and walk off to get my bag from under the coach. My bag seems to have made its way to the far end, I have to climb in to reach it. I drag it to the edge and then lift it out. It's quite heavy but I sling it over my shoulder anyway.

"Everyone gather round," Mr B says. I hobble over to the rest of the class. "You will be in pairs in the cabins, so listen carefully to your partners." He clears his throat. "Max and Sky, Milly and Caroline, Jade and Jessie and lastly I expect you both to behave, Brody and Emmie." What? Me with Brody? I guess out of all the guys I'd pick him. But I was hoping to share with Jessie.

Chapter 19

"How come she gets to share with a guy?" Jade whines, god I hate her voice, she's so whiny.

"Because I said so. Now go find a cabin," Mr B says firmly.

"Lucky Bro. I'd love to share with Cara de Angel." I bet you would. I rub my tummy, I've got a bump now. I slide my hand down my face, I'm fat. I was fat before, now I'm huge.

"Calm down Sky. It's cool because we are friends. Right, Emmie?" He looks behind him to see me. He frowns and closes the gap between us. "Give me that, what are you doing?" He grabs my bag. I go to speak but he stops me by putting his index finger up. "No lifting okay?" I nod in a huff.

We all walk towards the cabins, pairs of us disbursing into the cabins. Brody and I find one and we stand and look at it for a couple of minutes. It's modern, wooden. Small but cosy. "Well, this is it. Let's get settled inside. Then we can check out this party."

"What party?" I say when we are walking in the cabin.

"We are having a campfire party. It'll be fun. You in?" He had me at party, I love parties.

"Sure, nothing else to do." Except get anxious, and miss Damon.

We walk into the Cabin and its open plan. In front of us is one large bed. On the right is a door, I imagine it's the bathroom. On the left is a fireplace. In front of the fireplace is a sofa facing it. On the right of the bathroom door is a set of table and chairs. What catches my attention most is there is only one bed. I look at Brody and he is looking at what I am. The one and only bed.

"Seriously, only one bed? What are these teachers thinking? Don't worry, I'll sleep on the floor." He places our bags on the bed.

"Don't be silly. I'm sure we know each other well enough to share the bed. It's big enough." Not like we haven't shared a bed before. But it's definitely different this time.

"Sure. I'm going to take a shower," he says awkwardly. I nod as he retreats to the bathroom. Why did they put us two together?

It doesn't make sense. Oh well, Brody and I get on well. So it will be fine, right? I rummage through my bag to see what I can wear to the party. Soon my clothes won't fit, I'm dreading it. I decide to text Damon.

Arrived safely. Miss you already. Love you

I sit on the bed cross-legged. My ankles hurt.

I'm glad you arrived safe baby. Have fun. I love you.

Have fun? Camping? Yeah right. The door clicks open to the bathroom and I look up to see Brody in just a towel. My mouth drops open, he is still wet, his abs stand out more than usual. I can't help but stare. "Er, hey. I forgot to get some clothes." He flashes a nervous smile.

I clear my throat composing myself. "Don't worry about it," I say almost not audible. Pull yourself together Emmie. I decide I need a cold shower so I run into the bathroom. I slap my cheek to gather myself. Stupid Emmie. I strip and get in the shower. The cool water is good on my skin. It calms me a little. I use the soap and shampoo provided. The shampoo smells of coconut. It's different to what I usually use but it will do. I turn the shower off and grab a towel off the rails. I feel a sick feeling in my stomach. I forgot my clothes after all that. I run to the toilet and I vomit again. I rest my forehead on my arm. I'm exhausted. I wipe my mouth, stand up and rinse my mouth.

I stand at the door and call, "Brody, are you there?" I wait a few seconds but no answer. I clutch my towel tighter to me, feeling self-conscious. I walk out into the main room to find two figures entering the cabin. My face goes bright red and hot. "Er, sorry, I thought you left."

Brody and Sky both stand gawking at me and I hitch the towel up higher. As high as it would allow. "We've just got back. No need to apologise for a body as hot as yours." Brody winks at me. We are supposed to be just friends, what is he playing at?

"Hey, Cara de Angel. Looking good." He strokes the back of his head. Keeping his eyes on me. Brody shoves him as if to say back off.

"Seriously." I sigh and roll my eyes. "I'm going to go get my clothes and change in the bathroom." I turn to the bed and get the dress I chose and walk briskly to the bathroom.

Well, that was awkward. When Damon looks at me I melt, I feel special under his gaze like he appreciates every inch of me. But that? That felt like I was a piece of meat, I felt fat and ugly like I was some sort of freak show. I shake my head and start to dress myself. Once I'm finished I walk back into the main room. Brody and Sky are sat at the table with plastic cups in their hand. Drinking already? They both look up at me, they still look like they did when I was in my towel. Are they thinking of me naked?

"Are you ready to go?" Brody asks.

"Yup," I say casually, wanting to get out the cabin. Sky takes the lead and Brody puts his arm around my shoulder. I elbow him in the ribs and he winces and holds his ribs with his other hand.

"What was that for?"

"For gawking at me. We are supposed to be friends."

"We are friends, I'm sorry Emmie. I couldn't help myself, your body..."He swallows. "Besides you were gawking at me." He raises his eyebrow at me.

"I have an excuse," I joke, there is no excuse for what I did. I'm engaged. But who else is this close to an Ex and not look? It's hard okay.

"And what would that be? That I'm hot?" Full of himself today. I giggle. He is right though, he is hot.

"No, pregnancy hormones," I say casually. He laughs, and I mean really laughs. I have to elbow him again to shut up.

"Right, because that's an excuse. I will let you off just this once friend." Friend? I frown, I know that's what we are, it just sounds weird.

We follow the music to a small fire surrounded by people. Brody releases me and says to Sky, "I'm going to get a drink."

"Me too." Sky nods and they walk off to find alcohol.

Jessie skips over to me. "Hey, Bestie," She shouts a little too loud.

"Hey."

She frowns, "What's up?"

"Why did I have to be the one to share with Brody?" I cross my arms.

"What's the problem?" She holds her chin.

"Brody walked in the room in a towel. He kinda caught me checking him out." I find Brody in the crowd who now drinks beer.

"Emmie Salvatore! Do you still have feelings for Brody?" Is she stupid? Of course I do. That's why this is so hard.

"Of course I do. Choosing between them was the hardest thing I've ever done."

"Do you regret your decision?" No, Damon is my life. He is part of me now.

"No, I know I made the right choice but I will always love Brody."

"So what are you going to do? You've got the whole weekend with him." She takes a swig of her drink. Whatever she's drinking is strong. I wrinkle my nose at the smell.

"That's not the only thing. Our cabin only has one bed. And I kinda told him he could share it with me," I say awkwardly.

"Emmie! You're nuts, girl. I'm going to get a drink. This is too much information." Another drink, really Jessie? She walks off to where Brody is standing. He looks at his phone and frowns and then his eyes find mine. He scratches his head like he's in deep thought. I turn away and find a seat.

"You know your boyfriend is doing my head in and he's not even here." I turn and Brody has taken a seat next to me.

"Why?" What could Damon have possibly done now?

"He texted me to say I must make you eat because you conveniently like to forget." He hands me a plate with a burger on it. I examine it. "Don't worry, he told me to make sure it's veggie too. How he has my number, god only knows."

Damon is using his super powers again. He knows what I'm like with food. I hold the plate out to Brody, "I'm not hungry." I pout. Brody holds his hands up in denial.

"He said you would probably fight me on this. He also said I should hand feed you if I have to." Really? Shouldn't it be my choice if I'm not hungry? I huff at him. I'm mad at the both of them. "I'm going to get another drink. I'm watching you. I'll know if you don't eat it," and with that, he walks off. I frown at the food. I'm fat, I've got a bump, I don't need any food to make me fatter. I look up and find Brody glaring at me.

I roll my eyes and start to eat the damn veggie burger. I don't really taste it, but I eat it anyway. Brody has found Sky again. I finish the burger and set the plate where Brody sat. A figure stands in front of me. I squint to see who it is. It's getting dark now. Urgh, it's Jade. I groan.

"You better steer clear of me this weekend," she threatens.

"You're like a parasite that gets everywhere," I growl, I'm not in the mood.

"I'm warning you. If you go near Brody as well I will come after you." Well, that's going to be hard.

"And what are you going to do?" Cry baby.

"You'll find out if you test me. I'm Queen Bee." Still pulling that card? She stamps her foot impatiently.

"Jade, no one likes you. I'm sorry to break this to you. But you're not Queen Bee anymore. You haven't been since I came to school." There, that will do it.

"Urgh, I hate you. Just watch your back. I'm coming for you," she screams and walks off. Why do girls have to be so dramatic? If someone flirted with Damon I wouldn't be happy but I wouldn't confront them. If Damon was interested I wouldn't want to hold him back.

I decide to take a walk, I'm getting a headache with the thumping music. I realise I've probably walked too far from the party. I'm not sure where I am. I am at the entrance of a wooded area. I don't venture into the woods. I promised Damon I wouldn't do anything stupid. It's quiet and that's what I set out for. I close my eyes and take a deep breath, smelling my surroundings. Grass, bark and fresh air.

"Hey. I saw you come this way." I spin around and see Max standing behind me. Why do people sneak up on me?

"Hey, Max. You followed me?" I chew my fingers.

"I wanted to talk to you," he says slowly. I can smell the alcohol on him. He's drunk.

"Max, you're drunk."

"So… You're so hot, you know that?" He is slurring his words. I try and take an unnoticeable step back.

"Max, come on man. Don't do this." I feel uncomfortable being here alone with Max. I don't trust him. I shift my weight, think Emmie. Should I make a run for it?

"You know you turn me on. I know pregnant girls' hormones run wild. I know you like me." No, Max, I don't like you. And I'm pretty sure I've never given you the impression that I do.

"Max dude, you're my friend. You don't want to do this." I cringe.

He steps towards me and I freeze. My feet won't move. I'm screaming inside but I can't scream out loud. He grabs my face and pulls me hard into his body. I put my hands out in front of me to try and push him away. But he is stronger than I am. He puts one hand on my back and one on the back of my head. He forces my head towards his face. Or lips collide, he tastes like spirits. It makes me sick to the core.

I try and mutter, "Max, this isn't you. Please stop," but he just pushes hard on my head.

"Dude! What are you doing?" A voice shouts. Max releases me.

"Er, Brody." Max looks awkward.

"You better get out of here before I kick your ass," Brody demands.

"Sorry Brody." Max staggers off.

Brody looks at me up and down. I can't move, he walks to me and puts his hand on my head and pulls me into a hug. I wrap my arms around him. "Are you okay?"

"Yeah," I say but my voice is shaky. He strokes my hair. "I hate camping." He chuckles.

I pull away, "Is there nothing that doesn't faze you?" he says.

I shrug, "I'm used to it."

"You shouldn't be, that's the problem. I admire you, you know." Admire me? Why?

"Nothing good to admire about me."

"Oh but there is," he says matter of factly. He cups my face in his hands. His warm hands on my cold cheeks. His face leans into mine and his warm lips join my cold lips. For a second I respond, enjoying his lips on mine. But it feels so wrong. I pull away. I love Damon.

"Brody I can't," I say whilst looking at my hands that are knotting together.

"I know, I'm sorry. I've been drinking. I got caught up in the moment. I just find you hard to resist." Me, hard to resist? Yeah right, can he not see I'm fat?

"I'm sorry. I love you, Brody, I do. But I chose Damon. I don't want to hurt you." He doesn't seem hurt by this. He already knows. But I felt like I should explain myself.

"I know and I love you, Emmie. It hurts me that you chose him. Seeing you two together, I can see that you are made for each other. But you can't blame me for trying, right?" I hurt him because I'm a horrible selfish person. If I would just let him go it might be easier for him.

"I don't blame you for anything Brody. I'm just so glad you are still talking to me."

"I can't imagine my life without you so if this is what I have to do then I'm all in." All into this? But I'm hurting him. He pulls me in for a hug and I accept it. I'm cold and he's really warm. "Come on, let's get you back to the cabin. You're cold."

He places his arm over my shoulder and leads us back to the cabin. Thank heavens he's here as I don't know how I would have found my way back. He stumbles a lot but he gets us back to the Cabin.

It's warm in the cabin. He looks at me, "Are you sure you're okay?" Yeah, I am. I mean it unsettled me sure, but he was drunk. I forgive Max for that.

"I'm okay, thank you."

"I'm tired, so I'm just going to go to bed." He kisses me on the forehead and retreats to the bathroom. I gather my PJs from my bag and my toothbrush. Brody returns in his boxers. I don't look this time and he doesn't look at me. He just heads into the bed. I go to the bathroom to brush my teeth and change into my PJs.

I'm really tired too. I take out my phone and there is a text from Damon.

Goodnight Baby.

I text him back.

I miss you.

I stare at the screen. I really miss him and he is miles away. I return to the bedroom and put my phone on the side table by the bed. Brody is snoring softly when I return. He is lying on his stomach with his face on the pillow. I gently climb in next to him trying not to wake him and I lay facing him. I watch his steady breathing and try to calm myself. I drift to sleep.

I'm hot, really hot. It's really uncomfortable. I must have had a quiet night because Brody never woke me up. I feel a heavy arm around me. Oh jeez, it's Brody's arm. I should move, but I don't want to. "Hey, Beautiful," Brody says sleepily in my ear.

"Hey."

I turn to look at him but he keeps his arm around me. "We should get up," I say, not attempting to move.

"We totally should get up." Brody flashes a big white teeth smile, but he also makes no attempt to move. "I'm quite happy here though." He stares at my face. What's wrong with my face? He smiles. If there is something wrong with my face, why smile?

My phone starts to ring so I reach over and grab it. Shit, it's Damon, I feel so guilty. I push Brody's arm off me and stand up my back to Brody. "Hello," I say shakily. Guilty Emmie, that's what you are.

"Hey, how are you?" he says. I've missed his voice.

"I'm good. Time away from my family is good. But I miss you." I've really missed you, Damon.

"I miss you too. So has my smart mouth got in trouble yet?" Oh if you knew you'd never forgive me.

"Like you wouldn't believe." He chuckles. But I frown.

"Emmie, we really need to get dressed and go. We're going to be late," Brody almost shouts and he is sat right behind me on the end of the bed. I turn around and glare at him.

"Who's that?" Damon growls.

"That's Brody." I turn away from Brody again and cringe. Here we go.

"What's he talking about, getting dressed?" I could kill Brody right now. This should have been said face to face.

"Damon don't freak out," I take a deep breath, "but I kinda have to share a room with Brody."

I brace myself, "What?" he shouts. "What the hell?"

"It's not a big deal," I whisper.

"Not a big deal? You're sharing a room with your Ex. Who might I add, wants to get in your panties," he screams through the phone.

"Damon, do you not trust me?"

He pauses for a while and finally, he says, "Of course I do. I just don't trust him." I can handle Brody. I really think we put something to bed last night.

We need to go meet the class. We are running late. "I really do need to go. I love you, Damon."

"I love you too." He sighs. I hang up and look at Brody who is fully dressed now.

"You did that on purpose." I slap him around the head. He laughs at me. I thought I was scary? So why is he laughing? I grab my clothes and go change in the bathroom. I frown in the mirror, people do like to give me mixed thoughts. I'm so angry but I don't know who I'm more mad at, Brody or myself. But that's a stupid question, of course, I'm more angry at myself. Everything all boils down to my fault. I hope I can break the kiss to Damon gently. He knows when I'm lying or keeping things from him and I don't want to have to keep secrets from him. He knows me better than anyone. I don't have to waste so much energy putting my wall up with him.

I finish dressing, I'm in black jeans and a long sleeve black t-shirt. I prefer to wear darker clothes for two reasons, one so I can blend in and not stand out too much. And the second, black makes me look slimmer. I walk into the main room again and Brody is texting on his phone, sat casually where I left him sitting on the bed. He looks up and grins at me. He must have got up and left the cabin though because he has food next to him. He's eating a bacon bap, I wrinkle my nose at the smell. My stomach hurls and I run back into the bathroom. Damn, pregnancy is torture. Brody walks in quietly. He must have either finished the bap or left it in the other room.

"You okay?"

I finish vomiting and flush the chain. I stand and nod. I decide I should brush my teeth again. Brody just stands at the door staring at me. "It's just morning sickness," I mumble with the toothbrush in my mouth. We walk back into the main room.

"Please value my life and eat something." What is he going on about, value his life? Of course I value his life.

"What are you on about?"

"Your interfering boyfriend text me again, demanding you eat some breakfast." I laugh so hard. Damon wouldn't really kill him. Is Brody scared of him or is he joking? I can't stop laughing, it's the most I've laughed in a long time. Brody stands staring at me, he doesn't know how to proceed. But a smile finds his face and he bursts into laughter too. He grabs the muffin left on the plate and then he comes towards me, he bends down and lifts me over his shoulder. I scream, not with anger or fear but with excitement.

He walks out the cabin and down towards where we are meeting. We are both laughing when we reach the rest of the group. Everyone is staring, the teachers look pissed. Both of them with their arms folded. We are late I guess.

"Nice of you both to join us, better later than never. Mr Rivers put her down," Mr B says sternly. Brody does as he is told, but instead of putting me down gently, he pretends to drop me and then catches me at the last second. I slap him hard on his arm, he laughs and so do I. I was angry earlier but now I'm happy. Why? Brody hands me the muffin.

"Eat, let me earn my brownie points." He smirks. I do as I'm told and eat the damn muffin. What is it about everyone and food? Do they not know someone can go 3 weeks without food?

"Right listen up everyone, we are swapping pairs for this exercise." Mr B looks at his clipboard. "Jessie and Brody. Max and Milly. Caroline and Sky. Emmie and Jade." I look over at Max, he looks rough this morning, he catches me looking at him and he blushes. I break the eye contact to look at Jessie who looks really pleased. Is something going on between them two? If so, why would Brody kiss me? But he has a habit of cheating, well he never really cheated on me. We weren't official although we were definitely heading that way. In time, we may have got there. After a lot of time, everything always feels like a climb with everyone other than Damon.

Wait, did he just say Emmie and Jade? No way, I can't work with that drama queen. "No way, absolutely not," Jade says whilst she walks to Mr B. Mr D looks at me and raises his eyebrow. The strange things he does is creepy. He's hot yes, but why is he showing concern when it is not appropriate?

"I wasn't asking Jade. You are all going to head off in your teams. On the piece of paper Mr Dudley gives you, this is what you will be doing." Mr D heads around and gives out the papers, he lingers in front of me, I reach for the paper and he keeps hold of it.

He whispers, "Be careful." Why is he so worried? He doesn't even know the half of what Jade has done to me. Or is he worried I may get into trouble? Again, he doesn't know the half of what I've gotten into. He releases the paper, and I cross my arms.

"I can handle myself," I mutter so only he can hear me. He nods and walks back to Mr B. Well this is going to be fun. Is it wrong to have a pang of jealousy? I hate that Brody's going with Jessie. I really do feel like we are just friends now, but I still like being his favourite. I look at the piece of paper in my hand. The writing is typed, it's weird that I find that odd. Writing by hand would have sufficed. In big black writing, it reads COLLECT WOOD FOR THE FIRE. I look around me. There is nowhere in the distance that I can see we can gather wood. We have to travel a while to get to the forest. The thick forest anyway. I'm exhausted just thinking about it.

"This is going to be the worst day ever!" Jade exaggerates her 'ever'. She's like a childish kid.

I let my hand fall over my face, "Trust me, the feeling is totally mutual." Spending all day with Jade is not on my bucket list.

"What are you doing?" Brody nudges me.

"Collecting wood." I sigh.

"You're going to get cold up there." Up where? But then I remember we are going to have to walk a while. He takes off his leather jacket and holds it out. I put my arms in and he pulls it over my shoulders. It's too big for me, but it will do.

"Thanks."

"And what about me?" Jade says in disgust. I honestly wouldn't care if I got cold, it would teach me not to forget a coat. I don't like to rely on anyone that way.

"Emmie's pregnant." Brody shrugs. Not that he would really care about Jade anyway.

"I hate you," she mouths at me. Everyone has dispersed into their pairs except Brody, Jessie, Jade and I. Jade walks off so she's out of earshot, looking at her phone.

"Are you going to be okay with her?" Brody seems nervous.

I giggle, "What's she going to do, bite me? She's harmless." Jessie laughs too but Brody's mood doesn't shift. Is he worrying about Damon again?

"Well be safe." He hugs me quickly.

"You too," I whisper in his ear before he releases me. I start to walk towards our destination. Jade follows ten feet behind me. After about half an hour I have to turn and wait for her because she's dropped behind. "Jade, come on!" I shout.

I hear her cursing and moaning. "I'm tired okay," she says when she reaches me.

"Seriously, we will never make it back before dark if you don't move your ass." We both know we don't like each other so I don't bother to be nice.

"God I hate you. I need to rest." She stamps her foot.

"I'm the one carrying a baby. It should be me that needs to rest. Let's move." I turn and carry on moving through the open space. The wind is strong, it breezes through Brody's jacket. We don't have long to reach the forest.

After another 10 minutes, we make it to the forest. It didn't take us too long. I sit down on a fallen tree trunk and rest. "Jade, we made it," I call, I'm exhausted. I wonder what the other activities were that could have been better suited for pregnant women.

Jade enters the forest a few seconds later and she slumps on the tree next to me. "Oh good. Thank the Lord. Start gathering sticks then."

Is she kidding me? I didn't walk all this way with her to do this single handed. "I don't think so. You need to help." I glare at her.

She stands up and stands over me. Maybe trying to intimidate me. "You know what? I've had enough of you. Everywhere I turn there you are. You've ruined my life. I hate you." I sigh and stand up and walk over the tree trunk, putting space between us so I don't punch her.

"Well, I don't like you much either. But we have to deal with the life we have been given," I say calmly, with my back to her.

"Your life is great. What are you talking about?" she scoffs.

"My life may be healing now but it never used to be." I still don't look at her.

"What's that supposed to mean?"

I take a deep breath, I'm not looking for sympathy. I just want her off my back. "My Dad used to abuse me."

She gasps, "I didn't know." Of course she didn't. It's only been about 2 months since anybody knew. I don't go sharing it around the school, especially not to the Queen Bee.

"Well, how would you? I then got kidnapped which is how I met Rider."

"That sounds hot." Jade goes all gooey.

"Yes, it was actually. And then I was admitted to hospital with a head injury. I was in a coma. Rider finally woke me. Then my Dad kidnapped me for a week. Rider and Brody found me eventually. No one could get me to wake even Rider. I finally woke for Rider as I knew I needed him. Then you tried to have me killed. That topped it all off. Your boyfriend is a psycho."

I turn to look at her, something inside of her snaps. She steps over the log as I did. She's standing in front of me. She's all red like ketchup. "That is a pretty bad past. Although Rex isn't a psycho. How dare you say that?" I thought she knew what an idiot he was before he shot me. I guess not.

"Are you serious? He's got issues." I hold my hands up in defence. She shoves me hard. I lose my footing and instead of falling to the ground, I start rolling downhill fast. Shit, my leg slams into a tree. I hear a crack, but I keep rolling. My head hits the ground and I black out.

My head hurts, my leg hurts. I open my eyes and my vision is blurry. I blink a few times and my vision becomes clearer. I sit up, my face feels wet. I touch the side of my head with my hand and I see red blood dripping off my hand. I wince at the pain that shoots through my head. I examine my leg. It seems okay from the outside. I try to get up but as soon as I bear weight on my right leg, I collapse on the floor and cry out. I look around me, I don't recognise anywhere. I'm doomed, I know Jade won't help me and I know I can't walk. I crawl to the nearest tree and pull myself up without putting my right leg on the ground.

I look around again and see a small cave like feature about 200 yards in front of me. I will have to take shelter, it's going to get dark soon. Okay, you can do this Emmie. I start to hop to the cave. I fall constantly, but I get up each time, determined to reach my goal. It's strange because although I know I'm doomed, I'm not scared, I've been through worse. I guess I'm not around people so what do I have to be afraid of? I'm not afraid to die. But I'm afraid to lose Damon. I reach the cave finally. It's not big, but just enough to shield me from the wind. I'm really cold. I fall to the floor, my back against the cave wall.

I pull Brody's coat tighter around me. It smells of him, I close my eyes, drifting in and out of consciousness. I check my phone but the battery has died, I really want to hear Damon's voice. I'm tired, really tired. It's dark outside now. How long can I hold on for?

I hear a muffled voice, it's way in the distance but I can't make out the words. "Emmie!" the voice calls. It's Brody. I shout back, but my voice isn't as strong or loud as I planned. I'm tired. I close my eyes again.

"Emmie!" The voice is louder, closer this time. But I don't have the energy to respond. I didn't even think to put pressure on my head until now. But it's too late.

"Emmie!" Now that was really close. Unless I'm hallucinating.

"Brody," I whisper. I call again a bit louder this time.

A light flashes in my face making me blink. I hold my hand up, covering my eyes. "Shit, Emmie." Brody runs towards me. I close my eyes again. "Emmie, you are okay. Thank God." I feel his warm hands on my face. I gasp as he touches my injury on my head. "Give me your t-shirt," Brody says.

"No, I'm cold," I mumble. He chuckles.

"Not you Emmie." Then who? Who's with him?

"Here," a voice says. Sounds like Sky. I feel something wrap around my head. I bet I look a lovely sight. I groan as he ties a knot in the shirt around my head.

"Can you walk Emmie?" Brody says softly.

"No, do you think I'd be here if I could? I think I've broken my leg," I whisper, I want to scream. To give him attitude like I usually do. But I don't have the energy. "Brody, I hate camping."

"Oh, my beautiful. I promise no more camping." Humour doesn't reach his voice. But I feel like there should be. He slides his arms under my knees and my upper back and lifts me off the cold floor. "Don't fall asleep," he growls. My eyes are still closed, all I want to do is sleep. Instead, I focus on his warm skin, his beating heart. And then silence.

"Emmie, fuck sake." I jolt awake, I haven't heard him so angry with me. Not when I wouldn't tell him the truth. Not when I've put myself in danger. Not ever. I open my eyes and he is glaring at me.

This is hard not to sleep. "Don't shout at me," I whisper.

"Well do as you're told then, for once in your life." He sighs. "Sky, go run ahead and tell the teachers she needs to go to the hospital." I don't hear Sky's response, only heavy fast footprints that are getting further away.

"How did you find me?" I say weakly.

"Jade said you fell down a bank. She never mentioned it was a damn cliff. What were you doing so close to a cliff Emmie?"

"Wow, Jade helped me? I thought she'd leave me to die. I didn't see it."

"How could you not see it? Do you need to get your eyes tested?" He puts his warm lips on my forehead.

"Obviously," I roll my eyes.

"Are you okay Emmie?" I hear Mr D.

"I hate camping." I groan.

"She's okay." He giggles. I see him looking over me. He brushes his fingers on the dried blood on my face. I flinch at his touch and bury my face closer into Brody's chest.

"Everyone is loaded onto the bus. Jessie has grabbed your bits from your cabin." Brody carries me on the bus and hits my good leg on the door.

"Careful," I scold him.

"Emmie, you are heavy. I've carried you for ages. Give me a break," he says sarcastically. I know I'm fat.

"Maybe you shouldn't have made me eat that muffin then," I say after he sits down with me lying on his lap so I don't need to move my leg. He laughs at me. I giggle too for a while until the pain is too much.

"Can I borrow your phone?" I ask Brody.

He lifts me up slightly so he can grab his phone from his back pocket. I find Damon's number. Wow, he has been texting Brody a lot, and he hasn't exactly worded them politely. I roll my eyes and press call.

"What do you want?" I hear his irritated voice.

"Nice to hear your voice too," I say weakly. I'm so tired.

"Emmie?" he says startled. "What's going on? You don't sound good." I sigh, how does he always know? "Emmie?" He is growing impatient.

"I er fell down a bank."

"More like a cliff Emmie." Brody looks down at me.

"Pass me to Brody," he demands.

"Why?" I say exhausted.

"Because he will give it to me straight."

I hold the phone up to Brody. "He wants to talk to you." He takes the phone from my hand. I close my eyes, I'm warm and comfy now.

"Emmie, I mean it god damn it. Stay awake." I mutter in agreement with him.

"Look, don't have a go at me. She fell down a cliff... yeah she's not great. She's hit her head and probably broken her leg... I'm doing what I can... Yes, we are going straight to the hospital... Yeah, bye then." He shoves his phone back in his pocket. "God, he frustrates me."

"Hmm," I say. "Brody, I'm tired."

"I know beautiful, we are nearly there."

I focus on Brody's breathing, to try and keep me from the pain and from falling asleep.

"Brody, go," Mr D calls. Brody stands up and takes me with him out the bus. I feel other arms around me. And Brody disappears from my view. Instead, I smell my favourite smell. I will my eyes to open. I am met with a gorgeous pair of eyes. Damon doesn't smile at me. He walks fast into the hospital.

Chapter 20

"You are beautiful," I say exhausted. He grudgingly lets out a chuckle but it doesn't last long. I bury my face into his chest and shut my eyes, I'm safe.

"Emmie, open your eyes." The warmth is gone. The smell is gone, did I dream it? Maybe I'm not really safe after all. I'm cold, I hurt and I want to sleep but people keep disturbing me. "Emmie, open your eyes," the voice says again.

"Open your damn eyes, Emmie," Damon growls, my eyes fly open wanting to see him. He is standing to my right.

"How are you feeling Emmie?" I follow the voice, it's the Doc. He's trying to examine me on my left. I frown.

"I'm tired and cold." Damon grabs my hand and tries to warm me.

"You can sleep after I've done some tests. Are you in pain?"

"Well yeah. I feel down a bank and broke my leg and hit my head." I shrug.

"Emmie, it was a cliff," Brody's frustrated voice fills the room. I try to find him and he is sat in his normal chair. He looks tired. I'm tired, let me sleep.

"You don't do things by halves, do you? Did you lose consciousness? We will need to do an X-Ray and a CT scan." He uses his torch pen thing to look into my eyes. I pull away. It's too bright for my sensitive eyes. "Emmie, let me look," he demands. I do as I'm told.

"Yeah, I was in and out."

"She hasn't been able to stay awake. I tried my best," Brody confesses.

"Okay, I'm going to take you for the tests now." I hold onto Damon's hand tightly. I don't want to let him go.

"It's okay, I'll be here when you get back," he says, reassuring me. I frown and let go. I close my eyes, I want to go home. I hate camping. I hate my life. The best part is Damon, his beautiful face. His musical voice, well that's what it sounds like to me. His scent that sends me into a daze.

"Emmie, you are going to go into this machine. You need to keep still."

"Can I sleep? Is it safe for the baby?"

"Emmie, you can't sleep."

"And the baby?" Why has he avoided the question?

"Emmie, I promise you the baby will be fine." Then why did he avoid the question? But I do trust him strangely. He helps me onto the machine, he's careful not to touch me for long and I am grateful for that. I lie back and let the machine do all the work. I close my eyes again.

I hear muffled voices. I try to concentrate on them. "What the hell happened?" Damon growls.

"The principal split us up into pairs. Emmie was paired with Jade." Brody is calm, surprisingly.

"With Jade? And you didn't think that was a problem?" I can take care of myself, Jade was just lucky there was a bank. Brody's voice echoes in my head, 'Emmie, it was a cliff.' I'd roll my eyes if I was fully awake.

"Of course I did. But you know Emmie, she's stubborn." Hey, I'm not that stubborn. Am I?

"Yeah, I know," Damon sighs. "She's frustrating sometimes." You find me frustrating? I guess I frustrate everyone. It's what I do and what I'll continue to do. Damon said to be myself, but I'm not sure that's such a good idea.

"Well, they were collecting wood for the fire. But they had a trek to get to the forest. Jade said they got into a fight and she slapped her. Emmie fell down a cliff. Jade left her to get help. I found her eventually, she was cold and she couldn't walk. I was more worried about the blood she'd lost. You know she didn't even bother to try and stop the bleeding? She was in and out of consciousness." I still can't believe Jade got help. Maybe I judged her wrong.

"Oh my god, how does that girl get into so much trouble?" Sully? He's here too? When did he get here?

"And the baby?" Damon asks.

"Baby's fine. Somehow. I guess she must have automatically protected the baby," the Doc says. My head must be okay if he's letting me sleep.

"Thank God. Wait till I get my hands on Jade," Damon curses.

"I don't think so. She has me to deal with," Brody mutters. I force myself to wake up more.

"Seriously guys, leave her alone. She didn't mean to do this." I wanted to shout it but I don't know what it was, a whisper or a squeak? I don't open my eyes though.

"Baby, you're okay." Damon grabs my hand. He's so warm.

"Of course I am. Takes more than that to kill me off." I giggle a little bit but no one joins me.

"That's not funny," Damon growls.

I shrug, "I thought it was funny. I want to go home."

"You can't go home yet baby. You look tired. Sleep." Damon says softly.

"I'm cold," I say. Damon climbs in next to me and I cuddle up to him. I breathe him in again. It doesn't take long before sleep finds me.

I don't know how long I'm asleep for but I wake up feeling more rested. I open my eyes and Damon is in the same place just staring at me. His gaze doesn't bother me like it does when everyone else does it. It feels like I'm the most beautiful person he's ever seen. His eyes tell me he is delighted at what he sees. He strokes my face. "I don't know what I'd do if I lost you."

"You won't lose me," I say strong now that I've slept.

"How can I be so sure? You walk into danger wherever you go. Of all places, you fall down a cliff whilst camping." He sighs. He looks broken, but there's no way he is as broken as me. He'll be okay in a day or so.

"In my defence, I did say I hated camping." I giggle. He kisses me on my forehead.

"Yes, you did baby." He laughs quietly.

We both hear the door go. I am gobsmacked, the last person I thought would walk in. I guess she did save me, even if she did cause the trouble. No, I caused the trouble, I can't blame anyone else. Damon slides off the bed in a hurry, leaving me cold again. I think I need a hot bath. He stops Jade before she can reach me.

"I don't think so. You nearly killed her. Was this planned? We all know how much you wanted her dead." Damon blows hot and cold too quickly, it makes my head spin.

"It was an accident. I was just so mad at her for Rex and then she was getting her paws into Brody." Oh no, Jade don't do this. Not now.

"Jade it's fine, I know it was an accident. I forgive you," I say quickly trying to shut her up. Did Damon notice?

He frowns, "What do you mean getting her paws into Brody?" Of course he did.

"Well, they were really close. They shared a room and a bed together. I was jealous I suppose." Oh shit, mention the one bed bit why don't you. I put my hand on my forehead.

He stares at me, he's mad. But then he does have a right to. "You shared a bed with him?" he says quietly, I wish he would just shout at me. I hate it when he's like this, it's deadly.

"No big deal Damon. There was only one bed. We are friends, I wasn't going to let him sleep on the floor. Anyone would think you didn't trust me."

"I'm glad you are okay. I'll leave you to it," Jade says and makes her hasty exit. Yeah, you run, before Damon murders us all. What did you do? I roll my eyes. Brody enters the room after Jade leaves. He seems more awake now. He comes over to me and sits on the bed and puts his hand on mine. Wow, he's so warm. But this doesn't help right now, not with Damon on the loose.

"I know what happened between you two. Don't try to deny it." Damon points his finger at Brody, looking at his hand on mine.

Brody moves his head to look at me startled. He raises his eyebrow. "You told him that we kissed?" he says awkwardly. No! Of course I didn't, I was going to obviously but not while I'm in my hospital bed. Are you crazy? You know what? This is why I prefer to keep to myself. It's too much drama.

"What? You guys kissed?" Damon shouts.

"Damon, I'm sorry," I whisper, tears fall down my face.

"Dude calm down. It was all me," Brody confesses. Damon, please listen. Is this make or break? I'm not worthy to be fought for, but I need you. Like life or death and it kills me that I feel like this. It makes me too vulnerable.

"I can't believe this," Damon shouts. He's not listening, why would he? Damon turns for the door.

"Damon please don't leave me," I beg. I knew I would fuck things up. I watch as my life, my heart and my love walk out of the door. Brody hugs me tight.

"Emmie, I'm sorry. I thought he knew."

"It's okay, I'm the only one who should be sorry," I mumble through my tears.

"Damon," I sob into Brody's shoulder. He strokes my hair, trying to soothe me. I should run after him, beg him. But why would he want me? I don't want to force him to want me.

"He will come around Emmie. Don't worry." He's angry, but he's never been this angry with me. My heart feels like it's tearing into little pieces. He broke me, no I broke me. This is all my fault.

"I need him, Brody." He sighs.

"I know you do Beautiful." I can feel like he wants to say something more, but he keeps his mouth shut. I'm sure I already know what it is. But I choose to ignore it.

"Emmie, what's wrong?" Momma asks. Brody doesn't let me go and I'm glad because I feel like I may crumble into tiny pieces if he does. Momma stands in front of the bed.

"Momma," I cry.

So Brody can talk to my Momma, he moves so he can sit next to me and hugs me from the side. I curl up on his chest like I did with Damon. Although it's not the same, nothing will be the same. Nothing is worth living without Damon. I tried to keep myself safe for him, but now that doesn't matter. His opinion mattered to me which is why he could get me to listen to him. He understands me or did, I guess. At least I can go back to being alone. Like I've always been.

"Rider just walked out on her," Brody says softly, not smug like I thought it would be.

"Why would he do that?" Momma frowns.

"He found out that Emmie and I kissed over the weekend. He already was pissed that we shared a cabin and bed."

"Oh, Emmie. Sweetheart. It will be okay." She walks to the other side of the bed and climbs in next to me. They both hold me but all they're doing is keeping me from breaking. They aren't going to fix me. Time won't fix me, people won't fix me. I was healing with Damon, I know I was. But now I'm never going to heal and that's okay because I don't deserve to be fixed. I shouldn't have got so close. But everything about him drew me in. I cry myself to sleep.

I'm in my old bedroom. Dad is standing at the side of my bed, staring at me. He's mad. But I just feel broken. "Daddy," I cry.

"I told you not to do this. This is your fault," Daddy growls.

"Daddy, I miss you." I miss you so much.

He sits on the bed next to where I'm sat and he hugs me, he smells the same. Before this would make me feel sick to my stomach but now it gives me comfort. He rocks me backwards and forwards like he used to do when I was younger. This calms me.

Damon appears in the bedroom. "Damon," I sob. Daddy stands and walks straight to Damon and punches him in the face. Damon clutches his face, takes a look at me and punches Daddy back again.

"I don't want you, Emmie," Damon growls. "You are nothing to me."

"I know. I'm nothing. I'm broken, why would anyone want me?" I sob into my hands.

"I want you, Princess. I've always wanted you." Daddy smiles. Damon hits Daddy again. If he doesn't want me then why is he fighting Daddy? I scream at them both to stop. They are fighting each other.

"Stop!" I scream again. But neither of them do.

"Emmie, Jesus wake up." Brody? I feel my body shaking or rather someone shaking me. I wake up disorientated. Brody's eyes are in pain, why? "Jesus Emmie, you were screaming in your sleep." That's not news to me. I know I have verbal nightmares when I'm not with Damon. My heart sinks when I think his name.

*

Days passed, the Doc says I have a concussion but no swelling or bleeds to the brain. I have a boot on my leg to help heal the break. Damon never came back or contacted me. But I don't expect him to. Brody stays with me, I think he's worried about me. I'm not worried, in fact, I don't feel anything but numbness. Pain comes and goes when I think of Damon. But time seems to be passing around me.

"Emmie, if you eat something I'll discharge you," Doc says. I ignore him, just staring at the door. "Emmie, do you want to go home?"

"I don't have a home," I mumble. Not anymore, maybe I should have ignored Damon and continued to not be myself. I'm confused, why would he say such a thing and then leave me? I know I'm a bad person. I know, I know. But I thought he understood me.

"Why don't you call him? Or text him?"

"I won't force someone to be with me. I'm not good enough for him. He will be happier without me."

"It sounds like you genuinely believe that," Doc scoffs.

"Yeah, because it's true." I don't look at him. Just continue to stare at the door. I see Danny walk through the door. He frowns. I guess I've disappointed him too. All this disappointment is exhausting. He doesn't say anything just lays next to me so he's blocking the view to the door. I stare into his eyes and he looks at mine. I bet I look empty.

"Danny, I will discharge her if she eats something."

Danny sighs, "She's always had a problem with food. Leave it with me, Doctor." He doesn't break eye contact with me.

"Okay. Come find me when she's eaten." You'll be waiting a while then. Go run along. I frown. I may have to discharge myself at this rate.

"You know, I never understood the connection you have with him and right now I think he's done more harm than good." I don't answer him. This isn't Damon's fault. He strokes my hair. Usually, this would make me sleepy but I have no desire to sleep. I'm exhausted but I can't face the nightmares. They used to be flashbacks of Daddy hurting me, of Rex hurting me. But they don't scare me anymore. What hurts the most is watching Damon leave. Watching Daddy leave. I'm alone, all alone. It hurts more than it did before Damon. I have a huge gaping hole in my chest. I feel like I can't breathe. You'll heal in time they say. I'm broken, I'm different I know I won't.

Danny gets out his phone and taps his phone. I ignore him and continue to stare at his face. My brother, my constant. "Are you going to leave soon?" I ask.

"I'm your Brother, we may fight because you're stubborn, but I will always come back to you." His words comfort me. But Damon said he would never leave me, and so did Daddy. He reaches for my face again, I'm numb so I don't care if he touches me. I don't think I would care if anyone touches me in this moment. We stare at each other for ages. I hear the door go, but I don't look as I know it's not Damon and I don't care who else it would be.

"Special delivery," Momma sings, trying to lift my spirits no doubt. I

Ignore her. But Danny reaches over and grabs the delivery and then he's back with me again. Face to face. He fiddles with something in his hands and then he moves his hand to my mouth. He shoves something in my mouth. I trust him not to poison me. But I am shocked that he's resorted to hand feeding me.

"Chew Emmie," Danny demands. I consider spitting it out but Danny clamps his hand over my mouth. I'm forced to chew, I frown. I guess I know now why he had the special delivery. He got Momma to get my favourite. Chocolate spread sandwich, the good stuff too. He knows once I've tasted this stuff there's no going back. I grab the rest of the sandwich and continue to eat. Danny smiles.

"That's mean," I mumble with a mouthful.

"Hey, if it works then I will use it against you." He grins. I poke my tongue out at him and he laughs and so does Momma. We hear the door go again but I still continue to watch Danny and eat my sandwich.

"Wow, how did you do that?" Doc sounds impressed.

"I know my sister." He shrugs with a huge grin. You know some things about your sister, you will never know me the way Damon knows me. No one ever will. I will not be making that mistake again. I will grow old the way Daddy wanted. With my baby, will he want to have anything to do with the baby? Will I want him to? Seeing him and not having him will be torture. I don't think I can handle that. I push the thought to the back of my mind, I don't want to think about that right now. I still have time. Time is something I'm sure of, death would be too easy for me. I deserve to suffer, however, my family don't and that would kill them.

"Well, you are free to go then, Emmie. Take it easy." The door opens again.

"Hey, beautiful." Brody's calm voice surrounding me. Suffocating me, it shouldn't but he reminds me of something I've lost. I don't respond, I feel rude not responding but nothing is forcing me to answer.

"Let's get you home Emmie," Momma says. I don't have any urge to move. Danny frowns, trying to read me. He gets off the bed and looks at me questioningly. He seems to have found an answer and leans over to pick me up. I don't think I could walk anyway.

I zone out on the walk to the car, the car journey and the walk to my new room. Danny kisses me on the forehead and leaves my room. Brody sits next to where I'm lying. I didn't know he was with us. "I guess you are not going to school?" His lips turn down on each side.

"No, I can't." I curl up into a ball. Damn boot, it's in the way.

He strokes my forehead. "That's okay, rest up."

"I know I have no right asking. But will you come back after school?" He's my friend, I know I have no romantic desire anymore. I don't know if it took Damon to leave me or when our kiss happened. I'm not sure, but I know I still need him. I know he still feels the same way, which is why I'm a bad person for asking him to stay. But it's not like I wasn't clear about how I felt, right?

"Anything for you. I'll see you later." He kisses my forehead too and then he leaves. I'm alone in my room. I stare at my phone, but nothing changes apart from the time. Tick tock. I know I'm going insane again, but honestly what is there left to do? I haven't slept since I dreamt of my Daddy and Damon fighting, the horror of that was too real. Brody questioned me about it, but I vowed to myself that I would keep my distance from everyone. I can't let anyone in, the walls and windows are permanently locked tight. I hug my tummy.

"It's okay baby, Daddy will be back for you. I know him." I think I do anyway, unless he's like me and lets me see only things he wants me to.

I don't cry anymore, I'm all cried out. I stare at my door, the shut door. It's just me against the world. I've had enough of laying down, I'm going for a bath. I don't bother asking for help, Bro might not worry about seeing me naked but I mind. I walk to the bathroom not realising how heavy the boot would be. I lock the door behind me. I run the bath, I strip and take the boot off. I fall rather than lower myself into the bath. "Ow," I mumble. Water spills over the side.

"Emmie!" Danny calls. He bangs on the door and tries to open it. That's why I locked it. "Emmie, answer me."

"Go away, Danny."

"What are you doing? Why did you lock the door?"

"I'm having a bath."

"What was that bang?"

"I just fell...into the bath. So it's all good."

"Sis, I don't like the door being locked." He's stressing out, I knew he'd be nervous. But this much? Nah I didn't expect that.

"Well, I'm not getting out now. I'll probably fall out." I hadn't got that far yet.

"That didn't give me much confidence." I like to live life on the edge, what can I say? I'm not going to drown. I start to wash using my strawberry body wash. I smell normal again. Danny is quiet but I know he's still out there. Once I finished, I pull the plug. I then start to think about how to get out. I lift myself up and keep my right leg extended out in front of me. Lift it over the bath and oh shit I fall out the bath. I'm not as strong as I thought. Oh well, at least I'm out. "Ouchy."

"Emmie, what happened?"

"I um fell out the bath, but it's all cool." Loud thumps hit the door and then it's open and Danny is standing in the doorway. He grabs me a towel and puts it around me.

"Damn it, Emmie." He lifts me up off the floor and carries me to my bed. "Stay there, don't move." Where am I going to go? I roll my eyes. He walks back to the bathroom and grabs another towel and my ghastly boot. He dries my leg and puts the boot back on my leg.

"You broke my door." I glare at him.

"Yeah, well now I don't have to worry about you locking yourself in." He glares back at me. He shakes his head like he is shifting a bad thought. I poke my tongue out and he grins. He walks to some drawers and finds some clothes for me to wear. I didn't unpack so I guess Momma did it. I have no idea where anything is, but he doesn't seem to have much trouble. He helps me dress. "Try to get some sleep, Sis." I shake my head. I can't sleep. "Sis, you need sleep, you look exhausted. I know you haven't slept."

"Danny, please don't force me to do this too," I beg.

He lays next to me. "Please, just try. I will be here. You are safe." No, I'm not safe but I curl up into his chest and shut my eyes.

Why is it always my old bedroom? I'm alone in the bedroom. Standing in the middle of the room, I start to sink into the floor, a big black hole at my feet and I continue to fall. Damon appears in front of me. He smiles, not at me but at the black hole sucking me in. He continues to smile. Daddy appears next to me. He is sinking with me. Daddy holds me close. Is he trying to tell me something? That I should have gone down with him before? Things were more hopeful then. Even if I did lose myself. I'm in darkness, I can't see anything. But I feel hands touching me and I keep slapping them off me but more hands come. I want to be alone. I try to beat them off like they are bugs crawling on me. My heart is beating fast, please stop. I scream. Hands touch my shoulders and I open my eyes.

Danny is holding me, they are his hands. "You are safe." I want to scream at him that I'm not but I let him comfort me.

"Hey, beautiful." I look up and see Brody smiling at me. Danny strokes my cheek and leaves the room.

"Hey." Brody sits where Danny left.

"How are you?" I shrug. You wouldn't understand how I'm feeling so why bother explaining? "Have you eaten today?" Yes, I have, I was forced to eat a sandwich.

"What is it with people and food?" I say tersely.

"Because we need it." Brody lifts one side of his lips. Well, the only thing I need is him. I can't even think his name anymore.

"Good for you," I sigh.

"Emmie, think of your baby."

I explode, "Don't give me that crap. My baby is fine. Leave me be," I shout. Why do people have to interfere? I wish... I wish I was actually alone. Just me, then I wouldn't have to worry about keeping others happy. I could do what I want to do.

"I'm worried about you." He crosses his arms.

"Well, you don't need to be."

"Emmie, please."

"Don't Emmie me," I shout.

He holds his hands up in defeat, "I'll just go then."

"Wait, don't go. Please don't leave me," I say urgently. As much as I don't want him getting through my wall, I still want him at the door.

"Okay, beautiful."

Momma walks in and we both look up. "Hey, Sweetheart. How are you?" I shrug.

"I'm cooking your favourite, veggie curry." God, I can't stomach food. "Brody, you should stay for dinner."

"I'm not hungry," I say.

"Emmie, you need to eat," she scolds. Again, I have three weeks before I actually need to eat. I'm fine.

"That's a bit of a touchy subject at the moment, Esme." I slap him and he shrugs.

"Emmie, come on, be reasonable."

"I hate that word. Reasonable. Everyone uses it against me," I growl.

Momma chooses not to argue with me further, "Well you're more than welcome to stay for dinner Brody. Try and get her to join us for dinner." Brody nods and Momma leaves the room.

"You should be kinder to your Mom. She's trying to help you."

I sigh, "I know. All these emotions Brody. I can't take them all at once." I hold my head with my hands. Brody hugs me tight.

"I know Beautiful."

Someone clears their throat, I look up and Desmond is standing in the doorway. I scramble off the bed onto my feet. He scares me for some unknown reason, even when I feel numb. "Emmie," he says harshly, with his arms crossed. He is leaning against the door frame. To someone on the outside, he may look unthreatening. But to me, he unsettles me more than anyone has before. More so than Rex or my Daddy. My Daddy that was only protecting me. I believe that now, for me to believe that, I must be ill. If someone else told me the same thing in the same situation I would be worried about them.

"Yes," I stutter. I glance at Brody who is frowning at me. I feel terrified so maybe I look terrified, probably something he's never seen.

"Do you remember the rules of living under my roof?" How could I forget? The memory lingers in my mind over and over. But it was followed by a good one. The smell of him. I will not think his name, it will make my heart stop.

"Of course," I squeak.

"So you will join us for dinner shortly."

"Of course Desmond, I'll be there."

"Good. See you both for dinner." He smiles and leaves us. I sag with relief and hobble back to the bed.

"What was that?" Brody demands.

"What?"

"What's the deal with him?"

"I don't know what you mean Brody." There is only one person who could tell I was lying and he isn't here. He never will be. I had very mixed feelings about him telling if I was lying and now it doesn't matter.

"You don't listen to anyone. So why him?" I listened to one other person too. When he pushed me, anyway.

"It's his house. His rules." I shrug.

"Has he threatened you?"

"No." Yes, but ha, you can't tell if I'm lying. My inner-self wants to poke my tongue out at him.

"Good." He doesn't sound like he believes me but he chooses to ignore it.

"Dinner's ready," Momma calls from downstairs.

Brody helps me get up off the bed. Thank god Doc didn't put a cast on my leg, I don't think my body would be strong enough to get myself around on crutches. I nearly trip down the stairs but Brody catches me from behind. I haven't got used to this boot yet. But I've always been clumsy so I'm used to it.

"You aren't safe even in your own house," he huffs. But when I turn to look at him he is grinning at me. I choose to ignore him. When we walk into the dining room, Danny strides over to me and puts me over his shoulder and I squeal.

"Danny." I slap his back. He places me gently into a chair at the table.

"Just helping my Sister to her seat." He giggles and so do I. Danny hasn't shown me this sort of affection for years.

The food is already set on the table. Urgh, I can't stomach anything right now. Danny sits on my right and Brody sits on my left. Desmond sits in front of me. Being this close unsettles me. I feel my stomach churning. "Dig in everyone," Desmond announces.

Yes, you've got that right for once Desmond, I'd like to bury myself in a hole. I pick up my fork and start stirring my rice into the curry and then just play with it over and over. Danny places his hand on mine to stop my fork from turning, over and over. I look at him and he mouths, "Eat." My face sinks and he must have seen it because he frowns.

"Emmie, I don't know what Damon has done to you," I wince as Desmond says his name, "but I will not tolerate people not eating a perfectly good meal." I clutch the side of Danny's shirt to steady myself. I want to scream. Danny looks at me and grabs my hand from his side and holds it under the table and squeezes it to reassure me, I guess.

"Emmie, is there something wrong with the food?" Momma asks softly. I shake my head, no words will come out. I wouldn't know because I haven't even taken a mouthful.

"Guys back off, she doesn't need this." Danny looks at me again. "Emmie, just eat a few mouthfuls." Desmond is glaring at me and Danny. Why are people so concerned about food? I know people are starving in the world, if I could give them my food then I would. I take the fork in my left hand so I can keep hold of Danny's hand. I force myself to eat the food, I don't taste it, just chew and swallow. Just a few mouthfuls have left my stomach feeling bloated and heavy. I feel so tired again. I lean my head on Danny's shoulder whilst everyone makes idle chit chat. I just watch and listen. I close my eyes and focus on the voices.

"Emmie, it's rude to fall asleep." His voice drills through me as I wake suddenly. Danny has his arm around me, supporting me.

"She's tired, leave her be," Danny scolds. I am tired, so tired. "She doesn't sleep well anymore," he says like it's nothing new to him but maybe to other people.

"Because of him? Because of Damon," Desmond sighs. I shudder at his name being mentioned too often. Please stop saying his name.

Should I bother explaining? Is he worth it? Yes, I should, this isn't... this isn't Damon's fault. Wow, that was hard. "No, not because of him. It's because of Daddy. Because of Rex. Because people leave me," I say sleepily. I snuggle into Danny's chest and shut my eyes. They don't question me, unless they do and I can't hear them.

A chair squeaks against the floor making my teeth cringe. I am folded into Danny's arms and he is carrying me upstairs. I hear two sets of footsteps. Danny slowly lowers me onto the bed.

"Goodnight Beautiful," Brody mumbles in my ear, I can feel his breath on my ear.

"Night," I mumble back. Well, that's what I tried to say but I'm not sure if it came out the way I heard it in my head.

I am in the middle of the desert. Nothing but open sandy land. I'm all alone. I see a figure in the distance. I squint, it's him. It's Damon, he sees me and walks away. I run as fast as I can towards him screaming his name. But he doesn't turn back, he just gets further away out of my reach.

I'm now in Damon's safe house. No one is here. I call but no answer. I find a door that doesn't belong in the real safe house. I open the door, its light, too bright that I have to blink to adjust. There is a sign that reads 'congratulations' and money falls from the ceiling. I don't care for money, this isn't what I desire. It all goes dark and another door clicks open on my right. It's the same room and my family stands in the room. Buzzer sounds and red lights go off. Nope, this isn't what I desire either. Another door clicks open in the same place and I step inside. Daddy stands in the room. I miss my Daddy and this is close to what I desire most. But the alarms sound again. I move forward to the next room.

Damon stands in the room leaning up against the wall. My heart skips a beat. His beauty drawing me in. He is holding something in his hand. It's red and it's pulsing. It's a heart, I realise it's my heart. He smiles, not my favourite smile but enough to get butterflies in my tummy. His hand clenches around my heart and crushes it into tiny pieces. I drop to my knees and let out a scream. This hurts, he has my heart and he's crushed it into tiny pieces. He laughs an evil laugh. Like he is enjoying my pain. A voice comes through on a microphone.

"This is your biggest desire, yet it's something you can never have." They emphasise the word 'never'. "Take a good look Emmie, this is the last time you will see your biggest desire," the voice says.

Damon is still looking at me. "I will keep this, you will always be trying to find it, and find me. But know I will always be far away." I wouldn't take it back anyway, it only truly belongs to him. Only him, I don't want it. Damon's face multiplies all around me and continues to do so. So eventually it's all I can see. I curl up into a ball and sob.

"Emmie. You're okay." Danny is hushing me. My head is on his chest. His hand in my hair. I let out a sigh of relief that that wasn't true. Well, it was, but the dream itself wasn't.

"You okay?" I nod into his chest. No, seeing him so clearly in front of me tore me more apart.

"What time is it?"

"8.30 am Emmie. I have to go to work." He seems worried to leave me. I won't make him stay. I won't make anyone stay.

"Okay." I shift my weight off his chest so he can get up. He kisses my forehead and leaves. I close my eyes, I can't breathe. I can't think clearly. Pressure is building, I don't want this life anymore. All I can see is him spinning around and around. I feel myself drifting from my body before this scared me. But now I smile, the pain fading.

Chapter 21

When I wake, I'm lying on the beach in the sun. I take a deep breath smelling the salty sea. Feeling the sand between my fingers. There is no one on the beach. I am in a bikini, not something I would choose to wear. But I'm alone, so what does it matter?

"Emmie. Get in the water. We want to get you wet." I sit up on my elbows to see who is in the sea. Damon and Brody are ready and waiting in the sea. If this is my safe place, I can dream what I want? I never knew that. I get up and run into the sea. Water splashing up my legs, I run deeper into the sea and run into Damon's arms. He leans back so he falls into the sea and he brings me with him. He kisses me under the water briefly before we emerge above the water again.

Brody grabs my hand and pulls me into his chest and kisses me. I pull back and look at Damon. "It's okay, it's your dream world. I don't mind." Is this because I truly want him to have these feelings? I thought I put these feeling to rest. But I don't feel anything anymore. So what does it matter? I'm free here. I don't need to worry about protecting myself. It's not real anyway so I kiss Brody back.

I don't know how much time passes, I honestly don't care. The three of us have taken strolls in the sunset on the beach. Romantic meals together. We've gone to the cinema, shopping. I don't have to eat here, nor do I have to worry about other people.

I get odd moments with my body. I heard Desmond mention that he did kill that other girl, but I was a bigger prize. I'm a problem he has to deal with. I am not classed as his family. I don't want to be his family. I heard Danny crying when he realised I left. If I did feel anything I think I may have cried too. He has been a rock to me, and I left him. But he wants me to be happy.

I am on the beach with Damon and Brody. We are all in beachwear. I don't feel exposed but things change. I thought I was in control, but I'm not. I didn't think this, nor would I want to. I look down at my body and I am in a wedding dress. I don't understand. Damon grabs my right hand and Brody grabs my left. I look at each of them in turn and they both are wearing suits. My mouth drops open, they both look breath-taking. They both grin my favourite sexy smiles.

A man in a vicar outfit stands behind us. I flinch at the presence of someone else in my dream world but then I remember I don't care. I don't feel anything. "We have gathered here today to witness this wedding," the man says.

Okay…? So I know I'm still dreaming... So who the HELL is getting married? This is so weird.

"You are the most beautiful woman I've ever seen." I melt at Damon's words. If only his words were true. But I choose to enjoy this moment.

"I agree. You look beautiful baby." Brody's voice is always so soft and gentle. So which one will I be marrying in my dream world?

"Damon Rider, do you take this woman to be your wedded wife?" the man says. Okay, so Damon. He would obviously be my first choice.

"I do," he says without any doubt.

"Brody Rivers, do you take this woman to be your wedded wife?" Wait? I'm marrying them both? That's not even legal. But I remember that this isn't real. But it feels so real.

"I do," he says. I don't understand. Whoever is getting married, I will kill them. Why would they do this to me?

"Damon, if you would like to read your vows," the man says and Damon nods. I look into his eyes and he looks into mine.

"Emmie, the day you entered my life you turned it upside down. You were such a strong, smart mouth, beautiful woman. Who knew you would mean so much to me? You are having my baby and I want us to be a family. You keep me on my toes and you make me question my life." That sounds like something the real Damon would say and then I push that thought away because no he wouldn't, he doesn't want me.

"That was lovely. Brody, if you would like to read yours." I turn to look at Brody.

"Emmie, I've never felt like this about anyone. I admit I've had my fair share of girls. But you stand out from every single one. You take my breath away. I want to be in this little bubble for the rest of my life. I will have you any way I can. You are stubborn, strong and hot. You are one of a kind." Why does this all feel so real?

"Wow, these vows are making me cry. Anyway, that's it. You both may kiss the bride." I never said I do! But I guess it doesn't really matter now. They both take it in turns to kiss me. "I now pronounce you Husbands and Wife." The man whoops and cheers.

"Let's go on our honeymoon," Damon whispers seductively in my ear.

"Yeah, we want to take you to bed and show you how much we love you," Brody whispers in my other ear. We then appear in a hotel suite.

"Mrs Rider-Rivers, let's get you out of that dress." Mrs Rider-Rivers? That sounds so weird but I love it. Bearing both of their names. Damon undoes my dress, his fingers skimming my skin. Fake Damon doesn't affect me the way real Damon does, I feel nothing. The dress falls at my feet and Damon carries me to the bed. I am numb.

I think Danny may hate me because I don't hear or feel him with me anymore. I feel cold all the time. Even though I am in the sun here. Damon and Brody never leave me. I don't want to leave them. I don't know quite how long has passed since I came here. I feel pain from my body sometimes but I can push it away. We seem to still be on our honeymoon, none of us wants to leave. It's been great.

Sharp pain shoots through me. I clutch my stomach. This pain is unbearable. I don't feel anything here, what's going on? Damon and Brody are by my side. Holding my shoulders. "Baby what's wrong?" Damon's voice is shaky.

"You okay Beautiful?" Brody says, scared. He is never scared. Frustrated sometimes. But he's usually so calm.

"No, it hurts," I say through my teeth. Almost hissing. "I'm scared."

"Don't leave us, baby," Damon cries. What do you mean leave? I don't choose to leave, does he know something I don't? I don't want to leave them. This has been the best life I could ever imagine. I know it's just a dream but I want to stay. I know I'm going back... but I don't want to go back to a life without Damon.

I open my eyes, I feel disorientated. Where am I? The room is dark like a basement. I sit up but something huge is blocking me from sitting up easily. I look down, the thing blocking me is my stomach, it's huge. What the fuck. My leg boot has disappeared too. How long have I been out?

That means... he didn't come back for me. Pain punches me in the chest. I can't breathe.

I stand up off the metal frame I'm sat on. I feel stiff and aching like I've fallen off a cliff. I wince at the memory. Not many people can say they've added that to their CV. Pain sears through my stomach and back. My trousers are wet and so is the bed. I'm huge, like a bloody whale. Am I in labour? No, this is too soon, I haven't mentally prepared myself. No, this is all happening too quick.

The pain continues to shoot through my body, it keeps me breathing. Come on Emmie, pull yourself together. You need to get your baby out of here. I make my way down a hallway. The hallway has many doors all the way down like in a hotel hallway. It's dark and the doors are metal and rusting away. It's dirty and smelly in here like sewers. I try the first door for a way out. It's just another room but not just any old room. There is an armchair in the corner and my feet stick to the floors. I crouch down to examine the sticky stuff. I think... it's blood. I check my body and I have bandages scattered around my body.

What the hell has been going on? I must find a way out, so I try another door. The first thing I notice in this room is the bathtub. Above the bath is writing, red writing. Is it more blood? I suspect that it is. It reads, 'Daddy loves you.' I know Daddy loves me, but he wouldn't do this. He isn't alive anyway. Who else would do this? A puddle of blood in the bath. Who's been bathing me? How could I sleep through this?

I don't want to find out. So I try another door. This seems more promising. This room is also covered in blood but it only houses a cabinet and has another door. How am I still alive after all this blood? I examine the door but it's locked. Of course it is.

"What the fuck? Where the hell are you? You stupid bitch." I know that voice from anywhere, the voice that terrifies me. This is why his presence scared me because deep down I knew what he is capable of. "I will find you. Today is the day you are going to die! It's going to be great. I will make you suffer if you don't show yourself."

Today I die? No, not before my baby is safe. I can't let him find me. "I'm so glad you are awake. We will have so much fun together. No one will save you. They have all forgotten about you." His plan must be to distract me. Well, it's worked. I honestly wouldn't be surprised if they forgot me. I'm no one.

I search the cabinet in the corner and surprisingly I find an axe. Yes, this is good. Blood covers my hands. The handle is all sticky with blood. This is gory, like something out of a horror movie. I hit the door with the axe and my shoulders throb from the impact. An echo surrounds the room. Shit, he's going to hear me but I continue to hit the door, ignoring all pain.

"I found you. I have to say it was fun trying to find you." I spin around in horror. He looks the same. The same he always has to me. I need answers.

"Desmond what's going on? Why are you doing this?"

"You ruined my family. We have all moved on without you. Now I'm going to have fun killing you. Watch the life leave your face." If they've truly moved on, then he wouldn't need to kill me. I would just leave. I end up ruining people's lives without even realising. What did I do this time apart from existing?

"You wouldn't..." I hope, but I know he would.

"Oh, but I will Emmie. I am so happy you are awake because it means I get more fun with you. You just made my day." I haven't seen him so happy, so pleasured before.

"Ow." I put my hands on my knees to absorb the pain.

"What's wrong with you?" his voice is dull.

"Nothing," I lie.

"You're in labour. This is great. Things keep getting better and better. I will take your baby. Let them grow up and their fate will be the same as yours." Why? He's sick. Nothing gets past him, does it? I won't let my baby be in danger.

"No you can't have my baby," I yell. I will go down trying to protect Damon's baby. The last thing I have left of him.

"Fighting talk, I like that." He shrugs but moves closer to me.

"Don't come near me, you murderer." The flashback of him confessing his sins to me comes into my mind.

"She was a means to an end. But you, you are special because you are the prettiest girl I've ever seen. You are only alive now because I have a soft spot for you." Soft spot? I can't bear much of a soft spot if he's going to kill me. Why do people keep saying I'm pretty? Right now, I'm not going to complain if that's the only reason why I'm still alive.

I'm angry. " Oh, well if you put it like that then I feel lucky."

"I am going to miss you when you are gone." Well, the feeling is not mutual.

He comes towards me again. He put his hands around my throat, pinning me against the wall. He is sucking the life out of me. Before I know what I am doing, I hit him over the head with the axe. Blood splatters all over my face. He falls to the floor. I am covered in blood. I manage to get the door open. This pain is unbearable. I must get help.

Tears fill my face, I must find safety. I run outside and feel the sun on my face. I take in my surroundings. I'm not far from Damon's safe house, even if he won't help me, maybe Sully will. I need to feel safe again. It's been so long. I keep running, my body taking over. Autopilot taking me to safety.

I reach the safe house. I type in the code with shaky hands. What if he changed it? What would I do then? It clicks open, oh thank god. Thank you, thank you. I run to his office, I don't even know if he's here but I have to check. The office door is shut but I barge through. He is standing right there with Sully. I don't care if he doesn't want me. I need him. I run into his arms. He is stunned.

"Emmie?" he says startled. I am running on adrenaline.

"Emmie you're covered in blood..." Sully says worriedly. Yes, yes I am.

"Emmie. You are here?" he says like he doesn't understand nor expect me to be here.

"I'm safe. Please tell me I'm safe Damon." I feel safe, but I need confirmation from him. I need to know he will take care of me. Well, take care of the baby.

"You're safe baby," he said baby? Why?

"Good," Is all I can say before my legs give out but Damon's strong arms support me. I can relax, or drift asleep, whichever comes. I've been tense for too long.

He carries me in his arms to the car, I just watch his beautiful face. I breathe in his scent. He makes me dizzy. I've missed him more than I realised and that is stupid because I nearly died missing him. "Where have you been baby?" he whispers when we get in the back of the car.

"Mentally or physically?" I mumble, I want to stay awake. I don't want him to disappear again.

"Both I guess."

I don't know why I even consider telling him. Does he even care? "Physically, Desmond has had me locked in an abandoned scary building. Mentally I've been with Brody and you." I exaggerate the word you. "The fake you anyway. The one that wants me," I whisper.

"Wait, hold up." He stares down at me. I am lying on his lap. He strokes my face and I push him off. I can't let him get close to me again. Even though I know he's like weeds, he's buried at the roots inside me. "You think I don't want you?" What does he mean? Of course he doesn't.

"Baby, I love you."

"Don't lie, I can't handle the pain."

"I'm sorry I caused you pain. But I do love you." He goes to stroke my face again, I stop his hand. He frowns at me. "Please let me touch you."

"I can't, watching you leave me nearly killed me. I can't have you get close again. I won't." I can see tears in his eyes.

"I'm not going anywhere. Danny told me how bad you were. I'm so sorry." He's seen Danny? How is he? There are so many questions I want to ask. "He said your nightmares were the worst." I shudder at the memories of the nightmares. "You never told Danny about your nightmare?"

It doesn't sound like a question but I answer it anyway. "No, like I said, no one is getting close to me again."

"What were the memories, Emmie?"

What is it that makes me want to tell him? "My nightmares used to be of Daddy and Rex. But they changed when you left me. Some were you leaving and some were you telling me you didn't want me. Daddy stayed with me through them all." I sigh recalling the worst. "The worst one, the last one I had. I had many rooms with my desires in. They all led up to my biggest desire. You. You held my heart in your hand, where it belongs and then you crushed it. You enjoyed it." I pause for a second. "A voice told me you were my biggest desire and that I would never have you. You told me you would keep my heart, not because you wanted it but so I knew that I could never have it back. I would never be able to find you or my heart."

Tears fall down his face. "I've done more damage than everyone put together, didn't I?" I nod and bury my head in his chest. He strokes my hair and I let him.

We reach the hospital and he carries me inside. "I'm fat Damon. A big fat whale." I get the feeling he wanted to laugh but after my confessions, he doesn't.

"You aren't fat, baby." His voice sings through my body.

We reach the reception desk. "Page Doctor Grey. Now!" Damon growls. The receptionist jumps up and does as she's told, taking one look at me. I must look awful.

"Ah," I call out. The pain. Damon's eyes are in pain. I've never seen him like this before. I clutch tighter to him.

"Go into room 1, he will be there soon," she says. Damon doesn't thank her, he just takes me into the directed room.

He places me on the bed, I don't want to let him go but I decide I must let him go. The Doctor runs into the room and he stops and stares at me. "Emmie?" he gasps.

"Ah, yeah?" It's me, plain old me.

He closes the gap between us. He frowns and examines me. "It looks like Emmie is in labour Rider. Where did you find her?" I am here, you know.

"I didn't, she just ran into my office and into my arms. I've been dreaming of her for months. I was just giving up hope and then she appears like an angel." Like an angel? That's so sweet. But I'm no angel. Dreaming of me? Why? You don't want me.

"You think I'm an angel? If I didn't look like a damn whale, then it may have been cute." He chuckles softly.

"You don't look like a whale. You are beautiful." He looks at me the way I love. I shake my head. I find him hard to resist right now.

"Emmie, you are ready to start pushing." No, I'm not. I'm not ready for anything. If I could go back to my safe place, then I would.

"No, I can't. I want my brother." He was my rock before I left. I need him now.

"Yes, you can. You can do this," the Doc says. No, this is too soon.

"I'm scared."

"Come on Emmie, let's do this. Let's meet your baby." He opens my legs and I clamp them shut again. "Emmie, don't start this, I have to look to get the baby out." I don't want him touching me, let alone looking down there.

"Baby, let him do it." Damon grabs my hand and I squeeze it hard, but he doesn't say anything. He strokes my sweaty forehead. I want my brother, where is he? I push a lot, I am so exhausted. I cry out in pain but it doesn't help. Eventually, I hear a baby scream and then everything goes dark. Everything quiet. This feels like when my heart stopped. Is this death? It's peaceful.

After a while, I wake up in one of the bloody rooms. Desmond is sat in the arm chair. "What's going on?" I say.

"You're awake, oh good." Awake? What does that mean?

"I'm having a nightmare. Great." I put my hand on my forehead and let it fall in irritation.

"No, you're not, do you really think you could get out of here?"

"I did get out of here."

"You lost a lot of blood. You were hallucinating." I did get out, didn't I? Or was it a magical dream that I saw Damon again. I start to doubt myself.

"I did get out of here. I didn't dream it." Unless I wanted it to be real. It felt real but I know nothing anymore.

"You believe what you want. I'm still going to kill you either way."

"Please don't." I begin to sob.

"Here we go. Here comes the begging." He folds his arms, waiting in anticipation.

"I wouldn't beg you," I scoff, not for this scumbag.

"Oh, you will soon enough. What shall I do first? I want you in many pieces. Shall I take your foot first? Or a hand maybe? The possibilities are endless." He seems like he holds each possibility in his palms, weighing up the pros and cons.

"You aren't taking anything, you creep."

"I like a bit of fighting talk. That other girl didn't have much fight in her. She just kept her mouth shut. It was a bit boring actually." He moves closer to me.

His face is inches from mine. He grabs my face and his lips touch mine. I scream and thrash out. "Get the hell off me." Get off me. I continue to lash out.

"Emmie, you are safe," Damon says softly.

"Great. Lover boy is here," Desmond groans.

"I knew this was a nightmare."

"Well, I'm glad to see I haunt you in your dreams." You aren't my worst nightmare.

I open my eyes and Damon is staring at me. "Great. Just great," I mutter.

"What?" He frowns.

"Another dream." I take a deep breath. "Okay, do it," I wince.

"Do what baby?" he asks.

"Walk away. It will hurt and it will break me. Just get it over with."

He puts his hands either side of my head. I frown. "I'm not going anywhere," he whispers. Okay, this doesn't normally happen.

"Yet, why are you dragging this out? Did you want to torture me first?" A tear falls down his face.

"Emmie, please. You are not dreaming. What will change your mind? I broke you, didn't I?"

"I broke myself. I only have myself to blame. I did this. Everything comes down to my fault."

He slides in next to me and I lean against his chest and he wraps his arms around me. I feel like I'm home, his scent, his warmth and his touch. He kisses my forehead.

"Damon? Where's my brother? I want to see my brother." He sighs. "I want to know what's been going on."

"Well, I confronted your Mom. I'm sorry Emmie, she believed Desmond and his lies. She wouldn't even check to see if you were okay. Hell, they went on their honeymoon after that." Honeymoon? It was them that got married? "Shit, sorry baby, you don't know about the wedding, do you?"

"Actually, I knew someone got married."

"How?"

"I er lived it. In my dream world, I knew it wasn't real but then I was in a wedding dress standing in front of a vicar with you and Brody."

"You got married? To who?" he says, shocked.

I shrug and bury my face in his chest. "To both of you." He laughs and his chest vibrates making my head bob up and down.

"Damon, where's Danny?"

"He would be here if he could." What does that mean? If he could.

"What do you mean?" I whisper.

"After the wedding, he came to see me. He believed you were in trouble too." He sighs. "Of course he hated me for the way you were."

"Where's my brother, Damon?" Why does he sound like he is bearing bad news?

"I'm sorry, I tried to help him. I did." His voice is sad. Tried to help him? What was wrong with him?

"Damon? Where the hell is he?" I scream, why won't he just tell me? Please god, please tell me he's not...

"He fell off the rails when he realised what happened. He would pick fights with anyone. He got in some pretty bad ones too. Many times he went looking for trouble. Even came to mine. I wouldn't fight with him." God damn it, just tell me.

"That doesn't sound like Danny."

"It wasn't him Emmie. He was angry at himself. He nearly killed Desmond. Trust me, I wanted him dead too but if we killed him we wouldn't have found you. Desmond pressed charges." Of course he did. Sick son of a bitch. So he's in jail then? Hope courses through me.

"So Danny is in jail?"

"Not exactly. Your Mom got him out of jail. But he couldn't handle what he did to you. He started drinking at first. I tried to help him, but he didn't want help." It feels like someone's punched me. "He started taking drugs. He didn't hide it." Drugs, Danny? No way.

"Danny on drugs? And there was me thinking no one would care."

"Wait, what? Care about what?"

"Me leaving." I shrug.

"Emmie, how can you say that? Everyone was worried sick. Especially as you weren't with your body. Anything could have happened. I thank the Lord you are still here. Your Mom on the other hand..." I don't want to know about her right now.

"I'll get back to my Momma in a minute. First I want you to finish telling me what happened to my brother," I demand.

"He tried overdosing Emmie. I'm sorry. Lucky I caught him in time. Many things were going on in my head at that moment." He tried to kill himself? Did he succeed? No, Danny, my precious Brother.

"He overdosed? Oh my god Damon, my poor brother. Is he dead?" I cringe as I say those words.

"He was out of control. I didn't know what to do. No Emmie, he's not dead." Oh thank you, thank you. "He is in a drug rehab clinic. The problem is, no one can help him unless he wants to help himself."

"Is he getting better?"

"No, he has hit rock bottom."

"I need to see him."

"Are you serious? You've just got out of surgery. You are not going anywhere." I did? Huh, well I don't care about myself. I need to see my

Brother.

"Please Damon. I just want to see him. Maybe him knowing I'm safe will make him get better. We will be there and back in no time." I try to reassure him. "Or I can go on my own, besides I'm not even sure why you are still here."

"Emmie, I'm not going anywhere, you are not dreaming. I'm really here and I love you. You aren't going anywhere on your own." No matter how many times he tells me, it never sinks in.

I sit up and wince, I reach for the call button. I need to see my Brother now. "Emmie, what are you doing?" Damon growls.

The Doc runs in the room and then frowns. "What are you doing? Are you really causing trouble already?" Who me? No... Wait, yeah.

"I need to see my Brother." Damon rolls his eyes.

"Doc, please. She can't go. Can she?" The hell I can't. I try to stand up but Damon won't let me.

"I will go, either I get your approval or I'm going anyway. What's it to be?" I glare at them both.

The Doc laughs, "Okay, okay. As long as you are in a wheelchair at all times or carried. Do not exert yourself. We all know what you are like." Yes, thanks, Doc.

"Seriously, you are letting her go?" Damon growls.

"If you come straight back. You heard her, she will go anyway. This way she can be supervised." Yep, you heard me.

"Good. Doctor, how's my baby?" I really want to see my baby. But I need to know Danny is okay. It's my fault he's in that place.

"She's doing very well." She? I have a baby girl? "Considering you didn't have any vitamins or folic acid or anything. She's a healthy little baby. She's beautiful like her Mom. I will bring her up to you when you return." She's healthy, that's all I need to know.

"That's great. Her looks definitely must come from her Dad, not me."

"Why can't you see how beautiful you are? Is having every guy after you not enough?" Damon says disappointedly. I do not have every guy after me. I'm not that special if you left me.

"Every guy is not after me," I protest.

"You're clueless, aren't you?" Damon sighs.

"She's a spitting image of you Emmie. Definitely your looks." I frown, will she be an ugly baby then? I shake my head, no baby of Damon's would be ugly, it's not genetically possible.

"Please let's go, if I see my daughter I won't want to leave her." The urge to see my daughter grows by the second.

"Our daughter," Damon sighs. Our daughter? Sounds weird. The Doctor leaves the room.

"I need to change and wash. I probably look like something from a horror movie huh?"

He chuckles. "You'll give me nightmares for weeks running into my office like that."

I slowly get off the bed and head for the bathroom. I wash my face and arms in the sink. The water runs red. I don't look in the mirror, I don't want to be met by what I see. Damon walks in handing me a set of clothes to change into, Sully may have come back with them. "Do you need help changing?"

"By you? No." I shake my head.

"Why not me?" he asks.

"Because you can't see me like this. You won't ever see me like this again." He sighs. I know this is hurting him. He ignores me lifting my shirt over my head.

"Do you love me?" he asks.

"Of course I do." How can he doubt that? After all we've been through.

"Well, I will be here until you push me away. I'm not taking this shit. If I know you love me then we will work this out." I stand while he undresses me. It's strange, I don't feel exposed here, even now after all that's happened. He dresses me in the clothes. Work things out? I don't think we can. "Why exactly won't you let me love you?"

"I have this wall, I've kept it up for years. The only one that can see the wall is Danny. He can look through windows into my soul. But he only sees what I want him to see. But then there's you. You shatter the wall into tiny pieces. Which was fine because it felt like you were healing me. And then you left. But you lingered inside of me. The walls are up Damon and I can't let you hurt me like that again."

"I know about the wall Emmie, I know about your invisible scars." He puts his hand on my heart. "I knew about it from the beginning. I felt you dropping the wall. I knew I was healing you." He looks from his hand on my chest to my eyes. "I can fix you, I will fix you."

I can't resist him anymore, I reach for his face and I pull his face towards my lips. He knew? All this time? I still think I'm dreaming but I enjoy this moment. This connection we have. We don't hold back. But he pulls away, probably remembering about surgery. He lifts me up and carries me to the car.

Chapter 22

"Hey, Big Guy," I say when Damon slides us both on the back seat.

"Hey, Emmie. Er, where are we going?"

"Emmie wants to see her brother. She's been out of surgery less than an hour and she's out and about." He sounds really irritated.

"Well, I'm glad you are more yourself." He shrugs and drives away from the hospital.

"How would you even know?" I question him.

"I carried on watching you when Damon was an idiot." He thought Damon was an idiot for leaving me? "You never left the house, Brody would come and go. But yet you wouldn't see him. I was worried about you." He looks at me in the rear-view mirror.

"I wouldn't refuse to see Brody. He's my friend." Why would he think that I would?

"Desmond must have been keeping him away."

"I want to fill you in on your Mom, Emmie." He puts his hands on my face and I stop breathing. "Emmie, breathe."

"What about her?"

"I told her about Desmond, Emmie. She wouldn't believe any of us, not even Danny. She refused to see you just to check on you. Hell, she went on her honeymoon even after I told her." Desmond is crafty, I can't blame her for that. But choosing to believe him over me? My heart aches for my Brother, my constant, maybe him just seeing me will help him.

Danny has always been so strong for me, I can't imagine him weak.

"She picked Desmond over me?"

"I'm sorry. She was saying how you shouldn't be relying on everyone else to pick up your mess. She didn't want to see you. You disgusted her." Damon wouldn't lie to me about this. Momma and I haven't had the so-called Mother and daughter bond, is there something wrong with me? I can't blame her, I've only been a problem since she's returned.

"She came to the hospital earlier when you were in surgery. The Doctor told her to leave as she could be a danger to you. You know she could be in on it with Desmond." In on it with Desmond? I find that hard to believe, she's been nothing but nice to me. Although I remember the last meal we had. She sided with Desmond. Only Danny backed me up. My hurting Brother, what did I do?

"I can call her if you want to see her. But I told her I would let you decide what you wanted. What are you thinking?" I thought he knew what I was thinking? I frown.

"I don't want to see her, not yet. I want to see Danny." I cuddle up into his chest so he can't see my face. "I'm thinking... that there must be something wrong with me. And I can't blame her. And I hurt my Brother, I need to fix this."

"Baby, there is nothing wrong with you. And I can blame her, she's your mother. She should want to protect you. Keep you safe. We will see Danny soon, just don't get your hopes up okay?"

"My hopes?"

"He's in withdrawal. He is different, not the Danny you know." Danny will always be Danny to me. He can't change that much, can he?

Sully pulls up outside a big white building. It has a huge sign reading 'Centro de rehabilitación de Drogas' Translation 'Drug Rehabilitation Center'. This is all feeling too weird, he doesn't belong here. I open my door and slide my legs out. Sully lifts me up and smiles at me. "You didn't think I was going to let you walk, did you?" I frown. I have legs.

Damon makes his way to my side of the car. "Emmie, will you never do as your told?" Nope.

"I'm so confused."

"In what way?"

"What's been spinning around in my head is, you said I should be myself," I wince at the memory, "but you left me and said you didn't want me. Should I not be myself to not risk losing you?"

Damon takes me from Sully and sighs. "Thanks, Sully. See you soon." Sully nods. He looks puzzled too but retreats into the car. "I never said I didn't want you." He doesn't look at me, just carries me towards the building.

"Yes you did, it echoes in my head constantly." Loud and clear.

"No Emmie, I didn't. You must be thinking of a nightmare." It was him, he may have been fake but it felt just as real. "Always be yourself, Emmie. Always, I love you for who you are." Then why did he leave me? "To answer that question, I was an idiot, I shouldn't have walked out on you. I was just so mad that you kissed him. When we were trying to find you, Brody explained what you said. And what his friend did to you." How does he know I asked that question?

We reach a white reception desk and a young guy sits at the desk. He looks up and raises an eyebrow. He's dressed all in white. "Can I help you?"

"We are here to see Danny Salvatore," Damon demands.

"You are here to see Danny?" he asks nervously. "He isn't having a good day. Maybe you should come back."

"You listen to me, I'm his sister and you can't stop me from seeing him. I've just got out of surgery and I'm not leaving now. Do you know what I've been through to get here?" The guy crumbles under my glare and starts to straighten clipboards in front of him, all fingers and thumbs.

"You are his sister? He talks about you all the time. It's like I know you." His mouth drops open.

"You don't know me. Now take me to my Brother."

"You heard her," Damon says and looks at me and grins. The guy shuts his mouth and grabs a clipboard.

"Please sign in Emmie." Wait, I never told him my name, how much has Danny been saying about me?

"How much has he said about me?" I say while I sign our names on the register.

I look up at him and he is all red and flustered. "Emmie, he isn't in his right mind. So he has volunteered too much information."

"That fucker." Damon doesn't sound angry at all which is strange. How much did they connect whilst I was away?

"Shall I show you to his room?" the guy asks.

Damon snorts, "No thanks, I know where it is." How many times does he visit? He takes us down a hallway and stops outside room 19. He puts me down, he put me down? I thought I wasn't allowed to walk? He knocks on the door and walks in. I follow him but stand in the doorway. Damon walks over to Danny and they fist pump. I never thought these two would be friends.

"How are you?" Damon asks.

"I'm waiting for my drugs." He raises his voice, "The service is slow." He is acting strangely. He hasn't seen me yet. I don't like my brother like this. I walk carefully over to Danny and hug him. I've missed him.

"Oh, this is just great," he says frustrated. Is he not pleased to see me? Because I am pleased to see him. He pushes me away.

He talks to Damon and not me, "I'm seeing my bloody sister again. The downside about drugs." And then he looks at me. "I don't want to see you." He doesn't want to see me? That hurts. He shouts again, "Nurse. I need more damn drugs. That's it, don't hurry now."

"Danny," I try to hold back my tears. What did I do to him?

"Whatever you say, I don't want to hear it." This doesn't hurt as much as Damon leaving me but this is second worst. Danny is my constant, or was.

I turn to face Damon and hug him. "This is why I didn't want you to see him. He's not himself. Danny, Emmie is here."

"I thought he might get better if he saw me," I mumble into his chest. But I should have known, I saw Damon in my dreams, he was in my head all the time. I am anti-drugs and always have been.

I take a deep breath and turn to look at Danny. "Cut your crap," I raise my voice.

Danny looks shocked, "Excuse me? These damn drugs," he mutters.

"Danny, how could you do this to yourself?"

"Maybe because you left me," he growls. I hated leaving him.

"I didn't mean to. You were the one thing I regretted leaving behind."

"You never mean to do anything. But you hurt everyone around you." I know I do, I don't deserve these lovely people. Damon stands between me and Danny now.

"Dude, that was harsh." Damon despises people talking to me like this. But it doesn't matter because I already know this. It just makes my scars grow deeper I guess.

"This isn't my sister. So who cares?" I frown. I am your sister, I am here.

"Is that how you feel about me?" I whisper, clutching onto Damon's arm.

"Don't play this pathetic innocent act. You know that you hurt people. You do it on purpose, for attention." No, I never mean to hurt people, it just seems to be what I do. I never do it on purpose.

I decide to give up, my voice only a whisper, "I'm sorry I make you feel this way. I actually really wanted to see you. I've just got out of surgery and I came to see you. I put my life in danger again for you." I would give my life for my loved ones. Danny's expression turns softer, confused even, "Not that my life means much to me anyway. I left my beautiful daughter to see you." Well, I imagine she is. "Yeah in case you care, you have a niece. She was born about 3 hours ago. Not that you seem to care about anything right now."

"Emmie, easy..." Damon says. Me, easy? He attacks me with these harsh but true words yet me saying these words I must be gentle? My Brother would care about these things and I need to find him.

"No, he needs a reality check. I am still alive, thanks for asking. I woke up today after all this time because I was in labour. I woke up alone and scared. I was in a cold strange place. Rooms that were smeared with my blood all up the walls and puddles on the floor. I had to save myself. Desmond nearly killed me." I pause for a while. "And you know what? I knew I couldn't die there and then because I was worried about my family. I'd missed you. I could feel you around me for a while and then you disappeared. You gave me comfort. I love you, Bro, I can't watch you do this to yourself." I step forward but Damon puts his arm in front of me. Danny looks stunned. I push Damon's arm away and hug Danny again. My brother won't hurt me.

"Sis?" His voice is confused.

I squeeze him harder, "Yeah it's me." I feel his arms wrap around me and I relax. I have my Brother back.

"Sis I'm sorry. I can't believe you are safe. I tried so hard to find you. I walked the streets every night for you. I was lost. It is all my fault." No Danny, don't blame yourself. He strokes my hair. I start to hurt. Danny picks me up and carries me to a bed. I wince as he sits down with me on his lap. Damon follows and sits next to Danny so he can also see my face too.

"No, it's not. It's mine," I say as I lean my head on Danny's shoulder. Danny has his arms around my waist. I start to feel tired again. I can't even blame it on pregnancy anymore.

"Emmie, it's not your fault," Damon scolds.

"Of course it is. If I hadn't of left. If I hadn't let Brody kiss me. None of this would have happened." It all boils down to 'If I hadn't.'

"Now I know you're safe, sis. I want to get better for you." My strong Brother trying to protect me.

"Well good, I'm going to need my protective brother back. Seeing as Desmond may still be out there... I'm going to need you. Your niece will need you."

"Hey Sis, have you thought of a name for her?" I shrug.

I look at Damon who is also waiting for the answer to that question. "I have a name in mind, but we haven't discussed it yet. We should be in agreement on a name."

"You have a name picked? I'd like my sister's name in there somewhere." He has a sister? Isn't this something that should have come into conversation by now? I mean we are engaged, or was. I'm not sure anymore. I still haven't fully decided if I'm dreaming or not.

"Wait... you have a sister?"

"Yes. She's dying to meet you." Dying to meet me? Pah, yeah right. I'm nothing special, I'm no one.

If I am not dreaming I vow that we will get to know each other better. "Okay, so what's her name?"

"Her name is Alexa, Lexi for short. So what was the name you picked?" Okay, that's not so bad, I like that name.

"How does Lilly-May Alexa Rider sound?" I wait nervously for his reaction. His face is calm and he's processing the name.

"I couldn't have picked a better name myself. It's perfect, like you." I gasp at his affection. It takes me off guard. Maybe I am dreaming.

"That's a beautiful name. I can't wait to meet her," Danny says.

"What are you thinking?" Damon asks.

"I'm thinking... I must still be dreaming." Danny laughs, making my body shake, I shut my eyes to shut out the pain.

"You aren't dreaming. How many times do I have to tell you?" I shrug. Nothing he can say will prove this to me. Maybe in time, I can believe it.

"You have to sort your crap out first Bro. I'd better be going too as I haven't seen my daughter myself. I'm dying to meet her." I need some painkillers.

"You haven't met her yet?" I shake my head.

"No, I was rushed to surgery before I got the chance. I came here to see you first before I saw her. I know I won't be able to leave her once I meet her."

"Wow, Sis. Means a lot you coming here." I hope so too. I've missed you, Danny.

I slap him hard on his arm, "Anyway, can you not talk about me to the staff here? Especially the hot ones. I don't know what you've been saying, but I don't like it." I giggle, not able to keep a straight face.

"Hot ones?" Damon snorts.

"Sorry Sis, won't happen again. Like I said, I will get better now."

I take a deep breath, "Mhm. I better get going, I should be resting. My drugs are wearing off." Damon grabs my hand as soon as he heard that I was in pain.

"Let's go then," Damon demands.

I hug Danny tighter, I don't want to leave him. "It's okay Sis, I will come see you real soon." That isn't soon enough. I can't walk away from him, I feel tears free falling from my face as my head is buried in his neck. My Brother, my constant. Danny nods at something and then I feel different hands under my knees and on my back and then I'm pulled away from him. Damon holds me close to Danny for a second and Danny kisses me on the forehead and then Damon is marching out the room and out the building.

Damon doesn't say anything, I think he is mad at me. When we are in the car, Sully doesn't say anything either. Everyone seems mad at me. I look at my hands on my lap. Leaving Danny in that place was hard. I wish I could trade places with him, I owe him that. I know what it's like to feel trapped in a place like that. When I had my breakdown, I don't think I've ever got better since being admitted there. But hey, I'm good at hiding things.

Damon sighs and puts his hand on mine. "Stop overthinking things." I'm not overthinking, I'm just thinking. "Why didn't you say you were in pain? I need to trust you to take care of yourself." He is mad at me. But I know he is fighting himself to not shout at me. He is being patient with me. He understands me.

"I didn't want to leave my Brother. He took care of me when..." I can't even say it... when he left me. I needed him and I had Danny. Damon is hurt, why do I keep hurting him? I should just shut my mouth. I'm such an idiot. I put my head on Damon's shoulder but he lifts his arm up and he puts his arm around me. I'm exhausted, I drift to sleep.

I wake up to people arguing. I open my eyes and I see three bodies around my bed. Damon, I could identify him anywhere and there is also the Doctor. The other is a man stood near the Doc. He has black emo type hair, tall and slim. Early thirties I'd say, he is dressed in a policeman outfit. I blink, trying to find my bearings.

"How are you feeling Emmie?" the Doc asks.

"Tired and sore."

"On a scale of 1-10, how much pain are you in?" Physically or mentally? They never specify these questions.

"5." I shrug and narrow my eyes.

"Emmie," Damon scolds. How does he always know? I will never understand, maybe I should ask him at some point, maybe I do something that gives me away. I frown at him.

"Fine, maybe a 9 or a 10." The pain is unbearable, but still, I've felt worse. Like when Damon left, it wasn't physical pain but it felt like I had a huge gaping hole in my chest. It felt like my heart had shattered.

"Why the hell didn't you tell me?" he growls.

"I need to ask Miss Salvatore some questions."

"No. Not now," Damon shouts and sits on my bed to hold my hand.

"I don't think so. I need to examine Emmie. Give her some pain meds. And then you may be able to see her," the Doc says calmly, would he do this for all his patients?

"This is important." The policeman crosses his arms.

"And so is my patient." No, I'm not, but I don't want to speak to him right now so I am grateful. Wow, a Doctor arguing with a Police officer over me, it makes me feel warm and fuzzy.

"Fine, I'll wait outside," the Policeman huffs and leaves the room.

"You know Sully's been worried sick about you too. The effect you're having on my staff." He shakes his head. "They would all put their life on the line for you. And you go and say you don't value your life." Nobody can change the way I feel, what does it matter if people would try and protect me? Damon's probably made it their job to do that. But Sully is the exception to the rule, I can't figure him out.

"I only said that to get my brother to snap out of it." He looks hurt, maybe him thinking I didn't mean it will help him somehow. The Doctor starts to examine me.

"No you didn't, I can tell when you're lying." Shit, I forgot about that. How can I forget that?

"Doctor, I want to see my daughter." I've waited too long. I need her now. I don't like the thought of strangers taking care of her, they would have seen her before me.

"I need to do my checks and then I'll be sure to get her for you." No, get her now, who cares about these checks when my daughter is in this building?

"Damon? Could you get Sully for me? I want to speak to him."

"Sure, I'll send him and then I will need to make some calls." He sighs, probably reacting to my face. "I'm not going far, I will come back." I nod and he leaves the room.

"I must express my opinion, Emmie." He's a Doctor, I'd expect nothing less. "You must take it easy. Putting yourself in danger is irresponsible. You need to think of your daughter now." His words punch me, leaving me winded. I imagine he wouldn't dare say this in front of Damon but he obviously doesn't think I'm as fragile as Damon thinks I am. He injects some fluid into my IVs. I guess it's pain killers. Haven't I only thought of my baby? Keeping her safe? Maybe I didn't, I don't know.

Sully walks into the room and sits on the chair next to the bed. "Hey, Emmie." He smiles at me and then goes red. I still can't figure him out.

"Hey, Big Guy. How bad was he?" I know he gets angry and stressed when I'm in trouble. Was he even bad? He left me.

"Honestly he was hell. He blamed himself." Why? I was the one who kissed Brody? I did this.

"Well thank you for being there for him." Although they don't say it, they love each other.

"It's my job, Emmie." No, it's not. He cares more than most people.

"And was it your job to take a bullet for me?" I hope it isn't, I wouldn't be surprised if Damon put it in their job description. I frown at the thought.

"He would expect nothing less." And that worries me, Damon sees my life as more important than his staff. I couldn't live with myself if something happened to them because of me.

I decide that it wouldn't be in their job description "But it's not your job. And you care about him. I dread to think where he would be without you."

"I care about you too Emmie. We see the gang as family. You are our family now." Family? I can't imagine a gang thinking of themselves as a family. They think I'm family, I don't know what to say.

All I can say is, "I care about you too, Big Guy."

A smile reaches his face, "I better get back on watch but get better soon. And do as you're told. I'm not afraid to treat you like a child again. Hell, it was fun." Flash backs of when I first met him. Him carrying me on his shoulder. I smile too.

"Okay, I get it. We don't need your big muscles. Get back to work," I tease.

He laughs as he stands up. "Yes, boss," he says whilst saluting me. I laugh too.

"Get out of here, you." I giggle.

And he does, I watch him leave. "You are all sorted now Emmie, has the pain subsided?" I forgot he was even here working around me. God, my memory is failing me recently. I do feel better.

"Yes, thanks Doctor. I feel rather sleepy now. If I wasn't so tired I could run a marathon," I tease.

He gives me a deathly stare, "Emmie, I mean it, take it easy." God, everyone is so serious. I was joking. "Emmie you need to stay awake to meet your daughter. I'm going to get her okay?" I really do want to meet her, but why did they take so long? My eyelids are heavy but I nod and he exits the room. Moments pass whilst being on my own.

I start to panic that it was all a dream, I get out of bed and start to pace at the window. I feel the heat on my skin. My feet aren't on the ground anymore, I'm being lifted to the bed. I didn't even hear the door go. "What are you doing?" Damon looks at me, confused.

"Nothing." I don't want to hurt him again. Maybe I really should stop thinking that I could be dreaming.

"You thought you were dreaming again, didn't you?" I nod. He slides in next to me and pulls me towards him. "I'm not going anywhere," he whispers in my ear. "How are you feeling now?"

"Better, just really tired. But I need to stay awake to see Lilly-May."

"You'll love her. She's beautiful. So my family have invited you to our annual party." His family? What if they don't like me? It's a lot of pressure, and if it's a party there will be a lot of strangers.

"When is it?" I can get out of it if it's in the next couple of days.

"In a week. They are desperate to meet you and Lilly-May." I haven't seen her myself and they are the ones that are desperate?

"I'm nervous to meet them."

"They are lovely once you get to know them. My Dad has never approved of my girlfriends. I didn't often introduce them to my family as they would run screaming for the hills after." This doesn't give me a vote of confidence, in fact, I may run screaming for the hills without meeting them. "I have no doubt in my mind that they will love you. Let's face it, everyone loves you." No, they don't, my Brother loves me. I'm starting to accept that Damon does. But that's it.

"Yeah right," I scoff.

"I will spend the rest of our lives together proving that." Okay, that gives me confidence, but won't he get sick of me by then? I don't think it's enough time for me to get enough of him or for him to prove anything to me.

"Here she is," the Doc says, I must have been lost in thought not to hear the door go. I look up to see a small bundle in his arms. I sit up straighter but Damon continues to lean his arm around my shoulders. The Doc hands me Lilly-May. I just stare at her beautiful face, something clicks inside of me. Like we are bonded for life. Tears fall down my face, but these are happy tears. She is sleeping peacefully, her nose twitches now and again.

"She's... Beautiful," I squeak. "Damon... she's..." I can't finish the sentence, no words can describe her, no words are good enough.

"I know baby. She's perfect." He kisses my cheek and he strokes Lilly-May's head. This is my family, I will never let my baby feel any pain, no suffering. She will get what her heart desires, she will want for nothing. She will have the love of her parents.

Chapter 23

We are having our own little family reunion. Damon, Lilly and I. This must be my all time favourite moment. We are interrupted by the door opening, I scowl at the door. It's the damn police officer. "Miss Salvatore, can I speak to you now?" He has really bad timing. Damon huffs next to me but doesn't argue with him. I nod reluctantly.

"Why are you here?" I say.

"I have to follow up my reports and allegations. Your fiancé came to report you missing. I wanted to get the facts from you." I laugh gently, remembering Lilly is in my arms.

"You went to the police?" Damon is in a damn gang, does he really need the police?

"Emmie, you were missing, I didn't know what to do. But they turned out to be useless anyway." He shrugs. I can't imagine what was going on in his head that I was presumed kidnapped again.

"Miss Salvatore, can you tell me what you remember?" He takes out his pen and notepad. "Start from the beginning, please. Don't leave anything out."

"Well, Desmond, my Mother's fiancé." I choose to call her my mother rather that momma now. She betrayed me. "He always creeped me out." I shiver and Damon holds me close.

"How did he creep you out?" the policeman asks.

"Well at first it was subtle things like grabbing my arm, leaving a mark. Always reprimanding my behaviour. And then the day I moved into his house he..." I take a deep breath. "He threatened me."

"He did what?" Damon growls. Shit, I didn't tell him, I just said it all got on top of me.

"Carry on."

"Well, he gave me a list of rules to obey. And ones I wasn't all too happy about obeying." I look at Lilly for comfort.

"What were they?"

I remember them clear as day. "Rule number 1. I'd have to respect my Mother and him. Rule number 2. I would start being good at school. Rule number 3. No boys staying over. Rule number 4. If I'd stay out I would have to text my Mother or him. Rule number 5. I would help around the house. And finally, I'd have to do anything I could to please him."

"Why didn't you tell me about that?" Damon says, he seems to have calmed down a tad.

"What would you have done? I wanted to make my Mother and Brother happy."

"I wouldn't have let you go back there."

"And what would have happened when you left me?" He stays silent. And I don't say any more.

"So what happened next?" the policeman asks.

"Well, Damon left me." I close my eyes trying to block out the pain but it doesn't work. When I open them again they are both waiting for an answer. "I refused to eat anything, Brody tried and my mother tried. But the last thing I wanted was food. But Desmond interfered so I sat down at the dinner table. He had a go at me for not eating perfectly good food. Danny, my brother was the one who got me to eat a little. I fell asleep on his shoulder. And Desmond scolded me for falling asleep at the dinner table. I hadn't long been out the hospital, so I was exhausted."

"Danny left for work and too much time was spent thinking. I was numb to the world so I slipped into a self-induced coma, something I've done before. I wasn't scared, this time I was relieved. It didn't hurt anymore, the loss of Damon. I could still feel and hear certain things from my body. And I heard Desmond say that he did kill the girl he was suspected of killing."

"Did that not scare you? That you weren't with your body? Did you try to wake up?" the policeman asks whilst taking notes.

I shake my head, "Why would I want to wake up to a world without

Damon? In my dream world, he was there and he wanted me. I didn't want to wake up, even though I was probably in danger."

"Okay, carry on." Damon stays silent, I don't think he is liking this but he doesn't leave. Just continues to hold me tight.

"I got married in my dream world, I knew it wasn't real but I knew someone was getting married. And I hear that it was my mother and Desmond." I frown. "I tried to block everything out from then on. I felt cold all the time, sometimes pain but I could push it away."

I don't like rethinking about these moments, they were the worst moments of my life. I'm ready to start living my life with my family. "But I started to get these unbearable sharp shooting pains. Pain I've never felt before. I could feel myself slipping back to my body. When I woke, I was in a dark, cold, dirty room. The first thing I noticed was how bloody huge and fat I was."

Damon interrupts me, "You looked beautiful. You are in no way fat, even whilst pregnant." I chose not to contradict him.

"I was alone, and I knew I was in labour. I had to save my baby. Get my baby to Damon, and then it didn't matter what happened to me. So I started down the hallway, it had many rooms like in a hotel. I checked a few doors to find a way out. The first room had blood all over the floor." Damon strokes my hair and I look at Lilly again, she keeps me calm. "I checked my body and I had bandages all over my body. I left that room and found another. This room had a bathtub, above the bath read, 'Daddy loves you,' in blood. I couldn't make it out because my Dad was known as Daddy. And he's dead, I didn't know anyone else who I would call Daddy. But there was blood in the bath. Someone had been bathing me, I didn't like that thought so I soon tried another room. The room had another door but it was locked, I suspected it was a way out so I found an axe in a cabinet. It was covered in blood. And then I heard him."

"Heard who?" the policeman asks.

"Desmond, he was angry that I was up and about. He said that that day was the day I died. I started beating the door with the axe but the sound echoed through the building and he found me. He started saying things like I was more of a prize than the other girl and that he thought I was beautiful and special which is why I was still alive. He wanted my baby, bring her up and her fate would be the same as mine. I snapped, I couldn't let him hurt my baby. But he started to distract me, saying everyone had forgotten about me. I believed him, why wouldn't I?"

"Because we all love you," Damon says without hesitation. But why? I don't understand.

"He grabbed my throat and he was strangling me, I couldn't breathe. I panicked and I hit him with the axe. He fell to the floor, I didn't check to see if he was breathing. I just broke the door down and ran to the only place I felt safe."

"And where was that?" the policeman asked.

"In Damon's arms, I didn't care if he didn't want me. I needed him, I thought he would help me protect our baby. That's all I needed to know, that my baby was safe."

The policeman nods as he finishes his notes. Damon kisses my forehead and I sag with relief. "Thanks, Miss Salvatore."

"What will happen now?"

"Well, we have searched the location, there was no body. But we have taken samples of the blood and we have confirmed it as yours. Desmond will be charged with attempted murder if we find him." If? He's still out there? I gasp, my poor baby needs protecting from this mad man. "We are doing everything we can. I will be in touch." He nods again and leaves us in the room. Damon takes Lilly from me, I'm tired, but he still keeps his arm around me and I snuggle into his chest. I soon fall asleep.

*

Since I laid eyes on my daughter, she is all I've thought about. I never leave her. She sleeps in the bassinet bed next to mine in the hospital. The doctor has refused to let me go after previous occasions when I didn't rest. I think he secretly likes me around. I brighten up his day. I seem to be crying all the time. My emotions are still all over the place. Damon stays at the hospital with me at night. I don't know if he doesn't want to leave me or he thinks I don't want him to leave. Tonight is the party at Damon's parents.

Lilly-May is sleeping in my arms. "Emmie, I'd like to do one more check on the both of you before you go." I frown. He goes to take Lilly-May away from me and I move my arms away from his reach. "Emmie, you know I won't hurt her." I shake my head.

Damon frowns and scoops her out of my arms. I feel anxious when she isn't in my arms and in others. He passes her to the Doc. He strokes my forehead. "She's fine." He knows I don't like to let her go. Damon is the only one I will willingly give her to. Is that because I trust him implicitly? Sometimes I don't even let him hold her. He knows when he should and shouldn't push me. I watch the Doc as he examines Lilly. She starts to cry so I jump off the bed and grab her from the table that the Doc was examining her from and sit back on the bed. "Emmie, seriously. She's fine," Damon says. She stops crying when she's in my arms. And I relax too.

"That's okay, I was just about done anyway. Emmie, your turn." I glare at him. "You know, you are my hardest patient. And now with Lilly, you are worse. I didn't think that was possible." Damon chuckles but I poke my tongue out at them both. I'm all ready to leave this hospital. I want to see Danny. He hasn't seen Lilly yet. I let the Doctor examine me and he leaves the room when he's done.

"Move in with me," Damon says softly.

"What?" Move in with him? I never even thought about where I would stay. I haven't seen Momma yet. Nor do I have the urge to. And yet I don't feel sad about it. She let Desmond take me. She wouldn't come to find me, what sort of mother does that? I won't even leave Lilly for 5 minutes without worrying.

"I won't have you go back to your mom's. The only way to know you are safe is for you to live with me. I want you with me all the time. Besides, living apart hasn't really worked out has it?" No, I guess it hasn't, I've always wanted him to say those words. And now he's saying them I can't help but think it's because he doesn't think I'm safe on my own. I mean I still have Dad's house. I could live there. Danny should be discharged soon, I could live with him.

"Okay. I'll move in with you." Please, please don't be a dream. Don't wake up if it is. He smiles and kisses me. He grabs Lilly's change bag and we walk out of the hospital. In the car is a car seat. Well, I guess she should be safe. But when did he get this? I slide her in, she's sleeping now. I sit in the middle seat and Damon sits on my left. He puts his hand on mine and he brings it up to his lips and places soft kisses. I gasp at the familiar feeling I get. Maybe it wasn't hormones that connected me to him. It was just us.

We pull up outside the clinic to see Danny. I decide to leave Lilly sleeping in the car seat. So I get the seat out the car and carry her in the building. Damon tries to carry her for me but I refuse to let him. He must be getting annoyed with me by now. But I only trust myself to protect her.

We sign in and the same young guy smiles at me. "He is doing really well, Emmie," he says chirpily this morning. Well, that's good to know. We reach his room and he is reading a book on his bed. He looks up and smiles. He bounds up to me and hugs me. I hug him with one arm as I'm carrying Lilly. I hug him longer than I need to. He's looking better.

He takes my hand and pulls me to the bed and we sit. "You are looking better," he says with a smile.

"You too." I smile back at him. I've kept one hand on Lilly's seat that is perched on the floor. Damon sits next to me.

"So, are you going to let me hold my niece?" he says hopefully. I frown, he wants to hold her? What if he drops her? Damon puts his hand over mine on Lilly's seat.

"She will be fine." Why does he keep saying that? I'm her mother, I need to assess the danger. Damon pulls gently at Lilly's seat and I let go. I watch anxiously as Damon gets her out her seat and passes her to Danny.

Danny is careful with her but he has the biggest smile on his face. "She's beautiful Emmie." Of course she is, she's Damon's baby.

My heart is pounding out my chest. I sit watching Danny's clock tick by. I start tapping my leg but Damon puts his hand on my knee. "Danny, could you watch her for a bit?" I freeze under his hand. Watch her? I'm not going anywhere.

"Sure," he says calmly. I glare at Damon.

"Come for a walk with me. We won't be long. You trust your brother, right?" I shake my head, not in answer to his question but at the thought of leaving her.

"Sis, I promise, she's safe with me."

"No, Damon. Don't do this." What's there to gain from me leaving her? He grabs my hand and pulls me to my feet.

"She's sleeping, she'll be fine. Come." He pulls me towards the door and we head down the hallway. We reach a door that opens into a garden. Damon leads me out the door. I feel like I'm a magnet and I'm being forced back to her. Damon stops and pulls me towards him. Our fronts are touching, his arms around my back pulling me to him. I feel a different kind of pull now. One pulling towards him, the one that's always been there it's just been hidden since I met Lilly. He kisses me softly and then I can't resist him anymore. Our lips lock urgently like we haven't been this close for a long time.

I sag against him like I've found comfort. I now realise I am awake. I'm wide awake, I have Damon, Lilly-May and Danny. My family, I don't know what I did to deserve it but they are mine. I think I've been trying to keep Lilly close in case this was all a dream but I know this is real. So maybe I can relax a little bit. I smile at Damon's beautiful face.

"What?" He grins at me.

"I'm not dreaming, am I?" He chuckles.

"It's taken you a good week to figure that out." Yeah well, at least I've figured it out. We take a stroll in the garden hand in hand. There are loads of pretty pink flowers. Damon picks a handful and offers them to me. I smile and bring them to my nose to smell. "What are your favourite flowers?"

"Hmm, it's cliché, but roses."

"What colour?" he asks curiously.

"Pink are my favourite, the red and white joint second." He nods as if he will keep that to his grave.

"So your sister, what's she like?" I'm curious.

"She's annoying but pretty. She is the outgoing type. I am protective over my sister." I don't doubt that he is. I would be disappointed if he wasn't. "I don't know what else to tell you." He shrugs. "Shall we go back to Lilly-May?"

"Wait," I say and he stops in his tracks. I reach up and put my fingers through his hair. He groans and kisses me again. I love this man so much. I can't say more than anything anymore because Lilly tops that. But, well, I know I can't live without him. We both pull away, breathless.

"I need to get you home." It sounds like a promise and my heart is pounding, pounding for him. My body is yearning for him to touch me.

"I finally have a place to call home. Not just a person." I smile at him, I'm smiling too much. But I'm happy, so who cares?

"I'm glad to hear it, baby." He takes my hand once more and we walk into the building and into Danny's room. Lilly is awake and Danny is cooing at her. Danny looks up at us and smiles.

"She's got your looks, Emmie." I snort but choose not to say anything. There's no point wasting my breath with these two around.

"Let's get my two favourite girls home." I frown, surely his sister trumps me, but I roll with it. Damon takes Lilly off Danny and places her into her car seat. Danny hugs me tight, rocking me from side to side.

"I'll see you soon Emmie. I will be out soon." He said that last time. How much more time does he need? He's my Brother, he makes this look easy, this rehab stuff but I guess I don't see behind the scenes. I can only imagine how hard it is for him.

"I love you, Bro."

"And I love you, Sis." He releases me and we head to the car, I let Damon take Lilly.

We get inside Damon's house and I take my shoes off. I take Lilly into the living room. The room looks different, there's a travel cot in here. When did he get all of this stuff? I place Lilly in the cot whilst she sleeps. She will wake soon for a feed. I sit on the sofa and pull my knees to my chest. Damon stands in the doorway and leans against the doorframe. How does he look so hot doing that?

"Hey baby, do you want me to take Lilly-May while you get ready?" It's not time to get ready yet.

"No, I'll keep her with me. If that's okay." Although I know I've discovered the cause of my anxiety about leaving her, I'm not prepared to take the band-aid off yet.

"That's fine, of course. I'm going to get some work done. I want you to meet some of our new staff. So when you're ready, I will introduce you. If you need anything, Sully will be around, okay?"

"Sure, see you later." Our staff, he means his staff. Why do I need to meet his staff? He leaves me alone in the living room. I lay down facing the cot, I don't like to sleep in case I can't hear her cry. But sleep takes over.

I feel a hand on my forehead and I open my eyes sleepily. Sully is crouching down in front of me. "Emmie, I think it's time for you to get ready. I've fed Lilly-May so don't worry, she's sleeping now."

"How long have I been asleep?" I sit up and rub my eyes. Did I sleep through Lilly screaming?

"About two hours. Damon wanted me to let you sleep as long as possible, so he had me watch Lilly-May for you. Go get ready, I'll watch her." I frown. "She'll be perfectly safe with me." Did Damon tell him about my paranoia or did he tell my anxiety from my face? I guess I don't want to disturb her whilst she's sleeping.

Sully stands and helps me to my feet. I take one last glance towards Lilly and head for Damon's bedroom. This room is different too. There is a cot next to the bed. But also, a Moses basket, how does he know so much? A changing unit, a new white chest of drawers. This is a lot to process. I head for the bathroom and have a cold shower, the last time I was in here we made love in this shower. I bite my lip at the memory.

The cold water feels good against my skin. I reach for Damon's shower gel but notice there is some woman's shower gel. Does he think of everything? I wash quickly and get out the shower. I look in the steamy mirror. Do I want to look at myself? I rub the mirror with the towel that is wrapped around me. I look different somehow, has motherhood changed me? Or is it because I'm actually happy? I'm happy, relaxed and looking forward to the future. I don't think that's ever happened before.

I walk into the bedroom, what am I supposed to wear? I don't have any clothes. On Damon's wardrobe, there is a dress bag hanging on the door. I walk over in curiosity. There is a note on the front it reads, 'Wear me. Your Loving Fiancé.' I open the zip with hesitation. I've always chosen my own clothes, what's he chosen for me to wear? I pull the dress out the bag. Okay, he got the colour right, black. I look best in black. It doesn't look too bad, I guess.

I decide I should put it on before I make any rash decisions. Oh my god, I can't wear this. The dress is shorter than I would have chosen, okay, be careful not to bend over. I turn around and look in the mirror. My mouth falls open. It has lots of little straps, my whole back is visible. Why would he want me to wear this? It's rather low cut and shows off my boobs. There's another note on the mirror. 'Don't freak out, you'll look beautiful. Can't wait to see you in it. Here's a peace offering.' I look down in front of the mirror.

My bag of makeup. Okay, maybe I can forgive him, I will need my shield to meet people tonight. I finish applying the makeup and brush my hair. There seems to be random belongings of mine around the room. I look at the bedside cabinet and identify the picture with Daddy and I in it. I walk over to it to examine it. Underneath is my letter. He got me this from Desmond's house? How? Damon really does have superpowers. I smile, I go in search for panties and shoes to wear.

Okay, I'm ready. Emmie, I'm ready. My feet won't move, damn it Emmie, move. The door clicks open and Damon's mouth drops open. I frown.

"Okay, I thought you would look beautiful, but wow. You look breath-taking." He closes the distance between us and pulls me towards him. "Let's go before I decide to keep you here." I giggle. He knows how to make me feel special. We walk out of the bedroom together, he's already dressed in smart black jeans and a white shirt. His looks could seduce any women on the planet, so why choose me?

Chapter 24

We gather in the hallway by the front door, Sully passes me Lilly. I stand close to Damon and Sully's side. I feel incredibly safe with these two by my side. In front of me are two young guys, maybe early 20s. Why does Damon always recruit young people? Except for that idiot that hit me when he kidnapped me. I haven't seen him in a while. A guy with long black hair in a ponytail stands directly opposite me, he has his arms crossed. He is actually rather hot but I have Damon, why would I need to window shop? And there is another guy with black dreads. He doesn't appeal to me much but they both have their mouths dropped open staring... at me? Nah, can't be at me.

"Erm, what is everyone gawking at?" I say awkwardly. It looks like they are staring at me, all of them, even Damon and Sully. But they can't be.

"You look beautiful. You are obviously lighting up the room," Damon says, wrapping his arm around my back and I blush with everyone staring.

"Guys, stop eying up my fiancée," Damon demands.

"You look stunning Emmie." Wow, Sully isn't usually this forthcoming. I bet he's blushing. I look up and giggle, yep, he's blushing.

"You never mentioned how hot your fiancée was. Damn." The hot one with the ponytail is flirting with me? Be careful, Damon is territorial.

"Emmie, how can you not see the effect you have on us? Seriously, enough with the eye fucking of my fiancée." Damon is such a jealous person, I mean I'm seeing I guess... but I'm not believing.

"Damon, no one is doing that. Chill." Trying to get the attention off of me. I hate people looking at me, it makes me uncomfortable.

"How can you not see it? You're frustrating." Okay, I get it. I frustrate you more often than I please you. So why am I here exactly?

"Hey Sully, I see why you took a bullet for this girl," the dreads guy says. Really? Sully took a bullet for me because his orders were to protect me at all costs, don't get any ideas, wise guy.

"Can we get back to the meeting? I do not like feeling jealous of my staff. You know this. As you guys know, security has stepped up due to recent events. Of course, Sully, you are Emmie and Lilly-May's protection. That will never change." Why are you so jealous Damon? Have I given you any reason to be jealous? I mean there was Brody but I've put him to rest now, no one could come close to you.

"I'd take a bullet for her. Why does he get her?" the ponytail guy says. No, you wouldn't, don't lie. Is he trying to get brownie points, sucking up to the Boss?

"Because he is my right-hand man, he's proved his loyalty." And I feel safest with him besides Damon.

"You might need your right-hand man," Dreads says. Why are they fighting this? Damon would never let these guys be my first security guy.

"Enough you guys, Sully gets Emmie, end of. You two will be around more often. So don't worry, you'll get your chance to be around my fiancée. Just keep your eyes and hands to yourselves." Jesus Damon, why did you have to add the last bit? They aren't interested in me. They are probably repulsed at that sentiment. I mean look at me, I'm fat and ugly.

"Definitely can't promise anything," Ponytail says. Excuse me? What is he on about?

"That's why Sully gets this job. He takes things seriously. Anyway, you will all escort us to the party tonight. Sully, stay close to Emmie. You two keep your eyes peeled." Security at a party? That's going to be a downer.

"And who keeps an eye on you?" I look up at Damon on my right. He looks down at me and smiles.

"Emmie, I don't need protecting."

"Of course you do," I scold, what would I do if something happens to him?

"Knowing you will keep your eyes on me will make me feel better." Damon laughs and so does everyone else.

"Anyway, this is Dyno." He points at the hot ponytail guy. "And this is

Billy." He points at the dreads guy, okay I got it Dinosaur and Billy no mates. Yeah, I'll remember them. "Let's go," Damon says irritated. Okay, what did I do this time? I'm pretty sure I did nothing. But hey, he could take offence at my appearance?

Damon takes my hand and leads me to the car. Damon sits in the front with Sully and I sit with Lilly in the back. Dyno and Billy take another car behind us. Damon discusses with Sully the plan for this evening, he has made it very clear that Lilly and I are his main priority. I roll my eyes, yes, Lilly needs protection but Damon needs more protection than I do.

We reach his parent's house and it's huge. My mouth falls open, it's like the size of a palace. I can't get my head around someone needing a house like this. Even if I had the money, which I now do, I wouldn't buy a house like this. I need to decide what to do with that money. I still don't feel like I can keep this money, even if I do want to follow my Daddy's dying wishes. Well, that part anyway. Damon is at my door already holding his hand out to me.

I take his hand and he kisses me softly on the forehead, he seems tense. Is he as worried as I am? I mean he did say his parents make his girlfriends run for the hills. Nothing they can say will make me leave Damon. Only Damon can push me away, and he tells me he won't do that. Do I believe him? I don't know that either.

I walk around the car to get Lilly out but Sully has already unstrapped her from her car seat and is holding her. He offers her to me and I take her in my arms. We walk towards the house Damon with his arm around me, his hand caressing my naked back. The electricity pulsing through my body. Damon lets himself in through the unlocked door and leads us through the house into a big room where everyone has gathered.

The security follows closely on our heels. I scan the room, there are too many people. "Hey, they will love you, okay?" Damon reassures me. I nod but don't argue. "I'll take Lilly-May while you mingle." No way, I want to keep her with me. He takes her without my permission.

"Oh okay," I mumble, feeling defeated. I frown, looking at Lilly.

"Don't worry, I'll give her back." Damon chuckles softly, he strokes the side of my face, pushing hair out of my face. I watch as Damon leaves me standing anxiously on my own. A young pretty red haired girl approaches me. She's impeccably well-dressed, which shows off her amazing body. I frown with jealousy. Why can't I look like that? She smiles at me. No, she's also staring.

"Wow girl, you are hot. Why haven't I met you before?" I turn around to see if she's talking to someone else, that would be the logical thing. But no one is near me.

"Umm thanks?" I guess. If she means it, she may pity me. Her hair is in a bob but plaits running through the top of her head. Bright blue eyes.

"You have amazing legs. What I'd do to you if I got the chance." I look down at my exposed legs, Damon picked a dress that's way too small for my liking. I just see chubby legs. I'm confused, and what does she mean if she got the chance?

"Excuse me?" I'm startled.

"Sorry, I'm a bit forward. I have a particular taste of women and damn girl, I've never seen anyone hotter," she says matter of factly. I blush, she's gay, makes more sense but she can't have met many women then.

"So you're a lesbian?" trying to lighten the mood getting the topic off me.

"Yes, and proud." I giggle, she looks proud of it. Not many people flaunt it like this. I'm in awe of her, standing up for something she believes in. Takes guts.

"I can tell," I say sarcastically. I like this girl, she speaks her mind. Cuts through all the crap.

"So please tell me you like to party?" She emphasises the word 'please'.

"Of course, you could say that I'm the life of a party." I think of Jessie and I and the gossip spread around the school.

"I think we are going to be great friends. I like you. You have sass." I like her too but I don't see why she likes me. But again, I choose to ignore it.

"Yes, I think so too."

"Hey, bestie." I turn around to see Jessie. What is she doing here? She grabs my face and kisses me. It takes me a few seconds to process what's going on. I don't like kissing anyone else other than Damon but I go with it anyway. I smell and taste the alcohol on her breath.

"Damn, when you said you're the life of the party, you meant it. Save some of that loving for me, will you?" the pretty girl says. I pull away from Jessie, embarrassed.

"Someone's been drinking," I say to Jessie.

"We need to hang out more. I've missed you." I've missed her too.

"Well considering I've not been myself lately, it would be hard." Life keeps getting in the way, well, my hard life where I keep getting into trouble.

"We should all hang out at the mall or something," the pretty girl says. She seems excited.

Jessie squeals too, "Clothes shopping? Count me in." I roll my eyes at the enthusiasm to shop. I do love clothes shopping but there is one problem. Too many people, they get in the way and make me anxious.

"Great." The pretty one claps.

"Brody wants to talk to you by the way." Jessie looks awkward. Brody's here and why does he want to talk to me?

"Whoever this Brody is will have to wait. Let's go get a drink." She grabs my arm and leads me to a bar. She makes two cocktails and passes me one.

"All these security guards are driving me nuts. They watch your every move. I mean, they are hot. But all eyes watching…" I know what she means, it doesn't help my anxiety them all watching. But I do wonder why she's annoyed about it.

"Yeah, it is a bit much." But it gives Damon peace of mind so I don't mind too much.

"So what brings you here?" She takes a swig of her drink.

"I've come with my fiancé," I shrug.

"You're fiancé? He doesn't mind you kissing girls?" She's shocked. I remember the time he saw me kiss Jessie, he said he had mixed feelings about it but he didn't forbid the idea.

"Why would he? It's only a bit of fun. Anyway, don't all guys like it?" I smile, thinking about how it affects people.

"Of course they do. Turns them on big time. One of the guards is staring. Why don't we drive them nuts?" I look where she's looking, it's the hot one, Dinosaur. I smirk.

"I like your style," I say and she takes that as permission and her lips find mine. She's a better kisser than Jessie, maybe because this means something to her, to kiss another girl. Maybe I shouldn't have allowed it because I'll probably end up hurting someone else.

She pulls away, eyes dilated but she shakes her head and looks at Dinosaur, "Ha, did you see his face?" She laughs. I look too, his mouth has dropped open and he is looking flustered. He looks away at the crowd.

"Yes, priceless." I join her, laughing hard. I finish my drink and place my glass back on the bar.

"Anyway, I'm Lexi." No way, it must be a coincidence. Please be a coincidence.

"Lexi as in Alexa?"

"Yes, the one and only. Why?" She frowns at me, assessing my mood shift.

"That's funny." I laugh, of all the people I could have kissed it turns out to be her.

She crosses her arms and glares at me, "What's so funny?"

"I just kissed my fiancé's sister. I think he may be pissed at that one." I continue to laugh.

"Your Emmie? Girl, how did he get a hottie like you?" She's shocked. I think he deserves better than me but I am tired of pushing him away.

"Long story…" Really long. It will take like a year to explain, my life's so complicated.

"Well, you better explain it to me one day. Right now, I want to meet my niece." I frown, she wants to see Lilly. I don't trust her enough yet. But I nod and we go in search for Damon. We find Damon, Lilly and what I assume are his parents in the kitchen.

"Hey Bro," Lexi says. "Now I want to know how you bagged such a hot fiancée. But first, I want to hold my niece." Damon grins at her then looks at me as if to ask approval. I nod and he passes Lilly over to her. But I keep my eyes on Lilly. Damon walks towards me and puts his arm around me and kisses the top of my head. I close my eyes and breathe him in, forgetting the people around us. I still don't know how he makes my mind blank when I'm with him. It's just me and him.

"Honestly Lexi, do you have to? My staff are all eying up my fiancée, I don't need you as well," he says but I can't see his face as my face is leaning on his chest whilst I hug him. But I watch Lexi and Lilly in front of us.

"Wow, she's beautiful. What's her name?" Lexi is gently rocking Lilly. Did he not tell her already?

"Lilly-May Alexa Rider." He pronounces it slow and clear.

"Oh my god, you named her after me. I love you, Damon," she squeals, Damon and I laugh at her. I'm glad she is so chuffed with it, although I did it for Damon.

"It's so lovely to meet you, Emmie. We have heard so much about you." I'm assuming she is Damon's Mom. She is stylish for her age. She wears a lovely black dress that falls below her knees. She has silky black hair and she wears it in a high ponytail. Wow, I know where Lexi and Damon get their looks from. She's so pretty, Damon's been surrounded by pretty people all his life. Maybe he got bored which is why he chose me.

"Yes, it's nice to meet you, Emmie. You really are beautiful," the Dad, I assume, says to me. His Dad is rather handsome too. He just looks like an older version of Damon.

"Come on Dad, don't scare her." I close what little distance there is between Damon and me. My stomach to his side.

"Seriously Bro, how did you get this girl? I'm impressed. She's a great kisser too." Oh, Lexi, really? Damon tenses in my arms.

"Lexi, you kissed her? Can't you keep your hands to yourself?" he growls, but not his usual pissed voice, I guess he is nicer to his sister than most people.

"Can you blame me? I couldn't resist. And besides, I didn't know she was your fiancée. I mean, you've never had someone this good looking." I frown, I will never understand what these people see.

"Oh, Lexi," he sighs.

"Lexi, please be appropriate in front of our guest," Damon's mother says. To be honest, I'd prefer her to speak her mind, that's why I like her.

"Emmie, please tell us how you and Damon met. He's being very secretive," Damon's Dad says. I look up at Damon's face. He looks a little awkward. Does his family not know he's in a gang? I don't know what to tell them.

"I don't mean to be rude but I need to go feed Lilly-May. I'll be back soon though to answer your questions, okay?"

"Oh love, you scared her. That's fine dear, you go feed my granddaughter." I scoop Lilly into my arms and leave the room.

I sag with relief when I leave his parents. Damon's Dad appears in front of me and I start to shift my weight on each foot in awkwardness. "Emmie, could I have a private word with you please?" he says.

"Umm sure." What could this be all about?

"Follow me," he demands. He has the no-nonsense tone that Damon has.

We are heading for a room at the corner of the big room. Sully appears in front of us with his arms crossed. "Sir, where are you going?"

"That's none of your business," Damon's Dad accuses.

"It is when you're going with Emmie," Sully says calmly.

"What's it to you?"

"I am hired by your son to protect her. I intend to do my job."

"And you think I'm going to hurt her?" Hurt me? No. Threaten me? Maybe, but I can handle myself.

"Sully it's fine. We will be fine," I try to reassure him.

"I don't want to risk it." His expression has changed to worry, sadness. Like he doesn't care about his job, he cares about me.

"Just get out the way, will you? You heard her," his voice grows more frustrated but Sully doesn't step aside.

"It's fine Sully, you can wait outside and I'll shout if I need you okay?"

"Okay." He still doesn't look satisfied but he lets us through.

"Great," Mr Rider says sarcastically. I frown, leave Sully alone.

We enter a study, a computer sits on top of a large desk. He turns towards me, I stay by the door so I have a way out. I don't like being put in this situation, not with Lilly around. I lift her so her head lies on my shoulder as if to shield her from Mr Rider.

"What is this about Mr Rider?" I try to stand my ground, braveness overpowering me. I don't know where it came from.

"I've seen you with my Son. He seems happy with you." I like to think he's happy.

"Yes, we are happy."

"You can't make him happy. Look at you, you look... Well, I have to admit, you look like a pretty expensive hooker." A hooker? Wow, how rude. That makes me feel cheap even if he did use the word 'expensive'. I'm not pretty enough to be a hooker. It must be this dress that makes me come across that way.

"Excuse me?"

"My son deserves the best. He doesn't need you and the baby ruining his life." Ruining his life? Is that what I'm doing? Shouldn't he have the right to decide that for himself? I'm angry.

"Who the hell do you think you are, talking to me like that?"

"The person that's going to pay you a lot of money to leave him." Is he serious? I wouldn't take all the money in the world to leave Damon. I've been through the loss of Damon and money couldn't compare to Damon.

"I don't want your money." I'm repulsed.

"Then what do you want? There must be something?" The only thing I want is Damon, nothing will change that. I've never wanted for much in my life. Daddy always taught me not to be greedy.

"You are unbelievable. I don't want anything from you. You disgust me. Do you even care about your son's happiness?"

He looks at me like I've said something stupid. "Of course I do. This is why I'm doing this. Deep down he doesn't want this kid." How would he know? Damon hasn't given me any indication that he doesn't want Lilly. I've always questioned if he wants me but never Lilly. Everything inside me is boiling up. How dare he say this? I would never take anything to leave Damon. Since I've been back, I've been the happiest I've ever been. I have to admit, even better than the fantasy world. I am so angry. I feel so sick.

"Did I do something wrong for you to hate me?"

"Quite the opposite actually. I think you're beautiful. And I like your braveness." I think my head is going to explode. I'm so confused.

"So why are you doing this?"

"Because slappers like you won't make him happy. Why are you being so stubborn? All the others jumped at the chance to get hold of lots of cash." His words are punching me hard, leaving me breathless. A slapper? Is this how I really look? Wait, all the others jumped at the chance to get hold of cash? I feel a pang of sympathy for Damon. He always said they went screaming for the hill but they didn't, they ran with a wad of cash.

"Are you saying that you paid his other girlfriends to leave?"

He seems rather smug, "Of course, they all wanted something. So I just need to find out what you want."

Something snaps inside of me, I've heard enough. "You know what Mr Rider? You need to open your eyes. Your son is happy. I will never leave him. Not over money or anything else. So you can shove your proposal where the sun doesn't shine, you jerk."

I turn around to leave but he grabs my arm. I can't pull away because I'm holding Lilly. "How dare you? You're not leaving." How dare I? After he said all those cruel things? Making my self-esteem deflate even more. He sees me as a slapper.

He releases me and I glare at him, "Oh, bite me," I growl. I leave him speechless in his study. I'm angry, so damn angry. I need to leave.

Sully stands outside the door. And he frowns. "Emmie, are you okay?"

I shake my head.

"No, I want to go home. Now."

"Did something happen?"

He's upset that I'm upset. But I can't help but snap at him. "I don't want to talk about it." I walk away from Sully but he follows closely behind me, I try to find the way out but I'm met by Damon and Lexi. He frowns.

"Emmie, are you okay?" I glare at him.

"No, I'm going home," I growl. He looks to me and then to Sully who looks as confused as Damon.

"What happened?" Oh, just me not being good enough for your family.

"I don't want to talk about it."

"Okay well, I'll just say goodbye and then we will go." Why is he being so reasonable? I'm angry and he is calm.

"You don't need to leave on my account. You can stay if you want. I don't want to ruin your night." I don't know when he last saw his family, so he should spend the rest of the evening with them.

"Emmie I'm not letting you go home on your own," he argues with me but he's gentle.

"That's okay, Sully can come." I shrug.

Damon sighs, "Stop fighting me. I'm coming." I walk towards the door.

I hear Lexi say, "Wow Bro, she's a fighter. Someone still has raging hormones. Good luck. She's good for you, I can see." She calls to me. "Emmie, we need to meet up soon."

I turn around and call back. "I'd like that. Text me to arrange something." I'm sure she can get my number off Damon.

"I definitely will," she calls and then Damon kisses her on the cheek and turns to follow me. I walk ahead of him to the car. Sully somehow beats me to the car and holds open the door so I can put Lilly back in the car. Damon sits next to me this time, he tries to comfort me but I push him off. We sit in silence until we get home. I can tell Damon is frustrated with me.

Chapter 25

As we reach inside, Dyno and Billy make a hasty exit but Sully hovers, waiting for Damon's command to leave. I try to ignore them both, I head for the bedroom and feed Lilly. I stare at the picture of my Daddy, I never had to worry that I wasn't enough for him.

Lilly falls asleep in her Moses basket and I take the baby monitor with me and sit in the sitting room. Damon finds me shortly after, he crouches in front of where I'm sat and looks up at me with his hands on my knees. I scowl and cross my arms but I don't push him away.

"Are you going to tell me what the hell happened? Or are you going to give me this silent treatment?" He's nervous but also mad at me for not sharing things with him. But he remains calm, pleading with me. "Whatever I did I'm sorry. I love you, Emmie. Please speak to me." His words take me off guard. I can't believe he's like this. So worried that he's done something wrong. I love it when he begs me. Makes me feel like I'm worth fighting for. He tries so hard with me, and I just treat him like crap. This isn't even his fault. So why am I mad at him?

"I'm sorry," I say, ashamed of my behaviour.

"What are you sorry for?" he asks, confused.

"Being moody." I guess.

He smiles, "You are one feisty kitty when you're mad. My staff fled the scene so they didn't have to cover up a murder. Or maybe they thought they would be murdered. Who knows?" I laugh, if he was trying to cheer me up it worked. "Baby, please tell me what's bothering you?"

"I can't." I don't want to hurt him. What if he goes back to another girlfriend now that he knows? But I can't be that selfish, can I?

"Was it my parents? Did they embarrass you? They can be a bit overwhelming. But they loved you. My sister... well SHE likes you. Maybe too much." I can't imagine his parents liking me but Lexi did seem genuine.

"Did they say that?" I frown at him.

"Of course baby. So is that what this is? You're worried they didn't like you?" What is his Dad playing at?

"Not exactly."

"Emmie, just tell me."

"Fine, but don't get mad, okay?" I hold his face in my hands.

He grabs my hands from his faces and holds them on my lap. "Fine." He may say that but I can't imagine Damon not getting mad at something like this.

"Well, your Dad wanted a private word with me."

"Okay?" He looks at me questioningly.

"The things he was saying, Damon, I'm sure his intentions for you were good." Or maybe not, I'm not really sure.

"What the hell did he say?"

"You know you said your girlfriends fled after meeting your parents?" I look at his hands in mine and stroke his with my fingers.

"Yeah." He raises an eyebrow as if to say where the hell is she going with this?

"I know why. Damon, he paid them to leave you." He removes his hands from mine and his hands ball into fists.

"What the fuck? He wouldn't do that." He stands up now, pacing the room.

"Are you calling me a liar? Damon, I didn't want to keep this from you. I want us to be honest with each other." He doesn't believe me, I thought he could tell if I was lying. But maybe he's lying to himself.

He pauses to think for a while and then he's back with me again. Kneeling between my legs. "You are not a liar. I believe you, but what did he say exactly?" He grabs my hands and I look at them, not his face.

"Oh you know, just called me a slapper and a hooker. And I couldn't make you happy. You secretly don't want us. And that there must be something I wanted in return for leaving you. All the other girls wanted something. So I told him to shove his proposal where the sun doesn't shine." I'm not angry anymore, I'm just sad. Sad for Damon.

"I'm so pissed. Of course you are none of those things. You are my beautiful fiancée," he growls.

"I'm sorry. I hope you know that I never thought about it for a second. I love you. I wouldn't do that to you. But just so we are clear, if you ever didn't want us then we would leave. If that's what you wanted..." I don't know what I'd do, but if that's what he wishes.

"How can you say that? I don't want you to leave. You've changed my life for the better. I've never wanted marriage until I met you. I've never met anyone like you. And to stand up to my Dad like that, you have guts. I bet he wasn't happy with you."

No, he wasn't. "Thank God," I say to his response. "He wasn't happy, I told him to bite me."

He chuckles, "There's the girl I fell in love with." I smile.

"I really am sorry Damon." I stroke his hair. He puts his hands on the back of my knees and he lifts me up, I have to wrap my arms around his neck to stop me from falling back.

"You have nothing to be sorry about." He kisses me and then he sits on the sofa, bringing me with him so I'm sitting on his lap with my legs either side of his legs. I keep my hands on the back of his neck.

"I hope your staff aren't afraid to come back tomorrow. Am I really that scary?" I frown and he laughs at me. He drops many soft kisses all over my face and I giggle at him. He really does know how to cheer me up.

"Yes, you are. They're men, they can handle it," he says in between kisses.

"So what are you going to do about your Dad? I don't feel comfortable seeing him again Damon. He said some nasty things." He stops kissing my face, and I miss his lips on me.

"It's okay. I'm going to phone him in the morning. If you don't want to see him then I won't make you."

"I'm sorry your girlfriends left you because of him."

"I'm not, I wouldn't have met you otherwise." I beam at him like he's just said the most romantic thing ever. I love that he is so open with his affections, I need this. I feel like my scars are slowly healing. I don't know if they will stay gone but I know I'm better with Damon.

I giggle, "Thank you for kidnapping me, Damon."

He laughs, "Oh, anytime. I may have to re-enact that first day in my office. You were beautiful, strong and your mouth... I didn't understand why you weren't afraid of me." He frowns as if he's getting lost in thought.

"I'd love that," I say, teasing, trying to snap him out of this mood.

"Oh, Miss Salvatore, I bet you would. And so would I. Anyway, let's get to bed." He stands up but he keeps hold of me. Kissing me and walking out of the living room, turning the light off as he goes. He's so skilled at this, he makes me feel like I'm skilled. I don't have to try with him. It just comes naturally, every touch, every kiss encouraging me, making me feel special.

*

A month has passed and we have set a date for the wedding. It is set for March 19th. It's two months away. In the last month, I've been taking my end of year school exams. They gave me the option to sit them due to special circumstances. I don't think they could handle me at school for another year. I've passed them all with flying colours. My Dad would expect nothing less. Damon has told me anything I want for the wedding is mine. Although I'm not the big wedding kind of girl. I'm only getting married to him because it means a lot to him and that I want to bind myself to him as much I can.

My phone rings and I answer it. "Emmie." I roll my eyes, she's too excited.

"Hey, Lexi." I try to return the same enthusiasm.

"What you doing today?"

"Erm, you know, cleaning up puke, changing nappies."

"Okay, enough. I love my niece but that's too much information. Anyway, you are coming wedding dress shopping with me today." I curse silently at the phone so she can't hear me.

"No, I'm not. I mean, Damon's busy today. I don't want to drag Lilly out. Another time though." She sighs, disappointed on the phone.

"Okay, that sucks. Well, text me when you're free then."

"Sure. Bye Lexi." She says bye and I hang up. I sag with relief, I feel so mean lying to her. I decide to take a cold shower while Lilly is sleeping. I stand with my front facing away from the door. So much has happened, I feel safe and calm for the first time in my life. I feel arms around me, even though he's caught me off guard, I don't tense like I used to. I know it's him. I tilt my head to my right giving him access to my neck and he kisses me. He nibbles my ear, that makes me gasp.

"So, you are lying to my sister now?" he says, teasing me. I freeze for a second and turn to face him. He's not mad, he's just smiling at me, how does he know anyway? "I've got a surprise for you today." I wonder what it is.

"And what is it?" I feel his smile on my neck as he kisses me.

"You'll have to wait to find out." I glare at him, I hate having to wait for things. I put my hands in his hair and pull his head down to kiss him. Once his lips touch mine, I trail my fingers over his abs and he groans in my mouth.

"You know," he says breathlessly between each kiss, "this won't make me tell you." Damn it, he knows me too well. I pull away and turn my back on him, continuing my shower. He chuckles behind me. We finish showering, I walk to the bedroom wrapped in a soft fluffy towel. I walk to Lilly and she is still sleeping peacefully.

I dress in jean shorts and a black strap top. I love Spanish weather. I brush my hair and leave it down. Damon kisses me on the forehead after he dresses and leaves the room. Now, what do I actually do today?

"Emmie!" Damon calls from downstairs. He never calls, he always comes to find me. So what is going on? I walk casually to go find him. He's standing in the hallway by the door with another guy. I freeze to assess the situation. "Your surprise," Damon says, smiling at me.

It's Danny, my Brother. I run into his arms and he spins me around. This is the best surprise I could have hoped for. He sets me on the floor and smiles at me. I was beginning to lose hope that he was going to get discharged from rehab.

"I'm taking you out today," Danny says.

I shake my head, I don't feel safe going out anymore. "I can't, I have Lilly."

"I will watch her Emmie, go have fun." I frown. Was this their plan all along? Get me out the house? Danny grabs my hand and leads me out the house without letting me refuse. Damon is laughing at me from the house. He picks up his phone and makes a call. Danny opens my side of the door and lets me climb in.

We sit in silence with the radio playing softly in the background. "So when did you get out?"

"Today, I wanted to see you." He shrugs but keeps his eyes on the road.

"So where are we going?"

"The mall." He looks at me and grins. There are too many people at the mall, any of them could be Desmond or my mother. I trust Danny to look after me so I try to relax a little. He pulls up in a car park. I hesitate to get out the car, he reaches my side and opens the door and takes my hand. He seems like he knows where he wants to go so I let him take me. I'm stopped in my tracks when I see Lexi and Jessie standing outside a shop. Damn it, I hope she isn't mad at me.

They look up and they flash a smile at me. Danny pulls me forwards even though my feet feel like they are planted in the concrete. Lexi and Jessie hug me. I hate hugging people with the exception of Danny and Damon. "You made it," Lexi says.

I look up at Danny who is laughing. "What's going on?"

"I called my brother to see what was so important that he wouldn't let his soon to be wife shop for a dress." Lexi crosses her arms. "And you know what he said?" I shake my head because it's true, I don't. "He said he was bored stiff and he would be happy to look after his daughter whilst his fiancée went dress shopping." I frown, of course he would drop me in it.

"So when I called him, he asked if I could do him a favour. He knows you have issues with leaving the house. He thought you may be more comfortable with me with you," Danny says.

"So we are going dress shopping," Jessie says whilst clapping her hands. I roll my eyes and Lexi and Jessie pull me into a shop. They pull a few from the rack and show them to me, I'm horrified at some that they've chosen. Danny sits on the sofa that sits in the middle of the room. I skim the dresses with my fingertips.

"Emmie, look at this one." Lexi holds up a huge puffy dress which I shake my head at. I frown, will I ever find a dress I'm comfortable with?

"Can I help you miss?" a lady asks. "If you give me a description of what you're looking for maybe I can help," she says sympathetically.

"I'm not really sure, all I know is I want something simple. Not too puffy like most dresses. But at the same time, I want something elegant." I put my hand on my forehead. "I'm looking for the impossible, aren't I?"

"Give me a minute to see what I can find. What size are you?"

I shrug, "Size UK 16/44." Her mouth drops open.

"Er, I'd say more like a UK 4/32." She frowns at me. I shrug again, what? I've always felt fat. I never check sizes I just throw them on. She smiles and walks away. I sit next to Danny who places his arm over my shoulder.

"So, what do you think?"

"This is exhausting, I'm never going to find the right dress, Danny. They won't have made one for me." The lady comes back with a dress in her hand. She holds it out towards me as if she's trying to show it off to me.

"Try this one. What do you think?" I think that I'm never going to look good in something like that.

"Go on Sis." I stand and carefully take the dress from her. I walk to the changing room, Danny follows closely behind. He waits outside while I slide the dress on. I look in the mirror, it's a simple chiffon lace with beading under the bust. Sweep train, A-line Sweetheart dress. There are no shoulder straps which expose my shoulders. I manage to do up the zip at the back. Is this me standing in front of the mirror, I squint and look closer.

I shake my head. "Sis, have you fallen and hit your head in there? It's a bit quiet." I don't reply, just stare into the mirror. He walks in as he didn't hear a reply. He stands there staring at the reflection too. Tears fall down my face. This is the dress.

"Emmie?" Lexi calls. I ignore her. She stands behind Danny now. "Emmie. Wow." She puts her phone to my ear.

"Emmie? Baby?" Damon says softly. I sniff. But don't reply, I just stare at the reflection of this angel in the mirror. "Baby, are you crying? Talk to me."

"Damon," I sniff.

"I'm here baby. What's wrong?"

"I found it," I squeak.

"Found what, the dress?" he says concerned.

"Yeah. It's beautiful, it's like I'm staring back at an angel."

"You are my angel. And you'd look amazing in a dustbin bag, so I bet you look blinding with beauty with a wedding dress on. I can't wait to see you in it." I smile at his words. The price tag catches my eye in the mirror. I gasp. "What's wrong?"

"I just saw the price tag." I frown. It's too expensive. I may love it but I'm also not spending that much on a dress that I'll wear once.

"Baby, I told you money isn't an issue. Now I thought I'd have to pick one myself for you and tell you I liked it so you would wear it. But you've found one that you love, and I didn't think that was in your DNA to love a dress. Now please, buy it. If you don't, I'll get Lexi or even Danny to buy it anyway," he pleads on the phone.

"Okay," I whisper. Lexi takes the phone back.

"Of course Bro. I wouldn't allow such a thing. If it wasn't you that she was marrying, I'd drag her to a church right now and marry her myself." Yeah, but I wouldn't say I do.

"Everyone out. Sis, let's get the dress off so you don't soak it in your tears." Lexi leaves the room still on the phone. I nod and Danny leaves the room. I don't want to take it off. I feel beautiful for the first time in my life. First time I've truly believed it.

I unzip the dress and step out of it and hang it back on the hanger. I get dressed and take a deep breath and bring it to the front of the shop. The lady smiles at me. "I did it?" I nod at her, she did. She picked the dress. I place the dress on the table by the till.

"Shall we go get food?" Lexi asks.

I shake my head. "I don't think so."

"Why? What do you mean?" Lexi asks confused.

"You haven't found your dresses yet." They both look at me shocked. "I can't get married without bridesmaids." I smile.

They both squeal and clap. "What's your theme colour?" Lexi asks.

"Turquoise blue." I smile at them. I sit on the sofa next to Danny. He must be so bored with all this dress stuff but he doesn't say anything. Jessie and Lexi find dresses they like in my theme colour and try them on to model them for me.

We all agree with the second one. It matches some of the design on my dress, strapless. It is floor length at the back but the front opens up above the knee. It has heart sequins under the bust. I pay for the dresses with the card Damon insisted I had. He said, 'What's mine is yours'. I tried to refuse but he wasn't to be argued with. The dresses will be delivered in a week or so, she said.

We head to a small cafe to have lunch. I scan the menu, my stomach is in knots from dress shopping. I'm too wound up to eat. I've been eating more so than normal whilst living with Damon, he rarely lets me skip a meal. And I haven't needed to. I feel normal, relaxed with him. Life's easy with him. It's how it should be. But I sit staring at the menu just wanting to be in the comfort of my home.

"What can I get everyone?" the male waiter asks. He looks straight at me and winks at me. I frown, what is he playing at?

"I guess I'll have a strawberry and banana smoothie with a feta salad.

Please."

"Sure, can I get you anything else?" He lingers on anything.

"Is that all you are having?" Danny scolds. "Will you ever grow out of this not eating crap?" I shrug, it's not something you grow out of. It stays with you in the back of your mind.

"I'll get a double cheeseburger and chips with a coffee," Danny says. How can people drink hot drinks in this heat?

"I'll get a cooked breakfast with a strawberry milkshake," Lexi says.

"Can I get your number...? And also a jacket with tuna mayo. And a coke." The waiter looks flustered and I open my mouth at her forwardness. The waiter glances at me and then back to Jessie.

"I'd rather give it to your friend," he says casually as he glances at me.

"She's not my friend," Jessie says. I'm not? Ouch. "She's my girlfriend." I drop my mouth open again. Is she mad that he rejected her? I don't understand. "If you want to give it to her then she will share it with me. Or share you with me." She winks.

He goes red with embarrassment. "Girls, stop messing with the damn waiter, I'd like to eat sometime today," Danny moans. The waiter nods and retreats like a flash to the kitchen.

"What the hell was that?" I demand.

"What? I love you but how is it you have all the guys? I just thought he may like a threesome." She shrugs. "Something I've always wanted to try." I put my hand under my chin.

"Wait, have you?" She sounds surprised.

"No, not really."

"What do you mean not really? Spill."

"When I was in my dream world I um, kinda dreamed that I married Damon and Brody. After the honeymoon we..."

"Stop," Lexi and Danny say in unison.

"I don't want to hear about my sister having a threesome." He holds his hands up towards me. I nudge him with my elbow playfully.

"And I don't want to hear about my brother," Lexi says disgustedly.

"Well, I want to know more," Jessie says intrigued. "Who was better?"

I roll my eyes at her, "Jessie it was a dream, I didn't feel anything. I was numb, I just saw what I wanted to see. It wasn't real, and if it was I would have pushed Brody away."

"So you don't have feelings for him?" She sounds a little relieved that I'd push him away.

"I love him, he's been a huge part of my life. But I don't see him romantically, not since that night he kissed me." She nods. What's it to her anyway?

The waiter arrives with our drinks. He doesn't say anything, just returns to the kitchen again when he serves our drinks. I rest my head on Danny's shoulder. He takes out his phone from his pocket. He passes it to Jessie. "Take a picture of us? I want memories of my sister happy," he says and wraps his arm around my shoulder. I smile a genuinely happy smile whilst Jessie snaps photos. Then I poke my tongue out. Lexi laughs. I kiss Danny on the cheek for the last picture and he wipes his cheek.

Not like I slobbered on him. He laughs. Our food arrives and the waiter lingers while he gives me mine, I lean towards Danny when he comes too close. Danny looks up at me to assess my sudden shift towards him. He glares at the waiter and he backs off almost immediately and I sag with relief. This is why I love my protective big brother. I smile at him and he frowns back like he's still bothered by the waiter.

I eat the feta cheese but push the salad around on the plate. Danny leans towards my ear and whispers, "Emmie, if you love me you'll eat your damn food. Make your big Brother happy?" I frown at him, he's always been overbearing with the food thing. But he's never played this card. Maybe he's changed since rehab. And that sits heavy on my heart because I'd do just about anything for my Brother if he pleaded with me. I rest my face on my hand, shovelling the salad in my mouth. Good job I only ordered a salad, or this may have gone a different way.

The waiter comes over with the bill and I hand over my card. They all try to give me money but I fend them off. This will make Damon happy. And anyway, I'm a millionaire if I choose to accept it in my mind. The waiter goes to take my card but his fingers catch my fingers and I gasp and drop the card by accident. When people touch me, it still repulses me. He smiles at me and grabs my card from the table and inserts it into the card reader.

He hands me the machine and I'm much more careful this time. I hand it back when I'm done. He hands out the card to me and Danny reaches across me and grabs it himself. I guess he noticed why I dropped the card. The girls seem oblivious, which is good. Danny hands me my card and I return it in my pocket.

I say goodbye to Lexi and Jessie, I guess it's been good to spend the day with them. At least I can check dresses off my list. Danny grabs my hand and leads me back to the car. I'm exhausted and I end up falling asleep on the way home.

Chapter 26

Today is the day of my wedding. I've been up since stupid o'clock stressing. Damon believes in that stupid superstition that you can't see the bride before the wedding. So he stayed at the safe house. He would have paid for a hotel for me but he knows I'd feel safer here at home. The wedding is at noon. Jessie and Lexi will be here soon to help me get ready.

I'm pacing the bedroom when Danny walks in. He brings me in for a hug. "Big day, huh?" I nod into his chest. I've had a sleepless night without Damon, so I'm all anxious now, knowing people will be staring at me today. "I'm here to take Lilly-May for you. But I just wanted to let you know, I'm so proud of you. And it makes your big Brother happy to see you so happy." I frown.

"I'm terrified, Danny." Not happy. Not yet, not till I see Damon again.

"Of what Sis? Damon will be waiting for you. He will look after you for the rest of your life. What are you so afraid of?" I don't know. I guess lots of things that he won't show, that I'll make a fool of myself. But I just shrug. "Sis, he's crazy for you. Do you think I would let you marry him if I wasn't sure about him?" No, I don't think Danny would.

Danny walks over to Lilly's Moses basket and picks her up. She cries and I go and take her off him. I rock her gently, "Sis, you know I could have done that." Lilly falls back to sleep. "You have to relax a little." I shake my head, I can't relax. Not yet.

Jessie and Lexi arrive in my bedroom. "Emmie, you look awful. Looks like we have a lot of work to do," Lexi says. I frown, I always look awful. Do I look worse today? Is that even possible? "You get out," Lexi points at Danny. This is too much to process. I back up away from them. I'm stressing out, my heart is beating out my chest.

"Call your brother," Danny frowns as he's talking to Lexi. I continue to back away, keeping Lilly safe in my arms. Lexi does as he says.

"Bro," Lexi says. "No, Emmie's freaking out. Can you talk to her?" she says with a hurt look on her face. Lexi walks towards me and I continue to back away until my back reaches a wall. She holds her hands up in defeat. Stay away from me, please. "Bro? I'm going to put you on loudspeaker, she won't let me near her." She holds out the phone.

"Emmie?" Damon's soothing voice surrounds my body. Enveloping me into a bubble, his bubble. "Baby, you are safe." My heart yearns for him. I want him to hug me, his arms protecting me. Feeling his lips on mine. But instead, my heart is beating too fast. My body shakes and my breathing is too quick.

"Emmie, talk to him. You will see him in a few hours, he will be waiting for you," Danny says slowly.

"Baby, I will be waiting. I promise and I have to say it will be a long wait," he chuckles, trying to lighten the mood.

"Damon, I'm scared." He lets out a loud breath like he was holding his breath.

"You have nothing to be scared of, I promise." My heart slows and I sag with relief, just hearing his voice has soothed me. But I'm still anxious, I will have people staring at me walking down the aisle. Danny walks towards me and takes Lilly off me. Danny hugs me tight with one arm to avoid Lilly getting squished.

"You'll be one amazing bride. I'm so proud of you. See you soon," he whispers in my ear, kisses the top of my hair and leaves. My breathing is back to normal. Lexi has hung up the phone and is setting up the makeup. My phone beeps so I grab it from the bed and turn my back on the girls.

Good Morning beautiful. Did you miss me?

The number is unknown, who the hell is this person?

I reply, *Who is this?*

Well that hurts. I've definitely missed you.

Who the hell would miss me? I've only given family and friends this number.

I'm sorry, I don't know who you are? Wrong number maybe?

Must be a wrong number, I frown at the screen.

That seriously hurts Emmie. Don't worry, you'll find out soon enough. I'll make you regret leaving me. Have fun at your wedding. Watch your back.

My heart is pounding out my chest again. I think Danny and Damon are right, I may die of a heart attack with all this worrying. They know my name, so it's not a wrong number. Leaving them? I don't understand. It's not my back I'm worried about.

"Emmie, are we doing this?" Jessie says, frustrated. I turn to face them, throwing my phone on the bed. I'm not letting anyone scare me into not turning up for my wedding. Getting married to my soul mate. No, I won't be scared away. I sit on the edge of the bed and let Lexi and Jessie work their magic. Jessie does my makeup and Lexi does my hair. I told Lexi I wanted my hair down but she is welcome to do any style she wants.

After an hour or so they give me the all clear to get in my dress. After trying to reject their offer of helping me in my dress, they wouldn't take no for an answer. They didn't want me to ruin anything. They both stare at my body when I'm stood with only my panties on. I frown and they busy themselves with the dress.

"You have so many scars, Emmie," Lexi says. Again with her honest mouth, saying what she's thinking. My scars aren't that noticeable, but they are really close to me. "How did you get them?" Lexi doesn't know as much as Jessie. Well, in fact, Lexi doesn't know anything as far as I'm aware. But Jessie doesn't say anything, even Jessie doesn't know everything. They hold the dress open on the floor so I can step in. I step in and they lift it up and fasten the zip.

"My magic touch," Lexi says. She holds out a simple but stylish tiara. "I didn't think you'd like to wear a veil." She shrugs and I muster up a smile for her and she places it on my head. She drags me over to the mirror. My mouth drops open. The person in the mirror is even more of an angel than before. I can do this.

"Wow, girl. You look amazing. Rider is a lucky man," Jessie says, admiring her handiwork.

"You think?" I hope Damon likes it.

"No room for tears today Bestie," she scowls. I carefully wipe my eyes, I didn't even notice I was crying. Oops. "Brody will meet us there," she says. I frown, recalling that awful conversation.

*

I was at home and Brody came to visit me. "Hey, Emmie," Brody said.

"Hey, Brody. You okay?" I noticed how tense he was. Brody is always so calm.

"I wanted to ask you something."

"Okay?" I didn't know why he wouldn't just say it. He never normally has a problem with speaking his mind.

"Now I don't want to hurt you." Hurt me? I'd been hurting him since I met Damon.

"Brody, just spit it out already." I hate it when people beat around the bush.

"Okay, so I really want to ask Jessie out. Nothing has happened as I wanted to check you were okay with it first." I zoned out, he wanted to date Jessie? I suspected something was going on between them, but Jessie always claimed she hated him. "Please say something." What the hell did he want me to say? "Emmie..." It hurt to hear it. I knew I was being selfish thinking that. I wanted to be just friends so I should let him go, right? But with Jessie? I just didn't know what to do. "Emmie, please."

"Are you serious? You are replacing me with Jessie? Didn't take you long, did it? If this is what you both want, then who the hell am I to stand in your way?" I held my mouth in shock. I was upset but it wasn't fair to say those things. I had Damon, I couldn't be tied to Brody too. I wanted Damon with 100% of my heart.

"Please don't be mad. If you aren't comfortable with this then it won't happen. I care about you. You left me, remember?" He was being so understanding. I did leave him, it was all me. He was still holding out hope? Or just didn't want to hurt me. He had the right to move on.

"I'm sorry Brody. Ignore me. My hormones are still everywhere. I want you to be happy. I shouldn't get in your way." Part of me didn't mean those words but they had to be said.

"That is such a relief. Thank you. You are truly a great friend." Yeah, friend. He left happy, and he left me feeling like I'd lost a chunk of myself. But of course Damon came home and he filled the chunk that Brody had left.

*

"Emmie, we need to go," Lexi says, bringing me out of that memory. They've both changed into their dresses. They look stunning. They'll totally upstage me on my wedding day, but I choose not to let that bother me.

I leave the bedroom, taking each step with great care because I'm so damn clumsy. I take the last few steps of the stairs and I look up to see

Sully standing by the door. He's in a smart black suit. His mouth drops open when he sees me. I smile at him.

"Wow, Emmie. You look amazing. Like an angel." That's the word I used to describe myself in the shop.

"Doesn't she?" Jessie grins.

"You don't look too bad yourself in that suit. Look at you." I've never seen him in a suit before, he's always been in jeans. He blushes and I giggle.

"Jessie, Lexi. I'll meet you outside. I need to speak to Sully," I say awkwardly.

"Sure, but don't take too long. You don't want to be late," Jessie says and they both leave the house. I turn to face Sully and he is looking at me, trying to assess the situation.

"Emmie, are you okay?" he asks, concerned.

"Not really." I need to tell someone and Sully is the only one I trust apart from Damon.

"What's wrong?" he frowns.

I take a deep breath trying to get the right words out. "I'll tell you if you promise not to mention it to Damon. Not today."

"Emmie, if it's bothering you, and you think I can help then I will. Even if I can't tell my Boss. But you know he could help whatever it is." I feel reassured that he won't tell Damon, not today at least.

"Please, I don't want to worry him. Not today." He stays calm but I know he wants me to just spit it out.

"I promise. Please tell me."

"Okay, well, I received these texts this morning. Can you try to trace the number?" I hold my phone in my hand.

"Let me see them." I open up the texts and pass him my phone. He scowls at the screen.

"Emmie, this is serious. Sounds like they aren't messing around. Damon should know about this. He will be pissed if he doesn't know." Yes, he will be, but I'm hoping nothing will happen on my wedding day and then I'll be sure to tell him.

"Sully, you promised."

"And I'll keep that promise. Of course. But I'm not comfortable with it. I will tell him tomorrow though if you haven't." I nod, that's fair. "But I will be keeping a close eye on you today. Just to be safe."

I smile. "All eyes will be on me anyway. You all like gawking at me." He blushes again, this is too easy.

"Ha, don't let the Boss hear you say that."

"Ha, he would probably shoot you all," I laugh, teasing him.

"Emmie, come on!" Lexi calls from outside. I roll my eyes. That girl is so damn controlling.

"We better get you to your wedding before the Boss freaks out that you're not coming." He probably would freak out if I was late.

I laugh, "He knows I'm coming. But I know what you mean." Sully holds his arm out to escort me to the limo. Yes, the limo! Damon wanted me to ride in style. But he only hired the limo, Sully will drive it. Sully escorts me to the back of the limo and helps me slide in, making sure all my dress is inside. Jessie and Lexi have already cracked open the champagne. They hand me a glass and I take a huge mouthful. I need confidence.

It's only a short trip. Our wedding is on the beach, it's my ideal wedding location. Sully helps me out of the limo. I examine the beach, it's filled with many people. Mostly of people I don't know. I can't see Damon anywhere and that puts me on edge.

"Be careful you don't ruin anything," Lexi huffs and her and Jessie walk off towards the crowd.

"Sully, will you promise me something?" He isn't going to like it, but it will keep me calmer.

"I guess," he says awkwardly. He knows me well enough that it's going to be against Damon's orders but for some reason, he likes to put my feeling before Damon's.

"If anything does happen today, make sure you protect Lilly-May and Damon first. They come first." I don't care about myself, they just need to be safe.

"How can you ask me to do that?" He shakes his head. He's pissed. "Boss will never forgive me if I did that."

I stand my ground, "Promise me, Sully," I demand.

He crosses his arms and so do I. We stay glaring at each other for a while and then he lets his arms relax, "You are a stubborn woman, aren't you? Okay, I promise," he grudgingly accepts.

"Thanks, Big Guy," I say and quickly hug him.

"I will see you down there. Better do my best man duties." I like that

Damon chose Sully to be his best man. They are like brothers.

Sully walks towards the crowd and Danny walks towards me and hugs me tight. "Wow, Sis you look amazing. I'm so proud of you." He pushes away a tear from his eye. I must not cry, not yet.

"Where the hell is my daughter?" He's supposed to be watching her.

"Relax, she's with Lexi." I don't 100% trust her yet, not with Lilly, but I let it go.

"Make sure you stay close to her today, okay?" She needs all the protection she can get if something does go down, which I hope it doesn't.

He raises an eyebrow, "What's going on Sis?" I can't tell him. Not today, he'll probably drag me away kicking and screaming.

"Just promise me, Danny." I glare at him.

"Of course Sis. She will always be safe with me," he says in defence, and I trust him. He may not have protected me, but I think he's learned from his mistakes. Well, they weren't his mistakes, he is an amazing brother. "May I walk you down the aisle now? I figured that I was most fitting for the job." I never thought about it, but yes, he is most fitting for the job. I grin at him.

"Aww Bro. I'd love that." I really would. He holds his arm out and I put my arm in his. We reach the sand and I stop, I kick my shoes off, holding on to Danny for support. As we reach the crowd, they all stand and stop their chattering. They all stare at me.

I reach the aisle and I catch sight of him. My soon to be husband. I stop and take a second to feel relieved that he showed. He looks at me and his mouth drops open. He makes me think I could be beautiful every day, but today is different. Today he looks at me and I feel beautiful, I didn't think that would be possible. But I do feel beautiful, I feel worthy of this man. I don't know if it will last but it makes my decision to marry him worthwhile.

Music starts to play, I'm not sure where from. But Danny and I take our cue to walk down the aisle. I listen to the lyrics, I never choose a song for this bit. So I guess Damon did, maybe trying to tell me something?

'I was her, she was me. We were one, we were free. And if there's somebody calling me on, she's the one. If there's somebody calling me on, she's the one. We were young, we were wrong. We were fine all along. If there's somebody calling me on, she's the one.'

The music stops when I reach Damon and Danny grabs my hand and places it into Damon's. My hand is shaky but it doesn't seem to bother him. Danny smiles and nods at Damon and Damon nods too. Danny leaves us.

Damon leans towards my ear and whispers, "Baby you look absolutely beautiful. I didn't think it was possible for you to look more beautiful. But here you are proving me wrong again." Do I prove him wrong a lot? Damon is handsome in a suit, he is definitely the most beautiful one here.

"Thank you. You are looking good yourself," I whisper back.

The marriage officiant clears his throat. Everyone takes a seat. I don't look closely at their faces. I just try and focus on Damon's beautiful face. "We are all gathered here today to witness the marriage of Emmie Salvatore and Damon Rider. Damon, you may start with your vows." This all sounds like Deja Vu.

"Emmie, I promise to love you, care for you and protect you. I feel we have been through a lot together. I can't wait to grow old with you. You've given me a family, one that I'll cherish every day. You make me question life, make me want to be a better person, for you and for our daughter. I love you." He looks straight into my eyes while he says those words. "You are the most beautiful thing I've ever seen. I don't understand how you can love me but you make my life whole. My life was meaningless without you. You gave me our beautiful daughter. She obviously takes after you. You are one very stubborn woman and you keep me on my toes. You make me alive."

I think he has things the wrong way, this is how I feel. You don't know how I love you? You are amazing in every way, I am the luckiest person on the planet. "Thank you, Damon. And Emmie, it's your turn," the marriage officiant says, looking at Damon then to me.

His vows were beautiful. I look to our family and friends. Mrs Rider is crying. She looks proud of her son. Danny is smiling at me.

I giggle, trying to lighten the mood. "Well, I have to admit that's going to be hard to beat." The crowd erupts into laughter too. Great, that's what I was hoping for. "I know our life together has been somewhat rocky. I know I've put you through hell and back. You are my anchor, you keep me on earth. You make me keep living. I feel you know me inside out. And I have to admit, that scares me. But having you around me makes me feel safe, protected, happy. I know I'm always in danger or in trouble but I always know you will protect me. My head goes blank and all I can think of is you. You are my soul mate and I'm drawn to you like a moth to a flame."

Damon grins at me. "I think I can speak for everyone here and say that was a beautiful speech, Emmie. Damon, you are one lucky man," the marriage officiant says and Damon nods in agreement.

"Oh trust me. I know." He chuckles.

"Okay, Damon Rider, do you take Emmie Salvatore to be your wedded wife?"

"Obviously. I do." The crowd laughs at Damon's strong answer.

"Okay, Emmie Salvatore, do you take Damon Rider to be your wedded husband?" What a stupid question.

"I do." A million times yes.

"I now pronounce you husband and wife. You may kiss the bride."

"Finally," Damon says while he pulls me close and tilts me back and kisses me, my hair brushing against the sand. The crowd whoops and applauses but I don't want him to let me go, ever. And I think he feels it too. All tension is gone now. He does that to me. He pulls away and brings me back on to my feet.

"I love you Mrs Rider." Wow, that sounds odd. But I love it.

I grin at him, "I love you too Damon." He grabs my hand and leads me to the crowd. His Mom runs up to us with tears running down her face. She hugs both of us in turn. I freeze at her touch, but I've got to get used to this. I have a feeling a lot of people will want to hug me.

"Son, I'm so proud of you," she says wiping away her tears.

"Thanks Mom." Music starts playing softly in the background.

He leans down to my ear and says, "May I have this dance?" I picked this song so I'd better dance with him. I can't dance but I'm hoping he will lead me through this like he leads me through life.

"You may," I say and take his outstretched hand. He quickly pulls me into his chest and I gasp. He starts to move in time with the music.

He sings softly with the music. *"Every time our eyes meet this feeling inside me is almost more than I can take. Baby, when you touch me I can feel how much you love me and it just blows me away. I've never been this close to anyone or anything. I can hear your thoughts. I can see your dreams. I don't know how you do what you do. I'm so in love with you. It just keeps getting better. I wanna spend the rest of my life."*

He spins me around and then pulls me back to his chest. *"With you by my side. Forever and ever. Every little thing that you do. Baby, I'm amazed by you. The smell of your skin. The taste of your kiss. The way you whisper in the dark. Your hair all around me. Baby, you surround me. You touch every place in my heart. Oh, it feels like the first time every time. I wanna spend the whole night in your eyes. I don't know how you do what you do. I'm so in love with you. It just keeps getting better. I wanna spend the rest of my life. With you by my side. Forever and ever. Every little thing that you do. Baby, I'm amazed by you. Every little thing that you do. I'm so in love with you. It just keeps getting better."*

He spins me around again, I just want to stay close to him. But I try to enjoy his enthusiasm. *"I wanna spend the rest of my life. With you by my side. Forever and ever. Every little thing that you do. Oh, yeah every little thing that you do. Baby, I'm amazed by you."*

This is the best moment of my life.

Chapter 27

When the first dance song finishes others follow in its place, but Damon keeps hold of me. We are caught up in our own little spell. "Emmie, can I have this dance, I'd like a word?" I tense and look at who is talking to me. It's Mr Rider, I still don't want to talk to him, but I won't let him ruin this day.

Damon pulls me tighter into his chest, "Dad, not now."

"Please son. I want to apologise to Emmie." I can't imagine him meaning an apology but I guess I want to see what he has to say.

"Damon, it's fine. Go dance with your sister or something." I walk out of Damon's arms, and I miss his protection already. But I shake the feeling off.

"Okay, just shout if you need me." I nod and he walks to the crowd of people. I always need you, Damon, you just don't know it.

Mr Rider holds his hand out and I hesitantly place mine in his. Come on Emmie, you can do this, it's just one dance. His touch affects me just the same as anyone else's. It makes me recoil from him, as we dance, I try not to touch any other part of his body apart from his hand and his shoulder very lightly. He has his hand on my waist and I'm conscious of that fact. I look anywhere but his face.

"I want to apologise Emmie. It was wrong of me to say those things. I know now that you make him happy and quite frankly, he needs you." I shake my head, Damon doesn't need me. Not like I need him.

"And I need him." I frown.

"I know. I've always had an image in my head of who he would marry." Yeah, some skinny pretty blonde no doubt, one that looks like a super model.

"And I don't fit the bill, I get it." I try to find Damon in the crowd but I don't see him.

"I imagined a smart, beautiful woman who encouraged him to better his life." Nope, definitely not me. "I made a quick judgment on you and I'm sorry for that. You know he doesn't listen to anyone." Of course I know that. He's my husband. "But when I see you with him, I can see he loves you and he wants to do anything to make you happy. It's good for him that he listens to you. Hell, he's never listened to any of us. He's very hot headed." Yes, Damon does have temper issues, but I love him for it. He's compassionate and protective of things that are his. Does he really mean this or is he just making peace? "I don't expect you to forgive me but I had to say sorry. I hope you enjoy the rest of your wedding." My problem is I do forgive, maybe too easily. I don't know what to say.

"Thanks, Mr Rider."

"Call me Jerry." Jerry? So where is Tom? I laugh to myself, I really should stop giving people nicknames. I nod and he releases me and walks away, I sag with relief that he's taken his hands off of me.

"Emmie? Would you make your brother proud and dance with me?" I smile at Danny and I let him sweep me off my feet across the dance floor. He doesn't let my feet reach the ground, just continues to spin me around and dance around the dance floor. I squeal playfully and giggle. I love my Brother. He joins me laughing, and then I see him nod at the DJ and the song changes. He sets me on my feet so we can dance together. I haven't heard this song before but I listen carefully to the lyrics. He mouths the words as I hear them.

'You are my sister, we were born. So innocent, so full of need. There were times we were friends but times I was so cruel. Each night I'd ask for you to watch me as I sleep. I was so afraid of the night. You seemed to move through the places that I feared. You lived inside my world so softly. Protected only by the kindness of your nature. You are my sister. And I love you. May all of your dreams come true. We felt so differently then. So similar over the years. The way we laugh the way we experience pain. So many memories. But there's nothing left to gain from remembering. Faces and worlds that no one else will ever know. You are my sister. And I love you. May all of your dreams come true. I want this for you. They're gonna come true.'

I beam at him, what a lovely song. He hugs me tight and says, "I really do love you, I'd better go watch Lilly-May. Lexi is with her." I nod and smile at him and then he leaves.

"Emmie. You look beautiful." My hairs on my back stand up in repulsion to her voice. I turn around to see my mother smiling at me. Seriously? Is she stupid? I haven't seen this woman in months and she chooses to turn up now? Pray that Damon doesn't see you.

"What the hell are you doing here?" I don't want you here, not since you put Desmond before your daughter. When your daughter needed you.

"I wanted to see my baby on her wedding day." How did she even know? I didn't send her an invite and Damon certainly wouldn't.

"What gives you the right?" Keep calm Emmie, don't let her ruin this.

"I'm your Mom." She shrugs.

Okay, I'm angry now, she's not my Mother anymore. "No, you're not. You stopped being my Momma when you chose him over me. Who the hell does that?" I would never put Damon before my daughter, no matter how much I love Damon.

"Honey you have to understand I thought you were in a clinic." People are starting to stare at our outburst, but I don't care. I'm too angry.

"Didn't you think to check after countless people told you?" She never even believed Danny, her own son. Or chose to ignore him.

"I trust Desmond. You were in a clinic." That is present tense which means she still trusts him, which means he must still be alive. I step away in horror.

"I'm sorry, what did you say? You TRUST Desmond." Even now, she still believes him.

"Emmie." She steps towards me and I step back too.

"You've seen him, haven't you?"

"Don't be like this." Is she serious? Her husband tries to kill me and my baby and she tells me not to be like this.

"Come on, let's hear it dear Mother of mine. What was his excuse for kidnapping me?" I can't wait to hear what he's come up with.

"Emmie, he didn't kidnap you. You were in a clinic, you woke up scared and you fled." Of course he did. She really is stupid.

"You are deluded. You really are. I want you to leave," I scream, I don't want to see her face anymore. Not on my wedding day. Not ever really. I feel an arm around my waist and I relax at his touch.

"What the hell are you doing here? You are putting her at risk being here," Damon shouts. He's mad but I don't care if he gets her to leave.

I cross my arms, "In her eyes, I'm not. Apparently, I woke up in a clinic and fled the scene."

"You are insane. She was covered in blood."

"So how does he explain his head injury? How is he alive anyway?" I say.

"He was doing some work at home and a hammer fell on his head." I laugh hysterically, a hammer fell on his head? That's funny, that's the best he could have come up with?

I roll my eyes, "Yeah, that's what happened."

"You should leave Mrs White," Damon says calmly, Mrs White sounds too weird to me.

She glares at us, "I can see where I'm not wanted." Why am I hurt by her pain? I think it's just who I am. I hug Damon with my front on his side and continue to watch her. She walks away from us. I don't feel like I'm missing anything, the opposite actually. Since she was back, nothing seemed natural about us. Instead of my mother looking after me, it was my brother.

A few people scream, I don't think anything of it but Damon drags me away. Where to I don't know but Damon stops in front of a blonde guy. He looks familiar, like from a dream. Damon pushes me behind him. My heart beats double time, not because this guy has a gun in his hand but because of who he is. He haunts me in my dreams, he haunts my memories. It's Rex, the guy that held me captive and made me be his girlfriend. He smiles at me but I cower into Damon, clutching to him.

"Hey, baby. Did you miss me?" No, I didn't. But that may be because I see him nearly everywhere I go. When I go out in public I always scan faces to see if they are Rex, my mother or Desmond.

"It was you, wasn't it?" He must have sent those texts this morning.

"I'm hurt that you thought it would be anyone else." He doesn't look hurt. Why has he come after me now? I thought he was in prison.

"What's he talking about?" Damon says confused. He doesn't look back at me but I know he's speaking to me.

"I sent her a good luck wedding text this morning." Not really, more of a threatening message. But I didn't think whoever was behind it would come here.

"Why didn't you tell me, Emmie?" Because you probably wouldn't risk marrying me if I had. And I couldn't wait any longer.

"That isn't important right now." I know Damon wants answers which he will get if we survive this. But right now, he doesn't push it anymore.

"I'm not going to prolong this. I came here to shoot your husband. You are mine." Wait, what? No... If I thought this was the plan then I would have kept Damon out of harm's way.

"Do your worst," Damon growls, shifting his weight so he is covering my body. I can't let this happen. Rex draws his gun with a huge smile on his face. I cry out, I can't lose Damon. Where the hell is Sully? I know I said protect Lilly-May but I did say Damon too. I kick the back of Damon's knee and push him hard with my body and he tumbles to the floor and then I hear a bang, shortly followed is a sharp pain in my arm.

I drop to my knees, man this hurts but not as much as other gunshot wounds I've had. I fall to the ground, the pain too much and everything goes black.

I'm awoken to shouting, "Shit. What the hell happened?" Sully is panicked.

"That idiot Rex had a gun. Where the hell were you?" I feel Damon's hands on my face but I don't open my eyes yet.

"I'm sorry Boss, my first priority was to check the baby was safe." Yes, she was but you also promised Damon would be safe too.

"I get that but it's almost like you knew that was going happen." He did but don't shout at him, shout at me. I did this.

"I'm sorry Boss, Emmie showed me the text this morning. She didn't want to worry you. She made me promise to protect you and the baby." I think Sully regrets promising anything but I don't regret it.

"Why the hell would you promise that Sully? Your job was to protect Emmie. And now she's been shot again. Why didn't you tell me?" Damon is angry, I won't let him take it out on Sully. "Why the hell did you let this happen, Sully?" he demands again.

"Leave him alone," I scold, my voice is weak but they heard me.

"Emmie?" Damon says, relieved. I'm angry with him. Sully was only respecting my wishes.

"No, I'm Jessie," I growl.

"This isn't funny," he scolds me, no this isn't funny.

"Will you shut up? This isn't Sully's fault." I try to stand but Damon grabs me and lifts me into his arms as he stands.

"Emmie, you were shot," he says as he nuzzles his nose into my hair. I close my eyes and breathe him in. No, I'm still mad at him.

"Was I? I didn't realise," I mock him.

"Seriously? We're playing that card?" he glares at me and I glare back. I'm not worried so much about him finding me frustrating now that we are married.

"Just be quiet," I whisper as I bury my head into his neck and he sighs.

"I should take you to the hospital, Emmie." No way.

"You'll do no such thing. I haven't heard the best man speech yet." I'm not leaving yet, the pain is bearable.

"Emmie, you've got a bullet in your arm." Damon is hurt, but he knows I won't be argued with.

"Huh... that's what that is. The Doctor is here somewhere. He'll do something later."

"I'll go find the Doctor," Sully says awkwardly but I don't look at him, just continue to glare at Damon.

"Why the hell did you push me out the way?" He puts his forehead on mine.

"You're my husband now. I need to protect you." I can't live without you. Also, Lilly needs her dad.

"That's what I'm supposed to do for you. I don't know what I'd do if I lost you." Ditto.

"You're not going to lose me. Life has had many chances to take me and here I am..." Countless times has some force tried to take me and some of them I didn't mind going but now I'm happy and I want to stay with Damon forever. A lifetime isn't long enough for me.

"You're so strong. I will kill Rex for what he has done." I'm not worried about him, he obviously still has feelings for me which I could manipulate. But Desmond, no way, he scares me more than anyone has before.

"Actually, I'm more worried about Desmond." His face still haunts my dreams.

"I promise you, I'll get them both. I love you, Emmie." He walks over to a chair and sits down with me on his lap.

"And I love you, Damon." I stroke his face and kiss him softly.

"It could only be you who got shot on her wedding day. Seriously Emmie?" I break the kiss with Damon to see the Doc standing in front of us.

"What can I say? I was protecting my man." I smile but the Doc doesn't smile at me.

"And what about all the other times?" He raises his eyebrow.

I shrug, "That was nothing. Bad luck, I guess."

He looks at my wound from where he is standing. "You really need to go to the hospital."

"I don't think so. My wedding isn't over yet. Patch me up till later." I can wait a few hours, I can and I will.

"Just say the word Doc and I'll have Sully carry her there." I frown, if anyone's carrying me it would be my husband.

"Just because it's your wedding day and I have a soft spot for you, I'll patch you up. Are you in any pain?" Not really, not anymore.

"No, I'm just mad."

"Well good. You'll find that you will get discomfort soon, you're running on adrenaline. Come to me as soon as that happens, okay?" Yeah, yeah, whatever. I'll be fine.

"Sure, thanks Doctor." I shrug.

"I think it's about time you can call me by my first name. Call me Lucas. Besides, I've seen parts of your body men only dream of." Damon clears his throat, I look at him and he's pissed by Lucas's words. I can't imagine people dream of seeing parts of my body but I'm not going to argue.

Lucas grabs a chair and takes a seat, he cleans my wound and bandages it up for now. I bury my face into Damon's neck whilst he does it. "I'm done. Congratulations you two. You're perfect for each other." I smile at him and he smiles back. Lucas walks off, leaving us to it.

"Let's take our seats. I can't wait to hear these speeches." Instead of letting me stand, he stands up with me in his arms. He carries me to the table, facing the stage. He places me in a chair and he sits next to me, grabbing my hand. He grins. "You look so beautiful."

I roll my eyes at him, "Oh stop."

"You are so beautiful and you don't even know it." I'm starting to get the idea.

Mr Rider taps the microphone. "Can I have everyone's attention. It's time for the speeches." Why are they doing speeches, they don't even like me?

Mrs Rider goes first, "I'm so proud of you Damon. We never thought you would settle down. Emmie is a remarkable young woman. God knows how you got her but you better do everything you can to keep her. She gave us a beautiful granddaughter." Do everything he can to keep me? I thought they disapproved of me? Tears fall down her face, "I hope you enjoy your lives together and be as happy as we are."

"Don't cry dear," Mr Rider says to his wife and puts his arm over her shoulder. "The day I met Emmie I was shocked at her beauty. How could my son get a good-looking girl?" Enough with the Emmie is beautiful crap, it sounds like that's the only nice thing they can say. I frown.

"Yeah, he's never bagged such a hot woman before," Lexi calls from somewhere, I can't even see her through the crowd.

"Seriously…" I say frustrated, putting my hand on my forehead.

"What are you doing to my family?" Damon whispers in my ear. I don't even know what he means, they are just being polite.

"I was too quick to judge her. I mean, I don't fear anyone. But when she spoke her mind. Wow, she's some scary lady. Don't make her mad son! That's my advice for you!" The crowd laughs and so does Damon. I'm not that scary.

"Hey! I'm not that scary," I call to Mr Rider.

"Yeah, you are." Damon chuckles. I shake my head in frustration.

"But welcome to the family Emmie. We are pleased to have you," Mr Rider says and raises his glass and everyone does the same.

They both walk off the stage, Mr Rider with his arm around Mrs Rider. Sully stands on stage. "Well, I'm the best man. Definitely the BEST man here." Has he been drinking? He's not normally this confident, unless that's just with me.

"Really?" I smirk at him.

He looks at me when he makes his speech. "I remember the first day I met Emmie too. She was feisty, brave and she had a mouth on her. Although nothing's changed, she will still give you a run for your money. Damon and Emmie seemed to click the moment they met. It was really weird." Weird? Was it? "Emmie was very vulnerable and has had a bad past but Damon protects her. She looks safe whenever she is with him. Emmie makes him a better person, although she can be hard to deal with. We will be seeing more of each other so I pray to God you'll make it easy on us."

I burst into laughter, go easy on him? I already am easy on him, everyone else, no. It seems I'm not the only one that found that funny, everyone else is laughing too.

"These last few months, Emmie has been in trouble. Damon was hell on legs when she was gone. It's like he couldn't function without her and I know Emmie doesn't function without him. They were made for each other. So congratulations to you both. And Emmie, please don't kill me for that speech."

I laugh again, if he was aiming for a funny speech he succeeded, well I thought it was funny. I wouldn't kill Sully, he keeps me safe and he's my friend. "Thanks Sully, great speech," Damon calls to him and Sully winks at us as he walks off the stage. Danny walks on stage, his eyes lock with mine and I frown.

"Don't panic Sis, Lilly-May is with your mother in law." I really should write a prescribed list of trusted people to watch Lilly, it will be a short list. "She is very overprotective over her daughter. She has made me a proud Brother. I understand not all of you know what's happened to Emmie over her life. But when she was missing I felt like I'd lost a part of myself. Emmie is the magnet to my life and it seems to be the same for all of you." What is he talking about? I'm no magnet. But I love my Brother and I feel the same way about him.

"I honestly didn't like Damon at the start, he was a bad influence on her. But I learned that he wasn't the bad influence, it was her." Everyone laughs except me, I just glare at Danny. "She would always get herself into trouble and Damon was always there to save her. I don't know where she would be without him." Dead, most probably. But If I had never met him, I'd be broken. No one has fixed me like Damon has. And no one ever would. I'd be alone. "When Emmie was missing, Damon was there for me. He was a true friend, you could even say like a brother to me. I saw him hurt for Emmie, but yet he did what he could to help me. And he has done so much for Emmie and for me, I don't know how to repay him." I look at Damon who is smiling at Danny. I know Damon doesn't need repayment for that, he has a good heart. "As Emmie's brother, I am protective but Damon has protected her when I couldn't." He looks sad when he says those words and I'm left wondering what memories he's thinking of. "She is hard to handle but you do very well with her. I'm glad she's found you." I listen to Damon because I love him and I want to please him.

"Aww, thanks, Bro," I call. He's such a good Brother to me, one I don't deserve.

"Thanks, Mate," Damon calls.

"I know Mom and Dad aren't here but they would be proud of you. They don't deserve to be here. So I hope me being here is enough for you." You obviously didn't know Daddy as well as I did. He would be turning in his grave knowing I married another man and had a daughter. I don't want to disappoint him but I need Damon more than I need to honour Daddy's wishes. Damon squeezes my hand to bring me out of my daze. I focus back on the stage and Danny has left and in his place is Lexi.

I roll my eyes, this will be good. Lexi that has no damn filter, she just speaks her mind. I normally don't mind but it's a special day. "I met Emmie at one of our parties. I didn't know who she was but we got on really well. She was so beautiful, she's the soul of the party. She lights up a room whenever she enters. I have to say, I am jealous of my Brother. She's a catch and I have to say she's a great kisser." I feel like banging my head on the table continuously. No one could ever be jealous of Damon. Not because he has me.

"Yes, she is!" Jessie calls. She's referring to the great kisser bit.

"Really Sis? Please stop fantasising about my wife." His wife, I love that.

She giggles, "I can't promise that Damon. Anyway, I'm so glad she is my sister in law. She's great. She does have a temper though. But Damon knows what buttons to press and calms her down. His presence seems to relax her." Yes, it does, more so than it should. But I feel normal when I'm with him. Some days I forget my horrific past and live in the present and look forward to the future.

My shoulder is really hurting now, I bite the inside of my cheek to try to mask the pain. I will hear the rest. I lean against Damon's shoulder and he lifts his arm instead so I can cuddle up to him. "You okay?" he whispers to me. I nod.

"Anyway, I plan to spend a lot more time with them. Everyone will be happy to spend time with me." Oh, Lexi, you are great company, just in small doses. You are too excitable for me. But I love you anyway. Lexi leaves the stage and Lucas enters. Lucas making a speech?

"Well, I was asked to make a speech. The first time I met them, they led me to believe they were already married. And you know what, they looked happily married. He looked like he was going to bite my head off. She woke up from a coma for him. It was so romantic. The perfect love story." I loved him even then. He made me feel safe and I'm glad that I begged him not to leave me then because I probably wouldn't be here now, married to him. "Emmie has been admitted to hospital countless times. She just can't stay away. Her second coma, she wouldn't wake for anyone. Not even Rider. It hurt him. Physically, Emmie should have woken but some patients aren't ready. And she wasn't, Rider stayed with her all the time. He had left for a shower. And she went into cardiac arrest.

Her heart stopped beating because he left. She gave up living because he left." The crowd simultaneously 'aww', I forget that some people haven't heard this story. "He returned back to the hospital and she woke for him. It gave me a warm fuzzy feeling. It was so romantic. She returned many times after that, mostly because she was too stubborn to do as she was told. She makes my job interesting when she's at the hospital, to say the least." I knew it, I knew he loved me around. "And when she gave birth to her baby, she lost a lot of blood. I was so worried as she'd lost too much. But somehow, she pulled through. She's very strong. And when she woke all she cared about was her family. She didn't care about how she was doing." No, I needed to know everyone was okay. And I found out my brother was not okay. He needed me. "As soon as she woke from surgery, she was on her feet giving everyone mouth. Rider keeps her calm, and everything she has been through, she needs him. She's proved that many times. When Rider left her, she was broken. It hurt me to see how broken she was. She would stare lifeless at the door. She didn't think she was worth it. " Damon gasps and holds me tighter. "She blamed it on herself. She was just a zombie, I prayed for Rider's return, she was helpless. I mean jeez, she was shot today and here she is refusing to go to the hospital until this is over. Anyway, congrats guys." The crowd all 'aww' again. What can I say, my connection to this man is unique and different? But I've always been different.

Lucas exits the stage and comes to sit next to me. I'm starting to feel sleepy. "How are you doing Emmie?" Lucas says.

"Yeah, I'm okay." Not, but this isn't finished yet.

"Emmie, you look a bit pale," Lucas accuses.

Damon pulls my head away from his chest so he can examine me too, "Emmie, are you okay?"

"I'm fine. We are nearly done. Just keep listening," I growl, please. I don't have the energy to argue. I just want to make it to the end of my wedding.

"I think I should take you to the hospital," Damon says.

I shake my head. "You dare!" He won't do this to me.

"Doc?" Damon looks at Lucas questioningly.

Lucas sighs, "I'll keep an eye on her."

Chapter 28

A barman comes to us and gives me a glass of champagne and I gratefully accept. "Congratulations," he says to me and I smile at him. Damon puts his arm around my shoulder again and I watch the stage. It's Jessie and Brody's turn. Brody has his hand in Jessie's, they look so happy together. I'm happy that they are happy. But at the back of my mind, I hate that they are happy. They could have waited a bit longer and then I hate myself for feeling that way.

"Emmie is my best friend. Like sisters. We clicked the moment we met. I think everyone who knows Emmie loves her. I do hate her sometimes for how much trouble she gets into." Jessie grins at me. I pout in frustration to her comment about how everyone who knows me loves me. Change the damn record already.

"All the guys at our school were head over heels for her, including me," Brody says. I can't believe he is saying this in front of his new girlfriend. "She's so beautiful and she doesn't know it. She is such a badass. I was jealous of Rider at first and we both competed for her." Brody fought but Damon let me make my own choice. "Hell, all the boys competed for her. I saw how much Rider cared for her, and how much Emmie cared for him. I know she loved us both, and it tore her apart." It really did, I didn't want to hurt anyone. "But I knew it was a case of who she loved and who she needed. She needs Rider, she needs him to keep living. He keeps her sane and stable. He is good for her." I think so.

"Emmie will do whatever she can to help people she loves, even if it hurts herself," Jessie says. That is so true, I would. "She will put people before herself. Emmie is a self-hating person. She can't see how great she is." I frown, I haven't even let her peek through my window, how would she know? "When we told her we were dating, we could see she was hurt but she was so happy that we were. Who does that? She should have been kicking and screaming at us." I wanted to, but as you said, I put others needs before my own. "Yet she just hugged us. She is truly a great person and we love you. We are so happy you are happy and married." I am happily married.

Their speech was amazing. I love them both. I loved everyone's speeches. This was such a great day. Even if I did get shot, but I'd do it again to save Damon. I can't say that it hurts anymore. I just feel tired and achy. I want to sleep. I feel sweaty and clammy. This day was the best day of my life and I have the best husband. How am I so lucky? I close my eyes and lean into Damon's chest.

"Emmie," the Doc says.

"Hmm," I mumble. It's all I can manage.

"Emmie!" he shouts again. I can hear you Doc. My ears are fine.

Damon grabs my face in his hands and lifts my face so he can see me. My body is heavy so he is taking all my weight. "Baby, are you okay?" Yeah, I'm all good, I made it to the end of my wedding.

"Shit, she's going into shock. She needs to go to the hospital now," Lucas says. I'm not in shock, I'm happy. But I lose consciousness.

I hear Damon crying, I follow his pain. My heart aches for him. Why is he crying? I wake up and he is lying next to me with his head buried in my neck. I lift my hand to his hair and stroke him. I hate to cause him so much pain. He pulls away and his eyes are red with tears. I feel groggy but I'm awake.

"Baby, you are okay." I frown, of course I am. I wouldn't leave him now. Will take more than that. He strokes my forehead and I reach up to his face and wipe his tears. He usually does this for me. He takes my hand and puts it on his cheek. "You worried me. You can't scare me like that. Not on our wedding day." I don't like being in trouble, it puts me on edge that I could be shot walking down the street.

"I'm sorry." I really am, but I would have done it again to save him, we are all lucky he only got my arm. He was aiming at Damon's heart.

"Everyone is outside. They're all worried about you too." I want to see Lilly.

"Please, I want to see Lilly and my Brother." He kisses my forehead and he walks to the door and he holds the door open and peers his head through the door and he must have said something as Danny walks through with Lilly. Danny's face goes from terrified to relieved. He passes Lilly to Damon and I frown. I want to hold my daughter. Danny comes towards me and hugs me tight. The bed is already sat up so I only have to lean forward. He whispers, "Jesus Sis, I'm going to murder you myself if you keep getting into trouble." He doesn't let me go. I can't promise anything, I don't choose this.

"Danny, I love you but I want to hold my daughter." He pulls away and grins at me.

"Always so protective over her. She's perfectly safe." I will be the judge of that, anything could have happened while I've been out. Danny moves to the side and Damon slides Lilly in my arms. Okay, now she's safe again.

"Has she been fed?"

"Yes Emmie, I'm not a monster," Danny huffs.

I roll my eyes. "I'm just checking." She's sleeping peacefully in my arms. I've missed her. "Mommy's missed you baby girl," I whisper to her. They both stare at me like I may disappear in a blink of an eye. I glare at them, I know they care about me, I do, but I honestly wouldn't leave, not now.

"Do you want to see anyone baby?" Damon asks. I shake my head, whoever they are, they aren't my family. My family is right here in this room. I don't need anyone other than these three people. He walks out the room for a while. Probably to tell them all to leave. I can't face anyone right now.

Lucas walks in and smiles. Does he live here? He always seems to be working, I should know because I am here a lot. "How you feeling Emmie?" he asks.

"Fine, just sleepy." Danny goes to take Lilly from my arms but I push him away. He frowns at me. No, I won't let you hold her. She's only safe in my arms.

"Any pain?" I shake my head, I feel drowsy so maybe he overdid the painkillers. Damon enters the room and I smile at him.

"Baby, you look tired." I do feel tired. He sits on my bed next to me. "Maybe you should sleep." I shake my head. I don't want this day to end.

"You'll be in here overnight Emmie. So get some rest," Lucas says. I frown. I'm still in my wedding dress. As if on cue, Sully walks through the door with a bag. I smile at him and he returns the smile with a blush. He is predictable.

"How are you feeling Emmie?" Sully asks.

"Like I've been shot." I giggle but no one laughs with me. Such a tough crowd.

"Sis, you aren't funny you know." I roll my eyes, I guess not. Sully places the bag on the end of my bed.

"Is that all Boss?"

Damon nods, "Yeah, thanks Sully." Is it wrong for me to want Sully to stay too? He helps me feel safe. But I would never ask him to stay, so I watch him leave.

"Shall I give you some time together?" Danny says. I shake my head.

"Stay, till I fall asleep," I beg.

"Danny, could you take Lilly please?" I frown, no, why? Danny approaches with caution but I'm too tired to argue and he goes to take a seat next to my bed.

Damon stands and lifts me off the bed. What is he doing? He grabs the bag from the bed and proceeds to the bathroom. He sets me down on my feet.

"Hmm," he says as he looks at me. "If only we were at home," he sighs. "But I guess I'm just happy you are still with me." He closes the distance between us and he undoes the zip on my dress. I stand motionless and speechless watching his every move. He lets my dress fall to the ground, my amazing dress that makes me look like an angel. He holds his hand out so I can step out the dress.

He rummages through the bag and finds some PJs for me. He helps me into them as my arm is still sore. I used to hate being looked after like this but now he's my husband I like it. It's what husband and wife should do for each other. Once I'm in my PJs, he removes his blazer and his tie. He undoes his top buttons of his shirt. I can see his chest and I bite my lip, I reach up to stroke his chest hairs. To my surprise, he lets me touch him, he shuts his eyes in response to my touch.

He places his arm around my waist and pulls me tight. I fall against his chest and snuggle up to his chest. Damon kisses the top of my head. As he says, if only we were at home. But we aren't and that's okay because we are together and that's all that matters to me.

He picks me up again and we enter my room. Yeah, it should be named Emmie Rider's room. Wow, that sounds weird. He gently places me back on the bed. I face Danny and Lilly. Damon tilts the bed back so I'm lying flat. Danny looks at me and smiles. But he is stroking Lilly's face. Okay, maybe I do trust Danny 100% to look after Lilly. He looks mesmerised by her, the same look I see in Damon and I trust Damon 100%. Maybe I should lighten up a bit.

So that's two people I trust implicitly with Lilly. Damon lays behind me, talking softly to Danny. My eyes grow heavier and I drift into a peaceful happy sleep with my family. Damon, Lilly and Danny.

I wake in the night because my arm is hurting. Damon is asleep next to me and Lilly is in a cot next to the bed. I climb out of bed and go in search for a Doctor. I don't expect to find Lucas, although it would be nice.

The hallways are deserted. I can't find one single person. But then someone walks into the hallway. I look down at the ground trying not to make eye contact, my whole body is going rigid. I peek up to see if this person has a gun in his hand, he doesn't but my body still doesn't relax. The person stops in front of me. Shit. Who is this person? "Emmie? What are you doing?" I look up to see Dyno. I let out the breath that I was holding. I sag with relief.

"I was looking for a Doctor. Have you seen any?" He frowns at me.

"You shouldn't be wandering around here at night. You are lucky I'm here." Yes, I am. I smile to myself that Damon is still having me watched. It makes me feel safer, although I would prefer Sully to be here but he needs to rest sometime. "Come, I will take you to the Doctor's office." He doesn't touch me and I'm thankful for that but he stays close to me, which I'm also grateful for.

We reach a door and Dyno knocks. A voice replies to come in. Dyno waves me in first so I'm not left in the hallway on my own I guess, unless he's being a gentleman. Which I doubt it. I look around the room, it's light in here even though it's dark outside. The Doctor looks up from his desk and then I realise it's Lucas. What the hell is he still doing here?

"What are you doing here?" I say, he should be resting.

He looks up from his desk and frowns at me. He looks tired, his eyes red. "I could ask you the same. What are you doing in my office?" he says softly.

"My arm hurts, I was looking for a Doctor to give me more drugs." I smile at him and he raises an eyebrow at me.

"Well, you found a doctor." He grins. Well actually Dyno did, I probably would have got lost. Or walked into a gun most likely.

A phone rings and Dyno picks up his phone. "Boss?"

Oh, great, Damon's awake. He will be freaking out. "Calm down Boss, I found her on my patrols. We are in the Doctor's office." He hangs up without a goodbye.

The Doctor exits his office for a few minutes. I stand shifting my weight on each leg. I look at the plain walls, it's so white. I walk to the Doc's desk and see a photo frame. I pick it up and examine it. It's a picture of a pretty blonde woman. I wonder who she is. I put the photo back down. The door opens again, I'm expecting the Doc but it's Damon. Did he not think to knock? Guess he doesn't care about that where I'm concerned.

"Emmie, what the fuck are you doing?" Great, he's in a bad mood. Fun times. I turn to face him.

"I'm standing and looking at you at the moment," I shrug.

"Don't play stupid. You know what I mean," he growls. Damn, is my husband angry?

"Damon my arm hurts, I wanted more painkillers."

"You should have woken me." Maybe I should if he's going to react like this. "I was freaking out." Yeah, I can tell. I roll my eyes.

He closes the distance between us and he hugs me tight and sighs with relief, I guess. And I feel my body relax too. He pulls away from me. "You okay?" he asks. I nod. I'm okay now that he's here and I know Dyno isn't a psycho with a gun. "So why did your whole body just relax in my arms?"

Was it that obvious? I do that all the time when I'm in his arms, so why is he pointing it out now? "I've learned my lesson Damon, I won't be walking around on my own again." I will always try to have someone with me at all times.

"Why? Did something happen?"

"I thought Dyno was a psycho with a gun."

"Oh great, thanks," Dyno huffs. Damon looks at me questioningly.

"Don't take offence, I'm glad you were there." I hug Damon's waist and the Doctor returns to his office.

"Are you ready Emmie?" Lucas asks me, ready with a syringe. I nod and he injects my arm that I hold out to him.

"You should get some sleep now Emmie."

"So should you. It's not good to work such long shifts," I say.

"I'm fine, and besides, I wouldn't trust any of my staff to keep you in check."

"You don't think much of your staff, do you?"

"Emmie it's not my staff that's the problem. It's you." I frown, I'm not that bad, am I? Dyno snickers behind me but I ignore him.

"Right, come on Mrs Rider. Let's get you back to bed," Damon says before scooping me up into his arms. He really is too overprotective. I'm not going to trip over in the hallway. Okay, I might, but what's the worst that could happen? Well, I could break my neck I guess. So maybe he does have a point. But anyone could trip and break their neck, right? It doesn't take me long to drift back to sleep once the painkillers are working.

I wake up and Damon isn't next to me. I sit up in a flash and see Danny in the chair where he was last night with Lilly asleep in his arms. "You're fine Sis." I search the room and Damon isn't here. "He's just going to get some breakfast. Chill out, I will keep you safe. Not that you are in danger here." He presses a button on my bed so it sits up.

Breakfast? Is he serious? I groan. I take one glance at Lilly, she's safe. I get up and head to the bathroom. My bag is here as well. So I change into jeans and a t-shirt. I freshen up in the process. My wound is covered by a bandage, I peel it back so I can see the wound. It's not that bad, not as bad as when Rex shot me last time.

"Emmie?" Damon calls and walks straight into the bathroom. Oops, forgot to lock the door. Oh well, I'm finished now. "Come eat breakfast." I pout at him in defiance. "Don't test me, Emmie. I never saw you eat yesterday." I didn't eat anything but I was too preoccupied.

He grabs my hand and leads me into my room. We both sit on the bed. Damon and Danny are eating bacon baps. I turn my nose up to that. Yuck. Damon places pancakes in front of me. They are still warm. Where did he go to get these? It looks like he's showered and changed too. How long has he been gone?

"Eat," Damon scolds.

"Emmie, just take a couple of mouthfuls," Danny says. He knows me well enough with food. Once I taste something good, I'm usually all good. "You've always been funny with food. One day you must explain it to me."

I shrug, "Why would one need food when they are fat? It makes me feel sick thinking about food."

They both are shocked and their mouths drop open with food still in their mouths. I scowl at them, I don't need to see their chewed food. They both carry on eating. "Emmie, do you really think you're fat?" Damon asks.

"Wait, I remember at the dress store, the lady asked you what size you were. You said size UK 16/44. I thought you were joking," Danny says. I frown, I wasn't joking. I wouldn't joke about my weight.

"Things make more sense now," Damon says.

"Yeah," Danny agrees. What makes more sense?

"Baby, you are skinny, maybe too skinny. But then your eating issue doesn't help with that." Me, skinny? I shake my head. Do they need glasses or what?

I pick up my pancake and take a bite. "How could I miss that one?" Danny says sadly. "I miss Dad abusing you, and I miss that you have an eating disorder because you think you're fat." He shakes his head. Oh Danny, don't be hard on yourself.

"Danny, don't blame yourself. I only let you see what I wanted you to see. Just like I never meant for you to see me cutting myself."

"That's something else I'd like you to explain to me one day," Danny says.

What is there to say? "I used to cut myself, what more is there to say?"

"I want to know why you did it."

"I'm not sure you do." They've both finished eating but I've lost my appetite.

"I do Sis, I want to understand you more. The way Damon has the natural instinct to. I want to know what I missed." He's only going to beat himself up. But I feel like I'm closer to him than I've ever been. I don't know if it's because I trust him to bring my wall down for him or Damon is dragging it down for him.

"You remember when I ran away?" He nods. "A lovely lady took care of me. I trusted her, she was like the Mother I didn't have at the time. It was weird, I felt more of a connection with her than I do with my own. Even when she came back, nothing seemed normal. Shouldn't a daughter turn to their Mother when they need them? I turned to you."

"So what happened to her?" Danny and Damon ask in unison.

"She got me to tell her who my family was, she contacted Dad. Dad was angry, he didn't want to risk me going back there so he got her arrested for kidnapping me. I never saw her again. You were out at work. He gagged me and beat me. I didn't want to live anymore." I take a deep breath. "So I locked myself in the bathroom and slit my wrists. I felt numb, relief even. It felt good to feel what I did."

"I don't remember that," Danny says.

"Of course you didn't. Like I said, I only let you see what I want you to. Anyway, Dad kicked the door down. He was horrified. He held me like a father should. Part of me was glad that I did what I did to have my Dad back. But it helped me more than I would have thought."

"I caught you," Danny says.

"You did, but that wasn't the first time. Dad had caught me a few times before that. Part of me did it to have my Dad back. And he would be the Dad I needed and wanted for a while, but he obviously needed to control me the only way he knew how."

"So you didn't mean for me to see that?"

I shake my head. "No, but when you did I couldn't bear your pain. So I stopped for you, even though it was better for me to do it."

"How can cutting yourself be better than not?" Damon says.

"Because Dad never hurt me when he thought I was vulnerable. And it helped me cope." Damon grabs my wrists and examines them carefully. I have faint scars but they aren't noticeable unless you know they're there.

"But you don't do it anymore?" Damon asks.

I shake my head. "Why would I need to? Dad's gone. And I haven't done it for a couple of years now." He sags with relief.

"What was the name of this lady?" Damon asks.

"Addison, I called her Addi though. I don't know her last name." I miss her, even though I didn't know her long. She helped me with my insecurities.

"Well, now you've eaten something, even if it's only minuscule, let's go sign the marriage register and start our honeymoon." He smiles his sexy smile. And I smile back at him.

Lucas enters my room. "Are you ready to be discharged now, Emmie?"

"If you discharge me, will you go home?" I feel guilty that he's here still. He looks shattered and it's all my fault.

"Yeah, I suppose. I wasn't completely truthful with you last night." I frown, what is that supposed to mean? "Yes, it's true I don't trust you to behave. But I also only trust myself to give you the best treatment." I continue to frown. What's that supposed to mean? Does he not trust his staff or does he see me as more than a patient? If it's the first option, then I'm worried about all the other patients but if it's option two then I'm flattered. "So you are all set to leave. Don't do anything stupid while on holiday okay because I won't be there to help you." He grins. I'm sure Damon can keep me from harm's way.

Sully walks in the room and smiles at me. "Boss?"

"Her stuff is in the bathroom." He nods and heads for the bathroom.

"Well bye, for now, Emmie," Lucas says. I nod and he leaves the room. Bye for now? Sounds like he's expecting to see me soon. I really do hope not.

Sully returns with my bag and my dress, I frown at him. "Be careful with that Big Guy. One wrong move and your muscles can tear it." I cross my arms and he laughs at me, I'm being serious.

"I'll be careful Emmie." He leaves the room. I climb out of bed and reach for Lilly from Danny's arms. He lets me take her and we head out to the car. I place Lilly in her car seat in Damon's car. Danny takes the seat next to her and I sit in the front. Why is he coming with us? I'd have thought he would be bored with me already. Or at least repulsed by my confession earlier. Damon doesn't say anything but Damon and Danny have bonded since I was away with Desmond.

We arrive outside the registry office. Damon beams at me, "Shall we make this official?" I nod and we all get out the car. Danny gets Lilly from the car. Damon grabs my hand and we walk into the building. I am happy, happier than I've ever been. And what have I done to deserve this? Nothing. But I'm not going to complain, I can't wait to live my life and grow old with Damon.

Chapter 29

We've had a lovely honeymoon. Damon took me to Australia, we explored safaris, restaurants, beaches. Moonlight walks along the beach. It was perfect. It was just the three of us, and I loved it. But today we are travelling back, we have been in our own little bubble. I don't want to leave it but times up. It's been nice to spend 3 whole weeks with Damon. I thought he may have got bored with me. But it turns out he is just as disappointed as I am.

We walk towards the house, I have Lilly in my arms. Damon scoops me up into his arms. "Just crossing the threshold, Mrs Rider," he says looking down at me. I laugh but I'm careful because I have Lilly in my arms. He sets me down when we get inside. I take Lilly straight upstairs to her Moses basket. She was awake most of the flight so she will sleep awhile. I grab the monitor, I know I'll be able to hear her even downstairs but I worry something may happen. It's my way of being close to her.

I walk back downstairs and Sully is talking to Damon. I bound up to Sully and hug him, I've missed him. Although I've felt 100% safe with Damon on our honeymoon, I've still missed Sully as a person, a friend even. "Hey, Big Guy." I step back from his tight grip.

"I've missed you both," he says awkwardly, missed me? That can't be right. "Catching the sun I see Emmie?"

I smile, what can I say? I've made the most of the sun whilst being away. It's a bit hotter out there. "Of course, I love the sun."

Sully chuckles, "We know."

"How's it been here, Sully?" Damon asks. Talking about work already?

He puts his hand on his head in frustration, "All I can say is, I'm glad you're back." Sully was put in charge while we were away because he is the most trusted and capable. So why does he sound like something has gone wrong? I'm sure he could manage, if I have faith in him then Damon sure does.

"You can fill me in, in half an hour." Damon nods at Sully and Sully retreats.

I feel hot and sticky. "I'm going for a shower," I say to Damon.

He winks at me and I melt. "Can I join you?" My husband asking permission to join me in the shower, like I'm going to refuse him. He's never asked permission before.

"If you want." I smile innocently at him.

"Oh Mrs Rider, I do." He frowns and gets his phone out of his pocket.

"It's my Dad. I'll see you in there." He gives me a reassuring smile. I nod and leave him to his phone call. What could his Dad possible want just minutes after we've got back? I sit on our bed for a minute. Although I'm married to Damon and this is my house now, I still don't see this as home. I feel safe, yes and I'm happy, but it's not home. What is wrong with me?

I strip and walk into the bathroom and get in the shower. The cool water ricocheting off my skin. Damon and I have been inseparable and I miss his touch already. He has healed me more than ever in the last three weeks. It's felt like therapy to me.

Hands find themselves around me. He feels tense, I frown. Why is he tense? What did his Dad want? Maybe he changed his mind and he still doesn't approve of me. I wash quickly, I need answers and he will tell me. I just need to ask him and I'm not worried about him leaving me anymore. So once I'm done, I get out the shower, he follows me out instantly. I grab my towel and wrap it around myself. I turn towards him.

"What's going on Damon?"

"What do you mean?" I know him well enough now to know when something is bothering him.

"I know something's wrong. Just tell me. What was the phone call?" He sighs. It must be bad.

"It was my Dad." I know it was, you told me, remember?

"Okay, so what did he want?" I've convinced myself it's my fault, it must be. Why would he hesitate like this? Can his Dad not see he's happy? I mean, I can see he's happy, is that because I hope he's happy and imagine it? Or is he truly happy? I don't feel so self-conscious anymore, but when the odds are stacked against you like this, what's a girl supposed to do?

"He wants me to go see him in Canada. He wants me to go alone. I have to leave today." My mouth drops open. He wants him to go alone? Okay, it's definitely as bad as I feared. I back away from him whilst shaking my head. He's leaving me, we haven't been apart for so long. I don't know if I will cope.

"Wait, no. You can't leave me," I say horrified. I see the pain in his eyes. I don't think he is happy about this either.

"I'm sorry, baby. He said it was important." I bet he did, desperate to get rid of me. The quicker he can get this in motion the better for him I'd imagine.

"So why do you have to go alone?"

"I have no idea. But I don't have a choice. I have to go." I continue to shake my head, he walks towards me, putting his arms around me. He's always leaving me. I thought things would be different. I was a different person in Australia and now I'm back feeling helpless again.

"We just got back. What am I going to do without you?" Tears start to fall down my face. He continues to hold me. "Don't leave me," I beg. Last time I did this he didn't leave me. But something tells me he won't fulfil my wish this time. Why wouldn't he travel thousands of miles to see his parents?

"You'll be okay. I'll be back before you know it. Sully will be here. He will look after you," he hushes in my ear. I don't doubt that Sully would look after me, but Sully isn't my husband.

"Fine, just go." I wipe my eyes and storm out the bathroom. I'm angry and sad and hurt all in one. I dress in my PJs. Damon enters and he hugs me from behind but I shrug him off.

"Baby, please." I sit on the bed and bring my knees to my chest, hugging them. This will protect me. He sits on his knees in front of me on the floor looking up at me. He puts his head on my knees. I don't want to push him away, I love him being this close to me. But I feel he could have fought harder, stayed with me at least one night. "I have a surprise for you before I go."

A surprise? What could that be? I don't smile because all I want right now is him to stay with me. He stands up and gets dressed. I watch him as he does, even though I'm angry and hurt, I still like to watch my husband changing. Once he's finished, he extends his hand out to me. I take it and he leads me downstairs. Sully is in the hallway with a tall slim lady. Her back is to us so I don't see her face. Who is this woman?

Damon continues to escort me down into the hallway. "Thanks for coming," Damon says to the woman. So she was expected? Does he know this woman? I stand awkwardly next to Damon. And then she turns around her smile. I remember her from my dreams. She shakes Damon's hand and then she looks at me with besotted eyes.

"Thank you for what you did." She smiles at him and then she looks back at me. I'm dreaming again. Damn it. "It's so great to see you again Emmie. You are looking good." Me, look good? I don't think so but I trust her. I do. Oh, Addi it's so good to see you too.

Tears fall down my face. "Addi?" I sob. She nods and we both hug each other. Now, this is what I feel motherly love is. This is natural, this is what I've been missing. She smells of lavender, it's a welcome reminder. We both pull away from each other grudgingly.

"Shall we sit down and talk?" she says. I nod, I can't get any words out.

"Baby I need to go. But Sully will look after you okay? I love you." He's leaving right now. I frown. He hugs me tight. He whispers in my ear, "Enjoy your wedding present from me." He kisses me on the forehead and leaves. I stare at the door after he's left.

Addi grabs my hand, I slightly flinch at her touch because it isn't Damon's but I don't withdraw. "Let's talk." She smiles at me again. I nod and we walk to the living room and sit on the sofa.

"What's going on?" I ask. I have so many questions.

"Well, honey, Rider your husband got in contact with me." Again with the damn superpowers. I thought she was in prison. "I just want to say I'm sorry." I shake my head, what is she sorry for? She took me in when I had nowhere else to go. "If I knew your Dad did that to you I would have never contacted him."

"I miss my Dad. So don't be sorry, it's not your fault. He got you arrested, I should be saying sorry to you."

"Honey, do you know why he got me arrested?" He told me that he got her arrested for kidnap.

"He said you were convicted of kidnap."

She nods, "Is that all he told you?" I nod. "Well that is true, I was convicted of kidnap. But he did it because he was scared."

I shrug, "Yeah, scared I'd go back to you."

She shakes her head. "Yes that is also true, but he was worried you'd find out the truth." What truth? At the time, I would have chosen her over Dad. So why would some truth matter? "I didn't know at the time. My sister never told me about you. She told me about Danny but not about you." What is she going on about? How does she know Danny? "Emmie, you are my niece." My mouth drops open. She's my auntie? No way? It almost feels like fate brought us together.

"Why did my mother not tell you about me?"

She shrugs, "I don't know honey, I lost contact with my sister around the time you were born I guess. She told me she was having problems with Josh, your Dad. She stopped talking to me." So my Dad was worried about Addi because she's my auntie? I never knew my Mother had a sister. "Rider brought me up to speed on your life, he's one great man. I'm glad my niece has found someone she loves and to take care of her."

"I've missed you Addi." She holds me tight.

"I've missed you too honey." She strokes my hair. "Your husband found me in a prison in America. He got me out and he flew me to you."

I pull away, "You've been in there all this time? I'm so sorry." I should have done something.

"Don't beat yourself up. This is all your Dad's doing. He's a vicious man."

I shake my head. "But he's still my Dad, Addi. I know he was protecting me." It looks like she's biting her tongue.

"Rider told me about how you feel." She takes a deep breath. "So do you think Danny will want to meet me? And what about my great-niece?" She smiles, I have a feeling she's changing the subject but I don't mind. I don't want to argue with her.

"I can call Danny if you like? And well, Lilly-May is asleep but I can bring her down." I smile. I trust her with Lilly. She showed me kindness when my own Dad didn't show it to me. Besides, Damon has left me alone with her and well, I don't see Sully lingering anywhere.

"Yes please," she says excitedly.

"Okay, I'll go get Lilly-May and grab my phone." I stand up and look at Addi. "You aren't going anywhere yet are you?" I feel like all good things leave me. If she's going to leave me and never come back, then I won't go upstairs.

"Honey, I will stay until you want me to leave." She smiles. I nod and run upstairs to my bedroom. Lilly is sleeping peacefully. I scoop her in my arms, she stirs but she doesn't wake. I grab my phone from the bed and press call, holding it between my shoulder and my ear. I head downstairs.

"Hey, Sis. How was your honeymoon?"

"It was great."

"Is that all I get?"

"Bro, could you come over please?"

"Everything okay? Where's Damon?"

"Damon's gone," I sigh. I enter the living room and see that Addi is still here. I place Lilly in her arms and she seems to adore her.

"What do you mean gone, Sis?"

"He left, he's gone to Canada. His family required his presence. But he was told to go on his own."

"What does that mean?" He takes a deep breath. "Don't worry, I'm on my way," he says and hangs up. I put my phone on the sofa and sit next to Addi again.

"He's on his way."

"Are you close with Danny?" she asks.

I nod. "It's been me and my brother for so long. I mean, we weren't as close as I'd like. But that's my problem, not his. I wouldn't let him get close. But Damon is removing my walls, and I'm letting Danny in."

"Well, I'm glad you have your Brother. The last time I saw him he was a little baby. Like Lilly-May." She looks down at Lilly and smiles.

"So are you going back to America soon?" I frown. I don't want her to, she's just come back into my life again. But she must have family out there.

"No honey. You are my family. I have nothing left in America. Your husband has sorted me out with a house. I will be here for you as long as you need me." I smile. Damon is amazing, he did this for me. I love him, but I'm still mad at him for leaving.

"Good." I can't stop smiling.

"Emmie! Your brother is here," Sully calls. I stand up and walk out of the living room to meet him in the hallway. He looks at me confused, I guess he expected me to be sad. Well, I am, but Addi is here. He hugs me tight.

"Damon got me a wedding present." I smile.

"To soften the blow of leaving you?" I frown, it may seem that way. But this would have taken planning. "What is it?"

I grab his hand. "Not a what, a who," I say, pulling him into the living room. Addi stands up looking at Danny. I look at Danny, he doesn't understand. "You remember what I said at the hospital? When I ran away?"

"Yeah," he says.

"Well, Danny meet Addi." He looks down at me and raises his eyebrow.

"The lady that took you in?"

"And our auntie." I smile.

His mouth drops open. "Auntie?"

"Danny, I'm Addison. I held you when you were a baby. About Lilly-May's age. It was the last time I saw you. My sister never told me about Emmie though."

"She never mentioned an auntie." He shakes his head. I hug his waist and he puts his arm around me.

"It's like fate right Danny? Of all people to take me in it was our Auntie?"

He nods, "Yeah."

He grabs my hand and leads me to the sofa and we all sit. I sit in the middle of them both. He takes my head in his hands so I look at him. "I'm surprised you aren't breaking down." I frown.

"I did." I shrug. "But I know he's coming back." He puts his arm around my shoulder and we talk to each other, getting to know each other for hours, we take up the whole day. Danny orders pizza and I eat, much to his surprise, without arguments. I put Lilly to bed.

I get a text from Damon. *Hey baby. I hope you're not too mad at me. I'm just getting on the plane to come home to you. I love you x*

I'm still pissed with him. He hasn't been gone long but I miss him. I hate spending the night alone without him. I get really anxious and I don't sleep. I don't reply. I just enjoy the rest of the evening with Addi and Danny. I snuggle up to Danny, I've missed him. My eyes grow heavy and I grudgingly fall asleep.

I dream of our honeymoon. Our perfect honeymoon. Our long walks along the beach at night time. Kissing under a tree, seeing the moon between the branches. The moon bouncing off the sea.

My dream changes into a nightmare. I'm back in the hallway with the rusty doors. "Emmie where are you? You're going to pay for what you did to me. Let's play a game. I'll let you hide and I'll come find you," Desmond calls. He sounds excited. I try the first room to hide from him. What sort of game is that? I don't want him to find me? I want to get out of here. My heart beating out my chest. Why am I in this nightmare again?

"Well, that was no fun. I found you. Oh well, straight to the killing part I guess," he says behind me. He didn't even give me a chance.

"Don't touch me." I back away. "Don't hurt me."

"Ha, that's it, beg me. I like it when you beg." Beg? I've never begged him and never will. I have too much self-respect for that.

"Leave me alone," I scream at him.

"Emmie, wake up," Sully says. I look around and he isn't here. Wake up? Oh yeah, I'm having a nightmare but it feels so real.

"Run along now. I'll be here waiting for you when you come back. Don't worry. I'll be here thinking of more ways to hurt you." I shake my head. I don't want to come back.

"Jeez, Emmie, wake up," Sully says panicked. I jolt awake. My breathing is rapid and my heart is pounding. I'm all sweaty, lovely. Sully is sat on my bed with his hand on my cheek. "It's okay, you're safe. Are you okay?"

I shrug, "Bad dream I guess. I don't often get them when Damon is around." Was I that loud that Sully could hear me? I sit up and Sully hugs me.

"It's okay, you are safe," he repeats. "I heard you screaming." I look at him and I notice he is in his boxers. What time is it? "I thought someone got in the house. He releases me and I lean against the headboard. How did I even get to bed last night? All I remember was curling up to Danny. I guess he must have carried me to bed. "Do you want me to stay with you until you fall asleep?"

"What time is it?"

"4 am Emmie."

"Then yeah, I guess I should probably sleep a bit longer." I lay back down and Sully lays next to me. I stare into his eyes and he stares into mine. I drift into a more peaceful sleep.

When I wake I'm on my own. I never expect Sully to stay but it would have been nice to not wake up alone. I look at my phone there are no new messages from Damon. He should be back soon. I take a shower and freshen up. Lilly is crying when I come back so I feed her and change her. I get changed myself and decide I want to venture into town.

I grab Lilly's change bag and my phone and head downstairs. I put my shoes on by the door and I get a strange feeling someone is watching me again. I roll my eyes and turn around. "Where do you think you're going?" Sully demands.

What's it to him? "None of your business Big Guy."

"Of course it. We have two guys on the run looking for you. You can't leave on your own." I frown, I would push this more if I was actually going alone. But I won't put Lilly in unnecessary risk.

"Whatever, I just wanted to meet some friends." Well, none that actually make the effort with me anymore.

"Well please don't leave on your own. Do you really need to go out? Because I'll come with you if you do." Why would I put Sully in danger when I don't need to? I shake my head.

"No, it's fine." I don't know what I was thinking anyway. I hate going out now.

"Good, don't try and sneak out again. Just a heads up, I'm in the office watching on CCTV." He points to the corner of the hallway. Huh, I must have been really stupid not to notice cameras around the place.

"Okay, jeez. I get the message." I'm frustrated, I'm not sure who at. Sully, Damon or me? I kick my shoes off and storm off into the living room and sag onto the couch with Lilly in my arms. She's awake but she's smiling. I love her smile.

I watch a bit of TV. I decide to watch *Pretty Little Liars*. I manage to watch 2 or 3 episodes, I can't remember. I put Lilly in the travel cot in the room and grab the monitor. I go in search to find Sully. He's in Damon's office. I walk in, I don't bother knocking. He's on the phone, he looks upset and angry. What's happened? He looks up at me and frowns.

I came in here to ask him where Damon is. He should have been back hours ago. Maybe he went on a job? Sully hangs up the phone and he walks towards me. His eyes bore into me. What's eating him? He puts his hands on my shoulders when he reaches me. "Sully, what's wrong?"

He takes a minute to think. Why? "Emmie. What I'm about to tell you... Please try not to freak out." Freak out? What's happened? "Damon's plane... It's missing."

"No, it's not." I shake my head. What's he trying to say? I back away from him.

"Emmie, I'm sorry. Damon's missing. It's most likely he's dead." I continue to back away. Dead, he's not dead. Damon wouldn't leave me now. My back hits the wall.

"No, he's not. No," I whisper. Sully walks towards me and I sink to my knees. My husband is just missing, I can handle that. He isn't dead.

"Emmie, calm down," Sully says sternly. I rock on my knees, tears pouring from my face. He kneels in front of me and hugs me. I feel numb. "Where's Lilly? I'll watch her for you."

"She's in the living room. Sleeping," I blubber. I push him away from me, I stand up and run out Damon's office. I run to our bedroom. I lay on his side of the bed and grab our wedding present from Danny. He gave us a photo frame with a picture of Damon and me together. He also gave me a picture album. It's mainly pictures of me when I'm happy but also Lilly and Damon are in it too. I stare at Damon's face and stroke his face with my thumb. He's not dead. He wouldn't leave us.

I grab my phone from my pocket and dial. Damon's phone goes straight to voicemail, his beautiful voice. "Damon? Sully says you are missing. He said you are dead. I refuse to believe that. I love you. Don't leave us."

I dial the only other person I can think of. "Emmie?"

"Danny..." I sob. I can't stop crying.

"Emmie? What's wrong?"

"Danny...I can't...No..." I can't get any words out.

"You're not making any sense Emmie. Speak clearly." I don't bother to say anymore. I know nothing will make sense. "Emmie, I'm going to come to yours now. I'll be there soon." I need Damon, why did his parents summon him? I would still have him in my arms. The last thing I said to him was for him to leave. He can't die knowing that's the last thing I said to him. I need to get out of here. I can't sit and do nothing. I drag myself up out of bed and head downstairs. I walk briskly to the front door, tears still streaming from my face.

Dyno appears from nowhere blocking my path to the door. "Get the hell out of my way Dinosaur," I shout. I need to get out of here now. I need to find him, I need to do something.

"No, and my name is Dyno." He chooses to correct me at a time like this?

"Yeah... Dinosaur. Now move. I can't stay here."

"Emmie, calm down. You're not going anywhere." I am and he is going to get hurt if he doesn't move.

"I'm warning you."

"Just stop. I know this news has upset you but you can't get out of control like this." I'm always out of control. I'm so angry I punch him hard on the nose. He holds his nose, I see blood dripping from his nose.

"Who the hell do you think you are? You have no idea," I scream at him.

"Calm down. You don't need to do this," he says, holding his free arm out in front of him to protect himself from me, I guess.

"I won't tell you again." I walk towards him and the door goes. Dyno grabs the door handle without looking behind him. "Dyno, just let me through," I shout.

"Emmie?" Lucas is staring at me.

"What? Move out the damn way." Dyno holds my shoulders so I can't move towards the door.

"Emmie, you need to calm down," Lucas says. Calm down? My husband is missing, I need to do something.

"What the hell are you doing here? My wound is fully healed. You're not needed here."

"Sully called me. He told me what happened. He's worried about you…" I drop to my knees and Dyno releases me. My eyes are sore from crying.

"I'm fine, I just need Damon. This is all a dream, I need to wake up now." I start to slap my face to try and wake up. This is all a nightmare, it must be.

"If you don't relax I'm going to have to sedate you." He is not coming near me. I stand up and back away from them.

"You will do no such thing. Damon will kill you if you touch me." My sweet beautiful husband.

"Emmie, Rider isn't coming back," Dyno says. He is, he will. He will come back to me. I shake my head.

"Yes, he is. He's not dead. I'm dreaming. I need to wake up. He will wake me, it's okay." I'm talking mostly to myself.

"Emmie, you are not dreaming, this is real." Why should I believe him? Desmond tells me it's not a dream all the time when I'm in a nightmare.

So this must be a nightmare.

The door opens. "No, it's not, shut up. Go away." I start to pace in front of the stairs. I talk to myself again. "I'd rather be tortured by Desmond than this. Someone wake me up." That was less painful than now.

"Emmie? What's going on?" Danny? He walks towards me and I jump into his arms.

"Danny, wake me up," I whisper in his ear. He doesn't let me go. He just rocks me.

"What's wrong with her?"

"Rider's plane went down, he's MIA. Believed dead," Lucas says.

"He's not dead. He can't be," I mutter. Danny strokes my hair, holding me tight.

"She's having a breakdown again. I'm going to have to sedate her. She's too wound up." He can't sedate me, no.

"No don't do that. Just wake me up. I can't take this anymore. This is my worst nightmare ever!" I step out of Danny's hold. My back hits the wall. I'm trapped.

"Emmie look at me." I put my hands on my head trying to process things. Damon, come back to me. We are supposed to grow old together. Lilly can't grow up without her Dad, she needs you. "Emmie, please look at me." I look at him he doesn't try to come towards me. "You trust me right?" I nod to him. I do trust you, Danny. "So listen to me carefully, can you do that?" I nod again. "You're not dreaming. This is real. You need to calm down for me. You can believe Damon is still alive but he is still missing. You are going to need to take one day at a time. I will be here for you."

"No, no, no. I can't take this. I need Damon. Where is he?" I can listen, I just did. I heard the words that came out his mouth. I just don't understand them.

I take my phone again and stare at the screen. "He will message me soon. He won't leave me." Danny closes the distance between us. He hugs me tight, crushing my phone to my chest. He turns me so my back is to the Doctor. He nods. I feel a sharp prick in my side.

I can't breathe. Someone, please wake me. I've never felt pain like this. This is worse than labour. Everything goes numb. My legs give out and Danny and I fall to the floor. I am leaning against Danny, I close my eyes. "Is she going to be okay Doc?" I hear Sully ask.

327

"Hopefully she will be okay after some sleep. She's in shock. I can't imagine what she's going through. She's been through so much already. Knowing her, she will need to be sedated again. Just try to keep her calm. Call me if you need anything," Lucas says.

"She better not be like that all the time. She's hot but I'm not her babysitter," Dyno says. I feel hands stroking my hair. I know I'm close to unconsciousness but I fight it as long as I can.

"I will stay with her. I'll try to keep her calm. So he's missing?" Danny says.

"We have no radio contact. The plane is missing. It's very unlikely anyone survived. But we have men on it trying to find the plane," Sully says. Find the plane and you'll find Damon. Alive, I hope.

"She was so happy. And now this? Do his parents know?" Danny says.

"I've told them, they are distraught. They are getting the next flight." I don't want them here. They made him leave in the first place.

"I don't think Emmie will ever get over this," Danny says. I don't think I will either.

"Neither do I. But what can we do?" Sully says.

"I say lock her up. She's way too much trouble," Dyno says. I hope I broke his nose, if not, I will try again tomorrow. I don't hear anymore. Everything goes black and peaceful.

Chapter 30

I wake up feeling drowsy with a headache. I turn over on my side to see Danny sleeping next to me. I have no desire to get up. What is a life without Damon? I'm calmer now, is it because I got some sleep like the Doc said? Or is it because I was in shock? I don't know, I'm just tired and exhausted. Danny stirs next to me and faces me. "Hey Sis, how are you feeling?" he says softly, keeping his eyes shut.

I frown and don't say anything. What a stupid question. I won't ever be the same again, I just accepted the fact that Damon does want me and now some force has taken him away from me. Are we not meant to be together? Something has been trying to take my life, was I too stubborn and the force settled with Damon instead? Should I have sacrificed myself to save him? In hindsight, I would have done that for him. Danny strokes my hair and cheek. I just stare into his eyes, speechless. I feel numb. "Sis, I love you. Stay with us." Oh, Danny, I won't be leaving my daughter, although it would be easier.

Someone knocks at the door. "Come in," Danny says. I hear the door click open.

"Emmie, Damon's parents are here. They want to see you," Sully says gently like I may break. Well, I am breaking inside. I don't want to see them, they took Damon away from me.

"Now's not a good time Sully," Danny says. There will never be a good time.

"Emmie, please. Damon wouldn't want this," Sully says. Damon isn't here so who cares? Deep down I care but I can't do this now. Damon doesn't like a lot of things I do, he told me to be myself. And that is what I'm going to do.

"Sully, please. I need to keep her calm." I don't look at Sully but I hear the door click shut.

"I'm going to go see them. I'll take Lilly with me. She will be fine with me." He gets up and puts on his clothes and takes Lilly. Tears stream down my face when he's gone. I grab Damon's pillow and hug it. It smells like him. I need more than this. I go to the bathroom and find his hoodie he left on the floor before he left. I change into it and make my way back into the bedroom and take up my earlier position on the bed. Tears continue to fall.

Where are you Damon? My heart still aches for you. You must still be out there somewhere, I have to believe that. The door clicks open again. "Emmie?" Mrs Rider says. I ignore her, I told them both I didn't want to see them. She stands in my eye line and sits in front of me. She reaches for my hand and I withdraw. "Emmie sweetheart. Jerry and I want to start planning the funeral."

What, no?! Damon isn't dead. He will fight for us, why are they giving in so soon? I will never accept his death unless I see proof. I need to see his body to believe it. She looks tired, she looks awful. When I last saw her, she looked young and carefree. But now she looks as though she's lost a part of herself. She looks like a mother who's lost their child. "I want you to help arrange it. Damn it, Emmie. Say something."

Anger is boiling inside of me. I get off the bed and stare at her. She stands up too. "Damon is not dead," I scream. "I will not help bury someone who isn't dead. He will come back to me."

"Emmie, for god sake. Accept it, everyone else has. He isn't coming back."

"He is. Get out!" I put my hands on my head. I want them to leave. The door opens and Sully runs towards me.

"Emmie, calm down." He hugs me tight and I let him.

"He isn't dead Sully. They can't do this," I say in his ear and he hushes me. Keeping me calm.

"Emmie, it's helping you to believe he is still alive. But his parents need this. They are entitled to do this if they wish," he says. I nod into his neck.

"Emmie, we are going to stay here. We want to be close to Lilly-May." I shake my head. They haven't done anything to deserve to be in her life. Why would it matter to Lilly if they are close? She needs her Dad, not her selfish grandparents.

"No," I mutter into Sully's neck. He strokes my hair but he doesn't say anything.

"Well come find us if you want to help. I'm sure he would want your input."

My body shakes with anger. "Shh, calm down," Sully says. How dare she say that? If Damon was actually dead then of course I would put my input in. But I won't, I can't. My body feels heavy. Sully picks me up and carries me to the bed. He pulls the sheet over me. "Do you want me to stay?" He sits next to me. I turn to face him and nod. I curl up to his chest and fall asleep.

"Sis?" Go away, Bro. I'm tired. "Sis, you need to eat." I groan, no I don't. "Sis, wake up," he says a little louder.

"I can hear you," I snap and snuggle back into Damon's pillow. I feel weight shifting on the bed. He's sat in front of me. Sully's gone. When he asked me if I wanted him to stay I thought he meant until I wake up. That's what Damon would do.

"Sis, you need to eat. You've been sleeping for two days." I have? Wow. Feels like a few hours. "I will make you eat it." The hell he will. He goes to put food in my mouth and I pull away. Horrified. "Sis." I sit up and grab the plate. He smiles. But I didn't pick it up to eat it. I stand up and throw it against the wall and walk out of the room.

I need to see my daughter. I can't believe I slept for two days. My husband has been missing for 4 days. Time is precious. Damon's parents are lingering in the living room. Lilly isn't in here. "Emmie?" Mrs Rider calls, I ignore her and head to Damon's office. Sully is on the phone with Lilly in his arms. Dyno is sat on the couch. His nose is bruised, it's purply blue. I smile at him. They both look up at me.

I walk towards Sully and take Lilly off him. He lets me take her. I walk and sit next to Dyno. I watch Lilly sleep. She's so peaceful, so oblivious to the heartbreak around her. Sully gets off the phone and joins us on the sofa, sitting next to me so I'm sat in the middle. "Did your brother find you?"

I frown at him, "Yeah and he got a plate thrown at the wall to show for it."

"At least he doesn't have a broken nose," Dyno says. I smile at him, at least I did something right.

"I need to know. You must have heard something by now," I say to Sully. I can tell by his face that he doesn't know anything new but I had to ask. He sighs and shakes his head. I lean my head on Sully's shoulder. I don't know what I'd do without Sully.

"You really should eat something," Sully whispers. I shut my eyes. I'm always so tired. I keep functioning for Lilly, but I don't feel anything. Just numb to this world.

"I would keep your mouth shut. She throws a good punch," Dyno says. I don't say anything, I wouldn't hurt Sully, not intentionally. And I could have aimed the plate at Danny but I didn't want to hurt him either. I feel Lilly being taken from my arms. I open my heavy eyelids to see Sully holding her. She's safe so I fall to sleep.

I feel awful when I wake again. It feels like I wake, behave like a zombie and then sleep. It's an endless vicious circle. I get out of bed, I change my underwear and put denim shorts on. I change my top but place Damon's hoodie back on. I haven't taken it off since he's been missing and it still smells like him. It protects me. I walk downstairs I poke my head around the living room door and see Danny with Lilly and Damon's parents. They don't see me so I walk towards the office. I hear Sully and Dyno talking, I wait to hear what they are talking about.

"Sully, we got him," Dyno says pleased with himself.

"That's good. Rex will get what's coming to him." Sully is happy too. They caught Rex?

"My thoughts exactly. What are we going to do about him?" Dyno says.

"We need to ask him some question. I'll be down later to interrogate him." Interrogate him about what?

"So how is Emmie today? We can't have her running the gang. Not like this, even if she is next in line." I'm next in line to take over the gang? I shake my head, it's Damon's gang. He built this, he needs to finish it.

"She's not going to find that out Dyno. She's still sleeping. Danny is looking after Lilly-May at the moment."

I need to do something. I sneak out the back door, I'm hoping no one is watching CCTV at the moment. Lilly's safe so I will be there and back in no time. I jog to the safe house, I need a head start, they will come after me soon so I need to get there quickly. I tire easily, maybe I should have had a sugar fix first.

I type in the code in the keypad. I try to be as quiet as I can. If I am going to interrogate Rex, I'm going to need protection from him. I go straight to Damon's office, I don't see anyone. I walk to his desk and curl up on his chair for a while. He has new pictures on his desk. One of me and one of Lilly. This isn't the end. I open his drawers and rummage through them. Yes, a gun, this will do. I'm not sure how to use it, but it can't be too hard, right?

I take a deep breath and go to find Rex. What will I do when I see him again? I must be strong. I stand up and slide the gun behind me in my shorts. I make my way to the holding cells where Damon kept me when I was here. I don't see anyone guarding him. This gang is stupid and obviously falling apart without Damon. Who leaves a prisoner unprotected? Oh well, good for me I guess.

I grab the key hanging to the left of the door unlock it and go through the door. His mouth drops open when he sees me. "Hello pretty. Did you come to save me? I've missed you." He comes towards me, my natural instinct is to back away from him, but for my plan to work I must play him.

"Yes, I've come to save you. I've missed you too. But I want answers first." He puts his arm on the door, he's inches away from my face. He has the biggest grin.

"Whatever you want, it's yours." You can't give me what I want. I want Damon here in my arms alive. I also want you to back off.

"Did you mess with my husband's plane?" This must be what Sully and Dyno wanted to know, he wanted him dead.

"Yes. I wanted you to myself and here you are." I feel like he's punched me hard.

I wince, "Are you working with anyone else?"

"Err yes." He's awkward about it. Who could he be working with? "You are safe with me, but we had a common interest." I'm only safe with Damon and he's not here. You took his plane down. I want to go die in a hole but I need more answers.

"Who?"

"Desmond White." I gasp as he says his name, even his name terrifies me.

"The one that wants me dead?" Why is he working with him? How is it a common interest? Rex wants me to himself, Desmond wants to kill me.

He grabs my chin, "I won't let him hurt you." I'm not safe from Desmond.

"You can't promise that. You shot me." Twice.

"That was a mistake, you got in the way. How stupid could you be?" My loved ones tell me I'm stupid all the time. But I fight for what I believe in.

"Are you planning anything else?" Like, go after my daughter?

"No, now that Rider is dead I have you to myself."

I shake my head, Damon can't be dead. No. Rex goes in for a kiss. "Stay away from me," I say whilst grabbing the gun. I hold it to his head.

"I thought you said you were here to rescue me?" He goes to step away from me, shocked.

"Well, I played you. I knew you wouldn't talk to my men, so I thought I'd do it myself." Sounds weird to say my men but I feel like they belong to me now. Not just as their leader but as family.

He shakes his head, "You won't shoot me." Of course I will, he took Damon away from me. I haven't been functioning since he's been gone. I've had a breakdown, I'm not well. I'm out of control. My hand is shaking.

"People seem to underestimate me. You took down my husband's plane. You've ruined my daughter's life. I hate you. I don't really care what you did to me." You ruined my life more ways than one.

"Come on beautiful, I know you want me." He couldn't be more wrong. He's clutching at straws, I feel nothing for this guy.

"That's where you are wrong. I hate you." Hate is a strong word, I don't hate many people but he's one of the very few.

I aim at his head, put both hands around the gun and pull the trigger. The recoil is strong but I manage to hold it. It hit where I aimed and Rex falls to the floor. I can't move, I'm stuck here. I can't put the gun down even though I despise it. What did I do? I mean, I'm glad he is out of our lives but I took a life.

I hear fast footsteps coming towards me. My heart is beating frantically. "Emmie!" Sully calls. He hasn't reached me yet. I still can't move. "Shit Emmie!" Sully slowly moves towards me, careful that I have a gun. He looks at Rex and then to me. Why does he look so scared? "Emmie, put the gun down." I can't, I want to but I'm frozen. I need Damon. I can't carry on like this. Sully is right by my side, he holds his hands up slowly so I know what he's doing. He puts his hand around the gun, I feel the weight disappear. I feel a sense of relief. "Good girl," Sully says and puts the gun in his waistband. His arms catch me, I feel so helpless. "What the hell were you thinking?" he whispers in my ear. I was protecting my family.

"He deserved it."

"Emmie, you just killed someone." I know. I was already a bad person, I'm going to hell anyway.

"And I'd do it again."

"Emmie, you're never going to forgive yourself for this." He's holding all my weight.

I sigh, "I don't forgive myself for a lot of things. This one will just add to that long list."

"Let's get you home." He lifts me up so I'm in his arms. I feel like a vulnerable child. I wish I was home, my home is in Damon's arms. I let Sully take me back to Damon's house, will I be able to stay there knowing he may never come back? It's just an empty shell without him. I close my eyes and fall asleep.

I wake when Sully lifts me out of the car. Dyno is pacing when we enter the house. "What happened?" Dyno growls.

"Not now Dyno," Sully snaps at him.

"I was just cleaning up your mess. What sort of idiot leaves a prisoner unattended?" Sully carries me upstairs into the bedroom and Dyno follows.

"What's that supposed to mean?" Sully eases me onto the bed. Why am I always so damn tired?

Sully sits next to me and I curl up into his chest, "I killed him."

"You did what?" Dyno shouts. I close my eyes.

"You heard me," I mumble, I must stay awake.

"You crazy girl."

"Don't call me crazy. You are all idiots. I had to finish the job off. Why was there no one with him?" I'm barely audible but they hear me.

"We are here looking after you." I wasn't here, I was at the safe house.

"Dyno, enough," Sully growls and strokes my hair. Don't do that because I will fall asleep.

"No, we need information and now we are stuffed." Oh, dinosaur we are far from stuffed.

"Who said we didn't have information?" I say.

"What?" Dyno says in disbelief.

"I got what we needed. He would have never told you. I, on the other hand, could get anything I wanted out of him. But why the hell should I share this with you? I'm just crazy after all." I hate him, he's always so angry.

"You got information?" Sully says softly, looking down at me.

"Of course I did. I'm not stupid." I meant that more to Dyno, I don't want to be mean to Sully. He's taken good care of me. But how long will it last? Maybe I should leave here, start a fresh.

Dyno sighs and sits at the end of the bed, "I'm sorry, okay. Maybe you're not so crazy. What do you know?"

"Maybe I don't want to share with you."

"Emmie please," Sully begs.

"Fine, he said he took down the plane."

"That's what I thought. Anything else?" Sully says. My body tenses at the thought of Desmond. "Emmie?"

"He's working with Desmond."

He holds me tighter which I welcome. "Oh dear. This isn't good."

"Rex was only the little fish. Desmond is the big fish. Rex only wanted me to himself. Where as Desmond wants me dead."

"So what are we going to do?" Dyno asks Sully.

"Err." Sully doesn't have a clue. I imagine Damon is the genius in this gang, they are out of their depth.

"I'll tell you what we are going to do," I say. I just want to sleep but sleep will have to wait.

"I don't take orders from you," Dyno scoffs.

"Of course you do. I heard you, I'm next in line." Dyno's mouth drops open.

"Emmie," Sully warns.

"We are doing this my way, as you are all so incapable." They don't have a plan, so this will work.

"Rude." Dyno crosses his arms.

"Bite me," I say, closing my eyes again.

"What does Rider see in you? Seriously, I get you're hot but jeez you're hard to deal with." I'm not hot. I don't know what Damon sees in me, but I gave up worrying about it. It was too exhausting.

"Shut up. I have a plan, Big Guy you're not going to like it. But you follow my orders now." Sully has always done as I asked, I'm not sure why but he's always tried to put my wishes first. Sully tenses underneath me.

"Just because you are my Boss now doesn't mean I won't treat you like a kid. Makes me happy." He's trying to lighten the mood. But I'm not laughing.

"You dare. Anyway my plan… I get in contact with my Mother. She will lead me right to Desmond."

"Absolutely not. I won't agree to this. You are putting yourself in danger," Sully says without even considering it. I knew he wouldn't like it.

"It's actually pretty clever," Dyno says thinking it over.

"I said no," Sully snaps at Dyno.

"This isn't your choice. It's mine," I mumble, I'm so close to sleep. Sleep takes me without my permission.

When I wake, I am so thirsty. Danny sits on my bed with some orange juice. He smiles at me and hands me the glass. I gratefully accept and down the whole glass.

"Sis, please don't throw another plate. But you should take a shower, you are starting to smell." Jee, thanks Bro. I don't even care if I smell, to be honest. He grabs my glass and puts it on the bedside cabinet. He grabs my hand and leads me to the bathroom.

He runs the shower and he looks at me. He undresses me and pushes me in the shower. I can't imagine what I look like. Do I look vulnerable? Do I look scared, broken? Do I look a complete mess like I'm having a breakdown? I quickly wash myself and Danny turns the shower off and places a towel around me.

I shouldn't be letting my brother do this. I don't even care if I smell, I just want Damon back. Danny helps me dress and I lay back down on the bed. Again, I make sure I have Damon's hoodie on, it's still holding his scent. The door opens and Brody walks in. I don't feel anything when he walks in, not relief, sadness, happiness or anger.

"Hey, Emmie." He lays in front of me so we are facing each other. He frowns, I guess I look more broken than last time. Last time I could disconnect from this world but Lilly ties me here. I wouldn't leave her. "How are you doing?" He strokes my face but I remove it. I can't have him touch me.

"Please leave." I don't need someone else to try to make me snap out of it.

"Emmie. I'm here for you," he says, hurt.

"I don't need you. I just need Damon."

"Emmie, he's gone. He's not coming back. Has a week not meant anything to you?" Danny has left the room. I get off the bed to protect myself. A week? It's felt like a couple of days to me. Tears pour down my face. "Emmie, calm down."

I pace the room. I can't handle this. Why has he not come back to me? I punch the wall hard. Ow, that hurt. Yes, that's good, pain is good. I hit it over and over. I see blood on the wall but that doesn't stop me. Brody grabs me from behind and I scream. Danny and Sully run into the room. I struggle to get out of Brody's arms.

"Let her go," Sully says calmly. Brody does as he says and I fall to the floor. Sully kneels on the floor and he hugs me tight. "First aid box in Damon's office," he says, I guess to Danny.

Sully lifts me onto the bed. Tears continue to pour from my face. Danny returns with a first aid kit, Sully deals with my hand. "I'm not sure if you broke anything. Does it hurt?" I shrug because I don't feel anything. I'm just numb again.

"What happened?" Danny asks.

"She flipped out, I told her it's been a week and Damon's not coming back and she started punching the wall."

"You shouldn't say that in front of her," Danny growls.

"It's true, she needs to accept it." No, I can't, I'll have nothing left in me to fight then.

I fall asleep again. When I wake I hear muffled voices. "What happened?"

"She freaked out and started hitting a wall," Danny says. "Doc look, she's not eating. We need to do something. She sleeps all the time. She's getting worse, not better."

"She needs time. She's always been bad with food, right? How did you get her to eat last time?" Lucas says.

"I tried that, she threw the plate at the wall."

"I'll throw it at your head next time," I say.

"Hey, Emmie. Can I look at your hand?" Lucas asks.

"No." I shake my head. I don't want him touching me. He walks towards me and I back away off the bed. He continues to walk towards me and I scream. I grab things from my dresser, my hairbrush and I throw it at them. Perfumes, anything.

Sully enters the room, he walks straight up to me and hugs me tight. I freeze. I feel so out of control. But I know I don't want to hurt Sully. I feel a prick in my side again and everything goes black. I don't bother fighting it this time.

I wake up groggy but I feel better than yesterday. I need to find Lilly. I walk downstairs and she is in Addi's arms. Addi? I take Lilly off her. I need to know Lilly is safe. I feel like I've been drugged. I know I was but I feel confused. "Honey?"

"What are you doing here Addi?"

"Everyone is worried about you." I know they are but I can't do anything about that. She takes Lilly from my arms and puts her in the travel cot. She brings me in and hugs me. She's like a magnet, pulling me to her. But Damon's magnet is stronger, my heart aches for him.

I shake my head and back away. I grab my phone from my pocket. "Momma?" I sob.

"Emmie sweetheart." Her voice repulses me.

"Rider is missing. I need you." Not, I just need Damon. Addi looks confused.

"Of course darling. Do you want me to come to you?" No, you are not coming that close to Lilly.

"No can I come back to the house? I miss home."

"That makes me so happy darling. Yes, come whenever you can."

"Bye Momma." I hang up.

"What was that about."

"I need to lure Desmond out."

"I'm coming with you." I shake my head. "Yes, I am."

"Once I get to Desmond, then I'll let her see you, okay?" She nods in agreement. I wonder if Sully is in the office. I wave at a camera gesturing for him to come to me. I may just be waving at nothing but worth a try.

"Emmie?" Wow, that was quick. "You okay?" Sully says.

I nod. "You ready? I've contacted my mother."

He shakes his head, "I don't like this Emmie." I shrug and walk to the door.

"Where is Danny?"

"He's in the office. One second." Sully walks to the office and moments later Dyno and Danny appear with Sully.

"Bro, can you look after Lilly?" He frowns but nods and walks to the living room. I walk to the car and sit on the back seat. Sully slides in next to me, he normally drives. What's going on? Dyno climbs in the driver's seat and Addi sits in the passenger seat.

Sully grabs my hand. "You don't need to do this. We can find another way." I shake my head. This is what we are doing.

"I need to do this. I will be fine. I know you want to protect me but I have to do this. I'm willing to do whatever it takes to get revenge."

He leans towards my ear, "I know you are. You killed someone," he whispers so Addi doesn't hear him.

"I know, I don't want to think about that."

He leans away again, "Boss will never forgive me." Sully sighs.

"Sully, he's probably dead. And well if he's not, I'm sure he will understand," Dyno says.

"Boss and understand do not belong in the same sentence." We all laugh, even me.

"You're right," Dyno says amused.

We reach Desmond's house and I go to get out the car but Sully doesn't let my hand go. I look at him. "Be careful." I nod and he lets me go. I walk to the house. I knock on the door. My mother answers it with a smile.

"I've missed you, sweetheart," she says.

"I've missed you too Momma. Rider is missing Momma, what am I going to do?" I start to cry again. It's not hard for me to cry, I just have to think of Damon.

"I'm sorry baby girl."

"Where is Desmond?"

She looks awkward. "He's out." Out? Is that all I get?

"Oh okay." Damn this isn't going to plan.

"I could call him…" I smile and nod.

"I need my family around me." Yes, I do, I need Damon.

"I'm so happy you came back to us." She tucks a strand of hair behind my ear and then grabs her phone from her pocket.

"Hey, my love." She pauses, waiting for his response. "Emmie came home. Rider is missing, she needs her family." She turns away from me. "I know my daughter Desmond, she needs us." No, you don't, not even close. "See you soon my love."

She looks at me. "We need to go meet him."

"Why can't he come here?" Sully is going to be mad.

"It's not safe."

Sully will kill me. It's not safe for me to leave. "Sure, let's go."

Chapter 31

My mother leads the way to her car by the garage. Sully is parked on the road so my mother won't get suspicious. "Get in Emmie," she says. I hesitate, this could go many ways but I decide that I'm doing this for Damon and to keep Lilly safe, there is no doubt in my mind that this isn't the right thing to do. So I climb in the front. She pulls out the drive and I glance at Sully's car before we leave but I can't see anyone's faces.

It takes ten minutes to reach our destination. It seems to be an abandoned building. She smiles at me and then gets out the car. My heart is beating out my chest. She waits for me to get out. She stares at me up and down. "Baby girl, you look awful. Have you not been taking care of yourself?"

Tears start forming in my eyes from the constant reminder of my missing husband. She hugs me and I stand frozen, this is too much. I'm starting to think Damon won't come back, it's been too long. But I have to get this out the way first and then I will deal with that. "Come on baby. We are your family," she says and leads me into the building.

Desmond appears in front of us. Seeing him here, I suddenly don't feel so strong anymore. What the hell am I doing? He scares me just as much as before. Maybe even more so now because Damon isn't here to protect me. He is real, here, not fake like in my dreams. "Hey my love," my Mother says to him and he kisses her.

"Emmie," he nods at me.

"Desmond." I return his coldness.

"So Rider is missing huh?" Like he didn't already know, he was in on it with Rex. Why do I have to keep being reminded of this? At the house, I would shut them all out. Sleeping helped with that I guess.

"What am I going to do?" I sob into my hands. We hear the door go.

"Who was that? Did you bring someone?" Desmond growls.

Please be Addi, I'm not ready yet. I turn to my mother. "Momma, Damon gave me a wedding present before he went missing."

She looks confused. "A present?"

I nod and on cue, she walks towards us. Addi looks scared but she walks straight to me and hugs me. "Addison?" Mother gasps.

"Hey Sister," she says coldly. Why, I thought she wanted to meet her?

"What are you doing here? I haven't seen you in years."

"And whose fault is that?" Addi keeps her arms around me. "Josh had me arrested."

"He did? I didn't know that." She shakes her head. She looks genuine, she wasn't there when I ran away.

"When Emmie ran away I found her on the streets, I took her in. But I didn't know the situation then and got in contact with her Dad. He got me arrested for kidnap but mostly because I was her auntie. Why didn't you tell me I had a niece?"

"It was a bad time for me," Mother says. Addi goes to comfort her sister and Desmond drags me away while Addi is distracted. He pulls me into a little side room.

"I don't know what you're up to," he says holding his chin.

"I don't know what you mean. I wanted to be with my family." I really do, my real family anyway. Damon.

"You suddenly remembered who your family are?" I've always known who my family are, even when I was trying to be selfless.

I cringe at thinking this, "Yes Daddy." I hated calling my actually Dad this. But I love my Dad and now it seems more fitting. I remember he wrote this on the walls in the scary building.

He smiles, "Oh Emmie. I've missed you." Missed me? I thought he wanted me dead. He hugs me and I am frozen again. I feel sick but there can't be anything in my stomach.

"Now we can be a perfect family." What about Danny? He would never come back here and I thought he was the favourite. He never had trouble fitting in.

"I'd like that." Not. He releases me.

We hear screams in the building. "Momma?" I call. Not that I really care.

"Esme?" Desmond calls too. If that is my men, then they are bloody stupid. Yep, Dyno and Sully enters the room we are in with guns and Desmond pulls me towards him like Rex did. Shielding himself. I'm obviously his get out free card.

"What are you doing Daddy?" I say terrified, I am but I let him see this to try and reason with him.

"You're playing me, aren't you?" I shake my head. I am but he can't know that I'm a good liar.

"Let her go," Sully demands. I look at his face and he is terrified too. Oh, Sully, this was my fault, I let mother bring me here.

"No," Desmond says, he pulls me further back.

"I'm warning you," Sully says.

"I knew you were playing me, you stupid bitch." I didn't even do anything. I guess he's decided that I'm lying.

"You two are stupid," I say annoyed, this was working.

"Shut up," Dyno growls. He is worried too.

"All of you shut up. Well, thank you Emmie, for playing right into my hands." I place my hands on his arms, I won't be able to stop him if he tries to strangle me but I can delay it.

"If you touch a hair on her head, I swear to God," Sully says. He's out of his depth and he knows it.

"What you going to do?" Desmond laughs. Desmond has the upper hand.

"Are you sure we can't leave her here? She's a pain anyway," Dyno says. Please don't leave me here.

"Hey," I huff.

"She can stay with me. I know many ways to keep her quiet. The things I did. The things I want to do again." My body starts to shake. Dyno's face is shocked.

"You are sick," Dyno says.

"No, I'm just a guy that knows what he wants." Yes, I agree with that, he goes and gets what he wants.

"That's enough," Sully says. Oh, please help me Sully. Sully takes aim at Desmond, I shut my eyes hoping Sully can shoot straight. I hear the gunfire but no pain. Desmond drops to the floor and he pulls me with him. I scream and scramble away from him. Sully grabs my arm and pulls me to my feet. He pushes me behind him and I clutch his shirt. He puts an arm around my shoulder.

"Ow, you shot my leg you bastard," Desmond says. He kept him alive? Why?

"You're lucky I didn't want to kill you or I would shoot you in the head." I don't understand.

"You're an idiot. I played you. You'll finally get what you deserve," I say, still shaking but I say it confidently.

"I have to admit you are a really good actor. You had me fooled." Yeah, until these idiots came in.

"Guys take him to the safe house. Make sure someone is actually guarding him this time." I want to get out of here. I don't want to see him anymore.

"You're such a pain in the ass. Do you know that?" Dyno says, putting his gun away and grabbing Desmond.

"Oh bite me. Just take him away."

Sully faces me and strokes my face. "You okay?" I shake my head. I will never be okay. Not because of Desmond but because of my husband. He scoops me up into his arms and I relax a little. I fall asleep on the way back.

I'm at the beach in my wedding dress, Damon is stood with me. Oh, my god, I'd forgotten how truly beautiful he is. My mouth drops open and I hug him tightly. I can't let him go, not ever. I hear a gunshot. What's going on? Damon drops to the floor. I see Rex behind him with a gun. He shot my husband. I scream and reach for Damon. No Damon, you aren't dead. No!

"I love you, baby," Damon's soft voice says. I scream again, crying. I can't handle this. I see the life drain from his face. I shake him but he doesn't wake. No!

"Emmie!" My eyes fly open, they are wet and sore. I've been crying. Sully is staring at me. "You were screaming." He hugs me. I can't accept he's dead, I need proof. "You okay?" I shake my head, my answer will always be no. "I need to get ready, I will see you later."

Sully leaves me in bed. It's supposed to be Damon's funeral today but

I'm not going. I guess Sully feels he needs to go. I hug Damon's pillow and grab his picture. He's so beautiful. I don't know how much time passes before Dyno enters my room. "Rider's parents are ready. They want to collect you for his funeral." I'm not going to any damn funeral. Dyno sits next to me on the bed. I'm curled up in a ball, a sobbing mess I'd imagine. "Emmie, did you hear me?" he snaps.

"Get out Dinosaur. I've had enough of your crap. I'm not going to this stupid funeral," I shout at him.

"You are so annoying. He's dead Emmie. You need to grieve and move on." No, he's not dead. I get out of bed and throw Damon's pillow as hard as I can at his head. He protects his nose.

"Never. Now get out. I hate you," I scream. I'm becoming hysterical again. He stands up with his hands up.

"Well, I have to say that I don't particularly like you either. But I wouldn't say no. You're sexy when you're angry."

I scream. I hate him. I don't accept this, not from him. I want to bang my head on the wall but I refrain.

"I'm warning you, get the hell out. You are so stupid. I hate you. Get the hell out." He walks towards me and grabs me. I scream and struggle to get out of his hold.

"Calm down Emmie. Don't make me call the Doctor again." I lose days when he sedates me. No! I'm not going to be drugged for the rest of my life.

"I'm sick of all you drugging me. You all should just leave me to it. I will deal with this in my own way. Let me go!"

"He's not coming back, Emmie. Accept that. You can't go around giving everyone crap." I don't have the energy to fight him. I haven't eaten.

"Remember what happened last time you got on my nerves. Yeah, I broke your nose. Now get the hell out."

"Fine, but I'm calling the Doctor. He can deal with you." I scream again, he doesn't let go of me though.

"No need for that." My heart skips a beat at the sound of his voice. We both look up at the door. Dyno releases me and I drop to my knees. I'm too tired.

"Damon?" I whisper. He nods at me and I scramble to my feet and run into his arms. My arms around his neck and my legs wrapped around his waist. I'm home, my husband is alive.

"You're alive?" Dyno says, shocked. Damon strokes my hair and kisses my head. He just continues to hold me.

"Yes, now get the hell out. I will speak to you later," Damon growls, he's angry. How much did he see?

"Yes, Boss." I hear the door click shut.

"Damon." I sob into his neck. I won't let him go. I can't.

"I have heard you have been hell." He sits on the bed and pulls my head away so he can look at my face. "You look awful baby." I shake my head, I don't care about me. Where's he been?

"Are you really here?" He kisses me softly.

"Yes baby, I'm here." Tears freefall from my face. "Don't cry baby, I'm back now." He wipes away the tears, his touch sends pulses down my spine. I don't feel numb anymore.

"Where have you been? I've been so worried."

"I can see that. I will fill you in later." He sighs. "You haven't eaten anything? Not one mouthful?" He sounds mad. I shake my head. I'm fine.

"Oh, Damon. I can't believe you're here. Please don't leave me again." I hug him and Damon doesn't push me away.

"I won't leave you, I promise." He pulls my head away so he can kiss me. He lays down and brings me with him. I have missed this man. I finally feel safe and calm after this past week. He kisses me gently at first and then it turns more urgent and demanding. I can see he has missed me too. This is what I've needed. He pulls me closer. I would do anything for this man right now.

He goes to lift his hoodie from me. I stop his hands and he sits up again. "Why are you wearing my clothes?" He smirks at me.

"It smells like you, it's protected me."

"It protects you? How long have you been wearing it?"

I shrug, "Since you've been missing."

He puts his forehead on mine. "Well, you have me back now. You don't need this." He stands up and carries me to the bathroom.

He removes my clothes and his. "Danny said he had to shower you." I don't say anything, I was a zombie. He leads me to the shower. He kisses me on my lips. He washes me and I let him. I wouldn't let Danny touch me. But my husband can and he is healing me. We lose ourselves in each other.

I'm back in the bloody room with Desmond. "So you came back to me? You have been missed."

"I'm not afraid of you anymore," I say.

"Well, that's good because Rider isn't here to save you. He's dead."

"A life without Rider isn't worth living and if he isn't here then I'm not afraid to die."

"I'm sure I can find a way to make you scared," he shrugs.

"Try me." He grins at me and then nods towards the other side of the room. I look at what he is staring at. It's Damon's dead body. I scream. No!

"Wake up baby. You're having a nightmare," Damon says. I wake instantly. Oh, thank god.

"Damon?" He strokes my face.

"You're safe baby." I am now that he is here.

"I'm not worried about my safety. It's yours. You were dead."

"I'm here Emmie. I'm not going anywhere." I believe that, mainly because I'm not going to let him.

"Good. I've missed you." He kisses me.

"I've missed you too. I need to get up to get an update on everything while I've been gone." No, you can't. He will be so mad. I grab his hand.

"Don't leave me."

"I have to go to work sweetheart but I guess you can come with me. Get dressed and I'll see you in a minute." I nod and he leaves the room. I look under the sheets and I'm naked. I don't feel naked around Damon. I get up and change into something comfy. I then go to Damon's drawers and grab another hoodie. He may be here now but I still need the band aid on.

I walk downstairs to find Damon and Sully talking in the hallway. I go and hug Sully and he pulls me in tight. "You look better," he says in my ear. I smile at him when he releases me.

"Yeah, I'm good." Now that Damon's here. "Are we going now?" Damon looks horrified. "What?"

"Emmie, you haven't eaten anything. We aren't leaving until you've eaten something." I shake my head and back away.

"Emmie, calm down," Sully says. He grabs my hand before I get too far away. He walks towards me and strokes my cheek. "Emmie, Damon is here now. You don't need to do this."

Damon comes towards me and hugs me tight. "Baby, you are safe. I'm here, you just need to eat something," he whispers in my ear and it soothes me. He grabs my hand and leads me into the kitchen and gets me to sit at the table. Danny is sitting next to me with Lilly in his arms.

"I may need your help this time," Damon says to Danny. Danny shakes his head and holds one hand up.

"You are on your own. Last time I got a plate thrown at me." Damon frowns.

"If I wanted it to hit you, I would have hit you. You are lucky I didn't want to hurt you."

"Well gee, thanks sis," he says sarcastically.

"And what happened to Dyno?" Damon asks.

I shrug, "I punched him in the face."

"For what?"

"He wouldn't let me leave."

"That sounds reasonable." He shrugs.

"Not when your husband is missing it's not. He kept saying you were dead. I wasn't going to think about that." Damon looks sad.

"Emmie, he wasn't going to let you leave, the state you were in," Danny says. I poke my tongue out at him.

Damon places food in front of me, Danny and himself. He's made toast for everyone, is this to give me no choice to argue? I think it is. Damon sits opposite to me. He takes a bite out of his and glares at Danny. Danny picks up his toast and eats too, not saying a word. I just sit staring at mine, why is this so hard? I'm too wound up to eat. "Emmie, please. For me," Damon begs. He grabs my hand that is on the table. I take deep even breaths.

"This is hard Damon. If you hadn't returned." I shake my head. "I'd probably have killed them if they did this."

He tugs at my hand so I stand up and sit on his lap. I feel happy here. I feel safest here. "Why are you wearing my hoodie again?" I snuggle up to his neck.

"Just because you are back doesn't mean I'm ready to lose you again. This gives me comfort. Just because you are back, doesn't mean I'm fixed."

"How many more scars did I give you?" He kisses my hair.

I shrug, "It's hard to tell. I felt numb when you were gone. Now you are healing me again. But it will take time." Maybe a long time, we seem to take 5 steps forwards then 10 back.

He grabs his slice of toast and edges it towards my mouth. "I wouldn't do that," Danny says.

"Be quiet," Damon snaps. "Trust me," he says to me. I close my eyes and nod. I open my eyes again and bite the toast. I gag like I'm going to be sick. But I carry on chewing. Man, this has never been so hard. "Thank you," he says softly. He continues to feed me. Will I ever get over this? Once I'm finished, Damon slides me off his lap and leads me out to the hallway. Dyno and Sully are waiting for us. Dyno looks worried, well I will pray for him. Damon is going to be angry when he finds out. Sully drives and Dyno sits in the front with him. Damon and I sit in the back.

"Sully," I say.

"Yes, Emmie?" he says softly.

"Will you play some music please?"

"Emmie if I do that then you'll sleep. You don't make it through the day anymore." I frown at him in the rear-view mirror. He sighs and puts the radio on. Music sounds softly in the car and I lean on Damon. My eyes become heavy. Shit, and darkness takes me.

I hear faint voices. "You seem to know her so well now," Damon says.

"Well yeah, she wouldn't listen to anyone. She seemed to accept me," Sully says.

"She trusts you more than anyone else, other than me," Damon says.

"I thought she would listen to her Brother more."

"Think about it, Danny never protected her from her Dad. The worst part of her life. She wants to trust him but deep down she doesn't forgive him for that. Whereas you, you took a bullet for her."

"I never thought about it like that. Don't get mad Boss but she wouldn't settle most nights so I had to sleep next to her."

Damon sighs, "I'm glad she had you." That's all he says. He can't be happy about it but he accepts it. Damon lifts me up and carries me. I guess we have arrived at the safe house. I feel Damon walk a while and then he sits down. I guess we are in his office at his desk. I snuggle up to Damon and he strokes my hair.

"So what's been going on?" Oh crap. "And you, how dare you speak to my wife the way you did yesterday. You shouldn't touch her let alone restrain her like you did," He shouts, I guess at Dyno.

"Really? She's been hell," Dyno protests. "She broke my bloody nose."

"That's funny, it really is," Damon laughs.

"I will tell you Boss, but you are not going to like one bit of it. So don't kill anyone." Oh, Sully please leave me out of this.

"Just tell me, Sully," Damon snaps.

"Okay, so Rex was the one who tampered with your plane."

"I'll kill him," Damon shouts. I hold him tighter.

"Yeah well you can't, and you know why?" Dyno says. Oh, it would be him. "Emmie, did you want to tell him?"

I groan but I don't move. "Shut up Dyno," I mumble sleepily.

"What the hell is going on?" Damon is mad. He pulls my head away from him and we stare into each other's eyes.

"Your darling wife killed him." I tense, shit. What other parts of Dyno can I break for this?

"You did what?" Damon says in disbelief.

"I was a mess, Damon. He took down your plane. He deserved it." I still am a mess.

"Emmie… You killed someone." I don't understand, he kills people.

I sigh, "I know." I remember in my dreams.

"What the fuck have you done?" He stands up and puts me in his chair. I glare at him but he doesn't look at me. I curl up on his chair.

"Well, I did it because your staff are useless," I mutter.

"How the hell did she get to him in the first place? Why wasn't anyone watching her?" This is the time to get my own back.

"We were watching her. She sneaked out," Dyno says. Damon paces in front of me.

"Your staff are idiots, not only did they let me leave but they didn't have anyone watching him. I mean, seriously?" I say to get Dyno in trouble.

"I expected you to keep things running while I was away. It seems my wife has been better at it than you two." He doesn't talk to me, I don't think he has ever been this mad at me.

"Our priority was her and the baby," Dyno says, trying to cover his back.

"So Rex is dead?" Damon says, testing the waters.

"Yes, but Emmie got more information out of him. He was working with Desmond," Sully says.

"What? And where is Desmond?" Damon asks.

"Well, we have him here in the safe house," Sully says, he's keeping quiet about my involvement, I smile at him to thank him.

"That was a good call on Emmie's part I have to say," Dyno says and I cringe as he says it. Damn it, Sully doesn't look happy either. I'm going to kill him for this. He's digging me deeper in my grave.

"Are you trying to get us in more trouble?" Sully snaps at Dyno.

"What happened?" Damon stops pacing but puts his hands on his desk and leans towards them like he's ready to pounce.

"It was no big deal," I say.

He sighs and finally looks at me. "You put yourself in danger, didn't you?" I shrug. "Sully, how could you let her do that?" Sully didn't want to do it but I made him.

"I didn't have a choice. Technically she was next in line to lead the gang." Oh, Sully, I respect you. If you put your foot down, I may have listened to you. Just maybe though.

"I'm so pissed right now at all of you. So what was this genius plan?"

"Well, Emmie got in contact with her Mom. And they arrange to meet. The idea was for Desmond to come to the house. But Emmie changed the plan at the last minute." Sully glances at me. I did change it, I knew he would be mad. But I did it anyway.

Damon rolls his eyes, "Of course she did."

"So we followed them to where Desmond was hiding out."

"Yeah, I had played him and he believed I was there to make amends. And then these two idiots came barging in." I pull my knees up to my chest. Protecting me.

He looks at me, "You weren't hurt were you?" Pain reaches his eyes.

"No, luckily the Big Guy can shoot straight. As for him, he wanted to leave me there with him."

"Dyno you are on thin ice. I want to see him now."

"I'll come with you," I say. I don't want him to leave me again.

"No, you won't. Dyno will take you home." No, don't make me leave you. I'm still not fixed yet. I feel like he's pushing me away.

"He will not," I argue.

"Don't push me, Emmie. I'm so fucking mad at you. Dyno take her home."

Dyno nods, "Sure boss. Emmie let's go." Damon goes to walk out of the room and I try and close the distance between us. He doesn't look at me. He's never pushed me away like this, and it hurts.

"No," I sob.

Damon takes a deep breath. "Emmie, just go." Go where? You aren't being specific again? Go as in don't come back? Damon leaves me crying helplessly. Sully hugs me tight, hushing me.

"Emmie, just go home. He will calm down soon." He releases me and kisses my forehead. No, I can't go home, not when Damon hates me. Sully races to catch up with Damon, leaving me with Dyno.

Dyno steps towards me, "Stay the hell away from me. I hate you!" I scream at him.

"Well, I don't like you either. The boss is mad at me because you are such a stubborn woman." Damon is mad at you because you mishandled his wife.

"Bite me," I say and run out the office, out the safe house. I just run and run. I can't stay here when Damon is pushing me away.

Chapter 32

I don't know if Dyno followed me but he isn't following me now. I wander the streets for a while with Damon's hood up so no one looks at me. Well, some do look but my face is covered so I feel safer. I start to feel tired again so I decide to find somewhere to sit down. I find a small pub. Yes, this will do. I find a seat at the bar. I realise I don't have any money. Darn it.

A blonde guy stands at the bar. He cocks his head to look at me and then he smiles. "Can I buy you a drink?" Why would a guy want to buy me a drink? My family say I've been looking awful recently. I feel awful.

"Er, are you talking to me?" I smile back at him.

"Yes, you are the most beautiful woman in here." I blush at his compliments. What does he want? Because he is obviously lying.

"Then sure. I'll have a vodka please."

"Coming right up." The barman comes over. "Whisky and a vodka, make them both doubles." Double? Eh, I need a good drink. The barman passes me my drink and I down it. My phone is ringing, I look at the caller ID. It's Dyno, I bet he is worrying that Damon will shoot him after this. I press ignore, I can't go back to where I'm not wanted.

"My name is Dylan," he says.

"I'm Emmie," I shrug.

"Pretty name to match a pretty person." I blush again, damn it. "Another?" He eyes my empty glass. I nod.

"So what are you doing in a place like this, on your own?" What does he mean a place like this?

"Just because I'm a woman doesn't mean I can't handle myself," I say, slightly offended. I don't need a man to protect me. Well only from myself I guess because I put myself in stupid situations.

My phone rings again. Great, now it's Damon, I ignore him too. I don't need him telling me he wants me to leave again. Dylan gives me another drink. I down this one again. My head feels fuzzy. My body doesn't need a lot of alcohol. I guess it's because I haven't eaten a lot.

"Well, I'm sure you can handle yourself." He winks at me. No, I really can't. I don't know what I was thinking. "So would you like to get out of here?"

"No, she wouldn't, not with you." I feel him wrap his arm around my waist. Damon's angry, still. I sigh, why did he come here if he is still mad? This is so exhausting, I'm always making someone mad.

"Sorry, who are you?" Dylan says defensively.

"I'm her husband," Damon snaps, well I guess I'm still that then. If he didn't want me he would say... Ex-wife? Maybe? Who knows with Damon.

"Oh er sorry man," he says awkwardly.

"Leave now," Damon growls. What is eating him? I put my hands on my head.

Damon walks in front of me and strokes my cheek. He removes my hands so he can see me. I frown. "Seriously Emmie? What are you playing at?"

I shrug, "You told me to leave. So I did."

"I said go home. How is that telling you to leave?" He's still angry.

"You are so angry at me. You said just leave. You weren't specific, as usual. I don't want to be somewhere I'm not wanted."

He takes a deep breath, "Emmie, I love you. I'm so mad at you for what you did. And then Dyno tells me you ran off." He puts his forehead on mine. "I will always want you. Please never doubt that. Let's get you home."

"No, I want another drink."

"I don't think so, Emmie. I can see you've had enough." How can he? I guess I am slurring my words a bit.

"How did you find me?"

"I tracked your phone." He shrugs.

"You are a stalker."

"Your safety is important to me. Looks like I arrived just in time anyway." What's that supposed to mean?

"What are you going on about?"

"He was going to take you, Emmie. And you are so drunk you couldn't have done anything about it." I'm not so drunk. But I am hurt enough to go with him I guess.

"You're over exaggerating."

He stares at me, angry again. I sigh. "Damon, I'm tired." I pull him closer to me and hug him. He strokes my hair.

"It's okay baby, you sleep. I'll take you home." I shake my head.

"No, if I sleep you'll disappear or you'll be dead."

He picks me up and carries me in his arms. "I won't leave you," he whispers and I close my eyes, I'm home and I'm in my favourite place.

"Is she okay?" I hear Sully say.

"She's okay, drunk though. What's been going on with her?" Damon says, stroking my face.

"Oh, Boss. She's been bad. She's refused to eat, she slept for days at a time. She's fought us at every turn. She refused to believe you were dead."

"Well, thank you for being there for her."

"She's been okay with me, but she has been hell to Dyno. They don't get along at all. But don't blame him, he really has tried with her. The scary bit is when she does eventually fall asleep. Her nightmares, her piercing screams."

"Were they that bad?" He's witnessed some of my nightmares.

"Yes, I tried to comfort her but she would cry, begging for your return. I just hope now you're back she will be okay. Shouting at her like that probably didn't help you know." Sully doesn't normally tell Damon off but he seems to when he's hurt me.

"My poor princess. I will keep a close eye on her. I know, I just couldn't believe that she killed someone. She will never live it down." Was he so angry not because I killed someone but because he is worried about my guilt? Why didn't he just say?

"I know, I told her that. Apparently, there is a long list of things she will never live down. She hides her pain from everyone and I know she is hurting badly," Sully says, I seemed to let him inside my wall when Damon was gone. This helped me.

"I know. It breaks me to see her like that. Did I hear right, that the Doc has been coming?"

"Yes, when she found out the news she was in a terrible state. She couldn't breathe. She was crying, angry, sad all at once. Not even her Brother could calm her. Some days she would be okay, others she had to be sedated," Sully says.

"I wish I could have been here to soothe her. Did she not ask for Brody?"

"No, she never asked but Danny asked him over. He couldn't calm her down either. To be honest, the one she listened to most was me. Brody made her worse actually."

"What do you mean worse?"

"I guess she didn't want to hear from him that you weren't returning. She was screaming so I ran upstairs, she was punching the wall continuously. Brody restrained her but she was freaking out, I don't know if it was him touching her or she was just out of control. But I told him to release her and she let me comfort her. The doctor had to sedate her as she wouldn't let him near her. Only me."

"She punched the wall?" he says in disbelief. I feel him grab my hand to examine it, it's still sore so I pull it away.

"Yeah, she wouldn't let the Doc or Danny near her, she was throwing things at them." Yeah, I remember I threw anything I could find.

"Maybe I was a little harsh to Dyno then?"

"No, he shouldn't antagonise her," Sully disagrees. "I'm so glad you are back, I didn't know how much longer we could carry on. I thought I was going to have to send her back to the mental hospital." What, no? I wouldn't have gone back there. "So what did your Dad want?" Yeah, what did he want?

"I can't say but I can tell you it won't be happening." I have this gnawing feeling in my stomach like it's as I confirmed, they want to get rid of me. But my husband is fighting for me.

"Sounds serious."

"Yes sounds serious but I can't agree to it." That gives me hope. I fall asleep.

"Emmie, wake up!" Damon sounds distressed so I wake up for him. He is hugging me tightly, what's going on?

"Damon?" I mumble sleepily. I'm back in our bedroom. He releases me.

"I love you, baby. You're safe. You're shaking." He loves me? I know he loves me but I feel disoriented so it's a comfort to hear. "You were screaming, you sounded broken." I guess even with Damon here, my nightmares overpower him. I still feel safe with him so why are my nightmares returning? Maybe because I fear he may disappear? "Why don't we take a shower and then get some sleep?" I probably still look awful, and I'm covered in sweat from my nightmare.

I am already beginning to relax. Just his presence is soothing. My head is clearer now after I've slept a little. "You were so mad at me Damon. You made me feel..." I shut my eyes at the memory. I feel empty when he pushes me away.

"I know sweetheart. I'm sorry, I was mad at everyone, but mostly at myself. I promise it will never happen again." Why would he be mad at himself? He did nothing wrong.

"I deserved it, it's fine."

He shakes his head while he sighs. "Emmie no-one deserves to be spoken to like that. If anyone were to speak to you like that I'd kill them. I haven't quite figured out what to do with Dyno yet. Seeing him talk to you like that. And to restrain you. I wanted to kill him there and then." This is what I'm used to being told, that it's my fault. Will I ever get used to Damon showing me such kindness?

"Dyno is harmless, besides I did break his nose." Damon laughs. "I know I've been hell, but honestly he was just being an annoying big brother."

"So I shouldn't kill him?" I giggle.

"No." He grins at me.

"Let's take a shower then." He pulls my knees towards him so my legs are hanging over the bed. He stands up and lifts me up under my knees, I have to grab his neck for support. He places kisses down my cheekbone, jaw and my neck. I can't stop giggling, my husband really does know how to cheer me up.

The next day I wake in Damon's arms, he is holding me close to him. I carefully get up out of his hold, I don't want to wake him. I dress quickly, today I do not wear Damon's clothes. I wander downstairs and Lilly is with Danny again. I frown, this should be me looking after Lilly. I'm her mother, I feel like I'm neglecting her. I feel like I'm being pushed out.

I go to find Sully, he must be in Damon's office. I don't knock, after all this is supposed to be my house. Sully is sat on the sofa looking at his phone. I go and sit next to him; he moves his arm so I can cuddle up to his chest. "Hey, you," Sully says.

"Hey, Big Guy."

"How are you feeling?"

"Better. I just wanted to say thank you for everything you did for me. It means a lot. I wouldn't have got through it without you." I wouldn't let my Brother comfort me, only you.

"Of course Emmie, I would do anything for you. Have I not proved that?" But why? That's what I don't understand.

"Yes, I just mean I'm nothing, so why would you do this?"

"It's my job, Emmie." He's brushing me off again. We've been through this before, he does more than his job requires.

"It's more than that and you know it."

"I care about you, Emmie. Seeing you so hurt, was agony. And knowing I couldn't help you hurt me." He cares about me? I care about him too which is why I didn't hurt him.

"But you did help me more than you could know."

"Well, I'm happy to hear that I helped you in some way." I'd probably have needed to be sedated every day if it wasn't for him.

"You're lucky that I like you because you might have got a broken nose too."

He laughs, making my head bob up and down. "Well thanks for not punching me. Although he did deserve it. He shouldn't speak to you like that."

"It's okay, I deserve it."

"No you don't, no one does." Why does he talk like Damon? Damon always insists it's not my fault. Is it because they are close?

I change the subject because I don't want to argue with him. "So Sully, have you got a family at home?" I've always wanted to know.

"No Emmie, I don't. I don't have time for a family with this job." I frown into his chest. Damon found time but is that because he's the Boss? Surely Damon would give him time to do this? He deserves this, any girl would be lucky to have him.

The door clicks open and Damon walks in. He frowns at me and Sully. Is he annoyed that we have grown closer? "Hey, I missed you when I woke up. I was worried about you. Couldn't you sleep?" He sits next to me and lifts his arm. I shift my weight so I can lean into his chest instead.

"No, I didn't want to wake you. But I didn't want to be alone so I thought I'd find Sully. He makes me feel safe. You both do."

"You could have woken me," he says, slightly pissed.

"You've been through enough and needed rest. Please tell me what happened to you?" He pulls me onto his lap so I can face Sully too. He looks at my face and strokes my cheek.

"Okay, so we got on the plane as you know. And the plane started to get really choppy. The pilot informed us the plane was going to go down. We buckled up, I saw the plane catch fire." I hug him tighter and he does the same. "In that moment, all I could think about was you and Lilly-May. I couldn't leave you knowing that you were still mad at me."

"Damon, I was so worried that was going to be the last thing I said to you. I was so mad at myself. I punished myself. I couldn't believe you were dead because I wouldn't have lived with myself."

Sully looks at me and not Damon, "That's all she was worried about was the way things were left. She beat herself up every day." I see the pain in Sully's eyes as he says those words. I still can't figure him out.

"When the plane landed, Larry and I survived but the pilot didn't make it. The nose of the plane took the beating of the landing. The radios were damaged. Our phones were out of range. We were stranded on an island with no way of getting home."

"So what did you do?" Sully says.

"That must have been awful," I say.

"Larry and I searched the island and found a flare gun. We made an SOS on the beach and when a plane or boat went past we would fire the gun. But we were losing hope as we were on our last flare. I was so angry, scared and I knew I had to return to you. A helicopter flew by, we released the last flare. They saw the flare and landed on the island. We were saved. And then I came home to find everyone was going to my funeral."

"I wasn't going. They tried to make me, that's what I was arguing with Dyno about."

"And he's lucky that he wasn't killed for that. I was so disgusted with the way he was talking to you."

"I deserved it, you don't know what I was like Damon." I was hell, I know that. But it was all I could do at the time.

"Emmie, you did not deserve it. The amount of times I told him not to do it," Sully says.

"Why do you always see the worst in yourself? On a lighter note, I have a surprise for you today." I smile at Damon. I love his surprises, the last one was Addi.

"A surprise for me?" I clap my hands. I don't know what I did to deserve it but I'm not complaining.

"Yes baby, for you. My sister is coming to babysit." Everyone seems to have their time will Lilly apart from me.

"Oh, I don't want to leave her."

"She will be fine," Damon says. It's not just about her safety, I just haven't spent time with her.

But I let it go, Damon seems so happy. "Okay." Damon lifts me up and places me on my feet in front of him. He stands and grabs my hand and leads me to the front door. Lexi is already hovering by the door.

"Emmie, you are looking better. You're still too skinny though." Skinny? I scoff, I'm fat.

"Er, thanks, I think."

"Still as beautiful as ever though." I roll my eyes.

"Don't make me regret asking you to babysit Lexi," Damon huffs.

"Chill bro. Lilly is safe with me." I haven't come to that conclusion yet but Damon seems to trust his sister with his daughter. "We are going to have a great time. I'm going to be her best auntie."

I roll my eyes, "Lexi, you're her only auntie," I say.

"Still, there wouldn't be any contest." Lexi giggles.

"Anyway, we better go. Bye Lexi," Damon says, dragging me out the door. He seems so happy this morning. I'm curious as to what my surprise is.

We are in the car, I don't know where we are heading. "You know? I don't know how you cope not eating. I mean we found some food on the island. But I think that was one of the toughest parts for me. Obviously, the hardest one was being apart from my family."

"I don't know what you want me to say." I've never been good with food.

"I don't want you to say anything." He shakes his head.

"Will you teach me how to drive?" I say.

He laughs, "No baby." Why not? "If you really want to drive, I'll get Sully to teach you." Why Sully? Why won't he teach me?

"Why not you?"

"I love you, it will make me anxious. I'm with your Dad on this one." Daddy didn't want me in unnecessary risk. It's a car, how hard could it be to drive? I shake my head. He pulls up into a driveway and cuts the engine. He smiles his sexy smile that melts my heart. Damon leans towards me and kisses me. I'm breathless and he's hardly touched me. "Come," he says like he is a little child at Christmas. He gets out the car and I do the same.

"So where is my surprise, Damon? What are we doing here?" I'm confused, but it doesn't take much.

He pulls me towards him and holds me. "I love you, Emmie."

"I love you too." What is this?

"I want us to be the perfect family." Where is he going with this?

"And we are." Aren't we?

"But I want you to have a fresh start." I did when I moved in with him.

"What are you saying?"

"This, Emmie, is our new house." My mouth drops open. I look at the house. It's very stylish from the outside. It has its own porch.

"What?"

"The house is in your name. It's my gift to you." He bought me a damn house. My husband is over the top as usual.

"You bought me a house? Damon, it's too much."

"It's too late now. The house is yours. I want us to be a family here. It's a nice neighbourhood that Lilly-May can grow up in. I want you to be safe here and not have to worry about my lifestyle. I can go to work and come back to you and leave the crap at work." He says the sweetest things sometimes.

"Damon, I don't know what to say. It's amazing, thank you."

"I'm glad you like it. I've had it decorated, I hope you like it." He kisses me on the lips and we walk hand in hand to the house.

We walk into the house and the door enters into the living room. The back wall is made of bricks. The rest has cream walls. A large grey corner sofa sits in front of the back wall facing a large flat screen TV that hangs on the wall. At the far end of the room are sliding doors that enter the back garden and the porch.

"It's beautiful," I say. Damon leads me into the next room. We enter a kitchen, it's bright in here. Blue walls, in front of us, are also sliding patio doors. On the left are kitchen worktops. White cabinets and black worktops. Similar to Damon's house. American style fridge freezer. There is a breakfast bar in front of the worktops. I really do like it.

He leads me out through the sliding doors and out onto the porch. There is a chair swing on the porch. I am in love with the porch. I've always wanted a porch. The garden is a decent size, I think we will be happy here together.

He takes my hand and we head back inside and we follow the hallway up the stairs. We enter a very pink room. I smile, it has a white cot by a window. A grey sofa faces the cot. I love it. "She has her own room. It's so pretty," I beam at him.

"Only the best for my daughter."

We walk into the next bedroom but he doesn't stop and let me look, he walks straight through into the bathroom. It's a modern bathroom, grey tiles. A walk-in shower. Also a bath on the right, it looks like it has jets and everything. Nice.

He walks back into the bedroom and I follow him. It's not very wide but it's long. In the middle is a huge king size bed. At the far end of the room there are wardrobes the whole width of the room. On the left side is a window that looks out into the garden. I can see myself being happy here. I can see myself seeing this as home. "This is my favourite room. I can't wait to christen the bed," Damon says and I giggle at him.

"Oh, Damon. This has been the best present ever."

"Now, there is a spare room." What's he getting at? "So if we have guests, or we need security. They have a room." No security is staying here.

"Definitely not. I will not have your staff stay in my house. With one exception, Sully." I've had Sully close to me for a while now, I'm not sure I'm going to like his absence.

"Okay baby, it's your house. What is it?" I frown. How does he know I'm stewing over something.

"It's just Sully has stayed with me when you were missing."

"Yes, I'm glad he was there for you." I can't ask this, can I? I shake my head. No, I can't. "Baby, what are you getting at? Tell me."

"I don't want to offend you."

"Baby, just tell me."

"I feel safe when Sully is living with us." I look at the floor.

"Well, he will move in with us then. For as long as you need or want him here." I smile at him.

He lifts me up and carries me to the bed. He pulls my clothes off and I remove his. I love this man. And I know he loves me.

Chapter 33

I lay on Damon's chest we both stare into each other's eyes. I could stay here forever. He strokes my naked back with his fingers. "I have another surprise for you in the back garden." Another surprise? This is already too much.

"Damon, you've done too much already."

"You're my wife, I want to spoil you. Anyway, I'm sure you will love it." I'm sure I will, he knows me so well. He gets out of bed and starts to dress. I reach forward and grab his hand and I pull him towards me. He grins and climbs on top of me.

"What are you going to do with me now?" he says playfully. I put my hands through his hair and pull him closer to me. I kiss him softly but then I bite his lip. He groans. "I want to show you your other surprise. But you are torturing me right now."

He kisses me on my lips down my neck. I writhe under his lips. I slide my hands down his strong back and pull him closer to me. We lose ourselves in each other once more.

*

We walk together down the garden along a stony track. My feet plant when I realise his surprise. He wraps his arm around my waist and encourages me forward. He walks me into a barn. 20 stalls run down the barn. I walk to one of the stalls to see a beautiful black Friesian horse. He walks towards me and puts his head over the door. I stroke his face.

"No way Damon," I whisper and Damon walks up behind me and

strokes the horse too. I have no words for this.

"Is Emmie speechless?" I nod.

"Damon, how did you know?" I never told him about this.

"Brody told me. He said you told him when you first started school." I did and then he told me in my self-induced coma.

"I can't believe he remembered."

"So this is yours, there is staff here. You are their boss. You now own a business." Someone's boss? That sounds so strange.

"How can you afford this?"

"Perks of being a gang leader. I earn a lot of money. My parents are pretty wealthy too if you didn't guess." Yeah, their house is like a palace.

"I'm so happy Damon. Thank you." The horse nudges me and I fall backwards but Damon's arm catches me.

"Easy boy," I say to the horse. He goes to nudge me again but I am ready for it this time.

"You are very welcome."

"I don't know what I did to deserve all of this but I love you."

"You are such a sweet girl Emmie, you've had a shitty life. I couldn't protect you from pain and danger, but I want to give you the world. You deserve what your heart desires and I'm going to give it to you." He wants to give me the world? But does he know he doesn't need to? What I have is what I desire.

"You are the best husband ever."

"No Emmie, you are the best wife ever." The horse licks my hand and I wipe my hand on Damon's face. He is shocked but he's amused.

He picks me up and swings me around playfully and I giggle. He frowns, sets me down and pulls his phone out of his pocket. He looks at the phone and groans.

"Mom?" Oh no. What do they want? I walk towards the horse again. I never have to compete for a horse's love. Once they trust you, they are loyal to you.

"If you mean you and father, then no I won't." He sounds really angry with his Dad. He never told us what went down in Canada.

"Fine, we are coming home." Oh no, please say they aren't there. He hangs up the phone and puts it back in his pocket.

"What's wrong?" They've ruined our little bubble.

"My parents are at the house. We need to go." What could they possibly want that's so urgent? They must be desperate to get rid of me.

"Oh okay." He puts his arm around my shoulder and kisses my hair. I kiss the horses nose and leave with him.

We don't talk on the way home, I think he is stewing over something as well. Tension is rising inside of me. We arrive at his house, he doesn't get my door. He just storms off into the house. I follow a few feet behind him. I'm like the horse loyal to Damon, he has my trust. When we enter the house, we are greeted by Sully. He looks at me like I may break.

"Er boss, your parents are here," Sully says awkwardly.

"I know," Damon snaps.

I look over Sully's shoulder to see Damon's parents standing by the stairs. But it's not them that worries me. There is a pretty black haired girl. She's slim and beautiful, the complete opposite to me but what is she doing here?

"Who the hell is that?" I demand.

"I'm not sure," Sully says. Damon storms off towards them. I can't move, I'm just stuck frozen. I can hear Damon, he's angry but I don't hear the words that come from his mouth. Eventually, Mr Rider and the pretty woman walks off towards Damon's office with Damon. Mrs Rider heads for the living room.

"Emmie, relax." Sully pulls me in for a hug. I don't return the hug. I can't move.

"Easy for you to say." A pretty girl walks into your house with your husband's parents and he says I need to relax. I can't take this anymore, I walk out of Sully's hold and go to the living room where Lexi and Mrs Rider is. I walk straight in, grab Lilly from Lexi and storm off to my bedroom. I need to protect Lilly from them. I can't protect myself but I can do this for my daughter.

I put Lilly in her Moses basket, she's sleeping peacefully. I pace up and down the room, checking on her every time I walk past. Tears are pouring from my face, something big is coming I just don't know what it is yet. This woman is going to hurt me. I can see it coming, why won't his parents except me? Is it because I'm fat, ugly? I just don't understand, all my life I've been used to not being liked or wanted. But even I can see Damon is happy with me, why can't his parents see that?

I thought they would pick some blonde bimbo but they have chosen someone that looks similar to me, but obviously, she won't be broken. She's also skinny and not fat like me. And I also know she's far prettier than me. Sully walks in my room and frowns at me, yet another person I've disappointed. He strides over to me, puts his hands behind my head and pulls my head towards his shoulder. His big arms comfort me.

"Emmie, calm down," he whispers softly in my ear. He's rocking me gently side to side. I don't know why I let Sully so close to me, is it because he doesn't expect anything from me? Should I be letting him so close because I do have a husband? But I see him as a close friend, Damon hasn't mentioned it and he said he was glad I had Sully.

"Emmie, what's wrong?" Damon says. Sully releases me and I start to pace again. What did his Dad want? I reckon he won't tell me.

"She's stressed out," Sully says, no shit Sherlock.

"Why?" Damon asks.

"The girl that was here." Nailed it in one Big Guy. Was here, or is?

"Emmie, she's just a random girl. She has nothing on you." Random girl? She's not random if she's in my house. She has everything on me, she's everything I'm not.

"Your Dad doesn't like me, does he? He's trying to replace me." Damon closes the distance between us and pulls me close so I have to stop pacing.

"Maybe, but sweetheart you know I don't want anyone else." Maybe? That's a yes and he just doesn't want to hurt me. Oh, Damon, if your parents want this so much then you'll give it to them. Why should he fight for me?

"Seriously? That's why they are here?" Sully growls. Wow, he's mad too.

"Yes, I hate him," Damon says. This hurts, how am I supposed to compete with her? She's like a damn supermodel and I'm fat, ugly and broken. I have nothing going for me. Maybe I should have said no to marrying Damon. I wouldn't be in this position. Why is life always so hard for me? I think someone up there is trying to beat me down with a brick. "Can I have a moment with my wife?" Damon says to Sully.

He seems to think this over for a while. "Sure Boss," he says grudgingly. He glances at me and gives me a reassuring smile and leaves. Maybe I should just move into this new house with Sully. It will break me to lose Damon but it's going to break me to have to compete for my own husband.

"Nothing's changed. We are moving into our new house tomorrow.

We can leave all this behind us. I love you, Emmie." Damon, everything has changed, why can't you see that? I wish things would change, I wish life was easier for me.

"I love you, Damon. But I don't like competition." A bit of healthy competition is good but not when it's your own husband.

"Baby, there is no competition. You are my wife, the mother of my child. You are my life, my soulmate. There's no question." I feel like there is, his parents hate me.

"Are you guys okay?" I sigh, Mrs Rider stands behind Damon. He looks at her but keeps his arm around my waist. I feel safer like this, like he is marking his territory.

"What are you guys still doing here? I told Dad to leave." Damon is angry but he keeps his voice low because of Lilly, I'd imagine.

"Don't be silly darling. We are all going out for a meal. Clear the air." I couldn't think of anything worse, a meal and their company.

"Are you joking? You've upset my wife. And now you want to go for dinner? You are crazy?" I don't like the thought of Damon arguing with his parents over me but in this moment, I am grateful.

"Emmie, are you okay?" She doesn't sound sincere, like she doesn't really care.

"Sure." I clutch tighter to Damon. I'm not but I won't let her win.

"Good, we are leaving in 10 minutes. Shall I take Lilly?" She goes to walk towards her but I block her path, she won't touch my daughter.

"No, she's staying with me," I snap.

Mrs Rider huffs but doesn't force the issue and she leaves the room. "Are you serious?" Damon says and then turns to face me. "Emmie, I'm so sorry."

"Don't worry about it," I shrug but I don't look at him.

"I'll leave you to get ready." He kisses me on the forehead and leaves the room. I walk to the bed and curl up. I can't handle people hating me. They must be picking every little detail of me and hating every single blemish. I grab Daddy's picture. I miss you, Daddy, I know you always loved me. I wish you were here. I wipe tears from my face.

I get up and go to the wardrobe and grab the black dress that Damon bought me for his parent's party. Mr Rider said I looked like a hooker. I shake my head, he only said it because he hates me. Damon liked this dress on me so I'll wear it. I apply makeup, I need this. I just need to not cry, but I doubt that will happen. Maybe I should invest in waterproof mascara.

I curl up on the bed again with Daddy's picture. I hear the door click open but I don't look up. I see a flash of pink in front of me. Sully lays down in front of me. What would I do without Sully? My protector, bodyguard? "Don't cry, Emmie," he says, wiping a few stray tears. Damn it, I said I shouldn't cry. I didn't even notice.

"How am I supposed to compete with her? The pretty one that his parents love?" I mumble.

"You have nothing to worry about. Damon loves you. Besides, you are the prettiest woman I have ever met. And I know for sure Damon feels the same." I don't doubt Damon's love for me like I used to. What I worry about is how far he will go to keep his parents. I can't compete with his parents. Sully thinks I'm pretty too?

"Aww, thanks Big Guy. Can you do me a favour?"

"I'd do anything for you, what is it?" That's what he always says, I just don't know why he would.

"Will you come to the meal with us? I will feel better." I can stick close to Sully if it gets too much. I mean, why am I being tortured to go to a meal with his parents and this new fancy girl who hate me?

"Yes of course. Are you ready?" I didn't even have to beg, he just accepted. Maybe he is hungry, I should offer him my food too. There is no way I can eat, maybe not eat for a week after this.

I nod and he pulls me with him off the bed. I take Lilly in my arms and follow Sully out of the room. My heart is pounding out of my chest. I suddenly feel so self-conscious worrying about how I'm walking, what I must look like. We all gather in the hallway.

"Damon darling, would you ride with us?" Mrs Rider asks. What, no? I clutch Sully's t-shirt with one hand as I'm still holding Lilly.

"Er sure. I guess," he says. I don't look at him. I won't look at him, why would he agree to this? Sully looks down at me, he's worried. Is it my face he's reacting to? I must look horrified because that's how I feel.

"Great, let's go." He's going to be inches away from her in the car. Sully grabs my hand from his shirt and holds it and leads me to the car. I curl up in the front seat after I've put Lilly in her car seat. Lexi crosses her arms as she gets in the car. Is she mad because she got kicked out of her car?

"Sully?" I say.

"Yes, Emmie?"

"Can you teach me to drive? Damon said he won't teach me but he will let you teach me."

He laughs at me, I'd laugh too if I wasn't so worked up. "What do you need to drive for? I'd drive you anywhere you need to go." I bet he would but in situations like these, I may need a quick getaway. I'd like to be able to drive my kids around someday.

"Independence and quick getaways." I lift one side of my lips at him and he frowns.

"I'm not teaching you how to drive for you to run away," he says in disbelief.

"I never said run away," I protest. "I just meant when things get tough I can clear my head." I shrug.

"Answer is no Emmie, when you need to clear your head with moments like these, you'll probably do yourself serious injury." I pout at him, who cares? I look out the window, it's still light outside, I watch buildings go by and all the people.

"Emmie, wake up," Sully says, stroking my face.

"How did she even fall asleep?" Lexi asks.

"She sleeps a lot recently. She's still not well," Sully says softly. I open my eyes sleepily. I'm still not well? I don't think I've ever been right. I'm not normal, Sully leans over me to get my seatbelt. He grabs my hand and pulls me out the car.

"Shall I get Lilly-May?" Lexi says. I shake my head and get her myself. She needs to stay with me, she comforts me. Sully takes my hand again and we walk into a hotel, damn it, why did we have to go to a posh place? Damon and his parents have already arrived and they are at the bar.

Sully leads me to the bar. The barman winks at me. "Drink beautiful?" I look around, nope, he's talking to me.

I smile back, "Vodka please."

"Coming right up."

"Emmie," Sully says disapprovingly. Yes, yes I know I'm a bad mother. We've established that already. I pout at him.

"Here you go. It's on the house." I glance at Damon and he is giving the barman a killer stare. That girl is all over him yet he notices the barman flirting with me.

"Thanks," I say to the barman. I love going places and getting free drinks.

"Who the hell is she anyway? She's so ugly," Lexi says as she stands to my left and Sully is on my right.

"She's pretty," I object.

"She's the type he used to go for before you," she says giving the girl a disgusted look.

"Great, thanks Lexi." That gives me lots of confidence.

"Obviously he knows he struck gold with you. He loves you, Emmie," Lexi says, trying to cover her back. I know he loves me, I do.

"Yeah, I know. Your parents hate me." That's the problem, why did they let Damon marry me if they were going to do this?

"My Mom loves you." Her Mom does try with me I guess. I down my drink.

"Emmie!" Damon calls. I frown but look at him. "A word please," he says and walks past me and I follow. We are out of earshot and he spins and grabs my arm. "Emmie, please. I know you have been put in an awful position but I don't need you any more vulnerable. Please, no more alcohol." I look at the floor and not him, he's remembering yesterday how I ran off and drank with a guy. "Please Emmie," he begs again. He thinks I'm vulnerable?

"Fine," I snap. He puts his hands on either side of my face and I close my eyes. He kisses me gently.

"Thank you," he says and walks off back to her. Sully walks towards me and puts his arm around my waist and pulls me back to the bar.

"We are ready to go in," Mrs Rider calls. Good for you, I'm not.

"Sully, can you take Lilly in please? I need a minute."

"Er sure," he says and takes Lilly off me. They all make their way into the restaurant area.

The barman comes back towards me. "Another?" I nod gratefully. He hands me the glass with Vodka in it. I swirl the drink in my hand before I down it again.

"Hello again." I turn to see the blonde guy from last night.

"Oh hey," I say.

"You don't remember me, do you?" he says, hurt.

"Of course I do. I was just a bit drunk." I think his name was Dylan.

He looks at my empty glass, "Starting early. You are beautiful, you know that?" Starting early? It was earlier yesterday.

"Oh erm, no I'm not, but thanks."

"Let me get you a drink," he says and walks towards me. His arm touches mine. I move away slightly.

"I should really be going. I have a dinner with the in-laws." The dreaded in-laws and the dreaded food.

"You don't seem too happy about that." This guy seems easy to talk to.

"I'm not," I shrug.

"Then let me buy you a drink. Vodka and a whisky please," he says to the barman and the barman gives me my drink.

"So, I'm surprised your husband isn't here." He's too busy getting flirted with.

"No, but I'm here." Oh shit, Sully puts his arm around my waist. Sully's angry. "Emmie, what are you doing? We are waiting for you." I bet they are, finding another excuse to have a go at me.

"And who the hell are you?" Dylan says.

"None of your business, now beat it." Sully glares at him.

"I'll see you around. It was nice to see you again." I smile and nod at him and then he leaves.

"What are you playing at Emmie?" Sully stands in front of me.

"I needed a drink. This is hard."

"I can't imagine what you're going through. But I'm here for you. You can't go drinking with a stranger. And what did he mean by seeing you again?"

"That's Dylan, I met him yesterday," I shrug.

"He's the guy that tried to take you home?" he says, shocked. I roll my eyes, I guess Damon told him about Dylan. Overreacting as usual.

"He wasn't, Damon was over reacting."

"This is bad," Sully says, he looks worried. Why?

"Why? He's nice."

"Let's go to the dinner. I'll sort it later." I grab my drink off the bar and down it. Sully rolls his eyes. I let him lead me to the restaurant area. I keep tripping, I guess I've drunk too much already, oops. I see the table we are sat at. Damon is sat next to her, the supermodel. And well, he hasn't saved a seat for me. I sit next to Lexi and Sully which is opposite to Damon. Lexi passes me Lilly.

"Nice of you to join us, Emmie. We have been waiting for you," Mr Rider says, pissed.

"You okay baby?" Damon says.

"Sorry, sir," I say to Mr Rider. I ignore Damon. The waiter brings us our food. I guess they have all ordered. The waiter brushes up against me, probably by accident and I lean into Sully. I notice Damon's hands ball into fists on the table. He is looking at me and then to the waiter. I'm super sensitive. My food is vegetarian so I guess Damon ordered for me. He didn't need to bother because I'm not going to eat it. It's pasta.

"Dig in everyone," Mrs Rider says. I look at my food and then look at everyone else tucking into their food. Lilly starts to cry in my arms. I guess she's hungry. I grab the change bag from Sully and prepare her milk. I sit feeding her. Yes, this is good. Thanks, baby girl.

Sully leans towards me, "Emmie, please eat something," quiet enough that only I can hear him.

"I'm not hungry. I'll grab something later." I feel so sick at the thought of eating.

"Emmie, you've promised me that since Damon was missing. Just please eat something. I'm begging you." Don't do this Sully, please.

"Stop fussing. Jeez," I say nudging him gently.

"Emmie, we need to go shopping soon, invite Jessie," Lexi says.

"Er, yeah sure," I say.

"Hey Emmie, do you think I could hold Lilly?" the supermodel says. Is she crazy?

"Absolutely not. Her name is Lilly-May," I snap.

"Why can't I hold her? Damon, I want to hold your daughter." Damon? I thought only family could call him Damon? That breaks my heart even more.

"The answer is no. Only people I trust can hold her." I clutch Sully's t-shirt again. Lilly's finished eating now.

"Damon," she says, whining. God, I thought Jade was bad.

"My wife said no. She's very protective of our daughter," Damon snaps. I smile that he is on my side.

"Izzy can be trusted, don't be so mean Emmie," Mr Rider snaps. Oh, her name is Izzy? Nice to have been introduced. Mean? Okay, I'm being mean. Great.

"Dad!" Damon scolds.

I shake my head. "I can't do this anymore," I say. "Take care of Lilly-May. Don't let her touch her," I say to Sully. I stand and slide her into his arms.

I trip over my chair and walk away from the table. "Emmie!" Sully calls.

"Emmie!" Damon calls. I ignore them both and head for the bar. I need another drink. Well, I don't, but I'm going to have one.

"You okay beautiful?" Dylan says when I reach the bar.

"No," I say.

"You want a drink?"

"Sure, thanks," I say sweetly at him.

"Vodka and a whisky please," he says to the barman.

"Here, get that down you." He hands me the glass which I down straight away.

"Thanks."

"You wanna hit a club?" A club? I haven't been to a club before. Maybe it will be fun to try.

"Sure." I smile at him. He goes to grab my hand but I pull it away. He ignores my rejection and walks out of the hotel and I follow him. The fresh air feels good on my skin. It's dark now. He calls a cab and we both get in.

Chapter 34

Once we reach the club I feel drunk. I have no control. It's loud in the club and I seem to be swaying and the people are spinning. Dylan holds me for support, I don't like it but I can't do anything to stop him. "Here, get this down you." He hands me a glass, I'm guessing it's vodka, I really don't need any more but I take it anyway. I feel awful.

I wake up scared and panicked. I don't recognise this place at all. I get out of bed and I'm in my underwear. I'm so confused right now. I walk out of the bedroom to find a good-looking guy with long blonde hair, it's so long he has it in a ponytail. He's a big muscly guy. He wears jeans and a blue shirt that has all the buttons undone so I can see his abs. Wow. He glances at me and smiles, that smile is to die for. My head is all fuzzy. I don't feel so good. "Morning beautiful," he says.

"I er, what's going on?"

"Do you remember your accident?" My accident? I'm so confused. I don't remember anything.

"My what?"

"You had an accident a few weeks ago. You suffer from memory loss. I'm Liam, your boyfriend. You are Emmie. We are happy together. We have the same conversation every day." This is too much to process. Why can't I remember anything?

"I did? I don't remember anything."

"I know, it's hard that you don't remember me." Pain reaches his eyes.

"I'm sorry," I say. I really am, I don't remember him. I don't remember myself. I don't remember anything.

"It's okay sweetheart. I love you anyway." He loves me?

"I don't remember anything."

"We have been together since high school. We were high school sweethearts. We haven't been with anyone else. It's just been me and you." I like the sound of that, I just can't remember.

"I like the sound of that."

"I know it's going to take time for you to trust me. I hope one day you will get your memory back. We have had such a great life." I hope I do too. I don't like not knowing who I am. It makes me anxious.

"Well, why don't you tell me some things? See if I remember?" I feel at ease with this guy. So I guess we have been together for a while.

"I met you in high school. You were the most beautiful thing I'd ever seen. You were the cool girl of the school. I tried so hard to get your attention. Your parents died when we were at school." My parents are dead?

"They did?" I don't even know what they looked like. Why am I having a mental block?

"Your parents loved you so much. You were distraught when they died. We were together for a year when it happened. So you came to live with me. We are inseparable, our love for each other is pure. You have no siblings. My parents love you." Well, at least I have no siblings because I wouldn't remember what they looked like either. I'm so confused but it sounds like a perfect life. "You are my princess and you get your own way every time. I can't resist you. I love you." I go all gooey at his words. He is so cute.

"It sounds like I was very happy with you."

He smiles, "You are." He uses the word are instead of was. I don't remember anything so how is this the case? I feel so guilty that I can't remember, he seems to be in a lot of pain. I don't want him to be in pain so I close the distance between us and kiss him softly. It feels like it's the first time I've kissed this guy. But it feels...right, he returns the kiss with lots of love and affection.

He pulls me closer, wrapping his strong arms around me. He makes me feel loved. I feel safe in this guy's arms. His hands move down my body, caressing my body. This feels so good. He pulls away but he keeps his head close to mine, " Wow, that never gets old." I can't help but smile like a Cheshire cat.

"I really hope I can remember for you soon."

"Me too baby. Shall we go get dinner downstairs?" Yes, I feel like I haven't eaten in days.

"Yes, I'm hungry." I smile sweetly at him.

"Why don't you get dressed? Your clothes are in the closet." I take a look around, it seems like a hotel room. I walk back into the bedroom and walk to the closet. It has my clothes and his. I grab a dress. I look at myself in the mirror, I'm covered in faint scars. What the hell has happened to me? I slide the black dress over my head. I look at my hands, I have a ring on my left hand but it's not on my ring finger, it's on my middle finger. But it strangely looks like a wedding ring. I shrug and ignore it.

I grab some shoes and put them on. Liam joins me in the bedroom. "You ready princess?" I blush and nod at him. He takes my hand and leads me out the room. I feel this strange sense that I want to retract my hand. It doesn't feel how I expected it to but I let him hold my hand because I don't have a good reason to withdraw.

We walk to the elevator and we get in. The elevator is filled with mirrors, I don't want to look at myself in the mirror. Something is telling me not to, like a habit? I stare at Liam's face, he's happy and carefree. He hasn't done up his shirt, I can't decide what I think about that? Should I feel jealous that other people are looking at his abs? I just don't know. The elevator pings open and we walk off into the lobby area of the hotel. "I will go get us a table, wait here beautiful."

"Okay, hurry back." I feel anxiety coming knowing that he is leaving me for a minute. I don't know anything, I feel vulnerable, I only know him.

"Trust me, you are worth coming back to." Damn it, I blush again, he winks at me and walks off. I look around the hotel to try to find any familiarity. But I find nothing. Wait no, I see a pretty black haired girl. She looks familiar, but why? I hate not remembering anything, it's so frustrating. She's like a supermodel. I shake my head while she walks away.

"You okay baby?" Liam's back with me now and I relax.

"Yeah, I'm fine now you are back." He seems a bit confused but he strokes my cheek. I feel that strange feeling again that I should push him away.

"Good, are you ready to eat?"

"Yes, I'm ravenous." I feel like I'm starving for some reason.

"Good." He takes my hand again and leads me into the restaurant area.

He pulls a chair out for me and I accept gratefully. He hands me a menu. I look around the restaurant area. People don't seem to be staring. I feel like I'm used to people watching me.

"You look beautiful," Liam says, breaking my train of thought.

"Thank you." What else can you say when someone compliments you?

"Can I take your order?" the waitress asks.

"What would you like, baby?" Liam asks me.

"Can I get a glass of red wine please?"

"Make that a bottle," Liam says. A bottle?

"I'll have a cheese pizza please," I say.

"You didn't want a steak? That's what I'm having."

"I'm a vegetarian."

His mouth drops open in surprise and then he quickly shuts it again. "Of course you are, baby, you remembered something from your past. Well done." It seems like he didn't know that. But the question is how did I know that?

I clap my hands, "I'm so happy I remembered something, Liam." Even if it's something small, I remembered.

"Me too," he laughs.

"I'll go get your order," the waitress says. "If you'd like something else, just ask. Maybe my number?" My mouth drops open, can she not see we are together? I frown.

"Seriously? You are asking me that in front of my girlfriend? I love her, I'm not interested." Wow, he stuck up for me. I smile and grin at the waitress as if to say ha, he's mine. The waitress nods and makes a swift exit. He makes me feel like I'm the only woman in the room. "I won't have you feel uncomfortable." I have a gentleman as my boyfriend.

Our drinks arrive and I take a huge sip of wine. I know I'm missing my memory but I feel like I'm missing something. I can't put my finger on it but I know something is missing. "So do I work?" I say.

"No baby, I'm rich, you don't need to work." I don't work? I feel like a trophy wife.

"So what do I do all day?"

"You go shopping, you read books," he shrugs. I sound boring. Our food arrives, I'm so hungry that I dig in straight away. Pizza is good, I love pizza. I feel full quicker than I'd hoped for. I try my best to finish my plate but it's like my stomach is small and it can't fit much food in. Liam finishes his food in no time. The wine is good and Liam tops my glass up.

"So what do you do? For a job, I mean."

He raises his eyebrow at me. "Princess, I run a gang." A gang? Is my boyfriend dangerous? He doesn't seem dangerous. We've been together since high school, if I wasn't happy I wouldn't have stayed. "Does that scare you?"

I shake my head, "No." But it should, shouldn't it? I have a strange feeling like I've been through worse but from what Liam's said, nothing bad has happened to me. Except my parents dying. Maybe him being in a gang has made me feel safe and protected. I don't know.

He grabs my hand that's on the table and slowly strokes my hand with his thumb. I smile at his affections but I have that same feeling again. "Good," he smiles too. "Have you finished?"

I nod, "Yes, thank you." I feel like I should contribute some money but I don't have any belongings. "Liam, do I own a phone?"

He frowns, "Yes of course. Sometimes you forget it. What with forgetting your life too." He is being so understanding and patient with me.

My head is feeling a bit clearer now but I still can't remember anything. Liam raises his hand to the waitress and she comes bounding over. "Check please," he says. He said please, he really is a gentleman. Why is he in a gang when he is so nice? Liam settles the bill, I feel uncomfortable letting him pay for my food. He's my boyfriend and he loves me but I don't remember him.

He stands up and offers his hand to me. I take it and we head back up to his room. "Liam, do we live here?"

"Yes princess." Why do we live in a hotel?

We walk into our hotel room. "Do you want to watch a film?" I nod. "Some romance film?" He rolls his eyes.

"How about horror?" I love a scary movie.

"Horror huh? I'm up for that," he smirks at me. I walk to the sofa and sit down. Liam joins me flicking through films on the telly. He picks *Insidious* to watch. I wouldn't know if I've watched it before because I still can't bloody remember anything! This is starting to stress me out. Liam puts his arm around me and I cuddle up to his chest. Nothing feels familiar with him. But he's hot and he's caring and he loves me. I'm tired so I end up falling asleep on Liam's lap.

When I wake the next morning I'm in my underwear again. Maybe my boyfriend likes to look at me like this? I shrug, oh well. My head is feeling fuzzy again. I get up to go find Liam. I walk into the main room and Liam stands with a blonde guy. He looks familiar but I can't put my finger on it. I walk over to Liam and clutch his side, he lifts his arm. I feel protected like this, his friend freaks me out for some reason. "Good Morning, Beautiful," Liam says, looking down at me.

"Sorry, I didn't realise you had company." I try to cover my body behind Liam.

"Don't apologise. Close your eyes, Dylan." Hmm, Dylan, that sounds like a familiar name. But again, my head is fuzzy and I can't piece things together.

"I like what I see." I feel awkward with him staring at me. I don't mind when Liam does it I guess but he hasn't exactly been obvious like this.

"Close your damn eyes. Now!" Liam is angry.

"Okay, okay," Dylan says and covers his eyes. I relax a little knowing he isn't staring.

"As much as I'd like for my girlfriend to walk around in her underwear, you'd better get dressed. I don't want anyone else seeing you like that." I see Dylan's mouth drop open but he shuts it again quickly. I smile sweetly at Liam and head for the bedroom to change.

I settle for shorts and a top today. Something comfy. I find a hairbrush and brush my hair through. I feel tired and I've only just woken up. What's wrong with me? I go in search to find Liam. He is sat on the sofa on his own, I guess Dylan left. I walk towards Liam, he grabs my hand and pulls me so I sit on his lap.

"How are you feeling today?" My head feels fuzzy again.

"Confused."

He sighs, "Yes baby, you had an accident. You suffer from memory loss. We have this conversation every day." He seems like he has said it a thousand times. I frown.

"I know, I remember yesterday. My head is just fuzzy."

"Princess that's progress, you haven't remembered a day before."

I feel happier about that. "Really? Does that mean I'm getting better?" He sounds happy that I've remembered yesterday.

"I hope so, beautiful. Shall we go out for breakfast?" Yes, although I ate my pizza yesterday I feel hungry again.

"You don't need to go to so much effort for me." I almost feel like I'm putting nothing into this relationship.

"I want to and it's no trouble at all." Does he not have work to do?

"Well thank you, Liam." I don't want him to leave anyway. I feel like he is all I know. He stands which means I have to do the same. He still wears another open shirt. I really am starting to get jealous now but I'm not going to say anything.

We walk out of the hotel out into the sun. I soak it in for a second. I love the sun. He walks with his arm around my shoulder, he has a huge smile on his face and I can't help but join him. We stop outside a cafe. "This is perfect," he says and walks us in. We take a seat by the window. "What would you like?" he says like I should know what's on the menu. I don't even know what I'm supposed to like to eat.

"I'm not sure," I say awkwardly.

He smiles at me which reassures me. "How does pancakes sound?" Really good actually.

"Amazing, thank you."

"What drink would you like?"

"Latte please." He nods and kisses my lips softly.

"Wait here and I will go get it. Don't go anywhere."

"I won't." Where am I going to go? I don't know anyone, only Liam. He walks off to order.

"Hey Emmie, it's been awhile. How are you?" I frown at a girl about my age, she has short black curly hair. She dresses well too. She looks familiar but I don't know who she is and she is scaring me.

"I'm sorry, I don't know you," I say, my voice shaky.

"You don't remember me? That hurts. We went to school together." I don't remember anything about school. I feel awful that she thinks she knows me and I can't remember.

"I'm sorry, I don't remember." I shake my head. My head isn't clear.

"Seriously, you were nice to me. You said there was nothing wrong with being gay. You gave me the confidence to come out." I like to think that would be me, I mean, there isn't anything wrong with being gay. If I helped this girl in anyway then I guess I'm glad.

"I'm sorry, I still don't remember you." She looks hurt.

"Come on Emmie. I'm Milly." A name won't help me, if I don't remember her face I won't remember a name. I feel anxious now.

"You are upsetting my girlfriend, please leave. She said she doesn't remember you." Liam puts our drinks on the table and sits down, grabbing my hands, comforting me.

"Boyfriend? I heard she was married." She heard I was married? That can't be right, I've only been with Liam and I'm sure he would have said if we were married.

"Emmie and I have been together since school. We haven't been married. You must be mistaken. Now leave, you are upsetting her." I shake my head, this girl must be mistaken because I went to school with Liam and he would know this girl too if that were the case. But it worries me that she knows my name.

"Sorry." Milly ducks her head and walks out of the cafe. I relax a little knowing the crazy woman has gone.

"You okay baby?" I nod. Liam is the only person I know. That's the only thing I'm certain about right now.

"I'm confused, she looked familiar, yet I didn't know who she was."

"That's okay, it's all part of the memory loss. Here, eat your breakfast." Someone brings over our food as he says those words. Will I ever get my memory back?

"Thank you, it looks lovely." It really does and it smells delicious.

"You are welcome, princess." And I do feel like a princess around Liam. He seems so nice. This seems too good to be true. I still have trouble trying to finish my breakfast. It was tasty though. I finish my coffee. We take a walk along a row of hut shops. I wrap my arm around Liam's waist and he puts his arm around my shoulder. This feels natural.

We get back to the hotel and I decide I need a shower. I don't remember the last time I had one. That sounds bad. I strip and head into the shower, it takes me a while to figure out how to use it. It feels like the first time I've used it. But then Liam says it's all to do with the memory loss.

"Can I join you?" Liam asks.

"Sure." I should feel comfortable with him, he's my boyfriend. He climbs in behind me and wraps his arms around me. I turn to face him and he kisses me. His hands caressing my body. "Liam, can I ask you something?" I say whilst he is kissing my neck.

"Of course," he says between each kiss.

"I've got so many scars. How did I get them?" He pulls away to examine my body. He strokes each one and kisses them. I'm worried about the one on my hip. It has a D engraved there. Why a D? We haven't slept together yet but I can't deny this connection any longer. I start to kiss him, his eyes are in pain. I need to fix his pain. He lifts me up and I wrap my legs around him. My back is pushed up against the wall. He is muscly and strong. I put my arms around his back. Feeling his muscles. I lose myself with him and this moment. He never told me where my scars came from and I don't care in this moment.

*

Two weeks have passed since I remembered something. I feel happy, loved. It's a great feeling. I can't remember my past but I feel like I'm building a future. Liam seems to love me and doesn't mind that I can't remember. He's taken me on romantic walks along the beach. Romantic meals. I think I love him. He's so beautiful. I can't help but feel like I've lost something though. Makes me feel sad when I think about it, but Liam comes along and makes me smile again.

When I wake, I'm alone in bed again. It seems to happen quite often. I dress into something casual and go to find Liam again. He is my constant, I feel safe when I'm with him, maybe because he is the only thing I remember. I'm worried that my memory hasn't come back after all this time. I don't see any doctors about my memory loss, I find that a bit odd. I would have thought I'd need monitoring or something.

I find Liam in the main room again. "I love you, baby," he says when he sees me enter the room. I smile at him.

"I love you too Liam."

"You do?" I haven't told him this yet. Well not since I started remembering things. He seems shocked but pleased at the same time.

"Although I can't remember the past I know the now. I love you."

"That's great." He seems relieved in some way. But he should be upset that I don't remember the past surely?

"Boss?" Dylan says from behind me. I tense and move next to Liam's side and hold his shirt tight. What is it about him? Is it him or just men in general?

"What did I tell you about knocking?" Liam growls.

"Sorry Boss." He doesn't look that sorry. "Emmie." He nods at me and smiles.

"H-hey," I say.

"It's okay, you are safe." Liam wraps his arm around me, reassuring me. Does he know about my insecurities?

"I got the file you wanted." File, what file?

"Oh good," Liam says and takes the file off Dylan.

"It would be nice to get to know your girlfriend better, Liam." I clutch to Liam tighter, I like it being just Liam and I. I feel safe and normal.

"Back off Dylan," Liam snaps.

"Chill Boss." He chuckles and holds his hands out in front of him.

"Leave before I kick your Ass," Liam says. I don't think he would, he doesn't seem like a violent person.

"I'm going," Dylan says. He seems to respect his Boss though and he leaves. I feel like my body sags with relief.

"You are safe beautiful." I know I'm safe when I'm just with him.

"I'm sorry, just men make me uncomfortable. I'm going to watch some TV."

"Okay princess." He picks up the file and he sits at the breakfast bar and reads it. I search for something to watch on the TV. I settle for *Pretty Little Liars*. I'm on the last season. I don't remember watching it in the last 2 weeks. I just know I have watched it. Little things I remember or think I do. They don't seem to match Liam's story. So I don't tell Liam about these memories. I don't want to hurt him, he's been great.

"Baby, let's go out." Out where? I frown. I'm watching *Pretty Little Liars*. "Why don't we go to the beach?" The beach with my hot boyfriend? I bite my lip, hell yes! I nod and head to the bedroom to dress into a swimsuit. Damn it, why don't I own a swimsuit? All I have is a bikini. Shit, I guess this will have to do. I put it on and place shorts and a top over the top. I put flip flops on and find a towel in the bathroom.

I'm ready and waiting when Liam emerges from the bedroom. He wears his swim trunks that hang off his hips that makes me bite my lip. He wears no top, just his swim trunks. I can't look away. He kisses my lips and we walk out of the hotel room. It's not far to the beach from where we are.

I shake my towel out and lay it on the sand. Liam looks at me and whispers in my ear, "You must be hot in that. You definitely look hot to me." He chuckles and removes the top layers of my clothes. I'm self-conscious that people are looking but I don't care when I'm with him. We stand in our swimwear, he grins a playful grin and picks me up so I'm over his shoulder. I squeal and he slaps my ass and runs into the water. The water feels cold on my skin so I stay close to Liam until I get used to the water.

I'm not a sea person really. I'd much rather a pool. He grabs my hips and kisses me. He grins at me and lifts me up and throws me backwards. I fall into the water. When I reach the surface again, he is laughing at me. What was that for? I move my hair from my face and I splash him back. He chuckles and starts to swim away from me. I've always been a strong swimmer so I can keep up with him. But he's obviously fitter than I am so I tire quickly.

I stop and tread water for a while until he returns to me. "Is my princess tired?" I nod. I sleep well but I need a lot of sleep. He grabs my hand and swings me onto his back. I hold on to his neck tightly. He swims us back to the shore but he doesn't put me down. I wrap my legs around him and hug him tight. We lay together on the towels, soaking each other in. I could get used to this life.

"Liam? Why haven't you been working?" He never leaves me which I'm grateful for but is his gang not falling apart?

He sighs, "Since your accident, I don't want to leave you. You've made me realise how precious you are to me." What a lovely thing to say. "Shall we head back?" I nod. I prefer to be at the hotel just him and me.

When I wake up the next morning I hear shouting. Sounds like Liam is angry. I don't bother to change I just want to see Liam. He is alone when I enter, he looks really angry. "Is everything okay? I heard shouting." He doesn't say anything, he just hugs me tightly. It's almost like he can't bear to lose me. I try to comfort him the best I can.

"Yes, baby. Don't worry. Go put on something nice, we are going out okay?" Where are we going that requires something nice? He doesn't normally suggest what I wear. I don't like to see him hurting so I kiss him. He pulls me away and looks at me, I frown, he seems to be thinking something over and then he kisses me back. I wrap my legs around him and he holds my legs to support me.

He carries me into the bedroom, I can fix him this way. Making love to him will fix him, I'm sure. He seems to be putting extra passion in this than normal, like this will be the last time. I hope it won't be, it can't be, we've been together since school. He loves me.

We lay in bed catching our breaths. "Well, that was amazing as usual. You distract me you know. You need to get dressed." He seems better but he still looks sad.

"I'm sorry but you were looking too good to resist," I giggle.

"Oh, princess. I'll see you outside. Get dressed." He kisses my forehead and leaves the room with his clothes. What is this? I dress in a blue dress. He said to put something nice on so this will do I guess. He never told me the occasion, maybe it's some anniversary that I've forgotten about because of my damn memory loss. I hope not, I will feel guilty if that's the case.

I'm all ready so I make my way to find Liam. He seems to have watery eyes. Is he crying? I walk over to him and hug his waist. He kisses my hair. "I love you, Princess."

"And I love you, Liam." I don't like this. What does he want, reassurance? He takes a deep breath.

"You look lovely as usual. Let's go." We walk out of the hotel and into his sports car. I feel anxious that something is going to happen. I'm scared. Liam grabs my hand. He loves me so why is he sad? We've been so happy these past 2 weeks. Has he got fed up with me because I can't remember? I do hope not, I'm happy.

Chapter 35

We reach a playground, there is no one here which I find strange. Where are all the kids playing here? Liam gets out of the car so I follow. What's going on? I don't like this at all. I run to catch up with Liam and I hug his waist. He puts his arm over my shoulder, I feel better that he is returning the hug but he carries on walking until we meet two youngish guys. They both look familiar, one with bright pink hair, the other with sandy coloured hair. I clutch tighter to Liam and he strokes my hair. "Emmie, thank God you are safe." The sandy haired guy seems relieved.

"Emmie are you okay?" the pink haired guy says.

I stand behind Liam, clutching to him. "Liam, what's going on? I'm scared."

"What did you do to her? Emmie, it's me." The sandy haired guy sounds angry. I don't know you.

Liam turns around to face me, clutching my face. "You are safe, baby. Don't be scared. You know these people." I shake my head in his hands.

"No, I don't. Who are they?" I take a long look at them both, they look familiar but I don't remember anything, only Liam.

"Baby it's me, Damon, your husband," the sandy haired guy says. Husband? I'm not married. I'm so confused, I don't know what to think.

"I don't have a husband. I don't know you. I've only been with Liam since high school."

"What the hell have you done to her?" Damon growls. Liam ignores him and continues to try and comfort me.

"Princess, I lied to you. I drugged you and kidnapped you. You were married to this guy." He takes my hand, takes off the ring that I noticed and places it back on my ring finger. "You have a daughter with him."

I'm such a bad mother, how can I forget my daughter? "Lilly-May. How could I forget my daughter?" Was this what I thought was missing?

"Yes, Emmie our daughter," Damon praises.

"It's okay baby. I'm so sorry. But I do love you, I didn't lie to you about that." And I love you, Liam. I hug him around the waist and he returns the hug.

"Baby it's time to go home now," Damon says. I shake my head. I'm not leaving Liam, I don't know them. Why is he calling me baby?

"Liam, don't make me go. I don't remember them." I look him in the eyes.

"You will remember soon enough." Tears fall from my face. He's going to leave me.

"No please, I don't want to remember." I've loved my life with him.

"Your life isn't with me. It's with him."

"No. If you love me, you won't make me."

"It's because I love you that I'm letting you go," he says.

"If you won't come home to me, come home for our daughter," Damon says.

"Liam, I'm scared. I don't know these people." He strokes my hair.

"Please take her home," Liam says to Damon. I shake my head. No. Liam kisses me on the forehead and leaves me. I drop to my knees.

"Liam, don't leave me. Liam! Please!" I beg, sobbing on my knees. Damon grabs my arm and lifts me up. A strange current runs through my body. His scent feels familiar. They both pull me towards their car.

What am I supposed to believe now? Liam told me I have memory loss and now he's said he's drugged me. Damon sits in the back with me. His presence makes my body relax for some reason. The pink haired guy drives the car. We reach a house and the pink haired guy gets my door. I climb out the car. I don't remember this place at all. Liam just left me with two strangers, how could he do that? I follow them both into the house.

"Emmie, I'm so glad you are back," a brown-haired guy says. He hugs me and I freeze. He looks familiar but again I don't know who he is.

"Please don't hurt me," I say terrified.

"Why would I hurt you?" he says shocked.

"Danny, she doesn't remember anything. She has been drugged," Damon says.

"I'm your brother Emmie. You are safe." I don't have any siblings.

"No, I'm an only child. My parents died when I was at school. It's just been me and Liam." Danny looks shocked and angry.

"He's brainwashed you." No, he loves me.

"Please take me to Liam. I'm scared."

"You can't, you belong here. Let me take you to our daughter," Damon says. Yes, maybe Lilly will help me. I follow Damon into a living room.

"Emmie, you are safe, I'm so glad you are back. I've been worried," a pretty redhead says.

"Who are you?" All these people that know my name freak me out.

"Lexi, please give Lilly-May to Emmie." This Lexi is holding my daughter.

"What's going on?"

Lexi passes Lilly to me. She's changed so much. I've missed watching her grow. "She's got so big. I've missed you baby girl."

"She doesn't remember anything," Damon says to Lexi.

"Dadda," Lilly says and holds her hands out to Damon. She speaks? I've missed her first word.

"Yes princess," Damon chuckles. Lilly starts to cry for her Dad. She doesn't want me. I remember it was me and her against the world and now she's forgotten me. I pass her to Damon.

"Take her," I demand. Which he does and Lilly stops crying instantly.

"Emmie, don't worry about it. She will want you in time. She cried for you for ages." But she doesn't want me now. Nothing is keeping me here. I don't know anyone.

"I can't do this." I run for the front door. Tears fall from my face.

"Emmie are you okay?" the pink haired guy asks.

"No. Let me go, please. I don't know you people. I'm so scared."

"Please Emmie. Give us a chance to remind you who we are."

"Baby, please. Just give us a chance." Damon walks up behind me. "Here is your phone. It may help you remember. I also wanted to play something to you." I take the phone from Damon. I look through pictures. There are pictures of Damon and I. We look happy. Also pictures of Danny and I. The pink haired guy and me. Pictures of Damon, me and Lilly. I shake my head, I don't remember this. "It's when I was missing in a plane crash. You left me voicemails on my phone." He was missing?

He plays the voicemail, I sound so sad and upset. I beg him to return, that I couldn't live without him. My voice is shaky, angry, sad. How am I feeling all those emotions at once? But nothing's changed, I feel nothing. I don't remember.

"I'm sorry, I know that's my voice but I don't remember."

"I'd like to take you to the Doctor to see if there is any lasting damage. Will you do that?" I nod, maybe a Doctor will help me get back to Liam.

"I guess."

"Great, let's go," Damon says. Sully and Damon lead me back to the car. Damon sits in the back with me again. I have a feeling Damon is struggling to refrain himself to touch me to comfort me. But this wouldn't help me now. We reach the hospital and the pink haired guy gets my door again. They both walk in front, constantly looking back at me. We reach a reception desk. "Page Doctor Grey," Damon growls.

"Yes, sir," the girl says. We all take a seat. I tap my foot on the floor, waiting. I can't help but shake the feeling that I've been here before.

"Well, there is my favourite patient. What can I do for you this time Emmie?" a blonde doctor asks. I stand out of my chair. "What's wrong? Where has feisty Emmie gone?" Feisty Emmie? What is he talking about? "Come to room 1."

We all walk to room 1. "She was taken, she's been drugged. Brainwashed, she doesn't remember anything," Damon says.

"Do we know what drugs were used?" the Doctor asks.

"No," Damon says.

"Emmie, it's me, your Doctor. Do you remember me?" Does it look like I remember you?

"No. As my doctor, you should take my interests at heart. Maybe even call the cops?"

He looks shocked, "Why would I do that?"

"I don't know these people. Please, I need to see Liam."

"Emmie, you do know these people. Rider is your husband. I was there at your wedding. Who is Liam?" Stop saying that, I don't remember! Who is Rider? I thought I married Damon.

"Liam is my boyfriend. I've been with him since high school. I've never been married."

"Liam kidnapped her right? And drugged her? This is a very weird side effect. I mean it can happen but it's rare. I want to run some tests."

"Please don't touch me," I scream.

"You are safe here, I promise." No, I'm not. I'm only safe with Liam.

"Will she ever get her memory back?" Damon asks.

"You'd better hope she doesn't," the pink haired guy snaps.

"What's going on with you two?" the Doctor says.

"Did he not tell you? He married someone else while Emmie was missing." He married someone else? I don't remember our wedding or our marriage but doesn't mean it doesn't hurt that he replaced me. Was I not good enough for him?

"You did what?" the Doctor is angry.

"What can I say? It was love at first sight," Damon says half-heartedly. Love at first sight huh? Does that even exist?

"I'm sorry as you aren't family anymore you need to get out. She will probably be more comfortable anyway," the Doctor says. Why is he annoyed with Damon? He's a Doctor, why would he be so involved?

"Are you serious? You can't do that." Damon is shocked and angry.

"I allowed you in here before as she needed you. But you are making things worse. I'm sorry," the Doctor says.

"Fine," Damon snaps and he walks out the room with the pink haired guy.

"Please call Liam," I beg the Doctor.

"He kidnapped you and drugged you, Emmie. He isn't a good person." He is a good person, he was always kind to me.

"I had an accident 3 weeks ago which causes memory loss. This is all this is," I say defensively.

"Wow, he is clever. No wonder you believe this lie." What lie? I don't understand.

"What lie? This is real," I snap.

"It may feel real but it's not. Do you feel groggy? Head fuzzy?" I've always had a fuzzy head.

"Yes." I guess, but that doesn't mean anything.

"That's the drugs messing with your head." No, I shake my head. I can't believe this. "If what your saying is true then let me do the tests."

"Fine, whatever."

The Doctor chuckles, "Ha, that's the Emmie I remember." What he remembers and what I remember are two different things.

"So you keep saying, but I don't know you. Please call Liam. You should follow the patient's wishes. Please. I'm so scared. I don't remember anything."

"Emmie, this Liam drugged you, that's why you can't remember anything. I'm running tests for you. You shouldn't be scared. You know me very well after all the times you were admitted. And Rider loves you." Who is Rider? Why have I been admitted into hospital a lot? Maybe that's why I have so many scars.

"People keep saying that he married someone else, how is that love? I can't be that great if he left me."

"I think you are perfect." I turn to see Liam standing in the doorway.

"Liam?" He nods and I run into his arms. I feel safe now he is here. "Liam, I was so scared." He came back for me.

"You are safe now princess," he says softly in my ear. He carries me to the bed and he places me on it so I'm sitting on the edge.

"So you are the Liam that drugged her? You can't be here," the Doctor says.

"Please don't leave me." I grab Liam's hand. He strokes a strand of hair away from my face. "Please don't make him leave," I beg the Doctor.

"Rider wouldn't be happy to know he is here and I should call the police." Is this Rider supposed to be Damon?

"Don't do that, please. I feel safe now he is here. If you care about me the way you seem to, you'll let him stay."

"Fine," the Doctor sighs.

"I'm sorry I left you, and I'm sorry that I drugged you." I don't care about that right now. I'm just happy he is here.

"I don't care about that. I'm just glad you are here."

The doctor takes some blood. "Ow," I protest.

"Sorry, just taking blood." I know, I can see that.

"I shouldn't be here Emmie. What I did to you was wrong. But the moment I saw you, I knew I needed you. And when I found out what

393

happened to you, I couldn't tell you. You were so happy with me. I didn't want you to remember the pain you went through."

"Is that what that file was?"

"Yes Princess, I saw the way you went about life. You are terrified of men. You are always looking over your shoulders like someone's watching you. I needed to know."

"I love you," I say.

"I love you too, you say that now but when you remember you won't." I will love him.

"I will Liam. I love you."

"Right, I'm done. I'd like you to stay here until I get the results. Do you think you can do that?" It sounds like he's talking to a disobedient child.

"Sounds like you don't trust me, Doctor."

"You'd be right, you are such a stubborn thing." I can't see myself being stubborn. The Doctor walks out the room, leaving me alone with Liam. I grab his hand and pull him towards me so I can kiss him.

He grins and kisses me back. I reach for his abs that are showing as usual. We hear shouting in the hallway and Liam pulls away and stands in front of me. The door swings open and slams into the wall.

"What the fuck are you doing here?" Damon shouts. He is really mad. I clutch Liam's arm.

"It's okay sweetheart, no one will hurt you," Liam says, reassuring me.

Damon's face falls. "Emmie I'm sorry, I would never hurt you." That must be a lie if he married someone else when I was supposedly kidnapped.

"I don't remember you, so how would I know that?"

"I want you out," Damon points to Liam and I pull his arm closer to me.

"I'll make you a deal. A compromise so to speak," Liam says calmly.

"And why would I do that?" Damon snaps. Why would I marry this guy? He seems like such an ass.

"I will stay until Emmie gets her memory back. And then I will leave. I don't want her scared and alone." I don't want him to leave even if I do remember.

"I don't want you near my wife," Damon growls.

"She's not your wife anymore. Is she?" Liam says.

"Fine. Emmie, please don't be scared of me. You love me." In this moment, I don't love him.

"I'm sorry. I love Liam," I say and it looks like I've hurt him again.

"He drugged you, Emmie. Kept you from our daughter."

"Yes, it hurts that I missed her grow but it is what it is. She doesn't want me anymore."

"You're her Mom, she just needs to get used to you again." I shake my head. No, she doesn't want me anymore.

"He's right Emmie, you'll get your bond back with your daughter." He looks at me, trying to reassure me.

"How did you get her to sign those forms?" What forms? I don't remember signing anything.

"There you are handsome." It's her the one from the hotel lobby that looked familiar, she walks up to Damon and kisses him on the cheek. "Liam, what are you doing here?" She looks startled.

"I wanted to make sure Emmie was okay?"

"Hang on," I say.

"What is it, princess?" Liam says, stroking my hair.

"I remember her now. She was the one that made me run away." I remember the hurt I felt when I ran away. But why I ran away and who I ran from, I don't know. That's all I remember.

"Emmie, please, I'm sorry," Damon begs.

"I knew it, the first time I saw her. I knew that she would be the end of my marriage. You said she was just a random girl. You lied." I remember him saying those words but I still don't remember him.

"Emmie, I'm sorry. Do you remember now?" He looks truly sorry.

"No, I just remember her," I say, looking at the pretty girl.

"I must have made an impression then. Damon I'd like to go home now. And I'd like you to take me to bed." She wants my husband to take her to bed. My mouth falls open. This hurts and I don't even remember him.

"I want to see my Daddy," I say.

"Emmie, you can't," Damon says shocked.

"Why not? I remember my Daddy loved me. I want to see my daddy." I miss my Daddy, he was there for me always.

"Even if he was alive Emmie, I wouldn't let you see him. You haven't remembered that bit yet have you?" Remember what?

"My Daddy is dead? What happened?" I say with tears falling down my face. Liam grabs my face in his hands again.

"Maybe we should wait until you get your memory back. All these memories can't be good all at once."

"I want to know," I say to Liam.

"Baby he abused you for years, he killed himself. He nearly killed you," Damon says.

As if by magic all my memories come flooding back, my Dad abusing me, my Mother leaving me. Meeting Damon, kidnapped by Rex. Losing Damon. Desmond kidnapping me. Giving birth to Lilly, my brother in rehab. Marrying Damon, losing Damon again when he was missing. And now the pain of Damon divorcing me. Daddy must have been the trigger where it all started. I can't breathe. I fall to the floor. I remember everything and I wish I didn't. I'm broken, I'm worthless. I knew Izzy was someone to be feared when I met her. Can I really believe he loves this Izzy? I know Damon he loved me. Betrayal is all I see now.

"Hey, princess. Don't cry," Liam says.

"Baby I'm here," Damon says.

"Stay away from me," I say between each laboured breath.

"Emmie?" Damon says, he must have thought I'd come running back to him. Why would I if he married someone else?

"I remember okay. How could you? I love you and you married someone else, so easy?"

"I can't help if I'm irresistible." I want to punch her. But I can't get up.

"Shut the hell up Izzy," Liam snaps.

"I didn't sign," I mumble.

"You did baby, I don't know how he got you to sign. But you did," Damon says. Why does he keep calling me baby? What is he trying to do?

"I'm sorry Emmie. It was never part of my plan to fall in love with you. You were drunk, you were only too happy to sign. Although I guess you didn't know what you were doing." Of course I didn't know what I was doing.

"I don't believe this. You all lied. All this hurt inside of me. I can't handle it." I start rocking on my knees backwards and forwards.

"What happened?" the doctor asks.

"She remembers," Damon says.

"This isn't good. All her emotions at once. I've seen this look before. I'm going to have to sedate her." No, please no. Not again.

"No please, I can't," I whisper.

"You can't drug her," Liam protests.

"You can talk, you drugged her. This is different," Lucas says.

I stand up, no I don't want this. I run into the corridor and see Sully sat on a chair. He looks up at me and frowns. He stands up and I run into his arms. "Betrayal Sully. That's all I can see." I mutter into his neck. He holds me tight. I feel a pinprick on my side and everything goes black.

I wake up feeling groggy. I groan. "Back in the same crappy old life," I sigh. Lucas is sat on the end of my bed.

"Hey Emmie, how you feeling?" he says.

"Hey, I feel like crap," I say honestly.

"The sedative will be wearing off now. I wanted to speak to you before I let them all come back in." I don't want them all to come back in.

"Sounds serious."

"There's no easy way to tell you this but... You're pregnant." I shake my head and sit up like a flash. I can't be pregnant. No. I can't look after my daughter.

"What?" I squeak.

"You are having twins, Emmie." My mouth drops open. Twins! Is this some sort of sick joke?

"Say what? I'm a bad mother. I can't cope with twins."

"Emmie, you are not a bad mother. I've seen you with Lilly-May. You are an amazing Mom. Don't doubt yourself." I was protective over Lilly but now she doesn't want me.

"Who's the Dad? How far along?" I've been with Damon and Liam since Lilly has been born.

"Yeah Emmie, it's something called Superfetation. Your babies were produced at different times. One 4 weeks and one 2 weeks." My mouth drops open again. My life is too complicated, I have children inside of me with two different dads? This could only happen to me. I've been drinking with my babies inside of me.

"You are kidding me? That's just great. Pregnant by my ex-husband and my kidnapper. Fucking great." Well, technically they both kidnapped me.

"I'm so glad that you are back to your old self," Lucas chuckles.

"I'm not," I scoff.

"Shall I send them in now?"

I shake my head. "I don't want to see them. Please send Sully in."

"Sure," Lucas says and leaves the room. I can't face either of them right now. Of course I love them both. But Damon left me for Izzy when he promised me she was just a random girl. I thought he would fight harder than this. And Liam, he drugged me took me away from my husband and my daughter.

Sully walks in and smiles at me. "Pregnant again huh? Don't go missing this time okay?" He is really funny, not.

"I can't promise anything. These things have been out of my control." I move over, inviting him to lay next to me. He takes his cue and I curl up to his chest.

"You okay?" he says.

I shake my head. "No, not really. I don't know what to do? Damon left me while I was missing. And Liam drugged me and made me sign the end of my marriage."

"Just take one day at a time. You'll get there," he says softly. "I think we have got the answer to your sleeping issues. You must be exhausted because you're pregnant." I guess this does explain it.

"I don't know where to go from here." He hushes me and strokes my hair. I still feel groggy and I drift to sleep.

When I wake, Sully is still with me, holding me tight. Sully has never hurt me and yet I don't know why he is here. I don't know why he cares about me. I look over to the chair and Danny is sat there. "Danny?" I whisper. He stands up and sits facing me on my bed.

"I'm here Sis."

"Danny, how could he do this to me?" I married him because I was so sure that he loved me.

"I don't know Sis. I thought he loved you." He looks sad. Like he's ready for me to break. Danny said that he only let him marry me because he was sure he loved me. I was so sure too. I guess we were both wrong. My heart still desires him most, but now that I know he doesn't want me, how am I supposed to carry on?

The Doc walks in. "Emmie. I will discharge you today." Great, thanks Doc.

"Emmie, your belongings are at your new house," Sully whispers in my ear. That was supposed to be mine and Damon's home. Our fresh start, we were so happy together before his parents ruined it.

"Am I expected to move there on my own?" I'm not sure I can cope on my own. No one says anything so I guess that's a yes. "Home being the operative word. My home is with Damon and now I don't know how I will cope. My life is so hard to cope with. I liked not knowing who I was. I thank Liam for taking me away from my pain and then I remembered my awful life. Damon made me happy, everything was worth living. But now I'm not sure." I shake my head.

"Emmie, I know it must be hard and he is an idiot for leaving you. Maybe I shouldn't let you go home. So I can keep an eye on you." I can't stay here forever.

"What's the point?"

"The point is I know you'll be safe," Doc says.

"I'm not safe wherever I go. I think I've proved that." I walk into trouble wherever I go.

"Maybe speaking to Damon and Liam may help you." Why would it help me? Damon doesn't want me and Liam helped me lose Damon.

"What's there to say? Damon left me, he doesn't want me. Liam ended my marriage, took advantage of me."

"But there is a good situation in both cases. You love them both, you thank Liam for making you forget. You need Damon." That may be the case but Damon, my home, my anchor, doesn't want me and Liam, our relationship was based on a lie.

"None of it matters," I say.

"Let's go, Emmie," Sully says, standing up and taking my hand. We sit in silence on the way back to the new house. I get out the car before he gets my door. He leads us to the house, opens the door and then passes me the key. I shove it in my back pocket.

"Well, I'll see you later. If you need anything just call, and I'll be right over." He's leaving me? Of course, he is just like everyone else.

"Okay," I say and he leaves. I'm alone, all alone. My life is such a mess. I walk a few steps and collapse on the floor. I'm all alone, I repeat to myself. I curl up on the floor. Where is my Daddy when I need him? I'm alone.

Chapter 36

I haven't moved since Sully left. I don't know how long it's been. This is what I've always wanted to be, alone, all alone so I wouldn't have to worry about other people's feelings around me. I thought Damon and I were happy. Really happy, I just don't understand what changed. I guess it is possible that he fell in love with someone else so quickly because he did with me.

Yes, I fell in love with Liam in a short amount of time but that was all based on a lie. If I had my memories I wouldn't have even let him near me. There was that feeling I got every time he touched me but I didn't know what it meant at the time. It was another man touching me apart from Damon and now I'm pregnant with twins. I hated pregnancy last time, how am I going to cope? And all alone.

Someone knocks at the door but I don't move. "Sis?" Danny calls. But I'm too tired to answer him. I don't want anyone near me right now. "Sis, are you there?" Yes, I am but go away. If I stay quiet, he will think I'm out. Maybe. He stops calling so I guess he has left.

My phone starts ringing, I pull it out of my pocket. Danny is calling. I don't know why I expected to see Damon's number calling, how stupid could I be? He doesn't want me anymore. It won't be hard to convince myself that he doesn't love me because I never understood why he loved me in the first place. I guess he got fed up of how broken I am.

Someone is at the door again. I ignore it once again. "Emmie?" Lexi calls. "Emmie, are you there? I wanted a shopping trip." You may want one but you won't get one with me. Go find Jessie or something. I don't want to go outside, I'm not safe.

When I wake again I feel awful. My stomach is tying itself in knots. I can't move even if I wanted to. I'm so exhausted. "Baby, it's me. Open the door," Damon's soft voice calls through the door, he is all I've wanted to hear but now he's here I resent it. He doesn't want me so why is he here? "Emmie, if you don't open the door I will kick the door down." He sounds stressed and panicked. "Okay, you asked for it." God he's going to break my door just so he can what? Tell me some more that he doesn't want me. Great.

He gives the door a few good blows and the door slams open. "Shit Emmie." He crouches in front of me and strokes my face but I don't respond. He scoops me into his arms, I still feel like this is home. It's my favourite place in the whole world. "You are safe now baby."

I wish he would stop calling me baby. It makes it sound like he still wants me. He carries me to his car and he buckles me in. He kisses me on my forehead, it soothes me that he is still treating me normally but it is torturing me. Being so close to him and not be able to kiss him or touch him. I'm going to die alone, I would use the saying old and alone but because I walk into trouble, I may not reach that age. Without Damon to protect me it may be sooner than I had previously hoped for.

I wonder where he is taking me but if I know Damon, he will be taking me to the hospital. Maybe I should just live there, I seem to be there all the time anyway. Sure enough, that's where he pulls up. He carries me into the hospital. "Rider?" Lucas says, shocked. "This way."

Damon follows him, I'm not sure where because I have my eyes shut. Damon releases me onto a bed and I wish he didn't, I was safe and protected in his unwanted arms. "What happened?" Lucas asks.

"I don't know, I found her on the floor. No one has seen her since Sully took her home." Of course they wouldn't, they all belong to you Damon. Which means they don't want me either.

"You left her on her own? Really?" Lucas, I'd have done the same in company. "She was upset when she left. She didn't see the point in living anymore. When she had you she was happy and she had a purpose. But now she feels lonely. You left her. She feels worthless." I've always felt this way. I wouldn't do anything stupid, not with Damon's baby inside of me and Liam's baby will be beautiful too.

"Why didn't you tell me? Or keep her here?" What difference would it have made? I'm not your responsibility anymore.

"She didn't want to. I thought she would be okay." I'm am okay. "I'll be back soon with the tests." What tests? I didn't even feel him take blood.

"Oh, Emmie I'm sorry. I love you so much. I did this all for you." You broke me even more for me? Well, that makes me feel so much better. He can't love me if he did this.

"You can't love me that much if you left me. You did all this to hurt me? That's good of you," I mumble the words out. They are barely audible.

"Emmie I... I didn't realise you were awake."

"I wish I wasn't…"

"What? Emmie, please don't say that." I don't know what he expected. To me he is my world, he is the gravity that keeps me here. He makes my heart keep beating, he is that meaningful to me. We have tested this theory a couple of times. I can't function without him. Of course, if he doesn't want me then I'm not going to force him to be with me.

"Why, you don't want me? Lilly-May doesn't want me. Everyone hates me."

He grabs my face in his hands. "Emmie, I love you. Our daughter loves you. There are plenty of people in this world that loves you. You just can't see it." I see nothing for certain anymore. Damon has my heart and he has everything else of mine, my loved ones, my family and my life, he has it all.

"So you keep saying. Please leave." This is torture to hear he still loves me. It gives me hope when I shouldn't have any.

"Emmie…" He is hurting just as much as me, I can see it in his eyes. I wish I could comfort him but his new wife should be doing that so instead all I can do is push him away. "Please," he begs. Damon sighs and leaves the room, I have a feeling he won't be going far. I turn over to face the window. The little things I remembered when I was drugged like how much I love the sun, is it because I'm so stubborn that I couldn't truly forget myself? Even remembering I'm a vegetarian when I couldn't remember my name.

"Hey, Princess," Liam says.

"Hey. What are you doing here?" Liam comes to sit on the chair in front of me.

"Rider called, he said you aren't doing well. I wanted to see you." Why does Damon keep trying to fix me? Is this guilt? If it is I don't want his help.

"Why would you want to see me? I'm not important. I don't want to be a bother." I've been a bother my entire life.

"Sweetheart, you are not a bother. I love you. You are the most important thing to me. I'm here for you." I love Liam but it's nothing compared to how I feel about Damon. I guess I love him like I love Brody. I will always love him and he means something to me and I wouldn't change it. But I need Damon, I don't need the other two.

"You shouldn't be." The only thing I can do is push them all away. Protect myself and protect them. If I can't give them what they desire, then I shouldn't lead them on.

"Hey, beautiful." What is Brody doing here? I sit up so I can see them both but it wasn't just Brody who walked in the door, it's Damon and Sully too.

"What's everyone doing here?" I push them away and they all spring back to me all at once.

"The Doc wants to refer you to the mental health clinic. I just wanted you to know we are all here for you," Damon says. No, I can't go back there, it didn't even work for me last time. The only thing that has come close to fixing me is Damon.

"No, I can't go back there. I'd rather die."

"Emmie. Don't say that," Brody says. What do you even care? You are with Jessie.

"Please, anything but that, I'll try anything. Please," I beg.

"Okay just calm down, we will figure something out," Liam says.

"Don't make me go. Damon, please." Sully walks closer to me. I move over and he climbs in next to me. I curl onto his chest again. He soothes me, he doesn't expect anything in return. Damon looks angry but he doesn't say anything. I close my eyes.

"I can't risk you hurting yourself," Damon says.

"I won't, please."

"How can I trust you? I can't lose you." I don't look at his face I just keep my eyes closed. Trying to match my breathing with Sully's.

"Honestly, you already lost me when you married Izzy. But you can trust me."

"I've never trusted you to take care of yourself. Why will this be different?" How am I supposed to know? But I'm willing to try. Anyway, they are bound to leave me again so who cares? Brody has Jessie. Damon has Izzy. Liam shouldn't want me and well I can't figure Sully out. I'm sure he will be there but he works for Damon. If Damon orders him away from me, he will have to obey.

"We can all take turns to watch her. We are here for you Emmie. We need you better," Brody says.

"No, it's not happening," Damon says. He sits down on the end of my bed and puts his hand on my ankle.

"Boss, you need to consider this," Sully says.

"Damon please, if you love me you'll do this. Please." I know he loves me which is why this is so much harder for me.

"Fine," Damon snaps. Wow, that was easier than I thought. Why would he give me what I want?

"Great, let's go home," I say.

"Not so fast Emmie," Doc says whilst entering the room. I pout at him. "Your test shows you are severely malnourished. You are dehydrated. When did you last eat?" I'm not having this same fight again.

"Before I got my memory back."

"Emmie? The was nearly a week ago," Liam says, shocked. "Why haven't you eaten?" He doesn't know about my issues with food.

"Because I'm fat. It makes me feel sick."

"Emmie, you aren't fat. I never had trouble getting you to eat," Liam says.

"That's because I didn't even remember who I was. Let alone my problems with eating."

"Baby, how many times? You are not fat, you are like a twig. I'm always worried you'll snap in half," Damon says.

"Look, Doc, give me an honest answer now will you?" I say.

"Of course," he says.

"Tell them, how long can a person go without food?"

"Technically one can go without food for at least three weeks," the Doc says.

"See. It doesn't matter that I don't eat. As long as I have something between those times."

"Emmie, just because one can doesn't mean they should. It's really bad for your body." I frown, I've been fine. "Your mental state could be something to do with the food." I shake my head. My mental state is the problems with my life. Not my food aversion. "You can take her home.

But she must eat."

"Yes, she will eat," Damon says. Even he struggled to get me to eat last time. So I don't know how he will do it this time.

Sully gets up off the bed. "Great," I say and climb off the bed. I'm exhausted so I fall to the floor. "Ow," I say on my knees, brushing my hands off. Sully lifts me up off the floor. He looks me up and down and then bends down to carry me. It's not the same when he carries me but it gives me comfort. And right now, I'd rather him carry me than Damon who doesn't want me.

When we are home, Sully places me on the sofa. He walks off somewhere in the house. Damon, Brody and Liam hover around me. "So I'd better get back," Damon says.

"Yeah, to your wife. You should go." He crouches down in front of me and grabs my face. I wish he would be here for me.

"Emmie, come on. I'd be here if I could." I don't understand that answer.

"I get it, you don't want me." Why does he keep giving me false hope? Or maybe he doesn't and I'm reading too much into it?

"I've got to go. I'll come back later Princess," Liam says. This didn't take long for them all to scatter like flies.

"Okay. Anyone else? Brody, you going back to Jessie?"

"Yeah, I should," he shrugs.

Sully comes back with a blanket and he places it over me, moving around Damon on the floor in front of me. "Sully, are you going too?"

"I'm not going anywhere, Emmie. I won't leave you on your own." Sully seems annoyed. He sits next to me.

"I will be back later baby," Liam says and kisses my forehead and leaves.

"Bye beautiful," Brody says and also leaves.

"I will be back tomorrow. I will bring our daughter," Damon says.

"I miss her so much." Even if she doesn't want me.

"Goodbye mi chica Bella." I frown. He kisses me on the forehead too and leaves. He hasn't called me that in ages. Why is he doing this to me? Is it a secret message that there is hope? I must be mistaken, why would he come back to me?

"Can I make you some food?" Sully says. I shake my head.

"No, I'm not hungry. I don't want to fight with you, Sully." I curl up into his chest and he sighs. I can't sit here and do nothing.

I stand up and Sully frowns at me. "Where are you going?" Sully says.

"To the stables." I stand my ground. I head for the back door.

"Bloody woman," I hear Sully mutter.

I walk down the stony track and into the stables. I walk straight to the black horse. "Can I help you?" I turn around and see a young girl.

"I'm Emmie," I say.

"Oh, the Boss. Of course. I'm Billie" She goes to shake my hand and I grudgingly shake it. "If you need anything just ask."

I nod. I grab the head collar for the horse. "What's his name?" I say.

"Willow. He can be a bit bolshy sometimes so watch out." I don't blame him. I walk in the stable and put his head collar on. He licks my hand again so I wipe my hand on his neck. I slide the door open and walk out of the stable.

I tie him up outside and start to groom him. His coat is all shiny, he's been well looked after. Once I'm finished I take him in the school. I do some in hand work with him to get him to trust me. But he already seems to for some reason. Willow drops to his knees. What is he doing? Is he trying to get me to ride him? I shrug and slide onto his back and he stands up.

I never planned to ride him but when it's offered I won't object. He is very obedient to my legs. This horse is well trained. "Er, Emmie. You really should be careful up there. He isn't the safest of horses," Billie says.

"He's fine," I say. And he is. Does she not know I like to live life on the edge?

"Emmie. Get down off that horse now. Damon would kill you," Sully shouts. Damon isn't here.

"Fine," I snap. I slide off Willow and lead him back to the stable. Willow is safely in his stable and Sully drags me back home. Literally, drags me.

Once I'm back I shower quickly and get ready for bed. When Sully enters my bedroom, I'm curled up in bed. "Can I get you anything, Emmie?" Sully asks.

"No, I just want to sleep. Thanks, Sully, I love that you are here."

"I wouldn't be anywhere else. " He smiles and leaves the room.

I feel numb after this day. Damon is messing with my head. Liam is as hot as ever and he still makes me feel special. Brody is always there when I need him, except I don't need him. I just need Damon. Sully is the only one that stayed with me. I close my eyes and drift asleep.

"Hey Princess." My eyes fly open. Liam came back.

"You came back?"

"Of course I did. I just had things to do. But I'm back. Can I stay with you tonight?"

"I'd like that," I say.

"Good to hear beautiful," he says and strips so he's only wearing his boxers. He climbs in behind me and pulls me tight. I turn to face him.

"You are so beautiful. Have you been crying?"

"Hard day I guess."

"It will get better, I promise," he says and he hugs me tight.

He starts to kiss me. Do I want this? I don't know. "Liam," I say as I pull away.

"I'm sorry Princess," he says, hurt. I don't like to see him hurting. I'm holding back because of Damon, but he is at his house doing the same with Izzy. He is the one who moved on with someone else. He left me.

"No, it's okay." I pull Liam towards me.

"Are you sure?" No, but I'm not sure of anything apart from my love for Damon. But none of that matters right now. I nod and he kisses me once more. I'm not as comfortable with him now than when I had no memory. I ignore the impulse to push him away. His touch isn't as bad as any other guy. My love for him is stronger than the repulsion I feel when he touches me. As he touches me, I close my eyes wishing it was Damon's hands on me. His soft lips kissing my body. It's bearable when I do this. Damon's bright blue eyes looking at me like I'm the only girl in the world.

"Emmie?" I hear Sully call. I feel arms on me. "Emmie, can you hear me?" I shake my head and blink. I'm in the kitchen in my underwear and Sully is in his boxers.

"Yeah, sorry Sully. I don't know what happened."

"Looks like you were sleepwalking. You know you are safe here, right?" I nod. Sleepwalking? That's all I need. He strokes my face I close my eyes. I feel his warm lips on mine. Am I dreaming? Sleepwalking still? I feel myself kissing him back. I didn't know he felt this way about me. And I never thought about him this way.

He pulls away. "I'm sorry Emmie, I don't know what came over me."

He bows his head and leaves me in the kitchen alone. There is no way I can sleep now. I'm not even sure what time it is. I head outside onto the porch. It's light outside and the sun is warm already.

"Baby what are you doing out here? You are going to get cold," Damon says softly. I turn to face him.

"Damon this is Spain. It's hot all the time."

"Good point but I still don't like the thought of people seeing you in your underwear." What's it to him? He can't get rid of me and then not let anyone else near me.

"What are you doing here so early?"

"I could ask you why you are awake so early."

"I don't sleep well without you. Liam stayed with me but it's not the same."

He shakes his head "Emmie...I..."

"I get it you don't have to keep apologising. I get it, I do. I mean Izzy is beautiful." She is stunning in a way that I am not.

"I came here to say happy birthday Mi Chica Bella." Is it that day already? I missed it last year because I was kidnapped at the time by Desmond.

"Doesn't feel very happy right now." I've always hated my birthdays. My Dad would follow me around all day, he'd take me any chance he got. He would call it his birthday gift to me.

"Maybe I can help with that." What does that even mean?

He walks towards me grabs my faces in his hands and kisses me. It's not just a soft kiss it's an urgent kiss. It sends pulses down my body. He pulls me close. What the hell is he doing? This is what I've been craving for so long. But why now? I feel like he's been saving this for me. I love this man. Who was my husband.

He pulls away and smiles at me. "What are you doing?"

"I'm sorry, I just wanted to give you a good birthday."

"Messing with my head you call a good birthday? You married someone else."

"I'm sorry, baby," he says but he continues to stroke my face.

"I love that you are here but I can't be the other woman. You either want me and only me or you need to stop this." I can't have only part of him. I need all of him.

"I'm sorry."

"Stop apologising." He needs to stop saying sorry, it's doing my head in.

"Let's go inside. Please go and get dressed."

"Maybe I like walking around in underwear in MY house." I cross my arms. In my house, it doesn't matter that I am so fat and exposed.

"This was supposed to be OUR house." Why does he keep torturing me like this?

"Whose fault was that?" I snap and head inside. When I reach my bedroom, Liam is awake but he looks tired.

"Hey princess, what are you doing up so early?"

"I don't sleep well anymore."

"Come back to bed," he says, grabbing my hand.

"I need to get up. Damon is here with Lilly-May."

"Why so early?"

"I don't know." I shrug.

"He saw you? Dressed like that?" Liam says, pissed. It's nothing he hasn't seen before. Like I said, he doesn't want me so who cares? It's not like I knew he would be there anyway. "Fine, let's get up. Unless you are ready for round two." I laugh at him.

"Get up." I giggle.

"You're boring," he sulks.

I dress in a black dress. "You look beautiful as usual Princess." I smile at him.

"Are you getting up?" I say.

"Why don't you make me?" he says playfully. So, he's playing that game hey? I grab a pillow from the bed and hit him with it. He grabs my hips and pulls me on top of him. He is being irresistible. Playful. I continue to hit him with the pillow. He sits up so we are nose to nose. He is so beautiful, strong, I love to trace his abs with my fingers.

"I don't see you trying very hard." He bites his lip.

"You are distracting." I bite my lip too. He starts to kiss my neck softly. I tilt my head back to give him full access. He bites and sucks my neck. Hickey? Really, why is he trying to mark me?

"You are childish," I say, holding my neck with my hand.

"Just letting people know where I've been." So this is his game? Is he jealous about earlier that Damon saw me in my underwear? Marking me so that Damon knows what we have been up to, seriously? Damon doesn't even care, well I'm not so sure about that now. Liam kisses my lips softly, I'm mad at him. But I also can't resist him either.

"Emmie are you..." Damon's voice trails off. I push Liam away from me. I still feel like I'm cheating on my husband.

"Dude really?" Liam huffs while lying on his back. I climb off him and walk to Damon.

"Damon…" I'm so sorry. I really am.

"Our daughter is waiting for you," he says coldly. I just want to run in his arms and heal his pain.

"I'm coming," I say whilst following him out of the room. I hear Liam scrambling out of bed and following us downstairs.

I walk into the living room and everyone is there. "Happy Birthday," everyone calls. I clutch to Damon's arm, there are too many people in my house. He looks at me and then I remove my hands. Shit, it's just habit to reach for comfort in Damon. He sighs.

I walk away from Damon trying to get as far from him as possible. I want to see my daughter. I go in search of her. No way. When I see Lilly, she's in Izzy's arms. I never thought that Izzy would technically be her Step Mother. I shake my head, this hurts.

"What the hell are you doing with my daughter? Give her here," I growl.

"How dare you? I'm her Mom now." As long as I keep breathing she will be my daughter. And I will fight for her. I can't fight for my husband but I will fight for my daughter.

"You will never be her Mom. Give her to me." She's mine and I need to keep her safe.

"Give her to Emmie." Sully places his arm around me. He sounds pissed too.

"She can't be trusted, she has mental issues." I may be ill, but I've always taken care of her.

"What are you trying to say? That I'd hurt my daughter?"

"I wouldn't put it past you," she snaps. She doesn't even know me.

"What's going on here?" Damon growls.

"Nothing, I guess," I say, looking at the ground.

"Your stupid wife is trying to tell Emmie she is Lilly-May's new Mom and how Emmie can't be trusted," Sully snaps. Stupid wife? Does Sully not like Izzy?

"Izzy give her to Emmie now. Emmie is her Mom and she will always be." Damon's angry. He doesn't speak to Izzy with respect. Why is that? He has given me nothing but respect even now.

"Fine, but won't be long until we have our own." She passes Lilly to me. One of their own? No, I can't process that.

"Emmie I'm sorry, she knows you are her Mom. No one will change that." I shake my head. I still can't handle them together.

"I want her to stay with me. I don't want her near her." She can't get her claws into my daughter, I won't allow it. Before I know it, Lilly will be calling her Momma.

"Do you think that's a good idea?" Does he think I will hurt her too?

"Why, do you not think I'm capable of looking after her either?" I snap.

"That's not what I meant." Of course it is. I leave him again, I seem to try to create a distance and then he closes the distance. He's messing with my head. It's almost like we are drawn to each other without knowing it.

I walk to the kitchen to get a drink. But I'm stopped in my tracks when I hear Damon shouting. He sounds really angry. I stay behind the door so he can't see me but I can hear him. "What was that about?" Damon shouts.

"I hate her, always miss perfect. You all run around after her. You're my husband Damon, act like it," Izzy moans. Damon and I never argued like this.

"You are such a selfish bitch." Did that really come out of Damon's mouth? There must be a good reason as the Damon I know wouldn't speak to his wife like this. Damon is kind, caring and protective.

"Don't speak to me like that. I'm your wife." You've said that already, change the record.

"You are nothing to me. You know why I married you. Not out of love for you but for Emmie." Wait, hold up, he doesn't love Izzy? But he said it was love at first sight? Why would he marry her for me? Is this some sick joke to break me? I don't understand.

"Who cares, she thinks you married me for love." She seems pissed but she really doesn't care that she's hurt me. What is this?

"I did this to save her, she was kidnapped. The only way to get her back was to marry you. It was the hardest thing I have ever had to do. I will never forgive myself for doing this. You are pathetic to have to blackmail someone to marry you. You have ruined my life." What is he trying to say? I was kidnapped so that Damon would marry Izzy? Was this the deal to have me back? Even if it meant I'd be broken?

Damon married someone else to save me? No, he's been through hell marrying this selfish bitch for me? And then he finds out I have fallen for Liam? What have I done? Sleeping with Liam, kissing Sully? Getting pregnant by Liam. He's been throwing these hints at me and I've been too blind to see it. Does that mean he really does want me? I feel angry, I need to save Damon from this bitch.

I walk back to the living room. "Happy Birthday Sis. I love you." He hugs me gently as I have Lilly in my arms.

"Thanks, Bro. Do you think you could take Lilly-May for a bit?" What I plan to do, Lilly can't come with me.

"Is everything okay?" he asks, concerned.

"It will be, there's something I've got to do." I slide Lilly into Danny's arms.

"Sure Sis, no worries," he says, confused.

I walk back to the kitchen, hopefully they have finished arguing now. When I walk in Damon is still angry. But when he sees me his eyes light up. "Hey baby, are you having a good birthday?" I have to close the distance between us. We are alone and he kissed me this morning so it won't hurt if I hug him. When I hug him, he doesn't hesitate to hug me back and I'm relieved.

"Yeah," I say into his chest.

"Good, where is Lilly-May?" he says, stroking my hair.

"With my brother. Hey, my phone died, could I borrow yours?"

He doesn't release me, just gets his phone out of his pocket and puts it in my hand. "Sure, here you go."

"Thanks," I say into his chest. I walk out of his hold grudgingly, if I don't move now I never will. I smile at him and he smiles back. I walk back into the living room, I manage to sneak out the front door without anyone noticing. As soon as I'm out of the house, I run. I'm still so tired so I fall now and again. But I just keep running.

Chapter 37

I reach the safe house and I text Izzy from Damon's phone.

Izzy I'm sorry about earlier, it was a mistake. I really want to make it up to you. Meet me at the safe house. Damon. x

Hopefully she knows about the safe house. If not, my plan is stupid.

I'm so happy to hear that. I'll be there soon babe. X

Babe, is she crazy? She's so stupid. I enter the code on the keypad and walk in. I hear voices so I sneak around to Damon's office. Sounds like they are guarding the lock ups. Has Damon still got prisoners? I sit at Damon's desk trying to be quiet. I text Larry from Damon's phone.

I want you and Dyno to meet me at Emmie's house now. I don't bother with pleases because Damon wouldn't do that.

I hear footsteps outside the office door and I freeze. "It's Boss, he wants us both at Emmie's pronto," Larry says.

"I guess we better go to her house. God, she's so annoying," Dyno moans. He's annoying, he's only pissed that I broke his nose. How rude. The footsteps start again and they disappear. I relax into Damon's chair. He still has the same pictures on his desk. No new ones, just Lilly and me. I keep an eye on the CCTV because I'm sure Izzy won't know the code. Damon never told me the code, I just watched and remembered. I can't imagine Izzy has a good memory like that.

I rummage through his drawers to find his gun again and sure enough, it's still here. I start to become impatient, tapping my foot. I see her at the front door and I buzz her in. I cross my legs waiting for her to arrive in the office.

"Babe?" she calls. Urgh, really? He's mine! The door clicks open. She looks shocked to see me here.

"Where's Damon?"

"At my house, I'm guessing." I shrug. Where I left him, safe from her.

"What's going on?" She crosses her arms.

"I know what you did." No one hurts my husband and gets away with it.

"What are you on about?" She knows.

"Stop the crap. I know you forced my husband to marry you. You are a psycho bitch, do you know that?" Did she know Damon before or is she mental, she saw him and she wanted him?

"Do you think your words are going to hurt me? You are pathetic." My words? No, of course not. But I will hurt her.

"Do you know what happened to the person that got between me and my husband the last time?" Rex knows.

She rolls her eyes. "No, and I don't care."

"You should because I put a bullet in his head and you know what?" Her mouth drops open and she starts to back away towards the door. I stand up and walk around the desk. I perch on the edge.

"You d-did? And what?" I can see she is terrified now. Good.

"I did, but the thing is I wasn't pregnant then. Which means my emotions are raging. And hey, as you put it, I'm mental and need locking up so, sucks to be you. No one crosses me and gets away with it and especially if they hurt my husband."

"He's not your husband anymore, he's mine," she says defensively. He will always belong to me.

"When you are dead it won't matter."

"You won't kill me." She crosses her arms. I grab the gun from the desk and point it towards her. She holds her hands up.

"Oh Izzy, people do like to underestimate me. Rex didn't think I'd kill him, but I did. Poor Izzy. I'd like to think you will learn from your mistake. But guess what? I'm not going to give you a chance." I laugh at her.

"Please, I'm sorry. I will leave him, I promise." She says scared, tears stream down her face. It's too late for that now.

"You've hurt my husband, you forced him to do something he didn't want to do. So it's game over for you."

"Wait, Liam won't be happy if you do that." Why not? He loves me, he will be fine.

"Who cares what Liam thinks he will be happy about it. He loves me, he will support me."

"He won't forgive you for this. He loves me." They don't even know each other, do they? Is she trying to stall me? Why would anyone love her?

"You think anyone would care if you were dead? I think not."

"Liam is my brother." What? I guess it does make sense, Izzy wanted Damon so she got her brother to kidnap me. He loves me and he's tried to look after me since.

"What? Why didn't he tell me?"

"All part of the plan. He played you. He doesn't love you and if you kill me, you are dead too." I shake my head, she's trying to distract me. Liam will be fine, he loves me. And well, if not, Damon will protect me and so will Sully.

"Have you learned nothing about me? I don't value my own life, you crazy fool. Right, say goodbye, I've had enough of listening to your whining voice."

I aim at her head. "No please." I smile at her and pull the trigger. I'm not so frozen this time. I stare at her body on the floor. I'm ill and that's okay, I already knew that. Damon never told me what he did with Desmond and they were obviously guarding someone so I decide to take a look. I tuck the gun in my boot.

I grab the key from the left of the door and unlock the door. I peer in first and see Desmond laying on the bed. I walk in and shut the door. He looks up at me, he looks awful. "Emmie? Am I dreaming? You are as beautiful as ever." I don't feel beautiful, I feel exhausted, out of control.

"This is real, I guess." I'm never really sure what's real and what's not. He sits up slowly, wincing as he does. My god, Damon must have fucked him up big time. He must be torturing him slowly for all the things he did to me. He has fingers missing. He is covered in bruises and blood. He looks half dead. I kinda feel sorry for him.

"What are you doing here?" he asks.

"I just came to kill this annoying bitch. Whilst I was here, I thought I'd see if you were still alive. And here you are." I smile at him. His mouth drops open, this situation is reversed, I'm in control and he is scared and out of control. Well, I don't feel in control but I have got the upper hand.

"You killed someone? Emmie, what's happened to you?" A lot has happened to me since I last saw him.

"People like you did this to me. I feel out of control. All because of you, my Daddy, my Mother, Rex. The list is endless." I clutch my head, it's all too much.

"Look, Emmie, Damon has been torturing me for months. Please, I want you to do it." I can see he's been torturing him. Desmond deserves this for what he did to me and I don't blame Damon for this. But what does he mean he wants me to do it?

"Do what?"

"Kill me. I know Rider will kill me eventually. I don't want to see his ugly mug when I die. I want it to be your beautiful face. The one I love. Please. I'm begging you." Damon isn't ugly, he is the most beautiful man I've ever seen. He loves me? What about my mother?

I put my hands in front of me in defence. "My hormones are raging Desmond. I'd be only too happy, but are you sure?"

"You're pregnant?" he says, shocked.

"Yes. I'm having twins."

"I bet Rider is happy." I don't know if he is. I haven't spoken to him about it.

"I haven't spoken to him about it. He is only the father of one of them."

"What? How's that possible?" he says.

"It's very rare but it can happen. Anyway, I'm not here to discuss this with you. Are you ready to die?" I don't have all day. If he wants to die, then we will need to do it now.

"Yes, Emmie please do it, my beautiful Love." I lean down and reach for the gun. Desmond stands up and leans his face towards me. He doesn't touch me, just with his lips. He kisses me one last time and while he kisses me I aim the gun at his head and I pull the trigger. The recoil is strong in only one hand but it hits him where it was supposed to. He falls to the floor.

"I'm not yours." I'm Damon's and I always will be. I drag Izzy's body to the holding area where Desmond lies on the floor. I am so numb. I killed two people. I remember the scar on my hip. The D from Desmond.

He marked me and now I will mark him. I go search for a knife in Damon's desk. I come back and carve an E in both Desmond and Izzy. I want everyone to know that I did this. There is blood everywhere. I'm obviously not in my right mind. I put my hand in the blood and write Emmie on the wall.

My whole body is shaking. I wipe my hair from my face. I'm satisfied that I've done enough to ease my mind. Damon's phone is ringing, I take it from my boot and look at the caller ID. Larry is calling but I'm guessing it's Damon.

"Emmie? Where are you?" Damon says, afraid.

"I'm alone, all alone." Apart from two dead bodies.

"Baby, what's going on? Where are you?" Yes, I'm your baby Damon and I love you.

"I did it, Damon, I freed you. I did it. I did it all for you." I don't care what happens to me, I saved Damon, that's all that matters to me.

"You're not making any sense Emmie. Where are you?" Yes, come to me, Damon. Please.

"I'm where it all began." Where our life started. Where I fell in love with you. Where you took my heart. He hangs up before saying goodbye. I'm so tired I drop to the floor, my head is resting on Desmond's chest. But I don't care anymore. He doesn't scare me now he's dead. Nothing really scares me anymore. I've lived through the worst pain imaginable.

"Emmie!" Damon calls. I close my eyes, Damon came for me. "Emmie! Where are you?" he calls again. I'm here Damon. Look what I did for you. "Emmie, what the hell have you done?"

"I did it for you Damon. I found out what she did to you. I won't let anyone hurt you," I say. He grabs my arm and lifts me up. He holds my weight while he looks into my eyes.

"Emmie, what you did was wrong. Give me the gun." I forgot I was still clutching the gun.

"Why?"

"Baby, look at me, I love you, please give me the gun." I love you too Damon but why do you look so anxious? Maybe he is worried I may hurt myself. I don't want him scared so I hand him the gun.

"Good girl," he says. He hands the gun to Dyno and he hugs me tight.

"You are one crazy bitch, Emmie," Dyno says. I know I'm ill. I know this isn't normal but there was nothing stopping me. Desmond begged me to kill him.

"Leave us now. Call the Doctor," Damon snaps. He's with me, that's all that matters.

"Yes, Boss," Dyno says and leaves.

"I did it all for you," I say, he still seems angry.

"Let's get you home baby." He picks me up into his arms.

I frown, "Did I get it wrong? Are you sad that Izzy is dead? I thought you loved me. But you seem angry. Did you want Izzy?"

Damon kisses my hair, "No baby, I'm not mad that's she's dead. I love you and only you. It's always been you." I feel better knowing he wanted her gone too and I fall asleep in his arms.

I wake on his chest, we are in my bedroom. "Are you mad at me? Do you hate me?"

"I'm not mad, baby. I love you more than anything. I just should have protected you from this pain. You shouldn't have done this." He was trapped, I had to. This was the only way.

"I had to, it was the only way. It's just there may be a slight issue."

"What is it?"

"Izzy is Liam's Sister." Or was, should I say.

"What? And you killed her anyway?" he says, shocked.

"I didn't want to hear her voice anymore. She deserved it."

"I will sort it but get some more sleep."

"Are you leaving me?" I say, panicked.

"No, I'll be downstairs. I will be back shortly okay?" He prizes himself from my grip and stands up. He kisses my forehead and leaves the room. I need a shower, I need to wash this blood off me. I get out of bed and walk into the bathroom.

The water on my skin feels good. I feel like I'm washing away Desmond and Izzy. "Emmie!" Damon calls. God, he is as paranoid as Danny. I hear the bathroom door open. "Emmie, what are you doing?"

"Having a shower Damon." He grabs my arm and pulls me out the shower. Good job I was done anyway. He turns the shower off and grabs me a towel. He wraps it around me and I bury my head into his chest.

"Don't scare me like that. I thought you ran again." He hugs me tight.

"I won't be going anywhere if I know you want me."

"I will always want you. No matter what." That's what I thought when he married Izzy, I couldn't make it out.

"Damon, can you do me a favour?"

"Sure, name it."

"The file you have on me, the one Liam was able to get hold of, can you make it disappear? I don't want people knowing my life. I want people to remember me when I was happy," I say.

"That's reasonable. I can do that for you. Come, the Doctor is here." He takes my hand and leads me into the bedroom. I curl up in bed as the Doctor sits on the end of the bed.

"Hey, Lucas," I say. I'm always so exhausted.

"How are you feeling?"

"Tired, I'm always tired."

"Have you been sleeping?"

"No, I don't sleep. When I do, the nightmares are awful. Sully caught me sleepwalking last night. What's wrong with me Doctor?"

"Did you eat anything when you left the hospital?"

I shake my head. "Emmie, how could you be so careless?" Damon says. He left me, he was at home with Izzy.

"Damon, I feel so scared all the time. My anxiety is through the roof. Every time I think of food I feel sick."

"Emmie you really need to eat, for your babies. But not just that, for you." Lilly turned out fine.

"I don't care about myself. The pain, it reminds me I'm still alive. I want the pain to stop. Damon, you left me, I'm not worthy or deserving of a good life."

"I'm going to come see you every day. You'll have to be watched 24/7. I will arrange a counsellor for you. I will make you better but you need to help us okay?" I nod. "I will be back tomorrow. Get some rest."

"Thanks, Doc," Damon says.

"You owe me." How much does Lucas know? Lucas leaves the room.

"Do you want me to stay tonight?" Of course I do. Nothing would make me happier.

"I won't make you do anything you don't want to do." I won't force him to stay.

"Emmie, I love you, I want to stay with you but I don't know who you want right now." Is he thinking of Liam?

"I want you to stay with me. I feel safest when I'm with you. I don't sleep well without you."

He smiles, "Then I will stay with you." He strips to his boxers. He gets into bed with me. He grabs my hand and he plays with my ring. "You kept it on?" he says in disbelief.

"Damon, you know you own my heart, what proof do you need that I'm bound to you? You kept telling me you loved me. I didn't know what it meant at the time. But even then, I knew you loved me. I just didn't understand the full picture. You will always be my husband."

"And you will always be mine." Yes, I'm always his. "But you were with Liam." He shakes his head.

"You have to understand I thought you were with Izzy. Did you ever...?" I can't even say the words. "I recoil at his touch like anyone else, it's just my love for him overpowered that. Just so you know, when we had sex I wished it was you touching me."

"Well, I'm glad to hear that baby. I really am. And no baby, our married may have looked real but behind closed doors I never touched her, no matter how much she wanted me to. You know Sully punched me when he found out about my engagement."

"I'd like to say I'm happy about him punching you, but now I know the truth I'm not sure you deserved it."

"So when you were kidnapped, what happened?"

"I didn't remember who I was. I didn't know anything, but it was strange, I still had certain feelings I didn't understand."

"Like what?"

"I remembered I was a vegetarian, every time he touched me I felt this sense that I should push him away. He told me these lies that we were together and we were happy. So I thought that I should ignore those feelings. I still found myself looking over my shoulder when we went out. I only felt safe with him. But the main thing was I felt something huge was missing from my life."

"Do you remember what happened at the beginning?" I shake my head.

"All I remember was feeling hurt and betrayed."

"I still don't know how you knew," he says.

"Knew what?"

"You knew she was a threat. When I went to Canada my Dad told me I must marry another. And then when I returned to you, they said they'd already made contact with you. It must have been that guy at the bar. You were in a club, right? Sully said that you always know these things because you feel like you are on the outside of life. You see things others don't."

"Yeah but I don't really remember." Sully said that? That is so true. Maybe I've let him deeper than I thought.

"The guy sent me a video of you. You were out of it. He said that I must follow demands which was to marry Izzy and then they would return you. A divorce takes months to finalise but my Dad had connections. Danny begged me to get you back." Of course his Dad had connections. I bet he was only too willing.

"Part of me wishes you didn't."

"Why, because you love Liam?" he says offended.

"Not exactly, I liked not knowing who I was. Liam did give me a good life, even if it was just two weeks. I love Liam, yes, but it's like how I feel for Brody. I love them but I need you."

"I need you, baby." He needs me too? He holds me tight like I may break if he lets me go. I have my husband back. I slip into peaceful easy sleep.

I wake to shouting coming from downstairs. Damon left me, he doesn't normally leave me sleeping alone. I get up, I'm still only wearing a towel. I quickly put on some underwear and go find Damon.

"Something like that. Now get your nose out of my ass. You are lucky you are still alive after what you did to Emmie," Damon shouts.

"Making love to her, is that what you mean? Having her scream my name?" Liam is winding Damon up. I stand in front of Damon with my hands on his abs, keeping him away from Liam. "How much does it suck to not have her right now? I enjoyed her the other night. She was so good," Liam teases.

"Enough. Just enough." Damon is hurt and he shakes his head. I know he'd like to kill Liam right now but he must be holding back for my sake.

"Guys, enough, I can hear you from upstairs." I place my forehead on Damon's chest.

"Emmie please, what did I say about walking around without clothes on?" Damon's voice is hurt, I don't like my husband to be hurt. In my defence, I didn't even know anyone would be down here. I thought it would probably be Sully, they seem to be at each other's throats at the moment since Izzy.

"Yeah, save it for us in the bedroom," Liam says. I turn around and Liam winks at me.

"Get out!" Damon shouts.

"Guys, this is my house. Stop fighting over me." I don't deserve it.

"He has nothing left to fight for. He's with Izzy." He has everything to fight for, he loves me.

I giggle, "Till death do you part." I turn to face Damon and playfully bite my lip and he glares at me.

"Emmie," Damon growls.

"What's that supposed to mean?" Liam demands.

"Oops." I hold my mouth.

Damon grabs my arm and pulls me closer to him. "Liam, she had a breakdown yesterday. She's not thinking straight. She is under 24-hour supervision."

"I'm fine. I slept well, thanks to you." I look at Damon again. He looks terrified.

"You slept here? What about Izzy?" I don't know how much Liam cares about his sister but I'm guessing it's a lot because he kidnapped me for her and then after he fell in love with me he still continued this torture.

"Izzy isn't a problem anymore." I shrug.

Damon spins me around, "Emmie you need to eat, what do you want to eat?" he says quickly. He's trying to change the subject but one that I'm not interested in.

"No, what does that mean?" Liam says.

"There isn't any food in the house Damon." I don't store food in my house because I don't want anything.

"Yes, there is. I had Sully restock." Of course he did.

"Tell me what the fuck is going on?" Liam shouts, he grabs my arm and spins me around to face him.

"Calm down, Jeez," Damon says.

"We came to an understanding, that's all," I say.

"When did that happen?"

"When I lured her into the safe house and put a bullet in her head." Damon grabs my arm and pulls me behind him. What is it, grab Emmie day today? Damon has his body between Liam and me. I don't believe Liam would hurt me but I know how protective Damon is.

"What the fuck, you are joking..." Liam roars. Does it look like I'm joking?

"Of course she is," Damon says quickly.

"No, I'm not. I found out what she did. How she destroyed me, forced Damon to marry her. She didn't deserve to live anymore. Her voice was so whiny."

"Emmie shut up," Damon growls.

"No Emmie, carry on." All these mixed signals.

"Ha, bless her, she begged for her life. She underestimated me. People shouldn't do that. She told me you were her brother. I looked her in the eyes and shot her in the head."

"Emmie, jeez, shut your mouth already," Damon demands. Liam has gone quiet, he's as white as a ghost.

"I dragged her to the holding cell where I shot Desmond. I engraved an E in their bodies. Used their blood to write my name on the wall. I was satisfied that I did enough."

Liam shakes his head, "Emmie, you are nuts. Mental. Sick." I know I am, I'm not well. Does that mean you don't love me anymore?

"She's not well. She doesn't mean anything," Damon says, protecting me.

"Like hell she does. You killed my sister." He points his finger at me whilst shouting at me. I clutch Damon's t-shirt.

"Oh please, I did you a favour," I say. Sully comes running from nowhere and stands in front of Damon, protecting us both I guess.

"Boss, shall I kick him out?" Sully says casually.

"She is fucked up. She needs to die." I've wanted to die many times, it doesn't scare me to die.

"Yeah, that's not going to happen," Damon scoffs.

"What about your baby...?" I whisper but he heard me.

"You killed my sister Emmie. How am I supposed to forgive that? How could you?" An eye for an eye.

"I'd say I'm sorry but I'm not. All I can say is I snapped. After all the crap people have given me, rage took over. She ruined my life, Liam."

Liam's face softens, "Princess, I know she wasn't a good person. But she was my sister. Didn't you think I'd be upset?" He called me princess, maybe he still cares.

"You never seemed to like her. I thought I was doing everyone a favour. Please, Liam. I love you," I say, holding tighter to Damon's shirt.

He sighs, "I love you too princess."

Someone knocks at the door and Liam turns around to get the door. Lucas walks in the door with a huge smile on his face, why is he so happy? "How's my patient today?"

"Better, I slept really well." Damon was with me.

"Emmie, go get dressed," Damon snaps. I roll my eyes.

"I can join you if you like," Liam says, flirting with me.

"I'm a big girl. I can take care of myself," I say.

"Mmm, I meant..." Liam says but Damon interrupts him by coughing. I'm pretty sure I know what he meant.

"Emmie, get your ass upstairs," Damon demands.

I roll my eyes. " Okay. I'm going."

I walk out of the room but I hear them talking so I stop and listen. "How has she been?" Lucas asks.

"She slept well. She was peaceful. I just haven't succeeded with the food yet. This jackass got in the way." Damon really is being patient with Liam.

"I never had any issues getting her to eat. You just have to wine and dine her," Liam says, teasing.

"You are driving me nuts," Damon sighs. I love you, Damon.

"You need to get her to eat Rider," Lucas says.

"I can help with that, she can't resist me," Liam says. If Damon can't get me to eat, you can't.

"We don't need your help," Damon scoffs.

"We need all the help we can get," Lucas says.

"Not from him," Damon growls. I've had enough listening so I run upstairs to change. I settle for something comfy shorts and a top. I don't bother brushing my hair.

When I'm back in the living room, I sit on the sofa and curl up. "Damn princess, you look hot. Although you'd look better without your clothes."

I roll my eyes at him and glance at Damon who is angry.

"Emmie, I need you to eat something now," Lucas says.

I put my hand over my mouth, I feel sick thinking about food. "Excuse me," I say and run to the bathroom. Urgh, I hate being sick. When I finish, I wipe my face and walk back into the living room. Damon is sat on the sofa and I curl up on his lap, I'm tired already.

"You okay baby?" he says, stroking my hair.

"Yeah, I'm okay." Someone knocks on the door.

"Ahh, that'll be your counsellor," Lucas says.

"Boss, if you need anything else, I'll be at the safe house." He's avoiding me since our kiss. I hate that he is doing this. I miss him being so natural around me. Maybe he's decided we can't be friends and that he will treat me as an employer, so to speak.

"Thanks Sully," Damon says. Sully doesn't look at me, he just walks to the door, invites the guest in and leaves.

"Hey, Lucas," the counsellor says. He is young, really young and hot. Smart black hair, he's dressed in smart but casual clothes. He looks like a god with his hotness. But I stop staring at his looks, he will never be as good looking as Damon. I snuggle closer to Damon and he strokes my hair again.

"Hey Stefan, thanks for coming." They both shake hands.

"So who's the patient?" Stefan's eyes scan the room and then his eyes settle on me. I guess it's that obvious.

"Stefan, this is Emmie."

"Well hello, pretty lady." I roll my eyes. Why do people always say that?

"Doc, don't you think a lady shrink would have been better?" Damon says with disgust.

"Yeah, I agree," Liam says. Wow, something they actually agree on.

"Nice to meet you, Stefan. Wow, I can't believe you two actually agreed on something."

"We agree that you are beautiful." Liam winks at me.

"Maybe you guys should give us some privacy," Lucas says.

"Okay." Liam shrugs and leaves the room.

Damon grabs my shoulders so I sit up. He holds my face in his hands,

"If you need anything baby, I'll be in the other room." I nod and he kisses my forehead and also leaves the room.

Lucas and Stefan sit on the sofa. I pull my knees up to my chest to protect myself. "So let's get started, shall we?" Stefan says. He has sat closest to me.

"So Lucas told me about your past, I hope you don't mind." I do mind, I don't like people knowing my past. Which is why I asked Damon to get rid of the information. But information can't be lost in people's memories.

"Lucas loves to talk about me," I giggle and put my chin on my knees.

"A woman that speaks her mind. Nice." Cuts through all the crap.

"Best way to be." I shrug.

"So Lucas said you won't eat. Can you explain?" If this is what we are going to talk about then this is going to be waste of time.

"I don't know you very well, I don't think I should share my secrets just yet." I smile sweetly.

"Emmie, come on. Don't make me get Rider," Lucas says. I roll my eyes.

"So who is Rider?" The love of my life.

"My ex-husband." I cringe as I say it.

"I see. But you listen to him?" Of course. He is the only one I will listen to.

"Of course, he's the love of my life."

"So why did you divorce?" It feels like he is ripping my heart out. I close my eyes to shut out the pain.

"Let's skip that question. Carry on Stefan," Lucas says. Stefan glares at Lucas but doesn't say anything.

"Okay then, so who was the other guy?" Stefan sounds pissed with Lucas.

"That's Liam, he kidnapped me. I fell in love with him too." My life is so complicated.

"Huh. You have a lot of admirers." He smiles at me.

"You have no idea. 4 in total that I care about, I have no idea why they chase me." I sound like such a whore. But it's not like I'm sleeping with them all. I had chosen who I wanted but something keeps pulling us apart.

"Emmie, you are a beautiful woman. Why do you put yourself down? Does the long list not mean anything?"

Not to me. "I don't see what others see. My Dad drummed into me at a young age that no man would want me. Only him..." My daddy who loved me.

"So your Dad abused you?" I thought Lucas told you? Why ask me?

"Yes, I thought Lucas told you?" I snap. I don't like talking to him about this stuff.

"He told me the gist of things. So how do you feel about that?" How do you think I feel about that, you moron?

"How do I feel about my Dad abusing me?" What a stupid question. He nods. "I don't know, I was used to it. I guess that's how he showed he loved me. He always cared about me. He wanted what was best for me. Now he's dead, I don't get the same feeling anymore."

"What feeling?"

"Safe, like I was the only girl in the world. He was my Dad."

"I can understand why you feel that way. So you don't feel safe?" You can? Nobody apart from Damon understood and deep down he never understood how I felt but he always said the right thing.

"I did. For a long while with Damon." And then he went and married someone else.

"Who's Damon?" he says, confused.

"Damon is Rider's first name. Only family calls him Damon," Lucas says.

"Okay, so he loves you enough for you to call him that. So why don't you feel safe with him anymore?" Yeah, but he let Izzy call him that which hurt.

"Let's skip this question. Carry on Stefan," Lucas says again. Stefan turns to face Lucas.

"Why do you keep blocking my questions? Do you see me blocking your surgeries?" Oh shit, Stefan isn't happy.

"There are things she can't repeat okay and it's best that you don't know." How much does Lucas know? It sounds like a lot.

"You know what Emmie says is confidential. I can't pass it on, even to the police."

"But once you know, you can't un-know." Well, that's generally how it works Lucas.

"For me to help Emmie, I need to know everything." Everything? All my insecurities, all the abuse I've had, how I'm so fucked up?

"Right Emmie, please answer my question," Stefan says whilst turning to face me.

"He married someone else whilst I was kidnapped."

"Okay, so you feel betrayed?" Betrayed? And the rest, it broke me. I knew he loved me I just didn't understand what he did. He spent over a year making me believe he did love me. The best thing he did for me was marry me and now I don't have that security.

"I did at first. He was the only one that made me feel safe. So after he left me, I started feeling anxious all the time. My nightmares came back."

"What are your nightmares about?" Everything, my Dad, Rex, Desmond. Damon not wanting me, Damon dead. The list is endless.

"My past, when Desmond kidnapped me. When I shot someone. I see Damon dead on the floor. I see Damon with my heart and him crushing it because he doesn't want me."

"Okay, so who did you hurt?"

"His name was Rex. He kidnapped me. Used me for sex. He let his gang rape me. He was psycho, he thought I was his. I found out he took down my husband's plane. So I took revenge. He took me away from Damon."

"When you say his name was Rex?" he tests the waters.

"You killed him too?" Lucas says, shocked.

"Wait, so you've killed more than one person?" Stefan says, he's so calm. I like him.

"Well, I found out that Damon's wife blackmailed him to marry her. She hurt my husband. I needed to free him from her. So I lured her and I killed her."

"So you've killed two people?" I shrug.

"Not exactly."

"How many more Emmie?" Stefan says.

"Just one more. I killed Desmond yesterday too. After I killed Izzy, I went to see if he was still alive. He begged me to do it."

"Why would he do that?" Lucas says in disbelief.

"He was in pain. He wanted it to be me. He wanted to see his love when he died. He wanted his girl to do it."

"And how did you feel?"

"It was weird, I told him I wasn't his. But I felt good that he felt I was his," I say.

"Why?"

"After all he did to me, I felt special."

"Okay. So Izzy and Rex, you killed them both for Damon? So that means you love Damon." Yes, is he stupid? I've never questioned my love for Damon.

"Yes."

"I think we are getting somewhere. Why won't you eat Emmie?" You do? I don't feel any weight lifting unless I'm not supposed to.

"The pain, the aching pain I get. It makes me exhausted. Sometimes I don't want to wake up. It was okay before because I had something to live for. But now, I don't have the energy. I like feeling physical pain, instead of just mental pain."

"Is that why you always said you could handle the pain?" Lucas says.

"Yeah, you were never specific when you asked about my pain. Physically, the pain felt good but mentally, I felt like I was at 100 out of 10."

"So in a way, not eating is a coping mechanism?" Stefan says.

I shrug, "I guess. I would have killed myself before if it wasn't for Lilly-May and my unborn twins."

"You feel suicidal? And who is the Dad? Liam or Damon?" I've always felt this way, I was just all alone and no one saw me suffering.

"The world would be better off without me. But I can't kill my unborn babies or leave my daughter without her Mom. And both, ish."

"How can you say that? I feel you have a very large list of people who care about you. What do you mean both?" It means I'm so stupid and I end up having a rare type of pregnancy. It could only happen to me.

"Superfetation," Lucas says like Stefan should know.

"Wow, I've never witnessed that before. How do you feel about that?" He asks some stupid questions sometimes.

"Worried."

"About?"

"I love them both, I'm worried that one will leave me because of the other. They don't exactly get on well." More like they want to kill each other.

"Why do you think they don't get on?" Because they are both gang leaders, rivals most likely and they are staking their claim.

"I guess it's because they both love me and they are fighting for me. Damon doesn't like Liam for kidnapping me. Liam doesn't like Damon because he married his sister."

"Your life is so complicated," Stefan says, putting his hand on his head. I know, my life just keeps getting more and more complicated.

"Tell me about it. When Liam kidnapped me, he drugged me. I had no memory of before. He made up the perfect story of my life. I loved not knowing the pain I've been through. I knew I had issues, as I was terrified of men, except Liam. I ate like usual. I felt safe with Liam."

"How do you feel about him now?"

"I love him, sure. But I only truly feel safe with Damon. We've been through so much together."

"He brought her out of comas before," Lucas adds.

"Wow, so that's intense. So you love him that much?"

I blush, "Yeah."

"So you want to be with Damon?"

"I'm still undecided." Damon would be my obvious choice but he hurt me when he married someone else.

"How so?"

"Well, I still feel hurt by Damon's betrayal. Liam, I love him but he kidnapped me and blackmailed Damon to marry Izzy. Brody, the guy from the beginning, I love him too but he is with my best friend. And Sully, he's Damon's right-hand man, he is so protective. He took a bullet for me. We kissed the other night, now he hasn't spoken to me. My head is all scrambled. I feel out of control..."

"I can see how that can be confusing. But I think you know who you want. You are just scared of losing the others." That's what my mother said.

I sigh, "Always the same. I can't lose anyone else."

"For you to move forwards, you need to. Right, let me ask you

430

questions and you answer me." I nod. "When you think of home, what do you think of?" Well, that's easy. Damon.

"Damon," I say without question.

"When you are in trouble, which you seem to get into a lot, who do you wish to see?" Of course Damon. Always Damon.

"Damon." I shrug.

"What's your worst fear?" Okay, I get it. My answer will always be Damon.

"Damon dying, I see it in my nightmares."

"Well, you have your answer then. If the others love you like they say they do, they will still be there for you," Stefan says.

"I guess."

"So what now?" Lucas says.

"Emmie is depressed. Although I'd like to have her in a clinic, you insisted she's kept here. I am prescribing anti-depressants and some Diazepam for anxiety. I'd like to see you once a week." I need pills? How will this help me?

"Are you sure you won't miss me too much in a week?" I giggle.

"You have a great sense of humour Emmie. If you weren't taken by 4 men, I may try myself. You are a real catch." I frown, no I'm not.

"Hey, baby, are you all done?" Damon says and kisses my hair. He lifts me up and he sits down on the sofa with me on his lap. I relax a little and curl up into his chest.

"I guess."

"So what happens next?" Damon asks.

"I've prescribed drugs for her. She's to see me once a week. So, which one are you?" Stefan asks. Like he doesn't already know.

"This is Damon, my ex-husband." I exaggerate the ex. I don't like it.

"Talking about me, were you? Good things I hope. I don't like that term."

"I see. What term?" Stefan asks.

"Ex-husband." Damon sighs. I don't like it either.

"Boss, we could do with you down the safe house." Sully enters from the front door.

"So who is this one?" Stefan asks.

"This is Sully." I glance at Sully, he still doesn't look at me but he is blushing.

"The one that took a bullet for you." Stefan nods with approval, I think.

"I'd do anything for Emmie." Even now? After you've been avoiding me?

"I can see that," Stefan says and nods again.

"I will see you down there in a bit," Damon says and I clutch tighter to Damon. I don't want him to leave.

"Yes, Boss," Sully says and leaves.

"Are we done, princess?" Liam says as he enters the room.

"I'm guessing you're Liam?" Stefan says.

"I see I'm spoken highly of. We all know Emmie dreams of me." He winks at me. Hmm, actually I don't. Sorry.

"Do you never leave?" Damon curses.

"Emmie likes me around. You leave." Of course I like him around which is why I haven't asked him to leave.

"I see what you mean," Stefan says to me. He's referring to the fact that they don't get on.

"What's not to like, look at this body," Liam says, showing his abs off with his hands. I bite my lip.

"No one wants to look at your body. Shall I buy you a shirt?" Damon snaps.

"Emmie, would you like me to wear a shirt?" Liam grins at me. That's not fair because his muscles are to die for and any girl would be mesmerised by them.

"No," I whisper.

"See, Emmie likes it," Liam taunts Damon. They are like squabbling kids.

"I'm going to the safe house before I do something. Liam, would you come to help with our situation?" He goes to stand up but I hug his neck. "Hey shhh, I'll be back soon," he says, soothing me because of my reaction. He kisses my lips and sets me back on the sofa and I pull my knees to my chest again.

"What would that be?" Liam says, raising an eyebrow.

"Your sister," Damon says awkwardly.

"Wait, no! He can't," I say anxiously. He will see what I did to his sister and then he'll hate me.

"Why not?" Damon says, confused.

"I left her in a state, he won't want to see that."

"Do you feel bad Emmie?" Stefan asks. No. Why would I?

"Not really, I just don't want Liam to be hurt."

"Aww, I knew you cared princess. I can handle it. Don't worry. I'll see you later." He kisses my hair and leaves the house.

"I will be back later Mi Chica Bella. Shall I send Sully back to watch you?" Sully doesn't want to speak to me so I won't force him.

"He doesn't want to speak to me at the moment so I guess not."

Damon looks confused. "Why doesn't he want to speak to you?" I can't tell Damon that we kissed. Damon will probably kill Sully, he trusts him.

"Doesn't matter."

"Do you want him here?" Of course I do.

"Yeah. I don't want to be alone."

"Then he will come. See you later beautiful," Damon says and leaves the room. I'm left with the Doctor and the Shrink. Neither of them I feel particularly safe with.

Chapter 38

"I can see they all overwhelm you," Stefan says. Damon has always overwhelmed me. But having more than one guy is worse.

"Is it that noticeable?" I start to fiddle with my hands.

"Yeah. Anyway, I think we have made progress today. If you need me before our next session, then just call. Please try to eat something. With your medication, you'll start to feel better."

"Thank you, Stefan. You have helped me." I think.

"Good, I'm glad. Well, goodbye," Stefan says. I stand up and start to pace the room.

"Bye," I say.

"Just relax Emmie. We can stay until Sully arrives," Stefan says. Why is he always so damn calm?

"It's okay, I'll be fine." They don't settle me anyway.

"We all know what you mean when you say that Emmie. It means you won't be," Lucas says. That's so true.

"It's okay to ask for help Emmie. Help is good, you need to get better." I frown, but I need to be strong.

"I don't feel I'm going to get better."

"You will, I promise."

The door opens and Sully walks in. "You okay Emmie?" he says. I frown, he's talking to me now? He doesn't wait for my answer, he just closes the distance between us and hugs me tight. I relax in his arms.

434

"I am now, thanks for coming Big Guy," I whisper in his ear.

"Like I said, I will do anything for you," he reassures me.

"That's our cue to leave bye, Emmie," Stefan says.

"Bye Emmie," Lucas says and they both leave together.

"So why did you think I wouldn't come?" Sully says, releasing me.

"Because you haven't spoken to me since we kissed."

"Yeah, I'm sorry about that. I don't want to make things complicated for you."

"They already are," I say exhausted.

"I know. But I can see how much you love Damon. And since you found out that Damon was forced into marriage and that he does love you, I just thought…" He pulls me onto the sofa and I lay my head on his lap so I'm laying down.

"I love you, Sully, I just love him more." He strokes my hair and I close my eyes.

"I know Emmie. I know," he says and I drift asleep.

*

It's been a few days since the shrink came. He really did help me. I've been suffering in silence for years and all it took was Stefan to help me look forward. I am feeling less stressed, scared and anxious. But it's still there in the back of my mind. Lilly-May lives with me now. She is used to me again now. I don't let her out of my sight. She said 'Momma' yesterday. I still don't know what I'm doing about the guys. I'm just taking one day at a time. Izzy was declared dead. Which means Damon isn't married anymore. That's a relief but I honestly don't know how they got around that. Is there not an investigation or anything?

My phone rings so I grab it from the bedside cabinet in my bedroom. An unknown number, I don't answer them so I let it ring. I stare at the phone wondering who it could be. A text comes through.

Emmie Salvatore died 28th August 2017. May she R.I.P

What the hell? I throw my phone on the bed. Technically I'm still Emmie Rider. What is going on? I drop the phone in fear. 5 days away? I have no enemies, do I? They're all dead. What am I going to do? I thought all this shit was over. I'm better now. I don't want to die.

I dress in a casual dress. I head downstairs with the baby monitor, Lilly is asleep in her new room. Someone knocks at the door, I hesitate. Who could that be? I slowly walk to the door and open it. No one is at the door, but there is a wreath sat on the doorstep. I look around before I pick it up. No one is looking, I bring the wreath inside and place it on the table. I read the card, it says, 'Sorry for your loss. RIP Emmie.'

I drop to my knees, who is doing this? Tears fall from my face. My whole body is shaking. I crawl upstairs to grab my phone off the bed. I sit on the floor against the bed and ring Damon. "D-Damon." My voice is shaky.

"Hey, baby, what's wrong?" How does he always know something is wrong?

"You're not under attack, are you? I mean with another gang?"

"No why? What's going on?" I didn't think so, he runs his gang well.

"I'm not sure yet. Don't worry about it."

"No Emmie, tell me what's going on."

"It's nothing, bye, Damon." I hang up before he can say anything else. I throw my phone on the floor away from me. It feels like a ticking time bomb. Everyone is dead. What's going on? I don't understand.

I pull myself to my feet, my legs wobbly. I walk downstairs into the living room. I pace again wondering who could be doing this to me? I hear someone at the door and I start to back away terrified. The door opens and I see Damon. My whole body relaxes with him here. He walks straight over to me and hugs me. How does he relax me so much? "Thank God, it's only you," I say.

"Emmie, what's going on?" he says, pulling away, looking at me.

"It's nothing," I say, shaking my head.

"So help me, Emmie, if you don't tell me. Something is bothering you. Tell me." He's annoyed.

"I think someone has put a death sentence on my head. I thought everyone was dead Damon." His face drops like he never expected me to say those words.

"What do you mean?"

"I got a text this morning," I say.

"Show me."

"My phone is upstairs, I threw it on the floor." Damon releases me and runs upstairs to get my phone. He returns and passes it to Sully. I didn't even realise he was here.

"I thought everyone out to get you have been taken care of," Sully says. You and me both.

"I also got this wreath earlier. I have no idea who would do this." I point at the wreath on the table.

"Maybe Liam isn't as okay with this as we thought," Damon says.

I shake my head, "Liam wouldn't do this to me. Not to his baby."

"I don't know. You are not to go out alone okay?"

"Damon, I can look after myself." I roll my eyes.

"No you can't, you've proved that many times."

"Whatever. You can go back to work now." I pout at him.

"I'm taking you out tonight. I'll pick you up at 7 pm." He smiles at me. Taking me out? It sounds like a date.

"Well, in that case, I should go shopping."

"Seriously Emmie? Do you never listen?" Sully says.

"Well, why don't you come with me? Can go out for lunch," I say to Sully.

"Well if you are offering to eat voluntarily then who am I to say no?" Who said I was eating, it was just an excuse to get him to go shopping.

"Well, I'll see you both later. Have fun." Damon kisses me and leaves. The absence of him makes my heart grow heavy.

"I'll just go get Lilly-May ready," I say to Sully, he passes me my phone and I walk upstairs to get Lilly. My phone rings and I jump out of my skin. My heart beats fast. I glance at the screen. It's only Lexi.

"Hey, Lexi." I try to get my breathing back to normal.

"Hey Emmie, you sound better," Lexi says. She's still too excitable for me.

"I am much better." I feel better since I've been taking these tablets but I'm not fixed not by a long shot.

"I've missed you. Do you want to go shopping tomorrow? Just us girls? It's been ages."

"I'd love to Lexi but..."

She cuts me off mid sentence, "I don't want excuses. Just a yes." Damon won't knowingly let me go, not just girls anyway.

"Damon will kill me." She should know, it's her brother.

"My brother is a big softy really deep down. He will be fine and if it bothers you, don't tell him."

"I know he is but it's very deep down Lexi." How deep do you want to go? I personally don't need to reach very far to find his soft spot but I know not many people find that. But I've had to dig deep when I've made him mad. Which let's face it, I'm good at making him angry.

"So is that a yes?" Lexi says hopefully.

"Fine, I'll meet you at the mall tomorrow at 12 pm." I'm going to have to run there and find an alibi. She hangs up and I put my phone down my bra. I have no pockets. I get Lilly changed and ready and head downstairs with her.

"The pushchair is in the car already Emmie," Sully says. Wow, he's so helpful. We head to the car and I strap Lilly in. Sully starts the car and we head for the mall.

"So will you teach me to drive now?" I say sweetly.

"Do you want to kill yourself?"

"No." Stefan has had more progress than anyone. He is helping me move forward, although he makes me look to the past, he also makes me overcome them and move forwards. Where was Stefan 10 years ago? I may not feel so broken?

"Then sure, you want to have a go later?" I nod at him. I do, I do.

"Thanks, Big Guy. Anyway, how did it feel to punch your Boss?" I giggle.

"Honestly I was punching my best friend. I've never been so angry with him. Somehow I didn't break his nose like you broke Dyno's."

"Lucky punch I guess." I shrug.

A song I find familiar comes through on the radio and I turn it up.

'If you ever find yourself stuck in the middle of the sea, I'll sail the world to find you.'

Sully smiles at me and he starts to quietly sing the song.

'If you ever find yourself lost in the dark and you can't see, I'll be the light to guide you. Find out what we're made of when we are called to help our friends in need. You can count on me like one two three. I'll be there. And I know when I need, it I can count on you like four three two. You'll be there. 'Cause that's what friends are supposed to do, oh yeah. Whoa, whoa. Oh, oh. Yeah, yeah. If you tossin' and you're turnin' and you just can't fall asleep, I'll sing a song beside you. And if you ever forget how much you really mean to me, everyday I will remind you. Ooh. Find out what we're

made of. When we are called to help our friends in need. You can count on me like one two three. I'll be there.'

I lean on Sully's shoulder whilst he's singing to me. It feels like this song was made for us. *'And I know when I need it I can count on you like four three two. You'll be there. 'Cause that's what friends are supposed to do, oh yeah, Oh, oh. Yeah, yeah. You'll always have my shoulder when you cry. I'll never let go. Never say goodbye. You know you can count on me like one two three. I'll be there. And I know when I need it I can count on you like four three two. And you'll be there. 'Cause that's what friends are supposed to do, oh yeah. Oh, oh. You can count on me 'cause I can count on you.'*

His voice isn't as good as Damon's but he can still sing. And I love that he felt like he could sing this to me. He pulls up at the mall and we sit in silence for a while and then he grabs my hand. "You ready?" he says. I nod and we get out the car.

Sully gets the pushchair out the car and I get Lilly out. "Momma," Lilly says. Huh, she's awake.

"Hey, Baby Girl." I place her in the pushchair and strap her in. I push Lilly in the pushchair up the ramp escalator.

"Where did you want to go first?" Sully says.

"Primark?" I shrug. I don't really know what shops are about, Lexi usually just drags me in each shop and I don't get a chance to look at the name of the shop. Primark is furthest away so I guess that makes sense.

When we reach Primark, it's busy. I don't do busy shops, I get claustrophobic. I wander around the shop, looking at the clothes. I seem to have done the whole shop so I decide to go around again. Once I hit the same spot for the second time I decide to have another look around in case I missed something. "Really Emmie?" Sully says.

"What?" I snap. He wanted to go shopping with me.

"Nothing," he sighs. Wise Idea Big Guy. I poke my tongue out and him and he chuckles.

I pick up a few items this time. "Emmie," Sully says.

"Yes, Sully," I say.

"You may need a smaller size than that," he says, eyeing the dress I just picked up.

"Why? I don't want it too tight."

"Emmie, it will literally fall off you. Trust me, get at least 5 sizes smaller." I grab 5 sizes smaller and compare the size. I shake my head.

How am I supposed to fit in that? "Trust me," he says grabbing the smaller dress and hangs it over the pushchair. Of course I trust him, I wouldn't be out here in public if I didn't. I pay for the items and we head outside. "Emmie, we've been here hours and you haven't eaten. Let's eat. Please," Sully begs.

"Haven't bought any outfits for tonight yet. Please one more shop and I promise we can eat." Or he can eat. Whatever.

"Okay, Emmie." He sighs. I walk off towards another shop.

I hear him mutter, "Damn woman." I don't bother acknowledging that comment. I find three dress and decide I need to try them on. "I can't keep up with you Emmie. This is not what I had in mind," Sully says when he catches up with me when I'm about to go into the changing rooms.

"I'm nearly done. I want to try them on. Will you help me pick?" I smile at him.

"Emmie, you know I'll do anything for you. I'm sure you'll look great in all of them." I frown.

"Watch Lilly-May and I'll try them on." He nods and takes a seat.

I go try them on. The first one is a long black dress. You have to wear this one without a bra because of how low the dress goes. It does a V down my breasts. I glance in the mirror, I like it. I walk out to show Sully and his mouth drops open.

"Wow Emmie, you look amazing," he says, speechless. I smile and try on the next one. It's a nice shade of blue, it's knee length with white lace that hangs on my shoulders, the blue dress curves my breast perfectly. This one's not bad either.

Sully's mouth drops open again. "You look great," he says, staring at me. I shrug and try on the last one. The last one is a navy blue long dress. It has a slit up the dress to show off my legs. This dress also has a V shape that shows off my breasts. It has a small shoulder strap on both shoulders but also straps hanging over my shoulders.

Has Sully's mouth ever been shut? "Emmie, that one looks the best on you," he says, speechless again. People are starting to stare at me and I don't like it. "I love them all. You should buy them all. But wear this one tonight," he says.

I nod, I think I will. I head back to change. I never normally have the confidence to wear these sorts of dresses but I feel like I can now. I gather the dresses up and head back to Sully. We head to the till and I buy the dresses.

"Emmie?" Sully and I both turn around. I groan. "Emmie, is that you?" he says again.

"Yeah, who else would it be?"

"Still got that smart mouth of yours?" he says. He walks towards me and hugs me. What the fuck is he doing? I freeze.

"Can you step away please, sir?" Sully says. And he does, he lets go of me and frowns. You may be wondering who hugged me, yeah, it was Mr Dudley. Why would he feel the need to hug me?

"Who are you?" Mr D says.

"I'm her bodyguard," Sully snaps.

Mr D laughs. "Emmie doesn't need one. Her mouth can protect her." I grab Sully's arm and tip toe so I can whisper in his ear.

"Sully I want to leave." He nods at me.

"Well, we need to head back," Sully says to Mr D.

"Right of course. Well, it was nice to see you again Emmie." Mr D says and walks off.

"You okay?" Sully says when he is out of sight. Am I? After seeing my old inappropriate teacher? I shrug. He grabs my hand and leads me out the store. He pushes Lilly with one hand. We end up in a small cafe. He grabs Lilly a highchair and I place her in.

"You know," I say, "it probably looks like you are my date or something," I say, teasing him. He's said this a few times at the beginning.

He grins, "Yes I'm sure it does what with holding your hand and taking care of a baby." He hands me a menu. "So who was that guy?"

"That was Mr Dudley, my old teacher." I shake my head at the memory. "He always did little inappropriate things that made me uncomfortable."

"Your old teacher just hugged you." I look at my menu, yes he did. But why? Weird right? "What are you having Emmie?" I shrug. "I knew this was too easy." He sighs.

"I'll have a Strawberry and Banana smoothie and jacket and beans." I stick my tongue out at him. He seems to relax a little.

"I'll go order," he says, leaving me with Lilly on my own. I start looking around me, searching people's faces. Watching them if they linger too long on me. I glance at Sully and he's watching me confused.

I grab Lilly's food from her change bag. She's such a good baby, I hope that doesn't change. I feed her the baby food. And Sully returns with our drinks. Someone grabs a chair and sits next to me, my heart is beating out of my chest. "Hey, Sis."

I spin my head to look at him. I slap him hard. "Don't do that," I snap. He laughs at me. "What are you doing here?"

"Can't your brother do some shopping? I saw you so I thought I'd say hi." I hug him, I haven't seen him in a while and he returns the hug. "Missed me?" he grins when he releases me. I nod of course I have.

"Here's your order," the waiter says. "Can I get you anything else?" he asks. We shake our heads. "Anything for you sir?" he asks Danny.

"No thank you." I frown. He looks at me and sighs. "Don't worry Sis.," He says and grabs a tomato from my plate. "Now eat," he demands. He places the tomato in his mouth and raises his eyebrow at me.

I pick up my knife and fork and cut a small bit of potato and put it in my mouth. I gag but I continue to chew. "Good girl. So where is Damon today?" Working I guess. "Are you back together?"

I shrug, "How am I supposed to know? Probably not." He hasn't said the words and he hasn't touched me like that since I killed his wife. Liam has backed off slightly too but he still flirts with me. I don't like not knowing where I stand.

"He's an idiot then. Unless it's you that won't accept him back," he says curiously.

"May have something to do with the people I killed on my birthday," I whisper to him.

"What people?" he says in disbelief.

"Emmie. Not now," Sully snaps.

"Well, I killed Rex when Damon was missing. And then I killed Izzy and Desmond on my birthday." I shrug.

"Emmie. You need help."

"And I'm getting help Bro."

"Not from Damon, Emmie. I know he helps you but you need professional help." He sighs.

"And I am Danny. I've been seeing a shrink, he has prescribed me pills. You know to help me get better. And I feel better Danny, I do." I smile at him. "Except today." I shake my head.

"Why, what happened today?"

"I got a text today saying I will die in 5 days. I also received a wreath."

"Get up," Danny growls.

"Why?"

"You are going home." I shake my head.

"I'm with Sully, he will protect me."

"I'm not taking the risk. Move." I sigh, we have finished our food anyway. I look at Sully and he nods. Sully sorts Lilly out and puts her in the pushchair. Danny grabs my hand and leads me back to the car. I glance behind me to make sure Sully and Lilly are close.

"You are overreacting," I say to Danny. "Do you think Damon would take the risk?"

"Emmie, he divorced you and married someone else. I don't trust his judgement anymore."

"He had to, to save me," I protest.

"Emmie, he runs a gang, there must have been something else he could have done apart from breaking your heart." Sully unlocks the car and Danny ushers me into the front seat. "Stay safe, I will come over later okay?" I nod.

"I love you, Bro." He kisses my forehead.

"I love you too Emmie. I mean it, don't do anything stupid," he says. I nod again and he shuts my door and leaves. Sully gets in and starts the car. Lilly plays with her toys on her car seat. We head back in silence.

It seems as though Damon is home when we return. He is sat reading the paper when we enter the house. He looks up and smiles at me. "Hey baby. Did you have fun?" I frown, yes and no.

"Boss? Can you look after Lilly-May?" Sully says, once all the shopping is in.

"Yeah, why?" He looks at us both questioningly.

"Emmie wants to start driving," Sully says. I forgot about that. Damon's face falls...

"Well can you return her in one piece please?" Damon says. "We have a date tonight." A date now is it? He says go out and now a date.

"Sounds like you don't trust me," I say.

"Go, before I change my mind," he sighs. He takes Lilly from Sully, kisses me on the forehead and leaves the room.

"You ready?" Sully says. I nod and walk to the car. He sticks L plates on the car and then he holds the driver's door open for me. He reversed onto the drive so I only need to worry about going forwards.

He adjusts my seat for me. "Seatbelt Emmie." I do as I'm told. "Start the engine." I turn the key and the engine starts. "Put your foot on the clutch, that's your left pedal, Emmie." I put the clutch down. "Now put it into first gear. Now lift the clutch until you find the bite, you'll hear the engine lower its tone." Lower its what? I'm already confused. "There, did you feel that?" Yeah, I guess I did. "So that's your bite, that's what gets the car moving." He looks at me and I look up at him. "You ready?" he asks.

"Yeah, I guess."

"Now you know where your pedals are don't you?" I'm not stupid. I nod. "Okay, take the handbrake off." I do and the car rolls forwards. "Okay, easy does it, slowly bring your clutch up. Turn left out the driveway." I turn left as he said. I feel so out of control at the moment. It's rather scary. "More gas Emmie." More gas? I'm already going too fast. "Now take your foot off the gas and step on the clutch. Good, now change to second gear."

I manage to get it into second gear. "Sully."

"Yes, Emmie?"

"I can't do this. I'm going too fast. I'm not in control, I don't want to kill you because I can't drive the damn car."

"Emmie, calm down. You are fine, you are doing really well. Look, press your clutch down and put the brake on until you stop." I do as he says and the car stops. "Emmie, you are in control, if you want to stop then just do that." It almost sounds like he is talking about my life. Okay, I can do this. I place the car back into first gear and I get the car rolling again. I then put it into second gear and then third. This isn't so bad I guess. "You are doing amazingly well Emmie. How do you feel?"

"Shh, don't distract me. I'm trying not to kill you in an accident."

"Emmie, you are fine. You won't hurt me." I know I won't not willingly anyway. "Turn right Emmie."

We drive around for a while and I start to get tired. "Sully."

"Yes, Emmie?" I stop the car a little too quick and we jerk forwards but our seatbelts stop us. "Emmie, what's wrong?" I park the car and get out and walk to his side. He's already out and he puts his hands on my face.

"I'm tired, Big Guy." He sighs with relief I guess and puts his forehead on mine. He helps me back into the car and buckles my seatbelt. He gets in his side and heads home. He puts his hand in mine and I fall asleep.

"What happened?" I hear Damon say. He's so paranoid.

"She's fine, she's just exhausted. She really doesn't make it through the whole day anymore," he says. I guess Sully must have carried me in. I feel new arms and I'm taken into what must be Damon's arms. Sleep takes over again.

I wake and I glance at the clock and it's 6 pm. Shit, I need to get ready, I'm all alone when I wake which freaks me out. Damon normally stays with me. I get out of bed and run a bath. I get in the bath and relax a little. I feel my tummy, I have no bump yet which is good, I'm not looking forward to getting like a whale again.

The door clicks open and Damon stands in the doorway just staring at me. "You're awake," he says.

"What a genius," I say, teasing. He walks towards me and grabs my chin.

"You and your mouth," he says so close to my face. He kisses me and I grab his hair and pull him closer to me. He hasn't been this intimate since I've been back. I've hated not being this close with him but I won't force him to be with me. Part of me thinks that he'd rather have Izzy, I mean she's much prettier than me. "What you do to me," he says breathlessly. Does he feel this too?

He pulls away and makes distance between us. I frown, he just said that and now it's like he doesn't want to touch me. "Baby, what's wrong?" he says, sitting on the edge of the bath.

"Do you not want me like that anymore?" He frowns at my question.

"Of course I do. I just…" He shakes his head. "You are vulnerable right now, Liam may be happy to touch you like this but I guess I'm not."

"Is it because I slept with Liam?" I say.

"No, I don't blame you for that. What I'm trying to say is you are getting better from a breakdown, you can't know what you want right now." How would he know? Only I know what I want and I want Damon.

"But I blame myself for sleeping with Liam. I feel this yearning desire for you that I can't shake and when you push me away it feels like you don't want me."

"Baby, I will always want you and I hate that I did this to you. You were so comfortable in your skin, you believed that I loved you

445

undoubtedly but now you don't believe it."

"I need…" I close my eyes, "I need reassurance."

I feel his lips on mine and it feels like he's pulling his clothes off. He climbs in the bath and the water laps up over the bath. He pulls my knees apart and he hovers over me and then he's inside me. Yes, this is what I needed but it felt like I had to beg, but I don't care right now. It's me and him. He kisses me down my neck to my breasts and then he tugs on them with his teeth. "Damon," I say breathlessly.

"I love you," he says between each torturing kiss on my body. Everything is drawing me to this man. I've never understood this connect to him, everything in my body aches for his touch yet anyone else repulses me. I don't know what it's like for everyone else but it only feels right with Damon. Are we all supposed to have one guy that makes us feel like this? Am I lucky I found him? I thank everything that's holy that they brought me to him.

"Thank you," I say when I've recovered.

"You're thanking me?" he says confused, laying on me but he's taking most of his weight on his elbows.

"Yeah, I guess I am."

"Well, in that case, you are most welcome." He grins at me. "Come on, we need to leave soon." He gets out of the bath, making me miss his warm body on me. I get out and wrap a towel around me. We both head to the bedroom and he changes into some clothes. He stays with me but he hasn't moved his stuff in.

I go to find Sully to get my shopping but Damon stops me. "Where are you going?"

"To find my shopping."

"In your towel?"

"What's wrong with that? It's my house."

He sighs, "I'll go find your shopping," he says and leaves the room. I go to do my makeup, I know Damon doesn't like makeup on me but I do.

"Here's your shopping Ma'am." I throw my hairbrush at him but he catches it, damn it. "I'll leave you to get ready."

He leaves and I rummage through the shopping to find the third dress I tried on that Sully said to wear. I slide it on and go to the mirror. I guess I look okay for our date. I grab some shoes from the wardrobe and head downstairs. When I enter the living room, Sully and Damon are talking to each other, Lilly is awake in Sully's arms.

Damon looks up and his mouth drops open. "Wow." Sully looks up too and he seems to be staring too even though he's seen me in this dress already. "You look breath-taking," Damon says.

"Er thanks, you look good too." He's wearing a grey suit.

"Are you ready to go Mi Chica Bella?"

"Momma," Lilly babbles. I walk towards her and kiss her head. "Momma," she says again. I take her from Sully and she settles down. I rock her in my arms and after five minutes or so she drifts to sleep. I carefully place her back into Sully's arms. He strokes my face.

"Have fun," he says softly and I nod.

Damon takes my hand and leads me out of the house. "So how was the driving lesson?" Damon says when we are on the move.

"Well, all I was focused on was trying not to kill Sully if I crashed."

He chuckles, "Sully said it went well." Of course he would. He's probably just glad I didn't crash his car.

Chapter 39

Damon gets my door when we reach the restaurant. We walk in and my mouth falls open. It's so posh, like rich people posh. I shake my head, he knows I don't like these sort of places. "Table under Rider," Damon says to the waiter. He does a double take at me and I frown, yes, I know I don't belong here. Damon puts his arm around my waist, I look up at him and he is glaring at the waiter. What is his problem?

The waiter leads us to a booth away from everyone else, okay I can breathe now. He does know me better than I thought. I smile at Damon and he smiles right back at me with his sexy smile. We take our seats and the waiter gives us some menus. "Can I get you some drinks?" the waiter asks.

"I'll have vodka please," I say.

"No, she won't," Damon snaps. Jeez, I was only joking. "Baby, what do you want?"

"Vodka," I say.

"Emmie don't fucking test me. Would you like me to order you something?" he says. I shrug. "She will have an orange juice and I'll have a whisky."

"Sure, I'll be back to take your food order shortly," the waiter says and walks off.

"What the fuck was that?" Damon growls.

"What?" I snap at him, he's so uptight.

"Alcohol, really? You are pregnant and do you not remember the last time you drank too much? You promised me that night you wouldn't have

448

anymore."

"I was joking Damon, chill out. And you promised me that she was a random and yet you married her. She was all over you that day and you never pushed her away. And well, as for your parents they were horrible to me and you didn't stick up for me. I felt like an outsider, not your wife that day."

He sighs, "I'm sorry baby, I don't want to fight." Neither do I. "You know you are probably being difficult because of your damn hormones again." Probably, I was hell last time. I look at the menu to see what I can have.

"I know. I'm sorry, you don't deserve this crap from me anymore," I mutter.

"Can I take your order now? Here are your drinks. Miss?" The waiter looks at me.

"I guess I'll have the five bean chilli."

"I'll have the double cheeseburger," Damon says. The waiter nods and leaves us.

"Baby, I will take your crap any day if it means I have you," Damon says. I didn't expect him to say that. "Besides, you aren't that bad. I think you have the patience of a saint to put up with me." Put up with him? I know he gets angry sometimes but I don't blame him for that, he's protective and I like it.

"I wouldn't change anything about you. I love you the way you are."

"Do you?" He raises his eyebrows. "Well, that's good to know." I smile sweetly back at him. Oh, I do Damon, you are perfect to me.

"Are you still worried about Liam?" Everything seems to point back to Liam with Damon.

He frowns, "No baby, it's not. I don't always think about Liam you know. I guess you do," he snaps. I don't always think about Liam, I always think about Damon but not Liam. It feels like we will never get past this hurdle so why are we here?

The waiter arrives with our food and then leaves us alone. "I don't always think about Liam. I just don't think you have truly forgiven me." I don't blame him because I wouldn't. If he had slept with Izzy, I'm not sure I would have forgiven him.

"But I don't blame you for anything, there is nothing to forgive," he says, picking up his burger and taking a bite.

"Of course there is, I slept with Liam when we were married and I ended up getting pregnant with him because I managed to get some freak pregnancy thing and then I slept with him again after."

"You had no memory, I blame him for that, not you. That's what I'm saying about him taking advantage of you while you were vulnerable. He may have loved you but he was only thinking of himself." I didn't stop him so technically that's not true and I came on to him the first time.

I start taking small mouthfuls of the chilli, it tastes good, although I feel sick eating it. Will I ever get used to eating again? "You know, it's so nice to see you eat and starting to look better." I'm not sure I can eat all of this but I'll try.

"I feel better, even if I do have a bounty on my head." I still don't understand who would do this to me.

"As long as you don't do anything stupid, I won't let anyone hurt you." I feel safe knowing he won't let anyone hurt me.

"You know me, I can't promise that." I would love to promise that but sometimes it's out of my control.

"I'm serious Emmie, what would I do without you?" He will be fine, it's me that people have to worry about when he leaves.

He looks nervous. "Emmie, I love you." That's good to hear but I know he loves me.

"I love you too." What is this?

"I can't lose you, Emmie." I frown.

"You already did," I say because it's true.

"I want you back. I love you more than anything." He slides from his chair and kneels in front of me. He grabs my hand. "Will you marry me?"

What? He wants to marry me again? I don't know what to say. I never even thought about it. All I want to do is say yes, but the truth is, I can't. I married him because I couldn't lose him, I honestly thought that this would be the last time. I was so sure, but it was so easy for me to lose him, I'm not ready to go through that again.

"Damon I love you, I do. But no, I can't." I stroke his face to try to soften the blow.

"Why not?" He's hurt.

"I've married you already, yes it was the best time of my life, but I can't go through that again. I married you because you were the one. My life, and then my marriage ended so easy and quick. I can't have that happen again, Damon. I need to move forward, not back."

"You should move forwards with me. To marry me, this won't happen again."

"Before Izzy came along, you would have said the same thing then. Damon, my safety means more to you than my feelings. I need time, can you give me that?" If he had taken my feelings into consideration I would still be married to him, I may still be with Liam with no memory but I would have still been Damon's in every way.

"Emmie, I'd rather have you hate me than dead. Is that so wrong?" I could never hate Damon even when I thought he married Izzy for love. I will always love Damon.

"Yes it is, I would have rather died married and happy than to be here hurt and divorced and alone."

"How can you say that? You will never be alone Emmie." I'll always be alone.

"I've always been alone Damon. I just felt less alone with you. You made me whole."

"I will give you time if that's what you want but I can't give up on us. Everything we have been through. Don't throw it all away." He threw it away when he divorced me.

"All I want is time Damon. I never said stop trying. I love you, I'm just hurting." If anyone can get through to me it's Damon but right now I can't marry him. He stands up and sits back in his chair.

"Well, time it is. Let's go home, it's late." He calls the waiter over for the check. I feel guilty for doing this to Damon but honestly, I'd rather be dead and happily married than divorced. Him marrying me again won't cover the wounds of him doing this to me.

Damon settles the bill and we head for the car, he doesn't say anything, he must be angry with me for rejecting him. He was probably so sure that I would accept his proposal. I never even thought about marrying him again. Now I have though, I can't do it. When I think of Damon he will always be my husband but I can't do the whole wedding thing again.

When I wake in the morning, Damon and Sully have already gone to work. I texted Danny last night to come over to babysit while I go shopping with Lexi. I get out of bed and shower quickly. I put on a black mini skirt and a white strap top. This will do for shopping. I see to Lilly making sure she's fed and changed before Danny comes over. I leave her to play with toys in the living room while I sit and watch her on the sofa.

When Danny arrives, I hug him. He seems taken back by my affections.

"So where are you going?" Danny asks.

"I'm going to Lexi's house," I lie, the way he dragged me to the car yesterday he will never allow me to go back to the mall, especially unprotected.

"But you hate Lexi's parents." Yes, I do.

"Well, it isn't safe for me to be outside so I have to settle for this. Anyway, Dyno is waiting outside." Oops, another lie. "So I'd better go. Lilly will be fine for a while."

"Okay Sis, have fun," Danny says, kissing my forehead. I run outside and once I'm clear of the house I walk towards the mall. It will take me a while to get to the mall but I'm pregnant, not injured. I search the streets for any potential threats but I don't seem to see any. My heart is beating out of my chest. I'm always so anxious about being outside in the open. Now I'm on my own, it's worse.

I reach the mall and I find Lexi and Jessie where we had arranged. "Hey, guys," I say.

"Hey Emmie, I'm so glad you could make it. We are going to have so much fun." Fun with Lexi shopping? Yeah, not likely but it's nice to see them both. My phone vibrates so I take a look.

Oh Emmie, you make things so easy. I see you.

I search the crowd in a panic. I put my hands on my head. I'm such an idiot but they won't do anything in public, surely.

"Emmie, are you okay?" Lexi asks. I nod and put my phone away. "Okay, well let's go."

It felt good to be one of the girls again. We bought lots of clothes. Jessie informs us how happy she and Brody are. I feel a pang of jealousy, he was mine once. My life is crumbling around me. We start to make a move home. It's been a long day and I'm exhausted as per usual. We stand in the car park saying goodbye. "Bye Emmie," Lexi says and hugs me.

A black van drives towards us and I step back, pulling Lexi and Jessie with me. The van stops and someone gets out the van and they push us into the back of the van. I try to fight back but they inject me with something. Damn it, Damon is going to kill me. Everything goes black.

When I wake, I feel groggy. I've felt this feeling before, after I've been sedated. I look around and we are in a cabin type room. I see Lexi and Jessie lying on the floor. I push myself on to my feet and go to them. "Lexi, Jessie?" I shake them but they don't wake. They are still breathing though. I look around the room and find a note on the table.

'Oh Emmie, this is your fault. You got your friends into danger. Will they forgive you? The clock is ticking Emmie.'

What do they mean the clock is ticking? Are they talking about another four days until I die? A black curly haired guy walks into the room. He looks oddly familiar but I can't put my finger on it. "What's going on? What's wrong with my friends?" I demand.

"Settle down Emmie. They had the same treatment as you, we sedated you. You are obviously stubborn and you've woken up quicker than your friends. They will wake soon." He cocks his head towards me. I must be becoming immune to this sedation by now.

"What?" I snap.

"I think we should wait until your friends are awake," he says and leaves the room. I scream, damn it. I pace the room, I don't know him. Maybe he's working for someone.

"Ahh. Emmie?" Lexi says. I kneel in front of her and try to comfort her.

"You are okay." Well, not really but I will do what I can to protect her. I did this so I need to do something to save them.

"What's going on?" Jessie says. I grab Jessie's hand.

"I'm so sorry guys. I really am. This is my fault."

"What do you mean?" Jessie says.

"I shouldn't have gone out with you today. Not without protection at least." I stand up and pace the room again. "I have a death bounty on my head. Someone wants me dead. I have 4 days left before I die. I'm so sorry I put you at risk."

"You couldn't have known they would do this," Jessie says. Not this per say, I thought I would be okay. I never thought they would go after my friends too, I'm so stupid.

"Who is it?" Lexi asks. They both stand up and dust themselves off.

"I have no idea. I'm so sorry. But Damon will come for you, Lexi. And Brody will come for you, Jessie. I will make sure you aren't harmed," I say. But as for me, I am on my own. I'm due to die in four days so what does it matter? I just don't want to die knowing Damon will hate me for what I did to his sister.

"If Damon is coming for anyone Emmie, it's you," Lexi scoffs.

I shake my head and put my hands on my head. "He will hate me for putting you in danger and for disobeying him. I'm such an idiot."

"He loves you. It won't stop him from saving you." I know he loves me now, but he won't when he finds out.

The guy walks back in again and looks us all up and down in turn. I curl my lip up in disgust. "Who the hell are you? Let my friends go, you idiot," I demand.

"Emmie, keep your big mouth shut. You'll get us in trouble," Jessie whispers to me. I place myself between the guy and Lexi and Jessie. My mouth is what has saved me most of the time.

"We already are in trouble," I say to them. "Start talking," I say to the guy. The guy walks towards me and slaps me, hard. I clutch my face and the girls gasp. "How dare you?" I snap.

"Enough. Now, which one of you pretty girls wants to have fun with me?" He starts to look at us again and he bites his lip.

"Please don't hurt us," Jessie pleads. I look at her and she is terrified. Both she and Lexi start to slowly back up.

"Yeah, please," Lexi begs. They wouldn't be able to handle this and I don't blame them. I can't handle it. I've felt safe with Damon not having people force themselves on me.

"Well, one of you needs to obey. Maybe I should pick one. Maybe you," he points to Lexi. I shake my head, no not Lexi, not Damon's innocent sister. I can't let him hurt either of them. I'm dead in four days anyway, at least I will die knowing I've protected my loved ones. What's one more added to the dreaded list?

I close my eyes, swallow and then take a deep breath. My heart is pounding, I really am surprised I haven't died of a heart attack yet. "Don't touch them. Take me," I say.

"I guess you are the prettiest one and as you are the only one that volunteered… I have to say it may be wrong but I'm up for it." Of course it's wrong you moron. It's classed a rape technically. Although he probably would say it's not because I volunteered to protect my family.

He pulls my panties off. Wait, he's doing this in front of them? Is this guy for real? What's he trying to do? Humiliate me? Well, it's working. He pulls my top over my head. He looks at my scars. He traces the one on my hip like it's of some significance to him. It's the D that Desmond gave me. I close my eyes, his touch seems to be worst of them all but is that because it's been so long since someone else touched me without permission?

"I like this one. It's nice to see it in person." He likes the scar? Why? I don't get it. Jessie and Lexi stand there crying their eyes out quietly. They don't know what to do. I don't blame them either. They aren't used to this. As for me, I've had this my whole life. They both decide to sit on the bed curled up together, choosing not to look.

He removes his clothes and looks at my face. "Such a shame," he says. "If I had my way I'd keep you alive for my pleasure," he whispers in my ear. I stay completely still. He grabs my hand and leads me to the sofa. He pushes me down so I'm lying on my back. He gets on top of me and eases into me. He doesn't kiss me. I look up at him and I see him staring at the girls so I grab his face and pull him towards me. He grins and kisses my neck. I hate this so much, it's torture but I don't want him staring at the girls while he is doing this to me. It's creepy. Who am I kidding, this is all creepy.

He continues this torture for ages, minutes? Hours? I have no idea. I try to block it all out and then he finds his release and he sags on top of me. He's heavy, I try to move because he will be squishing my babies but he just lays on top of me until he has recovered. "Well thank you, sister," he whispers.

"What did you say?" I say, startled.

"You are hilarious Emmie. I know what you did. You killed my Dad. And I am going to give you the same fate." He gets up and puts his clothes on. Come to think of it, he does look a lot like Desmond. I knew he looked familiar.

"Wait, what? You just raped your step sister. You are sick," Jessie says, her voice shaky.

"She was very good actually. I wanted to stand in my father's footsteps. I did say it was wrong. But it made it better that it was wrong. Hey, I'm a man, this is what we do." No, only sick men do it. Damon wouldn't dream of doing this to a woman. I miss Damon so much already.

"You are Desmond's son?" I say. I sit up and cover myself with my arms. "Great, let's add another family member who has abused me." Daddy, Desmond and now him.

"Yes, I'm Denny. You are beautiful. And yes, I know you killed him. I saw the E on his body." He saw the E? Was he released with Izzy?

"Emmie wouldn't do that," Jessie says. They don't know but I have to defend myself.

"Sorry, Jessie, I did. He begged me to do it," I say gently.

"Why would he do that?" Denny snaps.

"He wanted me to be the last thing he saw. He wanted the love of his life to end his life. He was in pain." He was half dead anyway. I'm better now and I know it was wrong. I can't say I wouldn't do it again but I wouldn't jump into it so quickly.

"I don't believe you, our Mom is his love." Our Mom? She is nothing to me now.

"I think you are mistaken. He loved me, I didn't like it but he did. I was his girl." He told me and why else would he keep me for that long?

"Shut up now!" Denny shouts.

"I wanted to mark him like he marked me," I say.

"You killed someone, Emmie," Lexi says, scared.

"I'm sorry. I had to. He begged me. I was emotional. I'd just killed Izzy and he caught me at a bad time."

"You killed Izzy too? Emmie, I can't believe you," Lexi says. She shakes her head.

"You are crazy Emmie," Jessie says. I know I am. Tears fall from my face. I get up and grab my clothes and put them back on. My life is falling apart around me and I can't seem to stop it. I know people have to deal with things like this but has anyone ever gone through so much like I have?

"I was, I admit that. But I'm better now. Please don't hate me." I am better now, I know what I did was wrong. Stefan has been helping me and so has Lucas.

"Enough with this crap. I want you to meet the person that wants you killed," Denny snaps.

"So you aren't the one that wants me dead?" I say.

He walks towards me and grabs my face, "No, I was up for it at first, but now after having you, I don't think I can let you go." What is so special about me? I am ugly, I dread to think what would happen if I was actually pretty.

"So who are you working for?" I whisper.

Denny looks up at the door, "Come on in!" he says. I turn to look at the door.

"Hello, Emmie." I can't believe my eyes. I knew she hated me but enough to want me dead? My mother stands smiling at me. Why does she want me dead now? I'm her daughter, I don't understand. I drop to my knees, this can't be happening. Murdered by my own mother, am I really that bad of a daughter? Has this been boiling up for years or is it because I killed her husband?

Chapter 40

I sit on my knees in front of my mother. Tears stream down my face. Denny stands between my mother and me. I shake my head. "What the hell is going on?" I say.

"Your face is priceless," Denny chuckles. I glare at him, how could he find this funny right now? I just found out my mother wants to kill me.

"Hello, daughter," Mother says with a smile on her face. She looks as beautiful as ever, why did she have to give Danny all her looks? I can't hate my mother even when she wants me dead. What is wrong with me?

"You want me dead? I'm not your Daughter." She stopped being my mother when she chose Desmond over me.

"Ouch Emmie, we are family," Denny says, faking his pain.

"She stopped being my Mother when she sided with Desmond. Will you answer my damn question?" I'm growing irritated, I need to know.

"You killed the love of my life. You deserve to die. And you want to know something?" A life for a life, I get that. But I was ill, surely a mother should make allowances for that.

"Why would I believe anything you say?"

"Believe what you want. But you know your Dad told you I didn't want you anymore? He was telling the truth." All my Daddy ever wanted was for me to be safe. In hindsight, I can see that. So I am not surprised by this.

"What? You didn't want me?" This makes more sense how we never had that bond. I wish Addi was my Mom. If she didn't want me, why did she come back? She has been a hell of an actor, I will give her that. All the advice she gave me, trying to get me to eat. Crying when I was in hospital, she looked genuine. How could I miss that?

"No, I didn't. I hated you. I knew what your Dad was doing to you. I wasn't blind. And you know what, I'm glad he did. You deserved to be punished." I don't doubt that I needed to be punished, I know I was a bad person and I still am. I can't help who I am.

"You knew?" I say. She left me knowing what Daddy did to me. I really was all alone.

"How could you let your husband rape your daughter?" Jessie demands.

"Your Dad raped you?" Lexi says. I still haven't told her anything. I guess I won't get that chance now.

"Oh quite easily. You know, you were young at the time, but I tried to kill you." She's tried to kill me before? I stay kneeling on the floor, I can't move.

"What? I don't remember that." Danny told me she loved me, I guess he was wrong, she was a good actor. He could never tell what I was thinking until now.

"Your Dad caught me. He hurt me really bad. That was the day he kicked me out. He would do anything to protect you. He wasn't going to risk anyone hurting you." Apart from himself. He never told me that. He was probably trying to protect me. I miss my Daddy.

"Apart from him. Yeah, this isn't fucked up at all." My life is too damn complicated. Why should I keep fighting, it all gets worse every time?

"I came back to kill you. But everything kept getting in the way." She must have had many chances to kill me. Unless she wanted to make me suffer. Or Danny was always in the way. I just don't know. This is all too much for me.

Denny kneels in front of me and grabs my face so I'm forced to look at him. "Oh, sweet sister."

"I'm not your Sister," I whisper, I'm so exhausted.

"Yes, I am. Stop fighting me, Sis." He pulls me into a hug. I'm too tired to fight him so I just let him hug me and I lean all my weight on him.

"What about Danny?" I say, loud enough for Mother to hear me.

"I hated leaving Danny. I love Danny. But you, you always got in the way." She walks towards me but she doesn't come too close, she just sits on the sofa in front of me.

"Okay, we get it, I was the devil child. Now please let my friends go." I'm such a disappointment.

"And why would I do that?" Because they have nothing to do with this.

"Because if you don't, Damon and Brody will find them and ruin your plan." I know Damon will stop at nothing to find his sister. He loves her.

"They will come to find you too." She crosses her arms. Don't be ridiculous, Damon won't come for me, I've messed his life up.

"No they won't, Damon will hate me after this. You have nothing to worry about."

"Denny, what do you think?" Mother asks.

He lifts my face from his chest and looks into my eyes. "We don't need them. I think she's right. If he comes here, our plan is ruined." Yes, that's right. It will ruin your plan. He lets my head fall against his chest again. My body feels like cement. I feel so heavy.

"We aren't leaving you," Lexi says. I know I'm only going to get worse, they don't need to see me like this. Being away from my loved ones will help me during my last few days. I won't have to see their pain.

"Guys go. I'll be happier knowing you aren't in trouble. Please look after my daughter," I plead with them. My daughter needs to know that I loved her very much. She needs to grow up safe and happy.

"Ahh, my granddaughter, how is she doing?" Mother asks.

"Oh, so you care about my daughter, do you?" She cares about her granddaughter but not me? She will never get her hands on my daughter.

"Of course I do, she's family." She isn't your family, she never will be.

"I didn't think you cared about family?"

"I love my family, it's just you I don't like." I feel much better now. But I guess I already knew that. I don't feel like I have a family anymore. Something is tearing them away from me. I see them drift away from me.

"Well, it seems you are going to kill your much-loved family then." I peek up to look at her on the sofa in front of me. She seems confused. "I'm pregnant dear Mother. You are going to kill your grandkids."

"You're pregnant? With twins?" she says in disbelief.

"You are?" Lexi says, surprised.

"Oh my god, Emmie," Jessie gasps. Lexi's nieces or nephews. She didn't even know. Mother stands up speechless and walks out the room.

Denny lifts my head up, he stands and lets me fall. My head hits the ground, I just lie limp on the floor.

Lexi and Jessie run over to me when Denny leaves. "Oh, Emmie. I can't believe you are pregnant again," Lexi says, stroking my face. I close my eyes not wanting her to touch me but I'm too exhausted to push her away. I wish I could give Lexi and Damon these babies.

"When they let you go, please make sure Lilly-May grows up to know I love her. And tell Damon I love him so much, and I understand that he will hate me," I say. "If I knew I only had this long left then I would have accepted his proposal." Even if it's not what I wanted, I would have done it for him.

"Emmie, my brother won't hate you. He loves you so damn much," she sobs. I've never seen her cry like this. "He proposed to you again?"

"Yeah, but I said no," I whisper.

"Why? I thought you loved him?" Lexi says in disbelief.

"I do more than anything. He hurt me when he married Izzy. I can't ignore that."

"But he did it to save you," Lexi says.

"I understand that but like I told him, I'd rather be dead and married than here unhappy and divorced. Please just take care of them," I say.

"I promise Emmie," Lexi says. "But Damon will come for you." I won't hold my breath.

"You two come on. We are letting you go," Denny growls.

"We don't want to leave you," Lexi sobs.

"Please, I'll be happier knowing you're safe. Besides, Lilly-May will need her auntie," I say.

"She needs her Mom too," Jessie snaps. I have been a shitty mother, I've tried and I'd do anything I can to protect her but Lilly deserves more.

"Just go." I try to push them away but I don't have the energy. I don't feel their hands anymore and I hear the door shut.

I'm alone, all alone. I hold my tummy. "I love you, babies. Mommy loves you." So much.

"Emmie?" I hear mother say.

"Yes, Esme?" I whisper back.

"Are you really pregnant?" she asks.

"Why would I lie? What difference does it make?"

"I had to know whether you were making it up or if I'm actually going to kill my grandkids too," she says and then she leaves. So she still plans to kill me then? She is really sick, I can't believe that there isn't more to this.

I stay laying on the floor for ages, I just can't seem to move. I hope Jessie and Lexi got home okay, should I have trusted them to take them home safely? I hope I did the right thing. I hear the door click open again. I open my eyes to see Denny kneeling in front of me. He leans down and picks me up into his arms. He carries me to the bed and he lays in front of me. We stare at each other until I fall asleep.

When I wake I'm alone. I don't know how long I've slept for. "Denny!" I call. I don't move, I just lay where he left me. He walks in and sits on the bed facing me.

"Yes, dear sister? I'm glad you are awake, you've been sleeping for three days." How does my body shut out so much time?

"You care about me, right?" He hasn't known me long, but he seems to care about me. He hugged me and then he carried me to bed.

"Yes," he says without hesitation.

"I need my meds, Denny. I can't go without them." I can feel myself slipping already.

"What meds?" he says, thinking things over.

"Antidepressants and anxiety pills. I need them, Denny." He strokes my face.

"What do you need them for?" he says softly.

"Please Denny, I lose control when I don't have them." I'm scared of what will happen if I don't have them, I killed people before.

"I will see what I can do," he says reassuringly.

"Don't bother Denny. She's dying soon anyway," Esme snaps. I didn't even realise she was here.

"Please Denny," I beg.

"I think she needs them, Mom." He calls her Mom? Of course he does. Perfect little family.

"I said no," she snaps and leaves the room.

"I knew she didn't care about family. If she did she would wait to kill me."

"I'm sorry sis. If I could save you I would." What's that supposed to

461

mean? He is stronger than her, how hard can it be? I reckon I could take her if I wasn't pregnant. I'm so exhausted all the time.

"How hard is it Denny? She's not even strong. You could overpower her easy."

He holds his hands up in denial, "I'm not going to fight my Mom, Emmie."

"But you are going to let your Mom kill your sister? Nice."

"You killed my Dad, Emmie." I know and I'm sorry for that. I was ill, well probably am ill now after not taking my meds.

"You know what he did to me?" I say.

"Yes," he nods.

"And how do you feel about that?" That your Dad tortured me.

"I respect my Dad." Like father like son I guess.

"Do you know why I need the meds?" I say. He shakes his head. "Because of what my Dad did to me. What your Dad did to me. Being kidnapped by a gang leader and used by all his men. Waking up divorced without your permission. Killing 3 people. It's all piled up. And if I don't take my meds, I get messed up. I killed two people last time." I start to rock and Denny strokes my face again.

"Emmie, I'm sorry." Not sorry enough apparently. I don't want his sympathy.

"If you won't help me, get out," I say. Denny leaves without another word. I close my eyes again and I drift asleep.

"Sis?" I open my eyes and Denny sits next to me again. "You should eat something. You've been here three days." Tomorrow I die then. Great.

"What's the point? I die tomorrow."

He strokes my cheek. "You must be hungry."

"You know I have an eating disorder, I was okay on my meds. But I'm not in my right mind," I say.

"Please just eat something," he begs.

"My brother Danny, he tried to get me to eat once. I threw a plate at him," I shrug, well it wasn't at him. But he doesn't need to know that.

"You have many issues, dear sister." Yes, I do. He lays in front of me again.

"Tomorrow will be a blessing for me," I say. Tomorrow will be the end of my suffering.

"No, it won't be. I haven't known you long and I care about you so much already. You deserve a good life," he says, staring into my eyes. Why are people drawn to me? I feel like I push them all away but they spring back to me. I don't understand.

"No I don't agree, I deserve suffering. This is karma for all the bad things I've done. I'm sorry for killing your Dad. I just wanted to let you know that before I died. I think if things were different we would be great friends," I say. He puts his arm around me and pulls me closer.

"I forgive you," he whispers into my ear. Why? I wouldn't forgive him if he killed my Daddy. I miss my Daddy so much and he abused me. I can't imagine Desmond abused his son.

"I don't deserve your forgiveness. Was Desmond a good father?" I ask.

"Well, you have my forgiveness whether you like it or not. Yes, my Dad was amazing. He made a good life for me." I'm glad Desmond looked after his son.

"And what about your Mother?" I ask.

"She died when I was younger. I don't remember her. Esme has been like a mother to me. I love her dearly." I bet Esme loved that. Two precious boys.

"Why are you sharing this with me?" I say.

"Because you are my Sister. I feel like I can trust you." I frown, I am very trustworthy I guess. I'm loyal to my family even when they don't deserve it. "I wanted to apologise to you."

"Apologise to me? For what?"

"For raping you. Mom said I should do something like that. She knows how you feel about people touching you. She knew that you would do anything to protect your friends." He is whispering in my ear. I guess so Esme can't hear him. "Is that because of your Dad?"

"I don't know, I guess we will never know. I can only accept Damon's touch."

"Who is Damon?" he asks.

"My ex-husband."

"Ex-husband? My little sister was married?"

"I love Damon more than anything. I was kidnapped and for him to

463

get me back he had to marry someone else."

"That's so cute, what he did for you."

"Cute? He betrayed me. I'd rather be dead than divorced," I snap.

"I guess I can see why you need your pills." My pills haven't stopped me feeling this way.

"So I guess you haven't met the right one yet?" I say.

"Nope, no one has caught my eye, little sister."

"Well, I hope you find someone special like I found Damon," I say.

"Oh Sister, I don't want to let you go. I've just met you and I can tell you are one of a kind." I can agree with you there. I am one of a kind, there is no one like me, I'm broken, damaged, selfish, ugly and fat.

"It's okay. I'm ready." I'm not scared to die anymore. Since taking the meds, they made me value my life and I was terrified of leaving. But now I don't care again, I will have died to save my family.

"Sleep now, sister," he says, stroking my hair, my head on his chest. I match my breathing with his and I fall asleep.

When I wake I'm alone again. "Denny!" I call. I stand up and pace the room. I need Damon, I'm too wound up. "Denny!"

"Denny isn't going to help you anymore," Esme says, standing in the doorway.

"Where is he?" I feel calmer with Denny here.

"Oh, he is here. But he knows what side he's on." Was last night just to mess with my head? I put my hands on my head. I can't handle this anymore. I rock backwards and forwards on my feet. I die today.

Esme walks towards me and stabs me with a needle, I think on my side. "Ow, what did you do?" I say, dropping to my knees.

"I injected you with a drug that is going to kill you." This is not how I expected Esme to do this. I thought she would make me suffer. Torture me.

"Momma, please don't do this," I beg her, everything goes dark.

I feel arms around me, I feel so cold. I can't open my eyes, I can't move anything. I try to hear my heartbeat, my breathing, but it's not audible. "Emmie, I care about you. I did this to protect you. I love you, sweet sister." Denny? I try to reach out to him but I can't move. "You need to look dead, for Mom to believe you are dead and leave you alone. She will never stop if she thinks you're alive. I can only protect you so much. You need to fight the side effects of this drug Emmie. When the time comes, you have to fight to be noticed. But when you do wake. Which I hope you will. You have to stay dead. Mom can't know that you are alive. Dear sister, prove to me that you are a fighter. This is me protecting you. I hope you survive this. It's the only way. I hope you forgive me one day." I do forgive you, Denny. I do. He eases me to the cold hard ground. He kisses me on the forehead. "Goodbye, dear Sister." Bye Denny. I don't feel or hear him anymore so he must have left me. So what did he have Esme inject me with? I'm terrified, I'm not in control of my own body.

All I have is thinking time, Esme thinks she killed me and my babies. I have to carry on pretending I'm dead if I wake up. I hear a scream. Who is screaming? "I have an emergency," a woman says. She's crying, she can hardly talk. Is she okay? "I found a dead body." Whose dead body? Oh yeah, she's probably looking at me. I look dead. Why did he not just let me die? I block her voice out because it unsettles me even more.

"We believe her name is Emmie Salvatore," a guy says. My name is Emmie Rider! I may have got a divorce but I never changed my name back. I guess Salvatore will lead them to Danny. He is going to be heartbroken. I am lifted up and placed on something cold. I hear wheels turning, I guess I'm on a trolley bed. A sheet is placed over my body and face. Car doors slam.

I hate not being able to see, that's the worst part. Can someone not open my eyes for me? It's cold where I am now and it smells strange. I feel someone undressing me, no, no. If I'm dead, then I should be laid to rest. I'm so cold here. I feel someone washing me, is this what happens when you die? They make you look all pretty? I wish they didn't, I should put this in my wishes when I die. When I'm actually dead, I'm sure it won't actually matter. Has this ever happened before or am I the only one? Someone dresses me again, I'd better be wearing something nice. A sheet covers my body again.

"Come in!" someone yells, it makes me jump but I can't move. I hear feet entering the room. "I'm sorry, I know this must be difficult. But we need you to identify her body." Who is here?

"She can't be dead, not my sister," Danny cries. Oh, Danny, I'm here, please don't cry. I love you.

"She's stubborn. There is no way she's dead. This isn't her." Damon's in denial. Oh, Damon's here, I love you, Damon. I try to reach out to him but again I can't move.

"We had belongings that indicate that it is Emmie. But take your time. I will be outside if you need me," the stranger says. I don't think I had any belongings so what did they plant me with?

"I can't do this Damon, you are going to have to look," Danny sobs.

"It's not her Danny. But I will do it." Damon, I love you, will you tell that I'm not actually dead? I feel the sheet come away from my face. I smell Damon all around me. His head drops to my neck. "No, no, no. Emmie, no!" He cries into my neck. His touch feels good but he's never been so distraught and I can't comfort him.

"No, say it's not," Danny cries.

"It's her. I'm sorry Danny." Damon sobs into my neck still. Damon, it's okay, I will come back to you. I'll find a way, I promise you.

I feel a new hand in mine, I guess Danny has decided to look. "Emmie. What happened to you? You are the strongest of us all," Danny weeps. I am, I'm still here, I won't leave you. "She's so cold." I feel cold. I'm not strong, if I was then I wouldn't be suffering a breakdown.

"I love you, Emmie. I'm so sorry." Don't be sorry Damon, this was all me. Please, Damon, I'm alive. I will myself to move but nothing happens. I love you so much. "You are at peace now Emmie. No more pain. I will never forget you." I wish that were true but I am still in a lot of pain. I never knew they would react like this. Please don't forget me, Damon. I'm so irritated, I feel like scratching my skin raw.

"So have you identified the body?" the stranger asks.

"Yes, it's my sister," Danny sobs.

"Thank you, I'm sorry for your loss. Now time's up." No, don't leave me, Damon. I'm here, I'm alive god damn it.

"I don't want to leave her," Damon growls. He's still sobbing in my neck. My neck is all wet but I don't care.

"I understand this is hard but she doesn't know you are here. She's gone to a better place." No, I'm right here with you Damon. He removes his head from my neck and he strokes my face. I wish I could see his beautiful face but I know all I'll see is pain in his eyes. I feel his warm wet lips on mine. I'd kiss him back if I could.

"Goodbye Mi Chica Bella," he says and then the sheet covers my face again. I don't feel Danny's hands either. I'm alone. Denny said I need to fight when the time was right but it didn't work. What will happen now? My love thinks I'm dead. My soulmate, will I die a slow painful death? Denny will come for me if I don't wake surely? He wouldn't go to this much trouble. I think.

Chapter 41

It feels like years since I've been lying here. If I could twiddle my fingers or tap my foot to pass the time I would, but I can't. I'm just so cold all the time. Will I get buried alive? Nothing seems to be easing, I still can't move. All I want is to open my eyes but it doesn't happen.

"Can I help you, Sir?" the stranger says.

"I need to see Emmie Salvatore," the familiar voice says. Again, I am Emmie Rider.

"Are you related?" the stranger asks.

"Yes, I'm her uncle." I don't have an uncle so who the hell is it?

"Okay, you have 5 minutes sir." Why don't you make them show I.D or something? Some murderer could want to harm me, but then I remember I am supposed to be dead. I feel warm hands in mine.

"Oh Emmie, I can't believe you are dead." Wait, I recognise this guy, it's Mr Dudley. I hear him crying, why does he care so much? He was my teacher. I feel him stroking my hair, get off me. I want to scream at him. Punch him until he is cold on the floor. I'm ill, I know that. I haven't taken my meds. I don't even know how much time has passed. Do people normally touch what they think are corpses? I don't think I could, but I guess I've never been put in this position.

"Time's up sir," the stranger says.

"Thank you. I just had to see her. I didn't believe it," Mr D weeps. Oh, come on, you don't know me. Get the hell out.

"No problem," the stranger says. I don't feel anything so I guess he's gone. Thank God.

"You shouldn't be here Sir," the stranger says moments later. Who is here now?

"Please, I need to see her," Damon slurs his words. He doesn't sound normal, has he been drinking? Oh, Damon, I'm here.

"Sir, this isn't healthy. You're drunk. You should go home," the stranger says. I guess if I can hear his words slurring, I wonder what he looks like.

"Please let me see her. She needs me." Oh, Damon, I'll always need you. But I need you to take care of yourself first.

"Fine, you have 5 minutes," the stranger huffs. I feel Damon's hands around my face. I smell him again, my favourite scent. But it's mixed with hard liquor, he's really gone for it tonight. Where is Sully? Damon is too vulnerable, I dread to think of him walking the streets alone. Who is looking after Lilly? I guess now I'm starting to get a glimpse of what he means by he can't lose me. I never expected him to be this bad.

"Emmie, don't leave me. I can't live without you. Please come back to me like you did the last times. I am begging you. Emmie, are you listening? Of course you're not, you're dead." I can hear you, Damon, I'm here. I focus on my hand to lift it up to his face but my hand doesn't respond. "I felt the happiest man alive when I met you, my life only got better around you. And now you're dead. I can't let go, Emmie. Mi Chica Bella, I love you. I hope you are having a better life in heaven. You deserve to be happy."

If I could cry right now I would. Damon, what would happen if I did die? You need to let me go. I love that he is here, I do, but I need him sane for our daughter. "Boss, you shouldn't be here. Let's go home. Sleep off the booze." Sully? Oh, it's good to hear his voice. I've missed my best friend. I want to hug them both and end their suffering.

"I can't leave her. I can't Sully."

"Boss, she wouldn't want you to do this," Sully says, I can hear the hurt in his voice but is this because he can see his best friend hurting or is it me being dead? I can't imagine I made that much impact on his life. Right you are Big Guy, I want Damon to be safe and happy.

"When have I ever listened to what she wanted?" I know, which is why I'm declared dead and divorced. I'd rather be here dead and happily married. Saying that, he has always put my best interests at heart and I don't deserve him.

"Boss come on. Please. Let me take you home," Sully pleads with Damon. I think Sully is out of his depth. I wonder what he prefers, Damon like this or me having a breakdown? I reckon Damon would be easier to manage. I don't want Damon to leave, I feel safer when he is here.

"Fine," Damon snaps. His warm hands leave my face.

"Come on," I hear Sully say, he sounds close. Maybe he is assisting Damon. Bye Damon, bye Sully. I love you both. Stay safe.

Time passes painfully slow. I am lifted onto a softer surface. I hear something shut above me. Is this a coffin? I'm being transported? Where am I going? It's slightly warmer now but I'm nowhere near the temperature I'd like to be. I hear muffled voices and car doors. Denny, where are you? It smells like wood and linen here.

I hear what I imagine the lid of the coffin open. It smells of burning candles. "Here you are Priest." Priest? Are we in a church?

"Thank you. Her family will be arriving soon." My family? Is it my funeral? No, I'm going to be buried alive. I hear footsteps gathering in the church. It echoes around the room. Chatter fills the church and it's almost deafening as I haven't heard loud noises in a while.

"We are here today to say goodbye to the much loved, beautiful Emmie. I had the honour of marrying her to Damon a while ago. She was very happy, and all I thought was, what a lucky man. Emmie was full of life and she would do whatever it took to help and protect others. She never knew how great she really was," the priest says. This is such a downer. I'm not dead, I don't expect people to mourn over me. "Damon, would you come up now please?"

Damon clears his throat, I feel him stroke my cheek. "As you all know, Emmie didn't have the best life. But she always made the most of what she had. It hurt me that she never knew how much we all cared about her. I want to thank her for saving my sister that day. Protecting her. But what I'd give to have you still here." I will save my family no matter what the cost. I love you all. "Emmie was very stubborn. She never listened to me at all. But everyone kept saying she listens to no one but me. We have had a very rocky ride but I wouldn't regret one minute of it. Lexi said she was worried that I hated her before she died. I wish she knew that I could never stop loving her."

Oh, Damon, I can hear every word. I listened to you more than anyone. Damn it, move Emmie. I want to scream I'm alive but nothing happens as usual. "Thank you, Damon, if you would all like to sing this hymn."

I hear people rise from their seats. I hear music surrounding me.

'Amazing Grace! How sweet the sound that saved a wretch like me. I once was lost but now am found. Was blind but now I see. When we've been there ten thousand years. Bright shining as the sun. We've no less days to sing God's praise. Than when we've first begun. Through many dangers, toils and snares, I have already come. 'Tis Grace has brought me safe thus far. And Grace will lead me home. Amazing Grace! How sweet the sound that saved a wretch like me. I once was lost but now am found. Was blind but now I see. Was blind but now I see.'

The music cuts out and they all stop singing. Well, that was cheesy, who chose that song? "If you would all like to take your seats again. Danny, would you come up please?"

"I love my sister but she always found trouble. She infuriated me. I just wanted to say, the only time she was truly happy was with Damon. He healed her more than anyone could know. And she would want you to be happy." Yes, I want Damon to be happy.

"Thank you, Danny. Thank you, everyone. If you all want to come up and say your goodbyes. Then please do." Music fills the church again.

'Spend all your time waiting. For that second chance. For a break that would make it okay. There's always some reason to feel not good enough and it's hard at the end of the day. I need some distraction. Oh beautiful release. Memories seep from my veins, let me be empty and weightless and maybe, I'll find some peace tonight. In the arms of the angel, fly away from here. From this dark cold hotel room and the endlessness that you fear. You are pulled from the wreckage. Of your silent reverie, you're in the arms of the angel, may you find some comfort here. So tired of the straight line and everywhere you turn there's vultures and thieves at your back and the storm keeps on twisting. You keep on building the lies that you make up for all that you lack. It don't make no difference escaping one last time. It's easier to believe in this sweet madness, oh this glorious sadness that brings me to my knees, in the arms of the angel fly away from here. From this dark cold hotel room and the endlessness that you fear, you are pulled from the wreckage of your silent reverie. You're in the arms of the angel, may you find some comfort here, you're in the arms of the angel, may you find some comfort here.'

Okay, I love that song, I'd be blubbering if I could. "I'm sorry for your loss Rider. I'm going to miss her. This is my amazing wife Sarah." Wife? Lucas has a wife? He kept quiet about that one.

"Me too. I hate that she left me." I'm right here with you. Always.

"I'm sorry for your loss too. Lucas told me a lot about Emmie. I felt like I knew her myself. I really did want to meet her," I guess Sarah says. She sounds lovely.

"It's nice to meet you. I hope he knows how lucky he is to have you. I

470

lost my wife a while ago." Oh, Damon, I was lying to myself. You never lost me, I've always been yours. I will my hand to move. I think I got my fingers to move but I can't be sure.

"She's very beautiful," Sarah says. No, I'm not.

"You are glowing. How far gone are you?" Damon asks. Glowing? Since when does he use the word glowing?

"20 weeks," Sarah says.

"Only 20 weeks but you're..." Damon, don't be rude.

"Huge? Yes, I know, I'm having triplets." Triplets? Fuck that shit. One is bad enough. Does the Doctor have extra fertile sperm? Jeez.

"I wasn't going to say that at all. But congratulations. How did you guys meet?" Damon asks.

"I'm sorry you lost the babies too Rider. She was a patient of mine. It was love at first sight. Of course, it was forbidden. But I couldn't deny the connection." I thought I was his favourite patient.

"Ahh, Emmie would have been jealous. She thought she was your favourite patient." Oh, Damon, you know me too well.

"I have a soft spot for her too." I try to move my hand again. I don't know if I achieved it because I can't see. Damon, I need you, I'm here.

"Lucas..." Sarah whispers.

"Yes, sweetheart?" Lucas says.

"Corpses don't move, right?" Sarah whispers again. Did I move? Please say I moved.

"They can at earlier stages but not now. Why do you ask?" Oh, he sounds like such a smart Doctor.

"She moved Lucas," Sarah says. Oh, thank you, Sarah.

"Sarah, she's dead. You must have imagined it." I try to move again but nothing happens.

"Lucas, are you calling me a liar?" she snaps, go, Sarah.

"No dear. But she's dead." I try to prove Sarah right. I try to move my whole arm.

"I swear I saw her move. See that?" Please say he saw that.

"I did. I'm sorry I doubted you, sweetheart," Lucas says. Aww, they are so cute together.

"What do you mean she moved?" Damon's voice fills with hope.

I feel something cold and hard on my chest, it stays there for a while. Lucas prizes my eyes open, I can see. He shines that annoying pen light in my eyes. All too soon he lets my eyes shut. No, I want to see. "The stubborn girl is still alive. Get her to the hospital now!" Oh, thank you, Lucas. I'm saved.

"She's what?" Damon says shocked.

"She's alive, just. I don't know what's happened but she's not dead Rider." I feel warm arms around me, I'm lifted from the coffin. I smell Damon all around me again. I'm safe.

"But she's cold and she's not moving. What's wrong with her?" Damon says, nuzzling my face with his nose. He still reeks of booze.

"Boss, what are you doing?" Sully asks, he probably thinks Damon's gone mad.

"She's alive Sully," Damon says.

"What?" Sully says awkwardly.

"Take us all to the hospital," Damon says softly. I am placed on Damon's lap so I guess we are in the car. Oh, Damon, I love you so much.

"Doc, do you have any theories?" Damon says whilst stroking my face.

"I have a couple but the one I'm steering towards is that she has been injected by Tetrodotoxin," Lucas says.

"What is that?" Damon says.

"It's a drug to make you look dead, slows your heart rate and breathing. It usually lasts a few hours. Having a high dose can cause paralysis and cause her to stop breathing. She is very lucky she didn't die of this."

I feel us moving again. Feels like Damon is running with me in his arms. "Put her on the bed," Lucas demands. I am eased onto a soft surface.

"Wait, where are you going?" Damon says.

"Look, I need to do tests. I will come find you when I'm done."

"Fine," Damon snaps. The wheels of the bed start to move. Doors crash open.

"We need to warm her up," Lucas says. "Put her on fluids," he says again. I feel heavy things surround my body. Ow, something sharp went in my hand. I hear people rushing around me... Stop touching me. "Emmie, I think you can hear us. If you can, I'd like you to try to fight this." What do you think

I've been doing, you moron? "Someone go get Rider," Lucas snaps.

I hear slow beeps. Is that supposed to be my heart? I don't think I'm ever going to wake from this. It's torture not being able to move. At least someone knows I'm alive now. The door crashes open. "Ahh Rider, I'm trying to wake her up. Maybe your assistance will help."

I feel warm hands on mine. "Baby, come back to me. I love you so damn much."

"Sis, wake up now. Lilly-May is going to need her Mom," Danny says. Lilly? I hope she is okay. My baby girl, she doesn't settle without me sometimes.

The door opens again. "Oh thank god. You figured it out." Is that Denny? He came to make sure I'm okay.

"Who the hell are you?" Danny growls.

"Hey Bro," Denny teases.

Damon's warm hands leave mine. "I'm going to kill you," Damon shouts. No, he's my brother, he saved me.

"Wait a second," Danny says calmly.

"Why? Did you forget what he did to your sister?" Damon says. I guess the girls got home safe and told Damon.

"I want to hear what he has to say," Danny says. Warm hands find themselves in mine again. The bed dips, is Damon sitting on my bed?

"You are a feisty one, aren't you?" Denny says, is he talking about Damon?

"Start talking." Damon is irritated.

"How is she?" Denny asks. Another hand is placed on my head.

"Don't touch her," Damon growls. The hand is removed, did Damon remove it? Or did Denny move it voluntarily? "What do you care?"

"I love my sister. I hated her before we met but then I got to know her. I've tried to protect her." I think we bonded when I was going downhill fast.

"You raped your sister. How is that protecting her?" Damon snaps.

"My Mom told me to. She knows Emmie doesn't like to be touched. I actually wanted the red-haired girl. But when she offered herself to protect them it was hot, I guess."

"You are sick," Danny says.

"That's my sister you idiot." Damon sounds like he is going to kill someone.

"I have to admit, Emmie was prettier," Denny says.

"Keep talking," Damon snaps.

"Fine, Mom wanted to kill her. I formed a bond with my sister. I couldn't let her die. But Mom needed to know I was on her side. So I switched the drugs around. I gave her this drug to make her look dead. She's conscious, she's been awake the whole time. I told her she needed to fight when the time was right. This was the only way."

"You could have killed her. You could have told us. All the pain we went through." Oh, sweet Damon, I heard you hurting. I wanted to comfort you.

"Mom saw how broken you were. She had to believe she was dead." I bet she marvelled in me being dead. It's all she's ever wanted. I just don't know what I did.

"So we need to keep her dead and hidden?" Danny says.

"Yes, you do," Denny says. I don't want to spend the rest of my life hidden like some prisoner. No, I can't take that. No one can make me. I hear the machines crashing.

"Everyone out!" Lucas shouts.

"What's going on?" Damon says. He is scared again.

"Just get out Rider. Now!" Lucas shouts. Everything goes peaceful again.

Ow, this feels like when I gave up living and they shocked me to get my heart beating again. Why am I still alive? I still can't move so what is the damn point of this?

"Rider, you shouldn't be in here," Lucas says.

"Shut up. She needs me. I can't let her slip away. Not now. I have a chance, right?" I don't want to keep fighting Damon, I'm sorry. I've had enough.

"Fine, talk to her," Lucas says.

"Baby, I'm here. Come back to me. I'm begging you." I'm sorry Damon, I am. You don't know what it's like for me. Life is harder than it should be. I don't belong here. "Emmie. For fuck sake, wake up. Don't leave us." Damon is scared, he only swears when he is scared or angry.

"Emmie, wake up." Daddy? I'm sure that was Daddy. I will my eyes to open. I am greeted by Damon, Lucas and Daddy.

"Good girl princess," he praises. How is he here? He is dead. Unless he is not. I'm so confused, but I don't care what this is. I'm glad he is here.

"Daddy?" I say. Daddy puts his finger to his lips to shush me.

Damon and Lucas frown. "Hey, Emmie. It's Lucas." I know it is but Daddy is standing right next to you. Why is Damon not killing him right now?

"Oh, Emmie," Damon sobs. I lift my heavy arm to his face and he puts his hand over mine and he looks into my eyes. It still feels hard to move my body but at least I can move it.

"You guys are all downers. Cheer up," I say, exhausted.

"I thought you were dead Emmie. Give me a minute." I want to be but I won't ruin this moment for him. I peer over to Daddy who is glaring at us. He never liked other people touching me.

"I am dead Damon. Or at least we need to pretend." I pull my hand away from Damon's face and Daddy's face softens.

"I know baby. Denny told us. I'm going to kill him."

"No, he's my brother," I snap.

"What he did to you, Emmie. I can't let that go." He shakes his head. I won't have Denny hurt.

"Forget about him, Damon. We need to focus on Esme," I say.

"Emmie, how you feeling?" Lucas says.

"Alive, ish. I guess." Lucas lifts my bed so I'm sat up.

"Are you up for visitors?" he says.

"Sure," I say. I try to move my legs over the bed. Lucas leaves the room.

Damon grabs my legs and put them back to where they were. "What are you doing?" he growls.

"I want to walk around."

"Not happening," he says in his no-nonsense tone. I've missed Damon, even this side of him.

"Emmie, if you want to walk around do it," Daddy says. Why is everyone acting like Daddy isn't here? I shake my head, I don't want to push Damon right now. Daddy crosses his arms.

I see Lucas walk back in with a blonde-haired girl. He is holding her hand, I see what Damon means, she is huge for only 20 weeks. She's pretty, very pretty. I can see what Lucas sees in her. "Emmie, this is Sarah, my wife." I smile, she holds her hand out to me and I struggle to lift my arm so I assist myself with my other arm. We shake briefly.

"I'm so glad you are alive," Sarah says.

"I hear it's you I have to thank for that." I smile at her.

"It freaked me out when you moved you know." I giggle.

"Sorry. So, you're pregnant? You look amazing. I'm not looking forward to looking like a bloody whale again. Wait, are my babies okay?" I move my heavy hands to my tummy.

"I haven't had time to do a scan yet." Why not? They are more important than me.

"Don't worry baby," Damon says. Don't worry, is he crazy?

"I want to speak to my brother," I say.

"I will go get Danny for you."

I shake my head. "No, I want to speak to my other Brother." I want to see Denny.

"No, no way. Nope. Not a chance," he shouts. Oh, chill out, he won't hurt me.

"Damon!" He can't stop me seeing my brother.

"I said no. Your protection is going to be tight around here. I'm not risking your life anymore. I don't give a shit what you say. I'm not going through that again." What's his problem, anyone would think I nearly died?

"We will give you some time alone. Come on beautiful," Lucas says. They look awkward. They leave the room quickly.

"Damon, have you been looking after yourself? You stink... And I can smell booze."

"Emmie, I thought you were dead. I had to handle this in my own way." He looks sad. Broken even.

"Emmie, don't let him push you around. If you want to see Denny then do it. He saved you," Daddy says. I look at Daddy.

"What's going on?" I say to Daddy. I'm not sure what's going on. Can Damon really not see Daddy?

"What do you mean?" I look back to Damon who looks confused.

"Don't tell him I'm here. He won't understand," Daddy says quickly. I look at him again.

"He will understand," I say to Daddy. Damon knows me better than anyone.

"No, he won't," Daddy growls. Oh shit, Daddy's angry.

"Who are you talking to?" Damon says. I look back to Damon's beautiful face.

"No one," I say. Maybe Daddy is right. Daddy smiles at me and I smile back at him. I don't know why he is here but I love it. I've missed Daddy so much. He can guide me forwards, he made the right choices for me. I feel safer knowing he is here with me.

Chapter 42

Damon looks at me confused, he knows when I'm lying. Everyone has left us in the room alone, even Daddy. Damon lays next to me trying to warm me up. He kisses my hair. "Damon, I love you." I've missed him and my heart ached for him when he was hurting.

"I love you too baby. So much." He emphasises those words. He seems to still be hurting.

"I know, I heard you." I get flashbacks to when I couldn't move.

"What do you mean you heard me?" He sits up and looks at me so he can see my reaction, I guess.

"I was conscious the whole time when you identified my body. When you came back drunk. Damon, I never expected you to..."

"To what, hurt that you were dead? That's what you are thinking right?" He's mad. I nod, I didn't expect him to hurt so much. "I know you are off your meds but how can you think that?" I am off my meds but I'm not sure this is the meds.

"I don't see what everyone else sees, okay? All I see is a fat and ugly worthless human being." He sighs.

"Sometimes I wonder if you are blind." He shakes his head. My eyesight is just fine regardless of the fact that I'm seeing my Daddy. I don't need to see any more, I'd be fatter. Maybe he needs his eyesight tested. Lucas walks in with a scanner, I guess he has the ultrasound equipment.

Lucas walks towards me. "You ready for this Emmie?" I nod at him, is he stupid? They are the only reason why I'm still here. Lucas tilts the bed so it's flat and pulls the blankets down. I feel a sudden shiver and I grab Damon's hand to try to keep warm. "This may be a bit cold Emmie."

"Cold, are you serious? I'm already cold, moron." They both laugh at me, jerks.

"I'm glad you are back Emmie," Lucas says with a grin. I'm not, I wish Momma had killed me. All this heartbreak and abuse is too much for me. No one should have to go through this. But I deserve this, this is karma for all the times I've been bad.

"Ahh," I gasp "Steady," I say when Lucas squirts gel on my naked belly.

"Sorry, I did say it would be cold." Such a bloody know it all. Why is he so damn smart? I cross my arms in annoyance. I hear a heartbeat on the machine. I think everyone sighs with relief. "Two good strong heartbeats Emmie." I feel guilty, should I feel relieved that they are both healthy or annoyed that they are still alive? They were the only things keeping me here and I don't want to be here anymore.

"That's great news, isn't it Emmie?" Damon asks. He frowns. I nod. Of course it is Damon's beautiful baby that's still alive.

"I want to see Lilly-May." Lucas goes to wipe my tummy with a paper towel. I grab it from him and push his hands away. I wipe my stomach and cover myself. "And I want to see Sully." I miss my best friend.

"Sure, I'll get Sully to bring her in," Damon says, he gets up off the bed and leaves the room.

"Are you feeling okay Emmie?" Lucas asks. No, but I nod anyway. I resent him for getting my heart beating again. "You can go home tomorrow, okay? But I want you to stay here overnight." Fun times.

"Are you not fed up of my company already?" I snap. I hate being here at the hospital. It's so bright and unwelcoming.

"Do you need to see Stefan again?" He's easy on the eyes but no. I don't want to see him right now.

"No." Lucas frowns and walks out the room. Why are people so serious today? I lift my legs over the side of the bed with my hands. I ease myself onto my feet, I need to walk. Will I be able to? My heart starts to beat double time again. It feels weird beating this fast again. I feel my weight on my feet, I hold myself steady with my hands on the bed. My feet feel so heavy. I carefully walk to the window and feel the sun on my face. Each step feels like agony, each step gets easier.

I hold the window sill for balance, I stare outside for a while watching the cars, the people. My legs are shaky, I want to see Denny. Will he want to see me? Technically we aren't related, so it's not like he should want to see me. Maybe Damon is trying to spare my feelings that Denny doesn't want anything to do with me.

I turn and try to walk around the room. Who would have thought walking would be such a difficult task? It's like I've got to learn again, I reach the end of the bed when the door goes. I clutch the bed frame for support. Sully smiles at me and I stagger forward and jump into his arms. He lifts me off the ground and spins me around. I clutch his neck tighter. He carries me back to the bed and he places me back down so I sit on the bed.

He sits next to me and grabs my hand. "Don't do that okay?" he says. I've missed him.

"Do what?" What does he mean?

He looks at me like I've just said something stupid. "We almost lost you. Damon was a mess. He drank all the time." I figured as much. He reeks of booze but everyone copes in their own way I guess. He strokes my face and I close my eyes. "I want to kill them both you know." I open my eyes quickly. "Your brother, what he did to you." He closes his eyes. I know he is in a gang but I don't expect this from Sully. I see Sully as kind, sweet and protective. He just sounds like Damon when he says that. "If they succeeded in killing you I probably would." He opens his eyes again.

He removes his hand from my cheek. I lean my body on Sully and he pulls me towards his chest. He's so warm. The door opens and Damon walks through the door with Lilly. Lilly is awake and she looks around the room and she looks at me. "Momma," she says.

I smile and sit up. "Hey, baby girl," I say. She holds her arms out to me so I do the same. Damon places her in my arms. She's getting heavy. She starts bouncing up and down on my legs in my arms. "Careful baby girl." She's heavy and I'm weak. Sully puts his hands out in case Lilly falls.

Lilly starts to babble, she's really loud and she's hurting my ears. I've had silence for so long. Damon holds his hands out to take her from me, I nod. My arms are hurting. Lilly starts to scream when she is taken from my arms. Damon tries to rock her but she doesn't settle.

"I guess she's been without you too long and she doesn't want to let her Momma go." Damon frowns. I sit on the bed properly and Sully presses the button to put my bed to sitting position. Sully sits crossed legged at the end of the bed facing me. I hold my hands out to Lilly and once she's in my arms she stops crying.

I love her but I'm exhausted again. She starts to slap my face playfully and she giggles. "Careful with Mommy," Damon says. He slips in next to me and Lilly starts to slap his face instead but she doesn't move from my hold. Lilly's eyes start to droop. I take her in my arms and rock her slowly. She's being too stubborn, she just won't sleep. Her eyes keep opening to look at me.

"Come on baby," I say, exhausted.

"She's stubborn like her Mom," Damon says. I poke my tongue out at him. I shut my eyes, why am I always so tired now?

The next day Damon and Sully take me home. Once I'm home I head for the bathroom to take my pills. I open the medicine cabinet and take the pills from the cupboard, when I shut it again I see Daddy standing behind me. "Daddy?" I gasp and turn around.

"Hey, Princess." I walk towards him and I hold my hand out and he does the same. Our fingers meet, he's real. I can feel him like I can feel Damon.

"Daddy what's going on?" I don't understand. "You are dead."

"Yes princess I am. I'm here because you want me here." I hug my Daddy. He smells the same. It is a welcome smell to me now. I just wish I appreciated him when he was alive.

"You saved me from Esme all that time," I say into his chest.

"Of course, I love you Emmie. I couldn't have her hurt you," Daddy says. His presence soothes me. I pull away from him and go back to the sink to retrieve my pills. Daddy puts his hand on my shoulder and I turn around. He puts his hand on mine.

"No, don't do that," he says, looking at my pills. I frown. "You don't need them, princess. I'm here now, you don't need them."

"I should take them. I'm not well, I'm seeing my dead Daddy." I chew my fingers. He grabs my hand and pulls it away from my mouth.

"Trust me. I've protected you before," he insists. I nod, I open the tablets and flush my daily dose down the toilet. "Good girl princess." I trust Daddy, he always made the right decisions for me.

"Who are you talking to, baby?" Damon says, making me jump.

"Er myself, obviously," I say awkwardly.

"Have you taken your tablets this morning?" Damon asks.

"Emmie, lie. He won't understand. He doesn't understand you like I do," Daddy demands.

"He does understand me. He loves me," I say to Daddy.

"Emmie, he follows you around like a puppy. He doesn't trust you like I do. Lie," Daddy growls, walking around Damon, glaring at him as he goes. Is that what it looks like? Daddy is just confirming what I'm already thinking. I nod and shake the bottle and put them back in the cupboard.

"Emmie, are you okay?" Damon frowns. I nod, of course I am, I have Daddy with me. "Good, don't forget your appointment with Stefan today. We need to leave soon. Get ready beautiful."

"Okay." I roll my eyes. Jeez, I don't need to see the shrink again.

"Who is Stefan?" Daddy asks.

"My counsellor." I shrug at Daddy.

"You don't need one of them, Emmie. You aren't crazy," Daddy says irritated. Daddy should know, he's a doctor. I'm not crazy, Daddy just said it.

"Are you sure you are okay?" Damon says.

"Of course," I say. Damon looks at me curiously and then walks out the bathroom. I walk into my bedroom and find some clothes to wear. "I need to get dressed," I say awkwardly to Daddy.

He frowns at me, "Your point is?" I don't like anyone seeing me naked, that's my point.

"You can go now if you like," I shrug.

"Why do I need to do that Emmie?" Urgh, I guess he wants to stay. I shrug awkwardly and start to undress and dress in clean clothes. I probably should shower but I don't care. "Well, this one doesn't show off your figure but you look good in anything princess." I really don't care if I'm wearing a bin bag right now.

I walk downstairs to find Sully with Lilly. "Momma," Lilly says, struggling to get out of Sully's arms.

I smile at her, "I've got to go princess."

She screams, "Momma." Does this child even know any other words? I love her but I feel too much pressure.

Daddy looks over my shoulders at Lilly. "So this is the devil child?" I snap my head around to look at Daddy. Devil child? No, never.

"You look beautiful," Damon says. He pulls me towards him and he kisses me.

Daddy starts fake coughing, "How desperate? He doesn't deserve you.

Ahem, don't kiss him, Emmie. He's using you." I pull away and stare at Damon's face and then to Daddy's.

"He wouldn't do that," I say uncertainly to Daddy. I don't know anything anymore.

"Who wouldn't do what?" Damon takes my face in his hands. He looks into my eyes like he is trying to look through to my soul. He must see emptiness because that's how I feel.

"Nothing, let's go," I say and head for the door.

We sit in silence in the car. I listen to the music on the radio, I curl up and close my eyes. *'I will not make the same mistakes that you did. I will not let myself cause my heart so much misery, I will not break the way you did, you fell so hard. I've learned the hard way. To never let it get that far. Because of you, I never stray too far from the sidewalk. Because of you, I learned to play on the safe side so I don't get hurt. Because of you, I find it hard to trust not only me but everyone around me. Because of you, I am afraid. I lose my way and it's not too long before you point it out. I cannot cry because I know that's weakness in your eyes. I'm forced to fake a smile, a laugh everyday of my life. My heart can't possibly break when it wasn't even whole to start with. Because of you, I never stray too far from the sidewalk. Because of you, I learned to play on the safe side so I don't get hurt. Because of you, I find it hard to trust not only me but everyone around me. Because of you, I am afraid. I watched you die, I heard you cry every night in your sleep. I was so young, you should have known better than to lean on me. You never thought of anyone else. You just saw your pain and now I cry in the middle of the night for the same damn thing. Because of you I never stray too far from the sidewalk. Because of you, I learned to play on the safe side so I don't get hurt. Because of you, I try my hardest just to forget everything. Because of you I don't know how to let anyone else in. Because of you, I'm ashamed of my life because it's empty. Because of you, I am afraid.'*

The music cuts out and I look at Damon whose hand is on the off button on the radio. "I was listening to that," I snap. It felt so me, the way I'm broken. I'm empty even now that I have Damon. At the beginning, I never thought I'd feel this way about Damon. I would have taken any part of him that he would give me. Too much has happened for me to feel that way again. I'll have to live an empty suffering life.

"I know, that's why I turned it off." He glances at me. "I know you, even if you won't let me in anymore. You are taking these lyrics to heart." I frown. Is that how he feels? That I won't let him in anymore? "I want to fix you, but you won't let me." I can see the pain in his eyes. I see the pain in his eyes but I can't help him when I'm so broken. I can't give him me when I can't be me anymore.

He pulls up outside an office. Damon gets out the car and holds my door open. I get out the door and start to walk towards the building. Damon goes to take my hand but I pull away. He stops and I freeze too. He is looking at me like I stabbed him. I don't think I've ever rejected holding his hand before. He stops for what seems like hours, he doesn't say anything. Did I break him? He takes a deep breath and then walks again towards the building.

I wish I was a mind reader to know what he is thinking. I don't feel guilty not holding his hand, I don't feel anything but numbness to this life. I don't feel attached to these babies anymore, I feel disconnected from Damon. I'm disconnected from life. We reach a small reception area. The woman receptionist looks up.

"Can I help you?" she asks.

I frown, no one can help me. "Amy Silva is here to see Stefan," Damon says. Amy Silva? I know I'm dead but could I not have picked my new name? I want my life back.

"Miss Silva yes, Stefan will be out shortly," she says. Miss? He could have made me Mrs Silva. But then I rejected his proposal, so why would he?

Damon ushers me over to the seating area. Damon sits on my right and Daddy sits on my left. "Emmie, you don't need to be here," Daddy repeats. What does it matter? I tap my leg impatiently. Damon looks at me, I think he is being careful not to touch me.

"Amy," Stefan says and I look up and he is smirking at me. I stare at him blankly. He frowns.

"Can I have a word with you before you start?" Damon asks.

Stefan doesn't take his eyes off me, "Sure."

Damon grabs my face, I don't push him away, "Stay here," he demands. Where will I go? I nod and he follows Stefan into his office.

Daddy shifts his weight and puts his hand on my knee, "They're talking about you. They don't trust you." This isn't news to me in all honesty.

"Damon isn't as bad as you think." I try to stick up for Damon.

"No one is good enough for my princess. He hasn't protected you from danger." He has mostly, he's saved me every time.

"That's because I get myself into trouble." It's true, I always get in trouble, I never used to in Daddy's protection. I look over Daddy's shoulder to see the receptionist staring at me like I'm crazy.

"I never let you get into trouble. I had a way to keep you safe." I resented it at the time but I'm thankful for it now. I hate being so out of control. "Emmie, you don't need to be here." He grabs my hand and stands up. He pulls me up and he leads me towards the door.

"Emmie," Damon whispers sternly. I spin around. He is walking towards me. "I thought I said not to go anywhere." Daddy knows best. "Come on." He leads me into the office, Daddy doesn't let go of my hand.

"Hey, Emmie. Nice to see you again," Stefan says when we are safely in his office.

I shrug. "He's flirting with you. Shut him down," Daddy growls, why would he flirt with me? Daddy hates anyone looking at me, yes, that's what this is.

"No, he's not. Hi, Stefan," I say. Daddy lets go of my hand.

Damon kisses my forehead. "See you in a minute baby," Damon says and leaves the room. Stefan gestures for me to sit on the sofa next to him. He has a desk yet he is making this an informal chat. I guess that makes it more comfortable for me. I sit as far away from Stefan as I can, Daddy sits in between us.

"How are you?" Stefan asks.

I shrug. "Okay." I guess.

"So how you feeling after what you went through with your Mom?" He is annoying me already with his questions. How does he think I'm feeling?

"I don't have a Mom, Stefan," I say. Daddy smiles at me. I think this makes him happy. Stefan frowns at me.

"But you do Emmie, you have a Mom just like you have a Dad," Stefan says. Yes, and my Daddy is here with me, protecting me. He's taking care of me.

"Emmie this guy is a douche. He doesn't know what he is saying," Daddy says, annoyed.

"He is nice," I say to Daddy. He helped me before, he was the only one that realised I needed help. But somehow, I don't think he will help this time. I'm beyond fixing. "No, I don't have a Mom," I say to Stefan.

"Okay, so you have a brother. How do you feel about that?" Technically he's not my brother. I feel nothing anymore. I was happy that I found him, but now? It doesn't matter to me.

"I love my new brother but Damon won't let me see him." Damon forbid me to see him. Daddy says I should just see him if that's what I want. But I wouldn't have a clue of how to find him.

"Why, after what he did to you?" He didn't want to. Esme made him do it. It's not his fault, I don't blame him.

"He saved me. He loves me," I say. He did save me, everyone should be grateful for that. Unless like me they don't want me here.

Stefan shakes his head and squints at me, "Emmie, when someone does that to you, it's not love." How would he know?

Daddy puts his hand in mine, "Emmie, he doesn't know what he's talking about. I love you very much. You made me happy." I half smile at Daddy, I never doubted Daddy's love for me. I'm glad I made him happy.

"Please be quiet. I'm trying to think," I beg. I put my hands on my head and shut my eyes.

All these mixed thoughts are too much for me to process, I've tried to make my loved ones happy all my life and when they all demand different things from me I can't cope. "I am quiet Emmie," Stefan says.

"Not you and it is love," I say when I open my eyes.

"I know you've been treated this way all your life. This isn't how things are supposed to be. Is there someone here with you?" How is it not supposed to be like this for me? Nothing is changing. Nothing is easing. The pain gets worse.

"Yes." I shrug.

"Emmie, what did I say? He will think you're nuts," Daddy snaps. Crap, I've made Daddy angry again.

"Who is with you?" Stefan asks.

"Umm, no one," I say awkwardly. I'm not crazy, Daddy thinks he will think I'm crazy. He's a doctor, I trust his judgment on this.

"Emmie, you can trust me," Stefan says. I've only met him once before and I trusted him then but my judgement can't have been good then, could it? Daddy said not to trust him.

I put my knees to my chest. "He said I couldn't." Daddy sits glaring at me.

"So there is someone here and it's a he?" Stop forcing me to answer these stupid questions.

"Argh, Emmie, stop disobeying me. Or I will leave." No, he can't leave me. I grab his hand and he half smiles.

"I'm sorry, don't leave me." He can't leave me, I feel safer that he's here. He is guiding me.

"Then don't tell him anything," Daddy says disappointedly. I nod at him. I won't say anymore, I promise.

"Who is it, Emmie?" He is so nosey today.

I shrug, "No one." I hug my knees with one arm, leaving my other hand in Daddy's hand. Daddy smiles at me with approval.

"What's going on Emmie? I thought you trusted me." I did trust him. I do trust him. I don't know anymore.

"I do trust you." I squint at him.

"So why won't you let me help you?" Stefan says a little frustrated.

"I'm your Dad princess, you don't need him." I only need my Daddy. I nod at Daddy.

"He's telling you not to talk to me, isn't he?" Stefan sighs when I don't answer him. "Let's try something else. Do you feel safe now and are your pills working?" I don't care anymore.

I smile at him, "Yes, I'm better now." I have Daddy to help me, this is all I need.

"So you are getting on with your pills?" What is he getting at?

"Of course." I nod at him.

"God this guy is a bore," Daddy huffs. I agree, this is the last thing I want to be doing right now.

"Good. And your depression?" It's hovering over me like a suffocating blanket.

He needs to get off my back. "Better, I'm cured, thanks, Stefan." This is what he wants to hear, I'm sure.

"Emmie, you are far from cured. It takes time. We were working through the heartbreak. But now you've had more trauma, it makes it harder." I'm impossible to fix now. I'm beyond repair, this is all a waste of time. Please stop trying.

"I'm fine," I mutter.

"Of course you are. I'm here for you," Daddy says whilst he places his hand on my knee. I don't fit in anywhere anymore. "It's just me and you Emmie. That's all that matters." Nothing matters to me anymore.

"Is there anything else you want to talk about today?" Stefan asks.

Daddy snorts, "Of course there isn't, you idiot. You can talk to me, princess. Princess, you'll start to feel better soon. You don't need tablets for this. They won't help you. It's just masking who you really are." Masking who I am? So I really am this broken, worthless person?

Everyone is slipping away and there is nothing I can do about it.

"I know you are right," I mumble.

"What's he right about Emmie?" Stefan asks.

"Nothing," I say to push him away, stop trying to get to know me.

"I wish he wasn't so god damn nosey. So rude," Daddy groans.

"Are we finished?" I say.

"Yes, Emmie. I want to see you again in 2 days." God, was today not enough to make him back off? I said I was better, didn't I? I don't want this. I want to be alone.

"Why, you said once a week?" I snap.

"Emmie, we covered nothing today. I can't leave you a week." Why not? He's not going to help me anyway.

"Fine. Whatever," I say and get up and leave the room. Damon is sat on the same chair he sat in before he went in. He looks up and smiles at me.

"How did it go, baby?" he asks when I reach him.

"Fine. He said you should let me see my Brother." He didn't but I'd like to see Denny.

Damon's face screws up, he does this when he is mad. "I told you, you aren't seeing him." What's it to him anyway?

"Please Damon. If you love me, you'll let me see him." I use my puppy dog eyes to plead with him.

"Don't play that card with me, Emmie." Damon's face softens slightly, like he is crumbling.

"Please Damon, I thought you loved me." I know he loves me.

He puts his hands on his head, "I do love you."

I shrug, "Doesn't sound like it."

He grabs my hips and pulls me towards him and pulls me onto his lap. "Fine, you can see your brother. But you won't be on your own." I never expected him to let me see him on my own. I'm not that stupid.

I smile at him. "Thank you, Damon," I say.

He puts his forehead on mine. "Yeah, yeah." He sighs, I don't know why he tries so hard with me. I don't deserve it. "Why do you play that card, Emmie? I hate it." I've done it before and I know he hated it. It was when I was in hospital and I thought he married Izzy for love. I never understood then, but I do now.

"Because it works." I shrug.

He chuckles, vibrating my whole body. "Yeah, and you know it."

I giggle too, "Of course I do." Which is why I do it.

"I love you, Emmie." He seems to draw me back in so easily sometimes. I don't know how he does it.

"I love you too Damon," I say and he grabs my face and pulls me in to kiss me.

"I don't want him touching you," Daddy growls. I didn't even realise he was here with us. I am enjoying being this close to Damon right now so I don't pull away. "Emmie," he growls. "Fine, bye Emmie," Daddy threatens.

I pull away from Damon, "Wait, I'm sorry." I look at Daddy who raises his eyebrow.

"What's wrong?" Damon asks.

"Nothing. Sorry," I say to Damon. I climb off his lap and hold Daddy's hand. We head back to the house in silence again. Daddy is making me push everyone away. But somehow Damon seems to be pulling me back. It's like a never-ending yo-yo. I'm not sure which way is up. I feel like I'm drowning and no one can see me fighting for a breath.

Chapter 43

I sit on the sofa in my living room waiting for Denny to arrive. Damon phoned him to ask him over because I wanted to see him. Patience is not my forte. Sully sits next to me and I lay down with my head on his lap. "Do you never work anymore?" I say sweetly at him.

He laughs at me, "Who says I'm not working, Emmie?" Is his job still to protect me? I don't bother asking him to elaborate. I guess I don't really care. The door knocks and I sit up. Damon answers the door and Denny walks in. Damon and Sully seem to be watching him extra carefully. I climb to my feet and walk to Denny and hug him. He hugs me tightly back.

"Hey, sweet sister. I've missed you." I smile into his chest.

"I've missed you too," I say.

"What is it with all these guys touching you? Step away now!" Daddy growls at me. I do as I'm told and step away from Denny.

"Thank you for saving me," I say awkwardly.

He smiles at me, "You're my sister. I love you." I smile back at him. I wish it was a genuine smile for my brother but I feel nothing. This just seems like what I should do.

"He doesn't love you, not like I do," Daddy says.

I ignore him, "So does she still believe I'm dead?" Damon still had my coffin buried and my headstone was placed.

Denny nods, "Yes, she has no suspicions." How can he stand to be so close to Esme when she would go to those lengths to kill me?

"Good," I say weakly. Is it good? If she believes I'm alive, maybe she will come looking for me again.

"So does this mean you forgive me?" I already said that I forgive him.

"Tell him you don't forgive him," Daddy says. But that won't be true.

"Why?" I say to Daddy.

"He's not good for you. He cares more for your Mom. He won't be there for you. You are second best with him." That's true, it does feel like he cares more for Esme.

"No, I don't forgive you," I say to Denny. Sully and Damon gasp.

"So why is he here Emmie?" Damon says, shocked. Denny looks hurt.

"Tell him you never want to see him again," Daddy demands.

"But I do," I mutter.

"It's him or me, Emmie. Choose," Daddy growls. I shake my head. He wants me to choose?

"I wanted you here to tell you I don't want to see you anymore." I look at Denny and then look to the floor.

"What?" Denny says.

"You hurt me, Denny." Daddy is telling me to push you away and that's what I'll do.

"And I'm sorry for that." Denny looks sorry but it doesn't affect me.

"It's not enough." I shrug. I don't want to lose Denny. But this constant voice in my head is making me confused. I don't want Daddy to leave. He is the only one that gets me. I have to let Denny go. I walk over to Sully and I curl up on his lap.

"I won't give up trying to get your forgiveness," Denny says, heading for the door.

"Just go, Denny." I sigh into Sully's chest. I'm exhausted. I hear the door open and close. Goodbye, brother.

"Who is this idiot?" Daddy says, eyeing up Sully. Leave Sully alone, he is my best friend.

"Shut up," I snap at Daddy. Daddy crosses his arms in annoyance.

"Umm, okay?" Sully says awkwardly.

"Do you want me to leave?" Daddy says.

"No. I'm sorry," I say, why is he doing this to me? I feel like people want to stretch me in different ways but I don't stretch.

Daddy smiles, "Good girl princess."

"Did I do something wrong?" Sully says. No Sully, you've been amazing. I hug him tighter, don't make me push him away Daddy.

"Tell Rider," Daddy says. I don't understand.

"Tell him what?" I say to Daddy.

"Tell him about your kiss. Tell him you don't want to see him anymore." Why would I do that? What is Daddy trying to do?

"I don't want to," I beg Daddy. Please don't.

"Is she okay?" I hear Sully say. He strokes my hair.

"I don't think so. I think she's seeing someone," Damon says. Oh great, he must think I'm crazy now.

"Do you see that? They're talking about you. They don't care, so why should you?" Daddy says. I guess they are talking about me like I'm not here.

"Fine," I say. I turn on Sully's lap so I can see Damon. I hug Sully again. "Sully kissed me," I say to Damon. I shut my eyes to prepare for his anger. I feel Sully tense beneath me.

"What?" Damon shouts. Here we go.

"Emmie..." Sully whispers in my ear like he can't believe I said it. Daddy made me.

"He kissed me around the time I killed Izzy." I shrug. Sully tries to release me but I hold on tighter to him and he gives up trying to move. I need him for support right now.

"You did what?" Damon shouts.

"Come on boss. I thought you were in love with Izzy," Sully tries to soften the blow.

"I wasn't," Damon denies. Well, we all know that now.

"Yes, but how was I supposed to know that?" Sully says. Daddy holds his hand out to me and I take it, he leads me out of the room and upstairs into my bedroom.

"Get into bed Princess. You're tired," Daddy says. I nod, I dress in my PJs and then I curl up in bed. Daddy lies behind me. He strokes my hair, soothing me. I drift asleep.

"Emmie, someone is here to see you." I jolt awake and Damon is staring down at me. I groan and turn over to face Daddy. Daddy hugs me into his chest.

"Damon, I'm tired. Tell them to come back." I don't want to see anyone.

"Emmie. It's important," he says sternly. Nothing is that important to me that it can't wait.

"I said no Damon." I close my eyes again and I try to fall back asleep. I hear Damon sigh and he leaves the room.

"Good girl princess," Daddy says softly. I don't feel so good. I just let Daddy hold me.

"Hey, Emmie," I hear Lucas say. What is he doing here?

I turn over and Lucas sits on the bed looking at me, "Hey Doc, I told Damon I was too tired for visitors."

"This is important Emmie." I sigh.

"Okay." I can't see how important this is but okay.

"How are you feeling?" What sort of question is that?

"Tired, so tired." He woke me up for this meaningless conversation.

"Have you been taking your pills?" What is it to him?

"Yes of course," I lie. Not that he will be able to know.

"Emmie..." Lucas says sternly.

"He doesn't trust you, Emmie," Daddy whispers in my ear.

"What?" I snap at Lucas.

"Tell me the truth." How would he even know?

"I am," I snap again. Stop pushing me.

"Who's here with you?" Lucas asks.

"Another nosey bastard. I'm getting so fed up," Daddy moans. You and me both Daddy.

"They care about me. That's all this is," I say to Daddy to calm him down.

"No, they don't. Only I care about you," Daddy says softly in my ear.

Of course, Daddy is right. "I guess you are right," I say.

"Emmie, who are you talking to?" Lucas asks.

"Myself," I say.

"I want you to talk to me Emmie, and only me. Can you do that?" No, that's too difficult, too many voices surrounding me.

"No, he won't stop talking. My head is full. I can't concentrate," I say.

"Tell him to go. Just for a minute. I want to speak to you alone," Lucas says. Is he crazy? I can't ask Daddy to leave, he won't come back.

"I can't do that, he will leave me for good." I shake my head.

"He won't leave you. He's just bluffing. Do you trust me?" How would Lucas know if my Daddy is bluffing?

"Of course I do," I say, he has looked after me well.

"Then tell him to leave." Lucas shrugs.

"I don't want him to leave." I'm scared.

"Please Emmie, just while we talk. Can you do that?" Lucas says, reassuring me.

I shrug, "I guess." I sit up and look at Daddy. "Daddy, please leave for a minute." I shut my eyes waiting for his anger to follow.

"You can't be serious?" Daddy shouts.

"Please, just for a minute. I want you to come back though," I reassure him. I do want him to come back, he can't leave me.

"You've disappointed me," Daddy says. It goes quiet so I open my eyes and he is gone. I feel a sudden rush of anxiety and insecurity.

I look back at Lucas, "Is he gone?" he asks.

"Yeah, he's not happy though." I pray that he returns.

"So you see your Dad?" How does he know? Oh yeah, I said his name, oops. Daddy will hate me now.

"Yeah, he's here most of the time." I shrug.

"Are you not scared?" Why would I be scared? He protects me.

"No, he loves me. He always protected me. I know that now," I say.

"But he hurt you," Lucas rejects. You don't understand.

"He did it to keep me safe," I defend Daddy.

"Emmie, tell me the truth now. Are you taking your pills?" What Daddy doesn't know won't hurt him right?

"No, he told me not to take them," I say.

"Emmie, you need those pills." Daddy said I don't need them.

"Lucas, I feel so alone. I don't belong here. Dad is the only one who gets me," I say. I stand up and start to pace the room.

"Emmie, you aren't well. He's not real. This is your subconscious messing with your head." I stop in my tracks. Daddy was right, he said no one would understand.

"He told me you wouldn't understand." I back away from Lucas.

"I do understand, I'm a doctor and your friend. He's making you push us all away. But it's not him Emmie, it's you. In the back of your mind, you don't feel like you are worth it." Everything Lucas is saying makes sense but I can't believe it.

"I need you to get out. Daddy, come back now. Please," I beg.

"Don't shut me out, Emmie. I'm here to help." I shake my head. No. He is messing with my head.

"I'm glad you've seen sense princess." I look at Daddy and clutch his arm.

"No, you don't understand. Only Daddy does," I say, hiding behind Daddy. I see Damon enter the room.

"Hey Baby, you have more visitors." He frowns at me.

If the visitors are anything like this one, then I don't want to know. "Whoever they are, tell them to go away."

"Baby, you will want to see these people." Not likely.

"Emmie, please don't do this," Lucas begs. I'm a lost cause, just get out.

"Fine, I will see them. But Doc, you aren't needed here. I'm fine."

He looks sad. "Fine," Lucas says and leaves the bedroom.

"What's going on?" Damon asks.

"Nothing," I say. Daddy takes my hand and leads me downstairs. We walk into the living room and I see Lexi and Danny stood in the living room. Lexi is holding Lilly and they are both talking to her. Danny looks up at me and he smiles and walks over to me. He hugs me but I don't hug him back, I just continue to hold Daddy's hand and my other arm is limp.

"Hey, Emmie," Lexi says. What is this, gang up on Emmie day again?

"What do you want?" I snap.

Danny lets me go and holds my shoulders. "What's wrong Sis?" he says worriedly.

"Nothing, I'm just really tired. I need sleep." People keep disturbing me for no good reason.

"We have something to tell you both," Danny says and he releases my shoulders. I look at Sully who is again sat on the sofa. I sit on his lap again and face Damon, Lexi and Danny. Sully puts his arms around my waist. I rest my head in his neck, I'm so tired.

"Okay?" Damon says suspiciously.

"Don't be mad Bro," Lexi says. It must be bad if she thinks her own Brother will react badly.

"Just spit it out, Lexi," Damon says. He doesn't like people beating around the bush either.

"Danny and I are dating," Lexi says. My mouth drops open. But Lexi is gay, is she not? Why did she pick my Brother of all people to try and be straight with?

"What?" I say angrily.

"Don't be mad Sis," Danny begs.

Daddy is sat next to me on the sofa. "What sort of friend dates your Brother, Emmie? She doesn't care for your feelings. Danny is going to put her first from now on. There is always someone before you, isn't there?" I agree, there is always someone or something that is more important than I am. I understand, I do. Why would anyone put me first?

"But you are gay Lexi..." Damon says, speechless.

"There's just something about Danny I can't shift. I really like him." I've heard enough. Why do people keep piling this shit on me?

"Get out," I say.

"What?" Lexi squeaks.

"Emmie please," Danny begs. I guess they thought I'd be happy for them. How wrong could they be?

"I said get out of my house. I do not accept this. Nor will I ever. Leave. You can be happy together, fine. But you won't be in my life. Which hey, is fine because no one cares about me," I say. I turn and curl up into Sully's chest so they can't see my face. He strokes my hair to comfort me.

"Emmie, come on," Danny says.

"Emmie, be reasonable. Stop pushing everyone out. She's not well, guys. Don't take what she says to heart." Oh, you should take what I say to heart because this is what I mean. There is that word again, reasonable.

"I said get out! I don't want to see you anymore," I shout.

"Emmie, calm down," Sully whispers into my ear.

"Emmie, we love you," Lexi says. No, they don't. No one does.

"Get out before I kick you out," I say.

"I'd kick their asses if I could. You tell them, Emmie," Daddy cheers me on.

"Maybe you guys should go. I will speak to her," Damon says.

"Okay Bro," Lexi says.

Danny walks towards me and kneels in front of me. He puts his hands on my knees. "Emmie please, I'm your brother."

"Not anymore. I'm all alone. I just have my Daddy," I say to Danny.

"What do you mean?" Danny says in disgust.

"It's your Dad. You are seeing your Dad?" Damon says in surprise.

"Leave me alone. You don't understand," I say, I stand up and run out the house.

"Emmie, wait!" I hear Damon call.

I don't know where to go but I run barefoot in my PJs down the street. I don't bother searching the streets for potential threats because I don't care if I live or die anymore. Daddy has made me push people away, or I did according to Lucas.

I find myself at the graveyard. I walk over the grass and I find my grave freshly made. I sit in front of the headstone. It reads, *'If there ever becomes a time when we can't be together, keep me in your heart, I will stay there forever. Emmie Rider.'* There are no dates on here but I love the Winnie the Pooh quote. I'm glad Damon put Rider on here and not Salvatore. There are flowers here and I look at the note. It reads, 'beloved daughter and grandkids.' I grab the flowers and throw them away, like Esme really cared enough to place these flowers.

I put my face in my hands and start to sob. This is the day the Emmie we all knew and loved died. I can never be the person I was. I have so much pressure to be that person. "You know the answer then don't you princess," Daddy says.

The answer to what? "I do?"

"Of course you do. If you want to be with me forever. And you want to be that Emmie..." Daddy trails off his words.

"I'm scared, Daddy," I say, looking at him.

"You won't be scared once you join me, Emmie. I promise," he says and smiles at me, reassuring me.

"Okay, I trust you. There is nothing to keep me here." I smile back at him. Daddy stands and holds his hand out to me. I grab it without hesitation.

"Good girl princess," he says. We walk out of the graveyard up the street. We walk over the park and up the hill. This will all be over soon.

Daddy stops at the top of a cliff and he looks back at me. "Do it, princess. It will be quick and painless. Trust me." I peer over the edge. I'm terrified of heights. But I'm more scared of living this life.

"Baby, come away from the edge," I hear Damon say. I turn in horror that Damon found me. When I turn it's not just Damon here, I scan their faces Liam, Sully, Denny, Danny, Lexi, Addi, Brody, Jessie, Lucas and his wife Sarah. All my loved ones are here. Why?

Damon inches towards me with his hands up, trying not to startle me I guess. "What is everyone doing here?" I say. I don't understand.

"Baby, we love you. Don't do this," Damon pleads.

I shake my head, "I feel like you are all there pushing me over the edge."

"But we aren't Emmie, we open our arms for you." I don't see open arms. I don't see anything for sure anymore.

"Emmie, we love you. Why do you think we are here?" Liam says gently, he doesn't make a move towards me only Damon is trying to get close. Are they here to push me over the cliff themselves?

"Emmie, please come back from the edge. We can't lose you again," Sully begs. I look at my best friend's face. I don't feel anything that he is hurting.

"Emmie, I feel like I know you. You don't want this. What about the twins?" Sarah says. I don't feel anything for the twins anymore. I already know I'm a bad mother.

"Emmie, I will help you. You said you trusted me. Then please show me you do," Lucas says. Why is everyone doing this to me? I'm so confused.

"No, only Daddy knows me. He will look after me." Daddy strokes my hair.

"Emmie, I've only just found you again," Addi says. Why couldn't she be my Mom?

"Emmie, I beg you. With all my heart. I love you. Please, I know you more than anything," Damon begs. Don't do this Damon. I put my hands on my head.

"I'd like to believe that but Daddy says..." I trail off.

"Look at me, I'm broken without you. Please, I need you." Damon stop, I used to be broken without you, but you broke me beyond repair.

"Damon, don't do this," I beg him.

"No baby, you don't do this. I will do anything for you. If you go, I go," Damon says. What does he mean if I go, he goes? He needs to be here for Lilly.

"Don't be stupid," I say, repulsed.

Damon edges closer to me. "I'm not, I stand here in front of you. If you die, I die." He is crazy, he can't die.

I shake my head, "No Damon. You can't die. I can't see you die." The thought of Damon dead is too much for me.

"I can't see you die. I love you, Emmie." Damon steps closer to me and I take a step back. I'm balancing on the edge. Damon holds his hands up and backs away one step.

"If he wants to die, Emmie, then let him. You can't stop it. But just come on, just take a step this way," Daddy says. Daddy holds his hand out. I look at it and then to Damon. This is a difficult choice.

"No Daddy. Stop. I won't have Damon hurt," I say.

"Don't defy me. You need to do this," Daddy growls. Voices swirling around and around in my head. Which decision is the right one?

"Shut up Daddy. I can't lose Damon," I snap. I look again at Daddy's hand and then to Damon's face.

"Emmie, please, I can't lose you. I love you so much. Marry me," Damon says. Marry him? We have been through this. I don't want this.

"What?" I mutter. I look over the edge of the cliff.

"Marry me, please. I beg you. I need you to be my wife again. I feel so out of control when you aren't my wife." Out of control? Oh Damon, I always feel out of control. Begging me won't change my mind.

"I can't," I say.

"But you can Emmie. I promise nothing will get in the way this time. I will put your feelings first this time. Please. You are my life. I'm nothing without you." His words slice through me. They make me feel something for Damon.

"Damon, I can't be hurt like that again. It makes me vulnerable." Sully walks closer to Damon.

"Please, I want to protect you. Grow old with you," Damon begs. I don't like him like this.

"Just shut up already," I snap.

"Excuse me?" Damon says, confused.

"You had me at marry me," I shrug. Damon and Sully reach out their hands and I take them. They pull me away from the edge. Damon kisses me, he seems to make my heart beat for him. He releases me and he kisses my forehead. He goes to find Lucas.

"Sully?" I say and look up at him. He bends down and lifts me up.

"You're tired?" he whispers in my ear. I giggle and nod. He knows me so well. I snuggle up into his chest and fall asleep.

Chapter 44

It's been two weeks since Damon proposed. I started taking my medication again. I see Stefan once a week which helps. I feel like I'm moving forward with my life. I feel safe here, protected. Sully still stays here too. I feel safe with him and Damon around. But there is still this minor issue... Yeah, I still see Daddy. I thought once I'd take my meds it would stop. No one knows I still see him. I think something is seriously wrong with me.

"I told you before Emmie, I'm here because you want me here," Daddy sighs like it's the obvious answer. I like him here but I'm more stable now that I can push him away if I want.

I stand outside on the porch looking out into the garden. I pick my phone up and call Lucas. "Hey, Lucas," I say.

"Are you okay Emmie?" Lucas asks, I've never phoned him before and I'm sure when Damon contacts him it's because something is wrong.

"Can you book me in for an appointment?" I ask. I've never booked an appointment, we have always just turned up but I don't want to make such a fuss.

"What sort of appointment?" Lucas sounds suspicious.

"Does it matter? And I don't want Damon to know." I don't want my fiancé to know there could be something wrong with me, I've already put him through so much pain.

"Fine, I'll see you at 1 pm today." I shouldn't put Lucas in this position because he has been so good to me and Damon will probably kill him if he finds out he's been lying. But if it comes to that, I will deal with Damon.

"Thanks Lucas," I say and he hangs up.

I put my phone away and sit on the swing seat. "Emmie, I'm a Doctor. There is nothing wrong with you," Daddy says. Lucas told me that Daddy says what I want him to say. So this is him telling me what I want to hear, that there is nothing wrong with me. I do hope that's true.

"Sure." I smile at Daddy. I curl up and swing for a while but I get agitated waiting for this appointment so I go in search for Sully. I find him in the kitchen making some food.

"Hey, Emmie." Sully greets me with a smile.

"Hey, Big Guy." I return the smile. It's a genuine one for my friend.

"Where you going today?" Sully asks. Does he know something? He can't or he would demand to come with me and tell Damon.

"I'm going shopping with Jessie today. Could you look after Lilly-May please?" I ask him.

"Sure, no problem," Sully says. I'd take her with me but I don't want to take her to the hospital.

"What's Damon doing?" I need to know how much time I've got.

"He has an important meeting today. He won't be back till late." This is good, right? But I feel annoyed that he is back late.

"Oh okay," I say.

"Food?" Sully asks. My instincts tell me no. But Stefan has taught me how to cope with this. It doesn't always work but it has helped.

"Sure." I grin at Sully and he grins back. "You're a good cook, right?" I tease him.

"Why don't you decide that for yourself?" He chuckles. He serves the food and takes it to the breakfast bar and we sit down. He has made a cooked breakfast, he's made mine veggie but he has meat on his.

I pick up my knife and fork and start to eat, "Is this part of your job description?" I giggle. Sully shrugs, does that mean it is? What exactly is his job description? "That must be some monstrous job description," I say, annoyed.

"Emmie, it's not so bad. Damon trusts me more than any of his staff, you trust me which makes it easier. Anyway, I like my job." Sully smiles at me.

"Why? So you can have breakfast with your boss's fiancée?" I tease.

"Exactly." Sully grins. He doesn't blush as much anymore. I don't know if he still feels the same way or not about me but since I turned him down, he hasn't mentioned it and we have acted more like best friends. Am I holding him back? Should I push him away? Surely he would tell me if he didn't want me so close?

I finish my food, "Thanks Sully, that was...edible." I giggle. He laughs too. "I'm joking, it was great. Thank you. I'm going to get ready." I head upstairs to my room.

Daddy is hovering around me, I think he is anxious too. I text Damon.

I miss you already.

He gets up too early sometimes and now he is going to be back late. I put my phone on the bed and head to the bathroom for a shower. I miss Damon's presence, he trusts me to leave me now. He must have so much work to catch up on since I've been ill or missing. I've liked having him close to me.

Once I'm finished I head back to the bedroom and put some sweats on. I don't feel pretty today, I just need to get through this appointment. What does it really matter what I wear anyway? I sit on the bed and look at my phone.

I love you, baby, wish I was with you.

I smile at his text, I wish he was too. I put the phone in my pocket and head downstairs, it's still early yet so I settle for watching TV. Lilly is playing in the living room with Sully, she crawls to me and holds her hands out. I pick her up and place her on my lap. I put on something we can both watch, I click on Winnie the Pooh. I could happily watch this all day.

Sully's phone rings and I frown. He looks at me and gives me a reassuring smile and then leaves the room. What is that phone call? "Momma," Lilly says, distracting me from my thoughts.

"Hey, baby girl."

She points to the TV, "Pooh Bear."

I giggle, "Yes baby, it's Pooh Bear." She's such a clever baby. She starts to babble excitedly again. She wriggles out of my hold and she crawls back to her toys. She's such a high maintenance child. But I guess all kids are like this.

Sully walks back into the room and sits next to me. He kisses my hair. I guess he isn't going to mention the phone call. I guess it's none of my business. "I'd better go," I say to Sully.

"Do you want me to drive you to the mall?" Sully asks.

"No, it's okay." I'm closer to the hospital here than I would be at the mall.

"Bye baby girl." I wave to Lilly and she frowns. She crawls to me and I pick her up. "I've got to go," I say and kiss her on the cheek. I pass her to Sully and she cries. I close my eyes and walk out of the door. I hate to leave her like this.

I walk towards the hospital. What will Lucas say? "Emmie, don't panic. Why won't you listen to me? There is nothing wrong with you." Daddy is frustrated. If he was alive and he was real, then maybe I would believe him but he's not and this is just me wanting to believe that I'm okay.

I reach the hospital and I head to the reception desk. "I'm here to see Dr Grey," I say.

The lady looks up at me. "Your name?" she says curtly. A bit rude.

"Amy Silva," I say in the same tone.

"Sorry, you aren't booked in with Dr Grey," she says.

"Yes, I am," I snap.

I feel a hand on my shoulder and I look up. Lucas stands next to me. "Come on," he says. Why didn't he book me in? Unless he didn't know my fake name and he didn't want to put my real name down. He leads us to his small office. He sits at his desk and he gestures for me to sit on the seat in front of his desk. I gingerly take the seat.

"It's nice to see you, Emmie. But why are you here?" He frowns at me. He doesn't sound happy to see me.

"I need your help," I say nervously.

"With what Emmie?" he asks curiously.

Okay, here goes nothing. "I er, I still see Dad."

He doesn't look happy. "Emmie, why the hell aren't you taking your meds? You know what happens," he says, frustrated. I didn't come here to be accused, of course I'm taking my damn meds. "I can't help you unless you help yourself." I am trying to help myself.

"Lucas, I have been taking my tablets for two weeks now. I'm worried there is something wrong with me," I say, looking at my hands in my lap. Why won't he believe me? Unless he doesn't want to believe there could be something wrong with me too.

"Emmie, I'm not kidding around. You must take your tablets." He puts his hand on his head in frustration and then he lets it fall.

"For fuck sake Lucas. I'm telling you, I am taking them. I promise I am. I feel so much better. If you won't help me then I'll ignore this." I really would like to just ignore this.

"You promise you are taking your tablets?" Lucas asks, testing the waters.

"Yes, I swear I am," I say again.

He seems a little bit sad. I guess he would rather have me admitted that I wasn't taking my tablets. "Okay. Let me run some tests. You should have Damon with you."

I shake my head, "No, Lucas. Promise me you won't tell him," I say sternly. I can't have Damon know about this.

Lucas thinks it over for a while. "I promise. But why?" He isn't allowed anyway so he had to agree.

"I fear something is really wrong with me. But I don't want him to be in pain." I've put him through too much already. We are supposed to be moving forwards but instead, I always find something to ruin our happiness.

"Okay. Do you feel nausea?" Duh? I'm pregnant, moron.

"Sure, but that's morning sickness, right?" I shrug.

"Have you got any headaches?" Does he suspect something?

"Yeah, but that's just stress. I feel better Lucas. The meds help," I reassure him.

Lucas stands and paces the room. "Why didn't I see this before?" he says, he looks mad at himself.

"What's wrong Lucas?" I say.

"Come on," he says. He leads me down the corridor and puts me in my usual room. I sit on the bed and he takes some blood. "Come," he says again. What is he doing? He won't tell me anything. He leads me down the corridor again into a scanning area. "You've been in one of these before," he says and gestures for me to get on the bed. "Phone," he says and I give him my phone and my headphones.

I stay still while he does the tests. Why won't he tell me anything? Is something seriously wrong? I want to scream at him but part of me doesn't want to know. The machine is bright white. The bed starts to move out the machine again. I guess Lucas got what he needed. He isn't in the room when I come back out. A nurse enters the room and escorts me back to my room. She hands me back my phone.

I sit on the bed panicking. Why is Lucas making me wait? The door opens and I see Sarah walk in. "Hey Emmie, Lucas said you were in here. I hope you don't mind me popping in." So she's seen Lucas yet he won't tell me what's going on?

"Hey Sarah, not at all. Be nice to talk to someone." Instead of going mad thinking what could be wrong.

"Where is Rider?" she asks. Far away from here. He can't know about this.

"Working," I say, because it's true, he is.

"I would have thought he would want to be here. You know, for the scan," she says. If I were here for the scan then, of course I wouldn't deny him that but I'm not so I don't want him here.

"Oh yeah right. This isn't an official one. He will be there at the proper one," I reassure her.

"You worried or something?" she asks worriedly. I'm not worried about my babies, they are healthy.

"Something like that." I shrug.

"Well, I'm sure my husband will put your mind at rest." Somehow the way he reacted I doubt that.

"Hey, beautiful wife," Lucas says when he enters the room. I glare at him because he is so calm now. Before he was nothing but snappy, has something changed?

Sarah goes all gooey, "Hey you," she says.

"Can I have a word with Emmie please?" he says to Sarah.

"Sure, I'll see you at home Lucas," she says and he nods and smiles at her. He kisses her on the lips and she leaves the room. Lucas turns to me and gives me a sad look.

"Give it to me straight Lucas." I don't want him beating about the bush.

"Oh Emmie..." he says. I can see a tear run down his face. This really is as bad as I thought.

"Just tell me, Lucas," I snap.

"How do you always know these things?" he sighs. How am I supposed to know?

"Doc just spit it out. How bad is it?" My patience is growing thin.

"You have stage 4 cancer, Emmie." I gasp. Cancer? I feel numb. Why do I always get punched after I'm getting my life on track? Cancer? Stage 4? No. I knew it was bad. But I didn't expect this. "I'm sorry Emmie. Do you want me to call Rider?" Is he stupid?

"No, he can't know. Promise me you won't tell him," I demand.

"Emmie, you will need family around you." I'm strong enough to do this on my own. They can't know. I've been through a lot in my life. I'm stable and I need to let my family believe that they are moving forwards with me.

"Come on, give it to me straight. How long have I got?" I say. If it's stage 4 I can't have much time. I will need to marry Damon sooner than I planned.

"We need to do more tests. But with you being pregnant, we can't start your chemo. I'm hoping to operate. But without chemo, your chances are slim. Maybe we should consider abortion." Maybe we should consider abortion? These aren't his babies, would he be so willing to abort his babies if it was Sarah on the line? I think not. I can't kill my babies to save my own life. No way. Two lives for the price of one, no way. I will give up mine to save two lives.

"Are you out of your mind? Tell me I have enough time to carry the twins full term?" I growl. I can do this, I can carry them full term.

"I don't know without more tests, Emmie." Lucas shakes his head. What more tests could there be?

"How can this be happening?" I say. I put my face in my hands and start to cry.

"Please Emmie, tell Rider." No, stop saying that. I won't put him through this pain and besides, he will be on Lucas's side, he would say abort my babies too.

"No, he will think the same as you. He would rather me alive than my twins. I can't tell him I'm dying. This will kill him." I have to protect him.

"I'm going to do everything I can to help you. I can't let you die, Emmie," he promises. I believe he would try but like he said, without Chemo it seems impossible.

"So what now?" I say.

"I want you to stay for more tests." More tests? What else does he need from me?

"How long will that take?" Sully is at home taking care of Lilly.

"A couple of hours Emmie," Lucas says.

"I'd better ring Sully, he is looking after Lilly-May." I take my phone out of my pocket I look at the time, it's already 3 pm. Urgh. Lucas nods.

"Sully?" I say. I wipe my eyes to try and avoid letting on that I've been crying.

"Hey, Emmie. Are you okay?" No, I'm not. But I'm stable so that counts, right?

"Yeah. I'm going to be a couple more hours yet. Are you still okay to look after Lilly-May?" I focus on his soothing voice. All I want is to have my best friend and my fiancé comfort me in my time of need. But I always seem to live in that moment. I always need them. It's my turn to protect them while I still can.

"Sure Emmie. See you later," he says and we hang up the phone. Sometimes I wish Sully would shout at me and push me away. I don't deserve his kindness. I let Lucas do the tests and I put my headphones in and listen to music, yes, this will help keep me calm. I need time. I've been through worse. I can't have cancer beat my ass. I need to stay strong. I can do this.

Lucas walks back in the room so I take my headphones out. "Hey Lucas, have you finished with the tests?" He nods so I sit up straight.

"Yes Emmie, I have the results. I estimate you have 10 months to live," he says with sympathy. I calculate that in my head. Yes, I have enough to time to deliver the twins.

I put my hand on my chest and take a deep breath, "Oh, thank god."

"Emmie, I just told you you're dying and you say thank god. What's wrong with you?" he says, repulsed. I know he is hurting. I know it's too late for me but it's not for my twins. There are many thing wrongs with me, but mentally I'm better than I have ever been. The breakdown I had two weeks ago has been painfully pushed to the back of my mind. I can't believe I didn't care about my twins. Of course I care, I will give them my life. As for my loved ones, I don't want to push them away and I thank Damon that he got through to me.

"Like I said, Lucas, my babies are the priority here." I shrug.

"You are our priority, Emmie. Rider will kill me." I shake my head, I'm the one that is dying, don't punish my babies for that.

I giggle at his reaction. "Don't be ridiculous. He won't kill you. He may hurt you though." Damon won't hurt him, but he will be angry.

"This isn't funny." Lucas crosses his arms in annoyance.

I grin, "You're right, it's hilarious." My life is just one big joke. Someone is playing one sick joke on me right now. I'd say it was Daddy's revenge for Damon and Lilly but my life was bad before he died.

"Emmie, this is a lot to take in. You are going to deteriorate. You need support and help." I can hide this, I know I can. I've been alone for so long, this will be the most difficult thing I've ever done but I will do this.

"I'll be fine, it will take more than this to bring me down. I'm going to live my life to the full for these 10 months. I have you for support." I'm so lucky to have a friend as a doctor. I trust him with my life. My life is in his hands. I wouldn't say I trust him as much as Damon. I couldn't have him touch me like Damon does. Could I let Sully touch me like that? We are friends and I trust him. Would his touch repulse me like everyone else's? I wouldn't be willing to test that theory but I seek comfort in his arms now like I do with Damon. But I don't see Sully like that and maybe that's why I can let him so close. I trust him not to force himself on me.

I love Liam but how well do I know him? I trust him not to force himself on me. I know his touch repulses me but I don't trust him like I trust Sully. "Emmie, I want to operate. That's all I can do, it may increase your chances," Lucas says, bringing me out of my troubled thoughts. It doesn't matter if I trust them or not to touch me, I only want Damon. I am marrying Damon.

"Why bother?" I shrug. I'm dying, why risk the lives of my babies to give me false hope?

"We will have a chance to beat this if you do. We can start chemo once you've had the babies. But Emmie, 10 months is only an estimate. And I want to be able to tell Rider that I did everything I could," Lucas says. Is he really that worried about what Damon would do? Damon knows how stubborn I am, he would understand eventually. He promised me he would put my feelings first from now on.

"Fine, do the operation," I sigh. I believe he is giving me false hope but I should try to fight this for my family, right? It may be harder for me but I must try.

"Great, I'll call you when I can book you in," Lucas says, more hopeful. I half smile that I've made him slightly happier.

"Okay. Can I go now?" I ask. It's 5.45 pm and I'd like to go home to my family.

"Yes, but I want to see you once a week to keep an eye on you." That sounds reasonable. All these appointments, I'm going to need a diary. I see Stefan once a week and now Lucas once a week.

"Okay, bye Lucas," I say. I get off the bed and Lucas hugs me tight. We have more than a patient Doctor relationship, I know this is hurting him, we have been through a lot together. "I know you will do everything you can," I whisper to him. I have faith in him. If he doesn't save me then I know he tried. He releases me and nods.

I walk out of my room, I see patients around the hospital. I wonder how many of them are terminally ill. How are they feeling? Are the scared? Are they fighting their illness? I know some people refuse all treatment. I do feel like that isn't an option for me.

Once I feel the sun on my skin I relax. I've heard the sun can give you cancer. Did my much-loved Sun do this to me? Or is it genetic, or just something that happened? I should have asked Lucas. I can ask him next time. I'm sure I will have many questions after I've thought about this some more.

I walk back to my house. How will I react when I see my families faces? I have to be strong. I open the door and I find Sully sat on the sofa. He looks up at me and smiles. I give him a fake smile. How am I supposed to leave my best friend? I walk over to him and curl up on his lap and hug him tight. "You okay?" he whispers. He puts his arms around me.

"Yeah, just tired," I say. I am, it's been a long day.

"Hey, beautiful. Are you okay?" Damon says. He takes a seat next to us and I smile. My two favourite guys with me. I'm so lucky, most people don't find this in their life. I crawl over to Damon's lap and hug him tight. I bury my face in his neck. I love his scent. I thought he was going to be back late today?

"Of course I am," I reassure him.

"Good, how was shopping?" Damon asks. He strokes my hair and I close my eyes. Shopping? I said I was with Jessie because Damon is less likely to talk to Jessie.

"Oh right, umm it was good," I lie. Was it a good enough lie? When I was ill he couldn't tell if I was lying. Probably because I was such a mess I couldn't tell what was a lie. But I'm better now and Damon will be able to tell.

"Did you buy anything nice?" he asks curiously. He suspects.

"No, I have enough clothes, Damon." Clothes aren't important. Only people are. I need to make the most of my family with what little time I have left.

"Are you sure you are okay?" Damon says softly. He doesn't believe me but that's okay because I shouldn't have to lie to him.

"Yes, Damon. I've missed you." He works too much now. Unless I've just become too attached to him.

"I've missed you too baby. I need to ask something of you. But you say the word and it won't happen," Damon says sheepishly. What is he going on about?

"What is it, Damon?" I demand.

"We need to seduce a guy, a gang leader to join ours. But Lara couldn't make the deal," Damon says. I laugh at myself. Lara couldn't seduce someone? I find that hard to believe.

"So you want me to do it?" I say awkwardly.

"Just say the word Emmie, and it won't happen," Damon says. He wants me to shut him down. So why exactly is he asking me to do it? I can't imagine him putting me in danger for no good reason.

"Who are you, and what have you done with Damon?" I giggle. Sully laughs too.

"What do you mean?" he asks.

"The Damon I know wouldn't put me in danger." I shrug.

"If I had any other choice, I wouldn't let you do it and you will be safe, I promise. I'm not happy about it though," Damon says. I know I would be safe.

"Lara couldn't do it? But I thought all you guys want a piece of her?" I add. If Lara couldn't seduce them how am I supposed to do it?

"Emmie, I'm sorry for that. Please don't keep punishing me for it. It was one of the worst mistakes of my life. In that moment, I was so upset I would lose you. I needed to be close to you. Lara reminded me somewhat of you. I imagined it was you kissing me. I craved your touch. I got lost in the moment. I needed you even then." He imagined it was me? I can't see how Lara looks like me, she is a dumb blonde bimbo.

"Wait, you imagined it was me?" I say, shocked. I hear Lilly cry from her bedroom. I go to get up but Sully places his hand on my lap and he gets up to see to Lilly.

"Yes baby, I never wanted Lara. I craved you," he says. This changes things.

"Why didn't you ever tell me that?" It would have helped me in a way.

"I didn't want to hurt you anymore. Would it have helped?" he asks. It may have been easier, soften the blow I guess.

"It may have. I need you, Damon." I guess we will never know now.

"You have me Emmie, all of me." I put my legs either side of his and I kiss him. He puts his hands under my knees and stands up. I clutch my arms around his neck and he takes me upstairs to our bedroom. He drops me on the bed and I bounce a few times on the mattress. I giggle.

He undresses himself and once he is done, he undresses me. He climbs on top of me and kisses down my neck, down my breasts. I squirm under his lips. I grab his face and I pull him towards my lips. I need him now, I don't want to delay this. I need to make the most of life.

When I come back to my senses I am lying on Damon's chest. How am I supposed to say goodbye to this beautiful guy who is mine? Do I marry him to know he will lose me? I have no idea anymore. But I want this. He may be happier knowing I was his wife when I die. Who knows? This man seems to be made for me. He protects me, loves me, makes me happy.

"I will do anything for you Damon. What do I need to do?" I say.

He sighs, "Emmie...trust you to say yes." Of course I would. Damon can ask me anything and I will give him it.

"Why ask me if you didn't want me to do it?" I snap at him. Either he wants this or he doesn't.

"Our gang depends on this deal, Emmie. I just hoped not to put you in danger. Larry and Sully think you are both perfect for the job." Why would they think that? I've never done anything like this before.

"Why?" I say in disbelief.

Damon sighs again, "Because all guys love you, Emmie."

What is he thinking? "They do not," I protest.

"Even now you don't see it. He drinks at the hotel bar. You need to seduce him and get him to sign." Seduce him? How do I do that?

"I can try Damon. But why would he be interested in me?" I say.

Damon shifts his weight and I am now lying on my back and he is hovering over me. "Oh, baby, who wouldn't be? You are the most beautiful woman I've ever met." He is always saying this.

"Oh stop," I say awkwardly. I don't do flattery.

"No, you deserve to be swept off your feet Emmie. I love you. Why don't you put something nice on?" Something nice? I'm happy in my sweats. I frown. "Baby, I think you look good in anything but this isn't your usual taste. Is everything okay?"

"I guess. Fine, I'll change. What about Lilly-May?" I ask. Where will she be?

"Your Brother and my sister are coming over." Oh good, it will give me a chance to apologise. I nod and Damon gets dressed. I get out of bed and head for my wardrobe. I scan the dresses and pick the short dress I picked when I went shopping with Sully.

I slide it on and find clean panties. When I turn around Damon has gone. I apply makeup and brush my hair. Once I'm done, I head downstairs. I don't feel comfortable in these clothes anymore. Knowing I'm dying has made me uglier. Uncomfortable in my own skin.

"Baby, you look amazing," Damon says and closes the distance between us. He wraps his arms around me and whispers in my ear, "Shall we go before I keep you here to myself?" he teases.

"I'm up for that." I giggle. Being in Damon's arms forever is where I want to be. Forever and always. He is too precious to me to let him go so easily.

"Oh come on," Damon says. I pout and he chuckles.

"Hey, guys," Lexi says awkwardly when she walks through the door.

"Hey, Emmie. I've missed you," Danny says sadly. I've hurt them both and they are worried about how I will react now. Damon releases me.

"I'm sorry for what I said. I love you guys," I say apologetically. Lilly will need her auntie and uncle when I'm gone.

"You miss them because they haven't been here for you. Not like I have," Daddy says. It's true, they could have come over but I pushed them away, I should have held my hand out to them. I roll my eyes at Daddy.

"Are you sure you are okay with babysitting?" Damon asks.

"Of course, I miss my niece. She will be fine," Danny says. I trust Danny with her so it's fine.

"Okay come on, baby," Damon says, grabbing my hand. I take his hand and he leads me towards the door.

"Can I come? I'll help you with this plan. I know what guys want," Daddy says. I look back at Daddy. He won't help me with this plan, he doesn't like people touching me. It would never work if Daddy is there. I shake my head and close my eyes. When I open my eyes and he is gone, I know it will only be for a little while.

Chapter 45

Damon, Sully, Larry and I are sat in the car in the car park to the hotel. Damon fixes an ear piece to me. I try and cover it with my hair, it's small and not really noticeable. I'm nervous, how am I supposed to seduce someone? Damon, Brody and Liam have always done the chasing. I can flirt with the people I love. Strangers wouldn't want someone like me to flirt with them. What are these three thinking?

Damon always says people love me, maybe I should just be myself and hope for the best. Damon places his hand in mine. His touch drives me crazy. "Baby, are you sure you are up for this?" I know he has faith in me, but it annoys me that he is doubting this.

"Of course, I'm not sure I can help but I'm willing to try." I will try my best.

"Okay well, I've put in an ear piece. Your safety is important to me. If you even have the slightest doubt, just say and I'll come get you," Damon promises. I know he would. I trust him.

"Damon, I'll be fine," I reassure him.

"Sully will be on the inside watching you," Damon says. Well exactly, if Sully will be close what's the worst that could happen?

"I'll protect you, Emmie," Sully says. Of course he will. I have no doubt. We get out the car and Damon hugs me tightly and kisses me on the lips briefly. I want to be in bed right now, I want to forget today. I'm so tired even now, Lucas said I will deteriorate. Could I even get anymore exhausted?

Damon releases me and Sully starts to walk towards the hotel. I slip my arm in his and walk with him. Sully's strong muscles are keeping me upright at the moment. "You tired?" Sully looks down at me. I'm always tired. I nod. "Maybe I should take you home?" he says.

I shake my head. "No, I need to do this. What would I do without you if the gang goes down?" It's too painful to think of my life without my best friend.

"You are too stubborn for your own good. I would still be here by your side even if the gang went down," he says, reassuring me. He would, why? I know I'm stubborn, I'm dying and I'm going through it alone.

We reach the bar and Sully points to a guy sitting at the bar. "So that's him over there," Sully says. He moves his arm and points to a table in front of the bar. "I'll be sat over there watching you," he says. He hugs me and then walks to his table. I watch him and he nods to me.

I take a deep breath and head to the bar. I take a seat near this guy that I have to seduce. I look at him through my eyelashes. He has tanned skin, blue eyes with black hair. He is early 30s I'd say. He is pretty good looking. I look away before he can catch me looking. "You're doing good baby," Damon says through the ear piece. I haven't even done anything but his words give me confidence. How do I proceed? What do I do?

Do I say hi? This is so stupid, why did I agree to this? "Hey, sexy. Can I buy you a drink?" I look over to see the guy smiling at me. Wait, what? I didn't even do anything.

"No thanks," I say. I don't need a drink. I can't drink anyway.

"Huh, playing hard to get. I like that." He smiles and shows his perfectly white teeth. Great, this is working to plan.

"I'm not interested," I shrug. Just be yourself Emmie and they seem to come running. I have always rejected people like Brody. It just made him come at me harder. I'm hoping this guy will be the same.

"Emmie, what are you doing?" Damon growls into the ear piece. I roll my eyes. He says he trusts me yet he isn't trusting me now. Can he not see this is working?

"I'm going to buy you a drink anyway. So would you like to pick one?" the guy says.

"Fine, I'll get a vodka." I shrug.

"Emmie, I swear to god if you drink that I will drag you out of there on my shoulder," Damon snaps. I roll my eyes, of course I'm not going to drink it but this idiot doesn't need to know that.

"Spirit drink, I like that." The guy winks at me. "Whisky and a vodka," he says to the waiter. Nearly every guy I've drunk with had Whisky. I don't like it personally. I look behind me to see Sully watching us intently. He smiles at me and I turn back around to face this idiot.

"So what are you doing here pretty lady?" Trying to seduce you. Is it working? I hope so.

"I was planning on having a quiet drink alone. But here you are annoying me." I bite my lip and the guy raises his eyebrow. I'm giving off mixed signals, I just hope this is driving him crazy.

"Yeah, that's what this is," he says sarcastically.

"Emmie, what are you doing? You seem to be doing the opposite of what I asked," Damon says. I'm going to kick his ass. He is driving me nuts, I thought this ear piece was for my safety, not for him to second guess me. Does he want to try to seduce this guy? My guess is that he does not.

"If you'll excuse me I need the bathroom," I say to the guy.

"I will be here when you get back." The guy winks at me and I return a grin. A little waiting is good for any guy, right? I've heard that that is the key. The question is, am I worth the wait? I don't believe I am but in this case, I had better hope so.

I walk to the bathroom to find Damon is already in there waiting for me. He looks angry. I cross my arms and glare at him. "Damon, what the hell are you playing at?" I accuse.

"What are you talking about? Emmie, you are telling him to leave you alone," he shouts at me. I'm angry too, I know I've been ill and I haven't trusted my own judgement but my mental state is better than it has ever been.

"Damon, I know what I'm doing," I shout back at him. Damon doesn't scare me one tiny bit but I know this isn't the case for everyone else. I think even Lexi is scared to push him too far.

"It doesn't look like you do," Damon sighs.

"I admit, I've never had to do the seducing. But If I play hard to get he will come running. Trust me," I say. I walk towards him and put my forehead on his chest.

"I do trust you, Emmie." He sighs. It really doesn't feel like it right now. I think part of him is worried I'm going to get hurt, not that he doesn't trust me to do this.

"Well prove it and stop bugging me," I say sweetly. I remove my head from his chest.

"Yes, Boss." He chuckles. I roll my eyes and head for the door. He slaps my ass playfully and I squeal and walk out of the door back to the bar. Thank god the guy is still there. I slide back onto the chair I was sat at. The vodka I ordered sits in front of me.

"Oh good, I thought you weren't coming back," he says. He leans slightly closer to me, it takes everything I have not to back away.

"I considered it." I bite my lip and then look at his lips.

"Well, I'm glad you came back. I'm Gab," he says. Gab seems really desperate, how could Lara not seduce him? I'd bet she would be better at this than I am.

"Like Gabby? Ha," I mock, I really am bad at giving people nicknames.

"No, just Gab. What's your name?" He seems a bit pissed that I joked around with his name, oops.

"None of your business." I shrug.

"Oh come on, I bet you have a pretty name." I shrug.

I grab his tie playfully and look into his eyes. "Fine, it's Emmie." Oh crap, I probably should have used my fake name. Oh well, too late now.

"That's unique. You know you really are beautiful." He reaches up and cups my cheek with his hand. He looks into my eyes and smiles. Please don't touch me.

"Emmie, don't let him touch you. That wasn't part of the deal," Damon shouts, making me jump. He's been quiet for so long that I forgot he was there.

"Your eyes are dreamy," Gab says. He releases my face and takes a sip of his drink.

"Are they? Maybe you will dream about them now." I flutter my eyelashes at him.

"Oh I will, but I hope to dream about more than just your eyes." Ugh, typical bloke. Always thinking of something they shouldn't.

I sigh to myself but not out loud, "Oh really, like what?" I say innocently.

"Like this," he says and he cocks his head to one side. Like what? I don't understand. He grabs my face again and then his lips touch mine. I clutch the bar tightly to try and refrain from punching him.

"Emmie, shut him down. I'm calling this off. I can't have him do this to you. No way," Damon shouts. Gab pulls away and I sag with relief, why did he have to kiss me? This would have been so easy for Lara but for me it was painful.

"Wow, girl you can kiss." Gab winks at me. I wasn't even aware I was kissing him back, but if he's happy that's what counts right?

"I guess I have that effect on people," I say awkwardly. People always say I affect them, I just don't know why.

"Do you want to come up to my room?" Gab says. I look over to Sully who doesn't look happy. I want to get this over with.

"Sure." I shrug.

"Emmie, don't you dare. You are not going to his fucking room," Damon shouts. God, he is so angry today. Maybe he should have chosen someone that would follow instructions to help him. Gab slides off his seat and gestures for me to follow him. I wait till he is a few steps away.

I whisper, "Damon, trust me. I'll be fine."

"I trust you, Emmie, I just don't trust him. You are not going up there," he says.

I shrug. "Yes I am," I say and catch up with Gab. I look behind me to see Sully on his feet, he doesn't know how to proceed. I nod at him to reassure him. He curls his face up, he is torn. He wants to follow my wishes but he doesn't want to put me in danger. Gab leads me to an elevator and we step in. I feel my tension rising when the doors close.

He goes to kiss me but I put my hand on his chest. "All in good time." I smile at him. He bites his lip and steps away. What am I doing? I'm such an idiot. The elevator pings open and Gab gets out. We stop outside room 301.

"Room 301, hey?" I say to Gab so Damon can find me if he needs to.

"Thank you. I love you, baby," Damon says through the ear piece. I guess I did something right. He probably would spend hours trying to find me if he had to search every room.

"It's a stylish suite," Gab says, trying to stick up for himself. To be honest, if he was living in a cave it still wouldn't bother me. I'm not that sort of girl.

He opens the door and we walk in. He turns and looks at me. "So what are we going to do now?" He grins at me, looking me up and down.

I shrug, "Well that's entirely up to you."

He looks confused. "What do you mean?" he asks.

"I need you to sign and agree with my terms." I tilt my head to assess his reaction.

"What terms?" Gab puts his fingers on his chin like he is thinking.

"I need you to join my gang," I say, well Damon does but something tells me he won't sign if he has a guy as his Boss.

"You are in a gang? What's a pretty girl like you doing in a gang?" he says in disbelief. Yet another guy who needs their eyes testing.

I shrug, "Needs must." Why does anyone join a gang?

"So what do I get in return for joining you?" he asks.

"Me," I lie. He would never have me. I don't know this guy so I don't know what he is into. I just know that he likes me enough to bring me to his room.

"No Emmie. Get out now. This isn't worth it," Damon says. He is anxious, everything is fine. He is no Rex. This guy seems to have respect for women.

"Well, I guess you are a decent prize," he says, thinking it over.

I produce the document from my shoulder bag. I place it on his breakfast bar and he looks over my shoulder to look at it. He is too close for my liking. "So who is your Boss?" he asks. I feel his breath on my throat. I don't have a Boss.

"Who says I have a Boss?" All these lies forming.

"You couldn't run a gang this good," he says. I find that a little insulting. I reckon I could.

"People do have a habit of underestimating me." I shrug.

He shrugs like he believes me, "Okay, so I would work for you if I signed?" In a way, yes.

"Something like that," I say.

"Why are you lying to him, Emmie?" Damon says. Like I could answer him anyway.

"Well, where do I sign?" he shrugs. Wow, that was easy. I hand him a pen and get him to sign on the dotted line. My job here is done. I place the document back in my bag and head for the door. "So for my prize," Gab says, grabbing my arm. I pull my arm from his hold.

"What prize?" I say.

He reaches up and strokes my cheek. "You," he says, leaning closer to me. I grab his hand from my cheek and push him away.

"Emmie, get out now. I beg you," Damon says. He is breathless like he is running. Is he coming for me?

"You aren't having me," I say firmly.

"But you said." He looks pissed that I played him.

"I lied." I shrug.

"You can't come in here with your beauty and not give me what you promised," he says, frustrated.

"What are you going to do about it? Yeah, that's right, nothing," I say. I don't believe this guy would hurt me. Besides, Damon and Sully are around to save me if I need it.

"Why are you being such a tease?" he says. A tease? Wow, I affected him that much, did I?

"I'm not, I just got what I wanted for my fiancé," I say to try and get him to back off.

"Your fiancé?" he says, backing off slightly.

I nod, "That's right." I smile that he has backed off.

He steps towards me again I step back against the wall. "I'm sure he won't mind sharing I guess." You haven't met Damon, yes he would mind. I know first-hand that he doesn't like sharing. I wonder what he was like as a kid.

I hear banging at the door like someone is kicking the door down. Gab is unbearably close with his hand on the wall by my head. We both look at the door and we see the door fly open. Sully and Damon walk in. "Yes, he would mind," Damon growls.

Sully walks towards us and puts his hand on Gab's shoulder to push him away from me. Gab moves willingly away and Sully pulls me into his arms. I stand to his side, hugging his waist while I watch Damon and Gab. "Who are you?" Gab says with his hands up.

"Emmie's fiancé and your new Boss," Damon says.

"I don't work for you," Gab protests. I shrug at Gab when he looks at me.

"Actually you do. You signed," Damon says.

Gab looks at me, "You played me." I smile at him, yes I did and then he looks back at Damon, "She said I would be working for her." He sounds like a little kid that didn't get what he wanted.

"Why did you say that?" Damon tilts his head whilst he looks at me.

I giggle, he looks so hot when he does that. "Ha, Damon, who is in charge of you?"

"No one?" he says shrugging. I don't think he fully believes his answer. I raise my eyebrow. "Okay, I get the point. You have me wrapped around your little finger." I giggle again and he smiles like he is enjoying my happiness.

"I'm not working for you. Especially without what I was promised," Gab says. Damon punches Gab in the face. Gab doesn't retaliate.

"You're not having my fiancée but you have signed so you now belong to me." I guess he is warning Gab not to go near me. Damon looks at me, "Well done baby." I smile at him.

"Do you trust me to work with her?" Like he will ever see me again, Damon doesn't like me at the safe house.

Damon chuckles, "Ha, I will give you a little word of advice, Emmie can handle herself." I giggle too.

"What's that supposed to mean?" Gab says confused, yes, I know I'm a girl but I can still get revenge.

I smile, "Where do I start...I killed Rex. He was a gang leader who kidnapped and raped me. And then there was Rider's wife. I killed her for hurting Rider. Oh, and the best one was Desmond, my step father. Yeah. I engraved their bodies with an E and smeared blood on the wall." I feel awful for doing that now. I'm sane and stable. I went too far, I know that now.

"Wow, I err... don't know what to say," Gab says.

"My girl is badass and you will do well to remember that." I'm not always a badass. I wish I was a badass so that I could fight this cancer.

"Okay, I get it. I can still try though," Gab says. Why is he still interested? Are all gang members crazy?

"Like I told the others, you can try but you won't succeed." I shrug. "Sully?" He looks down at me and scoops me up into his arms.

"Long day?" Sully says. I nod. Major long day. I close my eyes and fall to sleep instantly.

When I wake the next day, Damon is still in bed. I have an appointment with Stefan today. I get out of bed and dress in sweats again. "Sweats again?" Damon frowns, I imagine he doesn't care what I wear but

I think he thinks it's deeper than just the sweats. He would be right. I shrug and go sit on his lap. He kisses me softly.

"Why are you still in bed?" I ask, he's not usually in bed at this time.

"Can I not have a lay in with my fiancée?" he says. Of course he can but he hasn't for a while. "Where are you going anyway?"

"Appointment, with Stefan." I shrug.

"Do you want me to drive you on the way to work?" I nod. As long as he drops me at the door it will be fine. "Let's go get breakfast," he grins. Food right now? Who needs food when they are dying anyway?

"Sure." I smile at him, not wanting to spoil his mood. He gets up and changes into some casual clothes. He grabs my hands and leads me out of the bedroom. He leads us into the kitchen. I sit next to Sully who is holding Lilly-May at the breakfast bar. "Momma." I take Lilly off him and I sit her on the table so the table is taking all her weight.

Soon I won't be able to safely hold my daughter and that scares me. I want to watch Lilly grow, I want to help her with her homework. I want to see her get married and have kids. I won't be able to do that. "You okay?" Sully says. I wipe my eyes.

"Sure," I say. Damon passes me some *Weetabix*. I start to eat the food and Lilly grabs the spoon off me. What a cheeky monkey. It seems my daughter has more strength than I do right now.

"Lilly, Mommy needs to eat her food," Damon says to Lilly, laughing, I guess he found it amusing too. I hold my hand out to collect the spoon and she returns it. I put my head on her lap and Lilly starts to play with my hair. Oh baby girl, I love you so much. Damon puts his hand on mine that is placed around Lilly and I look up at him. "You okay?" I nod. Sure, I'm just a mother who is going to miss her child grow up. I finish my food and I pass Lilly back to Sully. Lilly doesn't cry this time, she must be used to me leaving her all the time. I never spend enough time with my loved ones.

We head to the car and Damon stops in front of the car. "Do you want to drive?" Damon offering me to drive? I shake my head, as much I love him for trusting me with this, I'm dying. I know I should take every opportunity I can in life but this isn't that important to me. "You sure?" he asks. He probably expected me to jump at the chance, although I did well last time, I got exhausted quickly and I have a long day planned.

"Thank you for the offer Damon, I love you. But I'm tired," I say, I am tired and it is worrying because I haven't long been awake. He frowns but seems to accept my answer. He opens my side of the door and lets me climb in. I would much prefer to watch him drive anyway.

We reach Stefan's office. "Have a good day baby," Damon says. I reach for his face with my hands and I kiss him. I go to pull away but he pulls me back and kisses me for longer. I smile at him. These small gestures mean the world to me, it means he can't get enough of me and that fixes a tiny bit of my broken heart every time. I get out the car and take a deep breath. Just because I take my tablets doesn't mean I'm still not anxious outside in public on my own.

I walk into the building and head to the reception desk. "Amy, you can go straight in. Stefan is expecting you." I nod. But I need to make a call first. I guess I'm regular here so people know who I am.

I take my phone out of my pocket and press call. "Hello, Mr Declan speaking."

"Hi, Mr Declan. This is Emmie Salvatore, I would like to arrange an appointment." I didn't think I'd ever require his services but I need him now.

"Miss Salvatore, it's nice to hear from you again. I have a space today at noon," he says pleased to hear from me. He remembers me then?

"Great thank you for fitting me in. See you then," I say and hang up. I shouldn't be using my real name but I don't think he would have fit me in if he didn't know me.

I walk into Stefan's office without knocking. He looks up and smiles at me. I return the smile grudgingly. Stefan has helped me these past few weeks and I'm grateful. He gets up from his desk and sits on the sofa and I flop on the sofa exhausted. "Hey, Emmie."

"Hey, Stefan," I say.

"How are you today?" he asks.

"I'm okay. Mentally I'm great, I've never been better," I say.

Stefan frowns, "Why do I sense that you are evading the question?" he says. I'm not exactly avoiding the question, I'm just answering carefully. I shrug. "Something has changed, hasn't it?"

I shake my head, "No Stefan, that's the problem."

"What do you mean?" he says, confused.

I nod over at his desk, "Daddy is sat over there looking at your paperwork." Stefan snaps his head around to his desk but obviously, he sees nothing. Yet I see Daddy scanning Stefan's probably confidential files.

"I thought you said you were fine mentally Emmie? Why haven't you been taking your meds?"

I sigh, I wish it was that simple, "I am Stefan, that's the problem. I wish it was the fact that I wasn't taking my pills." I put my knees to my chest to protect myself.

"I think you need a second opinion, Emmie," Daddy says.

"I trust Lucas," I say to Daddy.

"More than me?" Daddy says disgustedly.

"When you aren't real? Yes," I say.

"You trust Lucas with what Emmie?" Stefan says.

"I went to him because I'm still seeing Daddy. He gave me a diagnosis," I say, resting my chin on my knees.

"And what is your diagnosis?" he asks.

"Do you tell Damon what happens here?" I ask.

"No Emmie, I'm not allowed to tell him anything."

"Good and you can't. Lucas diagnosed me with stage 4 cancer," I say. Stefan's mouth drops open.

"What?" he says in disbelief.

"Stefan, I was just getting my life on track and now I'm dying. I can't have chemo because of my twins," I say. He can't get his head around this either.

"And you haven't told anyone?" he asks.

I shake my head, "No. I can't put them through that pain. After seeing their reaction when they thought I died, I won't do this to them."

"But if you are going to die, Emmie, they should know." I shake my head. I've decided that they won't know. I will hide this. "So why did you tell me?"

I don't know, "I guess I needed to tell someone." I thought this would help me, but saying these words haven't relieved any pressure.

"Oh Emmie, I'm sorry."

"Don't be. This must be karma hitting my ass again."

"This isn't karma, Emmie. You are just an innocent girl with a shit life." He got that right, I have a shit life but I'm thankful for it every single day. I have Damon, Sully and Lilly. "Lucas must be going crazy."

"Yeah, he was crying when I left, he is going to try everything he can," I reassure him.

"I could do everything for you if you just follow me, Emmie," Daddy says.

"Your way I'd be dead anyway," I say to Daddy. I need to keep fighting for my family. Stefan looks at me in question to my comment. "He still wants me to walk off the cliff with him." I shrug.

"You are strong enough to fight him now," Stefan says. I know I am. I want to live. "Is there anything else you would like to talk about?" I shake my head. "Okay, I'll see you same time next week." I nod.

I walk out of the office and then I walk down the street towards my next appointment. Part of me wishes Lucas didn't tell me. Lying to my family every day for the next ten months will be agony. Will I be able to hide my pain from them? How much worse is it going to get? Will Damon ever forgive me for this?

Chapter 46

When I enter Mr Declan's building I feel more anxious, last time I was here he was very unprofessional and now I'm here without Damon. I must do this, I walk to the reception desk. "Can I help you?" she says. It's the same woman who flirted with Damon.

I clear my throat, "I'm here to see Mr Declan at 12," I say. She looks down at her computer.

She frowns. "Yes, seems to be a last minute booking, that doesn't happen often," she says still frowning. "Take a seat and I'm sure he will be out soon." I nod and take a seat. That was weird, he doesn't do last minute bookings? So why did he do it for me?

"Emmie?" I look up to see Mr Declan standing by his office door. I stand up and walk towards him. He shakes my hand again. Please don't touch me. He releases my hand and gestures for me to go into his office. I glance back at the receptionist who is still frowning. She looks at us confused, well at least she knows I'm here. I take a seat where I sat last time, I glance at the empty chair where Damon sat last time. But to my surprise, it's not empty like I expected. Daddy is sitting there with his legs crossed.

Mr Declan sits down and smiles at me. "So Emmie, what can I do for you?"

I take a deep breath. "I need to make a will." Daddy looks at me. Yes, Daddy, I am doing what you did for me. Giving my loved ones my dying wishes, except I will be including all my family.

Mr Declan frowns, "You are so young, Emmie. Why do you feel the need to make a will?" he asks.

"I'm dying Mr Declan. I need to leave my assets to my family," I say.

Mr Declan's mouth drops open. "Dying? Where is your fiancé? I'm surprised you aren't married yet," he says confused.

"I have stage four cancer. I'm pregnant which means I can't have chemo. My Doctor estimates 10 months. Damon doesn't know and I would appreciate your discretion. Not that it matters but we were married and then he married someone else." I shrug.

"I'm sorry to hear that." He does sound sorry but it's none of his business. "Your secret is safe with me." He doesn't bother bringing up the divorcing bit and I'm glad because it was a dark moment of my life. "Okay, so what are your assets and where are they going?" he grabs a pen and waits for me to say something.

"Well, I have 5 million pounds, a house and a car." I shrug.

"You haven't touched your father's belongings?" he gasps.

I look at Daddy who looks disappointed. "No, I was always meant to donate to charity but I get into trouble a lot." I shrug. "Oh and I own another house," I say.

"Okay, so where are these going?" I need Lilly well cared for.

"The money I want to be split between my children. Lilly-May Rider and my two unborn twins," I say. "My Dad's house I want to be given to my Brother, Danny Salvatore. I want my house to be given to Damon Rider and Sully Valencia."

Mr Declan nods, "Anything else?" I have nothing else to my name.

"Erm, I need you to keep this on the down low," I say, I'm supposed to be dead.

"What do you mean?" he says.

"Someone is trying to hurt me. I faked my death, I'm supposed to be dead. I need you to put my will under the name Amy Silva," I say awkwardly, hopefully he won't call the police or anything.

"You are one complicated woman. Sure, I can do that. Anything else?" he says.

I nod. "Do you have a pen and paper?" I ask sweetly. He nods and rummages in his desk and produces a note pad. He hands it to me.

I write, 'My dear beloved husband, if you are reading this then I am dead. I'm sorry this had to end. I want you to know I fought for you till the very end. Please don't be mad, I wanted to spare you from this pain. I love you so much.'

I write another. 'My dear beloved daughter, I wish I was there to watch you grow, to watch you fall in love, to see you get married. I know that I would be very proud of you whatever you achieve. You mean so much to me, I want you to know that I did what I could to be there for you. Don't let anyone take you for granted because you deserve to be treated like a princess. I love you baby girl.'

I write another, 'Sully, you are my best friend. I didn't deserve you and I wanted to say that I loved you so much. I could be myself with you and you made me feel safe and protected. I don't know what I would have done without you. I love how you thought of me and my feelings and not about my safety first, even though I know it killed you. You knew when to tell me not to be so stubborn and when to let me be. That's a fine art, my friend. I love you, Big Guy.'

Too many loved ones, not enough time. 'My dearest twins, I haven't met you yet. I am still keeping you safe in my tummy. I did all this for you so please live life to the full. I know you may feel guilty about me giving my life for you but I was never given this. This is my dying wish to protect my children. I love you both so much and I haven't met you yet.'

That should do. Daddy reaches up and wipes tears from my face. I smile at him through my blubbering eyes. "It's okay princess. I'm here," Daddy says. I nod and swallow, trying to compose myself. Leaving my family is impossible, we haven't had enough time together.

"Okay, I've typed it up. Please sign here," he says, pointing to the dotted line with Amy Silva written underneath. I sign on the line and give him the letters. "Okay well, this is all official Emmie. I'm going to do this free of charge for you," he says. Why, is it because I'm dying? I don't need his sympathy.

"Well thank you Mr Declan, I appreciate you seeing me." I stand and Mr Declan takes my hand and holds it to his lips. I close my eyes wanting to scream at him but I owe him. I couldn't have done this without him. He releases my hand I walk briskly out of his office.

I grab my phone, who do I call? Do I call Denny? But maybe he is with Esme. What about Danny? Or is he too busy with Lexi? Sully has Lilly. Damon is at work. I decide to ring Denny, he was my first thought, he can either not answer or answer, right?

"Hey, sweet sister," Denny says. I love the way he talks.

"Denny," I say happily. He is always so happy to speak to me.

"Are you busy?" I ask.

"Not too busy for my sister. Where are you?" he says.

"I'm in La Zenia. Meet me at Bar Argento in Cabo Roig?" It's not far from here.

"See you soon sweet sister." He hangs up. I start to walk towards the cafe. I haven't contacted him since I pushed him away but he never came back to me. He was there the day I had the major breakdown but he never returned. But then neither did my own flesh and blood Danny. I can't expect Denny to do something my own Brother didn't.

"They don't appreciate you like I do," Daddy says.

"Shut up," I snap. They love me, I know they do. I just pushed them all away. I reach the bar and I take a seat outside. Daddy sits next to me, I guess so I'm safer that I'm not alone. He isn't real, he is just what I want him to be. The chair on my other side scrapes against the concrete.

I look to see who it is. I smile when I see it's Denny. "Just me dear Sister," he says to my reaction. "I didn't think I'd hear from you again." He grins.

"I wanted you to know that wasn't me. I love you and I do forgive you. I'm sorry I pushed you away. I am, was, I mean, seeing my Daddy. He made me say those things." Denny frowns.

"But didn't your Dad...?" Denny stops what he was going to say.

"I really don't like this guy," Daddy growls. I glare at Daddy to keep him quiet.

"I love my Daddy. That will never change." I shrug.

"Can I take your order?" the waitress asks.

"I'll get a Latte please," I say.

"I'll have an Americano. And she will have a piece of chocolate cake with that." I glare at Denny, what is he trying to do, make me fatter?

"Sure, I'll be back with your order," she says and leaves.

"What are you doing out here alone Sister?" Denny frowns.

I can't say anything about today or yesterday. Of course, all I want to do is tell my family and have their support but I won't. "I had my shrink appointment." I shrug.

"But why alone?" he says again.

"Why not alone?" I say.

"I haven't known you long sweet Sister but you walk into trouble wherever you go. You could probably walk into a fight without even knowing it. Our Mother still goes out you know," Denny says. I'm not that stupid to walk into a fight, I may try to stop it though but that's who I am.

"I can take care of myself," I snap.

He holds his hands up. "Don't get defensive dear sister, I'm just looking out for my little sister," he says.

The waitress comes back with our order. My phone rings, I look at my phone and I sigh. "Damon?" I say.

"Hey Baby, where are you? Sully was worried you aren't back yet," Damon says suspiciously. Of course they are worried, I don't go out much.

"I'm just having coffee with my brother," I say. He will never approve of me seeing Denny alone. I hope this doesn't end up in an argument. I know he only wants me safe but I know I'm safe with Denny.

"Oh okay. Well, have fun baby. See you later," he says and hangs up. I sigh with relief he didn't ask questions, thank god.

I start to drink my coffee. "So, how is my niece?" Denny asks.

"She's really good, cheeky monkey though." She is too cheeky for her own good.

Denny laughs, "Does she have the better of her badass Mommy?"

I don't have the energy to run around after her all day. "Yes, she definitely has." I dig into my cake that Denny made me have. I've already got a bump I don't need to get fatter too. I eat it anyway.

"I'll go pay the bill, Sister." I frown, I asked him here, he shouldn't have to pay. "Let me do this for you little Sister," He says and walks off. What is he trying to do? I finish my coffee when he arrives back outside. "So sweet sister, we are close to the beach. Shall we go check it out?" The beach? I don't have a swimsuit. "Come on, live a little." I frown, I vowed to myself I would make the most of life.

So that's what I'll do. "Okay." I grin. I stand up and put my arm in his and we walk towards the beach. It's a lovely beach here in Cabo Roig. It's a ten-minute walk but once we arrive, it's worth it. Denny strips into his boxers and lays on the sand.

I sit next to him. He has such a nice body yet I'm here fat and ugly. My phone rings again. "Damon?" I sigh.

"When you say Brother, which one do you mean?" Ugh, so this is what he is getting at. I knew he wouldn't be comfortable with this. He obviously assumed I meant Danny.

"What does it matter Damon?" I snap.

"You are with Denny, aren't you?" he shouts down the phone.

"He is my brother Damon, you can't stop me seeing him. I'm safe. I'll see you later," I snap and hang up the phone. He can't tell me who I can and can't see. I'm angry. My phone rings again but I ignore it.

Denny sits up on his elbows to look at me. "Does he not scare you when he is angry sweet Sister?"

"No, not one little bit. Even when I first met him I wasn't but I know how he could intimidate people." I shrug. It's hot here so I remove my clothes so I'm wearing my panties and my bra. I feel uncomfortable but it's too hot. Denny reaches over to me and skims the D again and I instinctively grab his hand.

"Sorry Sister, it's just it makes me feel closer to my Dad." I frown, I'm so fucked up I can't stand him touching me. I'd like to give him this, but I can't. He stands up and bends down and he lifts me up onto his shoulder. If I don't want him touching my scar, then I don't want him touching me.

He runs into the water and then he lets me fall when we are deeper in the water. "Denny," I scream when I surface again. He is laughing at me. The water is warm today which is good. I wonder how long I can refrain from drowning today. I tire quickly now.

Denny sits me on his shoulders, he holds me steady with his hands on my knees. I close my eyes trying to block out him touching me. He is having so much fun and I'm ruining the moment. I need to make the most of life, I need to give my loved ones happy memories near the end.

"Emmie!" I hear someone shout my name. Denny and I both turn. Oh shit, it's Damon and he is super pissed. I groan and Denny lets me fall in the water. I cough when I surface again because I wasn't ready.

"Damn it," I groan.

"Looks like you are in trouble," Denny says. I shove him for stating the damn obvious but he doesn't even move. Where has my strength gone? But saying that, I never had much strength anyway.

Damon reaches us in the water, he lifts me up onto his shoulder and carries me out. He doesn't say anything and I know better than to say anything, he probably wouldn't answer anyway. I look to Denny. "Bye Denny," I say and wave to him.

"Bye dear Sister," he says and waves back. Damon bends down and grabs my clothes and my phone and starts to walk back up the hill. Part of me is thankful that Damon is carrying me up this hill, I'm not sure I would make it.

"Damon, I can walk," I say quietly. He chooses to ignore me. He must have tracked my phone because I said I was having coffee. My amazing fiancé has gone mad again with his phone tracking skills. In this moment though I'm angry with him. Denny would never hurt me again, I know this, why can't he let it go?

Damon puts me on the front seat of his car. He puts my seatbelt on and then he grabs my face and kisses me hard. I return the kiss automatically but I can't help wonder what this is all about. He pulls away and then walks around to his side. He starts the car and then he heads home, I guess. "Damon, are you going to talk to me?" I say. I don't want to argue, I need to make every moment count.

He doesn't say anything so I try something else. I place my hand on his thigh and I caress his leg, going higher as I go. I reach between his legs and he is obviously enjoying this. "Emmie," he gasps.

"What Damon? Why are you so mad at me?" I snap but I carry on the torture.

"I'm not mad at you, is that not obvious?" he says, glancing at my hand. I frown, no not really. He wouldn't speak to me, this is just payback.

"No Damon, it's not," I snap. He seems to drive a little faster. Why?

"Take your panties off," he says. Why? "Do it," he says softly. I do as I'm told, I slide off my nearly dry panties and let them fall on the floor. He pulls up at the back of what looks like the safe house. No one is around. He cuts the engine and takes off his seatbelt. He then proceeds to undo his jean shorts and pulls them down along with his boxers. He grabs my hand. "Come here," he says softly again.

I undo my seatbelt with my other hand and then climb on his lap. My back is against the steering wheel. He takes my face in his hands, "I love you so much. You get yourself into so much trouble and it drives me crazy," he says. He eases himself inside of me and I tilt my head back. He kisses my neck which makes my skin super sensitive to his touch. I'm too distracted to argue with him right now and I think he knows it.

I grab his face and kiss him, his tongue explores my mouth and we seem to form one. I love my overbearing protective soon to be husband, again. I will fight for you, my love. In this moment, this is too much for me to bear. Tears fall down my face but Damon has his eyes closed so it doesn't matter. Damon is a part of me and always has been, even death won't be able to separate us. I'm not scared to die, I'm scared to lose Damon.

We both try to catch our breaths and I rest my head on his shoulder. Tears still continue to fall down my face. I would do anything for this man and giving him his child may soften the blow. "Baby, are you crying?" I sniff and wipe my eyes. He grabs my face so I have to look at him. "What's wrong baby?" he says, concerned.

"I just love you so much, I don't want this to end," I say, leaning my forehead on his and our noses touch and he nuzzles my nose.

"We have the rest of our lives, baby." He smiles. Yes, but my life isn't that long. I want to scream and shout and beat the crap out of this cancer. It seems impossible to beat but does it not know that I will do anything to protect my family? I nod to Damon. "Get dressed baby, I don't need my staff seeing you in your underwear," he smirks. Oh, playful Damon. I smile back.

I climb back over to my seat and dress in my clothes. My underwear is still a little wet and slightly uncomfortable. I step out the car once I'm done and Damon grabs my hand and leads me into the safe house. I guess Damon has more work to do. We walk in the back entrance and Damon walks straight towards his office. I hold back and he releases my hand. I wander around the safe house.

"Emmie," Dyno says. I turn and frown at him. "What are you doing here?"

"Damon brought me here, I guess he doesn't trust me right now." I shrug.

"Why, what did you do?" Dyno asks curiously.

"I had coffee with my brother," I say, walking towards Damon's office.

"I guess that was your step brother then. Emmie, you shouldn't hang around with him," Dyno says. What's it to him anyway? It's none of his concern.

"He is my brother, I can see anyone I damn well please," I snap. When I walk into Damon's office, I freeze. Damon is sat at his desk and Lara the blonde bimbo is hovering around Damon. They are looking at something on Damon's computer. Larry is sat in front of the desk along with the new guy Gab. Why is he letting Lara get so close? He seems oblivious to her charm, she's obviously trying hard to fight for his attention.

I'm angry and feel insecure, I know Damon hasn't given me any reason to but I feel I must claim what's mine. Dyno grabs my shoulder and I pull out of his grip. I guess he is warning me not to go nuclear, I guess he should know first-hand what I'm like.

"Boss, I really think this is the best way to proceed," Lara says, leaning too close to Damon. I walk towards Damon's desk and I step between

Lara and Damon and I sit on Damon's lap. Lara backs off completely. Good, that's what I had hoped for.

"You okay baby?" Damon whispers in my ear. I nod and he puts his arms around me whilst I look at the computer to see what they are both looking at. "Gab, what do you think?" Damon asks.

"I think you have a beautiful fiancée. You should bring her here more often, she brightens the place up," Gab says and winks at me. I groan. "Chill Boss, I don't agree with Lara. I think we should threaten his family." I gasp, threaten whose family? Damon holds me closer, I know he is a gang leader and all but I don't expect this from my fiancé.

By the looks of this screen, it's floor plans to a building. It shows in red what they obviously seek. Gab wants to threaten this guy's family to get to it. I imagine Lara wants to seduce her way in. The plans seem to have high security in this building. I grab the mouse and I search the company written on the plans on google. I search their security systems.

"Damon, do you have an IT specialist?" I say.

"No, why?" Damon says looking over my shoulder. He is distractingly close.

"I think if you hack their systems, you'll have a time window where you can get to what you need," I say.

"But we don't have anyone to do that," Damon says.

"Sure you do. Me." I turn and kiss him quickly on the lips.

"And how are you going to do that?" Lara snaps. I stand up and grab Lara's hand and I shove it behind her back and she screams. I slam her into the desk.

"Let's get something straight, I don't like you. If you want to speak to me, you'll do so with a little respect. Okay?" I say into her ear.

"Okay, I'm sorry," Lara says and I release her. I take my usual position on Damon's lap. I catch him grinning.

"When you said she could handle herself, I never believed it. But now..." Gab says, shaking his head, but he is amused.

"Baby, what do you mean you can?" Damon says softly.

"Let's just say someone taught me how to hack systems in exchange for lessons." I shrug. At my old school, a guy called James taught me how to hack things. We were good friends but we both had something each other needed.

"Why did I never know this?" Damon says.

"It's been a while so I may be a bit rusty." I shrug.

"I don't think I've found anything you can't do yet." Damon places soft kisses on the side of my face and I giggle. Of course there are loads of things I can't do. I can't seem to be able to live. I want to live but I'm dying. I yawn and curl up to Damon's chest. I hear Damon softly talking to his team and I fall asleep. I feel arms around me and I open my eyes. I see Sully staring down at me. Why is he here? I guess Damon still has more work to do. I smile and then fall back to sleep.

Chapter 47

A week has passed since I offered to help Damon hack the systems. It all went to plan and he got what he wanted. I didn't ask questions because I really don't want to know. I am all dressed in casual clothes and ready to go out.

"You look good today. Where are you off to?" Sully says behind me. I turn and see him leaning against the wall. I bite my lip, damn pregnancy hormones are driving me crazy. He looks so hot standing there like that.

I swallow, "Hey Sully. I'm off to work," I say awkwardly, trying to disguise the fact I was checking out my best friend.

"Work?" Sully says horrified.

"Yes, I'm starting work at the stables today." I need to do something, all this sitting around waiting to die is torture. I need to do what makes me happy for the remainder of my short life. It will exhaust me but at least I'll be happy.

"What about Lilly-May?" Sully says. It sounds like he is clutching at straws to try and get me to stay at home.

"I've dropped her at nursery. Damon will pick her up on the way home," I say. She started nursery a few days ago. It was a scary time for me, I hate to leave her there with strangers. It makes me more anxious than normal. Damon says it's all good to help her grow up. It took him awhile to convince me.

"Okay, well have a good day," Sully says. I smile and walk out of the back door to the garden and then down the stony track to the barn.

I am met by a young black haired girl. "Hey, you must be Emmie," she says.

I nod. "Yes, that's me," I say, I don't offer my hand because I don't want her to touch me.

"I'm Meeka. So I wanted to speak to you about one of our horses," she says. "Well, he has become out of control and is unsafe for people to ride. No one will ride him." Well if he is unsafe to ride I don't blame them for not riding him.

"Okay, tack him up and I will meet you in the school." I shrug.

"Are you sure?" she says anxiously.

"Yes, I'm sure." She nods and leaves. People underestimate me. A tall black haired guy walks up to me. Oh my god, he is topless. I straighten my clothes to avoid staring. Stop it, Emmie. Pull yourself together. You don't want anyone other than Damon anyway. I know, I know.

"Ha, can I help you?" the guy says. He must have caught me staring. Damn it.

"Oh um sorry. I'm Emmie." I try to act casual.

"Oh, the boss. Nice to meet you. I'm Noah." He smiles.

"Yeah, er you too." Damn it, Emmie, he is just another person. Act normal.

"So what are you doing? Do you need a tour?" he says.

"I'll take a rain check. I'm about to ride a horse." I shrug. Damon will kill me but hey ho. I have ten months, what's the worst that could happen?

"Who are you riding?" he asks.

"I have no idea. The one that has become uncontrollable." I roll my eyes.

"That's Willow. Are you sure you want to ride him? He dumped me," he says. Willow? He was an angel when I last saw him. What happened? Maybe he dumped him because he is an ass.

"Honestly I will be fine. Why do people underestimate me? Just don't tell my fiancé," I say.

"I've met him. He's deadly." Noah laughs. But there is an edge to his laugh that shows he is slightly worried.

"He's fine. Anyway, I'd better go." I make my way to the school.

"Don't blame me when you fall off," Noah calls.

I roll my eyes and look back at him. "Confidence, yeah great."

I walk to the school and Meeka has Willow. Willow is pawing at the ground, he won't stand still. I walk up to Willow and stroke his neck. "Woah boy," I say. Willow stops pawing at the ground. He shoves me with his head again and it sends me flying into Meeka.

"You okay?" she asks.

"Yes, I'm fine," I say. I grab the reins off Meeka and she leaves the school. I do some more in hand training with Willow and he seems to calm down a little. Willow drops to his knees again, I guess he wants me to ride him again. You have to earn the horse's trust before they feel safe with you. Willow must remember me from before.

I slide my leg over his back and I hold on tight when he stands up. Once he stands he starts to run, crap. What is his problem? I pull the reins and he slows down. This isn't the Willow I remember, the other woman tried to tell me he was unpredictable. He throws me a buck and I get knocked off balance but I stay on. "Woah boy," I say.

"Emmie, get off the horse right now for fuck sake," I hear Damon shout. What is he doing here? Maybe Sully snitched on me or maybe one of my staff did.

"Steady boy," I say again. He seems to relax a bit more. I ask him to walk forwards and he does so. I push him into a trot and he is nice and relaxed.

"Emmie, don't make me drag you off that horse," Damon calls again. I roll my eyes, he is such a drama queen.

"Damon, just wait one second," I say. I push Willow into canter and I line him up for the jump in the middle of the school. I keep my legs on and my reins even and he flies over the jump. Well, that was fun, I love jumping. I take Willow over to where Damon is stood.

"Emmie, what the fuck was that? Are you trying to give me a heart attack?" Damon puts his face in his hands. He just needs to relax a little.

"Damon, this is my job, you can't go interfering," I say. Willow stands perfectly still while I talk to Damon.

"You're pregnant Emmie, you can't ride a crazy horse," he shouts. I know what I'm doing.

"Okay Damon, you are expecting babies. You can't be in a fucking gang," I say. I don't shout because I don't want to scare Willow.

"What?" Damon gasps. "Is that how you feel?"

Noah walks up to us and grabs Willows reins. "You okay Boss?" Noah asks. Boss? That's going to take some getting used to.

"Yeah, fine thanks." I smile.

"What is it with you and guys with no tops?" Damon growls. He must be thinking of Liam. It's not like I ask them to do this.

"Damon, don't be so rude," I snap.

"Wow, so I totally saw you on Willow. You were great. He seemed to really respond to you. A few more rides and he should be okay. Just so you know, he doesn't like to jump though. But wow, he jumped it nicely with you. You both seem to work well together," Noah says, impressed. I'm not living my life saying what if? I don't want any regrets. I want to say I did that.

"She is not riding that bloody horse again," Damon shouts, he reaches up and grabs my hips and lifts me off Willow.

"Damon, will you stop bothering me at work." I cross my arms. Noah takes Willow back to the stables.

"Emmie, what if you fell and something happens to the twins?" Damon says.

"Nothing will happen. I know what I'm doing," I say. I know what he is saying, I do. I will try to be more careful next time. If I wasn't dying, then I probably wouldn't push to ride. He doesn't understand because he doesn't know I'm dying and he never will.

"Let's go home," Damon sighs and picks me up. I know I over reacted and he didn't. I probably shouldn't be riding whilst pregnant. I don't blame Damon for anything, only he can tell me when I've gone too far and sometimes I need him to tell me.

Damon carries me back to the house and he puts me in bed. I am tired but sleep is probably out of the question. Damon leaves the room. My phone starts to ring. "Lucas?" I whisper in case someone comes upstairs.

"Emmie, I can book you in for your operation this afternoon. Can you do that?" I frown, I'm scared. Can I do that? I need to find a good excuse to leave for a day or so. "Emmie, I'll take care of you. I want to do this as soon as possible."

"Okay," I squeak. This is all too much, I've tried to push it to the back of my mind for so long that I haven't processed it like I should.

"4 pm Emmie," he says and hangs up.

I turn over and see Daddy laid in front of me. He strokes my face and tears start to fall. How am I supposed to say goodbye to Daddy? Lucas hopes that this will stop me seeing Daddy. What if I don't want to? "Some operation isn't going to stop me seeing you Princess," Daddy says. How would he know? He is just telling me what I want to hear.

I shuffle closer to Daddy and I cry into his chest. He strokes my back trying to soothe me. He has been part of my life for a while now and I can't lose him. I fall to sleep.

"Emmie?" Damon says and I wake suddenly. I am still curled up into Daddy's chest.

"Yeah?" I say, not moving.

"It's 3 pm. You should eat something." Lucas said that I shouldn't eat. He didn't give me a lot of time but I haven't eaten today anyway so it doesn't matter.

"I'm going out for dinner with Jessie, I don't want to ruin my appetite. I'm also staying at hers tonight," I say. I don't want to leave Damon but if I am to have any hope, I must do this.

"You never mentioned it," he says as he sits down behind me stroking my hair.

"Last minute plans," I say. I get up, getting a change of clothes and PJs and anything else I can think of that I may need. I grab Daddy's hand and we head downstairs. I must keep Daddy close until the very end. People don't understand my love for my Daddy but I love him and he is here.

"I'll drive you," Damon says. I shrug, Damon won't take no for answer so I'll get him to drop me off close to the hospital and walk from there.

"Thanks, we are eating at Alingui," I say. It's close to the hospital. He nods and takes out his keys from his pocket.

I won't be there to put Lilly to bed, I always do that. Stupid cancer. "Come on Princess," Daddy says, tugging at my hand. I get in the front and Daddy sits in the back. Tension is rising within me again. I hate lying to Damon, I hate myself.

We pull up outside the restaurant. I grab Damon's hand and he slides his fingers through mine. I can't say goodbye. Damon reaches his other hand to my face and he strokes my cheek. "Damon, I love you," so much. He kisses my lips quickly and I get out the door.

"I love you too baby," he says and I shut the door. I walk into the restaurant and wait for him to leave. Once he pulls away, I walk towards the hospital. I find Lucas waiting for me in reception.

I follow him into my usual room. "Here are your clothes, please change," he says. I look at the clothes, they are ghastly hospital gowns. I go to the bathroom and change. What am I doing? I say to my reflection. Am I doing the right thing? I hope so. I gather my clothes and place them in my bag. "I need to shave your head," Lucas says when I'm back in my room.

He never said he had to shave my head. I shake my head, this is a deal breaker. "You are not shaving my head."

"I need to Emmie." I shake my head. "I suppose if I shave the cut line we might be okay." Lucas frowns.

"I need my hair to cover this up," I say. He nods and proceeds to shave the cut line on my head.

"So are you ready for your operation? Are you sure you don't want anyone here?" Lucas says. I shake my head, he knows this.

"Yes, I'm sure," I say and Lucas nods, he starts to push my bed out the door. I lie down and watch the ceiling lights as we go down the hallway. My heart is pumping uncontrollably. "Are you sure I'll be okay?" I say to Lucas.

"You'll be fine, your babies will be fine. I've done this many times," Lucas says. He is so calm yet I am panicking. I grab the handrails on my bed tightly. "Trust me," he says, putting his hand on mine.

"I do trust you Lucas, which is why I'm here," I say. We reach a small room and Lucas stops my bed inside.

"I'm injecting you with the sedative," Lucas says, inserting the needle in my arm. I grab his arm, I'm so scared. Once he finishes injecting the sedative he puts the needle down and holds my hand. I guess it's too late to back out now. I feel the sedative working its way through my body. I watch Lucas's face until I see nothing but darkness.

I feel groggy, I feel awful. I open my eyes to see bright lights. I turn my head to look around. It's dark outside. How long was I in surgery for? I touch my sore head and I feel a bandage covering the wound. I feel a hand on mine and I panic. "Calm down Emmie," Lucas says. I feel disorientated, agitated even. I want to be at home with Damon. "Surgery went well. You need to stay here for a few days."

No, I can't stay here for a few days. Damon would suspect. "I can't."

"You must Emmie," Lucas says. "You need to calm down Emmie." I'm suddenly aware of an annoying beeping sound, I follow the sound. It's a heart rate machine. My heart is going crazy, I don't need a machine to tell me this. "I will stay with you tonight," Lucas says. That helps me.

"But you should be with your wife," I say. Sarah is lovely and she is my friend but I would kill any girl who would keep my husband away from me.

"I've called her already, she's fine. She would be more okay with it if she knew it was you. She likes you," Lucas says. I shouldn't let him do this but I need someone. I debated telling Denny, I reckon he wouldn't tell my family but I can't risk it. He would probably tell them thinking he is helping me. "Can I get you anything, Emmie?" I shake my head. What I need he can't give me. "I'm going to stay right here on this chair. All night, okay?"

"Lucas, you shouldn't have to do this," I say.

"Emmie, I can't have you go through this alone. I can see how terrified you are. Even badass Emmie is allowed to be scared." Lucas grins, I don't think I'm a badass. People think I am but deep down I'm terrified of everything.

"Can you read me something? So I can fall asleep?" I ask. Hearing his voice may calm me enough to consider sleep. If it were Damon, I would curl up on his chest and get him to sing to me. If it was Sully or Danny, I'd get them to hold me.

Lucas grabs a magazine on the side of my bed and starts to read some meaningless drama. I don't focus on his words but his calming voice. I don't deserve to be blessed with these loved ones. Daddy? I look around the room, Daddy? He isn't here. I close my eyes and I picture my happy place. Not so much happy place as such but somewhere with all my loved ones together.

I wake the next morning and jolt awake. "Ow," I say and clutch my head. Lucas jumps from his chair and sits on the bed in front of me.

"More painkillers?" I nod slowly. It feels like someone has scratched my brain out. Lucas leaves the room to get some painkillers. I need my phone, I search my bedside tables and I find nothing. I remember I left it in my bag. Lucas warned me I may have muscle deficiencies. I move my right leg over the side of the bed and then I struggle with the left. Is this going to be like before when I was given the fake death drug? I have to learn how to move? It must be a good sign that I can move though right?

I hear the door go and Lucas is quickly at my side. "Emmie, I don't know how Rider copes with you sometimes. You shouldn't be up and about yet," he says. I don't know how Damon copes with me at all.

"I need my phone Lucas, if Damon calls and I don't answer he will come looking for me," I say, reaching for my bag.

Lucas leans down to get my bag, he places it on the bed and lifts my legs back on the bed. Once I'm comfy he presses a button to lift the bed up so I'm in sitting position. Lucas then passes me my bag. I get out my phone and I have a text from Damon.

I missed you this morning. I love you, baby, see you later.

I wish I was seeing him later but that won't be happening. I press call.

"Hey, baby," Damon says. I still feel groggy and any sound seems to be too loud for me. I hold the phone away from my ear slightly.

"Hey, Damon. I love you," I say, I feel so vulnerable right now.

"I love you too baby. When are you home? Do you need me to pick you up?" I sigh, all I want is to see your face.

"Actually, Jessie asked me to stay another night. We don't see each other anymore and when I have the twins we won't see each other as much," I lie.

"Oh okay. I'm not sure I can handle another night without you baby. But if this is what you want I'll see you tomorrow," Damon says. He is sad and so am I. I hate this distance between us. You may not even see me tomorrow.

"I love you," I say. He may not believe it after all this separation but I need to tell him as much as I can.

"I love you too baby. Have fun," he says and hangs up.

"I'm going to do some work, if you need anything press this call button." He places a remote in my hand. "Get some sleep," he says. I half smile and shut my eyes.

When I wake I feel someone watching me. "Hey Emmie." The voice sounds familiar. I open my eyes and I see Stefan sitting on the chair. "I was in the hospital and Lucas told me. I thought I'd pop in. How are you?" he says.

"I feel awful," I admit, "I must look awful." I smile. "I'm scared, Stefan." I frown.

"That's understandable, people usually go through this with family by their side and they are still terrified. Yet you do it solo. I just don't understand you," Stefan says. What's not to understand? I love my family, I will do everything I can to protect them.

"Isn't it your job to know the patients?" I mock him.

"You are one complicated woman, Emmie." He stands up. "I must get going but if you need anything just call okay?" Stefan says. I nod and he leaves the room. I need a pen and paper. I press the call button.

Lucas comes running in. He frowns at me and I shrug. "Emmie?" he says disappointedly. I guess I scared him.

"Can you get me a pen and paper please?" I say sweetly.

"Jesus, I remember now why I don't trust you around my staff." He turns on his heels and walks out the room. I'm a troublemaker, I know this, and I don't care.

He walks back in a few minutes later with a pen and paper. "Emmie, please only use this button for real medical issues," he says, I nod and smile at him and he sighs and leaves the room.

I need my daughter well protected when I'm gone. I wasn't into christening Lilly but now I'm not going to be around she needs all the support she can get. She needs god-parents, the godfather is obvious, that has to be Sully, Lilly loves him already. I just don't know who the god mother should be, maybe Addi? She loves Lilly and without me, she may not feel welcome. If she is god mother, then maybe she will feel more comfortable.

I ring the church near our house to arrange a date. I ask the vicar for one as soon as possible and he made it for a month's time. 8th October. I write down Addi and Sully as god parents, I write the date. I decide to ring Damon again.

"Emmie?" Damon answers on the second ring.

"I just wanted to tell you I have arranged a christening for Lilly. I want to ask Sully and Addi to be godparents. I wanted your approval," I say.

"I didn't know you wanted to get her christened." I didn't but I need to do everything right before I die. "If this is what you want I think it's a great idea."

"I'm going to ring them both in a minute. Save the date, 8th October," I say.

"Noted baby. Is that all?" he asks. I guess he must be busy.

Or he doesn't want to talk to me. "Yeah. Bye Damon," I say and hang up. I need more time, damn it.

I call Sully. "Hey, Emmie," Sully says. I put the phone on loud speaker and put it on the table in front of me while I draw on the paper.

"Hey, Big Guy," I say. I need my best friend. "I wanted to ask you something."

"Ask away Emmie. Although I hate that you are asking me over the phone. Just come home," he says.

"I can't come home, Sully. I wanted to ask you to be god father to Lilly-May."

He doesn't say anything for awhile. "Can't or won't? Whatever is stopping you I can sort it for you." I wish he could, I would like to count on him like he sang to me in the car. "I would be honoured to be Lilly's god father."

"Can't Sully, don't ask me any questions because I won't answer them. Good, 8th October. I miss you, Big Guy." I sigh.

"You are scaring me, Emmie. Let me come get you," Sully begs.

"I can't Sully, I have to ring Addi. I love you, Sully." I have to tell everyone I love them.

"I love you too Emmie," he says and hangs up.

I wipe my wet eyes and ring Addi. "Hey," Addi says.

"Addi," I sob. Is this me panicking or is this my hormones?

"Emmie, don't cry honey. What's wrong?" Addi says. I wish she was my mother. She is so sweet and caring.

"Nothing, just pregnancy hormones. I wanted to ask you something," I say.

"Okay?" she says curiously.

"I am getting Lilly christened. I would like you to be godmother."

"Oh my god Emmie. Yes, a million times yes," she screams down the phone. I giggle at her reaction. I love that Lilly will have her, I really do.

"Good, 8th October. I'll send out more info later," I say. I need to make invites, I suddenly feel really exhausted. "I had better go Addi. I love you," I say. I don't think I have ever told her this but I do.

"You sure you are okay?" she asks, concerned.

"Yeah," I say.

"Well bye Emmie, I love you too." I hang up and begin to cry. Just a couple more days, I can do this right? I must do this. A nurse walks into my room.

"Amy, are you okay?" she says. Amy? Who the fuck is Amy? Oh yeah, that's supposed to be me. I don't like strangers coming into my room. "I have brought you your meds. Dr Grey assumed you wouldn't have brought them with you."

She places my meds on the table in a white pot. "Where is Dr Grey?" I say. Has he gone home?

"Dr Grey is napping at the moment. He told me to tell you that he will be paged if you need him." I frown, why isn't he going home? He must be desperate if has to nap at the hospital. I take my meds and Miss Know It All leaves. I struggle out of bed and head for the bathroom. I am unsteady on my feet but I take it slow.

I freshen up and change into my PJs. I'm more comfortable in these. When I return in the room I feel anxious. My head is hurting again. I won't disturb Lucas and I don't trust Miss Know It All. So I decide to find my healer. The sun, I walk step by step down the corridor. I get some dirty looks, is it the bandage around my head, my PJs or is it just me?

When I get outside the concrete hurts my feet, from the heat and the tiny stones. I ignore it and I take a seat on the bench outside the hospital. I curl up on the bench, I probably look like some sort of homeless person but I don't care. I feel safer in the sun. I shut my eyes and drift into restless sleep.

"Emmie," Lucas growls. I jolt awake.

"Ow," I say. My head hurts. Lucas lifts me up, I guess he doesn't care if I don't want to be touched right now. He is probably frustrated with me. I probably look like an angel with Damon around. He carries me all the way back to my room. Damon always makes it look effortless, and Lucas makes it look the same. They all must be strong to carry me.

He places me back on the bed. "You'll be the death of me," Lucas snaps. "I woke and I came to find you and you were gone. My staff said they saw you for your meds and then you were gone." I shrug. "Why did you leave?" I'm not used to angry Lucas, I've seen many sides to Lucas but this is new.

"My head hurts and I was anxious so I went to find the closest thing to calmness I could. The sun," I say.

"What is the damn button for Emmie?" he says and shoves the remote back in my hand. "And don't say for a pen and paper," he sighs. "This is scary for you Emmie, I worry about you. Especially as you are alone. Please stay here," he begs.

"I'm sorry Lucas, I wanted to let you sleep. I didn't trust Miss Know It All to not over dose me or my babies." I shrug.

"Emmie, my staff are highly qualified." I understand that but they could work for Esme or they might take a certain dislike to me. Who knows? "Stay here, I'll get more painkillers," he says. I check my phone and see a text.

Lilly misses you.

Damon says. I think he is growing tired of my absence. I miss Lilly so much too. I can't keep lying to my family. But how will I hide my head? I sleep most of the day when I'm not too stubborn.

I miss her too and I miss you too. I love you Damon.

Lucas walks back in the room. He injects me and I shut my eyes waiting for the painkillers to work. I fall back to sleep. I dream of Damon growing impatient and him leaving me.

Chapter 48

When I wake I panic that my dream is reality. My phone is ringing and that is what wakes me up. I grab it from the table in front of me.

"Hello?" I say. I never even looked at the time.

"Hey, baby. Do you want me to pick you up?"

It is light outside but that means nothing on the time. "Hey, what time is it?" I say.

"Noon, Emmie. Have you just woken up?" he asks. Yeah, I have actually, Lucas says it's normal to sleep all the time after surgery.

"Yeah long night, I guess."

"So shall I pick you up?" he repeats.

"I was hoping to stay at Jessie's again tonight." I screw my eyes up, his reaction won't be good.

"Did I do something wrong? It seems like you are avoiding me," he says. Tears fall from my face to his reaction. No Damon. I love you so much. I would never avoid you.

"Of course not Damon. I love you," I say horrified.

"Okay Baby. I love you," he says and hangs up. He didn't sound like he accepted it. Oh, Damon. Please, just one more day. That's all I'm giving Lucas. As if on cue, Lucas walks through the door.

"How are you Emmie?" he says.

"Damon is growing tired of my absence Lucas. It's worrying me," I say.

"I actually meant how do you feel. Emmie, lies aren't good in any relationship. Lies just cause strain on a relationship," Lucas says. It almost sounds like he knows first-hand what it feels like. I know he is right but this lie is for their own good.

My phone rings again and I fumble to get it. "Where the hell are you?" Damon shouts. I pull the phone away from my ear. What is going on?

"At Jessie's, why?" I say calmly but inside I am having a coronary.

"Why lie to me?" he snaps.

"I'm not lying Damon," I lie.

"Don't bother coming home. Why don't you stay with your new guy," he shouts. New guy? What new guy? Does he think I am cheating on him?

"Excuse me, what new guy?" I say scared.

"That guy from the stables. That's where you have been," he says like it's obvious. I'm not interested in Noah. He hangs up the phone leaving me speechless.

Lucas takes the bandage off my head and assesses my wound. "This seems to be healing well," Lucas says. He doesn't cover it again which is good. This hurts, I thought it was me and Damon forever. It's not like I can explain this. What am I going to do?

"Emmie, what's wrong?" Lucas asks.

"Damon thinks I'm cheating on him," I say, getting out of bed.

"What did you expect Emmie? You need to tell him." I shake my head, grab my bag and head for the bathroom. I lock the door and get dressed into my clothes and shoes.

I am hurting but I need to find Damon and explain. Did Jessie come over and tell him? She never sees me anymore, I thought she would be a good alibi. I walk back into my room grab my phone and head for the door. "Emmie, you can't leave yet," Lucas says.

"I am leaving and you can't stop me," I say without turning around I just keep walking.

"Emmie, you can't leave!" Lucas calls. I shouldn't leave but I am leaving. I walk home, every step seems like agony. I have to fix this, this isn't the end. I haven't been through hell for nothing. I refuse to believe it.

I try and run but my body doesn't cope with it. My breathing is rapid, I can't stop moving. I feel so ill. I feel sick. I stop and I puke on the street. I fall to my knees and continue to be sick. I feel so tired. Once I've finished I climb to my feet, I feel exhausted. When I reach the house, I lean on the front door for a minute trying to recover myself.

I open the door and call Damon. Sully comes to greet me. "Hey Emmie, I'm sorry, Damon went to work." I close the distance between us and I fall against him and he holds me up.

"But I need to see him," I say.

"It's not a good idea. He doesn't want to see you. Emmie, you look awful." I feel awful and it's only going to get worse.

"Did he tell you?" I ask. Sully lifts me up and carries me to bed.

"Yes, he did," Sully says.

"I didn't cheat on him, Sully," I say, who would want me anyway?

"Well, how do you explain then?" Sully says. He places me on the bed and he takes my shoes off. If Sully doesn't believe me then I have no hope with Damon. Sully is always on my side, or he hears me out before he makes judgement. I was undergoing brain surgery because I'm dying of cancer but I can't tell you that.

"I can't," I say exhausted.

"What's going on Emmie?" Sully sits and strokes my cheek, I've been yearning for my best friend and now I have him it feels different.

"I need to see him," I say.

"Just leave him to it, Emmie," Sully says. If I could I would run there and make him see me. But I don't think I can move another inch. I will have to deal with the pain.

"Where is Lilly-May?" I ask.

"Asleep in her room."

"Okay, thanks, Sully," I say, dismissing him. I want my best friend, not Damon's best friend. I can see the way it looks, I can. But my two favourite people should know me better than this. Sully gets up and leaves the room.

Daddy, where are you when I need you? You said you wouldn't leave me. I'm all alone. I cry uncontrollably. I hurt and I'm dying. One more day was all I asked for but some bloody God in heaven couldn't give me that. Why bring hell to me? I've had enough. I need to be tough for my family. I need to be their so-called magnet that they think I am. I just want to be in Damon's arms. I need him right now and he doesn't want to see me.

"Emmie, are you okay?" Sully says.

"Get out. I want to be alone. You don't believe me so I don't want to see you," I sob, you can come back when you want to be my friend and not Damon's.

"Emmie please don't do this," Sully begs.

"No, you did this. You were the one person I could trust and you don't believe me. So I don't want to speak to you."

"I'm sorry Emmie," Sully says and leaves. It seems like I've been crying for hours. Damn pregnancy hormones. I can't stop. I guess this past week has caught up with me. It's dark outside and Damon isn't back yet.

I crawl out of bed and change into my PJs. I guess Damon won't come home tonight. I trust him not to cheat on me, why can't he do the same? I continue to cry for Damon. I hurt all over. I curl up on Damon's side of the bed. I feel the bed dip behind me.

"You can count on me," Sully says. "I'm here to be your friend," Sully says. I turn over and cry into his chest. He strokes my hair and I gasp. "You okay?"

"Yeah, headache," I lie, all these lies piling up. He moves his hand from my head to my back. I don't know whether Sully believes me now or not but I won't push him away. Part of me wishes I never had the surgery. I cry into Sully's chest and I fall asleep eventually.

I wake to my phone ringing. "Damon?" I say without looking at the caller ID.

"No Emmie, it's Lucas." If he shouts at me this phone is going out the window. I feel like death.

"What do you want?" I whisper angrily. Sully is sleeping peacefully next to me.

"Emmie, please come back to the hospital." I can't go back now.

"It's Lilly-May's birthday today. I'm not going anywhere." This is her day and I won't ruin any of it.

"You really must come back, Emmie. Please," Lucas begs. I wish I could obey but I can't.

"I'll come back tomorrow," I say and hang up the phone.

"Emmie?" Sully says.

"Hey," I say whilst climbing out of bed. I hold my head, it's pounding.

"You feeling better?" he says whilst sitting up.

"No," I say honestly. I probably should go back to the hospital. "I'm going to get Lilly-May." Sully nods and I walk out of the room.

When I walk into Lilly's room she is already awake. "Momma," she says excitedly. I lift her out the cot and sit on the sofa in her room. I am struggling to hold her weight. It brings tears to my eyes. This is ripping me apart.

"Hey, Princess. Mommy loves you," I say. Lilly bounces on my lap. "You will never feel this pain I do baby. I may not be here to protect you but Daddy will. You will have uncle Sully, Uncle Danny. They will protect you. You will have auntie Lexi and Addi. They will help you with what you need." Tears fall from my eyes. I should be all cried out by now. "I'm going to miss you, princess. If I could be here I would. But you will have brothers or sisters to grow up with."

I stand up, I put Lilly in one arm and hold anything I can to keep us stable. A mother should be able to carry her child without fear of dropping them. I walk extra slow down the stairs holding the bannister as I go. I safely reach the living room and I sit on the sofa.

Lilly crawls all over the sofa and then she comes back to me with a pillow. Damon walks through the door and sits next to us. He smiles at Lilly. "Hey birthday girl," he says.

He holds his hands out to Lilly and she lurches forward towards him "Dada," she says and I gasp trying to hold on to her. Damon's hands skim mine when he grabs her from me. I withdraw my hands quickly, if he doesn't want to be with me then he won't want to touch me.

"You are going to be so spoilt today. Daddy loves you," Damon says once she is on his lap. He is so good with her. He can't even look at me. I had no doubt he would come for her birthday. But he has no intention of fixing things. Maybe he doesn't love me as much as I hoped.

I grab the arm rest of the sofa and push myself up. My body just feels so heavy. I drag my feet upstairs slowly. I can't have Lilly-May see me cry. I hurt, not only mentally but physically. I'm feeling tired all the time. My body is starting to hurt all over. I know it's only going to get worse. If Damon doesn't want me then maybe all this is for nothing.

"Baby?" Damon says behind me. I'm curled up in bed because I should be resting and I'm too exhausted to stand. Why is he using the word baby if he doesn't want me? "Don't cry Emmie," he says. He walks towards me and lays in front of me. He wipes my tears, it does no good because they just continue to fall.

"You don't want me anymore. You hate me. You wouldn't even look at me. You left me to sleep alone." Well, my best friend stayed with me but I needed Damon.

"How am I supposed to react to you cheating on me?" he says, hurt.

"I would never cheat on you. I hate myself for you thinking that." I feel awful, do I flirt with these guys to make him think that I would cheat? I don't think I do but there must be some reason that I've made him doubt my loyalty.

"So where were you, Emmie?" He strokes my hair and I screw my face up and grab his hand and I move it to a different part of my body. "You okay?"

"Headache, I was at Denny's," I lie again. My nose will be ten feet long soon with all these lies.

"Emmie, you forget I know you better than anyone. You're lying." He obviously doesn't if he is accusing me of cheating.

"Damon, please. I love you," I say. I can't tell him the truth.

"Let's just get through this day for our daughter." He sits up and takes his hands off me. I miss his touch and he has hardly touched me. Just his presence has soothed me.

"I can't lose you, Damon." I sit up too.

"You may have already lost me," he says and leaves the room. I get out of bed too quickly and I fall over. I punch the floor, I always fuck things up. I hit the floor again. I look at my knuckles, I'm sure this will bruise.

I stand up and get dressed. I don't even look at what I put on. When I walk downstairs all my loved ones are stood in the living room. I fall head first to the floor. Everything goes black.

When I wake, people are huddled around me. What the hell happened there? I hold my head. "Emmie, are you okay?" Damon says, helping me to my feet.

"What do you care?" I snap when I'm standing up. I brush myself off.

"Did you just pass out?" Sully says concerned.

"Again, what do you care?" I snap. I cross my arms.

"Don't give me that shit. I will always care about you," Damon says. I frown, I find that hard to believe if he is giving up on us so easily.

"Whatever," I say.

"Maybe we should take you to the hospital," Damon says.

"Don't bother," I snap and walk outside on the porch. I know what is wrong with me, I'm not having Damon closer to the truth.

"Baby, you passed out. Maybe we should get you checked out. There may be something wrong with the twins," Damon says behind me.

I sigh, "The twins are fine. Don't worry." They are my top priority. I turn to face Damon and I trip over my own feet I guess, or the floor. I fall again, my vision goes blurry.

Shit. "Ow," I say, holding my head. Damon lifts me back up.

"Right, that's it you are going to the hospital," Damon demands.

"I just tripped Damon. No big deal." I start to blink until I can see Damon more clearly.

"Fuck sake, Emmie. Move your ass to the car." He grabs my arm and I shrug him off.

"I don't want this Damon."

He seems exasperated, "Then what do you want?"

"Honestly? I want to curl up in your arms. I want you to tell me everything will be okay. And most importantly I want to marry you." That's what I want.

"You do?" Damon seems surprised.

"More than anything." I clutch the porch railing for support.

"What is a marriage without trust?" I trust him even when he married someone else.

"I trust you, Damon. Even after you hurt me."

"I need time Emmie," Damon says. If I had time I would allow you it but I need to grab everything I can before it's too late.

"Well, I don't have time Damon," I say.

"What's that supposed to mean?" Damon demands.

Shit, "Nothing Damon. I just want to move forward. Not back. I'm here begging you, Damon." I fall to my knees. "Marry me, Damon. You said I deserve to be swept off my feet. And for the first time, I beg you to marry me. If you love me, you will marry me. I need you, Damon."

"Emmie please, I do love you." He bends down and puts his hands under my arms and lifts me back up onto my feet. I feel shaky so I clutch to him for support.

"Then marry me. I married you last time for you, not for me. But now I want to marry you for me. Damon," I beg.

"Okay, let's do it. Today," he says. I smile like Cheshire cat.

"Really?" I squeak.

"But first look me in the eye and tell me you aren't cheating on me," he says. I don't understand how he could doubt me but this will be easy. This isn't a lie.

I look him into his eyes. "I promise you, Damon, I'm not cheating on you. Nor will I ever," I say truthfully. He lifts me off my feet and kisses me. Oh, I've missed you, Damon. He releases me too soon and takes my hand and leads me into the living room.

All eyes are on us. "Change of plan," Damon says and everyone looks confused. "We are getting married today," Damon says and everyone cheers. "Come on, don't make me wait," Damon says to everyone and they all scatter out the door. Damon seems excited and impatient for this. I am going to enjoy this day but how long will I last?

Damon takes my hand and leads me to the car. Sully has put Lilly in the car seat already and he sits next to Lilly. Damon and I sit in the front, my family all in the car. I can't stop smiling even though my head is pounding and my body is hurting.

I need to be Damon's wife again, I had to beg to get here but right now I don't care. He seems like a kid at Christmas so it can't be that bad, can it? We reach the wedding office and Damon opens my door and offers me his hand. We walk in together. I take a seat while Damon arranges things. I hold my head, if I wasn't hurting this would be perfect.

Sully sits next to me with Lilly. "Still got a headache?" Sully asks. I nod and smile to hide the pain I'm feeling. I should be sleeping yet I'm here marrying the love of my life again, some things are just more important. I lean my face on Sully's shoulder and I close my eyes. "Maybe the Doc should take a look, Emmie," Sully says.

"I'm fine Sully. It's just a headache," I reassure him. Lucas knows what's wrong with me and he knows how to fix me, I just wouldn't do as I'm told. I know where my priorities lie and I know where I would rather be.

"But you fainted Emmie. It can't just be a headache," Sully says softly. He is a bright cookie, he's right but I can play dumb for a while longer.

"It is Sully. I promise you I'm okay." For a while anyway at least. Lucas says I've increased my chances after having the surgery but the chances still look slim.

Damon leans down in front of me. "Baby I need your ring." I open my eyes.

He can't have my ring. "I've never taken it off, Damon," I say, clutching my ring finger. He puts his hands on my knees.

"You'll get it back baby I promise," he says. This ring means a lot to me, even when he divorced me I never took it off. Even if he didn't love me, I loved him. This ring is a part of me. I carefully slide it off my finger and place it in his hand and I curl his hand up so he is protecting my ring.

He smiles, gets up and kisses my forehead and he leaves me and Sully. He never told me about his wedding with Izzy. I hate to think about it, was it more significant than mine? I shake my head, no. I don't care, my wedding is significant to me and no one can take that away from me.

People walk out a room and confetti flies everywhere. I guess someone has just got married. I wonder if it will be their last wedding. This will be my last, even if something does go wrong I won't have time to fix it. I don't think I'd want to if something happens. This may not be Damon's last wedding, I hope when I'm gone he can move on. He needs to be happy and I won't be here to do that, he is young enough to start again.

All my loved ones walk into the room where the other couple came out of. Sully kisses my forehead and follows them in. I'm on my own in the hallway. Well, I guess this is it. I look down and see I'm in jeans and a plain top. I never even looked when I dressed this morning. I bet I look awful, I was crying all night.

Damon is standing in front of me now, he kneels in front of me and puts his arms on my knees. "Are you ready baby?" he asks.

I am ready, I've been waiting for this for ages. "Yes, Damon." I nod. He grins and puts his hand on mine. He stands up and pulls me with him.

I put my arm in Damon's and we walk together into the room with our loved ones. I hold onto Damon tighter for support. We reach the front with a small lady. The wedding begins. I am blessed to have all this support around me. I scan the faces of my loved one. I have my two brothers, Addi, my best friend. Brody, Jessie and Liam. Lucas and Sarah are missing but as much as I'd love them to be here I need to keep distance between my loved ones and the Doctor.

So we are officially married again, we signed the register again. We went back to the house and celebrated our wedding and Lilly's birthday. Lilly had lots of presents to open. She was very excitable. I got rather tired so I had to lay down. The next couple of days I snuck down the stables to ride Willow. He has turned into a reliable horse, Noah has said that no one else can ride him still, he will only allow me to ride him. Noah, Meeka and I have spent a lot of time together. We have taken the horses hacking. They promised not to tell anyone about me riding Willow.

Today is the day of the 20-week baby scan. I have a good-sized bump. I feel huge already, it's hard enough to get around without being pregnant. I lay fully clothed and ready to go to the scan. "You ready baby?" Damon asks.

I nod and he lifts me up and carries me down stairs, I've been so exhausted the last few days and Damon hasn't let me do anything for myself. I've told him it's just typical pregnancy and it's worse because I am carrying twins. He seems to accept it. It's not like he's a doctor and he suspects it's something else.

We reach the hospital and I get out and walk towards the reception desk. Damon puts his arm around my waist and supports me. I sit down while Damon signs me in, I wonder what mood Lucas will be in today. I promised I'd come back after Lilly's birthday and I didn't. Damon sits next to me once I'm signed in.

"Emmie," Lucas sighs. Okay, I guess he is still mad at me. Damon helps me up from my chair and supports me while I walk. "This way," he sighs again. We walk down into a small room, it's not my normal room but obviously meant for ultra sounds. Damon lifts me on to the bed.

"Ow," I say and Damon panics that he has hurt me. It's just my head, it's fine. Lucas looks me up and down.

"I can't wait to see our babies on the screen," Damon says.

"Me too," another voice says as the door opens. I look up and smile at Liam, I invited him because it's only fair if Damon is here then so should he be.

"Not you," Damon groans. Damon and Liam still don't get on, I don't think they ever will, to be honest, but that's okay because they coexist with each other for me.

"I'm the babies' father too," Liam says. He is the father to one of them, not both.

"Lift your top," Lucas snaps.

"Bad day huh?" I say sweetly.

"Just patients not doing as they're told. Lift your damn top, Emmie," Lucas snaps again. Okay, he really is mad at me. I lift my top up.

"They are both healthy. Do you want to know the sex of them?" Lucas says once he has checked everything on the machine. Personally, I don't want to know what sex they are. I can't get too attached but I have a feeling Damon and Liam will want to know.

"Yes," Liam says too quickly.

Damon looks at me and says, "Why not?"

"Emmie?" Lucas looks at me. He is leaving the ball in my court, if this was up to me I wouldn't find out.

"Does it matter?" I shrug. I won't see them grow anyway. Lucas looks sad because he knows my dilemma.

"Well, you are having two boys. Emmie, can I speak to you alone?" Lucas says. Two boys? Well, at least Lilly will have two brothers to help protect her. She needs them, they will be younger than her but I'm sure they can protect her when Damon can't.

"I'll meet you outside then baby," Damon says and he leaves the room with Liam.

I take a deep breath waiting for Lucas to hit me with his disapproval. "Emmie, you never came back."

"I got married, Lucas. Things are more important."

"What than your life? I don't think so Emmie," Lucas raises his voice. I love him for caring, I do but he doesn't understand, not even Stefan understands me and it's his job.

"I'm dying Lucas, I can feel the cancer spreading. I need to make the most of my life." I hurt all the time.

"You're dying Emmie? Cancer? Oh my god." I turn towards the open door to see Sarah standing there horrified. My mouth falls open and I look to Lucas. Lucas nods and pulls Sarah inside and shuts the door.

"Sarah please don't say anything," I beg.

"Of course I won't, it's not my place. But you really should tell Rider. I know how much he loves you." She looks at Lucas. "Is she why you are always at the hospital?" Sarah says with a tear in her eye.

Lucas nods. "I couldn't leave her on her own," Lucas says sadly.

"You are amazing Lucas, I'm proud of you," Sarah says and kisses him quickly.

"Sweetheart, I'll see you outside," Lucas says to Sarah. She nods and leaves the room. Lucas walks towards me and moves my hair so he can see the wound. "It's still healing nicely Emmie. It's been a week so I'll remove the stitches now. Would you like more painkillers?" I nod, I need more of something.

Lucas has the tools all ready, he must have planned for this. I love how clever he is. He is such a good doctor and I feel safe in his expert hands. He injects me with more painkillers. He carefully removes the stitches from my head. "Emmie, you really need to take it easy. It takes months to recuperate after brain surgery," Lucas says, concerned.

"I know, I'm tired all the time but my family need me, if I sleep all day they will suspect something Lucas," I say.

"You need to think of yourself, Emmie. You can't push yourself." He really is being gentle with me but I know he just wants to scream at me and keep me locked up.

"I'll try Lucas but what with exercising Willow and looking after Lilly, I have too many responsibilities."

"Who is Willow?" Oh crap, I'm supposed to keep this quiet.

"My horse." I shrug.

"Really Emmie? What is wrong with you? You shouldn't be riding. You are weaker than ever before." Lucas is exasperated.

"Willow looks after me. I don't have much time Lucas. This makes me happy," I say.

"It won't be the cancer that kills you, Emmie, it will be your own stubbornness." He finishes removing the stitches and I start to feel sleepy, the painkillers are working and I feel relief for the first time in a while. I smile at his comment, he is probably right. "You look awful Emmie. Promise me you'll take it easy." I nod, I'll try.

"Hey Doc, I wanted your advice," Damon says. It's lucky Lucas is finished. I sigh, Damon just doesn't let things go.

"Okay?" Lucas says.

"Emmie fainted a few days ago and she's been tripping over rather a lot. Is she okay?" Damon says worriedly. I walk into things and trip over my feet or the floor, I don't know which.

"Emmie." Lucas sighs at me. He knows I'm over doing things, I should be resting. It's probably because of the surgery, people have trouble with speech or getting their limbs to move correctly because the surgery would have interfered with their brain.

"Tell him I'm fine. Because I am," I snap. I look at Lucas to urge him to tell Damon I'm fine.

"Maybe I should run some tests just to check," Lucas says. He wants to be thorough but what is it going to tell him that we don't already know?

"No," I say sleepily.

"For fuck sake Emmie. Do as you're told," Damon growls. He always wants my health before my feelings. I don't need more tests.

"I said no." I'm putting my foot down on this one. Damon can't force me to do more tests, if he stays around to hear the test results I'm screwed. No one pushes me any further and I relax a little. I am pain-free for a while so I drift into peaceful sleep.

Chapter 49

Three months have passed. My whole body aches. I feel ugly and huge. I can't keep any food down. I'm weak, I have to keep going to the hospital for fluids. It took me 30 minutes to get ready this morning, just normal daily tasks seem impossible. I can't hold Lilly safely anymore and it breaks me. I walk downstairs I end up walking into the wall on the way to the living room. Oh, great, Damon is guarding the door. "Baby where are you going?" he asks as I'm waddling to the door. I'm covered in bruises from where I fall or the needle Lucas puts in my hand or arm for fluids.

"To see my brother," I say breathlessly. I feel like I've run a marathon.

"Let me come with you," Damon says, I know he is just trying to look after me.

"No, I'd like to go on my own." He can't go where I'm going.

"You aren't well. The pregnancy is taking it out of you. Get him to come here," Damon says frustrated. It's not the pregnancy. I'm dying. I hold onto him before I fall down. He holds my elbows for support.

"No, see you later Damon," I say and walk out of his hold. I feel like an old woman. It shouldn't be like this. I close the door behind me leaving him speechless in the living room. I walk around the corner of the street and I see Sarah's car waiting for me. I wouldn't make it to the hospital on my own anymore. She started taking me to my appointments the moment she found out.

It takes me 10 minutes to walk to her car, it should take me a minute. I hate this. I struggle to open the door and Sarah helps me from the inside. I fall in the car, I'm too exhausted to make it look elegant. "When I think you couldn't look any worse, you prove me wrong," she says worriedly.

"I'm fine," I say to reassure her. She starts the car and drives towards the hospital.

"But you're not Emmie. How have you kept it secret all this time? Damon must be suspicious," Sarah says.

"Sarah, he is a bloke, he thinks it's typical pregnancy with twins because that's what I told him." I can see it in Damon's eyes that he is worried about me.

"I had triplets Emmie, I didn't look like this." I don't know how she coped with triplets. I keep her away from her triplets and I hate myself for it. If it wasn't for her though I wouldn't make it to the hospital for my regular appointments.

"I know," I sigh. Once I give birth to these twins I'm hoping it may be easier. I won't have so much weight to carry around, I won't have to constantly worry about hurting them when I fall.

Sarah parks the car and helps me out the car. I feel like a Zombie in horrendous pain. Lucas is ready and waiting with a wheelchair. I groan, my life has come down to this, being wheeled around. With Lucas and Sarah, I can be weak. I can let my guard down, I can show my pain because they know.

Lucas pushes me to my room. Why is this room always available? Lucas lifts me on the bed and I wince at the pain. He hooks me up to the fluids and attaches me to the machines. My heart rate is slower than usual, my body is struggling to keep going. "Are you okay Emmie?"

"No, I feel like death. Literally," I whisper, shifting my weight to get comfortable. Sarah helps with my pillows. But at least I'm still alive.

"You've deteriorated rapidly Emmie. It won't be long now," Lucas says. He thinks I've pushed myself too much and I may not have the ten months he estimated. He said it was only an estimate anyway. I can say I lived my life to the full these past few months, that's what counts.

"Oh Emmie, you look awful," Sarah sighs, stroking my forehead. I still don't like to be touched but I'm too exhausted.

"Great, thanks friend," I say.

"You know what I mean," she laughs. Lucas injects me with more painkillers.

"Where is he?" I hear Damon shout from the hallway. I tense, what the hell is he doing here? I look to Lucas who also looks worried. He bursts into my room and he stops to assess the situation. Shit. "Where is he?" he demands again.

Lucas walks towards Damon to try and calm him down, Lucas doesn't like me stressed out. "Where is who?" I whisper. It's all I can manage.

"The guy from the stables," Damon demands. He thinks I'm cheating still. I'm not in a fit state to sleep around. I have trouble getting out of bed every day. I can't even hold my own daughter.

"Don't tell me you still think I'm cheating on you," I say.

"All these secret meetings. I'm not stupid Emmie." Damon isn't stupid. He knows something is up, he has just jumped to the wrong conclusion. I rip out my IVs and my monitors and fall out of bed. Ow.

Lucas leaves Damon and comes to help me back up. "Emmie, what are you doing?" Lucas says. I need to get to Damon, I need to tell him I'm not cheating.

"You are stupid actually," Sarah snaps.

"Excuse me?" Damon is shocked. Not many people confront him because he terrifies them.

"Emmie wouldn't cheat on you," Sarah says. She helps Lucas get me back on the bed. My knees are pulsing where I fell on the floor.

"Of course she is," Damon says.

"Damon, please don't do this," I say. I tighten every muscle to push away the endless pain.

"Are you okay?" Damon says. I don't look at him, I just screw my eyes shut to block out the pain. I can't reassure him right now. Not with his insecurities or my pain. "Shit Emmie. What's wrong with her Doc?" Lucas grabs my hand and inserts my IV again.

"Emmie, please calm down. Don't pull this out again." I nod.

"Just get out Rider. Stress is not good for her," Lucas says. I need Damon away, I can't have him see me in so much pain. I grab Lucas's arm and look at his face. "I'll get him out, don't worry," he says to me.

"Stress? Maybe cheating on me is causing her stress." If I could laugh hysterically I would.

"You idiot. She's not cheating on you," Sarah says angrily. "Look at her," Sarah shouts. I open my eyes to see Damon looking at me. Lucas get him out. "She's dying," Sarah says. Shit, I trusted her. I can't have him knowing.

"What do you mean, dying?" Damon says.

"Sarah!" Lucas scolds. I grab Lucas's arm again, I'm scared. "Emmie, calm down." Do I look terrified?

"Please don't," I beg.

"No, this prat needs to know. You should be ashamed of yourself accusing your dying wife of cheating." I groan. No. It's not supposed to happen like this.

"Lucas," I say again. I think he is torn, he wants Damon to know for my sake. But it's his job to keep this confidential. He looks down at me, he doesn't know how to proceed.

Damon walks between me and Sarah. He takes my hand from Lucas's arm and holds it tight. I'm so scared, I need to spare Damon's feelings. "Emmie, what's going on?" he asks worriedly.

"This isn't typical pregnancy pains. She got stage 4 cancer." I groan loudly. Why did she have to tell him? I hate that she told him. He strokes my hair and I flinch, my head has been tender since I had surgery.

"What the fuck. Why didn't you tell me?" he says under his breath. "What the hell are you talking about? You aren't dying." He is in denial. He has tears running down his face. He can see it, he is just trying to block it out.

"Emmie, take it easy. If you need anything we will be outside. Come on beautiful," Lucas says to Sarah. They both leave the room.

"Emmie, so help me if you don't start talking?" he says.

"I'm dying Damon," I say. The cat is out of the bag, there is no room for more lies now.

"No you're not," he says. He looks terrified, I lift my free hand and put it on top of his to comfort him.

"Yes, I am Damon. I have stage 4 cancer," I say gently.

"No, you haven't, this is some sort of sick joke. I think I would prefer you to cheat on me," Damon says. This is a sick joke that someone is playing on my life. Someone somewhere gave me cancer because I was too stubborn to leave this world before. I can't fight this.

"It hurts me to know you believe I would cheat on you," I say. It cuts me deep in my heart. A knife slicing at my heart.

"I'm sorry, why didn't you tell me? So all these secret trips they were for chemo, right?" I take a deep breath. This isn't going to go well.

"Not exactly," I say.

"You are having Chemo..." he insists.

"No, I'm not having Chemo Damon," I sigh.

He looks horrified. "What? Why the fuck not?" he growls.

"You can't have Chemo when you're pregnant," I say.

"Well get the babies the hell out and get treatment. How long have you known?" he shouts. He is clutching at straws. My poor strong protective Damon, he is out of control and he is panicking. Tears continue to fall down his face.

"This is why I didn't tell you, Damon. I knew you would choose me over the babies. I've known for over 3 months." I get ready for his reaction.

"I can't believe you would keep this from me. I'd rather have you than the babies Emmie. I won't live without you." I know and it hurts me that he would put me before our children. That isn't right.

"You are going to have to Damon. I was given 10 months to live but Lucas doesn't think it will be long. He said I've pushed myself too much. I just hope I can deliver the babies."

He gets on the bed and he curls around me his face on my neck, "Oh Emmie. I need you. Please. Get the babies out. I beg you," he sobs into my neck. It takes all my strength to lift my hand to Damon's head. I try to comfort him.

"I can't do that. I won't," I say.

"So the Doc is doing nothing?" Of course, Lucas has done everything he can.

"I had an operation when I found out. There was a tumour on my brain, which was why I was seeing my Dad." He sits up and looks at me dumb founded.

"You were seeing your Dad because you weren't taking your tablets," he says.

I shake my head. "No Damon, it wasn't, I was still seeing him after I started to take them."

"You were? Damn it, Emmie, this is what I was talking about TRUST! When were you going to tell me?"

"I wasn't Damon," I say. I shut my eyes and try and relax.

"Oh, so you expected me to find out when you were dead?" he

demands. Yes, Damon, you were never supposed to find out.

"Yes." I shrug. "I've written my will so everyone is taken care of."

"How is that fair Emmie? On me, on your family, on you?" Fair? I didn't want months of you suffering watching me die. I didn't want to see the look in his eyes that I can see now.

"I didn't want anyone to see me like this," I say.

"I love you, Emmie, I can't lose you," he says. I know he loves me which is why he is reacting so badly.

"There's nothing I can do," I say.

"Yes, there is, get the damn babies out." I groan, I'm not having this argument over and over.

"No Damon. I'm not trading my life for 2 others. Not my kids, our kids." I hate him for wanting them dead. "I had an operation, it was a difficult time for me. And then you thought I cheated on you. I left the hospital to find you. It was agony to walk home after surgery but I did and you weren't there."

I open my eyes and Damon does a double take. "How did you hide it?" he says. I lift my hair and show him the scar on my head. He examines it closely. "The headaches? The fainting? That was because of Surgery?" I nod. "It just gets worse Emmie. You had brain surgery and you discharged yourself from the hospital?" he says. "Is that why Doc was so mad at the scan?" he says. Oh, he noticed that, did he?

"Yes to all those questions, Damon. Lucas was super mad. I was in so much pain because I couldn't have you thinking I was cheating. I was supposed to go back after Lilly-May's birthday but I was scared you'd leave me."

"It all adds up now Emmie. The christening, the wedding. The riding. You did all that because you knew you were dying." He shakes his head and I nod.

"I ride nearly every day because it makes me happy. I needed Lilly to have people to protect her when I'm gone. I need you to know that I loved you before I died, I needed to be your wife again."

"You still go riding? Emmie, you are pregnant and dying," he says horrified, oops I should have kept that one quiet. Lucas walks into the room and gives Damon a wide berth. "I'm pissed at you Doc." Damon points his finger at Lucas threateningly.

"When aren't you?" Lucas sighs and I manage a giggle.

"Get the damn babies out and give her treatment," Damon shouts.

"Don't you think I've tried that? I don't want Emmie to die." Lucas holds his hands up in denial.

"Well try harder," Damon growls.

"I can't do any more than I'm doing. Once she delivers the babies, I can start treatment. But honestly, I don't know if she will reach that," Lucas says. I have to make it, I have to deliver these babies.

"So what do we do?" Damon panics.

"She needs to be kept calm and relaxed. No over doing things. She's only going to get worse." It feels impossible that I can get any worse. I only stress when Damon is accusing me of cheating.

"Can I go home now?" I say. I just want to sleep.

"Yes, Emmie but as I've said a thousand times, take it easy," he sighs. He removes my empty IV and machines.

"Yes, Boss," I joke and he smirks at me. Even when I'm dying I still have a sense of humour, I don't think that will ever change. Damon gets off the bed and carefully lifts me out of bed.

"I must be the weight of a whale by now," I joke to Damon but I see his jaw tense. He isn't in the mood for jokes right now. I put my arms around Damon's neck and curl up into him. Part of me is relieved that he knows. I don't have to spend so much energy hiding things. I would still do the same though, I would still go out of my way to spare his feelings. I drift asleep.

"Hey, baby," Damon says and strokes my hair. I open my eyes and see him lying in front of me. I smile at his big blue eyes.

"Hey," I say sleepily.

"Baby, it's my parent's annual party tonight. Did you want to come?" he says. Is he stupid? His parents hate me, I don't want to see their smug faces whilst I'm dying. They will only be too pleased to know that not that I plan to tell anyone else.

"Damon, I haven't seen them since before Liam took me. The things they said hurt me." They hate me and it's that simple.

"They are truly sorry for that but if you don't want to go, that's fine." I smile and shut my eyes that it's the end of the conversation. I can't imagine that they are sorry.

"I don't feel ready yet," I mutter. I don't think I ever will be.

"That's fine. I'll call them to say we aren't coming," he says.

My eyes fly open. "Damon, you should go. It's your family's party. You always go," I say. He shouldn't not go because of me.

"Baby, I found out you're dying. I'm not leaving your side. Ever," he says. He is bound to leave me at some point.

I roll my eyes. "Don't be so dramatic. Fine, we can go," I say. I don't want to give his family another excuse to hate me.

"I'll call Sully to look after Lilly-May," he says.

"Okay, thanks Damon." I smile at him.

"Why don't you get some sleep?" More sleep? That's all I seem to be doing lately. I'm missing everything.

"Please stay with me until I fall asleep," I say. He pulls me closer to his chest so my head is on his shoulder.

"Anything for you baby," he says in my ear. I dream of growing old and grey with Damon. Watching the kids grow up, watch them all marry, see my grandkids. I wish that were true.

I wake up to soft kisses all over my face. I groan, I was sleeping. I open my eyes to see Damon looking down at me. "Hey baby, we should get up," Damon whispers.

I thought he was going to stay only until I fell asleep. "You are still here?" I ask.

"Of course, I didn't want to leave you." He nuzzles my hair. That is so sweet but I have a feeling he is going to treat me like some fragile dying person instead of his wife.

He helps me out of bed. "I will leave you to get ready," he says and releases me slowly. I go to the wardrobe and find a blue lace maternity dress. It shows off some cleavage and it's knee length. I don't bother with makeup because I'm too exhausted to waste energy.

I lay back on the bed after I put on some flat shoes. "What's wrong baby?" Damon says when he walks back into the room.

I groan, "I'm fat, like huge. Huge like a house."

"Baby you look amazing." He chuckles. I don't find this funny right now.

"Don't lie now. I'm just fat," I say.

"You are beautiful. Don't doubt that." He lays on the bed in front of me and kisses me playfully.

"I guess we better go," I say but he continues to place soft kisses all over my face. I wriggle, he is making me laugh. "Damon," I giggle. He makes me feel like the only person in this world. Even when I feel low, he picks me back up again. I love this man.

He grins and then lifts me out of bed. "I'm going to get fatter if you don't let me walk anywhere," I giggle.

"Well I guess you are just going to get fatter then," he shrugs. I miss playful Damon, he doesn't come out to play anymore.

"Boss, you have a call," Sully says when we get in the living room. Damon sighs and passes me over to Sully. Damon hasn't told anyone about me dying and I'm grateful.

I smile at Sully, "Hey Big Guy," I say.

"You look nice Emmie," Sully says.

I snort, "Don't lie." I sigh. I snuggle up to his neck. I'm going to miss my best friend. "You can put me down if I'm too heavy," I say.

"I'm not lying and you aren't too heavy," he says. He decides to take me out to the car and he puts my seat belt on. "You look awful Emmie." Why do people keep saying this? Do they think I don't know? "You look like you are going to break." I feel like I may too.

"Lucky for you, you are my best friend or I may kick your ass." I giggle and he joins me. Damon slides in next to me.

"You ready baby?" Damon asks.

I grab Sully's hand and I bring it to my cheek. "I love you, Big Guy," I say. I still feel the need to tell my loved ones all the time.

"I know Emmie, I'll see you later. I love you too," Sully says and shuts my door. He walks back into the house. He must be fed up of me keep telling him that I love him.

"You know I never understood why you kept telling me you loved me all the time but I understand now. Sully doesn't understand, you should tell him," Damon says.

"No, he will treat me differently like you do." Damon frowns like he doesn't understand how he is different. "You treat me like I'm going to break Damon. Yeah, one day I will. But at the moment I need you to treat me like you always have done. Like your badass Emmie." I shrug.

"My badass Emmie." he smiles whilst he thinks it over. "I'll try baby," he says. I wonder how long it will last. We arrive at the ridiculously huge house again. Damon carries me inside and puts me down by the door. "I'd better go find my parents. I'll be back soon baby." He kisses me on my head and leaves me alone.

I don't feel too good. I'm going to go somewhere quieter. I walk into the fancy living room where nobody normally goes. I sit down on the sofa and lean against the armrest and close my eyes. "Hey, beautiful," I hear someone say. It makes me jump, I open my eyes to see a tall black haired guy gawking at me. He looks familiar but I don't know why.

"Don't sneak up on a pregnant woman, you idiot," I snap.

"Wow, chill out sexy." Sexy, is he trying to be funny?

"Who the hell are you calling sexy? I'm fat. Have you not seen I'm the size of a house?" I say. I put my hands on the armrest and push myself off the sofa. I use my hands to gesture how fat and ugly I look.

"Oh trust me, I can see you and I love what I see." Well, that was kinda sweet I guess. I blush slightly.

"My name is Blake, it's very nice to meet you." He extends his hand but I don't take it and he lets his hand fall. He is very handsome I have to say. But I can't hide the feeling that I recognise him. "So are you going tell me yours?"

"Ha no," I say and cross my arms. Blake smirks, waiting for me to say something else, I raise my eyebrow.

"Why not? That hurts." He chuckles, he seems like a right ass. I bet he gets all the girls. I imagine girls fall head over hills for him, but I'm not most girls.

"I'd rather remain a mystery." I shrug. He walks towards me, he is rather close but I stand my ground.

"I like your smart mouth and your beauty," he whispers into my ear. I roll my eyes. I'm not feeling it.

"What the hell are you doing here? I wouldn't have come if I'd known," Damon says angrily. I see Blake roll his eyes and then he moves away from me.

"Nice to see you too," Blake sighs.

"Is this idiot bothering you, baby?" Damon says when he reaches me and puts his arm around me. What is going on between them two?

"Actually we were having a very nice conversation. I was complimenting her beauty." Blake winks at me. I frown, who the hell is this guy?

"Leave her alone, I'm warning you," Damon shouts.

"What the hell is going on?" I say exhausted, Damon pulls me tighter so he is taking most of my weight.

"She's a feisty one. I like it." I groan. I'm not into this kinda flattery.

"Back off," Damon growls. I stand in front of Damon and I face him.

"Damon, what the hell is going on? Tell me or so help you," I say firmly. I wobble slightly and he catches me and holds me still.

"Ha, someone has you whipped Bro." Blake laughs. Bro? Damon has a brother? Why didn't he tell me he had a brother? I hate that word whipped. I'd like to whip that Jackass.

"Bro, say what? He's your brother?" I push Damon's chest but he doesn't move.

"I'm definitely the hotter brother don't you think? Just a matter of time before you come running Beautiful," he says. Damon looks hurt, he isn't fighting back. Why?

I turn around and smile at Blake, I walk closer to him and he smirks like he has won. I punch him as hard as I can in the face. I'm not as strong as I used to be so it probably wasn't the hard but Blake holds his face. "How dare you?" I demand.

"What the fuck?" Blake says shocked. I glance at Damon behind me, it looks like he is watching but he isn't processing.

"You may be his Brother but you are pissing off a pregnant woman. I love my husband, now whatever you have against each other I won't be in the middle of it. Do you understand?" I scold.

"Damn girl, you're scary when you're angry," Blake mocks me but he holds his hands up in defeat.

"Yes I am and you will do well to remember that," I say.

"I like you," Blake flirts. Does he not take a hint?

"Well, I don't particularly like you."

"Oh dear Brother, do you have nothing to say?" Blake taunts Damon.

I look at Damon again, he looks broken, "No," Damon says like he is intimidated. What did Blake do to him?

"Is that because you actually know I'm a threat?" Blake laughs. He is a jackass. I want to hurt him.

"I guess," Damon says. What has Damon so scared? Damon doesn't bow down to anyone like this.

"Oi you, what do you mean by that?" I say, pointing at Blake. He smiles at me.

"Well, all his girlfriends come running to me. I guess I'm hard to resist." He is full of himself. He needs knocking down a few pegs. I feel sorry for Damon, his Dad paid them to leave and the others Blake stole. I'm angry, I punch Blake again.

"Jeez, stop hitting me," he says, annoyed.

"I will tell you once and only once, I will not choose you over your brother. I love Damon more than anything. And your attitude is pissing me off. I'm his wife, not his girlfriend," I say sternly.

"Okay, keep your sexy knickers on. Or maybe you should take them off." Urgh, this guy doesn't know when to quit. I turn to face Damon and I trip over my own feet. Damon manages to catch me before I fall. So he is with us because he processed me falling.

"Are you seriously not going to stick up for me?" I say, pushing his chest.

"Emmie I..." My husband looks so vulnerable.

I turn around again but Damon holds me, supporting me as I turn. Even when he is vulnerable he still looks after me. This is the difference between Damon and Blake. Damon is sweet and caring and Blake is just an ass. "Leave now. I want to speak to my husband alone," I snap.

"I'll catch you later for a kiss sexy." He blows me a kiss and leaves the room. I turn towards Damon again.

"Damon, what's going on?" I sigh. I reach up to his face and strokes his cheeks.

"I hate him, Emmie," Damon mutters. That's obvious.

"Why did you not tell me you had a brother?" I say. He left it a while to tell me about Lexi.

"Because he's dead to me. The things he has done to me..." Damon says.

"Then tell me. Help me understand." I'm your wife, you should confide in me.

"He's always taken everything I care about most. If I knew he was here I would have never brought you." He looks at me. What is this? I would never pick that jackass over him.

"Why, because you are worried I would leave you?" I say shocked.

"Emmie, they all leave for him. You aren't going to be any different." I find that offensive. How many girlfriends has he had?

I shove him hard again, I'm so angry, "Are you serious? Does our marriage mean nothing to you?" I protest.

"Of course it does. That's why he's here. To take you away from me. Whenever I'm happy this is what he does." I put my forehead on his chest. What did he do to you? It's like he has invisible scars like me.

"I'm not like your other girlfriends Damon. I'm your wife," I reassure him.

"I know. He has a way of making people fall for him," he says. He should know me, I'm too fucked up to want another. I only want Damon.

"You know what Damon? I'm dying, I don't want to play the sympathy card. But I want to spend the next couple of months with you. I am fighting for you and you say I will leave you for your brother. You are unbelievable. Come find me when you are thinking clearly." I storm out of the room. I'm so angry.

Chapter 50

I walk into the big room where everyone is gathered. "Hey, Emmie are you okay?" Lexi asks. Danny is standing next to Lexi. I lose my balance and Danny catches me. I hold onto Danny for support. I'm too ill to be doing this shit.

"Hey, no, your brother is an idiot," I say exhausted. Danny continues to hold me which I'm glad.

"Yes, I guess Damon is," Lexi agrees.

"I was actually talking about your other brother," I say, annoyed.

"Oh, you met Blake then?" She smiles.

"Yes, I've had the pleasure of enduring his company," I sigh.

"He's not that bad," Lexi giggles.

"Well I thought he was, he's worse than your other Brother. He may have a sore face later." I smile.

"You hit him?" Lexi says, shocked. I shrug.

"Yes, twice. What can I say? He shouldn't piss off a pregnant woman." I shrug again.

"Oh, Emmie," Danny sighs. I think he is slightly amused though.

"Wow Bro, she's given you a shiner there," Lexi says. I turn slightly to see Blake but I stay in Danny's hold.

"Ha, it's only made me want her more." He grins at me.

Lexi looks disappointed, "Is that what this is all about? You are trying to get Emmie in your bed? No wonder she punched you. Watch Damon doesn't kill you, he is very protective of her." I would have thought the same but he didn't bloody do anything.

"He won't do anything. He knows I will always win," Blake snorts, crossing his arms.

"I'm fed up with you," I say, frustrated. He will never win.

"Seriously if you hurt my sister I won't be afraid to kick your ass," Danny says. At least someone is sticking up for me.

"Chill out, people are so uptight. Emmie, can I have a word in private?" Blake says.

I shake my head, "No you can't." I don't want to spend any more time with this idiot.

"Please," he begs.

"Fine," I snap. I wobble slightly when I try to support myself.

"You okay?" Danny says. I nod and walk carefully after Blake.

Blake enters the room on the far side of the big room where his Dad took me. It looks just the same, a small office. I hold the desk for support. "What the hell is this about you moron?" I demand.

"I think you are beautiful Emmie," he says. I sigh. I didn't come here to be lied to again. Why do people say this? I haven't even worn make up today.

I roll my eyes. "Good for you."

"Stop being a tease," he says. A tease? I'm pretty sure I am trying to push him away. No, in fact, I'm pretty sure I'm trying to kick him down the damn road. He walks towards me and I stumble backwards. My back hits the wall.

Nowhere to run, not that I can run. He puts both of his hands either side of my head against the wall. His face is so close to mine. I can feel him breathing on me. "What are you doing?" I say. I tilt my head away from him.

He puts his fingers on my chin and he moves my head to look at him, "I know you can't resist me, Emmie. No one can." That's a bit presumptuous. I can resist him, in fact, he repulses me just like all the rest of them.

"I'm not interested. Get away from me. I'm warning you." I don't know what I'll do because I'm dying. I can't fight him off, I'm helpless and he knows it.

"Oh Emmie, there is no one to save you. You are too beautiful for me not to have you," he says. I'm disgusted that Damon and Lexi have a brother like this. After meeting his parents though, I'm not that surprised.

"Ahem," Damon clears his throat. Oh, thank god. "Get away from my wife," Damon shouts. Blake doesn't move so I shove past him and run into Damon's arms. Damon strokes my hair and comforts me while I catch my breath breathing him in. "I'm sorry I didn't stick up for you before. But I'm here now," Damon says. Oh good, he has come to his senses and just in time too.

"I love you, Damon," I say into his chest.

"I love you too baby," he says. We have been through so much that he shouldn't doubt my love for him but I guess I let my invisible scars hold me back all the time.

"Damon, I'm so tired," I say, exhausted. My knees give way but he continues to hold me.

Damon lifts me up so he is holding me so I don't have to stand. "Oh don't play damsel in distress. It doesn't suit you," Blake scoffs.

"Are you okay baby?" he says to me. "And shut up, you don't know what's going on," he growls at Blake.

"Can we go home, please? I don't feel well," I say breathlessly. Lucas said no stress yet all tonight has been is stressful.

"Is this how you are going to play this? I have to say you are a good actor," Blake says, impressed. Can someone knock him out already? I would if I could.

"She's dying for fuck sake," Damon shouts. Damon, no.

Blake's whole face changes, "What do you mean dying?"

"As in dying Bro. Cancer," Damon says like it's obvious. I bury my head in his neck. Can we trust Blake not to say anything?

"Bro I'm sorry," Blake says. He sounds genuine.

"Leave now!" Damon shouts. Blake makes a hasty exit.

"Damon," I moan. Someone else knows.

"I will sort it later baby. Let's get you home." Damon walks back in the big room but walks out a back way and takes me back to the car. I fall asleep in the car.

Damon lifts me out of the car when we are home. He carries me straight upstairs and into the bathroom. He runs a bath and stands me up and undresses me. In sickness and in health the vows said. This is all too real. He checks the temperature of the bath and then lifts me in. It feels hot against my skin. I guess I was cold.

Damon washes me. This feels wrong in some ways and right in others. I close my eyes and let Damon wash me. I'm so tired. I open my eyes to see Damon looking at me. "Kiss me, Damon," I beg. "Please."

He takes my face in his hands and he kisses me like this will be the last time. He is making every moment count. He is making this meaningful, gentle and urgent all in one. He is making my head spin. "Please," I beg again breathlessly. He groans, he knows what I'm asking. He pauses for a while thinking it over. He lifts me out of the bath and wraps me in a towel. I look him in the eyes, pleading him. He lifts me again and takes me to the bedroom.

He carefully places me on the bed and takes his clothes off. He climbs on top of me, careful not to put too much weight on me. "You are very demanding. I should say no, but I can't resist you," he says. I smile, he says the nicest things sometimes.

He eases himself into me. He is being careful with me, taking it slow. He does all the work but I enjoy this just the same. I close my eyes and hold him to me as much as my body will allow. I hadn't planned this but I need him.

When I come back to this world, Damon is dressing me in PJs. I open my eyes to see him wearing his boxers. Well, that was fun, I smile at him. "You feeling better now baby?" he chuckles.

"Yes, thank you for taking me home." I smile, and thank you for other things.

"You are welcome, baby," he says and kisses me on my forehead.

"Boss, can you come downstairs please?" Sully calls. Damon lifts me up so he can get the sheet from underneath me. He tucks me into bed.

"Coming!" Damon shouts. I want him to stay with me but Sully sounded urgent. I curl up on my side and Damon strokes my hair before leaving. Why does Sully call Damon Boss? We are more like family now. Damon turns the main light off but leaves the bedside lamp on. He is so thoughtful sometimes.

I shut my eyes. I can hear lots of muffled voices downstairs. Who the hell is here at this time? I try to block out the noises, I'm so tired. After 5 minutes or so I hear footsteps outside the door. "Baby I'm sorry," Damon says.

"What's wrong Damon?" I say worriedly.

"Everyone knows," he says. What is he talking about?

"Knows what?" I say.

"That you are dying. They demand to see you." Damon sits in front of me and he strokes my face. Demand to see me? Who do they think they are?

"I don't want them to see me like this." I can't face them right now. I'm exhausted.

"They won't take no for an answer," Damon says. I imagine Damon has tried to get rid of them but I can't imagine they will leave after this news.

"Fine," I groan. Damon gets up and leaves the room. This isn't going to be good. I need to be strong for my loved ones. I hear the door open, I don't bother to look up as I'm sure I'll find out soon enough. I see Danny laying in front of me and I feel someone sit in the space behind my bent knees, their hands are placed on my legs.

Danny pulls me into a hug. I look at his face when he releases me. He has been crying, his eyes are all red. "Jeez guys, cheer up will you." I proceed with my sense of humour.

Danny sighs and strokes my face. "Emmie, I just found out my sister is dying. Give me some time," he says. Time is what I don't have, I wish I did.

"I hate that you know," I say. I hate them hurting because of me, it's not right.

"And I hate that you never told me," Danny growls. That is something I'm not sorry about.

"Are you in pain Emmie?" Lexi cries. It's too much effort for me to move and comfort her right now so I settle for putting my hand on top of hers.

"I'm not going to burden you with that," I say. They don't need to know how much pain I'm really in. How simple tasks are impossible.

"You don't need to be strong for us," Danny says. I do, it only makes it harder for me to see everyone hurting. I can't see my loved ones hurts.

"Yes, I do. I can't be weak. I've been strong all my life. I'm not having cancer bring me down," I reassure them. I vowed to myself that I will fight until the very end and I will.

"Okay well, we will leave you to rest. You have many more visitors to come," Danny says. Part of me wants my brother to stay but more of me doesn't want him to suffer so I let him go. He kisses my forehead for a while and then gets up.

"Okay, bye Bro. Bye Lexi. I love you, Danny, I love you both," I say.

"I love you too Emmie," Danny says. I hear Lexi crying, I don't think she can get any words out. I hear them leave the room.

"Hey, sweet sister." I smile when I hear Denny. My brother. He lays in front of me like Danny did. He strokes my hair. "I have this strange feeling that you tried to tell me. Or at least slipped up," Denny says.

"I wanted to tell you but I couldn't risk you telling Damon. I nearly slipped when I said I was seeing my Daddy instead of used to," I sigh.

"I remember. The coffee, the beach. Was that your goodbye?" he says.

"Not goodbye. Just giving you happy memories. I love you, Denny," I say.

"I love you too dear sister. I will come back soon okay?" I nod.

"I'd like that." You'll just have to make it soon. He kisses my cheek and leaves the room. I'm going to fall apart soon.

Brody and Jessie sit in front of my eye line. None of them lay with me. Jessie is crying and Brody looks sad. "Guys, come on guys, you are killing me here with your sad faces." I smile. I know this isn't a joking matter but I need to lighten the mood somehow.

"Emmie, this isn't funny," Brody growls.

"That was low Emmie," Jessie sobs. I shrug.

"Guys I may be dying but I will never change. I don't want you to see me any differently either." They need to remember me, not who I become.

"We love you, Emmie," Brody chuckles, but it seems more like a cry, not laughter.

"I love you guys. Now go home and start living your lives." I smile, they are blessed with this gift whereas I am not.

"We will be coming back soon," Jessie snaps.

"I wouldn't expect anything less," I say. I will have to fight everyone off after tonight. They leave the room. I shut my eyes, I really am exhausted.

"Hey, beautiful," I hear Liam say. I feel his hand move hair out of my face. I don't open my eyes. I don't think I can.

"Hey," I mumble.

"You look awful," Liam laughs.

"Well at least someone is acting normal around me," I say. People may have told me this but Liam is messing with me. He isn't acting like I'm going to break and I appreciate that.

"I know how strong you are. You aren't going to let this beat you and I wanted to thank you," Liam says like he truly believes it. I wish I could fight this but I have no strength.

"For what?" He has nothing to thank me for.

"I know Rider doesn't think the same but thank you for not killing my son." Liam seems really into this baby and I'm glad.

"Our son, Liam," I snap, he's more mine than his but I will settle for ours. "I couldn't kill them to save myself." It's a horrible thought.

"You are one crazy bitch you know that? I don't know whether to bow down to you or slap you silly," he laughs. Slap me silly? Who came up with that?

"I already ache all over Liam. I will accept the bow." I try to giggle but it is pathetic.

"Oh, princess. What will I do without you to brighten my day?" he says.

"You can go out and kidnap someone else's wife," I snap. He took me from my husband, precious time that I should have treasured.

"Oh Emmie, none of them would be as good as you," he sighs.

"Of course they wouldn't, I'm one of a kind." I smile.

"I'll see you soon princess," Liam says.

"I love you, Liam," I say. I love you all so much.

"I love you too princess," he says and I feel him get off the bed.

"Oh, Emmie," Addi says. I try and prize my eyes open for her. I look at her and she is so beautiful. "I think of you as a daughter you know," she says. I close my eyes again. They are just too heavy. She strokes my hair.

"I wish you were my Mom," I say. It's the truth, she has been more of a Mom to me than Esme has.

"Emmie, I've been thinking about this for a while," she says.

"Thinking about what?" I say.

"I want to adopt you. I've looked into it and it's doable," she says. I would love that but I don't have long left.

"I would love that, I really would, but it will take too long," I say, it will never go through by the time I die.

"Please, let me try," she begs.

"Okay Addi. I have an attorney that will probably help us," I say.

"You can call me Mom if you'd like. If you feel comfortable that is. Oh Emmie, thank you for giving me this." She sounds really happy. She grabs my hand and squeezes it tightly. "Can we go tomorrow?" she asks.

"Sure, Mom." I smile and she claps her hands. I love how she is so happy right now. I can give her this and this will be easy because I want this too.

"See you tomorrow Emmie." She kisses my head and leaves. I'm smiling inside, it's too much effort to smile but I am truly happy.

I open my eyes when I feel the bed drop. How many more people are here? I see his annoying face. I sigh and close my eyes, "Get out."

"Emmie, you are my sister in law. I want to make this right. If I had known I wouldn't have done this," Blake says.

"I don't need your pity. In all honesty, I would have respected you more if you would have done this if you had known. I don't want sympathy, I want things as normal," I say but I know things will never be normal.

"Okay well in that case, I think you look hot. Did you want company in bed?" Blake flirts, I can hear it in his voice. Damn it, he is so annoying.

"Not from you," I sigh.

"I think you should leave my wife to it now. You are lucky you are here anyway," Damon says. Please, Damon, I need sleep.

"I was just saying Emmie might like company in bed. From someone who could help with her needs," Blake teases Damon again. Damon is quiet, I guess Blake really does get under his skin.

"Well, I have someone in mind but hey that's not you. It's my husband. And if you want to continue to come over... You need to stop acting like a tool and make things okay with Damon," I snap.

"Anything for you sexy." I groan but I feel the bed move so I guess he has left the room.

"Just one more baby and then you can sleep," Damon says and leaves the room. They have saved the worst one for last.

"Emmie," Sully says when he lays in front of me. My best friend cries in front of me and I cry too. He pulls me to his chest. "I'm so sorry Emmie," he says.

"Of all people, I thought you had my back," I say to Sully. I needed him to be my friend, not Damon's. He should have believed me.

"I never expected this Emmie. I'm sorry." Sully continues to cry.

"But you expected me to cheat? Nice," I say. I don't want to punish Sully.

"That's not what I meant. You could have told me." I look up at his beautiful face, I reach up and wipe his tears. Oh, Big Guy, don't cry. Tears fall from my face too. I knew this would be hard.

"Yeah right," I say. He would have told Damon.

"I love you, Emmie. I'm with Rider on this one. We would rather have you." I close my eyes and sigh.

"Well, that's why I didn't tell you. I forgive you, Sully, because I love you. And my kids will need their Uncle Sully," I say.

"Thank you, Emmie," he says for me forgiving him. "Your headaches Emmie? When you ran into my arms when Damon stayed at the safe house. You left the hospital, didn't you? You looked so vulnerable. And the phone call when you asked me to be godfather, you were at the hospital weren't you, alone? I was worried about you that day," he sobs.

"I needed you. I wanted my best friend to come get me but it hurts me to see you like this," I say and grab his hair. "I was so scared, alone at the hospital but I knew I had to do it."

"I can't lose you," he says.

"And I don't want to leave you," I say. "I love you."

"You keep telling me you love me. I didn't know why you kept telling me. You knew. Is this why you keep telling me goodbye?"

"I don't ever want to say goodbye. I just need to tell everyone how much they mean to me. You, Damon and Lilly, are everything to me. I may be cruel to keep you so close. Usually, it's husband and wife and their kids that make a home. But my family wouldn't be complete without you."

"I feel the same way about you, Emmie. You are family to me now. I just need to learn how to be your friend as well as Damon's. You needed me and I was Damon's friend."

"None of that matters now. I'm dying and want to be here with my family," I say. He kisses my forehead.

"Can I have my wife back now?" Damon says. Sully goes to get up but I grab his hand.

"Please, let him stay until I fall asleep. It won't be long anyway," I say.

"Sure Emmie, whatever you want," Damon says. He slides in behind me and strokes my hair. "How could we miss it?" Damon says.

"We could see something Damon but she made us believe it was just pregnancy," Sully says.

"But I should have known. How could I accuse her of cheating when I know she hates other people touching her?" Damon says.

"We both believed it. We saw her breaking when she couldn't hold Lilly anymore. Pregnancy doesn't make you weak like that," Sully says.

"She's been brave, now we have to be brave for her," Damon says.

"Were you going to tell me?" Sully asks.

"Tell you what?" Damon asks.

"That she had cancer, or would you have hidden it from me?" Sully asks.

"It's what she wanted. I tried to get her to tell you," Damon says.

"I'm your friend and she is my best friend. I live with you, I don't see how you could hide this from me," Sully says angrily.

"She's my wife Sully," Damon says. I focus on Sully's breathing and Damon stroking my hair. I'm safe for now and I'm with my two favourite guys. I would stay in the moment, in pain, if I could. I would take the pain for the rest of my life if I could stay with them.

Chapter 51

When I wake in the morning Damon is wrapped around me breathing softly in my ear and Sully is gone. I need to get up, Mom will be here soon to go to the Attorney's office. I reach for my phone on the bedside table. I press call.

"Mr Declan's office," he says.

"Er, Mr Declan? It's Emmie Salvatore," I say.

"Emmie, are you okay?" he asks.

"I need your help. It's my last dying wish," I say.

"Come in at 11 am Emmie and I'll see what I can do for you," he says and hangs up. I text Mom to tell her the time.

"Emmie?" Damon says sleepily. I turn to face him.

"Yeah," I say. "You should go to work," I say.

"I'm not going anywhere," he says like I've said something stupid.

"I'm going to get worse, I'll be okay. Your gang needs you," I say.

"Emmie, I'm not wasting one minute with you. You need me more," Damon insists. I smile and he kisses me softly. "What was that phone call?"

"I made a will. Mr Declan helped me with it. Now I need his help with something else," I say.

"I don't trust him, Emmie. What do you need help with?" Damon asks.

"Addi wants to adopt me." I smile.

"Wow, that's great. Let me come with you."

"Okay."

"Boss!" Sully calls. What does he want so early? Damon kisses me and gets up. He dresses quickly and leaves me. I struggle out of bed and walk over to the wardrobe to get dressed. I settle for a baggy top and some shorts, I say baggy, it just hangs over my bump.

I fall on the way back over to the bed. Ow, I push myself onto my knees and wipe my hands. I see Sully running towards me. He picks me up. "Downstairs my lady?" he jokes. At least he didn't use the word, Ma'am. I giggle and nod at him. I wish my legs could be more reliable, I have to rely on people to carry me which I hate. Not the carrying concept but just having to rely on other people because I can't do it for myself.

Sully grins and takes me downstairs. Instead of putting me on the sofa, he sits down and brings me with him. I curl up on his lap and close my eyes. "Sis," Danny says. I open my eyes and look at him.

"What?" He is looking at me like I may disappear.

"You look a bit better today," Danny says relieved.

"I was exhausted yesterday, I'm only going to get worse Danny. Don't get your hopes up," I say, false hope is not good.

He comes to sit next to us on the sofa and he grabs my hand. The door goes and Damon goes to get it. I look up to see Denny walking through the door. "Hey, Sweet Sister," he grins. I smile back.

"Seriously, why are you both here?" I demand.

"I was worried, you looked awful last night," Danny says.

"You thought...?" I sigh, he thought I could be dead. That's why he came. "Look, I am going to get worse but I'm not going yet. I will deliver these babies and then it won't matter." I shrug.

"Won't matter that what? You die? Emmie, are you taking your meds?" Damon growls.

I groan, "Yes Damon I am. I'm just saying I'm being so careful not to fall on the babies, it's hard to carry around so much weight what with being fat anyway." Just because I take my meds doesn't mean I don't get these thoughts, I just don't feel like I want to leave anymore. I want to stay with my family.

"Emmie, you aren't fat," Damon sighs.

"You aren't fat Emmie," Sully whispers too. No matter how many times they say I'm not going to be convinced.

The door goes again and Damon gets up to get the door and

Liam walks in. Damon tries to shut the door on him but Liam carries on walking through the door. I roll my eyes at them. "Hey, Princess."

"Guys, I'm not dead yet. You don't need to hover around me," I snap.

"Emmie, we want to spend every moment we can with you. Let them have this," Sully whispers. I sigh, I guess I can give them this if it will make them feel better.

"Emmie, breakfast?" Damon says.

"No," I say. Is he crazy?

"Emmie," Damon sighs.

"Look, I can't keep anything down so why waste food?" I shrug.

"Emmie, try a biscuit, anything. For me," Damon begs.

"Fine," I snap. Damon leaves the room. I rest my head on Sully's shoulder.

"Emmie, Damon said you had brain surgery. Do you have a scar?" Danny asks. Yes, it's hideous but at least my hair can cover it. I use one hand to move my hair out the way so Danny can examine it. I feel Danny touch it and I wince. "Does it still hurt?" Danny says.

"It's still tender," I say.

"That's cool," Denny says. "Battle Scar. You should have shaved that part of your hair, you would have looked like more of a badass."

Damon walks back in the room. "I'd rather die than shave my head, Denny. When I was going to have surgery, shaving my head was a deal breaker. Lucas had more work cut out but he managed," I say.

"Emmie, it's just hair," Damon says frustrated.

"Not to me Damon," I say.

The door goes again and Damon passes me a pack of biscuits. He walks towards the door. "Oh, Emmie," Mom says as she walks through the door. All these people worrying that I may keel over. I try to open the biscuits but I am just useless. Sully reaches around me and rips the biscuits open. I grab a biscuit and start to nibble on it.

"Hey, Mom," I say.

"Mom?" Danny and Denny say in unison.

"I'm going to adopt Emmie, isn't that great?" she says excitedly.

"What would Mom say?" Denny says in disgust.

"You will still be my brother Denny. Esme wants me dead or she thinks I'm dead. Who cares? Addi has been more of a Mom to me than Esme has," I say to Denny.

"Is this what you want?" Danny asks.

"Yes, I'd say more than anything but right now I just want my life. This is my dying wish. Well, I have lots of wishes but this is one of them." I half-heartedly grin.

"What are your other wishes?" Mom says.

"For my loved ones to be happy. I want Damon to move on and find someone to be happy with. I want my kids to grow up happy. I don't want you all to mourn me, I'll be watching over you all. The list is endless," I say.

"Emmie. You are so frustrating sometimes," Damon growls. Which bit is he mad at exactly? He walks towards me and gestures for me to face him so I shuffle my weight to face him. He grabs my knees and I hold his neck for support.

He lifts me up and he heads outside. He shuts the door behind us and he presses my back against the door. He kisses me like he is angry, he is overpowering but I like it. He pulls away. "I'm so angry with you," he growls.

"That's kinda obvious Damon. What did I do this time?" I tease.

"The bit that annoyed me the most was that you want me to find someone else when you die." He shakes his head. "I only want you," he says, hurt.

"But when I die, Damon, you may change your mind. I want you to be happy," I say.

"I will never want anyone else, Emmie. If I died would you want to move on?" That's different, we have tested this theory already. I was out of control. I only accept his touch, it's him or no one. There is no one on this planet that will make me feel what I feel when he touches me. I let Liam touch me when I had my memories and it was painful. I can't say I enjoyed it, I love him and I wanted to make him happy.

"Damon, this is different and you know it. I may love more than one person because I am fucked up but I can only accept your touch. There will be no one else that comes close to you. Anyway, I couldn't survive without you," I say.

"Emmie, I love you. You aren't the only one that feels something different. I've been with a lot of women but when I'm with you...It's hard to explain but it feels like electrical pulses. Like gravity brings me to you.

No one has made me feel this way," he says. I hate that he had so many girlfriends.

I don't understand? He makes me feel this way. How could we both feel this way? It really is like we are made for each other. "You are a part of me Damon, I couldn't live without you."

He grabs my hand and he slides it under his shirt and places it on his heart. I can feel his strong heartbeat. "My heart belongs to you and only you," he says. He truly knows how to make me feel special. He kisses me again but this time he doesn't stop. I scrunch my hands up in his hair and pull him closer to me. He is careful not to push too hard on my bump.

I can't say goodbye to him. This is so hard, I'm terrified to be somewhere without him. I push his head away from me. "You okay?" he says breathlessly.

I nod, trying to catch my breath. "I can't keep up with you anymore," I say, finding it difficult to breathe. He strokes my cheek and I close my eyes.

"Sorry baby, I just can't control myself around you," he says, putting his forehead on mine.

"Don't be sorry. I love that you still want me like this," I say, finding it a bit easier to breathe.

"I will always want you. You'll just be more breakable. I'm glad that you tell me instead of suffering." He smiles. I place my head on his shoulder and hug him tightly. He moves away from the door and he opens it to walk through.

When we reach the living room everyone is still here and they look up when we arrive back in. Damon places me back into Sully's arms and Sully puts his arms around me. I cuddle up to him, he is so warm. "Damon, can you get her a blanket or something?" Sully asks. It's Spain, I shouldn't be cold. Damon nods and leaves the room.

Damon is a jealous guy but for some reason he lets me be this close with Sully. He doesn't like to share but he doesn't say anything. He doesn't give me any indication that he is uncomfortable with it. Even when he found out we kissed. I should ask him about it, I don't want to make him upset and I don't want him to endure it just because he wants me to be happy. Sully doesn't push me away either. He always says he will be here any way I want him to be.

Damon arrives back with a blanket and he has Lilly in his arms. He places the blanket over me making sure all of me is covered. "Momma," Lilly says, holding her arms out to me.

"I can't baby," I say, a tear falls down my face.

"Momma," Lilly demands again.

"Emmie, it's okay. I'll hold her weight," Sully says. I don't trust myself. Lilly screams, I look at her and then to Damon. Damon nods.

"You'll be fine Emmie," Damon says reassuring me. They know it breaks me not to be able to hold my daughter.

"Trust me, Emmie," Sully says.

"Why do you keep saying that? I trust you explicitly. I just don't trust myself." I sigh. I hold my hands out to Lilly and she giggles. I sit her on my lap and Sully has his arms around me and Lilly.

"Emmie, my niece is more stubborn than her Mom," Danny chuckles.

"Yeah, I know." I sigh. "She always gets what she wants and she knows it."

Lilly lays over my baby bump and she closes her eyes. I look at her beautiful face, I try to picture what she would look like grown up but I just see her perfect baby face. It looks like Lilly feels so comfortable with me like I feel with Damon. I could fall instantly asleep with Damon because he soothes me. I guess I do the same for Lilly, if I wasn't dying it would be a comfort to me.

"Emmie, we should make a move," Mom says.

"Where are you going?" Danny asks.

"I know an attorney who will hopefully help with the adoption." I shrug.

"Can I come?" Danny asks.

"Yeah, me too," Denny says. I roll my eyes. They want to come because they don't want to leave me. Sully said I should give this to them.

"Er okay but like I said I'm not keeling over anytime soon. I'm sure you'll get fed up with me soon," I sigh.

"Great, let's go," Danny says. Mr Declan isn't going to like all these people coming. Damon carefully lifts Lilly from me, luckily she doesn't wake. Sully stands, bringing me with him.

I throw the blanket off me when he stands up. "Emmie, you may need that," he says worriedly.

"Big Guy, I already look like death. I don't need a huge sign on my head saying I'm dying," I say.

"Who cares what people think?"

"I care, I tried to cover it up for so long, too many people know already." I hate it.

"Oh, Emmie," Sully sighs. He walks out towards the car. Lilly is already in her car seat sleeping peacefully. Mom is sat in the front with Damon. Sully sits on the back seat with me on his lap. I rest my head on his shoulder and I close my eyes.

All the time I used to think that I was a burden on everyone, that no one liked me, I wasn't worthy of them, but these people have shown me that I am worthy. Damon married me twice to prove that, Addi wants to be my Mom. Sully is my best friend and he took a bullet to save me. My two brothers want to spend every moment they can with me. If this doesn't change the way I see things, nothing will. I love them and I know they love me.

"Emmie, we are here," Sully whispers in my ear. I must have dozed off. Sully slides out the car bringing me with him. No one lets me walk anymore. If it's not Damon carrying me then it's Sully.

Sully carries me into the building, I look behind Sully and Damon is following with Lilly in his arms. She is awake now. Denny and Danny are with Damon. Liam didn't come with us, he doesn't think I'm as fragile as everyone else. Sully takes a seat when we get in and Damon signs us in. I can see the woman flirting with him again and I groan. I know he isn't interested but it still bothers me.

We are a bit early so we have to wait awhile. Mom seems really happy but she seems impatient. Damon is trying to keep Lilly calm, she's too excitable. Danny is watching her and Denny is staring at me.

"Emmie?" Mr Declan says. I stand before Sully can stand up. Mr Declan frowns when everybody else stands. I walk carefully and slowly towards Mr Declan. I wobble and then Sully's hands stabilise me. I reach Mr Declan and put my hand on the door frame to catch my breath. "Are these people all with you Emmie?"

"Yeah, sorry. They know, they found out yesterday and they won't leave me alone." I shrug.

"I guess you all had better come in then," Mr Declan says, frustrated. Sully puts his arm around me and supports me while I walk, I can see Mr Declan watching me while I struggle to walk. Sully sits down and gets me to sit on his lap. Damon sits next to us with Lilly. Mr Declan sits at his desk and presses a button on his phone. "Rosie, please bring in three chairs."

A few moments later, Rosie, the receptionist brings in 3 chairs. Denny and Danny take a seat behind us and Mom puts her chair next to mine.

"Emmie, you have deteriorated since I last saw you. You said ten months, you don't look like you have long left," Mr Declan says. Well, he didn't word that very well.

"My Doctor says I'm too stubborn. I pushed myself too much." I shrug.

"Who are these people?" he asks.

"Well, you know my husband Rider." I point to Damon. "This is my daughter Lilly-May." I stroke Lilly's face and she grabs my hand. "This is Addison, my auntie," I say, using my other hand to point to Mom. I turn my head to look at Sully and smile, "This is my best friend Sully." Sully grins back at me. "This is Denny and Danny, my brothers." I point to each of them in turn.

"Some of these people are in your will?"

"Yes," I say.

"What exactly did you put in your will, Emmie?" Damon asks.

"I guess you'll find out when I die." I giggle.

Damon's jaw tenses, "You know you really aren't funny."

"So what can I do for you today?" Mr Declan asks.

"Addison wants to adopt me. I haven't got long left as you know. Can you make things speed along a bit?" I say.

"As she is already family, it should run more smoothly. I know your Dad is dead but what about your real Mother?"

"You know when I said someone was trying to hurt me?" Mr Declan nods. "That someone is my real Mother."

"Emmie," Damon growls. "How do you know you can trust him?" Damon whispers.

"Okay, you are so complicated. Normally we don't need consent from parents because you are an adult." Mr Declan uses his computer for a few minutes. "What is your surname Addison?"

"Hale. Please can you get this done in time?" she says desperately.

"I will do my best. There is something about Emmie, I don't know what it is but I really feel the need to follow her wishes. Her Dad insisted I help her any way I can. He was a good man." Damon grabs my hand instinctively, he doesn't trust Mr Declan.

"He was not," Mom growls.

"From what I saw he was. He wanted Emmie well cared for," Mr Declan says defensively.

"You call abusing your own daughter a good man?" Danny snaps. I groan, why do my loved ones always share this information? I don't want people to know how disgusting I am.

"What do you mean?" Mr Declan asks.

"Nothing," I say. I curl up on Sully's lap, I'm tired and I hurt.

Sully strokes my face. "You tired?" Sully says softly. I nod and close my eyes.

"He beat her up, he broke her. Dad caused mental and physical scars. He raped her and said it was to keep her safe. She believes it even now. She has suffered breakdowns because of him. She has an eating disorder. When she had her breakdown, she saw our Dad. She thought he was protecting her. She can't accept anyone's touch apart from her husband's. You really think he is a good man now?" Danny says angrily.

"Shut up Danny," I snap. Sully continues to calm me stroking my hair.

"Dude, not cool," Damon says. He puts his hand in mine once more which is placed on my lap.

I hear the printer. "Emmie, is this true?" Mr Declan asks. "Are you okay?" he asks.

"She's tired," Sully says. "She gets exhausted quickly."

"It's true," I whisper. I don't know why he really needs to know.

"Emmie, can you sign here please?" Mr Declan asks.

"Have you got a clipboard or something she can lean on?" Damon asks. I make no attempt to move, I'm comfy here. "Danny, can you take Lilly?"

"Sure," Danny says.

"Here you go," Mr Declan says.

I feel Damon's hands on mine. "Baby, here is the pen." He places the pen in my right hand. He slides something hard underneath my hand. I feel the paper underneath my fingertips. "Baby, you'll need to open your eyes," Damon says softly. I look up and see his handsome face. He chuckles. "Look at the paper Emmie, not me."

Well, that's no fun. Damon guides my hand to where I need to sign. I glance at the name, Emmie Salvatore. "Will this be safe?" I mumble to Mr Declan while I sign my name.

"Unless your real mother goes looking, she won't see this," Mr Declan reassures me. "I figured you would prefer this in your real name." I do because it feels more real this way.

"I'll keep an eye on her Emmie," Denny promises.

"Now your turn Addison," Mr Declan says. Damon takes the pen and the paper from me and I resume my earlier position.

"Just sleep, Emmie," Sully says. This is important, I should stay awake but it seems impossible. Sully strokes my hair which makes staying awake even harder. I focus on Sully's shallow breathing. In, out, in, out. Peacefulness finds me.

When I wake I'm on the sofa with a blanket around me. I look around and everyone is still here hovering around me. Just staring at me while I sleep. "Hey, Sweet Sister," Denny says.

"Am I going to have to kick you all out?" I say.

"You looked terrible again," Danny says.

"Will it make it easier if I promise to tell you when I'm on my way out?" I sigh.

"Emmie, please stop making jokes about your life. No one finds it funny," Damon says.

I see Lilly playing on the floor with her toys. "Lilly?" I say. She turns to look at me. "Why don't you bring me Pooh Bear?" I say.

"Pooh Bear?" she says.

"Yes baby, Pooh Bear." She looks around the floor and picks up Pooh Bear. She walks over to me and gives me it. "Thank you, baby." She climbs up on the sofa and then climbs on me. She sits on my legs and plays with Pooh Bear.

Damon crawls across the floor and sits in front of us. He strokes my face. "It's okay baby. Don't panic," he says to me. I am panicking, she could fall and I wouldn't be able to stop it.

So much has happened in my life, bad things mostly. Although I'm dying, I am happy. I feel safe in my own home. Lilly is safe, I don't have a constant threat behind me. Soon my twins will be born and they will grow and learn like Lilly. I just hope Denny and Danny will continue to be here for them when I'm gone. Danny said it himself, I am the magnet to this family. Someone else needs to take that role. They will need to make it work without me.

Chapter 52

Two weeks have passed. I have gone downhill fast. Some days I can't get out of bed. Damon hates leaving me but the gang needs him. He always makes sure someone is watching me. He has given every family member a key in case of an emergency. "Emmie, wake up." I open my eyes, I am awake, I'm just being disturbed by this moron. Blake bends down and pulls the sheet off me.

"What do you want?" I snap.

"Get up," Blake demands. If I could punch him right now I would, I'm not a morning person and dying makes mornings worse. Blake has grown on me these past few weeks. He still annoys the hell out of me but he is trying.

"No." I try and pull the sheet back over me but Blake holds on to it.

"I'm not taking no for an answer. Get up." What the hell is his problem today?

I turn over on my hands and knees and ease myself out of bed. I love that Blake treats me like a normal person but I shouldn't be out of bed and Damon would kill him. I wobble but I hold the bed for support. "I'm up, now what do you want?"

"Get dressed and I will see you downstairs. Unless you want help, of course. Which I'm happy to do." I groan, I don't want help from him. I could do with help but I don't want him to see my naked body.

"Where is Damon?" I ask.

"Checking to see where he is, are you? Because you are considering it?"

he teases. I would never consider Blake seeing me naked.

"Of course not. I just can't imagine him letting you disturb me like this." I shrug.

"He doesn't know, he isn't here," Blake shrugs.

I roll my eyes. "Oh okay. Get out then."

"You are boring. Why did Damon ever marry you?" Because he loves me, why else?

"I have no idea. Maybe he felt sorry for me. Who knows?"

"Maybe you are right. He would be crazy to marry a Heffalump. Now get dressed." Urgh, a Heffalump? If I didn't feel huge before I do now.

"You are an idiot." Blake winks and leaves the room. I follow the wall to the wardrobe leaning on it for support. Once I reach the wardrobe I put my hands on my knees trying to get my breath back. I grab leggings and a baggy top and follow the wall line back to the bed. I take a seat and dress.

"Emmie, hurry the fuck up!" Blake calls. Damn it, does he not know how hard this is for me? Damon and Sully carry me everywhere. Even when I try to walk they don't let me. Last time I walked was when I walked to Mr Declan.

I finish dressing and make my way downstairs, I hold anything I can for support. I find Blake waiting by the front door. "Jesus Emmie, take all day why don't you! I know you are fat, but jeez." I roll my eyes and I start to cough.

"I know I didn't want sympathy but this is hard you know. You are a moron."

"Yeah, yeah. Let's go," he says and puts his hand on the door handle.

Where does he expect me to go? "Where the hell are we going?" Doesn't look like I have a choice anyway.

"You'll see. Come on." He opens the door and steps outside.

"I'm not well enough to go out Blake. Not without Damon. I tire quickly." I am anxious to go outside without Damon.

"You'll be safe with me. I promise." I only trust Damon and Sully.

He will probably push me in front of a bus or something, "If you mean road kill, then yeah I'm safe."

"I'll make you road kill unless you get your sexy ass out that door." Enough with the sexy.

"Fine. Force a dying woman out of her deathbed," I groan and walk out of the door. Blake isn't like his brother, he doesn't show kindness, he leaves me to struggle to get my own door. His car is rather high too yet he just sits and watches me struggle. "What did you do to your brother to make him completely surrender to you?" I say once I'm safely in the car.

"Still hasn't told you huh?" Blake says.

"What do you think?" I snap.

"Why should I tell you?"

"You owe me, you are dragging me out, I think if you are going to kill me out here I should get to know the truth."

"What do you mean, die out here?"

"I'm not well enough to even go out with Damon, let alone with you."

"You'll be fine, a little exercise is good for people." Is he crazy? Yeah, I think he is. I agree with him, exercise is good for people but not dying people. "Let's just say he took something from me when we were younger," Blake confesses.

What on earth could this something be that has made Blake retaliate like this? If they were younger surely it wouldn't be that important at this age. What was it, his favourite toy? Something tells me it is more important than that but I don't want to think about it right now.

Blake pulls up at the mall. Urgh, shopping takes it out of me when I'm fit and well. Blake doesn't seem the shopping kind of person though. Blake gets out the car and I follow his cue. "Blake?" I say when he walks off too fast. He turns to face me.

"Yes fatty?"

"Can you help me?" I don't like to ask him for help but I really do need it. He sighs and tries to support me while I walk. Even with his help, I'm still painfully slow.

"You know what? This isn't working," he snaps.

"Don't leave me here," I beg, I'm too vulnerable.

"Leave you? Damon would kill me. Change of tactics." He bends down and picks me up. He groans when he lifts me to let me know how heavy I am. He could have been discrete about it. Damon and Sully never do this.

Blake walks towards the mall. I don't feel safe in his arms but what else can I do? I have to live with someone else touching me. Why did he have to drag me out of the house? "Please don't drop me," I beg. He chuckles, this isn't funny. He walks towards the railings, we are on the second floor. He puts his arms over the railing so I am in mid-air. I am terrified of heights and this asshole is playing with my life. I grab his neck and I hold on for dear life.

"If I wanted to drop you, I would." He pulls me back over onto safe territory. I slap him as hard as I can. It just hurts me though. He sets me down by a shop entrance and he walks into an arcade. I follow him at my own pace.

I wish Damon was here to tell his brother what a jackass he is being. The arcade is loud and it hurts my ears. I've had nothing but peace and quiet at home. I see Blake and he is tapping his foot impatiently. "Come on Emmie. Move your huge body."

I'm so fed up with him. "I'm going to kick your ass. Can you get any ruder?!"

"Come on then, bring it sexy gal." He brings his fists up playfully.

I roll my eyes, I don't have the energy to beat him up as much as I'd like too. "What are we doing here?"

"We are having fun," he says. It doesn't feel like we are having fun, all he has done is pick on me.

"I need a wee. Damn pregnancy." Blake looks annoyed.

"Oh just great, that will take you a week just to get there. Do you need a hand?" It probably will take me a week.

"Absolutely not. I can manage. I don't need you perving on me while I go to the toilet." I cross my arms.

"I'll hold your bag while you go. Don't need that slowing you down. You are already as slow as a snail." It's only a small shoulder bag where I hold my phone and my house key. I pass it to him and head for the bathroom. Why is he suddenly being so courteous all of a sudden? I decide I don't care. I just need to make one step at a time.

When I return, Blake hands my bag back and I put it over my head again. "I really think I should go home now. You'll be carrying me everywhere."

"I don't think so. We haven't started having fun yet." I don't think I will have fun, he is already having fun taking the piss out of me.

"You can't stop me. I'm sick Blake."

"Actually I can. Come on, let's play some games." Yeah, he can. I'm not getting anywhere fast without him.

He helps me to a car racing game. I sit down and he takes a seat next to me. He puts some coins in the machine and he sets it up. "Ready to be beaten?" Blake teases.

"Not by you," I snap. I take the steering wheel, I can't reach the pedals so Blake moves my seat forwards. 3,2,1 go. I put my foot on the gas pedal, I am pretty good at these sort of games because I used to play with Danny a lot on his *Xbox*. Of course, Blake is good, typical bloke and their racing games.

"Come on little girl," Blake torments me. I'm second and he is first, I come up along side him and I ram his car. He goes swerving off to the right. Ha serves you right. I win just in time. He stares at me. "How did you do that?" I shrug. "I want a rematch," he says and he puts more coins in. We play again and I let him win so he won't make me play anymore.

He takes us over to an air hockey table. "Wait here," he says.

"Where am I going to go?" I call. He heads off to the bar area and I hold onto the table for support. He brings back a chair.

"Don't say I don't do anything for you." He places the chair where someone would normally stand playing this game. I take the seat and grab the puck and get ready.

Blake takes the first shot. I am so exhausted, If I was on form I probably would have won by now. I'm too stubborn to let him win. Playing in here with Blake has been fun. It has got my mind off things but I am exhausted. We like to offend each other and give Banter. But it seems that is just the way we are. He is the only one who doesn't try to walk on egg shells around me.

"Come on, let's go sexy ass," he says when he has had enough.

"Where now?" I groan.

"Upstairs to the bakery." Best news I have had all day.

"Yeah, doughnuts."

"You really should watch your weight."

"Fuck you." I'm dying, who cares?

"If you want, I wouldn't say no." I roll my eyes and head to the elevator.

"I want doughnuts," I call back to Blake.

I hear him walking up behind me and he scoops me up into his arms so we get there quicker. He puts me down in front of the elevator and presses the call button. It pings open and we walk in. Blake drags me in before the door shuts on me. I collapse against the wall, I'm shattered.

"What is it with me and getting horny in elevators?"

"Well keep your hands to yourself," I say. Not like I'm going to help him with it. He didn't even need to share that with me. The elevator jolts and I fall forwards. Luckily Blake catches me, well more that I fell into him and he was just there. The lights go out and then a dim light comes on.

"What the hell was that?" I panic, holding on to Blake tightly.

"Chill out, don't worry your pretty little face. It will be nothing," Blake says casually but his face is saying something else.

Blake shifts his weight so he can start pushing loads of buttons and keep hold of me but nothing happens. The elevator has stopped. I can't be stuck here. I put my hands on my knees trying to catch my breath. I'm terrified. "Calm down Emmie. You are fine," he says again.

"No, I'm not, I hate confined spaces. You are a moron."

"That's it, let it all out. How is this my fault?"

"I don't know. Ow." I reach up and grab Blake's shirt.

"What?" Blake says alarmed.

"Ahh," I scream. This hurts.

"Emmie relax, if you have your babies in here I'll kill you myself. Just calm yourself." I've only ever felt this type of pain and that's when I woke up and I was in labour. "No signal. Great."

"I need Damon," I say, terrified. He will make me feel better. I will feel safe.

"You'll have to make do with me, Emmie." Make do? I'd make do with Sully. He makes me feel safe, but I don't feel safe with Blake.

"He calms me."

"Emmie breathe. Look at me." I look up and look into his eyes. I take a deep breath.

"Blake?"

"Yes, Emmie?"

"My water's just broke." I see Blake looking down and seeing for himself, I can see he is panicking.

"Emmie for fuck sake. I told you to calm down." I can't calm down, not without Damon or Sully.

"It's a bit hard when I'm stuck in an elevator. Please get me out of here. I'm not strong enough to deliver the babies." I'm exhausted.

"Yes, you are Emmie. You are the strongest person I know." How would he know? I haven't known him long. I don't feel strong right now. My knees give way and I fall to the floor. Why does nothing ever go to plan?

"Shit Emmie." Blake kneels down in front of me. He looks as terrified as I feel.

"I need to take a look down there Emmie. I'm going to get your bottom half naked." I close my eyes, I don't want him looking down there.

"Trust you to find a way to make this kinky."

"Oh Emmie, you know me too well." He chuckles but it isn't his usual carefree laugh. I have no energy. Walking around the mall has exhausted me. Tears are streaming down my face. I'm so scared. The babies are early. I can't do this without Damon. Blake peels down my leggings and panties. "Oh, Emmie if you weren't in labour this may be hot." I groan, of course, he would think that. This is the only time I would let him do this.

"Don't make me kick your ass," I mumble.

"Okay chill, Emmie. Deep breaths." He grabs my hand and I squeeze it tightly.

"It hurts Blake." I hurt everywhere.

"I know Emmie. I'm sorry." I don't blame this on him. Someone up there is still playing with my life.

"I'm so tired." I can't keep my eyes open. I shut them and try to block out the pain.

"Emmie, don't you dare fall asleep," he says. "Emmie!" He lets go of my hand and he shakes my shoulders.

"No need to shout, god damn it." I'm not deaf. Just tired. "Ahh! Make it stop." Please, Blake.

"Oh man up Emmie. Don't be a pussy." Blake sighs.

"You try giving birth," I snap.

"Oh no, Emmie. You are on your own." I know, I'm all on my own. Damon nor Sully is here to help me through this. Blake takes my hand in his again and he strokes my forehead, getting my hair out of my face.

"Emmie, I think you need to start pushing now." How would he even know? I can't even hold my own weight, how am I supposed to push two babies out?

"No, no way." I can't do this without Damon.

"Emmie, I think you need to."

"I can't." Please don't make me do this.

"Emmie, man the fuck up. You can do this." I can't.

"Once I get out of here, I'm going to smother your face with a pillow." He is pissing me off.

"Oh Emmie," he chuckles. "Now push!"

"Ahh!"

"Hello, is anyone in there?" a voice asks.

"Yes, we need an ambulance. A cancer patient is in labour." I groan, why do people always share too much information?

"Try to stay calm," the man says. Calm? I'll give him calm.

"Calm? Are you nuts?" I mumble.

"Ma'am, please. We are trying hard to get you out." Try harder so I can ·punch you for calling me Ma'am.

"Please call my husband. I need him." Just to hear his voice may be enough.

"What's his name, Ma'am?" Again with the Ma'am. I shout out his number, I made sure I memorised his number in case of an emergency.

"Okay, Ma'am. I will call him." I need Damon to know I love him.

"Blake, tell Damon I love him," I say sleepily.

"Tell him yourself," Blake scoffs.

"Please tell me what you did to make Damon fear you? Why he gives up on me so easily?"

"Emmie, now isn't the time." Of course, it is. I may not survive this. I need to know.

"Please," I beg.

"Fine, I loved winding him up. He had a high school sweetheart. He was obsessed with her. Of course, he was too young to know what love was. But she fell in love with me, but just so you know I loved her too. And I started a trend." Obsessed with her? That's the bit that stands out to me. "He was crushed. She died in my arms." Died in his arms? They both lost their love?

"What happened?"

"I was meeting her in an alleyway in secret behind his back. A gang came from nowhere and shot her." An alleyway? Well, that's romantic.

"Why?" Was she targeted?

"I have no Idea. That's why he joined a gang. He wanted answers. He wanted revenge." The gang was fuelled by his first love? He has risked so much to get revenge. She must hold a huge part of him. If he truly loves me then why is he still running his gang? Is he not over her?

"And did he get revenge?" That is the question that could be make or break.

"No, he didn't. He never found them. He has hated me ever since. I hated him too because I loved her too. So that's why I take everything he cares about. Because I lost the love of my life." But Blake took her away from Damon first. Who was this bitch that cheated on Damon? Who am I kidding? If he hasn't got revenge yet it means he is still trying and that hurts.

"But that wasn't his fault."

"I blamed him," Blake says.

"Ahh!" I scream. This is too much.

"Baby, I'm here. Talk to me, baby," Damon's soft voice surrounds me. This calms me slightly.

"It hurts Damon," I cry.

"I know baby, stay strong. You can do this." I can't.

"I'm so tired Damon."

"Emmie, I have the Doc on the phone for you." Lucas? Where is he? I need him now.

"I just want to sleep."

"Emmie, you can't sleep yet," Lucas scolds. But I need to sleep. I'm exhausted.

"It's too soon Lucas. I'm not giving birth." Please, do something.

"I need you to look how far gone you are." How does he expect me to do that? Idiot.

"I've already done that. I really think she needs to push. But she doesn't have the energy," Blake says. He's right, I don't.

"Okay, Emmie. You need to push. Remember what you've been living for. It was this moment." He knows I fought to save the twins but as much as I want to, I know I'm not strong enough.

"I can't Lucas. Please don't make me," I beg. I have nothing left.

"Baby, I'm here. You can do this. Do this for me. I love you," Damon says. I'd try and do anything for you Damon and it kills me to know I can't do this for you.

"I love you, Damon," I mumble. He needs to know. "Tell Sully I love him too."

"Blake, you need to keep her awake," Lucas says. No, you don't. I just need to sleep, leave me alone.

"Easier said than done," Blake snaps.

"I think a C section is the only way. You must get the doors open," Lucas says. Yes, get the doors open.

"The fire brigade is on the way," Damon says. They need to be here now.

"Just keep talking to us, Emmie." No, I'm too tired.

"Emmie! Fuck sake. Emmie!" Blake slaps my face, ow.

"Emmie? Answer me, baby," Damon says.

"I need sleep. Stop shouting," I whisper.

"Damon, tell them they need to hurry. She's exhausted." They know it's an emergency. What do you want to do, air lift them here?

"Fuck. Okay, I'm on it," Damon panics.

"Don't leave me, Damon." I need him here with me.

"I'm not going anywhere, baby." Good, I close my eyes thinking of the future I would like to have. Watching Lilly-May and the twins grow up. Having Damon by my side all the way. I can imagine Damon being really protective over Lilly-May when she's older. And Lilly-May would be embarrassed in front of her friends. Having my best friend with me, protecting me. I feel everything going black. Peaceful.

"Emmie. Emmie no," Blake says. I can hear him but I can't respond. I feel nothing, I see nothing. I can only hear.

"Get her to hold on. If you let her fucking die, I will kill you," Damon shouts. He is scared, I can hear it in his voice.

"Emmie. Come on," Blake says.

"Emmie," Damon calls.

"Doc?" Blake asks.

"Yeah..."

"She's bleeding." I am? Get my babies out then, do what you've got to do.

"Is she breathing?" I must be breathing if I can hear them unless I'm dead and I'm somehow watching over them.

"Is she fucking breathing Blake? Answer us," Damon shouts again. If he is in a gang revenging his first love's death, why is he here so angry that I'm dying? I don't understand.

"Yes, she is but its only slightly. What do I do?" Well, that's a good sign, right?

"Move her onto her left side. But be careful." Blake be careful with me? Yeah right, I wouldn't be here if he was being careful with me.

"Emmie, you are so fat and heavy. What now?" I know I am, you don't have to tell me that.

"Make sure her airways are clear and keep her warm." Does it matter? I can't feel anything anyway.

"How am I supposed to keep her warm?"

"Use your imagination," Lucas says.

"Fine, body heat it is." I can hear him moving around but I can't feel him. Is he hugging me to keep me warm?

"Keep your hands off my wife," Damon growls.

"If you want me to save her shut up. Go find the fire and rescue team or something."

Am I still too stubborn to leave this world? I should be dead, Blake said that I'm barely breathing. I'm anchored to this world, anchored to Damon. Even when I feel like I can't hold on anymore I prove myself wrong. What will happen? Can I hold on longer? I do hope so. I'm still fighting for you Damon.

Chapter 53

"Bro, I'm sorry," Blake says. Is he crying?

"Are you?" Damon says in disbelief. He sounds sorry Damon. What he is sorry about I don't know.

"Yeah, I actually really like Emmie. I was trying to help her. She warned me countless times that she shouldn't be out. Especially without you. I'm sorry." Don't be sorry about that Blake, if I didn't want to go out then you wouldn't be able to make me. I walk into danger all the time.

"You didn't force her Blake. Emmie doesn't do things she doesn't want to do. She's good at putting herself in danger." I would giggle if I could, Damon knows me too well.

"Hello, this is the fire and rescue team." It seems closer than Damon but further away than Blake.

"Hello, please hurry," Blake calls.

"Stand away from the door sir. We are coming in." I don't even think he is by the door, as far as I know, he is trying to keep me warm.

I hear metal colliding with metal and a sound of screeching. "Emmie!" I hear Damon, he seems closer now.

"Rider, get her on the bed," Lucas says. Is he here, did he come all this way to get me? "I'm her Doctor, she has stage 4 cancer and her pregnancy is superfetation," he says to someone?

"I'll meet you there," Blake says. I hear car doors slam, unless it was the ambulance.

"Get me some morphine," Lucas says. I don't feel anything Lucas, it's fine.

"Will she be okay?" Damon asks. "I'm here baby."

"I can't answer that," Lucas says. "I can only do what I can do and then it's up to her." I'm still here aren't I? I focus on sounds around me. The faint sound of Damon crying, the sirens on the ambulance. The beeping of what must be the heart rate monitor.

I zone out until I hear Damon again, "I'm not leaving her."

"Rider, I need to get her into surgery. Let me do my job." I hear the wheels turning on the bed. Doors slamming open. Everything crumbles around me, all my senses gone. I'm lost.

When I come around I feel awful, I feel really sick. I use my hands to feel around me. My hands find hands on either side of me. I grab them both not caring who they belong to. I open my eyes and see Damon and Sully either side of me. I smile at them both. I made it.

"Emmie, you look rough," Blake says disgustedly.

"Fuck you."

"As I said you are most welcome. You are still fat." I look down and my bump is still there but it's half its size.

"I didn't get my doughnuts." I was promised doughnuts.

Damon and Sully both laugh. "Emmie, I'm sure your body would thank you for that. Your body was obviously rejecting the doughnuts." Blake is so rude to me sometimes. One doughnut is not going to hurt.

"Baby you aren't fat. You scared me you know. I got home and you were gone. Loads of things were going through my head," Damon says.

"I'm sorry but this Moron dragged me out of bed." I didn't mean to worry him.

"You know you are the slowest person I know," Blake sighs.

"I looked everywhere. I thought you'd been taken. I know you can't walk far." Damon ignores Blake's snide comments, I wish he would just punch him and put Blake in his place. He would if it was anybody else.

"Thank you for coming for me. I relax when you are around. All I wanted was to be in your arms." It helped me to know Damon was close by.

"I would walk the earth to get to you." I smile at him.

"Better you than her. You'd die of old age before she gets anywhere,"

Blake jokes.

"I will put you through that window, Brother or no brother," Sully says. "Keep your cruel jokes to yourself." I smile at Sully who is glaring at Blake. I don't think he understands why Damon won't say anything.

"Emmie, the babies..." Damon sighs.

"I don't want to know," I snap.

"What why?" Damon says surprised. I have protected these babies at the cost of myself but I can't get too attached. They can't know me just to lose me, it's not fair.

"I can't get attached, Damon. I fear I haven't got long."

"Don't be ridiculous. Babies are out early. You are having Chemo." Is that what this sick feeling is?

"I'm not strong enough."

"Stop being a grumpy shit," Blake moans.

"Blake, stop picking on my wife. Seriously." Wow, Damon is sticking up for me for once.

"I'm going to get something to drink. Do you want anything?" Sully asks, stroking my face.

"A doughnut?" I grin.

"Sure Emmie," he says and leaves the room.

"Er Damon?"

"Yes, baby."

"I need a wee," I say awkwardly.

"Oh here comes the marathon. It will take you longer to get there than a tortoise." Real funny Blake, I wish I would get better so I could give him a run for his money.

"Whatever," I snap.

"Come on baby," Damon says, lifting me out of bed. I'm in a different room so I don't have a bathroom in here. We have to use one in the corridor.

When we enter the corridor, there is a brown haired girl, early 20s. She is dressed in shorts and a tight top, she's really pretty. "Damon?" she says shocked. Pretty and she knows my husband, great. Damon sets me down on my feet.

I struggle to hold my own weight. "Alex? Is that you?" Who is Alex?

"What are you doing here?" Alex says. She walks up and hugs him and he returns the hug. I stumble backwards to get out there way. She steps away from him.

"I could say the same to you," Damon says like he has just seen a ghost.

"Er are you okay there?" she says, looking at me. I realise I'm out of breath and shaking trying to hold myself up.

"Who me? Yeah just fine. Don't mind me." I'm just Damon's dying wife that you are all over. Carry on. "Blake!" I yell. If Damon is too distracted, then maybe I'll have to endure Blake taking me to the toilet.

"What do you want Emmie? Do you need me to hold your hand while you go to the loo? I'm surprised you got this far, to be honest," Blake moans.

"It seems Damon has catching up to do. Can you take me?" I never thought I'd ask him to do this.

"Of course. Anything to get you naked." He winks at me. Blake lifts me up.

"Blake?" Alex says. God damn it, who is this girl?

"Alex!" Blake says, putting me down a bit too quickly.

"You know what? I'll take myself," I mutter. I walk slowly to the bathroom. Who is that girl, why are they so mesmerised by her? Blake mentioned a girl they loved but she's dead, right? Unless she's not and that's why Damon could never get revenge because she's not dead.

I go to the toilet and then I fall on the way out. At least I don't need to worry about hurting the twins anymore. I smile, it doesn't matter. Nothing matters now. The babies are safe. If this Alex girl is Damon's first love, then he can move on with her. I try to get up but I can't move, I still feel heavy.

"Oh, Emmie. How clumsy can you be?" Blake says. I look at the door and Blake and Damon are rushing in.

"Shut up Blake. I asked for your help and you turned me down. Hey, I could have even let you watch..." Even though I want Damon to move on and be happy, part of me doesn't want him to and not with his first love either. The one that's made him so focused on revenge, the one that he has tried to hold on to. It makes our relationship feel fake and wrong somehow.

Damon lifts me up off the floor and he nuzzles his nose in my hair. I'm comforted that he came to find me but my husband shouldn't be love struck by someone else. If she is who I think she is, does he want her now and not me? "Well I'm here now, I'd like the floor show," Blake says.

"Too late, you missed your chance." Because you were flirting with some long lost girlfriend.

"Are you okay baby?" Damon says.

"I guess I'm okay after you both abandoned me."

"I'm sorry, baby."

"I hope she was worth it."

"What do you mean?" he says, confused.

"She was actually. Her name is Alex," Blake says, trying to make me jealous. Of course I am. I'm threatened by this girl, how could I not be? "She was the girl I told you about."

I knew it but how is she still alive? "But you said she was dead."

"Turns out she's not," Damon says awkwardly. "Why did you tell her anyway?"

"Oh okay," I say, feeling defeated.

"Is someone jealous Emmie?" Blake teases. Blake ignores Damon's question.

"Why would I be? I'll be dead soon. You can both then do as you please," I say defensively.

"Emmie, what are you going on about?" Damon sighs.

"It's okay Damon," I say. I just want you to be happy.

"What makes you think we are interested?" Blake says. He tries to make me jealous and now he is denying he is interested, what is he playing at?

"She was your first love. You've been fighting for years over her. Why wouldn't you?"

"Jealousy doesn't suit you. Now, are you finished? As much as I love being in the ladies' toilets. I'd rather take you to bed." Blake heads for the door. What is his problem?

We walk back out into the corridor and Alex is still there. "Hey Beautiful, you are still here," Blake says, glancing at me. I bury my head on Damon's shoulder in annoyance.

"Of course I am," Alex says.

"Er hey, I'm Emmie," I say.

"Alex. Are you sure you are okay?" I'll never be okay. I've never been okay. I just find ways of coping.

"No. I'm going to go find the Doc." Damon puts me down on my feet and he lets me go.

"Do you need a hand there clumsy?" Blake teases.

"What I could do with is a new body," I sigh.

"What do you need a new body for? You have one hell of a sexy body." I roll my eyes.

Alex looks pissed. Good. "Oh, Blake. I thought you said I was fat?"

"Oh, you are. But hey it will go soon. Your ass though. Damn." I turn to look at my ass. I just don't see what everyone else seems to see.

"Stop hitting on my wife, will you?" Damon is angry.

"Can you blame me?" Blake says. At least they are fighting over me at the moment and not Alex. Even if that is selfish of me.

"No," Damon sighs.

"Hey guys, I was hoping to have a catch-up," Alex says, I think she is fighting for their attention. I'm not playing this game. They either want to be by my side or they don't. I go to find Lucas but my ears perceive me, though they both want to catch up with her.

I find Lucas in my room. Sully has come back with my doughnut. He sees me alone and frowns. He picks me up and I hug him tightly, I never have to fight for my best friend. With a girl anyway. He places me on the bed. "Emmie, are you okay?" Lucas says worriedly.

"No, I hurt. I fell over."

"Emmie, you shouldn't be up and about yet." I grab my doughnut off the table and start to eat it.

"I needed a wee," I say with my mouthful.

"Why didn't you ask Rider to take you?" Lucas asks.

"I did, and then I asked Blake. But they were both mesmerised by a girl."

"Why didn't you wait?"

"Why do you think? I would have wet myself."

"Who was this girl?" Sully asks.

"I'd be surprised if you didn't know. Her name is Alex." I turn my nose up at her name.

"Emmie, she's dead." Sully shakes his head.

"No, she's not. She's out there fighting for their attention. Damon has his first love back."

"Even if she is out there Emmie, he is different with you. He needs you," Sully says, trying to reassure me, he knows I feel I'm not good enough for Damon.

"I can't compare to his first love. I'll be dead soon anyway." I shrug.

"Emmie, don't say that. Please. I can't lose you." I move over so Sully can lay next to me and I can curl up on his chest. He doesn't hesitate, I finish my doughnut, now I feel fat.

"Where is Rider?" Lucas says. I'm pretty sure I just said.

"Who knows? With his high school sweetheart."

"And you are okay with that?" Lucas asks.

"I'm dying Lucas, of course I don't like it. But I want him to move on after me."

"Emmie, come on, you need to fight this. You are strong." I am not strong. Inside I am weak. I am insecure, I'm jealous. I'm terrified.

"Doc, I'm so tired. I can't even go for a pee on my own. Let alone fight cancer." I don't need to act like a lady when I'm around loved ones.

"I know it feels hard now but if anyone can do it, it's you." Yeah, yeah. So people keep saying. "Do you want me to take you to see the twins?"

"No," I snap.

"I couldn't keep you away from Lilly-May. What's different?" Lucas asks.

"I'm dying. It will be easier for everyone if I don't know them. It will just make it harder when I die."

"Emmie. Come on. Where has your fight gone?"

"It gets chipped away Lucas, My Dad chipped most of it away and then Rex, Damon leaving me, Desmond, Damon marrying someone else, killing people, Esme wanting me dead, having my breakdown, Cancer, Lucas." The list is never ending.

"But you have so much to live for, Damon is here, Sully is here, your loved ones, your babies, you have a family home, you are mentally stable now. You are being adopted. Think of the positives, not the negatives," Lucas says, frustrated. I try and see the positives but negatives drown the positives. I snuggle up on Sully's chest, I'm pain-free for the minute and I'm safe. I fall instantly asleep.

*

A few weeks have passed since the elevator drama. Lucas says I can stay at home, dying at home is preferable. I go in a few times a week for Chemo. I am so exhausted that I stay in bed all day. Liam and Damon go to the hospital to watch over the twins. I still haven't seen them. I don't want them to get attached to me. Only to lose me. It is so hard. I just want to hold them in my arms.

"Hey Mi Chica Bella." Damon is trying to cheer me up. He and Sully have tried to help me move forward with my life but I'm terrified of moving forward only to lose it again. Having chemo is making me feel weaker, if that was even possible.

"Hey, Damon." I want to push them all away, I want to detach from them all. Knowing I'll lose them is clawing at my heart, it's ripping it out. Damon won't let me push him away, he wants me to know he is with me until the very end. He is still in denial, he thinks I'm strong enough to beat this and everyone else hopes the same.

"How are you today?" He lays in front of me bringing me to his chest, to my favourite place. I don't know where Alex's favourite place is but I feel safe and protected and in heaven when I'm curled up on his chest smelling his scent. I keep thinking about Alex.

"Tired." Always tired, I hate missing Lilly grow. I hate not living my life with Damon and Sully.

"Did you want to go see the twins today?" He keeps badgering me to see them. I don't know why he won't accept this. Everyone must think I'm a bad mother, I know I am.

"No Damon." It's the same answer every time you ask me and that will never change.

"How about some fresh air?" he says hopefully.

"No Damon." I sigh. I don't want to go out, I don't want people to see me like this. I was self-conscious before and now I have a big neon sign on my head.

"Okay baby."

"Please, explain it to me," I say. He looks at me confused. "Blake told me his side of the story. I need to hear yours. I need to know how you are feeling. About Alex," I say.

He frowns at me. "Baby, of all the things you could ask me you want to know about my ex?"

"Please," I beg. "She's not just your ex, she's your first love and I need to know what that means."

He sighs, "What Blake said is true, I loved her. She was my first love, she was everything to me. My parents loved her." Ouch, stab me through the heart again. "She was my first in nearly every way, my first kiss, my first love, my first intimate relationship."

Tears fall from my face, "And you started the gang to get revenge."

"Don't cry, baby." Don't cry? She was his first in every way, how can I compare? "I did and I put everything I could into getting revenge."

"So how do you feel about her actually being alive now? If she was your first love you must be over the moon that she is still alive. All your hard work has paid off, you run a successful gang."

"Listen, baby, I know what you'll be thinking." Of course he does. He always does. "You worry that I'll want Alex now I know she's alive, right? I will always love Alex but you'll always love Brody and Liam, right?" He's right he has never hated me for still loving them so I should return that understanding. "If you want to know the truth?" Yes, even if it will hurt me. "I probably would be happy to know Alex is still alive if I hadn't met you. The moment I met you everything changed, I stopped focusing on Alex and I focused on you," he says.

"But why did you carry on the gang when you met me? I don't understand."

"The gang is my family, it's something I enjoy doing. Without my gang, I probably would have lost you ages ago. All the resources I have are because of the gang. You see, although I love Alex she never made me feel the way you do."

"I still don't understand." Am I being stupid? Is the cancer messing with my brain or did Lucas steal my common sense when he removed the tumour?

"Remember what I said about the electric pulse? The gravity drawing me to you?" Yeah, I do remember that, how could I forget? It was one of the most romantic things he has said to me. "I didn't want marriage with Alex, I still don't want marriage with Alex. I only want you to be my wife. You are the mother of my kids. I was always careful not to get Alex pregnant, it wasn't something I wanted."

"Sully told me something at the beginning. I didn't understand it then but I do now."

"What did he say?"

"He said he has been with you since the beginning, he said I was different. He said that you were the happiest that you've ever been when you are with me. You are protective over me and you weren't with the rest. I thought he was telling me what I wanted to hear."

"Well, he is right, baby. Now can we please put this to rest? Yes, I was shocked that Alex is alive. Spending years believing someone is dead and then they are not. Blake is welcome to her but if I know my brother, he isn't interested in Alex either. He wants you."

"Why would he want me?" I saw the way he flirted with her and then looking at my reaction. He kept saying I was jealous, I was jealous. But it's because I'm selfish and insecure, I have no claim over Blake and I don't want him like I want Damon but I still don't want Alex to have him.

"Why wouldn't he want you, Emmie? You are beautiful, you are funny, you are clever, you are brave and strong. You are unique and one of a kind. To us, you are some beautiful goddess. You dazzle us with your beauty." What the fuck is he talking about? Has he been drinking or what?

"I thought you said I wasn't funny."

"When you joke about you dying, that's not funny but you have a good sense of humour other than that." He sighs, "Your list of admirers grows by the second, Brody, your old school friends, Liam, all my staff, my brother. Luckily I'm getting it through my head that you only want me."

Hallelujah, how long has it taken him? "It's taken awhile to get it through your thick skull." I giggle.

"Thick skull, hey?" He shifts his weight so he is looking over me. He places soft kisses all over my face and I laugh uncontrollably. It makes me breathless but I don't care. I feel like I have put Alex to bed now that he has explained it to me.

"I've got to get up baby. Shout if you need something," he says. If only he could stay in bed with me all day. If I wasn't dying, I'd find other ways to keep him here. He kisses me and leaves the room.

I love Damon, he makes me feel special, I don't know what I'd do without him. It's a horrible thought, part of me is thankful for Alex. If Damon didn't love her and she didn't die, he wouldn't have joined a gang and he wouldn't have kidnapped me. It's not the most normal way to start a relationship but I'm not normal and I don't care. I start to drift again.

"Get up!" I jolt awake. Why is he is such an ass?

"Leave me alone," I snap. Damn Blake trying to get me out of bed again. Does he not remember what happened last time? I guess that can't happen again but I could die walking down the street because he doesn't look after me as well.

"Get the fuck up fatty," he says again. He pulls the sheet off me again. If I ever get better, I'll hurt him so bad.

"I'm not fat anymore." I will always be fat but I don't have a bump anymore.

"You'll always be fat to me Emmie. Now get up." So why does he like me then if I'm fat to him? Damon must have it wrong, he doesn't want me.

"Fuck you."

"Oh, Emmie, how I would love you to. Now get out of bed before I drag you out." I really should stop saying that because he always turns it back on me.

"I hate you," I mutter when I climb out of bed. He grins and helps me stand up straight by holding my shoulders.

"That wasn't so hard was it fatty?" He smiles at me and pats my arms. He is such a damn pain in my ass. Yes, it was hard, I'm dying, you moron.

"What do you want moron?" I groan. He doesn't let me go. It's easier when he holds me steady.

"Get dressed. If you don't I will do it for you." He will do no such thing. I am covered in bruises. I don't even like Damon looking at me.

"You wouldn't dare!" I shout.

"Emmie, any chance to get you naked I'd take it. I have permission from Damon so…" he shrugs while he grins.

"Damon wouldn't agree to that!"

"He called me here." He shrugs again. Damon would never agree but Blake is doing my head in so I will do anything I can to get rid of him.

"Fine, get out. I'll get dressed." Blake winks at me and releases my shoulders. I wobble and hold onto the bed. I lean on the wall to get to the wardrobe. I put on a dress and some tights. Normally I'd just wear the dress but I get cold. I shove on some shoes and I head downstairs.

I trip down the stairs but it doesn't matter because it's just me. I only fall a few steps anyway and I laugh. Sully comes running towards me. "Why are you laughing?" he says, confused and picks me up off the floor.

"My life is funny Big Guy. To someone up there." I stop laughing and hug his neck. He doesn't say anything, just holds me tight and takes me to Damon.

"What happened?" Damon asks.

"She fell down the stairs," Sully says.

"That's new, are you too fat to see the steps?" I groan into Sully's neck.

"Are you okay baby?"

"I'd be better if I was in bed. And this idiot didn't force me out of bed." I nuzzle Sully's neck and I see him blush again, oops.

"Jesus Emmic, I could have walked to England and back in that time. Can you not move your fat ass any quicker?" I groan. Why did I say he was growing on me? He is just a jackass.

"Fuck you, Blake. Now I'm up and dressed what the hell do you want?" I say irritated.

"We are going out."

"No, we're not." I wouldn't have wasted so much energy getting out of bed if this was the plan. Lucas keeps telling me fresh air will be good but there are too many threats outside.

"Don't give me that face, grumps. Now get your fat ass out the damn door." I hold tighter to Sully.

"Damon!" I say frustrated.

"Don't look at me. I can't protect you with this one. You are on your own." I look at Sully and he gives me a sorrowful look like he won't help me.

"I see how it is. You are both ganging up on me." Did Damon call Blake here to get me out of bed? I'm so annoyed at them.

"Move!" Blake shouts. Sully sets me down on my feet and helps me walk towards Damon. Damon holds my waist and Sully lets me go. We walk to the car and Damon lifts me into the car. Blake gets in the back and starts tapping the seat. I know I'm slow, there is no need to keep telling me, it won't make me any faster.

Damon gets in his side and leans over to do my seatbelt. "Blake, are you wearing your seatbelt?" I ask.

"Yes, Emmie. Why?"

"Shame, I would have got Damon to slam the brakes on." That would have shut him up for a while. Damon laughs loudly. I look around to Blake and he looks pissed. That's pay back. I wonder where they are taking me, at least I have Damon with me this time.

A few minutes later Damon pulls up outside the hospital. I haven't got chemo so what the hell is this? I don't move, I just wait for an explanation. Damon opens my door and lifts me out. Damon doesn't go to the usual reception desk, he follows signs to the neonatal intensive care unit. "Stop!" I shout. Damon stops in his tracks. "What the hell are we doing here?"

"Baby, you need to see the twins." I don't need to do anything. Why are they forcing this?

"Are you deaf Damon? I said no. Put me down." He does as I ask. He sets me on my feet but he holds me steady.

"I'm sorry Emmie, you need to speak up. We didn't hear you." Blake grins and cups his ear.

"I said no!"

"Damon, did you hear something? Sounds like someone's whining like a baby."

"Did you know you are so annoying?" I say irritated.

"Who me? That's very hurtful," he says, clutching his heart. My heart bleeds for you, not.

"Fine, I'll do it," I say and head down the corridor. Damon obviously knows where he is going.

"Fuck sake, Damon just carry her," Blake says irritated.

"No. I want to walk." Blake rolls his eyes. Damon holds open a door to the side of us and encourages me in. When I walk in it's a small side room. With two plastic covered cot beds. I see Liam sat with his hand through one of the beds.

He looks up and smiles at me. "Hey Princess." He looks happy that I'm here. Liam holds his hand out to me and I walk slowly towards him. He sits me on his lap facing our baby. "This is our baby Emmie. He's a fighter, the Doctors are worried about him but he is better. He is strong like his Mom," Liam says.

"He is tiny," I say. I knew he would be but him being this small worries me.

"Hey, he is a little fighter. Put your hand through here," Liam says, removing his hand from the incubator. "Go on," Liam says, grabbing my hand and encouraging me to put it through the hole. He is hooked up to a load of wires. My poor baby boy. I put my hand in and touch his hand.

"Do you want to hold him, Mom?" I turn to see a nurse looking at us.

I shake my head, "No," I say horrified. He looks so delicate.

"You'll be doing him good if he has skin on skin contact with his Mom."

"Emmie, our son needs you," Liam says.

"I could drop him," I say terrified.

"If you lay down on the bed I'll bring him over to you," the nurse says.

"Baby," Damon says, grabbing my hand lifting me off Liam's lap. "You'll be fine. Don't panic," he says, reassuring me. I shouldn't be doing this but they say it could help him get better.

I walk over to the bed and I face the bed while I pull my dress down so no one can see me. I remove my bra. Damon covers me with a blanket and helps me on to the bed. The blanket lays over my naked top half. Damon holds my hand, reassuring me. "I'm right here," he says. The nurse comes over with my baby and slides him up the blanket. I did this with Lilly but she was much bigger and she wasn't hooked up to a load of leads.

"Would you like to hold your other baby too?" the nurse asks. My eyes widen. What is she trying to do, give me a heart attack? "They don't move much at this age, it will be perfectly safe."

"Okay," I whisper. She smiles and goes to get my other baby. She moves Liam's baby over slightly so Damon's baby can fit on my chest too. Damon and Liam perch either side of me, looking at their babies. Liam's baby has blonde hair and Damon's baby has brown red colour hair. At least they aren't difficult to identify.

Was this their plan to get me to fall instantly in love with my twins? I knew with Lilly I couldn't leave her after I met her and this is the same. I don't want to leave my babies alone here. They are both beautiful but then they have good genes, Liam and Damon are hotties. What am I supposed to do now?

Chapter 54

We stay for an hour or so in the neonatal intensive care unit holding my babies. I grow tired so I ask to go home. This is too much for me for one day. The nurse carefully puts the twins back in their incubators. Damon holds the blanket up whilst I put my bra back on and pull my dress back up. I feel incomplete without my babies on my chest.

I give them one last goodbye and we leave the room. Blake gets fed up and carries me himself. "Blake!" I shout.

"What, fatty? If Damon won't carry you then I will. No matter how fat you are." Most patients are pushed around in wheelchairs but I refuse. I give up trying to argue, it doesn't really matter, does it?

Blake throws me into the front seat. "Ow," I say, moving my body getting comfy. Blake shrugs and gets in the back. Damon gets in his side and does my seatbelt up.

"Have you thought of any names, baby?" Damon asks.

"I can't name them," I say, horrified.

"Of course you can. They will need names eventually Emmie."

"Give me time Damon, this is hard for me. Can you take me home now? I'm tired."

"Sure thing baby, you've done great."

"I don't think so. Emmie, you are a lazy shit," Blake says. Lazy? I'm dying. I never used to lay around all day. I even rode Willow until I couldn't anymore. I really miss riding my horse.

"Stop picking on me."

"We are going to have some fun," Blake says. "Take a left here Brother, then take the next right. Straight on at the roundabout." I sit in silence, frustrated. Why do I let Blake get to me? He just winds me up. "Pull up here Bro."

Damon does as Blake asks. Blake gets out and opens my door. He doesn't let me protest, he just lifts me out the car, probably so I can't refuse. He carries me over the road and to the beach. He wants to go to the beach? Really? Why doesn't he ask Alex to go to the bloody beach with him? Blake puts me down on the sand.

"What are we doing here Blake?" I say, crossing my arms.

"You are going to have some fun. Besides, it means I see more skin." He is such a jackass.

"I haven't got my swimsuit, Blake."

"That's okay. Underwear is fine. Live a little." I lived on the wild side with Denny but he is my brother. I wanted to live my life to the full. I've already done everything I wanted to do.

"No Blake." He steps towards me and pulls my dress over my head. My bruises are showing. My scars are showing and it looks like everyone is looking. "Blake!" I scream. Trying to cover my body. He seems to do a double take and that only puts me off more.

"Oh don't be such a spoil sport," he says. I can't handle people seeing me like this. I put my face on Damon's chest trying to hide myself. I'm mortified, tears stream down my face. Damon strokes my hair trying to calm me down. "Emmie?"

"It's okay baby. Blake, give her clothes back," Damon says.

"Why would I do that? Emmie, you have a sexy body. You shouldn't be afraid to show it," Blake says, this only makes me more uncomfortable.

"I was ugly before. But now, I can't deal with people looking at me," I mumble into Damon's chest.

"Emmie, you aren't ugly," Blake says, confused. I am.

"I am, now give me my clothes." I turn around and snatch my dress from Blake and put it back on. I run away from them, I don't know how I am running, I can't even walk. Is this adrenaline? My lungs are on fire. I don't look back, I just continue to run.

I end up running into a guy. "Oops sorry," I say breathlessly.

"Don't be sorry Emmie. Just get in," the guy says, opening his van door. What the hell is going on? How does he know my name? The guy pushes me forwards and I tumble into the van. What the fuck is going on? He injects me with something, everything goes black.

When I wake I'm in some sort of police station. Have I been arrested? What the hell happened? Where am I? If someone wants me dead all they had to do was wait. I hear a baby cry. I know that cry, I could identify it anywhere. I push myself off the floor.

"Lilly-May!" I cry out. I hold the rails of the bars and try to force it open. "Lilly-May!" I scream again. I wish I had more strength.

"Momma!" I hear my daughter cry.

"Who the hell has my daughter?" I shout. Hearing her cry pains me. I don't care for my own life but Lilly-May's life means everything. I will go down kicking and screaming to protect Lilly.

"I never believed you were alive when they told me," I hear Esme's voice and then she appears in front of me. I lurch towards her but these damn bars are between us.

"When, who told you?" I growl. Why didn't Denny warn me that she knew I was alive?

"The Brotherhood. The gang I work for." I laugh hysterically, Esme in a gang? That is funny.

"You in a gang?" That's the funniest thing I have heard all day. "Give me my daughter now!" I demand.

"Bring my granddaughter in!" Esme shouts.

"She's not your granddaughter," I snap.

"But she is Emmie. I'm your mother whether we like it or not."

"You are dead to me. I have a new mother now."

"Who?" she says, offended.

"Addi. She has adopted me."

"I didn't give permission for that," she snaps.

"I know a good attorney and I'm an adult. You don't need permission."

"Momma," Lilly says. I turn my head to see Lilly in Denny's arms. What is he doing helping her?

Esme unlocks the door and Denny walks in. He passes me Lilly and I sit on the floor with her. I still can't hold her. "Hey, baby," I say. I hug her tightly. My poor baby girl. I cry, this is low to kidnap my baby. "Mommy loves you." So much. "Denny, how could you?" I look up at him but keep Lilly close.

"I'm sorry Sis, I didn't know," he says.

"The gang informed me that Denny here was a traitor. And hey, they were right. So you are now going to be stuck in here." Esme shuts the door and locks Denny in here too.

Denny looks horrified, "What?" he says.

"You heard me. You betrayed your Dad." No, he didn't. Desmond loved me most in the end.

"No, I didn't," Denny protests.

"I know you swapped the drug, Denny. The gang told me. You've been lying to me this whole time." Who the hell is this gang? They seem to know everything about my life.

"You know what, you are crazy? What sort of person does this to her kids?" Denny sits next to me and puts his arm around me. I rest my head on his chest. My brother chose me.

"She had everything. Always the favourite. I'm sick of it." Esme turns her nose up at me.

"That's what you are supposed to do for your kids," Denny says. He always loved Esme but I think he loves me more now.

"Well, I never wanted her. Danny was all I wanted. She was a mistake. I hated her the minute I found out I was pregnant." She looks at me. "Your Dad loved you." I know my Daddy loved me. I just figured it out too late.

"There is something wrong with you," Denny says.

"No actually, there must be something wrong with you," Esme says to Denny. She probably thinks I'm some sort of disease and if someone gets too close they'll catch it too.

"So what is it? You want me dead?" I say.

"That's all I've ever wanted." She laughs, how is that funny?

"Did Denny not tell you?" I laugh. Now that's funny, all this when she could have waited.

"Tell me what?" She stops laughing.

"I'm dying of cancer Mother dearest."

"That's funny." She chuckles again. She really is sick and twisted, I wouldn't wish this on my worst enemy.

"You think me dying is funny? You didn't have to kill me yourself. And besides, I am in so much pain, if you hate me so much wouldn't you like me to die slow and painfully?" If I can delay this, Damon can find Lilly and she will be safe.

"That's not such a bad idea," she says, thinking it over.

"So let us go," I say, it's a long shot but I don't care.

"Oh no. I want you to die alone, Emmie. Or should I say, Amy Silva." How does she know that?

"Well take Lilly-May back to Damon. Please," I beg, as long as Lilly is safe that's all that matters.

"She's not going anywhere," Esme says and walks away. I look at Lilly and cry, I need my baby to be safe, I've never been so terrified.

"I'm so sorry Emmie." Denny moves in front of me and puts his legs either side of me and pulls Lilly and me in for a hug. I rest my head on his shoulder.

"You chose me in the end. What more could I ask for?" I'm happy. He was loyal.

"I will get you out of here." It doesn't seem likely. I love Denny but he doesn't have any control anymore.

"Just get Lilly-May out. Please," I beg.

"I'm going to get you both out," he promises. I'm happy that my brother is with me. I know he wouldn't let anything bad happen to my daughter. I turn around and curl up on his lap, I'm so tired. Lilly is sleeping in my arms. Denny puts his arms around me and sleep takes over.

I hear a gunshot and I wake instantly. I feel disorientated, I look around and I'm still curled up on Denny and Lilly is still sleeping. She really will sleep through anything. "What was that?" I say.

"I don't know," he says.

I see a figure in front of the cell. The cell is unlocked, I look closely and it's Damon. He got to us fast. Unless I was out awhile. Damon kneels in front of us and hugs us. Lilly still lays asleep. "I love you both so much." He kisses us both on our forehead. Damon takes Lilly from me. I see Sully coming through the cell.

He looks relieved. All the adrenaline seems to have faded now. I have nothing left in me. Sully comes towards me and picks me up. I place my legs around his waist and clutch his neck. My best friend is here.

*

Since that day. I have stopped looking back. Since my Mom took Lilly-May, I have become more protective. I started living my life for my family. We have lived happily as a family for 5 years now. The cancer has gone. The twins are healthy and grown up. I decided I'd call them Caleb-James and Thomas. Damon has become the most powerful gang leader in the country. Brody and Liam decided it made sense to join Damon's gang.

We walk down the shoreline bridge in Torrevieja. Damon and I are hand in hand. I love him so much. We watch the kids run around playing together. "I love you, baby," Damon whispers in my ear.

I smile at him, "I love you too Damon."

"Can we get ice cream! Please?" Lilly says excitedly. I can see a beautiful brown haired seven-year-old girl. She looks like Damon and she has Damon wrapped around her little finger.

"Yeah please, Daddy," Caleb says, crossing his arms. Damon is more strict with the boys.

"I want chocolate Daddy," Thomas says. Tommy is Liam's child but Tommy gets confused so we decided Tommy would call Damon and Liam Daddy.

"You need some lunch first," I say.

Lilly puts her arms out to Damon and he lifts her up, releasing my hand. "Please," Lilly begs. I don't know why I bother sometimes because Damon always gives in to Lilly. Always.

"Of course you can guys," Damon says.

"Damon, you can't keep giving them everything," I say frustrated.

"I can and I will." He laughs. I promised that Lilly would get everything she wanted because I never did but he takes it too far.

"Yay chocolate!" Tommy cheers. My beautiful blonde haired six-year-old. They just turned six a few days ago. He looks the spitting image of Liam.

"I'll beat you all there," Caleb says and runs off again.

"That's cheating. Mommy, he cheated." Tommy jumps up and down having a tantrum.

He is so cute, "Oh Sweetheart, go catch him up. Go on." I giggle. He nods and goes running after Caleb.

"They're so childish Mommy. They're so young and silly," Lilly says and I look at her crossing her arms in Damon's arms.

I giggle. "You are still young too princess," Damon says. He isn't amused.

"No, I'm a big girl," she sulks. Damon is in no hurry to see Lilly grow up. I think he dreads the day she finds boys.

"Daddy doesn't want to see you grown up. You have no rush to grow up." Damon says.

"Yes, I do." She wriggles out of Damon's hold and runs after the twins.

"She's growing up too quickly," Damon says, frustrated. He is out of his depth and he knows it.

"Yes, she is. Just wait till the boys come," I giggle, teasing him.

He stares at me like I've just said something ridiculous. He's angry, he hates the thought and I knew he would. "You are joking, right?"

"What?" I play innocent.

"She can't have boyfriends. No way." He sounds like the kid now. I'm going to have my work cut out in a few years. Damon will refuse Lilly to date and Lilly will beg me to change his mind. I don't think I could change his mind about that.

"Of course she can. It's all part of growing up. Come on," I say, grabbing his hand walking after the kids. The kids are waiting patiently outside the ice cream store when we catch up with them.

We walk in and join the queue. The twins are jumping up and down they are too excited. This is why kids should not have so much sugar, Damon. "You two are idiots," Lilly says.

"Lilly-May, don't be rude." I wonder where she heard that word.

"She takes after her Mom," Damon says. Well, she wouldn't have heard that word from me, I'm always careful around my kids.

"Sorry Mommy," Lilly says. They are good kids, they know how to behave.

"Right, what does everyone want?" Damon says.

"I would like Vanilla flavour," Liam says. He comes and hovers next to me. I wonder why he chose to pick that flavour. "What do you think Mommy? Do you like good old fashioned vanilla?" I wish he wouldn't flirt with me around my kids.

"Seriously Liam?" I roll my eyes.

"Daddy! Yay," Tommy cheers and jumps into Liam's arms.

"I still don't get why you have two Daddies. That's not fair," Caleb sulks. I know it's confusing but you'll understand later in life.

"I only want one Daddy," Lilly says, taking Damon's hand. "Hey, Uncle Liam."

"Hey, everyone. So, what flavours?" Liam smiles.

"I don't want ice cream, I want chocolate Daddy," Tommy says in his arms.

"Chocolate it is son." Liam is just as bad giving Tommy what he wants. I'm at a loss here.

"I'd like strawberry," Caleb says.

"Chocolate flavour for me," I say.

"Mint for me," Damon says.

"I want mint like Daddy," Lilly says. Lilly loves her Dad, she wants to spend all her time with him. Whatever Damon has she wants.

"Not a Daddy's girl at all," I sigh.

"Of course she's a Daddy's girl." Damon will do anything to protect Lilly and that's the way it should be. Parents should always put their kids first. We sit down and eat our ice cream. This is what I fought so hard for, my perfect little family.

Later that night I am woken up by Lilly. "Daddy?" she says terrified. I keep my eyes closed but I listen out just in case she needs me, but she is Daddy's girl.

"Yes princess?" Damon says sleepily.

"I had nightmares again," Lilly says.

"About what baby?" Damon says worriedly.

"The scary monsters under the bed," she says. If only monsters under the bed were all I had to worry about I wouldn't be so fucked up.

"No monsters will get you, princess. They are all scared of Daddy," he says. If I wasn't tired I would laugh because everyone is scared of Damon.

"I can't sleep, Daddy." I'm so lucky that Damon is such a great Dad. Takes some of the pressure off of me.

"Come here and sleep with Mommy and Daddy," he says. I hate it when he does this. I know he wants to protect Lilly but she is big enough to sleep in her own bed. I feel Lilly next to me and she snuggles up to me.

"Goodnight princess," Damon says.

"Night Daddy."

When I wake, Lilly is still with us. I'm always worried I'm going to crush her when she sleeps with us. Damon stirs next to me. "Damon," I say.

"Yes, baby?"

"You know you are too soft. She will never sleep alone if you keep giving in," I say.

"My baby girl was scared," he says. Or she just wanted to stay in Mommy and Daddy's bed. If Damon wants to believe his baby girl needs him then I won't burst his bubble.

"Yeah, you are too soft. Daddy's girl." I was always a Daddy's girl but I didn't have a lot of choice in the matter. I am still a Daddy's girl.

"Mommy, I'm hungry." Caleb jumps on top of me. Caleb seems to be the one that clings to me more.

"Okay, I'll be down in a minute," I say and hug him.

"I want pizza," he says. Damon is such a bad influence sometimes.

"Not for breakfast baby."

"Daddy, me want pizza!" Caleb looks over to Damon and crosses his arms. He is sitting on my tummy with his legs either side of me.

"Of course..." Damon says.

I cut him off before he can say anymore. "Don't you dare finish that sentence. You are not having pizza for breakfast. Now go downstairs please," I say sternly.

"Fine. I'm having chocolate then." Caleb pokes his tongue out and runs downstairs. Too much like his Dad.

"You let them get away with too much," I say, annoyed with Damon. I try to lay down rules but he doesn't support me.

"I'm the good cop." He smiles at me. The sexy smile that I can't resist.

"Yeah and you make me the bad one," I say and get up and head downstairs. Sully is eating breakfast at the breakfast bar. I walk over to him and put my arms around him. He lifts his arm so he can hug me back.

"You okay Emmie?" he says, smiling at me.

"Just Damon being a m-o-r-o-n," I say, spelling it out instead of saying it because there are children present.

"When isn't he Emmie?" he chuckles. I shrug. I step out of Sully's hold and make breakfast for the kids.

"Mommy, I want cupcakes for breakfast," Lilly runs in excitedly.

"Lilly-May you are not having cupcakes for breakfast," I say.

"Daddy said I could," she says and looks at Damon who has just walked into the kitchen fully dressed.

"Seriously Damon? Really?" I say frustrated and Sully laughs. I glare at them both.

"Here you go, princess," Damon says, giving Lilly a cupcake. I'm going to kill him.

"Is Daddy coming today?" Tommy asks me.

"Yes, Tommy. You are also staying the night." Unfortunately, Liam is coming over.

"Can I go too? It's not fair he gets two Daddies," Caleb sulks.

"You'll have to ask uncle Liam when he gets here." Liam is patient with Caleb considering he is nothing really to do with him.

"Can we go to the park?" Lilly says with her mouthful.

"I have work princess." Damon shrugs.

"Can I go to work with you?"

"No princess." Damon doesn't want the kids at the safe house which is good because I wouldn't allow it anyway.

"Whatever." Lilly crosses her arms. She likes to go everywhere with Damon.

"Don't sulk princess. Mommy does that," Damon says and Sully laughs.

"Hey. I wonder why we need to sulk. Oh yeah, that's right, Daddy's stupid," I say in annoyance.

"Well, I'll see you later. Have fun at Daddy's Thomas." They all hug Damon and then Damon comes over to me and kisses me. He looks at Sully who gets up to follow him. Sully comes to me and hugs me. I love my best friend so much. He releases me and follows after Damon.

"I will, thanks Daddy," Tommy calls after him.

"Mommy?" Lilly says.

"Yes, baby?"

"I'm a big girl now." Oh, princess you have a long way to be a big girl. She's growing up too fast.

"Don't let Daddy hear you say that. But carry on," I giggle.

"How come Tommy has two Daddies?" How am I supposed to explain this one? I can't say because Mommy is fucked up that she loved more than one person.

"That's a bit complicated baby," I say.

"Please tell me," she says sweetly. I'm pretty sure she learned that one from me.

"Mommy did something bad," I say.

"It's not good to be bad Mommy." When did she get smart?

"I know princess. You know how Mommy loves Daddy?"

"Yeah." She nods.

"Well, I also loved Uncle Liam. We made Tommy, me and Uncle Liam. But Daddy loves Tommy just as much as he loves you and Caleb." I guess this will have to do.

"Is Tommy not my brother?" she says sadly.

"Yes, baby, he is your brother."

Liam walks into the kitchen and he winks at me. "Hello, Mommy."

"Oh, Liam." He is so frustrating sometimes.

"You are looking good." I'm in my PJs, how is that looking good?

"Mommy told me that she loves you, that's how you made Tommy," Lilly says. Kids are so inappropriate sometimes.

"Did she now?" Liam says amused.

"I actually said loved." I'm pretty sure I did. I will always care for Liam but we have grown apart.

"Yeah, yeah, whatever you say," he still flirts with me though.

"Hey, Daddy! Can we go to the park now?" Tommy says, running into Liam's arms.

"Yes, buddy."

"Uncle Liam?" Caleb bows his head so he isn't looking at Liam. He looks sad and awkward.

"Yes, Caleb?"

"Please can I stay the night too?" Caleb asks.

"Of course Caleb, as long as you are good."

"Yay, thank you Uncle Liam," Caleb says, cheering.

"Why doesn't Mommy get dressed so we can go to the park."

"Okay, kids. I won't be long," I say.

"Does Mommy need help?" Seriously? He is so annoying.

"No Liam, she does not."

I leave the room and run upstairs. I feel fitter than I have felt in years. I can still remember how exhausted I was during the cancer time of my life. I was in pain and I'd get exhausted. I did what I promised I would though. Karma hit Blake in the ass, or I did, whatever you prefer. He doesn't annoy me so much anymore.

I get dressed and run back downstairs and find the kids all ready and waiting. Sully taught me how to drive in the end so now I can drive my kids around. We take my car and head for the park. When we arrive, the kids run to the play area and Liam hangs back with me and we sit on a bench inside the playground.

"So I guess he is working?" Liam says.

"How did you guess?" Damon is always working. He has the most successful gang in the country so the gang demand a lot of his time. When he gets home, he is with the kids.

"Do you need company?"

"No Liam." Not from you. I crave my husband.

"You are still as strong as I remember." I've been through a lot in my life but since that day that Esme kidnapped me, I have been safe. Five years being safe has been peaceful. I love my life, I won't complain.

"Of course I am. I'm still the same person." Just life events have changed me.

"You battled cancer, Emmie." They were all terrified at my weakest moments. For a few days, they all camped out in my bedroom. All of them, Brody, Jessie, Mom, Danny, Lexi, Denny, Liam and Blake. My best friend stayed with me too, he stayed by my side as did Damon. I wouldn't expect anything less from my husband.

"Yeah and I nearly died. But I pulled through."

"Not many people could do that Emmie. He isn't here, Emmie." Why does he even care? We wouldn't work. We never really did even when I had no memories.

"He's busy at work. He comes home and he is the best husband and

Dad ever. So don't come here giving me shit." It's none of his business.

"I was just saying, if you were mine, I wouldn't leave you. You are too sexy for that." I will never be yours, Liam. I was made for Damon.

"When are you going to get a girlfriend?" I can't wait for him to move on. It's been six years.

"All the while there's a better offer, why would I?" I sigh, I may be here but he will never have a chance, I've told him often enough.

"And what offer would that be?"

"You Emmie. I can't get over you that easy." Why would it take six long years for someone to get over me? I'm nothing special.

"I'm happy with Damon. You need to move on. Can you do me a favour?"

He frowns at me, "I guess?"

"I have an appointment. Could you watch the kids? I'll be an hour, max," I say sweetly.

"How could I say no to you?" It's a gift, I have a way to get around Damon too. I kiss him on the cheek and head for my car without the kids seeing me leave. I drive to the prison. I need answers, I need to know. Damon will kill me for what I have planned but I don't care. This will always be holding me back otherwise.

I reach the prison and I take a deep breath before getting out of the car. I'm terrified but I need to do this. I get out and walk into the prison. "Can I help you, Miss?" an officer asks.

"My name is Emmie Rider. I've come to see my Mother, Esme White."

"Oh okay. Follow me." I follow him to a side room. "I need to pat you down Mrs Rider." My eyes widen, no one has touched me in five long years. "Just routine," he reassures me.

"Please be quick," I beg. He nods and I hold my arms out, shutting my eyes, blocking him out. He keeps to his word, it only takes 30 seconds or so. He takes my belongings as I'm not allowed to take them with me. He escorts me into a meeting type room.

"I'll bring her in. Wait here," he says and I nod. It's a dark, dirty room. I sit at the table waiting for Esme to come in.

She walks in, she looks awful. Her hair is greasy and tied back, not the usual curly black hair I'm used to seeing. Her orange jumpsuit does nothing for her. I laugh at her, karma is a bitch. "That's made my day. You look awful."

"It's not easy to look your best in these clothes," she says, annoyed, taking a seat opposite me. The officer she's with stands behind her.

"Your age doesn't help either," I tease.

"What the hell do you want?" she snaps.

"I don't know." I shrug.

"Well, why don't you get on your merry way. I don't want to see your face." Oh cheers, Mother dearest.

"I want to know, why do you hate me so much? I mean, I could never hate my daughter. I just don't get it." I know people don't like me. I know I am a burden but I would never turn on my daughter.

"Does it really matter?"

"I just want to understand." I need this, she owes me this.

"I loved your Dad," she says. Well, I'd be surprised if she didn't love him at some point.

"Okay, so?"

"He always wanted a daughter and when he found out I was pregnant with you, he was so happy. He pushed me out. He always hovered around me to speak to you in my tummy." This explains nothing.

"And?"

"After 3 months of not speaking, I told him I wanted a divorce. He beat me." I can't say I'm truly surprised after what he did to me but she never mentioned this before.

"He did?"

"I was afraid to leave him. So when I gave birth to you, he took you off me. I loved him even then. I tried so hard for his attention."

"All this because he didn't pay you enough attention?" Doesn't seem a good enough reason to me.

"Your Dad said I had something called postpartum psychosis." Post what-y? What the hell is that?

"And what is that?" Where is Lucas when you need him?

"He said it's an illness that can occur after pregnancy. Can cause depression, delusions, hallucinations. Can cause the Mother to commit suicide or kill their baby." All this because of an illness? I don't think I'd ever favour killing my baby, I'd favour for suicide. But I can't judge because at my lowest I was prepared to die with my babies inside of me.

"So you have an illness?"

"Your Dad got me better but after having these thoughts, I still wanted you dead."

"So that's what this is? It was all triggered by me." I was the cause of her illness. No wonder she hates me so much.

"Oh, bingo. You have it in one. You caused my illness, you caused me to lose your Dad." Tears stream from my eyes. All this because of me. I see the door open and I see Damon looking angry as hell.

"Damon?"

"I can't believe you would come here," Damon shouts.

"She wanted quality time with her Momma." Esme rolls her eyes.

"No, that's not what this is. How did you know I was here anyway?" I protest.

"I have my connections, Emmie. I have people on the inside here. Your name popped up and then they called me. Now come on, I'm taking you home." He is super mad. Oh dear. This is going to be fun trying to calm him down. He grabs my hand and pulls me off the chair. "If you ever contact her again, I will kill you," Damon says to Esme and he drags me out of the room.

"I haven't had to worry about your safety for five years Emmie. Why are you going looking for trouble now? Do you miss the high or something?"

"No Damon, don't be mad."

"Mrs Rider, I'll need to give you another pat down." Why? I thought that was only done on the way in.

"You will not touch my wife," Damon growls and grabs my belongings and leaves the prison. I guess he must have been on Damon's payroll because he didn't argue. Damon takes me to my car and he gets in the driver's seat.

"Where is your car?" I say.

"Liam has it. Seeing as you left him at the park." I was only gone for an hour. Damon is so uptight. Damon starts my car and drives home. "Am I going to be able to trust you?"

"Damon, I promise I won't get into any more trouble," I say. He stays silent the rest of the journey home. I got what I wanted now I can move forwards with my life. This is what I've waited for. It makes more sense now.

Damon parks the car in the drive and storms off into the house. I walk slowly after him. When I get inside, Sully is on the sofa watching TV with Lilly. I guess Liam has taken the twins to his house already. Sully looks up assessing the situation and frowns. I walk over to him and sit on his lap. "What's going on?" Sully whispers.

"Damon has over reacted as usual," I say loud enough for Damon to hear.

He snaps his head around and glares at me. "I have not over reacted Emmie. You go to see Esme in prison on your own."

"What's going to happen, Damon? She's surrounded by officers," I snap.

"Emmie, you shouldn't have gone on your own," Sully says, agreeing with Damon.

"Does it matter? I got what I wanted."

"What did she have to say for herself then?" Damon growls.

"Daddy, why are you upset?" Lilly says worriedly.

Damon takes a deep breath and walks to Lilly. He picks her up and sits down placing her on his lap. "I'm sorry, baby. I won't be mad anymore." He kisses Lilly on her head and Lilly goes back to watching the TV.

"She's been suffering from an illness. She blames me because I'm the cause of her illness. And I was the cause of her losing Daddy."

"What do you mean, cause of her illness?" Sully asks.

"She developed an illness. It can occur shortly after pregnancy. Causes depression, hallucinations and delusions. In some cases, suicide or killing babies." I shrug.

"Your Dad was a Doctor Emmie. Did he not diagnose her?" Damon says.

"Of course he did. He tried to help. Esme said he did but she still had these thoughts after." Probably because I'm a hateful person.

"I guess this makes more sense. But this isn't your fault Emmie," Sully says. It feels like it is and Esme seems to think so. I get off of Sully's lap and head upstairs and have a shower. I need to do something to get this repulsion feeling off me. Was it the officer touching me after so long or was it visiting Esme in prison? I have no idea but I know I will never have to go back there.

I am happy, I've been happy for 5 years now. Nothing bad has happened which seems very unlike me. Damon has relaxed a little over the years. He is still protective but he isn't always worried about my safety. He only has to worry about the kids which is how it should be. I walk back into my bedroom.

Damon is sat on the bed looking at me. I feel comfortable in my own skin around Damon, even naked. He holds his hand out to me and I climb onto his lap and put my legs either side of him. "Hey, husband."

"Hey, Mi Chica Bella. How was your day?" He knows how most of my day was because he came to get me like I'm a little kid.

"It was okay. But it's just got better." I smile sweetly at him and he raises his eyebrow.

"Oh, mine too," he says and kisses me.

"Eww," Lilly says and Damon releases me. I sit and face Lilly but I stay on Damon's lap.

"Oh, Lilly-May what are we going to do with you?" I giggle. She comes over and climbs on my lap. I hug her and Damon puts his arms around us both. There is no little girl on this planet that is loved more than Lilly but I'm biased. She is our little princess and if anyone hurts her she will have to deal with me and Damon.

"I want a boyfriend Mommy. I want to be like you and Daddy," Lilly says. I laugh so hard, she's too young and Damon won't allow it.

"Maybe one day baby. There is no hurry. You'll give Daddy a heart attack. Why don't you get ready for bed baby?" I notice how Damon is keeping quiet.

"Okay. Daddy, can you read me a story?" Lilly asks, looking at Damon. He doesn't say anything, I look at him and he looks in shock.

"He will be there in a minute," I reassure her. She nods and runs out the room.

I shift my weight on Damon's lap so I am facing him again. "You know this is going to happen. She has a good few years yet. But it will," I say.

"No one will touch my princess," he promises. Part of me thinks he wouldn't be like this if it wasn't for what I went through. I like how he is protective of her but I resented my Daddy for denying me boyfriends. I couldn't handle to be close to anyone but everyone around me had boyfriends. I wasn't normal.

"I know she is definitely a Daddy's girl. I know what this is really about Damon."

"You do?"

"Yes, you are worried someone will hurt her like people did to me. But it won't happen. You'll be there to protect her." I will too, her brothers will.

"If I couldn't protect you, how can I protect our daughter?" I have faith in Damon, if my Daddy was a real father to me I wouldn't be in this situation. Damon is nothing like my Daddy and I am grateful.

"Our daughter doesn't run into danger like I did. She is smart Damon." I'm not sure if me in danger is in the past tense but that's where I'd like it to be.

"I guess you are right," he sighs.

"I'm always right," I giggle and he kisses me all over my face making me giggle. He lifts me off his lap and he goes to find Lilly. I get dressed in my PJs and head downstairs. I pause outside Lilly's door and I can hear Damon. I stop to listen.

"Lay down princess," he says.

"I want the story about Mommy," she says. What story is this one?

"Okay, Princess. There was once a beautiful girl. She was perfect in every way. She lit up my life. She was brave, smart and beautiful. She took my breath away. She was my princess. I knew she was the one when she walked into my office," he says.

I've never heard this story before from his mouth. I guess it's cute that he tells Lilly about it. I head downstairs to get a drink. I curl up on the sofa with Sully. We watch the TV series *Prison Break*. Damon gets jealous when I watch shows or films with cute guys in them. I don't know why he gets jealous because he knows it's always him.

Damon joins us twenty minutes later. I sit in the middle of them both. "Michael again, really?" Damon sighs.

"I didn't put it on this time and anyway you can't deny this show isn't good." I cross my arms.

"It would be better if the main actors weren't so good looking."

"Damon, stop being pathetic. You can't tell me you don't watch certain shows or films because of the women in it," I snap. He doesn't say anything because he knows it's true. I curl up into his chest and we watch many episodes. What I did to be so lucky to have these two by my side, my beautiful kids and my health, I have no idea.

When I wake, I am in bed. Damon must have carried me to bed last night. "Morning beautiful," Damon says, kissing my face.